THE McKANNAHS

A WESTERN ADVENTURE NOVEL

By

Rick Magers

SEQUEL — The McKannahs ~together again~
Available direct from the author in 2011
magersrick@yahoo.com

by

Rick Magers

DEDICATION

To the loyal readers of western novels.

If you stop reading them …we stop writing them.

If that happens, a valuable piece of Americana
will be lost forever.

Rick Magers
Member WWA
Western Writers of America

2nd edition 2010

TABLE OF CONTENTS

Illustrations

1

~ Tragedy: a new beginning ~

Oliver Newman McKannah often had visions. This one frightened him—flames always did. He watched his 13 year-old son Sean walk to the door of their Dublin, Ireland apartment. The boy stepped into the hallway, turned and smiled before closing the door then disappeared—forever.

Sean Brennan McKannah was born in a very small apartment only a mile from the shipping port of Dublin. It was a foggy fall day in 1780 as he slipped easily into the hands of the midwife. The stout, middle-aged woman secured his tiny feet in one callused, work-worn hand and hoisted him aloft to smack him briskly on his pink, bare bottom. She became alarmed, when after three attempts, he wasn't crying out against the abuse he was receiving at the hands of this giant creature. She turned him toward her and was shocked to see his miniature eyes staring straight at her. She swore later that he had a look of contempt on his doll-size face as he swung his little fists at her.

His father Oliver Newman McKannah stepped forward. "There'll be no cryin' in that lad, Missus Brennan." She scowled at the large, ruddy-complexioned, thirty-nine-year-old canal worker that had waited for what turned out to be almost his entire lifetime for the arrival of his son. She did not approve of men in the birthing room, but as all who knew Oliver were aware; he would be there.

During the following weeks, Mrs. Brennan spent considerable time in the McKannah household. It was a busy period on the canals that ran throughout Ireland, and Oliver was often away from home for several days at a time.

Myra Ellen Waithe-McKannah had a difficult time delivering her first, and as it turned out, only baby. Mrs. Brennan often spent days with her as she struggled to regain her health, deteriorated by this late-in-life childbirth. Fate intervened and prevented Mrs. Brennan from being in the apartment when tragedy struck

Oliver Newman McKannah was born in the final year of the 1739-41 famines that killed a third of Ireland's one-and-a-half-million people. Looking into his son's face, Oliver saw the same determination that was needed to survive the starving, diseased world into which Oliver was literally dumped onto the dirt floor of the mud and straw house of his parents.

His own parents and only brother had not survived the famine, and Oliver knew better than many that the stubbornness he saw in this child could make the difference between survival and death. Among the gifts he'd wish for his newborn son, courage and stubbornness would head the list.

Myra Ellen Waithe-McKannah was only one year younger than her husband but still far beyond the age to be having her first baby. She beamed proudly as Laura Brennan placed the little man in her arms. He was looking directly into her eyes when the harbor foghorns began blowing again. She later said, "His little eyes widened and I swear he tried to lift high enough to see where the noise was coming from."

Oliver would always confirm his wife's words. "It's quite true. I was also watching and saw the look in his eyes. I knew the sea had called m'boy to her."

Whether to prove the legacy he had heard about for all of his childhood, or simply because he loved the sound of foghorns that blew constantly, Sean made his first trip to the docks as an adventurous eight-year-old boy. Over the next five years he was never beaten by his parents, but often severely scolded about his regular disappearances from school to prowl among the wharves and ships in the harbor. His determination to return and talk with the seamen, plus his charming ways, made him a favorite youngster with the sailing ship's captains and crews. He loved their stories of travels to far places.

Consequently his dreams were not those of other boys—ships, always ships. Always with sails full of wind, searching for new adventures in new lands. A sad twist of events would soon place him within his dreams. He would be granted the opportunity to make his dreams come true at a very young age, but at a very high price.

His Sunday disappearances were so common that no one noticed him leave after dinner. He always honored one request made by the father that he idolized. "Don't ever be away from home after dark or your mother will worry herself into a grave." When Sean rounded the corner of his street he saw the flames and rushing people. When he arrived at the apartment house he lived in, it was totally involved in monstrous flames, reaching high into the sky. He stood helplessly watching as his family passed from this life to the next. Sean Brennan McKannah was totally alone. A kind neighbor took the thirteen-year-old boy in for the night because she knew that he didn't have another living relative that he knew of. Sean was wise beyond his years, partly due to an inquisitive mind, and also by his parent's patient tutoring about the ways of the world. He realized that his neighbor's kindness was not without sacrifice because she had a young family to feed, and in these difficult times that was a task not to be taken lightly.

The fire took his parents and everything he had on earth. The morning after found Sean talking to Captain Patrick Olin Mullholland. Sean had known the robust, boisterous sea captain for two years, and always looked forward to seeing Captain Mulholland's ship SEA DUCHESS come into port. Captain Mullholland carried cargo mainly around the British Isles, but told Sean the last time that he talked to him, "Aye lad, we'll be gone awhile next trip. We're takin' a load of wool to China." After listening to Sean's story, the captain said simply, "Get aboard lad, y'gotta 'ave a home."

Five days later a well-fed Sean McKannah stood on the rear of the cargo schooner watching his homeland for the last time.

After a horrendous battle between Sean's land-loving body and his sea-loving mind, the mind finally won. With his seasickness behind him he began to love the roll of the huge ship as it made its way across the Irish Sea to Liverpool for a load of wool. After a short trip to Cardiff, Wales for another load, Sean commented to the First Mate, "I love this wonderful ocean."

The Ship's Mate smiled, looked out at the gently rolling waves, then back to the young boy. "It's a wonderful life lad, but I must warn you, (Sean was too young to realize what the mischievous twinkle in the old man's eye was) she'll get a wee bit rougher 'fore we get to where we're heading."

The ship finally made it to the Cape of Good Hope off the tip of South Africa, and after thirty-seven days of beating against waves that would have swallowed the apartment building that his parents had lived in, Sean then knew the full meaning of 'a wee bit rougher.' From that day on until he left the ship four years later, the crew accepted him as a full-fledged seaman. He fought off seasickness, and it was obvious that he was frightened at times, but he never once shirked his assigned duties.

The seas calmed considerably as they headed for the Strait of Malacca between Sumatra and Malaysia. They stopped briefly at Singapore to hire a local pilot to guide them up the South China Sea to Hong Kong. Captain Mullholland insisted that Sean not go with any of the crew, as he knew quite well where they were heading for their two-day leave while the wool was being off-loaded.

Patrick Mullholland had been to Singapore a few years earlier on another merchant ship, prior to buying Sea Duchess, and knew many of the captains and crewmembers in the harbor. Captain Mullholland took Sean around and introduced him to many characters, some only a few years older than him. Most were traveling the world's wet roads in search of adventure and fortune, much the same as Sean. As Patrick took Sean around the seaport town he noticed how everyone liked the huge sea captain because of his easy ways and honesty. Even at such a young age Sean realized how fortunate he was to have been befriended by someone like the captain.

An hour before dawn on the third day, the young Oriental harbor pilot instructed the crew to begin hoisting the sail then pull the anchor back into the vessel. The young Oriental man spoke fairly good English, so Sean asked him why they left while it was still dark. "Wait, you see." Once the ship was well rigged out in canvas, the sun began peeking over the horizon. "Look," the pilot said to Sean as he pointed astern.

Sean counted eight sets of sails in the distance behind them. "Very busy time, we get in first, boat get stuff off first, we go home." The young man smiled then added, "You see?"

"Sure do," Sean answered with a grin, "why be last when you can be first?"

"Yep," The pilot grinned, "Bess way."

Once anchored in the harbor at Hong Kong a swarm of small boats surrounded Sea Duchess, and her remaining cargo was unloaded faster than Sean would have believed possible. Of greater surprise to him was how quickly the bales of cork to deliver to Australia were transferred from the many small boats that were soon alongside. In one day the vessel went from half loaded to empty, then back to fully loaded and ready to leave the following morning. Back in the harbor at Singapore, Captain Mullholland yelled for the pilot.

"Yes, Captain Bull Hollerin."

The crusty old captain turned around and looked menacingly at the little man. "Mullholland," he grumbled, "how many times I gotta tell ya that?"

Oh yessir, I very sorry sir," he said with a serious expression on his face. When the captain snorted and turned, he grinned at Sean then walked along behind the old man and imitated his gorilla-like walk.

Patrick turned abruptly and the little pilot almost ran into him. “Here,” he thundered, “this is a bit extra for the two days you saved me by getting us in and out fast.”

“Thank you very much Captain, when you come again you ask for Jolly Roger, Okay?”

“Jolly Roger?” Patrick said as he looked at the little man. “That’s a pirate insignia.”

“Yep,” the Chinaman grinned, “when I first start I charged too much because I new in business. One captain say, ‘You should have a Jolly Roger flag on your boat because you a damn pirate.’ He smiled widely. “I Jolly Roger now.”

“Well,” Patrick said with a grin, “pirate or no, you did a damn fine job n’ I want you to be my pilot each time I come.”

“Okay that good. I tell all other pilot they get shot by your crew when they come out to this boat.” He watched as the crew lowered his tiny rowboat from the deck back into the water. He untied the oars and waved before rowing back to shore. “See you next time Captain Bull Hollerin.”

The crew unloaded the cork in Sydney, Australia then Captain Mullholland hired ships carpenters to make repairs. All of the crew had four days to see this burgeoning new city that had been born only half a dozen years earlier. Captain Mullholland then headed out across the Tasman Sea for the South Pacific Ocean. The long run to one of the world’s most splendid natural harbors at Yerba Buena Cove was an uneventful one. Yerba Buena would eventually become San Francisco, California in the newly forming country of America. Patrick turned to Sean, “How’d you like Australia?”

“I liked it very much sir, just like home.”

Patrick looked down at Sean with a quizzical expression, “Really now, lad?”

Sean grinned, “Yep! Hollering at each other about politics and sports, while drinking beer.”

This was Sean’s first hollow run, as they called a run without cargo, so he asked Patrick, “Why did we put all those rocks in the bottom of the boat, don’t they have rocks where we’re going?”

Patrick laughed, “Them’s to keep us down in the water so we don’t flop over on our side when the wind blows. Wasn’t anything we could bring this time, but we’ll see if we can get an order for som’n on our next trip.” Patrick looked down at Sean a moment then explained. “I forget that there’s a lot about this that you don’t know anything about, lad. When the ballast stones; that’s what they’re called, start takin up too much room, the towns use ‘em to make their muddy streets more passable.”

“Furs Lad, fine furs. I’m gambling that my information’s correct. I was told we can buy furs here for a few pence that’ll bring us more’n a quid at home.”

"How long'll we be there?"

"Might be as long as a few months, but it'll be worth it if we can get those furs, 'cause we'll all make a nice pot o' money," he ruffled the young boy's hair, and grinned at him, "you too lad."

"You've been there before, sir?"

"Nope, but I talked to an old captain that's been there twice. A Spanish ship dropped anchor inside the harbor just a few years ago." He wrinkled his brow in thought. "Hmm, lemme see, seventy-five I think it was. The boat was the San Carlos, and the word got around about the beautiful harbor, then a year later some settlers from down at Monterey came up and built a mission called the San Francisco de Asis." He paused and looked down at Sean who was listening intently to every word. "That's who will send the word out for the trappers to bring their furs."

When they finally arrived at the north coast of California, Sean looked across the beautiful harbor to the rolling hills that were to become his home in three years. A month after he and Captain Mullholland went to the mission, trappers started showing up alongside the ship in their canoes loaded with furs. Sean was intrigued with these wild looking men that wore animal skins and carried more weapons than the British soldiers back home. What took hold of his imagination though, and wouldn't let go, were the Indians that came with the trappers. He had never heard about the Native Americans that inhabited this new land. The captain allowed only two men from each canoe at a time aboard the boat. His crew stood guard along both sides, and one man stood ready at a grapeshot swivel-gun on the highest deck, from which he could fire to either side if necessary. Patrick had heard stories of these wild men with their savages coming aboard vessels looking for weapons, whiskey, and anything else they could carry off. "Not aboard this vessel," he informed the trappers, "so keep your little boats out away from my ship till the one trading is back in his, and has pulled away."

Sean had never seen Patrick so aggressive toward anyone. He had a good crew and seldom had to raise his voice to any of them. He heard the Captain's order to his First Mate, "No warning shots if they try to come aboard, shoot to kill them." He said it loud enough for the trappers to hear, so from this trip on, the trappers remained a safe distance from Sea Duchess.

Sean could tell that a couple of the Indians were not much older than he was, and also that they had never been on a big ship before. They moved about the gently rolling vessel like crabs, unsure of their footing. He also noticed that they were as curious about him as he was of them. He remained quiet, but kept as close to the negotiating as possible, without getting in the way. Patrick had been informed that many of the trappers would speak only French, so he brought Devon Manieuex on deck to translate. Sean thought the Indians were only labor for the trappers, but soon realized that they had a stake in the furs too, as they used sign language to convey what they wanted.

The items the trappers wanted most were good weapons, shot, and powder. Patrick informed them that he had no idea what they would want, since he'd never been to this port before. "I brought only a few weapons, steel knives, pots, kettles, and basic food items like coffee, tea, flour, cooking oil, oil lamps, and things like that. I'll write down what you want, and we'll be back in a few months with everything we can locate."

The trappers didn't come out to the boat for trouble. They wanted supplies, so this arrangement seemed to satisfy them. Captain Patrick Mullholland had an air about him that made men trust him, and for good reason; he was an honest Irishman.

Several of the trappers in larger canoes brought so many furs on board that after they had taken all of the supplies they could, they let the captain log them in with a credit against items they ordered from the next trip. Before departing the sailing vessel, many of the mountain men produced letters and asked the captain if he would have them delivered if he ported on the coast of France. Captain Mullholland agreed, and the men left the ship feeling good that loved ones back home would know that they were still alive.

Although many of the trappers were Northeastern *voyaugers,* and spoke only French, there were several who were fluent in English. Sean listened very carefully to their brief stories about the difficulties of getting the furs. "Hostile Indians, white thieves, snow storms, earthquakes, huge bears, and wolves." Sean was hooked. Long after they left and were heading south toward Cape Horn to round the tip of Chile and begin the long run north between Africa and South America, Sean lay night after night in his bunk. He dreamed of an adventurous life in the high mountains of the new wild country he had just visited.

After Sean confided his dreams, Patrick said, "Lad, it's a tough life up in those mountains I'm sure, but I believe I'd do the same thing you're thinking of if I had it to do again." He cocked an eyebrow at the young boy, "Don't get in too big a hurry though lad 'cause you'll learn a lot that'll help you by listening to these trappers we'll be trading with."

"Oh don't worry sir, I know a boy wouldn't stand a chance out there but," he winked a gleaming eye that the old captain loved, "in a couple of years I'll be grown."

The next couple of years went by quickly for the young Irishman. The trips aboard Sea Duchess didn't make him wealthy, but he had amassed a stake much larger than most young men his age ever dared dream of. When they returned from the first trip to America, Sean asked the captain about an idea he had nurtured since the stop at Australia. "They don't have much of anything sir and I'm thinking I can go to the farms around Dublin and buy seed potatoes to take with us."

On the last day of loading the ship for her second trip to America, the young boy showed up with a cart loaded with six barrels of seed potatoes. Captain

Mullholland looked at the barrels then turned to Sean, "Lad, you're gonna do well no matter where you go. Tell you what we'll do. You've supplied the potatoes, so I'll supply the ship. We'll give the crew some wages for their effort, then you n' me'll split the gain."

"That's more than I expected sir, I figured to just get a percentage." His extended hand was shook sincerely by Captain Mullholland. "Thank you," Sean said with a smile.

When word spread around Sydney, Australia that there were Irish seed potatoes available, Sean McKannah was a busy boy. His potatoes were set on the dock next to the ship, so Captain Mullholland could keep an eye on the young entrepreneur whom he was becoming very attached to. The Sydney sun set that first day in port on six empty barrels, and one tired but proud young boy who was fast on his way to becoming man. Not a wealthy man, but in his young mind, on his way to becoming rich. So many people came looking for potatoes after they were gone that Sean promised to have many more on the next trip.

As the ship plowed her way toward San Francisco, Patrick opened a small wooden chest and placed the profit from his share of the potatoes in it. After replacing it beneath his bunk he stood and looked at the sea from his cabin window. The old sea captain's struggle to reach his present station had been long and difficult. He thought of his own industrious attitude as a youth—and smiled.

During the next three years, Captain Mullholland made as many trips as he could while planning his retirement. The profits had been high on the wool he carried to Hong Kong, and also on the materials he had been supplying to the new settlement in Sydney, Australia and Yerba Buena. His retirement funds were broadened considerably by the culmination of a deal he'd worked on for a year. A long time friend at the HEIC—Honorable East India Company—was finally able to supply him with a substantial amount of their finest weapons to be offered to the settlers in America.

When the trappers of the northern wilderness saw the India Pattern Brown Bess Muskets for the first time they fell in love with them. They weighed less than ten pounds, and were almost fifty-five inches long. They muzzle-loaded a .753 slug and were more accurate than anything they had ever seen. The captain's eighty rifles; brought on his third trip, were all of the advertisement that was needed. On Sean's final trip, Patrick notified the trappers that the two hundred rifles he had with him were the last. "I'm retiring to the country cottage in Cork, Ireland that my spinster sister has been preparing for the two of us." It was just as well, as the friend he had at HEIC had informed Patrick that he could no longer sell him rifles. He did inform Patrick however, that one final batch could be provided if all of the pistols available went as one lot. They were an assortment of old, but serviceable, pistols that the captain could purchase cheaply.

After inspecting the pistols in the storage basement of the building, Patrick decided to make one more trip. He was also anxious to see how young Sean McKannah was doing in his new trapping venture.

The morning after Captain Mullholland dropped anchor in the foggy harbor at Yerba Buena, he was called to the deck by his first mate. "It's the lad, Cap'n," he said as he pointed toward shore. He handed Patrick the long glass so he could see for himself.

"Aye, it's him alright Cap'n, but not a lad any longer. Just look at those shoulders." He handed the glass back to his first mate who held it beside his leg and rested it on the deck.

"Aye Cap'n, I had to look twice to be certain the big bloke in the front of the bloody canoe was Sean."

Patrick reached for the glass again, and focused on the canoe. "Yeah," he said then grinned at his mate before replacing the glass to his eye, "'tis him n' smilin like a bloody Cheshire cat." He stood by the gunwale after helping the mate drop the boarding net over the side of the ship then watched as Sean and his friend came alongside. The old man beamed when Sean came directly to him and put his muscular young arms out, and hugged him close. When Sean stepped back Patrick said, "My God lad, you've filled out, where's the scrawny little boy we sent off last year to seek his fortune?"

"Gone for good, Cap'n." Sean grinned, "I came as soon as I heard you were in the bay. I just got back from Clear Lake two days ago, so this is good timing."

Patrick Mullholland leaned forward with a twinkle of mischief in his kindly blue eyes, "Planned m'crossing that way, lad." He stood erect and added; "Timing's everything in life ain't it?"

"It sure is Cap'n," Sean said with a sly grin, "and I've had m'share of it. Meeting you was good timing, and meeting Frank was too." He turned to the young man that had boarded Sea Duchess with him and motioned him forward. "This's my partner, Francisco de Rivera Santiago," he put his hand on the shoulder of the dark complexioned young man about his own age. "Frank this is Captain Patrick Olin Mullholland, who stepped into my dead father's shoes n' carried me through some rough times."

Patrick took the black-haired young man's hand, and looked deep into his dark eyes. He was very pleased with what he saw. *No lurking danger or shadowed crevices to hide the truth in.* "Pleased to meetcha lad," he said as he pumped his hand. He later told his First Mate, 'Whatcha see's whatcha get with that young Spaniard.'

Patrick was surprised when Frank, as Sean later explained the young Spaniard liked to be called, said in perfect English, "The pleasure's mine sir. I've learned through Sean's stories to admire you already." He smiled as he pumped Patrick's skillet-size hand, "Would you mind if I look around your vessel sir, while you're visiting with Sean? This one is so beautiful lying in the water that I'd love to see her insides."

"Why certainly lad, my First Mate'll show you around." He turned to the six-foot-six-inch tall, two-hundred-and-seventy-five pound man standing nearby, "Mr. Winslow, would you show Sean's young friend around the ship please?"

The red-haired, red-bearded hulk with bushy red eyebrows strolled casually over. "Mr. Winslow indeed," he said with a sly smile, "thousands of miles it's hey Ollie getcher arse over here, but with company aboard it's Mr. bloody Winslow. C'mon lad I'll show you the rum locker if ye like."

"Forty-three years together," the captain grinned at Sean, "worse n' a bloody wife I reckon." He motioned for the two of them to go up to the high rear deck and as they did, Sean greeted his old shipmates. Once seated Patrick said, "I'm dyin' t'hear of your adventures n' how you're doing with your trapping?"

"Well," Sean began, "when I left the boat I went to the mission to find Frank. You remember; I met him when he came out with that crabby old trapper, doncha?" When Patrick nodded yes, Sean continued. "He wanted to make his own way in the world and not be a burden to his uncle, so we decided to go partners on the trapping supplies. He said that the old trapper went right by some good looking trapping areas not too far north, 'cause he wanted to go into the high mountains for some reason. Frank and I went up to Clear Lake to give it a try. It's only about a hundred miles north of Yerba Buena, and Cap'n there's beaver streams running all over the place. The first trip up there we paid for all our traps and supplies, so we kept quiet about the place. We had three more great trips, then on the fifth trip, wow!"

Captain Mullholland looked at his young foster son in his new wilderness garb of leather pants, buckskin jacket, and knee length moccasins. Sean McKannah slowly shook his head from side to side while recalling the incident, and the old man waited patiently for him to continue.

"Cap'n, you ever heard of a grizzly bear?"

"Well lad," he replied as he removed the new knitted hat his sister had made for him, and scratched his graying red hair, revealing the toll charged by time's passing. "Trappers talk a lot about the bears n' other animals in this wild country, but I don't remember anything called a, whatcha call it? grizzy."

"No sir, it's called a grizzly bear and believe me there's nothing else like it on God's green earth." He was staring beyond Patrick as he described the creature he and his friend had encountered in the high forests north of San Francisco. "Cap'n I'm not stretching it a wee bit when I tell you that the one me n' Frank ran up against was half again as tall as Frank and you can see that he's a few inches taller'n me." He pointed at the sturdy lap-sided oak lifeboat on the deck below them, "And Cap'n that bear would weigh more'n that boat down there on the deck."

Patrick was always eager to listen to the stories the trappers told while they were on board to barter their furs and gold coins for his supplies. The tales were often so bizarre compared to anything he had ever heard that he didn't know whether to believe them or not. He knew that Sean would rather swallow his tongue than lie, so he was eager for the young man to continue.

"We were up on a high ridge that was kinda flat and clear of trees. It was about three soccer fields wide, with the forest on one side running down from the heights. The other side of the ridge fell off real steep with treetops pokin up from down below and almost touching the side of the mountain. Kinda looked like a guy could reach out and touch the tops of 'em, but Cap'n if you slipped off that ridge it'd be a long fall to the bottom." The young man shook his head then looked at Patrick, "Ain't ever seen trees as tall's them up there. Anyway, we had just finished setting our traps, so we decided to have a look around. Frank and me were talking about setting up a permanent camp instead of living in the tent while we were up there. Like I said, I was walking along the edge of that ridge, just kinda looking at the tops of them big trees. Frank was ahead, over on the other side close to the forest; not more'n a few lengths of this ship away. All of a sudden this huge grizzly bear came charging out of the trees." His eyes opened wide and he shook his head again, "Cap'n you ain't seen anything like it; not even in your nightmares. He was actually closer to me when he charged out, but for some reason he took off after Frank, so I yelled. He turned and saw that huge bear, then began running, but I could see the grizzly was gonna catch him. I brought that old musket you gave me up and put a ball in that monster. I knew it was a hit 'cause it stopped and shook its huge head then started biting at its shoulder. Cap'n when that thing stood all the way up and looked right at me, I think my blood started freezin in my veins. I just stood there with that empty musket wondering if I oughta try to reload when it got back down on all four paws and started running right at me." He kind of shivered, and a 'phew' came with his next breath.

"My God lad," Patrick said with alarm in his voice, "what in the world did you do to get away?"

"Well sir, I had wandered a little ways from the edge of that drop-off where the tree tops stick way up near the top of the ridge. I turned toward 'em and started running, but I knew I would never outrun that grizzly. Cap'n you wouldn't believe how fast that thing was comin at me. I had no time to think, so I just reacted from instinct, I reckon."

"Lad, you had unusually fast reflexes, even as a young lad and your instincts were always good."

"Saved me arse this time I'm sure. I dropped the musket and ran as fast as any frightened man ever has and believe me sir I was scared. Before I got to the edge I looked back, and that beast was no more'n three meters behind me."

"My God."

"Y'know sir, He was mine too that day, because I was sure praying to Him, about the time I got to that drop-off. I didn't look back when I went flying out toward those treetops, but I betcha that grizzly wasn't more'n a step behind me, 'cause he hit m'leg with one of his claws as he followed me out into space. Look at this."

Patrick's mouth dropped open as he leaned closer to look at the healed wound. "Phew lad, too close," he shook his head slowly from side to side, "too bloody close."

"I sure chose the right tree to land in 'cause as I grabbed the limbs I was leaping at, the grizzly hit the ones just below me and they wouldn't support his weight. I wrapped my arms n' legs around them branches," he laughed as he imagined what he must have looked like, "like a bloody circus monkey. I looked down and watched that bear falling down through the trees, still growling and swiping with them huge paws that have claws almost's long as my knife blade." He shuddered again, "Still see 'em in m'dreams, I do Cap'n; nightmares that is."

"Phew, I'm sure you do. It's a credit to yer swift thinkin that you're still here to be dreamin atol, lad."

"And me swift feet."

"How the devil didja get back up on the ridge?"

"Frank had seen what happened and come running with the rawhide rope he always carries wrapped around his waist." He raised his buckskin shirt to reveal a similar one around his own waist. "Carry one m'self now."

"Ya reckon the bear was killed?"

"Don't see how anything coulda survived that fall to the bottom, but if he did I don't wanna run into him, 'cause he's gonna be one mad grizzly."

Captain Mullholland stood, "C'mon lad, I've got a gift for ye." As they entered the doorway to the hall that led to the captain's quarters, the First Mate and Francisco were about to come on deck. "C'mon lad," Patrick said, "I've a gift to give you too." Sean's friend turned and followed the two men as Brian Winslow went onto the deck to prepare for the arrival of the trappers to trade their skins.

Once inside his quarters, Patrick opened his small storage room and produced a wooden box about two feet square. He handed it to Sean saying, "Maybe these'll give you a better chance if you meet that grizzy again." He stood smiling as Sean laid the box on the bunk and opened it.

"Oh lordy, they're beautiful." He picked up the entire affair and held it out for Frank to see.

"They're French St Etienne Modele 1777's. I've actually got several pistols that're fancier, but these are the toughest I've ever seen lad." He pointed to the solid brass frame. "They're made to stand up against real abuse. The French royalists had 'em as regular issue during the 1789 Revolution." He turned to Frank, "They're the only two I could get lad, or I'd give you a pair also, but you can take your pick of the others." He returned his attention to Sean as he pointed to the butt of the pistols. "Lookit that solid brass butt-cap holdin' the walnut stocks." Patrick gave a short jerk of his head, "Lad, I do believe you coulda knocked that grizzy cold with one 'o these n' still shot him dead." The old sea captain stood clumsily smiling, as his young friend wrapped the leather holsters around his slender waist then placed the two pistols in them.

Patrick was somewhat surprised when Sean stepped forward and embraced him. "God love you Cap'n, this's the nicest gift I'll ever receive, thank you." He stepped back and pulled both pistols out. Holding them at the stern window he said, "These things are really balanced." He replaced them, and turned to Patrick, "How many pistols were you able to bring?"

"C'mon lads n' I'll show 'em to you before the trappers get into the lot." He turned to Frank, "And you can 'ave your pick of any two o' the bunch, lad." They walked past two doors along the hallway then he produced a large key and unlocked the third. "There's five boxes of 'em lads, so 'ow about carrying one of 'em onto the deck so we can 'ave a look. I'll call a coupla men while you're bringin' the one." He left the small arms room to summon a couple of his crewmen. After all five boxes were on deck and opened, the crew began laying them out for the trappers to inspect.

"Come with me a moment Sean, I've something else t'show you." The captain put his hand on Sean's shoulder and the two friends; one approaching the end of his life—the other just beginning his, headed back toward the captain's quarters. Once inside, Patrick locked the door then went to the closet again. He came out with a rifle as beautiful as any Sean had ever seen. "This's part of the reason I bought all the pistols to bring for one last trip." He grinned, "This was supposed to be finished before you n' me made that last trip together, but m'friend at East India couldn't get it completed in time." He handed the rifle to Sean, "Anyway, 'ere she is lad."

Sean took the rifle from Patrick, and just stood looking at the beautiful weapon. It was one of the same Brown Bess Muskets that they had been trading to the trappers, but it had been carefully worked over by one of the best gunsmiths in England. Many of the iron parts had been replaced with brass, and the new walnut stock had solid gold inlay work that spelled SEAN McKANNAH 1798. His mouth was hanging open as he turned it over to see his name in gold on the other side also. Tears were already beginning to fill his eyes when he looked up at his friend. He tried to speak, but was unable to get a sound to come from his throat full of emotion. He just stood silently looking from Patrick to the rifle and back again.

Patrick was on his knees reaching beneath his bunk. When he finally stood, he was holding the small wooden box into which he had placed every bit of the profit from Sean's potato venture—which was considerable. "Yer as much a son as I was ever likely to 'ave lad, and I saved every bit of the potato money so you'd 'ave a chance at a good start in your new country." He handed the box to Sean, who now had tears running freely down his cheeks. "You'll also find a packet of English pound notes in there; a thousand of 'em. I checked, and they're accepted most everywhere here in this country." He smiled broadly, "But, with all that's happening lately with all these people comin 'ere, I'd exchange 'em for gold first chance y'ave."

Weak at the knees, Sean lowered himself onto the captain's bunk and sat there weeping quietly as he held the small box. When he finally had control of himself he looked up at the captain. "I've been very lucky to have been given two wonderful fathers. Thank you so much sir; I'll never forget you." He removed a rag from his sleeve and wiped his eyes, "Thank you."

While the door was still locked Sean removed his shirt, and then untied the money belt Patrick had given him when he first left the ship. As he placed the bills in it, Patrick commented, "Still 'ave the money belt, eh?"

"Yessir! I exchanged most of my money for gold then buried it beneath a big tree that must be two hundred years old. I figure it'll be there till I decide what I wanna do, and I carry just enough in here to get the things I need." After replacing the belt, and pulling his shirt back over his head, he reached in the pocket of the leather pants. "I carry enough for a few days at a time." He showed Patrick a few bills and coins, "Then I get more outa the belt when I'm all alone." Sean began wrapping his leather rope around the outside of his tunic.

"Smart lad," Patrick said as he led the way out of the cabin. "I noticed that you and Frank carry your rope outside now."

Back on deck they found Frank, looking over all of the pistols on the deck. "I've never seen most of these," he said. "What kind is this one?" He pointed at a very plain muzzleloader.

"That's a German Calvary pistol, and it's supposed t'be one of the most accurate ever made."

"And this beauty?"

"Ah, y'like that one, 'eh?" Patrick smiled as he reached down and picked up one of the twenty like it. "This is a Memory, lad. It's made by a London gunmaker named," he paused and grinned.

"Memory?" Frank replied with a question mark in his voice.

"Right as rain you are lad, Memory is his name. He only made these a few years ago, but for some reason they didn't go over too well." He turned the end of the barrel up and pointed to the flared out end that resembled a bell. "Might be this slightly swamped barrel?" He handed it to Frank, "Who knows? Men're more fickle about their guns than women are about their shoes."

Frank held it out in front of him, and sighted down the barrel. He lowered it and looked closely at the ornate metal work, and the solid brass barrel.

"They're beautiful weapons ain't they, lad?"

"Yessir! If you don't mind, I'd like a pair of these."

Patrick smiled. "They're yours then, just pick out the pair you want."

After choosing the two pistols he wanted, Frank thanked the captain then shook hands with Oliver 'Ollie' Winslow and thanked him for showing him the vessel. "Excuse me sir," he said to Patrick, "what are all of those that are the same type in the three boxes?"

"Those are what I'll make me profit on this trip." He reached down and lifted one from the first box. "This is a British masterpiece lad." He sighted down the short barrel. "Tower Sea Service Pistol. See this GR beneath the lock plate?" He held it out for both men to see. "And this cross on the tail?" Again he held it out for them to inspect. "TOWER," he spelled out the letters. Means she was assembled in the Tower of London at the great armory. Bloody good pistol even if she is a bit of a plain chunk o' steel." He sighted out to sea then lowered the barrel. "Looks like our first customer comin there." He put the pistol back with the many others and yelled to his First Mate, "Getcher crew hoppin Ollie, a customer's about on top of us." Sean and Frank both said goodbye and began the climb down the boarding net to their canoe. Before turning toward the shore, Sean looked hard at the man he had come to think of as his father—knowing he would probably never see him again. No words would come, so after a long period of silence he turned and began paddling.

"Your Uncle Luis wants us to come out to the ranch?" Sean yelled to Frank who was in the front of their long canoe. The wind was beginning to howl across the bay, making conversation difficult.

"Yes," he turned his head to answer, "he asked us to come and talk to him before we make any plans." Sean shook his head and no more was said until they had the canoe pulled onto land and turned upside down near the trader's new log building, recently built at the junction of the bay and river. Each man had the new weapons strapped around his waist, and Sean was carrying his new Brown Bess musket as they entered the small building.

"Wow!" The tall thin owner of the trading station said, "Looks like it was a good trip out to see Cap'n Patrick, eh?"

James Poorsmith had always dealt fairly with the trappers and was liked by everyone, especially Sean and Frank. Even though they were young and very inexperienced, he had treated them with respect from the first day they came to him for outfitting as trappers. Sean removed one of the St Etienne pistols from its holster and handed it to James. "It's not loaded," he said and stood smiling as the middle-aged man who was to become one of the biggest men in the Hudson Bay Trading Company, admired the fine weapon. When he handed it back he said, "Fine pair of pistols, and that rifle's new too, isn't it?"

"Yessir," Sean replied as he passed it to James, "she's a Brown Bess n' I really like the balance of it. I can't wait to pack 'er full to see how accurate she is."

"You'll be pleased," he said, handing the rifle back. "I've fired them a lot, and they're one of the best muskets available, so I bought a mess of 'em from Patrick." He reached for the pistol that Frank was holding out to him, "I hate to see the old man retiring, but he's getting on in years; especially to be fighting that ocean to get all the way here from Ireland."

"He gave me these pistols as a gift too," Frank said.

"Well, well. You must have made a fine impression on the old fella 'cause he doesn't give much away." He smiled at the young Spaniard and handed the pistol back. C'mere," he motioned for the two men to follow him into the small room attached to the rear. "Let's load those weapons and you two take some spare ammo too, since you're going all the way to your uncle's ranch." When they were finished he said, "Traveling is dangerous these days with all the people moving in." He closed and locked the ammunition room then turned to Sean. "You men going back up to check your traps soon?"

"Dunno?" We gotta go out n' see what Frank's Uncle Luis wants first."

"Good. That'll work out fine 'cause I'm closing for awhile to go out and look at the supplies Patrick brought." He leaned down and brought a package up from the shelf. "Give this to your Aunt Carmen." He passed the two-pound package wrapped tightly in sailcloth to Frank. "It's sugar from an island called Cuba down in the Caribbean Ocean."

"Where's that?"

"Down south of Mexico I guess?" James was scratching his head. "Wish I had one of those maps like Patrick's got on the wall in his cabin."

"It is south of here," Sean replied, "but not south of Mexico, it's more the other way, over toward the other side of America. We was gonna stop there one trip, but Patrick decided to get on home."

"Probably knew about those waters from talking to captains like the Dutchman that brought me this sugar. He said there's about a million little islands through there, with shallow places everywhere."

"That's exactly what he said," Sean answered, "and we had a big load of furs on board, so we couldn't have carried much stuff anyway. But I sure woulda liked to have had a look at some of those islands."

James Poorsmith put his hat on and came around the counter. "Well gentlemen I'm off to barter with that Irishman." He grinned at Sean, "Can I borrow your pistols to take with me?"

Sean grinned back, "It's your wits you better be takin with you, sir."

All of James Poorsmith's horses were gentle, and had been broken to sell to the trappers and others moving into the area.

"If I'm off somewhere when you get back," James said, "rub down the two horses you're borrowing then feed 'em good." He waved as he headed for his canoe, "See you fellas later."

"Here," Frank said, as he tossed Sean a rope harness to put over his horses head then headed for the horse he'd picked to borrow for the ride out to his uncle's ranch.

Sean approached the tan gelding slowly with the saddle, while talking to it.

"How about a nice ride south to see some of your old friends?" The horse stood motionless as he slipped the harness over its head then slid the padded ring up over its nose. With the rawhide reins in his left hand and the pommel in his right he easily jumped up in the saddle. Frank had already reached the gate and was leaning down to open it. "Go ahead," Sean said, "I'll close it."

They were soon on the trail heading south, on the seaward peninsula toward Luis Javier de Carvojol's ranch at the foot of San Benito Mountain. It was a little more than a hundred miles from Yerba Buena.

"Whadaya think your uncle wants with us?"

"I know what he wants," Frank said somewhat glumly, "me to move to the ranch and start learning how to be a horse farmer."

"Yeah, I know that, but how about right now?"

"I don't know, unless he's had some word about my sister Bella."

Sean was silent a moment then said, "Her name's Issabella isn't it?"

"Issabella Magdelena Ruiz Santiago." He turned and grinned, "Too long, so I always called her Bella."

"Hmmm, pretty name; long but pretty."

"Pretty name, ugly girl." Frank turned a solemn face to his friend, "A very, very nice girl, but poor thing's ugly as a mule." Sean remained quiet. *Poor thing. It's easy to be a homely boy, but an ugly girl, mmmmm poor thing.*

A few miles from the trading post, the two young men rounded a curve in the trail. Twenty yards ahead, a man emerged from the forest and stood in the middle of the trail with his hands on his hips. Sean's eyes went immediately to the pistol that was shoved into his belt. Quietly, and with little motion Sean cocked the new rifle. When they were almost to the man, another stepped from the woods holding a pistol. It wasn't pointed at either Frank or Sean, but it was a mistake he would not be allowed to correct.

Sean squeezed the trigger then dropped the musket and drew his first pistol. The second man had his pistol almost up and aimed when Sean's ball hit him six inches below the chin. The Brown Bess Musket fired a lead ball that could knock a horse to its knees from a fair distance. The lifeless body of the first man was carried ten feet backwards then flipped completely over. He came to a stop laying face down with his arms outstretched as though in protest. The first man had his pistol out of his belt when the ball from Sean's pistol hit him in the chest, just below his throat—a fine, large target. The St Etienne pistol fired a ball almost as big as the musket, but with much less powder behind it. The road bandit simply staggered backwards, pawing at the hole in his heart. Before the powder had cleared, both bandits lay dead.

"My God! My God!" Frank repeated several times as he sat looking down at the two cadavers—which moments earlier had been men.

Sean slipped from his horse to retrieve his musket then jumped easily back up in the saddle. Frank was staring from the dead men to Sean and back again. Disbelief took command of each feature on his brown young face. His dark eyes were opened wide and his mouth was opening and closing, but nothing came out. It had all happened so fast that Sean hadn't had time to become nervous. He placed his powder and ball bag between his legs to begin reloading both weapons. When he was finished he looked at his still shocked friend. "Amigo, there's a good chance that you n' me would be laying down there dead right now." He paused to let his words get through the haze that surrounded Frank. "If they only wanted to rob us, then it's their tough luck to pick me, 'cause I've worked too hard to let some scum like those two walk away with my money." He nudged his horse, "Let's get moving."

After a short distance Frank looked at Sean. "It all happened so fast."

Sean just nodded his head, "It always will."

They made Coyote Lake before nightfall and prepared a small fire to heat coffee water and warm themselves against the evening chill. As the water heated, the two men gathered enough wood for a good fire. Sean went to the horse he had hobbled and patted its head, then rubbed the neck beneath its mane, "I'm gonna buy you from James if he'll sell you, amigo."

When he returned to the fire, Frank handed him a tin cup of coffee then leaned back against his saddle with his own cup. "You like that horse doncha?"

"You probably didn't notice, but that horse didn't shy or startle a bit when I fired that damn musket right near his head." He shook his head a little and looked at the horse grazing nearby, "Yeah, I really like him."

"Maybe James'll sell him to you?"

"I hope so. Only the second time I've ridden him, but he's my kinda horse."

"Sean," Frank asked as he looked hard at his friend, "you ever been in anything like that before?"

Sean washed a mouthful of hardtack down with coffee, "Yeah, once. Cap'n Patrick was coming into Singapore Harbor real slow one night on a full moon, and four long skinny boats came out from the shore, really fast. We figured later that they probably thought most of us'd be sleeping or relaxed since we was so near the anchorage where all the other boats were. Devon Manieuex," he turned toward Frank, "you met him out on the boat; short, fat, bald headed little guy."

"Yeah, I spoke in French with him."

"Well, he spotted 'em and gave us time to be ready, so when they tried to board us they got a helluva surprise."

Frank's eyes were wide as Sean painted the scene for him. "Did you guys kill them all?"

"No!" Sean never exaggerated his stories, but he did like to keep his listeners in suspense to build the tension. He leaned forward and poured a cup of the strong black coffee that he loved. He looked over the top of the tin cup and could see the excitement in Frank's eyes, so he lowered the cup and continued. "There musta been four, maybe five men in each boat, and they all came up on grappling hooks they threw up over the gunwale. Patrick had given each man two pistols, and a couple had swords too. We could see 'em easy in the moonlight, so as soon as they popped their heads up over the gunwale we let 'em have it." He couldn't resist a pause when he saw Frank easing himself closer and closer as he spoke.

When he could stand it no longer Frank asked, "What did they look like?"

"The first one that came up right in front of me was a pretty scary lookin' guy till the pistol went off right in his face. Another guy right beside him had his leg up over the gunwale when I let him have the other pistol load right in the gut." He pulled the long knife from its sheath and turned it so the firelight would hit the blade. "Patrick gave me this when I first came on the boat and I've kept it sharp, ever since he showed me how." He replaced it then continued, "Another of those pirates was holding on and getting ready to climb up over the gunwale when I came down on his hand with the knife. Later I only found two of his fingers, but I'm pretty sure I whacked 'em all off. When I turned around to see what was happening on the other side it was all over. No, we didn't kill 'em all, but I'll bet there weren't more n' two that got away with everything they brought with 'em. Me and Devon each got a souvenir from that night." He leaned forward and grabbed the coffeepot.

Frank was so caught up in the story that he couldn't wait. "What kinda souvenir?"

"Well," Sean said, and then sipped the hot coffee, while letting Frank stew for a moment, "I had those two fingers in rum for awhile, but I finally tossed 'em overboard. Ol' Devon kept his and said he'll keep it in a big jug of rum on the mantle back home in Dublin."

"Fingers too?"

"Nope."

"Holy Jesus Sean, what was it?"

"Well, Devon always was trying to advance in his position on Sea Duchess, and that night he sure got a head."

Frank sat waiting to be told what the souvenir was for a full minute, until it finally came through. "Ahead! A head! He actually cut one of their heads off?"

"Yep, slicker n' a whistle. He had that sword as long as I'd known him. He often carried it in a leather sheath on his belt. Wasn't a long one, but he kept it sharp enough to shave with, and as soon as he heard them guys were comin he run below n' put it on. Said he shot two of 'em like I did then when that third guy came leanin' over the gunnel he just whacked his head off."

The two young men were on their horses long before dawn the next day heading south. Since there was no apparent reason to be in a hurry they stopped several times to let the horses rest, and stretching their own legs felt good. When the sun was sitting on the horizon they had reduced the time to arrive at Frank's Uncle Luis's ranch to a half-day ride. The country they were passing through was rolling hills with many great oaks and sparse vegetation. They spotted one oak on the top of a small hill that was twice the size of any other tree around, so they headed for it. After hobbling the horses so they could graze, Sean began gathering wood for a fire as Frank assembled the necessary items for a meal and coffee.

James Poorsmith had given them a few pieces of jerked venison, and as it soaked in a pot of water on the fire beside the coffee water, the two friends relaxed and chatted. "We're on your uncle's land right now, ain't we?"

Frank looked around in the failing light, "Mmmm, probably so. If not, we're pretty close. It's so hard to tell around here because everything looks the same." He stood up and looked south, "If it wasn't so hazy we could see San Benito Mountain, then I'd know where we are."

"That one time I was at his ranch it seemed like we were on his property for half a day before we saw the hacienda. How big is this place anyway?"

"Two hundred thousand acres."

"Mmmm, that's sure a lot of land."

"Yeah, and he has another ranch the same size in the south about three hundred miles from here." The coffee and jerky water finally boiled, so the meat was set aside to soak as they drank coffee. "What's he planning to do with all the land?"

"He's bringing in grape plants from all over Spain and Italy to start a big winery, and then he wants to create a horse ranch on the southern property."

"Holey moley, a two hundred thousand acre wine factory. Oughta be able to supply the whole world with wine, huh?"

Frank laughed, "It'll only take about two hundred acres for the entire winery he says, but he's sure a lot of people are gonna start coming this way, and he plans to develop the whole place into a big town for them to live in."

"Hey, from the amount of people that're here now, compared to the few that were here when me n' Patrick first anchored in that bay, he just might be right."

"I think he is. My dad and him made a lot of money almost the same way in Spain before uncle moved here."

Sean was silent a few moments before speaking. "You told me once that your parents got sick n' died?"

Frank stared into the fire for a long time before answering. "Yes, they both died of influenza. A lot of people in our town died of it that same year."

"What is that, a disease or something?"

"Yeah, I guess so 'cause when people get it they don't usually live long."

"You said your family got you n' your sister outa there right away, huh?"

"Yeah, mama's sister sent us to Aunt Maria in Mexico City on the next boat." Franks words were choked and Sean saw tears flowing down his cheeks, so he remained quiet. After a long pause, the young Spaniard continued. “I found out later that Auntie Angeline and Uncle Antonio both died right after we left.” He sobbed then wiped his eyes on his sleeve. “They were both so good to all us kids.” He turned a sad smile toward his friend, “If it wasn’t one of the local kids birthday, they’d make up a phony kid and say it was his birthday then throw a big party for him. They were so very good—our parents too. So many good people died that year, and a lot of the no-good ones were still there when we left. We all knew who they were, and I’ll bet they’re still there, cheating and stealing from everyone.”

“Sure seems to work out that way,” Sean offered, “my Mom n’ Pop never hurt anyone, they just worked and worked all the time then when that fire burned the apartment building, a lot of those no good ones you mentioned came and stole what little there was left.” He shook his head slowly from side to side, “Probably still around there doin’ the same thing, just like you said.” He turned to Frank, “Enough of this depressing stuff. Tell me som’n, why do you think he wants both of us to come all the way out here?”

“I been thinking a lot about that amigo and it must either be that he wants us to go to work for him, or he’s got some bad news he wants to tell me.”

“Nah, if it was bad news he wouldn’t have asked you to bring me along. Must be a job he wants us to do for him or som’n like that.”

“Well one way’r the other we’ll know by about noon tomorrow.”

It had been awhile since Sean’s only trip to Luis Javier de Carvojol’s hacienda, and he had forgotten how beautiful it was. As they approached it he kept looking from left to right at the low rolling hills of grapevines. “He’s sure been getting the grapes in the ground since we were here, huh?”

“Yeah! He already had thirty thousand of them waiting in that greenhouse back there behind the barn, to be planted, you know.”

“No, you didn’t mention it while we were here.”

“He said he was gonna start putting them in the ground right away, and had a ship coming from Italy with a lot more.” He turned and looked out over the acres of short stubby vines, “Musta got here, huh?”

“Schrreee,” Sean whistled, “that’s gotta make a lot of wine.”

“Not for me,” Frank said, “never could stand the stuff.”

“Me either. Those guys on the boat couldn’t wait for their ration of rum at the end of the day, and couldn’t believe I didn’t want mine.” He made a face, “Yech! That stuff tastes worse’n that medicine Patrick makes everyone take when they get the runs. Come to think of it, that’s probably just rum and some old rotten fish heads. Yech,” he stuck his tongue out and crossed his eyes. “At least that’s what it tasted like.” Frank laughed till tears ran down his dark face.

“My mama used to make some awful tasting stuff too, that we had to take when we got sick. We always tried real hard not to let on, but she always knew when we weren’t feeling good. Out would come that horrible stuff and you're right, yech." He imitated Sean by crossing his eyes, and stuck his tongue out too.

Both young men laughed hard then began eating the jerked venison that had been soaking. Frank handed Sean a piece of hardtack, then poured the liquid from the jerky into his empty coffee cup. After soaking it a few moments Sean took a bite. Around it he mumbled, "Y'know Frank, I never get tired of this stuff, but darned if I ain't getting tired of that horse." He leaned over and rubbed his rear end then turned toward his friend, "How long's it take a guy to get used to ridin one o' those things?"

"I like jerky okay too, but I can't tell you how long till your butt ain't sore. I guess mine ain't bothering me because I rode horses a lot when I was younger." He grinned at Sean, "Musta toughened up my rear end huh?"

"Sure hope mine toughens up soon."

"Something that I really wanna learn," Frank said, "is how to make those acorn cakes that lady at the camp we stopped at on the way to our traps made us. Mmmm boy, those were good, and looked so darn easy to make too."

"Yeah," Sean smiled at his friend, "women got a way of makin that kinda stuff look easy, but you try it and kaplop."

"Yeah, I know that, but she showed me how they wash all that stuff outa the acorns, then grind everything n' put berries and nuts in, then cook 'em real slow like, on a stone in the fire coals."

"Well amigo," Sean said as he rolled up in his blanket with one pistol in with him, and the other plus the rifle beside him on the grouund, "you cook 'em, and I'll darn sure eat 'em."

The following day both men waved to the groups of Mexican workers tending the grapevines as they rode toward the sprawling hacienda. When a bell began ringing, Frank turned to Sean, "Good timing amigo, that's the noon meal bell." He nudged his horse into a trot, "C'mon, I'm starved."

"Me too," Sean responded as he caught up with Frank. As they were tying the horses to the rail in front, Sean asked, "Does your uncle feed all of these workers?"

"Yes, anyone who works here gets the noon meal. They fix their own morning and evening meal, but he insists they have a big noon meal then a two hour siesta before returning to work."

"Hmmm, never heard of that, but I like the idea."

"Most of these people have been with him since he came here ten years ago."

Sean grinned at Frank, "Darn, he must have a good cook."

"He does," Frank grinned back, "but mainly it's because he pays 'em good and they have nice little houses to live in over behind those hills." He pointed at a couple of low hills to the east.

"They build their own houses on his land?"

"Yes. When he hires them he supplies the material and some men to help, and then before starting to work they build a house to live in."

When Sean heard the noise of people laughing he turned to see a very large group of people running toward the hacienda. "That's darn good thinking; kinda like having all family working for ya, huh?"

"That was my reasoning when I began putting this operation together."

Sean turned to see Luis standing on the porch. He was a short man, not over five and a half feet tall, and very trim. His light skin accentuated the dark eyes, and his gray hair and goatee made him look very sophisticated. The only other time Sean had met Frank's uncle; he had been impressed that he dressed as a workingman during the day and as a gentleman in the evening. He stood on the porch now in worn boots, canvas pants, and a dirt-stained shirt. When the man stepped forward and took Sean's hand, "Nice to see you again Sean," he also remembered the small, callused hands of a man that was no stranger to hard work.

As he shook his hand Sean said, "You've sure been busy since I was here, Mr. Carvojol."

In a very evenly moderated voice, the middle-aged Spaniard replied, "Progress is not accomplished by the idle, Sean." He then smiled warmly and motioned toward the door. "Come inside, Marriah has a wonderful lunch prepared." He then held the door as Sean entered. "I'm always happy to see you Francisco," he said as he shook his nephew's hand. "I have some wonderful news for you, but it can wait until after lunch."

"I just love your ranch," Sean remarked as he admired the tall, carved plaster and wood ceilings in the foyer.

Before entering the long hallway that led to the dining area, Luis said, "You'll meet the man who supervised the entire construction. He's up from my properties in the south to get the men here started correctly on some additional rooms we're adding."

Even before the door to the dining room was opened, the smells were making Sean's stomach react. He couldn't recall when he last had a real meal, so when he entered he just stood and stared at the huge table full of food. It was the same as the last time he and Frank had visited, but the grandness of the spread was still a shock to him.

Luis went immediately to the tall, thin, dark-complexioned man standing near the window. "Miguel, this is the young man I was telling you about. He is Francisco's partner in the trapping business."

The middle-aged Mexican stepped around the end of the table and took Sean's outstretched hand, "I've heard a lot about you Señor McKannah." A genuine smile and a firm handshake put Sean at ease immediately.

"You built this place for Mr. Carvojol didn't you, Mr…he turned briefly to Luis, but Miguel spoke up.

"Miguel Alvarez Donalo, and no! I didn't really build it, but I supervised the construction during trips here from the main ranch in the south."

"Do the talking when those bellies are full of this food. Come, start eating." The voice was loud and familiar to Sean. He turned toward it and there was Luis's cook, Marriah Angelica Espinoza—all three hundred pounds of her. He recalled a similar reaction the last time he ate there. When she came into the room and said 'quit talking and eat'—everyone did. Even seated, Luis's head was only slightly below the less than five-foot tall Cuban-born woman's coal black face. *She's nearly as wide as she is tall*, Sean thought.

Sean would not have known what formal dining was, even if he had been seated in front of it, but he did know that this was not it. The food was incredibly delicious, and served on plain clay platters being passed from one to the other around the table, much the same as it had been on Captain Mullholland's boat. This was a friendly gathering of hungry people, and he felt comfortable digging in and satisfying an intense hunger. As the platters came to him, Sean took some of everything. One large sweet potato, fresh corn-on-the-cob, green beans, a huge stack of tamales and another stack of tortillas. Tortillas, like the tamales were new to him but he loved them from the first bite. Then came the last platter, which was full of delicious looking fried meat. After the first taste he asked, "What is this delicious meat?"

Before Luis could answer, Marriah, who was standing near the door to the long covered passageway to the separate kitchen house, spoke. "Conejo, you like?"

"It's terrific, Marriah." He swallowed the piece he was chewing then asked, "What's conny oh?"

The huge black lady smiled, "Conejo. Co-nyea-ho," she enunciated the syllables slowly. When he still had a questioning look on his face, she brought her short ham-size arms up in front of her as she wriggled her nose. Still nothing from Sean, so she began hopping around near the door, her weight literally making the table shake. "Mmmm," she mumbled to herself loudly, "what that little thing called?"

Luis was enjoying the entire display, so he remained quiet as the huge woman thundered around the table.

"No comprender?" she said as she looked at Sean while still holding her hands up and wriggling her nose.

Sean tried to think what it might be until Luis laughed then said, "Rabbit, Marriah, they're called rabbits."

"Oh si, si, señor Carvojol." She grinned at Sean, "I member now, rabbids. "Delicioso, no?"

Around a mouthful he answered, "Yes ma'am, very delicious."

After lunch Louis spoke to his nephew, "Francisco I must speak with Miguel for about an hour, so he can get the men started on the new construction. Please show your friend around until I can get together with you both." He smiled then added, "I have some very, very good news."

"My God." Sean exclaimed later as they looked at the new horses in the stable, “These are the most beautiful horses I’ve ever seen.”

“Yes! I wonder where he got them?”

After a long walk around the hacienda grounds Sean said, “Let’s go back and look at those horses again.”

As the two young men were admiring a huge red stallion, the stable door opened. “So you’ve seen my new horses, huh?”

“Yes sir, they’re fantastic. Where did you get them?”

“That’s part of what I want to talk to you and Sean about. Come, let’s have lemonade on the verandah and I’ll tell you all about my latest venture.”

Seated in the shade of the overhanging roof Sean commented, “Señor Carvojol, this’s the most beautiful place on earth, I think.”

The small Spaniard looked around slowly then said, “Yes! It is lovely, isn’t it; I must be careful not to take it for granted.” He turned as Marriah came with a large pitcher of fresh lemonade. “Ah, thank you, Angel.”

“Theez nice,” the gigantic woman said with a smile, “I peek from tree yescrday.”

After she was gone Sean asked, “Is Angel her nickname?”

“No, her middle name is Angelica so I started calling her Angel many years ago and now everyone calls her that.”

“Wow!” Sean said after a sip, “This’s the best drink I ever tasted.”

“We raise good lemons, but it’s the regular sugar delivery from Cuba, which my supply man sends us that makes it so good.”

Both of the young men sipped and savored the drink, stopping only when Luis spoke. “First is the good news Francisco. Issabella is coming to California to live with Aunt Carmen and I.” He paused as his nephew smiled wide.

“Oh Uncle Luis, that is great news. When will she be here?”

“She is already on board the ship and will be in Yerba Buena by the end of this month.” He smiled at the young man; “You will want to meet her when she arrives, yes?”

“Yes! Oh yes. How will I know when she arrives?”

“Before you and Sean leave tomorrow give me the location where a message will reach you. The ship’s captain will notify me when they stop at Friar Serra’s mission at San Diego and I will send a message so you will know what day she will arrive in Yerba Buena.”

After sketching the location of the Hudson Bay Company Trading Post, Frank wrote James Poorsmith on the bottom of the crude map. “Me and Sean will be waiting here for your message.”

Luis looked intently at the piece of paper then said, “I know Mr. Poorsmith quite well, but I didn’t realize that is who you are dealing with. I will send a rider with the message and a list of building supplies that I need delivered here.”

"Yes Uncle Luis, he helped us greatly when we first began." He looked inquisitively at his uncle, "How do you know him?"

"He arranged for the delivery of most everything that we used to build this ranch." He had a slight smile on his face when he looked at Frank. "Has he never mentioned my name?"

"Just casually, but nothing about doing business with you."

"That does not surprise me. You young men can learn much in that small lesson."

Frank looked blankly at his uncle then at Sean who was grinning slightly replied, "Don't offer any information you're not asked."

"You are a wise young man Sean." He looked hard at Frank, "You can learn much from your friend."

"Yes, I know. Oh my God," he looked at Luis then at Sean before saying, "I haven't had time to tell you what happened on the trail here."

Luis listened intently to the story about the bandits. When Frank finished, Luis looked hard at Sean. "I have lost much of my family and am losing more soon. I will remain in your debt Mr. McKannah for saving my nephew." He leaned toward Sean, "Would you accompany him when he brings Issabella to my ranch?"

"Yessir, that's no problem 'cause he n' I are together all the time anyway."

Luis shook his head slowly up and down, "And for that I am very happy." He finished his lemonade before saying, "Now for the other reason I asked you to both come here."

Both young men leaned forward in their chairs to hear what he had to say.

"Those horses you saw in the stable are the reason. Miguel bought two horses some time back from two Mexican boys that caught them east of my southern ranch. They are incredible animals, bred I suspect by the Indians. They go into Mexico and steal horses that were bred with our Spanish horses. I believe that when bred with the wild mustangs, they produce this wonderful species." He leaned toward the two young men, "What do you think of them?"

Sean was the first to speak. "I don't have a long history of riding horses Mr. Carvojol," he paused when Luis raised his hand, palm toward him.

"Please let that be the last time you use Mr. Carvojol. Call me Luis, as I call you Sean." He smiled warmly, "Please continue Sean."

"Well Luis, I must have a natural feel for 'em though 'cause I been able to pick out a good'n from a not so good'n since I first started riding." He pursed his lips in thought then continued. "Those're the best looking horses I ever saw."

"Yes uncle," Frank said, "I agree; the very best."

"That is exactly what I said to Miguel when he and Juan rode the two of them up here for me to see."

"There's eleven of 'em in there now," Sean commented. "How'd you get the others?"

"Miguel took three men and went east looking where the boys said they caught them. It was much farther than they said, but he finally located a small herd farther north, which is why they brought them here. He thinks there will be thousands of these horses closer to my south ranch, once he has scouted the area." He paused and sat back to let his words sink in. "He will have two men scouting to the east of South Ranch soon.

"Will it still be in New Spain?"

"Yes Sean, it's a short distance from an area called Chihuahua, so it's still in New Spain Territory. New France territory is east of there."

"How far is it, Uncle Luis?"

"Where Miguel believes they will be found is about five hundred miles. The area is near the San Pedro River, a day's ride from Apache Pass."

"I've heard that name Apache before," Sean said, "they're Indians aren't they?"

"Yes, and fierce ones, but the Mexicans in the area say they seldom roam that far south."

"Wonder why they call it Apache Pass?" Frank asked.

"Probably an area where a battle between Indians and Mexicans occurred. They have fought each other for a long time, but the Apache have moved farther north, because their numbers are dwindling. I'm told they still raid into Mexico to steal the Spanish horses, but they don't bother with wild mustangs because the ones they steal are already broken to a rider."

Sean leaned forward again and looked intently into Luis's eyes. "You wanna go there and get a bunch of 'em, huh?"

"Yes, you are a very intuitive young man, Sean." He leaned back into his chair and studied the young Irishman.

"Well Luis," Sean finally said, "I assume that's part of why you wanted us both to come here."

The Spaniard took another puff on one of the Cuban cigars that he loved, before leaning toward the two young men. "Yes it is, and I have another reason that I'm going to be very honest with you both about. I'm not in as good health as I might appear, and I want Frank to learn the ranching business so I will have someone to inherit my efforts. All of my family is dead, and my sister is in poor health. That is why Issabella is coming to live with my wife and me." Luis looked out across the landscape to the south for a few moments. "I have long wanted to raise horses and this is the opportunity I have hoped for."

"Uncle Luis, I know that you have wanted me to come here and learn the ranching business, but Sean and I are learning the trapping business, and we're doing very well at it."

"Frank, I think this's an opportunity that we oughta listen to." Sean looked at Luis, "I assume I'm here 'cause you want me along too."

"Yes, because if this works out I will need someone I can trust to operate this ranch for me. I'm going to move to the south away from this cold damp weather that causes me much trouble." He looked hard at Sean, "I'm hoping that you will be interested in that position later."

Sean turned to his friend again, "Frank we can always go back to trapping if we don't like horse ranching."

After a short pause Frank turned to Sean and grinned, "You've always said we oughta get all the adventure and experience we can while we're young, so why not?"

Sean grinned back, "Trappers on Monday and horse ranchers on Tuesday."

"Very good gentlemen," Luis said, "I will give you each two hundred dollars in gold to settle your affairs while you await the arrival of Issabella. When you get here with her we will visit for a day or so then you can begin the journey to South Ranch. Carmen will take charge of Issabella, so you can prepare for the trip with Miguel to get the horses."

2

~ Ugly sister—Wild mustangs ~

When the two men arrived back in Yerba Buena, the first thing Sean did was go to the Hudson Bay Trading Company's building to talk with James Poorsmith. "Sure I'll sell him to you Sean," James said, "sounds like you n' Frank're off on a good adventure. Got any idea how long you're gonna be gone?"

"Nope, not till we get enough horses to stock the ranch, I guess. Thanks a lot for selling me that horse, James; it's the best one I've been on yet."

"No problem, that's what I have them for. Tell Mr. Carvojol that I'll be down eventually to take a look at his horses." He smiled and shook his head slightly as he pursed his lips in thought, "I think there's gonna be a big market for horses and tack in this area before too long."

"That's what Uncle Luis says. Do you know when the Santa Maribella de la Cordova will arrive from Mexico?"

"Yeah, I do. A fast little Corvette sailed in from Mexico yesterday to deliver mail and take some prisoners back. The Captain said there are two big freighters coming heavily loaded, and the Cordova's one of them. It runs in here regularly." He turned to the counter and fingered through a pile of papers until he found the one he was looking for. "Yeah, here it is, hmmm lemme see. Okay it's due to anchor out in the harbor on the twenty-eighth." He looked at a calendar behind him that he'd made from birch bark. "This's the twenty-second, so she'll be here in about a week. Why, are you expecting someone?"

"Yep," Frank smiled, "there's a good chance that my homely sister who's coming to live with Aunt Carmen and Uncle Luis might be on it."

James was silent a moment. "A person can't help how they look Frank, and I sure hope you don't refer to her that way when the girl can hear it."

"Oh no sir. I love her dearly and wouldn't hurt her for the world." He turned to Sean, "Guess we oughta be getting up there n' gather our traps and gear while we're waiting on Bella, huh?"

"Yeah, might's well."

Frank turned to their friend. "Mr. Poorsmith have you got someplace we could stash our gear till we get back up here?"

The tall skinny man in his early forties ran a hand through his sandy brown hair as he looked at Frank then Sean. When he finally spoke he was looking hard at Frank. "Francisco, I've known your uncle a long time and I watched you grow into a man. Luis has had big plans for you since you came from Spain. I would suggest," he looked at Sean who he realized from the first was the driving force of the young team, "that you sell your gear while it is in good shape then buy new if this venture with the horses doesn't work out."

"I've also been thinking that's the best thing to do," Sean interrupted, "because we're gonna be gone long enough for that gear to turn into a big pile o' rust laying around in this salty air." When Sean finished he turned to his partner, "Whadaya think, Frank?"

"Yeah it's probably the smart thing to do." His boyish grin made the other two smile. "Uncle Luis never does anything half-way. They say he came from the old country to establish a little land for his family and before long he had this two hundred thousand acres up here, and another two hundred thousand down south."

"Okay," James Poorsmith commented, "I'll be on the look for someone to buy your gear. I hope you get a good batch of pelts because I can sure use them right now to fill an order for shipment to Mexico on one of those freighters."

"Only one way to find out," Sean said.

"Yep, I'm ready to head back up to the mountains if you are."

Sean and Frank had been camped on the side of a hill overlooking the bay for two days. "Hey." Frank yelled from the edge of the clearing, "That looks like the freighter, from the description the guy at the dock gave us."

Sean quickly joined him and looked through the small folding telescope that Captain Mullholland had given him. "Sure does. You'll be able to read the name in a while but she sure fits his description."

The two men continued watching the Spanish freighter work its way into the beautiful, deep-water bay of Yerba Buena. "Them beans're done," Sean said, "so let's have some hardtack with 'em and by then we oughta be able to tell for sure if that's the one she's on." After a lunch of beans, jerked venison, and hardtack, washed down with strong black coffee, Sean walked to the edge and studied the ship through his glass. "Here, take a look n' see if that don't read what we're looking for."

Frank steadied the telescope then read aloud, "Santa Maribella de la Cordova." He turned to Sean and smiled, "She's here." He pushed the small scope back together and handed it to his friend, then continued watching the ship. Sean filled two tin cups with coffee and walked to him.

"Been a long time, huh?"

Frank paused before taking a sip, "Mmmm, this is still June isn't it?"

"Yep, and must be about time for me to be having another birthday."

"No kidding, when?"

"The twenty-fifth of June."

Frank began recalling the years. "Bella and I were sent from Spain to Mexico by our Aunt Angeline and Uncle Antonio in 1791 after our parents died of influenza. We lived with Uncle Luis' sister Maria in Mexico City till I came here in the summer of '96', so it's been two years since we've seen each other." He turned back to the bay and looked at the ship over the rim of the tin cup. "I can't wait to see my little ugly duckling."

Sean felt a slight pang of sorrow for the homely little girl that he had never even met. "You n' her are close, huh?"

Frank hesitated a moment then turned to Sean with tears in his eyes, "Oh yes amigo, very, very close." He returned his gaze to the ship that was now preparing to drop anchor, "I can't wait to see her."

The two young men broke camp and headed down toward the dock as the small fleet of rowboats headed out to bring the passengers and supplies to shore. The dock that served as seawall wouldn't be completed until the following year. The first of three boatloads of people had nothing but men on board. The second was full of men and two older women. Frank was straining to see if his sister was on the third boat, as the crew pulled at the long oars. "Oh thank God, there she is."

Sean watched as the small boat docked and the passengers were helped up onto the small makeshift wooden pier. When he saw the slightly overweight young woman with heavy work boots on her feet climb clumsily up onto the pier, he searched her face for similarities to his friend. He quickly returned his attention to the remaining passengers. *Two old women and one pretty young girl,* He thought, as his eye's returned to what he was certain was Frank's sister. *That must be her.* He moved behind Frank and followed behind as they approached the chubby young woman.

When the beautiful young girl that Sean had mistaken for a child yelled, Francisco, Sean instantly knew that his friend had played a joke on him. He began beating Frank's head with his leather hat. "Ugly duckling, huh?"

After wrapping her arms around Frank, the girl looked at the handsome young man standing behind him. She turned her deep seagreen eyes toward Frank and asked, "Why was that redheaded boy hitting you with his hat?"

Before Frank could respond Sean said, "There was a scorpion on his head Issabella, and I quit being a boy a long time ago." He removed his hat then added with a wide grin, "My name's Sean Brennan McKannah."

Issabella liked his smile and forward manner, so she returned his smile, displaying a mouthful of teeth like her brother—pearl white and perfect. "Hello Sean Brennan McKannah, do you know the rest of my name?"

"Nope, just Issabella and I wouldn't know that except your Uncle Luis has been talking so much about you." He nodded his head at Frank. "All he's talked about was his ugly duckling sister coming from Mexico."

She looked at her grinning brother then back at Sean. "I'll find out about that later." She released her hold on Frank and stepped around to face Sean. "Issabella Magdelena Ruiz Santiago." She held out the most delicate hand Sean had ever touched then added, "But my brother has called me Bella for so long that is all I am called now."

Sean shook her hand gently then asked, "Is Bella what you like to be called?"

"Yes." The five-foot tall, light-skinned beauty with thick, luxurious brown hair, replied.

"Then Bella it is."

"Are any of those your trunks?" Frank pointed to three large trunks being put on the pier by the crew of the rowboat.

"They are all mine," she answered, "I brought everything in the world I own because I never plan to go back to Mexico."

As the three young people walked toward the trunks Sean asked, "Didn't you like it in Mexico?"

"Yes, I liked it okay but my Aunt Maria is very ill, and she is the only relative I have there." She looked at Frank, "I do not think she will live very long."

He pursed his lips and shook his head, "I wish I could have come for a visit because she was always so nice to me."

After looking the trunks over good Frank said, "We didn't know how much stuff you would bring so we didn't rent a carriage yet. We better go and get one now before they're all taken."

As the three passed a pair of wharf rowdies on the way to the stable, one of them whistled at Bella. "Hey little puta, when you finish with those two boys come back and spend some time with a real man."

Frank had seen Sean's lightning moves before, so he wasn't surprised when he jumped between the two of them and hit each a few times before they even knew they were in a fight. With the one on the ground moaning he grabbed the talkative one by the neck and was holding him up as he pulverized his face. When the one on the ground was about to get his pistol out from his waistband he felt Frank's boot hit the side of his head—just before the lights went out.

Sean had the other young man at a run toward the water, with his hair in one hand and the seat of his filthy britches in the other. He literally propelled the man through the air and into the bay. When he returned Sean said, "Might help him recognize a lady if he ever meets another one."

Bella had never seen anything like it before, and was silent as they walked to the livery stable. She watched Sean at every opportunity when she thought he wouldn't notice, but her brother had been watching her, and when Sean was beyond earshot he said, "He's a very good man, Bella."

"Hmmm," she mused, "is he always that violent?"

"Only when someone messes with him or someone he cares about."

"You and your sister ride together in the wagon so you can visit," Sean said when the trunks were loaded onto the cargo carriage, "and we'll tie your horse to the rear. I'll follow, and then scout ahead when necessary."

As their carriage headed down to the trail that followed the bay out of Yerba Buena, Frank and his sister noticed the two men leaning against bundles of redwood being readied for shipment to Mexico. They had bathed their wounds but were still a mess. Each had a flintlock pistol in his belt so Frank turned to watch. He enjoyed the look on their faces as they saw Sean's Brown Bess pointed straight at them as he passed. Frank could also see their eyes going to the pair of St. Etienne pistols hanging in the leather holsters on Sean's hips. Frank quit watching when he saw his friend bring the horse sideways as it sidestepped following the carriage so the rifle remained on the two wharfrats until they were beyond pistol range.

They weren't far from the growing new city they were leaving, when Sean came alongside. "It'll be dark in an hour, so I'm goin ahead and find us a good spot to camp for the night." He looked at Frank and grinned, "How's your memory?"

"Just fine," he said grinning as he patted one of the pair of Memory pistols Captain Mullholland had gifted him with, "both of 'em." He and Bella watched Sean ride ahead and disappear over the hill. Frank turned, "Do you like my friend?"

"Yes, he has a nice, friendly smile. Where is he from with that red head of hair?"

"A place called Ireland on the other side of the ocean."

"Hmmm, I've read about that place. Now," She turned to him, "what about that ugly duckling sister you were telling him about?"

They were still laughing about Frank's joke when they came over the top of the hill. Bella gasped when she saw Sean in the distance surrounded by Indians. "I don't think there's any problem," Frank said, "we know a lot of the natives around here." He kept the horse at a steady pace as they neared the group. He turned to Bella and smiled. "That's Quintin. He's a subchief of the Pomo tribe that we've traded with north of Yerba Buena where they live. I wonder what they're doing way down here?"

Frank stopped the carriage next to the group of Indians and lifted his hand in friendship, "Quintin."

The young Indian walked to the carriage and signed 'Hello my friend.' He then signed, 'You have a squaw now I see.' Frank knew the Indian would want to negotiate for hours to purchase Bella if he knew she was not married, so he signed 'Yes, I bought her from a boat captain.' The Indian leaned forward to look closely at Bella then signed 'Too skinny, you must make her eat more pig fat and acorn cakes so she can have many babies and work hard.'

'Yes,' Frank signed, 'soon she will be as wide as she is tall and I soon will have my own tribe.'

Quintin laughed as he related the conversation to his friends who were still talking to Sean. They all looked at Bella and laughed along with their leader. The Indians were soon walking north along the trail that the three young people had just came south on. "What were they all laughing about?" Bella asked.

"If they knew you were my sister and didn't have a husband, they would have wanted to camp right here for a couple of days and try to negotiate a deal to buy you. I told them I had traded a pig for you to be my wife."

"Hmmm," she mumbled, "but why were they all laughing?"

His grin widened, "They said she is too skinny, go get the pig back."

Frank was aware of her feisty nature so was surprised when she just smiled, "So they like their women fat, huh?"

"Yeah, and able to work all day n' have lotsa babies."

Sean had chosen a spot on top of a flattened hill, so they unhitched the horse and put it on a picket among good, thick grasses. Sean gathered wood for a fire as Frank rubbed down the carriage horse as it grazed, then his own. He removed Sean's saddle then put the horse on a long ground picket and began rubbing it down. Bella leaned against the carriage and watched at how efficiently the two men worked together. When Frank was finished, Sean had bacon sliced and was frying it while coffee water heated. As they ate beans and bacon with the hardtack Bella asked, "Why did we stop up on top here instead of down there among those lovely trees?"

"Storm season's here," Sean answered, "and the trees draw lightning, plus you never wanna get trapped in a flash flood."

"Hmmm, I see."

Sean watched the lovely head of chestnut brown hair flow back and forth. *Prettiest woman I've ever seen.*

"What were the Pomo doing way down here?"

"Trading."

"What in the world would they have to trade with?" Bella asked.

"Baskets," Her brother answered, "they make baskets that all the tribes around here, plus the settlers want. You can fill one with water and it won't leak a drop. You can also boil water in 'em to cook vegetables, crabs, n' stuff."

She looked skeptical at them both, thinking they were joking with her again. "Boil water in a basket?"

"Sure can," Sean said, "works as good as a tin pot."

"Hmm, that's interesting, and I hope I get to see one."

"You will, 'cause everybody's got 'em."

"What were they trading for?" Frank asked.

"They brought four donkeys loaded with baskets and got two of those plank boats the Chumash make."

Frank commented around a mouthful, "They already have crews paddling them home, huh?"

"Sure do, they left yesterday. Quintin and his bunch stayed to party with the Chumash. He said they like coming to their camp down here because of the berry wine they make." He grinned at Bella, "Said they all had big storms in their heads this morning."

When Bella saw Sean's grin, she felt a slight shiver go up her spine.

Frank wanted to sit up and talk with his sister but Sean could see her eyes trying to close after they had finished eating. "Let's get you a bunkroll set up beneath the carriage," He said as he stood. "I'm gonna go off a short distance and get some rest m'self." As he was getting her a canvas ground blanket, and situated it beneath the carriage he said over his shoulder, "There's another good reason I like it up on top like this. I can see n' hear anyone coming long before they," he turned a roguish Irish grin toward her, "or **it**," he emphasized the last word, "gets too near."

It was the third time she had seen Sean's handsome face twinkle with the natural Irish humor he inherited from his parents. A butterfly fluttered in her stomach.

Sean sat against a tree in the darkness and dozed on and off through the night. Even dozing, he remained alert to possible danger. He rubbed the sleep from his face with both hands as he watched the sun come up over the mountains. He always preferred an early start, but he could see the weariness in the young woman's face when she arrived, and knew how much a long sea voyage could take out of a person not accustomed to it. He quietly re-picketed the horses in fresh grass, then rubbed them all down as they ate. When he returned from the last horse, he was surprised to see her sitting next to a small fire, with Frank still sleeping nearby.

"Good morning," he said quietly.

"Yes, it is isn't it." Her smile warmed him more than the early sun on his back. "Does he always sleep like this?" she nodded her head toward her brother.

"Only when he knows I'm on watch." He sat down cross-legged next to the fire then added, "I sleep the same way when I know he's standing watch." He watched as she used the small mortar and pestle to grind coffee beans.

"This isn't your first time out in the wild, is it?"

After pouring the grounds into the tin pot she looked at him with her beautiful green eyes—he barely heard what she was saying "…would take me with him fishing in the mountains near our home in Spain."

"Uh, uh," Sean stammered, "your daddy?"

She pursed her lips and looked sternly at him, "You weren't listening."

"Uh, no I wasn't. Sorry, I was thinking about which way we gotta go this morning."

By the look she had seen in his eyes she felt certain that he had been thinking about her so she repeated, "My Uncle Antonio always insisted I go when he took Frank fishing in the mountains near our home in Spain. He showed us how to start a fire, make coffee, and even how to catch, clean and cook the fish."

"Frank told me about your Aunt and Uncle. They sound like great people."

She looked straight at him for several seconds before speaking. "Yes they were, and I miss them very much." After shoving a few more sticks beneath the coffeepot she said quietly, "And I always will."

"Ahhhh, what a lovely smell to wake to in the morning."

"Ain't morning," Sean said, "darn near afternoon."

"Huh, what," Frank began scrambling to untangle himself from his blanket, "afternoon?"

"Will be in a few hours," His sister grinned at him.

The late start put them near Coyote Lake about two hours before dark. "There's one of the most beautiful lakes I've seen, just ahead," Sean said, "let's spend the night there. We can have some fresh fish, and there'll be plenty of berries."

"Hey great," Frank answered before Bella could say a word, "I'll make us some acorn cakes while my fishing little sister gets us some dinner."

"Ah ha, big brother remembers who caught all the fish?"

"How could I not remember? The way you always rubbed it in."

"No patience for fishing, that boy," she said to Sean.

"I already knew that but we're about to find out another thing about him."

"What is that?"

"If he paid attention when some Indians showed him how to make acorn cakes."

"They'll be good," Frank said with a laugh, "I plan to start selling them to the Indians."

"With the baskets I'll make."

"Do you know how to weave those baskets?" Sean asked Bella as she was pouring his coffee.

"About as good as he can make those cakes, I bet." Her laughter warmed him more than coffee ever had.

An hour later, Sean had the horses picketed in good grass and was putting together a circle of small stones to build a cooking fire. He cut Bella a long pole and tied one of their fishing lines to it. She quickly caught several grasshoppers for bait as Frank was busy collecting acorns. Before dark, Bella had cleaned eight large perch as Frank pounded the meat from a hatfull of acorns. He washed the tannic acid from the nutmeat, as the Indian women showed him, added a little flour, and then mashed the berries into the thick, mush-like dough. While Sean moved the horses to another grazing area, Bella began frying the fish. Frank tested the flat rock he had placed in the fire earlier and found it hot enough to begin cooking his cakes. As they began shrinking and bubbling around the edges he slid his long hunting knife under each golden brown cake to turn it.

As Sean was picking the last of the flesh from the fish bones he said, "I wonder if Luis will let Bella go with us to get the horses?" He grinned at his friend.

"Uncle Luis might, but never Miguel. He is very protective of young people and would never allow it." Frank went back to eating, but spoke around a mouthful, "This's eating like we ain't had yet."

Bella was putting some of the honey they had bought at the trading post on her second acorn cake. "Francisco, I would never have believed you could ever cook anything so delicious, taken from the woods."

"Yep Frank, these cakes are every bit as good as that Pomo squaw made."

The Spaniard beamed, "No compliments please, just toss coins to the cook."

The three travelers got an early start the next morning and were under way before the sun came blazing through the forest. A couple of hours before dark, Frank said, "We're definitely on Uncle Luis's ranch." He pointed ahead, "That's San Benito Mountain."

As they approached the ranch itself, Bella asked, "What are all these little trees?"

"Wineberry trees. Uncle is going to start a winery."

"Grapes? My goodness there must be thousands of them."

"You know how Uncle Luis is?"

"Yes! Daddy too; they always did everything in a big way."

Luis and Marriah were standing on the porch as the carriage approached.

The rotund Cuban cook had left Mexico two years before Bella moved there, so she had never seen her. Luis spoke of her so often that she felt as though she had known her all of her life. Her Uncle helped Bella from the carriage and as all before her had, she immediately liked the huge black woman that was hugging her. "Oh my goodness," she said in very broken English, "Hermosa Princesa! Hermosa Princesa! You here now." She took her by the hand and headed for the front door, "We eat now. Oh my, Oh my, you so skinny."

"Yes," Luis said, "let's eat before this poor woman has a heart attack. She's been cooking all day and running to the porch to see if you were on the horizon." He issued instructions for two of his men to tend to the horses and carriage after setting the trunks on the porch. "Come boys, and I hope you brought an appetite because she has a feast prepared."

"I could eat half a cow before it stopped running," Sean replied.

"Yessir, me too Uncle, I'm starving."

"Good, Good, very good. She will be pleased." He held the door open for the two young men that were going to play an important part in the years he had left to live.

The visit to Luis' North Ranch was a pleasant experience for all three of the young people. Sean was quick to realize that Frank's uncle was very busy, so he suggested that they leave for Luis' South Ranch. Luis understood, and made a mental note to keep an eye on his nephew's young friend. He seldom saw such astute observation in someone as young as Sean. He smiled at Issabella. "Yes, I believe that would be a very good idea. Your Aunt Carmen probably hasn't stopped walking the porch, hoping to see you coming over the hills."

Sean scouted the trail ahead as Bella rode with her brother in the carriage. "I wish I could have spent more time visiting with Uncle Luis," she said, "but I can see he is very busy with his grapes and the new winery he's building."

"Don't worry," Frank answered, "he'll be down to South Ranch soon, because he loves the horses more than he does the grapes."

"I'm looking forward to seeing Aunt Carmen," she said, "it's been so long."

"I'm looking forward to seeing her too. I haven't seen her since I left to go trapping over two years ago."

"Mmmm," She mumbled as her brow wrinkled in thought, "the last time I saw her or Uncle Luis was when they visited Aunt Maria in Mexico, one year after we were sent from Spain."

"Phew. That was a long time ago. I was only ten, so you musta been eight. Do you remember her well?"

"Oh yes," Bella said with a laugh, "very well. She scared me a little when I first met her."

"Heh, heh, she's a pretty stern lady."

"But I remember her as very kind, and she treated me like her daughter. She insisted Aunt Maria have tutors teach me English." She looked around at the terrain before continuing, "She said I would one day live here in this new country."

"I think Sean was correct."

"About what?"

"He said Uncle Luis and Aunt Carmen have been planning our lives since we lost our parents."

She was silent for a long time before speaking. "Except for Aunt Maria we are the last of his blood line so it might be true."

"And I guess Aunt Maria won't be around long will she?"

"No, she is a very sick woman." She pointed ahead, "Here comes Sean."

Frank nodded. *She is always very happy to see him returning from scouting the trail ahead. I think love's flower is beginning to bloom.* He turned to her and saw the look of happiness on her face and knew he was right.

"Hey amigo, hi Bella," Sean greeted them as he reined his horse to walk along beside the carriage. "There's a nice area among the trees ahead up high enough, and there're no storm clouds, so let's spend the night there and get an early start tomorrow."

"Sounds good to me," Frank answered, "I think we've made good time today."

"We have. Does the trail stay this good all the way to South Ranch?"

"Mmmm," Frank said, his brow wrinkling in thought. "I've been trying to remember but it's been a long time and I was on horseback, but I think it was a good trail most of the way."

Two hours before dawn Sean had a small fire going and was putting the coffeepot on. As the other two shook off the night's ground aches, Sean went to the horses with a little grain and water. Under the cloak of morning darkness all three took care of their necessary toilet demands and when the coffee was ready so were they. "Uncle Luis said it is almost three hundred miles to South Ranch," Bella said, "how many days do you think it will take us to get there?"

Frank continued sipping coffee as he thought about it then asked Sean, "Whacha think, about ten?"

"Yeah, that's what I figured at first, but if we don't have any problems or bad weather I'm starting to think maybe a day or so less."

"Hmm," She mumbled, "longer than I thought it would take."

Frank looked across the top of his tin cup; "It'll be worth it when you see the beautiful ranch."

"I'm not complaining, I just didn't realize this country was so wild and undeveloped." Her grin lit up the entire camp for Sean. "I thought," she giggled, "we would be traveling on a road with cantinas like we did in Mexico."

"Probably ain't any people between here n' the ranch," Sean commented. "Except a few Indians of course," he added with a grin.

"Will we meet any more of them?"

"Probably not," Frank answered, "they stay away from the trails 'cause they've had some bad dealings with white men."

"Like what?"

"Our government in Spain," Frank said, "has been establishing missions all along the coast and it has pushed some of these Indians from their own land. There have been some small battles and some killing."

The weather stayed warm and clear so the three young people made good time, and encountered no problems until they were within a day's ride of Luis's South Ranch. They were traveling along the flat route, east of what would eventually become known as the San Bernardino Mountains. Bella was the first to spot the riders. "Look," she pointed to the east, "someone's coming."

Sean was driving the carriage while Frank scouted ahead. Frank soon came at a gallop from the direction the riders were approaching. "Five men coming this way," he said as he brought his horse beside the carriage.

"Take these reins," Sean said and handed the leather ribbons to Bella. He then jumped from the carriage and went to his horse that was tethered behind. He had named it Cuch after a character in an old Irish fable that he'd loved as a child. "Frank," he yelled, "take the right side and don't let 'em get around behind us."

Sean positioned himself at the left, just ahead and a short distance from the carriage horse then turned in his saddle and yelled to Bella. "Stop the carriage and hold tight to the reins so they don't run away when these riders approach." Sean could see the fear and uncertainty in her dark eyes, but he also saw strength as she nodded her head, before taking a good grip on the leather reins.

The five riders approached in a tight knot, so Sean knew they were all a bunch of weak men, uncertain of their own individual worth—and drawing strength from close contact with each other. When they were close enough to hear, Sean yelled, "That's close enough, whadaya want comin' up on us like this?" He had nudged Cuch sideways to the men and the Brown Bess was now pointing straight at them.

The scruffy looking man on Sean's side spit a stream of tobacco. "A closer look at that little beauty you got there in that buggy." He turned and grinned at his scruffy looking friends, "To start with." He kicked his horse lightly in the flank with his spurs and began to slowly move ahead.

Sean brought the barrel of the Brown Bess around to cover the huge bearded man. "Stop," he commanded in a tone that should have warned the fool trying to get behind him.

"Kiss my ass you Mick bastard, I want that woman."

The slug from the Brown Bess knocked the man from his horse and placed him on the ground—his blood changing the color of the sand black. Before his rifle hit the end of the tether, Sean had both St. Etienne's out of their leather holsters and pointing at the four men. Frank's Memorys were only a split second behind him and were covering the four men with shocked expressions on their faces. It had happened so suddenly that not a one even made an attempt to draw a pistol. "You wanna die here with him or head on to where ever you were going?" Sean's calmness even frightened Frank and his sister. The four men knew they were facing certain death, so they all raised their hands. "Can we get him up on his horse so's we can bury him?"

Sean nodded with his head toward the mountains. "Move on, the buzzards n' animals'll take care of him." Without taking his eyes from the men he said to Frank and Issabella, "You two go ahead while I keep an eye on these guys. I'll catch up to you." He sat and watched as the four men galloped west while Frank and Bella continued on along the trail. When he could no longer see the four men, he jumped down and rolled the body over and pulled the pistol from the man's holster. While looking at it he said quietly aloud, "Damn fool! I'll bet he never cleaned this thing once." *Probably wouldn't even have fired.* He unbuckled the holster and bullet belt then pulled it from beneath the dead man. After hanging it on Cuch's saddle horn he returned to the body. "What's this?" He pulled a gold chain from the corpse's vest pocket and was surprised to see a beautiful gold watch on the end. "Looks like you made a score back down the trail som'rs." He shoved the watch down into his pocket then climbed back into the saddle and retrieved his rifle to reload it. Without another glance at the cadaver he headed toward his friends in the distance.

"Here," he said as he came beside Frank who was now driving the carriage, "this gun'll clean up and probably be all right." When Frank finished putting the gun and holster behind the seat of the carriage Sean said, "I'm gonna scout up ahead to be sure those guys weren't running with a bigger gang." He touched Cuch with his spurs and galloped ahead.

Bella remained silent as her and Frank moved ahead, but finally spoke. "My God, he didn't say a word." She turned a wide-eyed expression to Frank. "He just shot that man."

"Yeah he did, Bella."

"Did what?"

"Say som'n to the man."

"What?"

"He said stop."

Her eyes opened bigger and her mouth dropped open. "That's all?"

"That's all you get with Sean. The guy shoulda stopped." He turned a serious face to his sister, "He probably saved your life." Frank turned his head in the direction the men had gone. After turning back he said, "And mine too, for that matter."

She remained silent for a long time. "Yes, they must have figured a woman would be in a carriage like this."

"Yes. That's the only reason they woulda been heading toward us. Men usually stay clear of each other out here."

"Hmmm, I can see why."

An hour before darkness Sean said, "We oughta camp out here and go on in tomorrow. I don't like coming in on anyone after dark, even when they're expecting us."

"Yeah, I agree. This's wild country to be traveling at night anyway."

Bella smiled at Sean, "My eyes will be closed anyway as soon as I lay down." She stretched as a quiet yawn escaped. "I am so tired."

"We got us a buncha bacon left so we'll have ourselves a little celebration for the last night on this trail."

Bella sipped her coffee as the bacon sizzled in a tin skillet. She was watching Sean clean the dead man's gun. "I think you probably saved my life back there."

He stopped and looked at her. "Those men were up to no good comin' right at us like that."

"Yes, I see that now. Frank explained it to me." She reached over and touched his arm, "Thank you."

She had only touched him a few times and each touch sent a funny feeling into his stomach. He had never been with a woman, and all he knew, about what went on when a man and woman were alone, was what he'd heard from his shipmates on Sea Duchess. He liked the feeling, but it also made him restless and uneasy. He paused a moment to let the butterflies in his stomach settle down before speaking. "I don't like killing a guy like that, but when I looked into his eyes I saw an animal looking at you."

"I saw it too, and it terrified me."

Frank chuckled, "I don't guess I'll ever get used to how fast you figure things out and react. I about jumped outa the saddle when that Brown Bess went off."

"I noticed," Sean said, "that you would have already had a Memory in each hand when your boots hit the sand."

"I'm gettin' quicker, huh?"

"Yeah, sure are."

Two hours after the sun was up they were still a couple of miles from the ranch when Bella pointed ahead. "Riders."

Sean had already seen them and had his small folding telescope out. "Good ones this time."

Miguel Donalo and four Mexican ranch hands approached, smiling. "We didn't expect you for at least another day." Miguel smiled as he removed his sombrero. He looked at Bella as he bowed in the saddle. "Welcome to El Cielo de los Caballos, Senorita Issabella Magdelena Ruiz Santiago."

"Just Bella," she said with a big smile, "and you are Miguel Alvarez Donalo, the wonderful man my Aunt Maria said came from Mexico with my Uncle Luis to settle in California."

Miguel smiled appreciatively and returned his sombrero, "Come, breakfast is being prepared as we speak." He turned his beautiful black stallion and headed off at a run while waving his arm for them to follow.

They all complied, and soon the carriage horses were flying as Bella held the reins. Sean raced along beside her and could tell by the look on her face that she was thrilled. *What a woman*, he thought.

Carmen Esmeralda Maria de Ginorella married Luis twenty-five years earlier in Spain when they were almost exactly the same age—twenty. Her family also controlled great wealth although they were not as influential as Luis' family, which had very powerful government contacts in Spain.

But wealth and power had nothing to do with Luis and Carmen's relationship when they met. All who knew them recognized the signs of a true and lasting love. After twenty-five years together it was still there, but their inability to produce children left a hole in their lives. When her nephew Francisco came from Luis' sister in Mexico to live with them, her dreams of a child to raise were almost satisfied. He was fifteen years old and a joy to be around, but she also saw in him the same fierce need to be independent that had been so obvious in her husband. He always displayed courtesy and concern for the aunt and uncle that had taken him in when his Aunt Maria's health began to fail. She could tell that the boy loved his uncle, but was pawing at the ground to be able to run free. On a trip to North Ranch, Frank met an old trapper heading into the high country. The old man's stories were fueling the dreams that lived in the young Spaniard's head. He asked his uncle for permission to accompany the trapper into the wilderness.

Luis hated to see the boy leave but he knew that forcing him to stay would lead to disaster. Luis encouraged his nephew, but emphasized that the ranch would always be his home anytime he wished to return.

When Carmen was told that the boy was going into the mountains to become a trapper, she was distraught. Now, two years later as she stood watching Issabella's carriage approach, she felt her dreams of having a child to raise being re-kindled. She had met Bella only one time on a trip to Mexico to visit Luis' sister, shortly after the two children came from Spain. When she looked into the eyes of the nine-year-old girl she saw her own sister, now dead of influenza. Carmen wanted badly to bring the children to California but Luis said, "We are going to be very busy building our ranch. We will have no time for them here, but in Mexico they will have my sister Maria and her husband Alonso to give them the attention that all young people need."

Carmen knew he was right but as they left Maria and Alonso's hacienda for the ride to Mexico City and the boat trip back to Yerba Buena, she looked out the rear of the carriage at the beautiful young girl who waved until she could no longer see them. Tears ran down her face as she watched the same girl, now a woman, approaching her porch.

"Aunt Carmen," was all that could get around the tears in Issabella's voice.

"Oh my beautiful Issabella. Oh my! Oh my!" Carmen said it over and over as they stood on the porch embracing.

Frank and Sean tied their horses to the rail and stood waiting as the two women held each other and cried. When Carmen looked across Bella's shoulder she said, "Francisco is that you? Can this handsome man possibly be the skinny Francisco that went into the mountains to catch animals?" She kept her arm around her niece but opened her other one for Frank to come into. "Oh Lord," she said as she looked up to the sky, "thank you for bringing them safely back to me."

After a rapid burst of Spanish, with Sean could only catch an occasional word, Carmen stopped and looked hard at Sean. "You are the Irishman that went into the mountains with our Francisco." She released the two and stepped down from the porch holding out a delicate, but well-used hand. In perfect English she said, "Sean McKannah, correct?"

She smiled and he knew where Frank and his sister got their smile and perfect teeth.

"Luis has sent letters when someone was coming this way and he has talked a lot about Frank's partner, Sean. Come!" She took his hand in hers and led him to the porch. "Mi casa su casa!" Carmen smiled. "Our home is your home from this day forth."

The following morning, the two men joined Miguel as he prepared the supply wagons for the trip east to bring back the wild mustangs. "How many wagons will we need?"

"Two," Miguel said, "one small cook's wagon and one big one for the gear we will need when we locate them."

"How many men will go with us?" Frank asked.

"There will be eleven of us. We three; Echevarria the cook, and seven very good horsemen."

With the two men helping him, Miguel had the axles of both wagons greased by the time Carmen's cook was ringing the huge dinner bell, which hung on the front porch. "Lunch is ready." Miguel said, and they all headed for the water pump to wash up.

Sean was surprised at how many people worked at the ranch and now came at a run for lunch. "Wow!" He exclaimed, "Do you have this many guys working here all the time?"

"Yes," the foreman answered, "and the newest man has been here for over two years."

When Sean noticed that all of them headed around back; he asked, "Same eating situation as at North Ranch, huh?" Luis' huge land parcel near San

Francisco was called simply North Ranch for so long that it became known by that name. His ranch in the south was actually named Horse Heaven, but most referred to it simply as South Ranch.

"Yes, one huge table for the hands on the enclosed verandah out back, and a table for the family inside in the dining room, but we all eat the same food at lunchtime."

"Breakfast and dinner's up to them, huh?"

"Yes, if they don't want to bother with breakfast or dinner, at least they can look forward to a good lunch."

"And," Miguel smiled as he held the door open, "they all make excellent wages. They all have enough money saved in five years to return to Mexico and open a business—but they never leave."

"Hmmm, no wonder. Sounds like they have a darn good deal here."

"They do. That is why we take great measures to select good men," he turned to Sean, "so they will stay with us."

Three days later, Magdalena Hidalgo, the cook, was in the kitchen three hours before dawn preparing a big breakfast for the eleven men. An hour later they were all digging into huge stacks of tortillas, chicken tamales, fried eggs, a pot of menudo, and a sauce that Sean would later say, "That's what I'm gonna use to clean the rust off of that old pistol."

"That is a sweet sauce," the trail cook Echevarria *ECHY* Obregon said smiling, "compared to mine." The five-foot-tall fiftyish man smiled wider, "Caliente."

All of his friends and workmates at the long table shook their heads up and down as each emitted whooeee. Several shook their hands in the air. "*Muy caliente*." A couple added seriously, "*Pero bien*." Another said, "*Sabroso*."

Sean had been learning Spanish from Frank, so he knew bien meant good, and sabroso was tasty. He smiled at Magdalena, who stood a little shorter than Marriah, and was a good fifty pounds heavier. "*Muy sabroso*," he said as he pointed to the sauce and smiled, then waved his hand across the entire table of food, "*todo esta sabroso*." She smiled at the compliment and returned from the kitchen a few moments later with more tortillas.

An hour later the small caravan was heading east toward the canyon country where the mustangs had been seen.

Frank nodded, “I’ll go out on the right and do the same.”

When the two returned, they saw Miguel and Laz riding in. Everyone was very relieved to see Miguel grinning. “We’re gonna camp with my sister and brother-in-law tonight.”

Frank and Sean crowded in on him as he explained while they moved toward the Gila River. “My sister married a Kawevikopaya when our parents died. She was only thirteen and didn’t want to go to an orphanage or a mission.” He turned and grinned. “She had been beneath the skins with him before, so when he asked her to go with him, she said yes.” He furrowed his brow in thought, “Mmmm, that must be,” he paused in thought, “hmmm I’m forty so she’s thirty-eight. Holy Maria, she’s been with Montezuma twenty-five years. It must be five years since I have seen her.”

“Montezuma?” Sean asked.

“Montezuma Wappanaja. He’s chief of a band of Kawevikopaya Yavapai. They’re actually Tonto Apache and are sometimes called Mojave Apache. They’re probably going north a little ways to find Mescal.

“That some kond of animal?”

“No,” Miguel smiled, “a plant they eat and make a drink from, plus they have a way to make fiber from it for their ropes and stuff.” He chuckled adding, “Montezuma says he has kept Molina all these years because she makes the best mescal.”

Miguel and his men arrived at the Gila River as Montezuma’s band of thirty Apache was setting up camp. While the Mexicans were hobbling their horses in a grassy area to graze, Miguel asked Sean and Frank to accompany him to Montezuma’s camp; a short walk away. As they approached the Indians, Sean watched with interest as several men, women, and children were tying together a dome shaped hut. Others were already covering it with brush and sticks.

“Hola Montezuma,” Miguel called.

A short stout Indian turned and smiled when he saw who was calling his name. He came to the tall thin Mexican and put his arms around him. “Cunado Miguel.”—Brother-in-law. The two men spoke in rapid Spanish that left Sean catching only a word here and there. When Miguel introduced them, Frank replied in Spanish while Sean could only smile and nod. The chief’s one remaining eye, beside the patch covering the empty socket of the other, bore intently into Sean’s eyes. The one eye kept going back and forth from one to the other as if in search of something he had lost.

He held the man’s stare until the Indian shook his head up and down slightly and spoke softly to Miguel, “Bien hombre.”

One of the women—short and wide, came with a wide smile from the group working on the chief’s hut. Sean and Frank could tell it was Miguel’s sister when she came to him and put her arms around his neck as he stooped to hug her. She smiled at both men then pulled Miguel by the hand to a group of women waiting nearby. Frank said to the chief, "We must go take care of our horses before it is too late."

Montezuma gave each man a sharp nod and signed 'tomorrow.' He smiled broadly when Sean signed back 'I look forward to seeing you with the rising sun.'

An hour before dawn, Sean was standing in the darkness surveying the camp. When he saw the fire begin to blaze at the chief's camp he walked over. "Hola."

He recognized the one eyed chief's voice when he called into the darkness. "Caballo rojo ven aqui."—Come red hair. He wondered how the man knew it was him in the darkness. *Recognized my voice I guess, same as I did his.* He passed the small bag of coffee beans he brought to Montezuma then signed, 'Do you like the bitter drink?'

'Yes, very much but we do not often get the beans.' The two men were still talking in sign language an hour after dawn when Miguel walked over to join them.

"Looks like rain coming so we better get across the river." Miguel spoke Spanish to his brother-in-law and sister then listened as Montezuma spoke at great length in his language. On the way back to their camp he told Sean, "Montezuma says there are many good horses where we are going, but to watch out for a small band of young Chiricahua Apache that are causing much trouble for everyone."

Miguel and his men crossed the Gila River without incident and headed west toward their next camp. The seventh night away from the hacienda found them camped just north of Montezuma Peak—a short ride from a small settlement that would eventually become Phoenix, Arizona. The next morning they came to the Gila River again and followed it for two days until it turned east. On the tenth night they camped on the bank of the San Pedro River. "We are very near the horses," Emiliano *Emil* Huerta said. He pointed to the mountains in the northeast. "When Miguel and I came here the first time, we found them in the Table Lands of those Mescal Mountains."

Sean and Frank had nicknamed all of the Mexicans so each could remember them when they first arrived at the hacienda, and now everyone was referring to them by those names. "Emil," Miguel said, "can smell horses a mile away."

"Anyone standing downwind," Emil said with a grin, "can smell horseshit a mile away, but I can smell the horses when they are near, no matter which way the wind blows." The six foot tall, too-thin man dug a fresh chew of tobacco from his leather pouch and filled his lip. He looked toward the mountains, "I don't smell them but they are there."

"Well," Frank said, "we'll be crossing the San Pedro in the morning, so we'll soon find out."

The following morning Sean stayed to the rear and kept an eye out, while Frank went ahead of the wagons that were crossing the river. He followed the cook's wagon across then rode to a nearby hill with Miguel to look for signs of horses or unwanted company. "Emil is going ahead," Miguel said, "and when we get to the Table Lands I'll be surprised if he hasn't located a herd."

"What are those mountains to the south of us?" Sean asked.

"Those are the Santa Catalina Mountains. I've been up in them and I know there are horses there, but they would be very difficult to catch because there are no canyons near the flat plateaus like there are in the Mescals to trap them in." He pointed toward the flat areas in the distance. "See those low, flat places?"

"Yeah."

"Those are the Table Lands and just behind them are several dead end canyons where we hope to run the herd into. That's where we can separate the stallions we want to take home for our breeding stock." He pointed at another flattened area near the base of the mountains. "We'll set up camp there and tomorrow locate a good canyon to set up our trap."

"I'm really looking forward to seeing how you guys go about this."

Miguel smiled at Sean. "My people have been catching horses this way for a long time. I went with my father when I was six years old to catch horses to take to Mexico City and sell them to the government for their soldiers. He broke one for me to ride and I had him for many years."

"Do you think Luis has a good idea here?"

"A very good idea because these mustangs will produce excellent horses when bred with the mares he has coming from Spain."

"Wow!" Sean said, "Bringing them all the way from Spain, huh?"

"Yes! He has thirty high quality mares coming now, and they should be here soon after we get back."

"Ain't that gonna take a long time to build up a herd with just thirty mares?"

"Ha, ha, ha," Miguel laughed quietly, "Senor Carvojol is a very smart businessman. He has arranged for a hundred more mares to be delivered from Mexico in a month. That is why we built so many corrals at the ranch. The ones from Spain will produce a very high priced horse crop and the Mexican ones will be our main stock to supply the settlers that are already coming to California."

"Sounds good, now all we gotta do is provide the stallions."

"I have great faith in Emiliano."

"Yeah, Emil sure seems to know what he's doing."

As the men started setting up the camp, Emiliano came riding in from the north. He dismounted and spit a wad of spent tobacco on the ground. His smile was a breath of relief for Miguel. Twenty years together, he knew the man—he had located horses. "Not three miles from where we stand is a very large herd, with one big black stallion in charge, and many younger stallions."

Miguel grasped the tall, skinny man's hand and patted him on the back, "Muy bien amigo, muy bien."

Everyone at the fire t hat first night was enthused and talking about the coming roundup of horses. Sean asked Miguel, "How do we go about getting the horses into a canyon?"

"First we locate the right canyon," Miguel answered, "then we use the material we brought to fence off a section in the rear part of it. After that we run a long fence out from one side of the front that can be carried across to close off the canyon entrance. Then we must carefully circle around to the other side of the herd so we can start them running toward the canyon. "We will have Victoriano *Victor* Madero waiting near the entrance to the canyon. He can ride the belly of a horse, so when the herd gets close, he will slide down to the horse's side and they will follow it into the trap."

"Sounds pretty easy."

"It is, but we must conceal the fence wire with brush and small bushes so they don't see it or they will veer away." He smiled, "It is also going to require some very good riding to keep them coming toward it."

"I'm still learning," Sean said," but Frank and your other men are the best I've seen on horses."

"Yes," Miguel commented, "they are all very good." He looked at Sean hard a moment. "You try very hard Sean, and I think you are soon going to be a very good horseman."

"Thanks Miguel, I really am trying hard, but when I see these guys on a horse I know I have a lot to learn."

"Knowing that you have a lot to learn is the first step in learning."

Emiliano located the perfect canyon by late morning the next day, and by noon they were all working on the fencing. An hour before dark everything was set and ready to bring the horses to the corral. "It will be a half-day ride to get around to the other side of the herd, so we all better get to sleep early, because we move out a couple of hours before sunrise. I will take the first watch after we eat."

Sean took the last watch and was surprised when he headed toward the cook's wagon to wake Echy. Before he got near it he saw the little man lighting the fire to start breakfast. "How do you always get up at the exact time, Echy?"

The man continued getting the huge coffeepot ready and answered Sean over his shoulder. "I set my mind to whatever time I know I must get up then tell myself over and over that many people are depending on me."

Sean squatted and watched him shake the salt from the cow belly into a container for later, and began to prepare the menudo. "Ever been late?"

"Yes, but only one time." He looked up from the tripe sizzling in the skillet and grinned. "I was the cook for my father and ten men taking cattle to

Mexico City." He removed the skillet and began adding the other ingredients to simmer. "I was eleven years old and stayed up all night looking at the stars that first night out. The men had to work all morning until noon with nothing to eat, so my papa made me go two full days with not one piece of food. He said I must learn what it is like to work hungry."

"You musta snuck something to eat?"

"Not even a crumb. My father said if he saw food in my mouth he would remove it from my belly." He stood up and removed a knife with a blade over a foot long, "He pulled one like this from a leather sheath and shook it in my face." He began breaking three-dozen eggs into a pot.

"Think he woulda done it?"

"I have thought about that a lot over the years. I think he loved me but he was a very tough man."

"Well Echy, I reckon he helped you establish some pretty good working habits, huh?"

"Sure did. How about getting the guys up? Coffee's about ready."

All of the men ate a big breakfast knowing there would be no eating again until the horses were either in their trap, or the men were sitting around a fire bitching about how, 'We let them slip away.' As Echy began straightening up the cook wagon and washing the dishes, eight men rode north into the darkness. Victoriano Madero had stood silently watching as the men climbed into their saddles, and then he went to his horse to double check the tack. Riding low on the side of a horse directly in front of a band of wild, frightened mustangs was not a good time for a saddle cinch to slip. Satisfied that all was in good order he too climbed into the saddle and headed toward the Aravaipa Canyon area north of the camp where their trap was set.

Lazaro Alvarez led the band of horse catchers in a wide arc around the canyon lands where the wild herd was grazing the day before. The word Apache had stuck in each man's mind, so when the sun arrived, each looked in every direction as they proceeded. "What's up Laz?" Sean asked.

Before the man could answer, Miguel rode up and asked in Spanish, "Are we close to them, Lazaro?"

Frank joined the three men and sat silent with Sean as Miguel and Lazaro spoke quietly in Spanish. Lazaro started moving slowly ahead as Miguel turned to Frank, "Explain that to Sean while I tell the men." He turned and rode toward the five men sitting quietly nearby on their mounts.

"Laz says to watch the black stallion that is their leader, and if he tries to break away when we start them running toward the trap, we must shoot him or they will all follow."

Sean nodded and brought the Brown Bess up from the leather scabbard that Benito *Benny* Costillo had made for him. Satisfied that it was primed and ready, he returned it. Miguel and the five men came beside them, and they all headed in the direction Laz had taken. "When Laz comes to us with word that they are still there," Miguel said, "we must form a barrier to keep them against the mountain. The trap we set in the canyon is less than two miles away, and they should follow the black stallion into it if we do our job well."

An hour of slow, careful, quiet riding later, Lazaro came slowly toward them. "They are all still there," he said to Miguel in Spanish. Sean grinned at Frank because he understood. "We will ride slowly in a long single line," the scout continued, "and get as far as we can before they sense something is not right. When the black stallion alerts them they will run for their lives, and we must ride like the death demons they think we are." Miguel nodded and turned to ride along the line and explain the plan to each man.

Lazaro knew they were very fortunate that the wind was blowing from the south. The men were laying on their horse's necks as they watched the herd of mustangs grazing to their right, near the mountain walls. The nine riders were almost even with the herd, and only a hundred yards out, when the black stallion raised his head and looked directly at Sean. *My God! I hope I don't hafta shoot that magnificent animal.*

For a full minute the leader of the herd looked at the strange horses while trying to decide if they were here to join his band. Suddenly his nostrils flared and he sensed an unusual odor. Alarms went off inside his head—*humans*. He had dealt with them before and knew they were bad. He reared up on his hind legs and screamed to his subordinate young stallions to start the mares running.

Silence and stillness was suddenly a mass of screaming riders and thundering hoofs as the air was filled with the disturbed dust of the desert floor. The black stallion made one brave attempt to challenge the human demons holding he and his band against the walls. The waving sombreros and screaming men was more than even this courageous beast could cope with. He led them straight to the canyon trap where Victoriano Madero was waiting.

Victoriano's ears picked up the sound of hoofs long before another man could have possibly heard them. When the black stallion came thundering around the bend he was in position and ready.

The beautiful black stallion saw the strange horse ahead and received a mass of signals in its brain. Everything was happening too fast to take time to decipher it all so he instinctually followed the horse—hoping it would lead his band to safety.

Victoriano lay tightly on the side of his horse and led the mustangs directly into the canyon. The riders rode to the wooden stakes holding the fence wire that was secured to the canyon wall, and pulled them from the ground. They rode as a unit, carrying the poles and wire to the other wall where they dismounted and began pounding the stakes into the desert floor again.

~ The herd of mustangs was trapped ~

"Now the hard work begins," Miguel said as he squinted beneath the sombrero so he could see the herd. "Just look at that black stallion looking for a way to lead his herd out of the trap."

"That is excellent," said Alvaro *Al* Carranza, "he is a determined leader and the others will follow him home once we have broken them all."

Sean understood, when Emiliano said. "I guess that's a job for me." He enjoyed watching the Mexican bronco riders at the ranch trying to out-do each other. Each said he was the best at breaking wild horses. It was a friendly competition between men that had ridden together for many years, but it was always an intense situation when they discussed handling horses.

"Ha," Alvaro said with a loud laugh, "you must get glasses for your old eyes, Emiliano." He turned and grinned at the watching men, "That is a horse not a burro."

"We still have some daylight to work by," Miguel said, "so let's start culling out the stallions so we can release the mares."

"I have counted twenty-nine stallions old enough to break," Antonio *Tony* Cardenas said as he walked up, "and another sixteen very young males that will follow us home."

"Very good," Miguel said with a huge grin, "much better than I could have hoped for. All the more reason to get those mares out of there and on their way so those young males will depend on the stallions instead of their mothers."

All ten men climbed in their saddles and waited as Echy opened the fence. They went in at a gallop with Echy riding on the back of Miguel's horse. He was dropped at the fence that was stretched across the narrow opening at the rear of the canyon. As the men got a couple of lariats on a stallion he would open the fence to let them through, then again to let them out once the lariats were removed from the horse's neck.

Everything went smooth, and by late afternoon all but the black stallion was in the rear of the canyon. Echy named the huge stallion SATANAS after watching him dodge the many lariats. He was a master at using the mares to shield him from attempts by the *demon humans* to throw the ropes over his neck—and then kill him.

Everyone watched as Victor lay against the side of his horse once again and eased toward the black stallion. The men kept the stallion busy watching them when they realized what Victor was attempting. The man was too close when the stallion finally saw him, and he was suddenly wearing a lariat. Instantly there were three more around his neck and all of his struggles were in vain. He too was led into the rear canyon. He reared up on his hind legs and kicked at the enemy ferociously, but the lariats remained on his neck.

When the fence was opened to allow the mares to escape—they remained, waiting for their leader. Several shots were fired to get them out and heading back to the tablelands where they came from.

"We gonna let the stallions back in the big corral?" Sean asked Miguel.

"No! They will be more subdued in the morning if left confined in that small area tonight."

"Breakfast was early the next morning and by daylight the men began taking turns digging a six foot deep hole that the center pole would be buried in. Sean and Frank both took their turn at the shovel to dig and the scoop to remove the loosened dirt. They removed the dirt from the hole but neither man knew what the hole was for.

A couple of hours later, the pole was sticking over six feet out of the hole as it was being tamped solidly into a rock-steady position. When Miguel was satisfied that it was solid enough he said, "Okay let's get one of them in here and get started."

When Benny opened the fence a little, Laz rode in and flushed a young stallion into the large corral. Victor was waiting and had a lariat on its neck instantly. When he rode to the pole and wound the rope around it, Sean realized the need for such a secure pole. The riders prodded the stallion around and around the pole, until it was on a rope not two feet long. Tethered so short it could do nothing but stand there as two horsemen crowded in on it. One was carrying a small, light saddle. When he threw it on the horse's back, little Benny rushed in and displayed a talent no other could master. Before the horse knew there was a human beside him so close, the cinch was tightened and Victor was in the saddle. The bronco tried to buck the intruder from its back, but being tied so close to the pole made it a futile attempt. One of Benny's heavy leather ropes was placed around the horse's neck for Victor to hold, and the lariat was removed. For a moment the stallion stood motionless.

Victor wasn't fooled for a moment, and when the bomb went off beneath the horse, throwing them both into the air, he was prepared. It was the first time anything had ever been on the young horse's back, but it wasn't the first time Victor had been on a wild horse. Sean's mouth hung open as he watched a show he never dreamed he would see. Frank had seen many horses broken to the saddle while he was at the hacienda, but they had all been subdued a little before being ridden. His eyes were also wide as he watched.

There were times the horse was almost standing on its nose and at other times it was on its hind legs dancing around in circles. "A barnacle on a ship," Sean said.

"What?" Miguel asked.

"Victor." Sean said as he shook his head from side to side. "He's like a barnacle on a ship. No matter how big the seas are y'ain't gonna get rid of it."

After watching the men take turns riding the stallions Sean said, "I'm gonna ride the next one." When it had been wound close to the pole he crowded Cuch up next to it. Al threw the small saddle on as Benny pulled the cinch tight. Sean slipped over to the stallions back as he had seen the others do. He wrapped the thick leather rope around his gloved hand and hugged the stirrups tight to its belly with his high-heeled boots. When the lariat was removed, the horse calmly walked backwards a few feet. Sean was no bronco rider but he was no fool either. He wasn't about to fall for the horse's ploy, and relax. He was looking at Laz sitting on the fence, and instantly he was three feet in the air and looking at Miguel on the fence at the other side of the corral. When the stallion's feet hit the soil Sean thought his spine would come out the top of his head. Another leap and they were facing Laz again. The men cheered as the horse did spins, stood on its front feet then on its rear ones. When it went too far to the back and fell sideways on the ground everyone held their breath. Sean deftly stepped from the saddle but remained astride the beast until it regained its footing. When it was on all four feet again the men cheered like never before—Sean was still in the saddle. A few token runs around the corral and it stopped. Echy rode up and slapped a smear of white paint on its rump to mark it.

Sean slid from the saddle as Benny untied the cinch. The stallion joined the other fifteen horses carrying the white mark of defeat.

"Let's eat some lunch then break a few more before dark," Miguel said.

"That was some ride," Frank said as they all headed for the cook's wagon, "you looked like an old pro."

Sean simply grinned.

"I'm gonna try one after lunch."

"Might as well Frank, 'cause this's all gonna be yours one o' these days."

"Y'know, I'm beginning to think you're right."

After lunch and a short siesta, Frank rode two with no problems, and Sean rode two more.

"That's enough for one day," Miguel said, "it's getting too dark. We have only three more plus the black stallion to go, so we will be ready to head home by tomorrow."

The men built a large campfire and sat around later than usual talking about the horses. "You are learning, old tobacco eater," Alvaro said to Emiliano. The six-foot-three-inch, two-hundred-pound man pointed at skinny, six-foot-tall Emiliano. "Old man if you keep at this you will soon be a good rider of burros."

"Amigo, if you keep putting your big lard ass on these poor beasts we will soon only have old swaybacks to offer Uncle Luis' customers."

As the men gathered around their fire, laughing about the day's events and their upcoming departure for home the next day, an unwanted pair of eyes was lying nearby watching. The fifteen-year-old Chiricahua Apache was returning from a trip to visit with his sister when he saw the fire, and changed course to investigate. He was part of the band of young renegade Apache that Miguel's brother-in-law had warned him about. As he lay in the darkness watching the laughing men, he thought, *if I could slip into their camp and kill one of them I would be recognized as a great warrior when I returned to my Chief with a fresh scalp.* The young Indian watched for an hour and realized that these were not traveling settlers but trail seasoned old Mexicans who would not be easy to sneak up on. He decided to move away from the camp and watch them when the sun came up, so he could tell his Chief what they were doing and how many there were. He was soon positioned among some boulders, dozing and awaiting the arrival of the sun. Long before the sun came up, he was awakened by the sound of voices. He reached into his traveling bag and pulled out a strip of jerked venison to satisfy his hunger. He was able to get an accurate count of the men in the camp—eleven. He lay motionless and watched. The young Apache was one with the land; even his color blended in.

When the black stallion was all that remained Miguel said, "Let's get him to the pole and get it over with." It took Miguel and three other men to get another lariat on the horse's neck. The magnificent animal put up a brave fight, and when Benny moved in behind him he kicked out with his rear legs. Unfortunately for the horse that's exactly what the diminutive Mexican was hoping for. The second time the horse kicked out at Benny he tossed one of his rawhide lariats on the animal's leg. With ropes on both ends, the animal was helpless and easily led to the pole. Laz and Al crowded in on him and when Laz tossed the saddle on the beast's back, Benny pulled the cinch tight. He removed the lariat from the horse's rear leg as Antonio removed the lariats that had been on its neck since first captured. Al had the thick rope around the animal's neck and slid easily over onto his back. He leaned forward and talked quietly to the horse. His friends all said, "Al can talk to a horse and they understand what he is saying."

"Easy now Satanas," he whispered, "I am going to help you be a better horse." He nodded to Venus at the pole, who then cut the lariat and freed the horse. Everyone held their breath, including Emil, when Satanas, as all now called the black stallion, slowly backed away from the pole. The horse walked majestically ahead a few paces as though this was a normal happening. Al was not fooled by the horse's clever ploy, and had his heels buried deeply into the horses flanks. Suddenly the animal went straight up with all four feet off the ground and when it came down it changed ends in a blur of motion. It charged straight for the pole and Al had to lift his leg to keep it from being crushed against it. The horse bounced from the pole and charged the wall fifty feet away. It changed course at the last second and Al had to lift his leg again as the horse smashed against the nearly vertical stone wall. Al could sense the frustration in the huge animal, and continued talking to it as it leaped into the air—repeatedly. The men sat on their horses and watched as it repeated its jumps around the corral. "I have never seen a horse jump and buck so many times," Victor said.

"I've never seen anything like this in my life," Sean replied.

That Mexican can ride as good as an Apache. The watching young Indian's dark eyes were moving slowly across the men below him.

"Open the fence," Al yelled to Echy.

Frank helped the cook untie the rope and pull the fence wire back so Al could ride through. A few more token bucks, that were half-hearted at best, and the stallion stopped. "Let's you and me go for a nice ride and show these people what a fine fellow you are." Al leaned far forward to talk close to the horse's ear as he stroked its sweaty, glistening black neck. With Al gently nudging it in the flanks, the horse reluctantly walked through the opening. After a brief resting period it was ready for round two and began running as fast as it could. "The poor beast doesn't know," Victor said, "that it has a tumor on its back."

"Ha, ha," Laughed Emil, "it can roll in cactus and still Alvaro will be on its back."

Before the horse and rider were out of sight, the horse stopped running and was easily turned back toward the camp and approached the watchers at a brisk trot.

Miguel walked to Al. "The wagons are ready to roll. We're leaving the wire here for the next trip so if you're ready to ride that devil we'll release the stallions and see if they're gonna follow him."

"Let's head home," Al responded.

"You wanna change saddles?"

"No, we'll leave this one on him till tonight."

The Apache watched as the twenty-nine stallions and sixteen young males came running from the corral. They stopped a short distance away and several began to whinny. The black leader's whinny settled them down and in a short time the men were heading for home.

As soon as the wagons and men were on their way west, the young Apache began the one mile run to where he had hobbled his horse. He was not the slightest winded as he quickly removed the rawhide straps from the horse's feet and effortlessly leaped on its back. With his short hunting bow tucked neatly in the quiver along with his arrows, he urged the horse south toward his Chief's camp. He had over eighty miles to go to deliver information that he knew his young, self-appointed War Chief would act upon if he could deliver it in time. *If this horse drops beneath me, I will continue running until I arrive at our camp in the hills.*

The hills that the young band of renegade Apache made their base camp was the Baboquivari Mountains near the state of Sonora Mexico. As the sun was setting, Miguel's wagon train and herd of stallions was making camp. The Apache boy removed his buckskin trousers to line a shallow hole he had just dug in the sand. The naked youth then began carving a cactus to get to the water inside, so he could get his horse and himself a drink. Moments later, after drinking a small amount, he stood by as his horse drank the remaining water. He then removed his bow and arrows from the rawhide quiver and poured some of the grain into the hole then filled his own mouth as the horse ate. Ten minutes later he poured the remaining water from the cactus into the hole. After each had a small drink, he pulled his buckskins on, and once again they were both heading southwest.

"We're moving along good," Miguel said as he sat on his horse with his leg over the pommel and watched Al hobble the black mustang, "but it's always a lot slower going home than it is coming."

Without looking up Al said, "Gotta move kinda slow n' easy anyway, so we don't spook 'em, boss." He looked up at the tall, slender man he had worked with for twenty years then added, "They're scared to death, so it wouldn't take much to set them off." He finished with the horse's feet and stood. "Only thing keeping them together is their trust in this magnificent animal."

Miguel watched as the big Mexican began whispering in its ear as he gently stroked the stallion's neck. He could hardly believe that the horse, now making gentle whisper-like sounds, was the Satanas they had battled only the day before. As Miguel rode back toward the fire next to Echy's cook wagon, he thought, *incredible horse incredible man*

Long after the sun had washed away the day's shadows, the young Apache knew his horse was going to drop dead if he continued. It wouldn't have mattered, if the animal could have continued running at a good pace, but it was beginning to slow and was having trouble with its footing. It had put in a run through the night that would have made a Pony Express Rider in the coming years proud, but had spent its energy doing it. The boy stopped the horse and slid from its back. He knew they would each need water and food if they were both to survive the miles left to cover. He removed his buckskin trousers again and lined a shallow hole. Another cactus yielded enough water for them both to quench their thirst. He chewed his mouthful of grain as he watched the horse eat the remainder he had emptied from his quiver. With the buckskins back on, he removed the simple halter from the horse's neck so it wouldn't get caught in a tree or fall beneath a hoof to stumble the beast. A long look at the terrain ahead convinced the youth that camp was about twenty miles away. As he tightened the strap holding the quiver to his back he spoke to the horse. "You will find your way to the camp after you have rested, but I must run swiftly now." He turned toward the Baboquivari peaks in the distance and began setting the pace that would soon put him standing in front of his Chief.

Sean guided Cuch beside Al and Satanas. "That's a fantastic horse."

"Yeah, and I hate to remove something like this from nature."

"I know whacha mean, but we might be saving it from being killed by a cougar or some hungry Indians."

"Yes." The man said with a halfhearted grin, "That's what I keep telling myself."

Sean nudged Cuch into a gallop toward Miguel, riding ahead of the men and horses. "I was talking to Frank awhile ago Miguel, and if you agree we'll spread out on each side to keep an eye out for trouble."

"That's a very good idea. I've been thinking about those renegade Apache that Montezuma spoke of."

"Me too, there's som'n about that word sticks with ya, huh?"

"Some, like Montezuma are very good people, but when the Apache is bad," he turned to Sean and raised his black, bush-like eyebrows, "he is as bad as man gets."

Before Sean rode to the south he said, "If you hear either of us fire a shot, start looking for cover." The Mexican nodded and watched the Irishman he had come to like very much, ride off into the scrubland toward the foothills below the Momoli Mountains.

The nearly exhausted young Apache finished telling his nineteen-year-old chief what he had seen. The short, muscular Indian wearing nothing but a loincloth and knee length deerskin moccasins spoke. "You did very well. We can trade those horses that are now ready to be ridden, to the white traders for guns when they come again."

Within an hour from the time that the boy had ridden in with news of the wagons, men, and horses heading west, the band of Apache were heading northwest for Montezuma Peak. The chief had told his men, "We will slip into their camp and slaughter them in their sleep." His youthful inexperience would cost he and his followers dearly. He underestimated the wilderness-wise, trail-hardened group of nine Mexicans, one Spaniard and an Irishman with an incredible memory.

Sean McKannah's ability to memorize became apparent at age four when he watched his father do an impromptu Irish jig, as his mother clapped her hands and laughed. When the father sat down and returned to his ale, Sean amazed them both by walking to the middle of the room and imitating the dance perfectly. Six months later he was sitting on the floor at his father's knees listening to him recite an ancient Irish poem. Both parents' mouth dropped open when Oliver Newman McKannah stopped, then after only a moment's hesitation the child at his knees stood and walked to the center of the room. With one hand over his heart, as he had seen his father do many times and the other stretched out, he began. Not a word was missed and the tempo was correct. From that day until the fateful fire that robbed him of his parents, his mother worked tirelessly to further develop the boy's incredible memory. Myra Ellen Waithe-McKannah was partly to blame for the grief that the small band of Apache Indians was riding into.

As Sean McKannah rode south, he angled to the west. His mind was unfolding a roadmap of the terrain he had memorized on their way to the Mescal Mountains. He stopped several times to survey the area running parallel to the route home. He and Frank continued scouting for two days and saw nothing to alarm them. On the third day, Frank was three miles north of the wagons while Sean was in the Sand Tank Mountains. He was looking through his telescope at the valley between the ridge he was on, and the Sauseda Mountain range to his south. An hour of looking produced nothing to alert him until he made one last sweep of the valley before moving on. The riders he saw were too far away to count but he estimated that twenty or more men were riding in the direction of where the wagons would soon be. He continued watching to determine who they were and exactly how many.

Sean watched, as the same young boy who brought the news to his camp came riding from the north with his chief and small band of Apache. He had never seen the young Indian, but he knew where they were going. *Those Indians are heading toward the Gila River where Miguel and the men are going. He'll camp near the canyons of Montezuma Peak tonight.*

Sean waited until he could count the nearly naked warriors, before he stood and fired a shot into the air. He quickly re-loaded his St. Etienne pistol then headed toward his friends at a gallop.

"We will continue to the mountain," the young chief said, "and wait for nightfall." He patted the long knife in the sheath on his loincloth belt. "No one knows we are here and when they feel our blade on their throat in the darkness tonight it will be too late." When he heard the gunshot he knew he was wrong. Youth and inexperience was working against him.

The distant gunshot turned Miguel in his saddle. He was not a man to weigh the odds or delay action when action was needed, so he waved his arm toward the others and charged toward Alvaro. "Let's get them into those canyons ahead until we see what's happening."

The young Apache Chief didn't have to say a word, or even wave his arm. When he burst forward at a full gallop, the others knew they were going to attack the men with the horses.

Sean was laying forward on Cuch and moving toward his friends at a speed he had not yet asked of his horse. As he emerged from the foothills of the Sand Tank Mountains he looked to his left and saw the small band of Indians running their mounts hard toward Montezuma Peak. The roadmap in his mind began unfolding to show the small canyons at the base of the mountain, so he knew exactly where Miguel would head the horses. As Sean charged forward he recalled the high mounds just ahead and knew he could get in a position unseen by the Indians angling toward him. When he stopped Cuch and tied the reins to a small bush, before coaxing the horse to lie down. He had just enough time to take aim on the closest man to his position.

Sean had fired the Brown Bess Musket many times in practice to prepare himself for an emergency such as the one facing him now. He knew the weapon could reach out and knock a man down at seventy yards. He waited until the man in the sight at the end of the thirty-eight-inch-long barrel was no more than thirty yards away. He held his breath and slowly squeezed the trigger. Without waiting for the smoke to clear, he was instantly on Cuch and heading toward his friends.

Frank was now back from the north end where he had been scouting, and recognized the sound of the Brown Bess. He was relieved when he saw his friend's horse running at full speed toward him. He joined the other men herding the wild mustangs into the canyon ahead.

The nineteen-millimeter slug rushed down the long unrifled barrel and sped toward the boy who had brought the message to his Chief. It struck him in the chest with such force that it lifted him from his horse's back and sent his body beneath the hoof's of his friend's horse running directly behind him. It didn't matter to the boy because he was dead by the time he was entangled with the hoofs, but it had deadly consequences for his friend. His horse stumbled with its front hoofs knocked from beneath it and the young rider was thrown over its neck as it went down. The sixteen-year-old Apache's neck was broken instantly as he hit the ground.

Sean McKannah would never know that he had killed two people with one shot from a Brown Bess musket.

Sean thought *that's one less renegade Apache charging the horse train of Miguel Alvarez Donalo.* Things were not going good for the inexperienced young chief.

As Alvaro Carranza urged Satanas into the canyon, the mustangs followed with the sixteen young males close behind. Miguel and the men positioned the two wagons at the entrance of the narrow opening to the shallow canyon. Sean was lying prone on Cuch's neck when he galloped through the opening between the cook's wagon and the canyon wall.

The young Chiricahua Apache Chief was convinced by what the young boy had told him that he was up against a small band of horse wranglers that would be easy to defeat, even though his original night plan had been thwarted. Each Indian had an arrow ready as they raced by the opening. Three never even had a chance to shoot the arrows before the eleven men fired almost point blank into them. The young Chief now had only nineteen men with him when he brought his horse to a stop and ran on foot to the boulders just beyond the canyon entrance.

When Sean heard many gunshots he looked quizzically at Frank then turned to Miguel. "I didn't think they had guns."

The Mexican leader shrugged his shoulders and looked over the front of the wagon.

Miguel recognized the voice yelling in Spanish, "Brother-in-law, it is I."

He yelled to his men, "Hold your fire, it is Montezuma." He yelled back as loud as he could, "Montezuma old friend, you are a long way from the Gila River."

The short, stout, fifty-year-old Kawevikopaya Yavapai Chief rode slowly around the cliff toward the entrance to the canyon. Twenty young Indians from his camp followed him as he passed through the opening. "They are all dead, and it is a good thing too, because they were the ones who have caused all of the trouble for our people."

Miguel walked to the old man sitting on his horse. "Our cook fixes good food; will you and your men eat with us?"

"Yes," the one eyed man said with a smile, "but be warned, we are a hungry people."

Montezuma Wappanaja and his men followed Miguel into the canyon to begin preparing a circle of stones for a fire. Alvaro said, "I will go to the horses and be sure there is no way out of the canyon.

The Indian chief could see the Mexican's horses behind the wagons. "I can see that you found the horses, cunado Miguel?"

"Yes, and they are even better than the ones I caught the last time I was here; especially a big, black one." As he told his brother-in-law and the Indians with him about the capture of the stallions, Al was talking to the black stallion to reassure it that all was well.

Emil and Venus arrived but a short time later with two bags of grain and a canvas to line a feeding pit. When the three men had the pit full of feed, they returned to the supply wagon for water bags to carry back to the horses. With the horses fed and watered they returned to the cook's fire. Echy had finished a huge pot of menudo, which was simmering, and he was busy making 100 tortillas. They each took a tin cup from the wagon and filled it with coffee then sat listening as Montezuma explained how he and his men had arrived at such a good time.

"We were on our way to this area to set many rabbit snares for food and pelts, to make winter clothes, when we heard the shot fired. I thought it might be time for you to be returning, so we came swiftly to investigate."

"I'm very glad you did, cunado Montezuma," Miguel said as he nodded his head. "So the dead ones are the renegades you spoke of when we came through?"

"Yes," the old Chief said with a tinge of sadness in his voice, "and I am glad we came, but I do not think you and your men needed our help." Miguel and the others remained silent until he continued. "Their leader, who I myself just killed with this rifle, was Managus Wannahanjas." He sat staring into the afternoon fire a moment then continued. "He was my sister's boy but was trouble since a young child. A year ago his tribe threw him out because he was stealing from his own people. Many of the other young bad ones went with him, and they have been causing much trouble ever since." He looked hard at Miguel. "They will cause trouble no more and it is a good thing for everyone."

Sean was getting better with every conversation he was able to hear in Spanish, so he said to the Chief when he finished speaking, "Especially us. Thank you for your help."

Montezuma looked hard at Sean a few moments. "Who are you?"

"A friend from far across the big water, who has come to make a life on this land."

As the Indians ate, Echy was beginning to think he was going to be forced to make another huge pot of menudo and another fifty tortillas. He was relieved when they finally stood and followed the Mexican wranglers' example, and put their tin plates on the rear of the wagon.

Montezuma stood and handed his plate to one of his men then turned to Miguel, "Thank you for the food, cunado. Now we must continue to the area where we will set our snares." He waved his arm toward the area where the dead bodies lay and spoke rapidly in his own tongue. His men silently departed as he spoke again in Spanish. "I told them to leave the dead ones alone so their spirits could leave in peace for the other side. Now they are going to remove their scalps so we can show their people that they fought bravely. We will find the one your man with red hair killed and take his scalp also."

It didn't take the Mojave Apaches long to locate the two bodies and put together what had happened. As they rode toward their snare setting grounds the Chief spoke. "The young one with the red hair will be a great warrior because he has the spirits with him."

"Yes," the Indian riding beside him said, "two enemies with one bullet."

Miguel decided to remain in the canyon until morning because of the late time when all was finished. The men all appreciated the opportunity to get a good rest and slept soundly except when on watch. At dawn, Echy had the horse hitched to the cook wagon and led the group into the scrub terrain toward the Gila River. Tony followed in the supply wagon and the rest helped Al, who was once again aboard Satanas leading the stallions and the young males out of the canyon. Each man looked at the scalped bodies as they passed and knew very well it could easily have been them lying there in the morning sun, if the group of young Apache had been wiser and waited, then quietly slipped into camp after dark.

Frank turned to Sean as they passed the bodies, “Might have been bad if you hadn’t spotted that group and prevented them from sneaking in among us at night.”

Sean nodded his head, “That’s probably what they had in mind.”

Miguel hoped to see his sister again for a short visit, but once they crossed the Gila River he could see that Montezuma’s camp was no longer there. *They must have moved his people into the hills before he and his hunters went out to set snares.* They moved more swiftly toward the ranch, as the wild horses became accustomed to following their leader.

Several days later they entered the ranch and immediately began separating the stallions into different corrals according to their individual traits that Al had been observing on the trail home.

It took three hours to separate the stallions, and during the entire time Sean kept looking toward the hacienda, hoping to get a glimpse of Issabella. Since the day she arrived he had thought about her constantly. The time it took for him and Frank to get her to South Ranch gave him an opportunity to see what she was really like. By the time the three young people arrived at the hacienda he was feeling things happening inside that were completely new to him—having never been with a woman. His only experience, on a close-up basis, was during the time he spent at Luis’s North Ranch watching Marriah Angelica Espinosa, Luis’ huge black Cuban cook, and the short time here that he observed Carmen Esmeralda Maria de Ginorella—Aunt Carmen as Frank called her.

“I really like your sister,” he said to Frank as they worked together to get the mustangs into the right corrals, “but I sure don’t know anything about girls.”

“Amigo, you came to the wrong guy for help in that department ‘cause I’ve never really had anything to do with ‘em.”

After a few moments of silence Sean asked, “Do you think she likes me?”

Frank paused to think about it before speaking. “I guess so from what I remember of our trip together here, but I can tell you one thing I’ve learned from just watching the one’s around me—they’re a bit strange.”

“Yeah, they sure don’t think like we do.”

"No they don't amigo, and they're like a friendly old dog." Frank turned a charming boyish grin to his friend. "When you ain't expecting it, grrrollf." he made a loud noise that sounded to Sean just like a wolf. "They have their teeth in you for doing something you don't even understand."

The two young men laughed and went back to work separating the horses, as Al pointed them out.

Sean's glances toward the hacienda all afternoon proved fruitless. He never got a glimpse of Issabella. That was not the case with the young girl inside the hacienda. She stood for two hours at the window, behind the curtains, and watched the red headed young Irishman she had found charming the minute she saw him at the waterfront in Yerba Buena. "I didn't know you had such an interest in horses," her Aunt Carmen said as she passed her.

"Oh yes, Tia Carmen," she used the Spanish phrase she had as a child instead of the Aunt Carmen she now used. She knew that her aunt, a very astute observer of people, was aware why she was standing at the window so she turned and grinned. "Especially the ones with red manes."

During the brief time Luis' wife had to observe Sean, she had developed a strong liking for him. *That young Irishman reminds me of Luis as a young man: a true gentleman.* Her thoughts strayed; *Luis is still a gentleman.*

Someone else had developed a very strong liking for Sean. Miguel had watched him closely since the first day he arrived. He watched him now casting furtive glances all afternoon toward the hacienda. *That young man's as rock solid and trustworthy as they come.* He looked at the window where he had seen Bella standing. *She will do no better than Sean.* "Hey Amigo," he said to Sean as he rode up next to him, "Marissa will have a fine dinner waiting after we finish; will you eat with us?" He watched as Sean glanced at the hacienda. "She will be going nowhere." When the young man turned a redder than usual face toward him and offered a short, "I, uh, but," Miguel held his palm out to Sean, "I would like to talk a bit with you."

"Oh yes, sure Miguel, of course." He smiled at his Mexican boss, "I've heard that your wife is the best cook in California."

"We should be finished in an hour, and then you will be able to judge for yourself." He spurred his horse toward a young stallion that was giving Emil trouble. As he assisted his number one tracker he thought of Sean. *That's another reason I like that Irishman, he's always eager to please.*

Forty-five minutes later the two men were on their horses heading toward Miguel's house, a quarter-mile away.

"Hello Sean," the short, stout, thirty-five-year old Mexican woman said in English, "you bring big appetite?" Her smile was just as he remembered from the one other time that he had met her—wide, white, and sincere.

"Yes ma'am, sure did and I'm gonna have to get a bigger horse if I don't hold it down." He returned her smile.

"You two sit on the porch and I'll bring you some lemonade to sip while I finish dinner." She disappeared inside the small wood house with twelve-foot-wide porches all around. A short time later she was back with a large pitcher of lemonade. "And Sean," she said while looking at him with coal black eyes that always seem to twinkle, "call me Marissa."

"Yes ma'am, uh," he stammered; never having had a personal relationship with a woman, "I mean Marissa."

"That's better." She turned and went back to her cooking.

After a long satisfying drink Sean said, "Miguel you sure have a nice wife."

"Yes," he answered with a smile, "I know it and I also know how lucky I am to have her." He took another sip of lemonade. "That's what I wanted to talk to you about, Sean."

When the young man just turned and waited he continued, "It is very obvious to me that you are more than just a little interested in Issabella."

Sean blushed at the realization that his attentions hadn't gone unnoticed. "I uh, well uh," he stumbled across his tongue, "she uh, well what I mean is I uh, I never have been around women much," he took a long slow drink and Miguel just waited for his mind to clear and the knots in his tongue to untangle. Sean cleared his throat. "She's the nicest person I've ever been around."

The tall, forty-year old Mexican foreman leaned toward Sean. "I am going to tell you something very briefly that will help you in your pursuit of Senorita Santiago."

Sean looked directly into the man's brown eyes, partially hidden by bush-like eyebrows, and waited to hear what Miguel had to say.

"Do not press yourself on the young lady. Casually notice her and compliment her, but do not overdo it. Do not look for things to compliment her on. Just wait until something is very special." He grinned at Sean, "And she will go out of her way to make herself special very often because I have noticed she is watching you as much as you are watching her." He nodded his full head of bushy black hair. "Then very casually say something like, 'That is certainly a pretty dress you have on today.' She will like that because she probably tried on ten different ones to look her best, just for you." He smiled when he saw Sean's mouth hanging open. "Flies will soon be camping on your tongue."

Sean snapped his mouth shut in embarrassment, turned and looked at the hacienda sitting on top of the hill, then turned back to Miguel. "She's actually been watching me?" When Miguel just smiled and nodded he said, "Wow!"

Their relationship continued along these same lines during the next month as Miguel and his men built corrals to hold the next herd of mustangs they planned to get on the upcoming trip. Bella never ventured into the work area down near the barn, but spent long hours on the verandah watching the men work—especially Sean. When he was sent occasionally to the main house by Miguel to inform Maggie the cook, that they would be a little late for lunch, he always waved, and with a wide smile always spoke. "Hello Bella, are you enjoying the show we're putting on?"

"Yes, and I didn't realize you were such a good rider."

"I have your brother to thank for that," he said, being careful not to stare at her. "I had never ridden a horse until I came to California."

She smiled and moved along the porch to where he was tying his horse. "Frank was riding horses when he was still just a little boy. He also taught me to ride."

His occasional trips to the house were the highlight of her day because his days ended so late that she rarely saw him otherwise. "Why must they work seven days a week, Aunt Carmen?"

Carmen knew the turmoil the young girl was in and tried to console her. "This is a very busy time dear, but when they have enough horses they will not work such long hours."

It didn't help, so it was a very sad girl that watched the wagons and men depart to the east, barely a month after returning. She stood beside her aunt in the dawn light and watched until she could see them no more. "Do you like Sean, Auntie?"

"Very much," she replied and put her arm around her niece's shoulder, "and I believe you are very lucky to have met such a nice young man."

In a voice only slightly above a whisper the young Spaniard said, "But I hardly got to speak to him while he was here."

"You will dear," her aunt said, "you will."

The second trip went as easy as the first with much less excitement. Around the campfire on the final night before heading home Miguel said, "Twenty-five Stallions and nine young males, not bad at all. One more trip like this and we'll have enough to begin breeding."

"Beautiful horses," Al said, "but none like Satanas."

"Yes," Venus agreed, "the big brown leader is a good one, but nothing like Satanas."

"He's tough though," Sean commented as he pulled his trouser leg up, "look at the bite he gave me when I tried to turn him by raising my boot up next to his face."

"Ha, ha," Emil laughed, "your first bite?"

"Yep."

"There will be more," Laz said with a big smile, "a lot more if you keep dealing with these beasts."

Many days later, a tired group of men herded the mustangs into the corrals of the hacienda. It would be dark in an hour, but Sean's heart beat faster when he saw Bella standing on the porch.

Sean thought about Bella during every spare moment he was away, and had made up his mind to overcome his shyness and inhibitions around women, as soon as they returned. The first night they were all busy until long after dark getting the new horses in the corrals. “We will straighten them all out tomorrow,” Miguel said, “but they are separated enough for tonight. I hear a soft bed calling me and that’s where I’m heading.”

‘Me too’s’ echoed through the group of tired men. Sean looked at the main house’s lights and promised himself, *Tomorrow I talk to Aunt Carmen.* He was already beginning to feel like family.

The next day ended a couple of hours before dark, so Sean hurriedly bathed and put on his best trousers and shirt. As he began pulling on his boots he stopped and looked at them, then recalled something Miguel had said to him one night as they sat alone around the campfire near the mustang canyon. ‘Women have sensitive noses and keen eyes that seem to see everything. Always bath and put clean clothes on before approaching one, and always take time to clean your boots.’ He had listened carefully to every word the man said, and remained quiet as he looked thoughtfully into the fire. ‘I’ve never understood it,’ Miguel continued, ‘but they seem to think a man in dirty boots is not showing them sincere respect.’ He shook his head then grinned at Sean, ‘Or something like that, I guess.’

Sean located a rag and wet it to wipe months of dust and grime from his boots. After the third time wetting the rag and rubbing, the boots still looked grungy. He held them next to the oil lamp. *Hmm maybe they’re right. These things sure don’t look very respectful.* Something in his mind made him look hard at the oil in the lamp. “Oil,” he said aloud, and got the unlit lamp from a nearby table. After pouring a small amount of oil on a dry rag, he began rubbing it into the boots.

Carmen answered his knock. “Yes Sean, can I help you?”

“Uh, yes ma’am, uh I mean yes Aunt Carmen, I hope so.” She could see his nervousness and stepped out of the door onto the porch. It was still light enough to see that in a very short time he had bathed and changed clothes.

“My you certainly look nice,” she smiled sincerely at him then added, “and new boots too.” She fixed him with friendly, but decisive eyes. “Now what can I help you with?”

He had been turning the rim of his hat in his hands and now had it going around at a good rate. “I’d like to ask your permission to sit with Bella on the verandah for a little while.”

Her smile warmed him and made him feel more at ease. “We had better ask Issabella that question. Come, she’s in the parlor holding yarn for Magdalena.” When she saw he was about to enter, still spinning his hat, she pointed to one of many pegs on the outer wall and said, “Hat.” After the door closed, she motioned for him to follow her to the parlor. “Issabella, you have a visitor.” *As if she didn’t know*, Carmen thought.

Issabella came into the hall and feigned surprise. She recognized his voice the moment he had spoken to her aunt. "Why Sean, what a pleasant surprise. Are you going to a rodeo all dressed up like that?" Her smile made it apparent to him that she was pleased with his appearance. "And new boots too."

"Nope," He grinned, "same ole work boots, but I cleaned 'em up."

When the two of them just stood silent, Carmen spoke. "He has something to ask you."

"Yes?" Bella said with a question mark in her voice.

"I was wondering," he said in a much more confidant voice due to her casual attitude, "if you would like to sit on the verandah and watch the sunset?"

"One of my favorite things to do," she said and placed her arm through his.

Carmen watched her lovely young niece walk out the door. *Those two people are going to have a good life together.*

Sean was the first to be awakened by the crackling roar of the flames. He stumbled sleepily from the bunkhouse in his long johns and ran toward the blazing inferno. A split second later Frank was running with the ranch hands to open the doors of the blazing barn, so the horses that had busted out of their stalls could escape. Nine of the eleven horses had already busted down their flimsy barriers and went running out. Sean was frozen to the spot that he had first reached. Frank ran into the flaming structure and released the remaining two horses. Still Sean remained frozen to the ground. There was so much excitement happening in such a short time that no one but Frank noticed Sean standing frozen in one spot—helpless.

By the time Carmen and Issabella came from the hacienda he was helping Frank and the others round up the frightened horses. Together they watched the structure burn to the ground. It wasn't nearly as large as the apartment house, which Sean had lived in as a child, but in his mind as he stood watching, the flames brought back a long buried nightmare.

After the horses were all in the corral, Sean walked slowly to the bunkhouse for his pants, then returned to the porch and sat down heavily—his head hanging between his knees. He looked up and saw Bella walking toward him.

When she sat beside him on the edge of the porch he said, "Oh God."

She put her arm around the shoulders of the young man she knew to be very courageous. "Frank told me about your parents. I am so sorry you had to see this too."

He looked at the smoldering embers across the clearing behind the main house and shook his head slowly from side to side. "God I hate to see a building burn. All I could see was my Mom n' Dad in there screaming."

Miguel called on the six men that worked on the ranch making repairs, building corrals, cleaning out stalls, and anything else that needed doing. Each man had his own family, and had built a house to live in. Most had been with Luis many years. The most recent was a replacement for a man who had died, and he had been at the ranch many years. He spoke directly to the man that he'd made foreman over this crew of workers. "Angelo, we must keep working with these horses and we will be soon leaving for one last trip." He turned and let his eyes roam across the ashes then continued, "Hire as many people as you need from the nearby village and build a new barn twice as big with many more stalls. Make arrangements for the material you will need and give Mrs. Carvojol the information and she will arrange for payment." With little else said, Angelo Antonio Baranaja instructed his five men to begin cleaning up the burned down barn as he climbed on his horse and headed toward the village to hire a crew.

Two weeks later, the wagons were once again heading east at dawn. Miguel was not surprised to see Angelo's crew of over a dozen men already at work on the huge new barn. Sean was riding beside him. "Angelo's a good man."

"Sure is," Miguel answered.

4

~ *Old game—New problem* ~

Six days later, two telescopes were being used to observe people. One was in the hands of a short fat man that was bald on top with long hair on the sides and rear, pulled back and tied in a ponytail. He had a red gourd-like nose that seemed to be a beacon, hanging below two lifeless gray eyes with no eyebrows.

The other was in the hands of a young Irishman. The first telescope was watching Miguel and his men as they crossed the Gila River. Sean was watching the man holding the telescope.

"I was hoping Montezuma would be here again," Miguel said to Echy, the cook.

"Those folks must move around a lot I guess?" Echy replied as he eased the wagon up out of the river and onto the trail to the mustang canyon.

"Yeah, they have to go where they can find what they need to survive."

"Buncha damn Messykins," the short, fat man said to his brother, who was lying beside him on the small cliff. His six other men lay against boulders in the shallow valley behind them. "Lemme have a look-see," his brother said. He took the glass and put it to one of the two milky-blue eyes crowded too close to a beak-like nose that ended in a downward curve making him resemble a buzzard.

All who knew the two escaped prisoners had in some way commented about their mother's infidelities. 'Ain't no way them two boys came from the same daddy.'

The Buzzard and the Gourd were being transported back to Mexico City a while earlier, to be tried for the murder and robbery of a cantina owner—and then shot by a firing squad. Well aware of the fate that awaited them, the two men were constantly watching for an opportunity to escape from the cargo vessel where they were temporarily imprisoned. The small ship was lying at anchor in preparation to off-load supplies the next morning to the people of the new settlement called El Pueblo de Nuestra Senora la Reina de Los Angeles—The Town of Our Lady the Queen of the Angels.

Their moment came that night when a careless young cabin boy unlocked the wrong door in the hold of the ship. The following morning his lifeless body was found on its stomach with the head turned nearly all the way around with sightless eyes staring up at the ship's First Mate.

The two desperate men swam to the river's bank then made their way to the Mission San Gabriel Arcangel, where they killed a priest and his two assistants before looting the place and heading east on stolen mission horses. During the next year they gathered a group of societies refuse around them.

Sean studied the man now holding the telescope. *Don't like the looks of these guys at all.* He had left the camp two hours before dawn, following his uncanny Irish intuition. He rode east, stopping regularly to listen for any alien sounds. By listening carefully to Lazaro Alvarez, a superb trail scout, Sean was fast becoming as good as they come. The roadmap that his memory was unfolding for him pointed to a small cliff in the hills ahead. When the sun arrived awhile later, it found him lying on his stomach trying to determine where the sound of horse hoofs he heard earlier came from. A patient search of the surrounding hills paid off when he saw a flash as the sun hit the telescope in the cliffs across the valley. *Whoever it is ain't got brains enough to shield that lens with a cut of leather. Apaches'll have his hair on a stick one o' these days*—He continued watching.

With his milky eye still glued to the eyepiece, the Buzzard said, "Betcha they're a buncha Messakins goin' back home 'cause they caint make no money what to eat with."

"Yep," The Gourd agreed, "that's what I figgered." He held out his hand,

"Gimme that glass back n' go tell them morons t'keep quiet back there." He continued watching Miguel's group.

Sean remained lying with his eye to the eyepiece long after the two men disappeared from the cliff across the valley. His patience was rewarded when the group emerged from the east end and rode casually northeast toward the foothills. He silently counted the men as they rode away from him. *Eight men. Might just be a bunch o' guys lookin' for gold'r som'n, but I'm gonna keep an eye on 'em anyway.*

"I figger them Messykins are gonna make the base o' Montezuma Peak by dark time," the Gourd said, "so when they get their camp fixed and have et n' are all relaxed, five of us'll ride in whilst the other three sneak up in the dark." He flashed a gray, hairy toothed grin at his brother then laughed, "When Ethan and his two guys slit a couple o' their throats the five of us'll start blastin the others."

The Buzzard matched his brother's morbid, gray grin. "Dang shame there ain't no wimmin with 'em."

Sean rode along beside Miguel explaining what he'd seen. "No," his boss said, "I don't recall ever seeing anyone like that. You say he had eight other men with him?"

"No," Sean replied, "seven others and him."

"Hmmm," Miguel mused then looked at Sean, "you're certainly correct about eight men riding around in this area—strange."

The Gourd was right. By dark the wagon train was camped in front of the same canyon where Montezuma and his band of Tonto Apache had arrived to finish the renegade Indians. As Echy prepared food, Benito Costillo walked toward the area where the renegade's bodies had been lying when they last saw them. Awhile later he returned to the campfire. "Not a trace of them."

Antonio Cardenas looked up from the fire through wizened old eyes—no one knew his age. "Mother Nature always cleans up a mess left by man."

Miguel went to each man and explained what Sean had seen. "Be sure to keep your weapons ready." It was all he had to tell this band of trail-wise Mexican vaqueros.

Sean and Frank ate then moved away from the fire. In the darkness each man removed his boots and spurs to replace them with leather moccasins. They had checked their pistols while it was still light. Silently each moved to a pre-determined spot and allowed his eyes to become accustomed to the darkness. Sean had unfolded the map inside his head and knew where the intruders would approach if they wanted to surprise this camp.

"Hello the camp." The voice came from outside the canyon. Sean and Frank both heard it but neither man turned toward the fire. Their eyes were adjusted to see any movement in the darkness nearby. They watched and waited.

"Yes," Miguel yelled to the darkness.

"Can we come to the fire?"

"How many are you?"

"Five hungry riders."

Alarm bells went off in the heads of nine vaqueros sitting around the fire—they had all been told that there were eight men. Sean and Frank remained motionless and unmoved by the news. It was exactly what they had expected. The gourd was leading his men into a trap he had set himself. Less than a split second after Frank heard Sean's first pistol discharge, he squeezed the trigger on his own pistol that had been following the man sneaking toward the camp. Two almost simultaneous shots were heard as Sean and Frank dropped a third man.

The resulting barrage of shots left four of the five men that had been allowed into the camp dead, and the Buzzard leaning forward hugging his horse's neck and crying, "Please don't shoot, oh God please don't shoot me."

Old Antonio walked to one of the bodies and reached down to remove the long hunting knife he had thrown. He occasionally entertained his friends with displays of his prowess with knives. He could juggle three of the razor sharp weapons then throw them one-by-one into a six-inch circle thirty feet away. Victoriano Madero walked to the horse that the Buzzard was still hugging. He had reloaded his pistol and pointed it at the crying man. The half-Mexican—half-Pomo Indian said, "Turn around in that saddle."

The Buzzard stopped blubbering. "Wha, huh, uh turn around?"

"Either that or I'm going to blow you out of that saddle." The look on Victor's face convinced the Buzzard to obey him. He turned around then kept looking down as the man tied his feet together beneath the belly of his horse. Old Tony just stood quietly watching. He had seen the half-breed mad only a few times in the many years he had worked with him. "Put your hands behind you and grab that saddlehorn." The terrified man did as he was told. When Victor finished tying the Buzzard's hands securely to the saddlehorn he smacked the horse on the rump to start it running into the night. A shot into the air from his pistol sped the beast on a journey it knew not where—carrying a crying, terrified man. The two men standing near the entrance to the canyon heard a couple of, 'Oh my God's,' then nothing but the distant thundering of the horse's hoofs. The old man bent down to clean the blade of his knife on the man he had retrieved it from then looked at Victor.

"The Apache will have fun with that one."

Sean and Frank approached the fire cautiously. "Anyone hurt?"

"Yes," Tony answered, "seven guys hurt dead and one galloping across the desert crying."

Sean looked at Frank who just shrugged his shoulders and turned to the fire. "I'm ready for a coffee." Frank was getting tougher as time passed.

The third and last trip of the year went better than the other two. Wagons and men arrived back at the hacienda with thirty-three stallions, and one huge, beautiful, sandy-colored leader and eighteen young males. Long before they arrived they could see the top of the new barn looming on the horizon.

When they were close enough to see the new structure it was plain to see that it would soon be completed. Angelo's hired crew plus his own five men were putting the finishing touches on it. They all stopped to watch the arrival of the new horses. When they were inside the main corral and his men started separating them, Miguel rode to Angelo. "Very, very good, amigo." He sat and looked at the structure. "We must keep this a guarded secret old friend or you will be in such demand I will lose you."

"I am already in great demand," the diminutive, forty-five-year-old man who had started with Miguel and the Carvojol family many years earlier, said with a stone face. "I have two children in college in Mexico City, two more here that are becoming more demanding as we speak, and a wife that doesn't understand why I cannot be with her all the time." He smiled up at Miguel. "Can a man be in more demand than that?"

"No," the tall, lanky hacienda boss replied, "and you love it."

"Very true," Angelo said as he turned to go back to work. He shook his head up and down as he walked away, "yes, very true."

Between the second and this last trip to get horses, Sean spent every evening but three sitting on the verandah with Bella. Those three evenings were spent riding guard around an imaginary perimeter surrounding the hacienda. After the incident with the gourd and his band of thugs, Miguel decided that with so many people moving into the area it would be wise to begin a regular night patrol to prevent anyone from sneaking up on them.

It didn't take Sean long to realize that while a man was on the north side of the property a group of men could be arriving on the south side, unseen by the guard. He approached Miguel the following day with an idea. Miguel liked it, and The Tower of El Cielo de los Caballos was created.

Angelo and his crew began construction immediately and within a month a guard tower stood in the center of the hacienda. It was fifty feet high and had a staircase going up inside the framework. The platform on top was ten-feet-square with walls four-feet-high and a roof supported by corner posts. Angelo's ingenuity created an almost bulletproof area the guard could stand behind. He built two walls; one six inches behind the other. The space between was filled with sand and a cap put on top. The last thing he did was even more brilliant. The final ten feet to gain entrance to the tower was a slightly leaning ladder rather than a continuation of the stairs. After climbing through the opening the guard would pull the end of the ladder up then secure the rope inside until it was time for him to be relieved.

All of the men thanked Sean for his suggestion. They not only disliked the night patrol, but also knew, as Sean did, that it was not effective. The huge bronze bell, that Miguel had arranged to be delivered, would awaken everyone in the event the guard in the tower saw something at night that looked like trouble.

Once again the first night back was consumed with horses, but the following evening found Sean knocking on the main house door. When Maggie, as all referred to the cook, opened it Sean greeted her in freshly washed clothes and lamp-oiled boots. "My, my," the dark Mexican behemoth said with a huge, sparkling white grin, "you so handsome it make me wish I am twenty years younger."

Sean was getting very affluent in Spanish and understood what she said. *All four of you,* He thought then responded in Spanish with Irish poetic prose. "One day a handsome knight will ride in and carry you off to live out your years in splendor." *On a very large horse,* he thought, and had to fight to keep from smiling at his own humor.

Her face lit up as she replied, "I will call Issabella."

During the next year, two things grew by leaps and bounds. The horses that were captured in the canyons bred eagerly with the mares delivered from Mexico and Spain. They produced a type of horse unequaled in California at the time. The other thing was Sean and Issabella's love for each other.

Luis Carvojol made two trips to his southern ranch to see the fruits of his dream and investment. "The winery at North Ranch is nearly finished," he explained, "and I hope to soon be able to turn its operation over to Manuello Calaveras until Sean decides whether or not he wants to assume the ranch's responsibility. We should get our first crop of grapes next year, then if all goes well I can move here permanently."

The dignified Spaniard handled all of the business except what he specifically authorized a few people like Miguel and Manuello to handle themselves. He never ventured into the area of emotional family situations. "That is Carmen's area of expertise," he said when queried on the subject. He could however recall the emotional feelings he had racing through his young mind and body twenty-five years earlier, when he had fallen in love with Carmen. He was well aware what was happening between his niece and the young Irishman he was so fond of.

"They have never spent one moment together, except on that verandah," Carmen informed Luis when he quietly inquired about their relationship. "But," she continued, "it is a very serious relationship." She locked her coal black eyes on his then smiled, "Much like another relationship I recall many years ago in Spain."

The small man stepped forward and put his arms around his wife, and then smiled down into her eyes. "I was so proud that you were still a virgin on our wedding night."

"And I was also proud," she said as she lay her head on his chest, "that you were such a gentleman."

He gently pushed her far enough away to see the twinkle in his eyes, "It was not easy."

She smiled, "And it is not easy for them, but I would stake my life that she will also be a virgin on her wedding night."

His second visit to Horse Heaven was five months later to view some of the new foals. He arrived in a four-horse coach driven by two rugged looking Mexicans. Another tough looking Mexican accompanied him inside the coach. He later told Carmen, "There are so many stories about trail bandits, that I had the coach built and hired these three men to take me to Yerba Buena, here, or anywhere else that I must travel."

When he stepped from the coach, his beautiful vivacious young niece immediately met him. "My goodness," he said with a smile as he accepted her hug, and then stepped back. "Can this possibly be my little Issabella?"

The bold young woman locked her arm in his and walked toward the house. "Uncle Luis, Sean wants very badly to talk to you." She turned and looked at him, "Will you please find time for him?"

"Hmmm," he said as he looked off into the distance. "It certainly must be important. Hmm, let me see, what would be so important that my niece meets me with his name on her lips." He frowned then said, "I know what it must be. He wants to buy one of those beautiful black and tan foals we just produced." He pulled on his gray goatee then turned to Bella as they arrived at the porch. "Either that or he wants to marry my beautiful niece."

Her look of shock was real and he smiled when she said, "How could you know?"

He leaned forward and affected a conspiratorial air, "I heard about it in Yerba Buena." When she gasped he added with a smile, "And on the way here, in several small villages."

The young girl blushed. "Was it that obvious?"

"Perhaps only to two people like your aunt and I who were also young like you and Sean when they first met."

Behind the screen Carmen added, "And just as much in love."

"Yes come in," Luis answered a short time later to the knock on the door of the room that served as his library and office. He walked forward and shook hands with Sean, "I've been expecting you." He led the way to two large seats facing each other in front of a large fireplace. "Please have a seat Sean; can I get you a drink?"

"Nossir. Thank you, but I don't use the stuff."

"If you don't mind, then I'll pour myself a small brandy to help the fire warm these cold old bones." Before sitting with his brandy he held out a hand carved walnut box and opened the lid, “Cuban cigar?”

“Nossir, thank you, but I don’t do that either.”

“Well now,” Luis said after he had his cigar lit and was sitting back in the chair, “how can I help you?”

Sean remained silent for a few moments and just looked at Luis. Finally he abandoned all of the flowery Irish speeches he had prepared and said simply, “I’m in love with your niece sir, and want to marry her but I wanted to ask you first.”

Luis knew what the young man was going to ask so he had prepared an answer before Sean entered. “And what about Issabella, does she love you and want to marry you?”

“Why uh, I uh, Yes. I mean I’m sure she does but I never asked her because I thought I would ask you first.”

“Then my answer is no.” He looked sternly at Sean and waited.

Sean was absolutely devastated. “No?” His tone was one of disbelief.

“That is correct, no. If you’re asking me first I must tell you that I am already married and very happy with my wife, but I am sure Issabella wouldn’t mind being asked second.” He turned a smiling face to the door and yelled, “Would you my dear?”

Carmen pushed the door open, and Bella rushed in to hug Luis then looked at Sean who was still sitting with a bewildered look on his face. “He loves to tease,” she said as she released Luis and reached for Sean’s hand.

Carmen was standing just inside the open door with her hands on her hips and a hard look in her black eyes. “Old devil.”

Luis turned in the huge chair and grinned, “A little harmless fun.”

Sean recovered his composure and gently put a callused, leathery hand on each of her shoulders and held her at arm length. With his Irish poet’s heart he said, “Issabella Magdelena Ruiz Santiago you have it in your power to make me the happiest man on earth.”

With a sense of humor gifted to her by her dead father and the uncle she loved, the beautiful young girl gave him a mischievous look then said coyly, “And how would I be able to do that?”

“By marrying me.”

“Oh well then,” she responded casually, “sure, why not?”

Her Aunt Carmen stepped ahead and smacked her briskly on her bottom. “You’ve been around this uncle of yours too much.”

Luis set his glass on the small table beside his chair and stood. He put an arm around a shoulder of each of them. “I am sincerely happy for both of you.”

Sean grabbed his hand when he removed it from his shoulder and shook it firmly. “Thank you Mr. Carvojol, thank you very much. I’ll always take good care of her.”

“I know you will Sean, and it is still Luis.” He smiled at him, “Even more so now that I am about to become your uncle-in-law." When Sean released his hand Luis indicated the chair behind and said, "Please have a seat. I am required back at North Ranch in a few days, so let us take a moment and make a few plans." He looked up at a radiant Bella, "When would you like to have your wedding?"

Without hesitation she responded, "October twentieth, on my birthday."

Luis paused for a few moments thinking then said, "Excellent choice. It will be cool and a perfect time for a grand fiesta wedding."

"A fiesta?" She said with a huge smile.

"Why of course, do you think for one small moment I would allow my favorite niece to have just an ordinary wedding?"

She affixed him with her devilish eyes, "I am your only niece, Uncle Luis."

"Oh so you are," he grinned, "well you would be my favorite if I had a dozen."

On the day Luis was to head back north he stood on the porch with Carmen and Issabella. "I will return in early August to see how the new foals are shaping up. Please get together with Magdalena and plan the details of the fiesta, then have one of the men deliver the invitations to your guests." He walked to his waiting coach and waved before boarding. The two women stood watching until it was out of sight.

"Who are you going to invite?"

Issabella looked inquiringly at her aunt. "Hmmm, that will take some thought."

In the late afternoon on August 3rd Luis' coach pulled back into Horse Heaven. His three men attended to the horses and checked the coach thoroughly then went to visit with the other men. Luis asked Sean to please come to the main house for dinner. "I have something very important to discuss with you."

Sean arrived in clean, but slightly ruffled clothes and boots that were beginning to smell like lamp oil. Small talk circulated during dinner with Frank telling Luis all about the new foals and how well everything was going. As Luis listened to his nephew Francisco he thought, *He is taking to this horse ranching just as I had hoped.* He studied the confident young Irishman who could now open up his dreams. *Sean, you deserve a lot of the credit for Francisco's advancements.*

Luis stood after the meal was finished, "Let us go to the verandah and talk, while Magdalena clears the table."

"Mmm it's so nice out tonight," Carmen said, as she locked her arm in Luis'. They walked slowly around to the north side then he turned to Sean and Bella who were also walking arm in arm.

"I have instructed Alejandro to survey out twenty thousand acres on the northeast corner of North Ranch for you two." He was interrupted with hugs from Bella and a very sincere 'thank you' from Sean. "There is more," he continued. "Sean told me," he glanced at his niece, "that he is going to raise sheep rather than be foreman of North Ranch, so I have contacted some very influential people in Spain about getting a parcel of attached land granted to you. I think we should hear something before the wedding."

"That would be wonderful Luis," Sean replied, "thank you."

"A man worries," Luis said with a philosophical tone, "about his daughter," he looked at Bella, "or in this case his niece and wonders if she will be fortunate to find a man to love her as he does. Carmen and I feel confident that she has and we want to do everything we can to help you two succeed." Bella left Sean's arm and put both of hers around her uncle. He smiled at her then continued. "I must return day after tomorrow so I want you to spend tomorrow with Carmen here in the house. You will be discussing the type of house you want built, so Miguel can begin ordering the material as soon as he and I return to North Ranch."

"You're building us a house?" The look of incredulity on Sean's face was humorous to Luis.

"Yes," he answered, "I refuse to have my favorite," he looked into her radiant face, "oops, only niece living in a sheep-camp." He added with a smile, "Although I am sure she would."

"Twenty thousand acres," Sean said quietly, almost to himself, "wow!"

"There is a large clearing," Luis said, "with a beautiful view. I would suggest you have it built there so you will have plenty of room to expand as you require a larger barn and other buildings." He pulled another Cuban cigar from his vest pocket and once it was lit said, "Tomorrow evening I will ask Miguel to spend some time with you so he will understand the type of home you want he and his crew to build."

"When is he going to begin?" Bella stepped away and asked.

"He will return with me and begin laying out the stakes immediately, so he will be ready to begin as soon as the material arrives."

"My goodness," she replied, and then lowered herself to the deck with her legs dangling over the edge. She sat silently looking out at the night sky then repeated, "My goodness."

"I'm certain Frank can handle everything here in Miguel's absence," Sean said.

"He has come a long way," Luis slowly shook his head up and down as he ran his hand over his gray goatee, "and I thank you for the help you have given him."

"Very little to do with me," Sean commented, "there was always a very strong minded man in there waiting to come out."

Four days before the wedding-birthday fiesta, Luis' coach arrived with Miguel and Luis each smiling out the side openings; Luis at Carmen on his side, and on the other side Miguel at his wife Marissa. As Miguel embraced his wife, Bella came running toward them but waited until he released her. "Oh Miguel, how's the house coming?"

With a very sober look he answered. "We plan to begin soon."

Her mouth dropped open and the look on her face caused him to laugh. After regaining his composure he smiled. "Everything is completed except some finish work on the inside, and we will be working on that right after the fiesta."

Her eyes narrowed and she said sternly, "You've been spending too much time with that uncle of mine." She then stepped forward and put both her arms around him. "Thank you Miguel, no one could ever build a house as well as you."

Without thinking he said, "It will be ready for you to move in by the time you get back from your honeymoon."

"Honeymoon?" She said with a large question mark in her voice.

His eyes grew instantly huge as he looked through the coach at Luis. "Oh no, you didn't know." He shrunk back and looked at his wife who was frowning as she shook her head. He bit his upper lip with his lower teeth as he sucked air in. "Oh my goodness Issabella, don't let on that you know or it will spoil his surprise."

Her brow wrinkled in thought as she repeated, "Honeymoon!" When she saw the look of dread on his face she hugged him again, "Not a word."

He sighed and grinned, "Thank you."

"Where are we going?"

"When?" he said and walked away with Marissa on his arm. He turned and grinned.

"Devil," she said quietly and wagged a finger at him.

The fiesta was held on Issabella's nineteenth birthday. Over a hundred local people who knew at least one person associated with El Cielo de los Caballos were praying to their own personal saint for good weather. It was a rare occasion when a celebration occurred in their rural area, so they wanted nothing to dampen the gala affair. Their prayers worked, because on the first morning of the two-day festival, the sky was clear, the weather was unusually mild, and there was a light breeze. "This is the nicest day I can remember," Echy said to Victor, "for uh, mmm, I can't remember ever having a nicer day during this time of year."

By noon on the first day, every ranch hand was sporting some of the finest garb they had ever worn, as they walked among the many booths Carmen had set up to serve refreshments. "You've done a marvelous job my dear," Luis complemented his wife as they stood on the verandah. "Where did you find so many people to come and work for you?"

"Ha ha," She laughed, "in your absence these last few years, our little community has grown."

"Hmm, yes. I've been too busy to think about it but I have seen many small communities spring up as I traveled between here and North Ranch."

She squeezed her arm tighter to his, "And many, many more to come."

There were as many children as adults, and all were enjoying the fiesta. Carmen had instructed her hired staff to begin making Piñatas several weeks in advance. She supplied the material and told them, "Work on them at home as you have time but leave a hole to stuff them with prizes and candy." There were now dozens of the colorful hanging papier-mâché baskets in shapes that ranged from donkeys to huge fish for the children to hit as they were blindfolded and given a long stick. When the basket was finally hit, a barrage of nuts, home made fudge and taffy wrapped in paper, oranges, apples, and small gifts fell to the ground to be divided between the smiling children.

Bella watched from her room as Magdalena helped her into the beautiful wedding gown that Carmen had ordered special from the best seamstress in the community. "One day we will have so many children we can have our own fiesta." She turned and smiled at the huge Mexican cook who had fallen in love with the young girl and treated her as the daughter she was never fortunate enough to have.

Frank and Alvaro escorted the priest; recently arrived from his trip from the mission near the coast. "My goodness, I have not yet seen this many people gathered together." He looked over the top of his eyeglasses at Frank, "Even during my services at the mission."

Tall, muscular, Alvaro Carranza—a slightly irreverent man, leaned down to look at the priest. "Perhaps you should have Piñatas, music, and beer." His humor was met with an icy stare from the over-fed little man, and a huge grin from Frank.

When Issabella appeared on the verandah in her dove-white wedding gown, all three of the hired bands stopped playing festival music. At a signal from Miguel they started playing a wedding march they had rehearsed together. Sean had been positioned near the priest with Frank as his best man. Bella had chosen eleven-year-old Arial, daughter of Angelo and his wife, to be her lady in waiting. Arial beamed with pride, as she stood alone in the new pink dress Carmen had made for her. When Bella finally arrived she went to the child first and hugged her. "I feel beautiful but second to you."

The wedding would be talked about for many years as the most elegant affair ever to take place in the area. After Sean and Bella had circulated among the guests for a couple of hours, Luis approached them. "Happy birthday Issabella, and congratulations to you both."

"Thank you for everything Luis." Sean replied.

She put her arms around her uncle, "You will always be the daddy in my heart."

Luis had to strain to keep from choking up. When he was in control of his voice he said, "Please come to the verandah a moment, I have something to show you."

On the porch he said, "Wait here a moment." He returned a second later and had a large scroll in his hand. "This came the day before I left to come here." He handed it to Sean.

After unrolling it and studying the document he turned to Bella then to Luis. "Oh my God." He stared and read the Spanish words to be certain he hadn't misread them. "Two hundred thousand acres are awarded us by the Government of Spain, Bella." He looked again at Luis, "Oh my God Luis; thank you."

A smiling Luis produced another large brown envelope. "These are tickets to Mexico City and back on the luxury freighter San Carlos. It belongs to a very good friend of mine." He handed the envelope to Sean, "There is enough cash for you both to enjoy a wonderful honeymoon, and your house will be ready when you return to North Ranch."

My coach is ready to take you to the coast near El Pueblo de Nuestra Senora la Reina de Los Angles, where it will be waiting for you. Get your things and you will be on it by this time tomorrow afternoon."

Bella hadn't said a word to Sean about the honeymoon that Miguel had let out of the bag. She knew he would only need a few minutes to pack his clothes. Since she knew about it, Issabella only needed a short time to gather the necessary things before leaving. She had begged Miguel but he wouldn't tell her where they were going, but he did tell her to pack her things because she would be leaving soon after the wedding. When she was standing on the porch in her traveling clothes, with two large suitcases, in less than half an hour Luis thought *my goodness that is the fastest I have ever seen a woman pack for a trip.* He never found out that because of Miguel's slip-of-the-tongue, she spent half of the night selecting the clothes she would take—to where she had no idea.

Luis' coach and three bodyguards were waiting at the side of the house, away from the festivities. Without so much as a wave, the two young people were whisked away and were heading for a twelve-hour trip to the coast.

Sean and Bella were met six weeks later; by the same three men—to begin another long trip by coach. This time however, it was to their own house sitting on a clearing with trees on every side. The thing they loved most about it was that it sat on their own two-hundred-and-twenty-thousand-acre ranch.

Their honeymoon trip to Mexico City would remain the highlight of their lives. They returned with a souvenir that would always remind them of the wonderful trip: during the years of hard work ahead. It departed with them from Mexico City and arrived with them in the harbor of Yerba Buena as a tiny creature about the size of a pollywog. It emerged from her womb nine months later on July 28th 1802 as Patrick Oliver McKannah. Broderick Luis McKannah arrived on December 5th 1803, and then came Ian Brennan McKannah on the first day of April 1805, followed by Simon Lamar McKannah May 5th 1806. The child they thought would be their last was born on February 12th 1807 and was named after Sean's grandfather, Jesse Devon McKannah.

Bella and Sean agreed that five children constituted a good family, but were delighted when the daughter they both wanted very much arrived. Everyone was happy when the midwife handed Issabella her little girl, five days after Christmas 1807. They named her Aleena Myra Carmen McKannah. Bella had carried the name of Sean's mother and her aunt in her head for years—hoping for a daughter.

The young Irish orphan and his lovely Spanish wife had created six human beings that would leave their mark on the new country.

5

~ *Dangerous trails* ~

A week before Christmas 1818 Jesse was a bloody mess when he and Aleena walked to the porch where Issabella was enjoying a cup of tea. He was only eleven years old but walked like an old man. Aleena had his two books tied with hers and was carrying them all. When Bella finally looked up and saw her youngest son, she jumped from her rocker shouting, "Oh my God, what happened?"

When she was at his side helping him up on the porch, his sister answered her mother. "Three boys were teasing me and saying I better hope Santa Claus brings me a new face for Christmas." It wasn't the first time the nearly six-foot-tall, homely little ten-year-old had been teased about her stringy brown hair and long narrow nose with too-close-together eyes sitting unevenly at the top of it. It was however the first time it had ever happened close enough for Jesse to hear. Before the three boys even knew he was nearby, one was on the ground with a busted nose and the remaining two were engaged in the fight of their young lives.

Mr. Adderly was summoned from the basement of the combination school-home that Sean and his neighbors built for the teacher years earlier. He was tending his home brew during recess, and arrived as Jesse took Aleena's hand.

"C'mon sis, let's get the buggy n' head home." The schoolteacher looked around in confusion as the two McKannah children drove away.

Two of Jesse's older brothers, Patrick and Broderick, had taken the school day off and heard the commotion on the porch. They came to investigate. "Still trying to whip the world huh, little brother?" Patrick loved Jesse but couldn't understand why he would rather fight or walk alone in the woods than get an education, so he could move away from the wilderness and live in the city.

"Because there ain't a thing in any of them cities that I want." He gave the same answer each time he was confronted.

"Oh Jesse," his mother said soothingly as she wiped the blood from his face, "I wish you wouldn't fight so much."

He remained silent for a moment. "Mama, I don't ever fight with anybody till they mess with me or Aleena." She was finished, so he stood and looked at his sister standing near the door. "She's just a little girl and I ain't ever gonna let anybody talk bad to her."

"She's a little girl, huh?" Patrick growled, "And you're a grown man now."

"Grown enough to whip your butt any day of the week."

Patrick stood and said menacingly, "Oh yeah."

"Sure!" Jesse said as he motioned with a sore arm, "How 'bout right now in the yard there?"

"Stop this foolishness," Bella yelled. "Patrick! Broderick!"

"Yes ma," the two older boys answered in unison.

"Go find something to do." When they paused a moment, she screamed loudly, "**Now**."

Jesse went to his sister's room later to see how she was feeling. After chatting a while about nothing in particular he stood to leave but turned at the door, "Wanna ride over to Chalponich's village with me tomorrow?"

"Sure," she said, "whacha gonna do over there?"

"Learn how to make a boat to ride down the river in." His sister's mouth dropped open and was that way as he closed the door behind him. He heard her through the door say, "Make a boat?" He smiled and headed for the rear door to go watch his father and the crew shearing sheep. He was certain she wouldn't be thinking about the cruel words of the boys at school now. He knew she wasn't a pretty girl and often thought *why couldn't she be pretty like mama?*

Christmas Day 1818 came and went. Aleena included Santa Claus in her prayers each night, even though she knew that he was just a fable. She added quietly, "If it's possible God, could you please just forget all about the stuff I ask Santa for and make me pretty." By her eleventh birthday, only five days later, the melancholy young Capricorn had given up hope of suddenly becoming pretty. The tenacious, inquisitive girl set her sights on becoming a schoolteacher and forever stopped hoping to be a pretty woman.

By Jesse's twelfth birthday, a little over a month later on February twelfth, changes had taken place. After several more boys had to have busted noses tended to, and had donated teeth to his plan of having all comments about his sister stopped—they did.

A few days before Jesse's thirteenth birthday he was in the barn watching Manollo and Sean putting the finishing touches on the coach that Uncle Luis had built for Patrick and Broderick to go off to college in.

"Daddy."

"Yes Jesse."

"How come this coach's smaller than Uncle Luis' if Patrick and Broderick gotta go all the way to that school in it?"

"Ain't goin' that far in it," Sean responded and kept working.

Jesse knew not to bother his dad too much when he was working, but his curiosity got the better of him. "How they gonna get there then?"

"Get that other bucket of grease Jesse n' bring it here. This ain't gonna be enough to finish these wheel hubs."

Jesse remained quiet as he watched the two men finish with the wheels. "Well." Sean said, "I reckon she's ready to go." He turned to his son. "C'mere." Jesse followed as his father went to the wall at the end of the barn. "Manollo just finished this awhile earlier." He pointed to the crude map on the wall with California, Mexico, and Texas, roughly outlined in homemade charcoal. "Here's where we are," Sean pointed at an X a little over a hundred miles southeast of what would become San Francisco. He picked up a thin stick that Manollo used when showing Sean the route that Luis had explained to Manollo the last time he visited. He placed the stick on another X on the Texas-Mexican border next to the Gulf of Mexico, which was labeled simply, OCEAN. "This's where they're going."

After looking back and forth between the two X's Jesse said, "That school ain't anywhere near where I thought it was."

Both men laughed then Sean turned to his son and smiled. He held the stick out in front as he walked to the other side of the barn. He tapped the stick against the wall. "Here's that Harvard school they're going to."

Jesse looked at the place on the wall where his father was touching the stick, then back to the X on the barn wall in front of him. "They're gonna take a boat ain't they?"

Sean walked slowly toward the boy realizing there was no way he could have known their plans. He stopped and just stared at him a moment. Finally Manollo spoke. "I always said he could think on his feet." The Mexican foreman grinned at Jesse then turned to Sean, "He might not be the best with them school books but he can figure things out."

There were no two men on earth that Jesse would rather have praised him than these two. He worked at keeping a straight face so his emotions wouldn't show. He busied himself with the charcoal map. "Boy, that's gonna be a long ride just to get to the place the boat'll pick 'em up."

Sean was aware of his son's intuitive ability to see things others didn't, so he quickly recovered from his temporary amazement. "We figure about fifteen hundred miles to the boat, then maybe three thousand or a little less to where that college is."

A noise behind them turned their faces to the big open double-doors as the two older McKannah boys came walking in. "Hi daddy, hi Manny, hi wild boy," Patrick said, as they approached. Broderick just gave a little wave and said, "Hi."

Jesse jumped from the stall rail he'd climbed up on. "I'm gonna go clean out a couple of the horse stalls." As he walked away he thought *there'll be a lot less horse poop in there.*

A week later, Jesse lay silently in the hayloft and listened intently as his father and Manollo explained the workings of the coach to his two older brothers.

"The wheels on this coach," Manollo said, "are the same as any others, just bigger. I don't think you'll have any problems with them but," he pointed to the wheel attached to the side of the small riding compartment, "we've put a spare on each side to allow you to replace a broken one instead of waiting until repairs can be made."

"Good thinking," Broderick commented, as he looked the attachment device over. "What did you do?" He questioned as he leaned in to look closer, "Run another axle all the way through to mount 'em on."

"Yeah," Sean grinned, "that was my idea. When Luis left to order the axles and other parts to be made down in Mexico at his friend's factory, I told him my idea and he liked it. Ran the spare axle right through the compartment behind the seat, so there won't be any worry about one of the darn things falling off on those rough trails you'll be traveling on to Matamoros."

"Look up here now," Manollo said as he climbed up to the driver's bench.

After Patrick was seated beside him, and Broderick was standing on the frame, the Mexican pointed out several things.

"This is a foot brake." He placed his foot on the iron shaft sticking through the floor. "Instead of the hand brake on the original one Luis had made. This allows you to keep both hands on the reins. Don't apply it until the horses are almost stopped." He pushed it in a couple times to demonstrate.

Sean climbed up on the other side. "The two drivers who are going to Matamoros with you will do all the driving, but once you get it off the boat in Boston you two'll be running all over the place in it," he grinned, "chasing girls I'm sure."

Takin' the thing all the way to the school, Jesse thought, *just so those two jerks can chase girls.* He remained 'Injun silent', as his friend Miguello, Manollo's son liked to say. His view through the crack in the hayloft floor gave him a good view of the coach and the men around it.

About seven hundred miles south of Horse Heaven, a tall thin man with his Mexican father's black hair and eyes, but his English mother's fair skin, was sitting in a cantina in Chihuahua, Mexico. His name was Pablo Eduardo Zala, but to all who knew him he was called simply 'Culebra'—snake. His smile was his deceptive trademark as it spread across his youthful face. Fifteen years earlier he had developed the pleasant smile, complete with twinkling innocent looking eyes. The Federal Policia, at an ambush they set for his bandit parents, orphaned the ten-year-old boy. He quickly learned to fend for himself in a land with only the very poor or the very wealthy.

The poor were of no use to young Pablo so he developed a method to bring the wealthy close to him. The sparkling black eyes were held wide open to emphasize them against his pale complexion, as a child's innocent smile spread slowly across his face. Old man or old woman, it mattered not to Pablo. In his early book of rules all that mattered was that they look rich and be alone. He talked in a voice barely above a whisper, which invariably caused his prey to lean down to hear what he was saying. By the time Pablo was thirteen he had left eleven dead men and two dead women emptying their life's blood in many small towns across a wide swath of his homeland.

When his unsuspecting victim's ear was an inch from his lips they suddenly felt a razor sharp, nine-inch blade entering their chest. A few quick left and right movements and their heart was no longer supplying their body with blood. It was changing the dusty soil beneath their body into red mud as he swiftly emptied their pockets or purse of valuables.

He was careless on only one occasion when he allowed his deadly deed to be witnessed. The young boy that saw him kill the old woman, described him as an old man with two shiny pistols on a bandoleer of bullets. As the policia searched for the 'Bandoleer Bandit' young Pablo was moving swiftly across Mexico on stolen horses, which he regularly abandoned for fresh ones.

By the time Pablo was twenty he had assembled a band of young men that had similar attitudes—eat or be eaten. All seven of the bandits each had two things in common. They didn't care who the next victim was, and they would kill without hesitation.

A young bank teller in Durango sentenced himself and his three co-workers to death during a robbery, by the gang that was now being called Culebra's Bandidos. In a foolish bid for fame, he came up with a small pistol and was still trying to cock it when a lead slug entered his left eye. It departed the back of his scull, taking a large portion of his small brain with it. With shouts of encouragement to one another all seven of the deadly bunch emptied their guns into the four bank workers. One bandido, a half-Mexican/half-Apache they had nicknamed 'Cortado' [cut] because of his insatiable need to cut anyone or anything that ever got in his way. He even took time to lift the scalp from a dying young woman on the floor before departing the bank.

With their guns reloaded they rode out of town, killing two more people and a dog on the way.

Culebra sat at the small table in Chihuahua talking to a young man. "These traveling Gringos are from a wealthy family?"

"Yes," the nervous young man answered, "and they are on a very important mission."

Culebra leaned far forward to lock his eyes on the fidgety man. "And you got this information where?" He left the question mark hanging in the air as he stared intently, waiting for an answer.

The young informant tried to keep his watery gray eyes on the eyes of the man he knew as 'The most dangerous bandit in Mexico'. He didn't succeed and answered in a shaky, nervous voice. "I have a reliable contact in California where their people ordered special parts for some kind of buggy to carry them to a ship in Matamoros." He grinned and the young man's blackened, rotting teeth sickened Pablo.

"And you are certain that these two men are now traveling toward Chihuahua?"

"Yes, because I was told about when they would leave California." He offered another gray grin, then continued when he noticed Pablo's stare become more intense, "I had some of my people keep an eye on the route they would use."

Pablo paused to stare even more intently into the frightened young man's eyes; knowing very well that he was a master of intimidation. When he answered, it was in a quiet, deadly tone of voice. "And this was when?"

"Five days ago at dawn."

"This morning began the sixth day?"

"Uh, uh, yes," his informant stammered, "yes! Dawn tomorrow they will be six full days on the trail."

Pablo sat motionless for several moments, which seemed much longer to the nervous young man that was wishing he had never started selling information to this deadly 'Culebra'. He couldn't hold back an audible sigh of relief when Pablo reached into his pocket and brought out a very large roll of bills.

After peeling off several bills of large denomination, Pablo smiled his lethal, trademark smile. "Your information has always been reliable, Antonio." He once again locked his eyes on the informant as he handed him what would amount to a year's wages for a Mexican worker, "I hope this will increase my wealth as it has yours."

"It will," the man said as he stood to leave.

After he had taken a few steps he heard Pablo call his name so he stopped and turned, "Yes?"

"It better, amigo!"

Antonio climbed on his horse. *I am going back to Guadalajara to fleece the sailors. I do not think anyone will live long working with that man.*

Pablo sat for an hour, thinking about the information he had just purchased. He always kept a low profile when he was in a town of any size, because he was now aware that he was wanted in every corner of Mexico. He politely ordered his second glass of tequila from the small, withered old man behind the bar. By the time he finished it, the information was filed away in his head. He paid his bill, left a moderate tip on the table, and walked into the night.

When he rode into his camp, which was well concealed in a stand of trees beside a river, the false mustache had been removed, and the skin darkening salve had been wiped from his face and hands. The man sitting at the campfire was not the man named Jose that the bartender had, only hours earlier, done business with.

"The little fieldmouse show up?" His half-Apache/half-Mexican, right hand man smiled wickedly as he passed Pablo a hot coffee.

"Yes Cortado and I believe we have fallen into a very good thing."

"A ripe bank ready to pluck?"

"Much, much better than that," Pablo replied then grinned, "we are going to snatch a couple of young Gringo's from a wealthy family that will pay a large amount to get them back."

The half-breed sipped coffee and stared into the fire. After awhile he turned back to his boss, who appreciated his only friend's subtle way of thinking everything out before committing. "Yes amigo, I think you have brought us into a very good situation. When they give us the money we will give them their children back." Another wicked grin—"In pieces."

The stop in Nogales revealed several small problems with the coach. Luis' friend who owned the hacienda put his best two men on it so Patrick and Broderick could rest. Emiliano Huerta was not about to let his guard down, so a guard was posted around the clock, with himself and his five men taking two-hour tours outside the hacienda. He had been most of his life with Luis, and considered him more a brother than an employer. He planned to see to it that the two young men in his charge reached the ship that was to carry them to the school they would attend—or die trying.

By noon on the second day the coach was ready, so Emiliano made the decision to continue. Neither of the young McKannah boys offered any opposition because they had found nothing to keep them there—no young girls.

Camp was made before dark every night that they were between Luis' pre-arranged stops. Emiliano wanted the entire camp area checked out before stopping. "We do not want to come into an area after dark, as we are strangers and there are dangers we might encounter."

When they reached Hermosillo they had been eight days from Luis' Horse Heaven ranch. The coach was performing better than any had hoped. The only changes made at the Hermosillo hacienda, was re-rigging the horse teams.

When the coach pulled out two mornings after they arrived, everyone was rested and in good spirits. Emiliano and his men were alert, well rested, and looking forward to the trip to Chihuahua. It was a good thing—they would need all of their wits, courage, and strength to survive the encounter that lay only a short distance ahead.

The coach carrying the two McKannah brothers toward Matamoros rumbled steadily along the dirt supply trail used for over a hundred years by traders moving across Mexico. There were seven men also on the move. Another of Pablo's young paid informants rode into Chihuahua two days earlier with the information he was hoping for. "They are at a hacienda in Hermosillo, and will be taking the trail you suspected toward here."

Pablo looked into the boy's eyes so intently that it frightened him. "How many men are with the coach?"

"Six, Señor Pablo," he answered in a shaky, nervous voice, "two gringos and four Mexicans."

Again, Pablo looked deeply into the young Mexican's eyes. After a full minute the man was sweating profusely. He thought *I wish I had never met this crazy, pale, pasty-faced bandit.* Pablo held up his hand with the thumb and forefinger locked down into his palm. "How many?"

"Huh?"

"How many?" Pablo repeated as his stare intensified.

"Uh," the boy stammered, "you mean how many fingers?"

Pablo remained as rigid as a statue as he held the fingers toward the young man, and said nothing, still staring—never blinking.

"Three fingers, Señor Pablo." He was very relieved when the man lowered his hand and smiled.

Pablo handed him a wad of bills bigger than he had seen in his fourteen years on earth. As he was putting them in his purple baggy pants pocket Pablo said, "It is very good you learned to count little Chico, or your boots would be filling with your blood right now."

The boy turned to leave the alley where they had been talking but stopped when Pablo called to him. "Hey, little Chico."

"Si señor."

"Live to be an old man and do not ever call me Pablo again. Call me only Culebra."

"Si señor. Si Señor Culebra." Aboard his horse heading back toward Hermosillo he thought, *no man will ever live to be an old man if they keep dealing with that crazy snake.* He smiled wide as he patted the wad in his pocket. *I now go to Uncle Hernandez in Mexico City to buy my own fishing boat.*

Pablo returned to his camp in a wooded area outside the city. Cortado poured him a cup of strong coffee, and when Pablo was seated at the campfire he asked, "Are the rich gringos coming to join us?"

His evil grin warmed Cortado. "Yes amigo, they are on the trail now."

"How many men are with them?"

"Four," Pablo answered, "two driving and two scouting the trail ahead."

The grin spread across the scarred, half-breed's face. "Fat rich gringo children. Ha ha, this will be our easiest money."

"Yes amigo, I think we have found our life's work." He took a deep drink from the tin of coffee then added, "We will meet them on the trail tomorrow just before dark, so other eyes will not see what is happening."

Pablo was correct about this new venture being his gang's life's work. One thing he couldn't have known though was the instructions that Emiliano had given his two best scouts. Before leaving Horse Heaven he called to Jaime Pelez. He was a short, thin, thirty-year-old man. Emiliano also summoned Pomada Estido, the twenty-five-year-old, five-foot-tall half-Apache/half-Mexican nephew of the south ranch cook. "You are the best scouts, so I am going to rely on your eyes to be sure we do not ride into trouble without being aware of it."

Jaime spoke for them. "Señor Huerta, you can rest well when we two are out front." Pomada seldom spoke, so he just nodded his head.

Emiliano, always a serious man said, "We will all rest when the two McKannah boys are on the boat." He looked at both men then added, "Never let anyone ahead know you are watching our trail."

With serious faces, both men nodded. As they walked away Emiliano thought, *They will carry their load well.* His eyes went to the bandoleer across Jaime's shoulders that held his two pistols, then to the two long knives on his waist belt—knives that he could hit a moving target with. He then glanced at Pomada's pistol and long knife, but the tomahawk swinging at his side held his attention. He had seen the half-breed sneak within twenty feet of a deer, and then bury the weapon in its head. *Two deadly men when needed.*

The misinformation about the exact amount of men accompanying the two McKannah boys that Pablo had received from his informant would be costly.

Pablo's black eyes burned brilliantly against his pale skin as he spoke to the two men he had selected as lookouts. "Position yourselves on top of that ridge

I showed you, and wait for the coach to pass. It is two miles from here, so wait ten minutes then fire your rifle two times in the air. We will be only three miles away, and will hear the shots. They will think it is only a late hunter getting something for his table." His eyes always burned as with passion before each dangerous encounter, and they were on fire now. "Potillo."

"Si Culebra," the short stocky Mexican bandit said as he looked into his leader's eyes.

"Do you understand all I have told you?"

"Si Culebra, I know what to do."

"Bring the watch from your pocket."

The man stammered as he fidgeted with the pocket of his filthy, red silk pants. "Uh, Uh, maybe it's in this other pocket." He began sweating as he shoved his hand in the other pocket."

Only Pablo's eyes showed any change of emotion as the man shoved his thin hand down into each pocket. Cruelty burned deeply within them, but his face remained as though made of stone until his lips moved. "Is this what you are searching so convincingly for?" He held the gold pocket watch and chain by the waist clip as the watch turned.

"Umm, er, uh, I must have lost it." The man stammered as sweat ran from his face.

"Potillo," he said through stone cold eyes, "Cortado saw this on the dresser of the puta he was with the other night." He held the watch out as he stepped forward. The sweating man took the watch chain, but before Pablo let it go he said, "A couple hours of fun with that puta could have cost you your life amigo. If we were not about to soon be engaged in a new endeavor—it would.

The sweat-soaked man took the pocket watch and looked at the face to be sure it was working. As he put it in his pocket and was fastening the clip he said, "Gracias, Señor Culebra, muy gracias." He was smiling as Pablo quietly spoke.

"I bought those watches so we can time our operations, Potillo." Even though the foolish man had never seen a cobra he knew what the eyes were like as he looked into his leaders. "If you ever do anything like this again I will take your liver for those savages to eat as you watch." Pablo nodded in the direction of his gang at the campfire.

An hour before dark that same day, Pablo and his four men were hidden in the brush at the side of the road, and were waiting for the rifle fire to signal the coming coach. *I hope it arrives before dark, but it really doesn't matter.*

The coach was about to arrive—but like a fire-breathing demon. On the ridge above the trail, Culebra's two men lay dead as he waited for the rifle signal. One man's head was almost severed and Potillo had a tomahawk wound in the side of his.

Jaime Pelez was the first to spot the two bandit's horses hobbled below the ridge. He called Pomada Estido by imitating the ever-present prairie hen. He and the young half-breed had been on scouting missions together several times during their years at South Ranch, so he knew his call would alert Pomada. Moments later the small, stout horse that his friend favored, emerged silently from the wooded area south of him. Jaime pointed toward the two hobbled horses a half-mile away. Pomada nodded and slipped from his saddle. Their two horses were quickly secured and the two men stealthily headed for the top of the ridge.

The two bandits were so intent on hearing the approach of the coach that they didn't hear the two men as they moved to within a few feet from them. The first noise the one man heard was Jaime's knife coming toward his throat. The brief noise Potillo heard was the tomahawk entering his skull. The scouts gathered the men's muskets, pistols, and shot bags. Jaime turned to his friend, "I will climb down the face of this ridge to the trail while you bring the horses around amigo. We must not take the chance that our coach will pass."

Pomada only nodded and was off at a trot toward their horses. Twenty minutes later he was riding toward Jaime, who was leaning against the cliff. He was leading Jaime's horse and the two dead Mexican bandit's horses. Ten minutes later, Emiliano and one other man preceded the coach. By the time the coach arrived, Emiliano had been told about the two dead bandits.

"We spotted a group of men that were acting suspicious, so we watched. The two men who we later killed rode away toward this spot so we followed. When we saw them, we realized that they were somehow to alert their gang who are waiting ahead to ambush you."

"How many are they?"

"Only five now," Jaime answered.

Emiliano shook his head slowly up and down. "You two have done an excellent job, so now let us prepare our own ambush."

Pablo was certain the rifles would have fired by now, and was becoming concerned. He glanced at his four men. They were spread out, and standing next to some trees in the shadows of a falling sun. He heard the approaching hoofbeats of horses and his mind raced with confused thoughts. *Is this the coach or just another farmer's wagon trying to beat the darkness home?*

"I will ride with you two." Emiliano turned to Jesus Molina, who was still sitting beside Antonio Palas in the driver's area of the coach. "You are the best with the team of horses Jesus, so you drive alone." He motioned to Antonio with his head, "Tony, you ride ahead of the coach with Echy." Emiliano turned to his friend of eleven years. "Echy, have that shotgun of yours ready for anything as the coach proceeds." He then went to the coach and spoke to the two McKannah boys who were leaning out listening. "Get those shotguns out and be ready for anything, but stay down low until we see what is waiting ahead." He then said barely loud enough for all to hear, "Be careful because it is quickly getting dark, and we do not want to be shooting each other." He turned to Jesus, "You and Tony wait fifteen minutes after we leave, then you can move ahead slowly with the coach." He climbed into the saddle, and turned to Jaime and Pomada. "Lead the way, amigos."

Moments after hearing the approaching coach, three of Pablo's men were silently dying with one brown hand over their mouth and the other hand holding a knife which was opening a gaping wound in their throats.

When Pablo heard the slight commotion he turned and looked directly into the eyes of Pomada Estido as he opened the throat of another of Pablo's men. There was enough light filtering into the wooded area that the half-breed got a good look at the tall, thin, pale man standing next to a tree only twenty feet away before he turned to run.

Pablo cast off all thoughts except escape when he realized he had walked into a trap. After looking into the eyes of the man cutting his friend Cortado's throat, he turned to begin his escape. His foot was coming down to touch the ground for only the second time when he felt the knife entering his side. He stumbled from the blow, but regained his footing as he reached behind and pulled the blade out. His bearings were temporarily thrown off by the unexpected confusion. He was running parallel to the road as the two men ahead of the coach rounded the curve just ahead of him. Echevarria Alondo knew the running man was not one of his own so he raised the shotgun that he always carried and fired.

Pablo saw the error he had made by following the road and turned toward the dense woods. A few steps and he stumbled. It saved his life. Several of the pellets hit him in the buttocks and legs, but only enough to slow him down slightly. Even so, he was faster on his feet than most uninjured men. The tall half-Mexican/half-Englishman had another trait to his advantage—he was a born survivor.

Even though Echy and Tony turned their horses into the woods and gave almost instant pursuit, Pablo wasn't seen again by anyone who stayed alive—until he surfaced far to the north.

Patrick and Broderick climbed from the coach and watched as Emil and Tony rolled one of the dead men over. Neither had ever seen a man with his throat cut so their eyes widened as they leaned forward to better see the wound. "Holey moley," Broderick exclaimed, "a little more and his head wouldn't be attached to his body."

"We could not take a chance with these desperadoes Señor Broderick, because we were not certain this was all of them." As he spoke, Jaime was cleaning his knife with a cloth dampened in a pool of water from the recent rain.

"This is a puzzle," Emil said as he walked up. "They certainly must have known we would be passing through here in order for them to be waiting in ambush."

Jesus Molina walked to the body and looked long and hard at it, and then he straightened to his thin, six-foot-two-inch height. "I think I know who these men were." When Emil and the two young McKannah boys looked at him questioningly, he continued. "Pomada told me he got a good look at the one that ran away. He was tall and very pale. On my last trip to Hermosillo to visit with my aunt and uncle, they told me about a young man that was fast becoming Mexico's most dangerous bandit." They all listened as he went on to describe Pablo Eduardo Zala, and the trail of infamy he was leaving as he moved from one coast of Mexico to the other. "If it really was him then I wish we had killed him for the sake of the people he will meet in the future."

Emil turned to the silent Pomada. "Will you know him if you ever see him again?"

"Yes. Until the dirt covers me in my grave, Señor Huerta, because that man had the evil of Satan in his eyes."

"Let's get moving," Emil said softly, "and see if we can locate a spot to camp so we will not have to travel all night."

6

~ Long trip to school ~

Pablo lay in a well-hidden cave that he had located earlier several miles from Chihuahua. He licked his wounds like the wounded animal he was. Two stops along the way had supplied him with a good horse and enough supplies to wait until he healed enough to travel on to the destination that now burned in his brain. He also left two women, two men and five dead children behind. He wanted no witnesses because he hoped the Mexicans who had wounded him would think he had died. The knife wound in his side had not penetrated a vital organ, and the pellets could be dug from the skin. Painfully he dug with his knife in his buttocks without being able to see. In a sick, twisted way he enjoyed the pain as he twisted his thin, limber legs enough to watch as the pellets came out on the knife blade's tip. On his small smokeless fire, a pot boiled leaves that he had gathered along the way. He knew which leaves and herbs would fight the infection. As each pellet was removed, he bathed the wound with the liquid. Several times each day he wiped the oozing wound in his side with the same solution. One week from the day he entered the cave he was feeling well enough to travel.

The man who rode into Chihuahua had hair lightened with bleach taken from his last victim's home. His pale face and hands were now light brown from tobacco juice and berries. The stolen horse was turned loose because he knew how easy it would be to steal another when he decided to head north to complete his mission. At the moment though, he was looking for someone. By midnight on his third night of searching the many cantinas, he was rewarded. Sitting at a small table in the rear of a dingy, smoke filled, dirt floored cantina was his prey. The young man was sitting with two whores. At two in the morning Pablo was waiting in the alley across the dirt street. The young man staggered out and headed for the cheap room he had been sleeping in since receiving the wad of bills from Pablo for the information about the coach and <u>six</u> men. As silently as the deadly jaguars that roamed throughout Mexico, Pablo followed. Twice the young man fell after staggering sideways in a futile attempt to regain his balance. A deadly grimace crossed Pablo's face.

He was certain the young man was passed out within minutes after entering the door to his tiny room, but he waited in the shadows a full hour before tripping the primitive latch and opening the door. The deadly *culebra* stood motionless for ten minutes as his eyes adjusted to the darkness. When the hand clamped over the young man's mouth, the boy's eyes opened. The drunken fog surrounding him prevented the boy from seeing the man he had earlier told himself that he never wanted to see again.

The long blade of the knife went in slowly as Pablo held the boy still. Hands that groped for the hand holding his mouth suddenly went to the knife as it slowly and painfully entered his stomach for the second time. Pablo pulled it part way out and waited for the boy to grab the blade before continuing. He kept his knife sharp enough to shave with so he knew fingers were falling. As the boy held tight to the blade with what fingers were remaining, Pablo slowly shoved it back in then leaned close to the boy's ear. "There were more men with that coach than you told me little Chico."

The young informant now knew who was torturing him to death and wished he had not stopped to visit the whores before going to his Uncle Hernandez in Mexico City to be a fisherman. All turned to blackness as Pablo shoved the blade up to slice into his young heart.

The next day at noon the bandit was on a big chestnut gelding heading north toward California. His thoughts were still of a large ransom.

Emiliano instructed Pomada to scout ahead of the coach. He then assembled the rest near him as they rumbled down the bumpy trail looking for a spot to camp for the night. Patrick and Broderick returned the shotguns to the compartment, each silently thanking Luis for his afterthought, even though they weren't used. Two hours later, Pomada was in the middle of the road waiting for the coach. "There is a very good place to camp only a mile ahead, and there are no people anywhere in this area."

A guard was posted and everyone was agreeable to eat cold tortillas and beans so they could get some rest. The morning sun came up as Jesus Molina prepared breakfast. He often filled in as cook, so everyone was glad to see him working up the mixture for fresh tortillas. One by one each man went to the coffeepot, but also lifted the lid on the huge pot simmering in the coals. Each comment was almost identical, "Mmmmmmmm, menudo."

An hour later, seven men were sitting at the small fire complementing Jesus on his cooking abilities. Emiliano was still chewing on one of the three tortillas he carried with him when he relieved Echy on guard duty. He stood at the edge of the small lake after circling their camp. He liked this spot better than any they had stayed in because the lake guarded the rear of their campsite, and he knew everyone was tired. He suggested they spend another day and night so they could rest before continuing, and all agreed that it was a good idea. It was an idea that almost cost Broderick his life.

Back on Sean's ranch, everything was going along fine until the priest brought bad news. He was in charge of the church that Sean had recently financed the construction of. "Good day Father," Sean said when the buggy stopped, "what brings you here this time o' day?"

The tall, gaunt, Irish priest from Dublin, Ireland stepped solemnly from the buggy. Sean had arranged and financed his passage, so he could take charge of the small wilderness church that the community had constructed. "Aye, tis bad news it is that I'm carryin' today, Mister McKannah."

"Well Father, hold onto it till we get inside and get you a glass of water."

"Yes, yes, lad. M'face is scorched, m'lips are cracked, and I do believe my brains are boiling. Thank you very much, I 'ad no idea that this new land was so hot."

Issabella was always happy to see the new priest and smiled as she handed him a glass of cool water. She leaned against the porch rail as he drank. Her face changed to intense distress as he explained.

"Ralph Ledderman and his son Elijah were found murdered on the trail while they were coming back from Yerba Buena. A young Indian boy saw the men who did it, so the new sheriff organized a posse to go after the two of them." Sean and Bella remained silent as the priest drank the remaining water. "They were the same two young men that robbed and killed a fisherman before leaving Yerba Buena. The sheriff said they have been trapping in the mountains and coming to town regularly for a year, causing trouble each time."

Simon and Ian were entering the ranch on their horses as the priest was leaving. They each waved and yelled to him as he passed. When Simon was told the news, he was devastated. "Elijah has been my best friend since we were little children. Oh my God, this is terrible. Oh my God, poor little Elijah.

He was gonna be a school teacher and take Mr. Adderly's place when he got his education." He held to the porch rail and lowered his head, "Oh my God, poor little Elijah." He turned to his father, "Will they catch them guys, pa?"

Later that evening as Ian was in the bunkhouse with the Mexican ranch hands playing cards; Simon was lying in his bunk thinking of his lifetime friend. Tears came as he squeezed his eyes shut. His thoughts were not those of a fourteen-year-old boy. *If they don't catch those guys Elijah, then I sure will.*

At fifteen he would back up his words with action, and begin a career that would make him a legend among hunters of men—and the Texas Rangers.

An hour before dark, Broderick was standing at the edge of the lake looking at the sliver of moon above the distant trees. He wandered along the bank of the lake until he was about a half mile from the camp. It felt good to stretch his long legs after so long on the trail in the small coach. He always had a long hunting knife—which his father had given every boy—in the leather sheath attached to a leather belt around his slender waist, and his pistol also shoved under it. Neither weapon would have helped him against the animal that had watched him from the time he left the camp area. As Broderick approached the boulders that lay at the northern end of the lake, two yellow eyes watched and waited. Two black eyes also watched the huge cat and Broderick. Pomada was the only man in the group that could track a jaguar unheard and unseen. He had spotted the cat stalking Broderick only moments after watching the young man walking away from camp.

Broderick stooped beneath a large boulder to pick up a flat rock to skip across the placid water. The jaguar prepared to spring on the unsuspecting young man, but before he could unleash the powerful spring in his rear legs, a terrible pain in his neck followed a loud noise. Pomada's slug tore the cat's spine in half at the base of its skull, and he fell twitching at Broderick's feet.

The half-Apache/half Mexican that Broderick had liked and known most of his life, was quickly at his side checking to be sure the cat was dead. "Holy Mother of Jesus, Pomada, how did you know that jaguar was after me?"

"I see you walking away so I watch, because there are plenty jaguar in this land."

By the time they had the dead cat stretched out, Emiliano and Antonio were there. Emiliano had yelled for the others to take cover not knowing what had caused someone to shoot. "My God! That is a big jaguar," he said then leaned down to raise the huge, limp head. "Good shot amigo," he looked up at Pomada, "severed the spine." He yelled for someone to bring a horse, and soon Echy was there with his big mare.

A rope was tossed over a limb so the horse could pull the dead cat up for skinning. "This thing is at least eight feet long to the tip of his tail," Broderick said as he watched the three men expertly remove the skin from the carcass.

"And I would wager that it weighs over three hundred pounds." Emiliano commented.

Back in the camp, the hide was stretched out with the flesh side up, and the excess flesh was scraped away. "Everyone must piss on the inside after we have scraped all of the remaining flesh out."

"Yes," Jaime answered, "this will make a wonderful gift for Aunt Carmen, so we must preserve it until we get home and can properly tan this beautiful hide."

The urine preserved the luxurious pelt until they returned and it could be tended to properly. Carmen shuddered at the story, but loved the gift.

During the time Simon was brooding about the murder of his friend and dreaming of revenge, he was also laying the foundation for his future. For his fourteenth birthday his father presented him with a brand new flintlock revolver. "This's a new type of pistol," Sean explained to his son as they walked toward the area where they all practiced shooting. "I saw it at James Poorsmith's new trading post last month while I was getting supplies." He stopped at the oak table he and his men had constructed just for this purpose then handed the pistol back to Simon. "Look it over real good son, it's a real clever invention."

Simon inspected the weapon that would become legendary in his hand in a few short years. "It's a," Sean paused as he read from the piece of paper he had written all the information on as James recited it from his own notes, "Collier flintlock five shot revolver, and was invented about two years ago by an American guy living in London, England." Simon continued his inspection as Sean read everything he had written. "James said he already has orders for more'n a hundred of 'em, so he wants me to tell him what you think of it after you use it awhile."

The rest stop in Chihuahua was relaxing for both the McKannah boys and their escort. It was a beautiful hacienda, owned by one of their uncle's oldest friends from Spain, and they were given royal treatment during their two-day stay. The wealthy Spaniard's men checked the coach from end to end. The food was excellent and served on silver trays. The wines were from his own vineyard, and were stored in a cellar twice the size of Luis'. The two young McKannah boys thanked the elderly couple for their hospitality then climbed aboard the coach for the three-hundred-mile trip to Monterrey. Before the coach was even out of the hacienda gates they were dreaming of the one thing that had been missing at each stop on their long journey—girls.

When the coach came to a stop inside the next hacienda; owned by the Admiral of the Spanish Navy's nephew, they knew that their prayers had been answered. Girls! There were several young maidens sitting at a fountain in the middle of the courtyard. *Girls*, the word ran simultaneously through Patrick and Broderick's minds. They turned to each other and grinned, "This is... they laughed as they both started to say the same thing. "Yeah," Patrick finished, "this is gonna be a good stop."

And it was. Their youthful, lusty dreams were not fulfilled, but it was two days they would forever remember. It seemed to them that beautiful young girls for miles around must live at the huge hacienda. By late afternoon on the first day of their arrival, a giant festival was in progress. The owner had been planning it since Luis' messenger arrived with the news that his two nephews would be arriving. The sixty-room hacienda was filled with young Spanish and Mexican ladies and gentlemen. The boys were pummeled with questions about their future plans after leaving Harvard. The McKannah boys were amazed when they saw how handsome their usually ruggedly dressed guards looked when they appeared in new clothes provided by their host. Emiliano and his men were told to relax because the four-corners of the fortress-like hacienda were guarded twenty-four hours a day by armed guards. "In these troubled times," their host said, "we cannot afford to let our guard down."

Mexican vaqueros and McKannahs each talked about the enjoyable time they all had at the hacienda during their trip's last hundred and fifty miles to Matamoros.

Two days after arriving at the Gulf of Mexico, the coach had been loaded on the deck of the cargo vessel, and the sails filled with wind to begin the long journey across the largest body of water the boys had ever seen.

Emiliano negotiated with a local man to exchange the team horses that had pulled the coach, for grain to feed their own horses, and supplies for themselves. The six men watched the ship sail toward the morning sun then Emiliano said, "Amigos you all fulfilled your task with excellence, but now we must return to El Cielo de los Caballos."

Everyone laughed hard when Jaime said, "Can we stop for a week or so at that hacienda in Monterrey?"

Days later, with their sea legs now under them, Patrick pointed ahead and asked the seaman standing with him and his brother, "What is that green in the sky ahead?"

"It is the sun bouncing off the trees on Cayo Hueso. That is why we always try to approach the island when the sun is shining."

"Well Broderick," Patrick said, "there it is. Key West; wild women, good whiskey, and dry land."

Broderick turned to the sailor, "Why do you call it Cayo Hueso?"

"When it was first found Senor, it had many human bones on it, so they called it The Island of Bones—Most call it Cayo Hueso—Key West."

"Hmmm," the tall thin redheaded boy mused to himself, *lotta pirates probably stopped here back then. Probably still do at times?*

7

~ *Deadly adventures* ~

"But why a gambling hall?" Ian's mother just stared into her short, too-thin, blonde young son's piercing blue eyes, and shook her head.

"Ma," the young boy who had just turned fifteen in April said, "it's what I've wanted to do since I picked up my first handful of cards." He sat patiently on the edge of the couch that his mother and father had built, padded, and covered. Ian watched as she paced back and forth across the huge family room. He was the one boy Issabella always thought would be a priest or a businessman, but never a gambler or gunfighter. She talked more to herself than to him as she paced.

"Two sons at a school half way around the world, one chasing after a gang of murderers, (she had her own way of finding out what was really going on around the ranch) a daughter that keeps talking about going back with her brothers when they come home for a break from school, and now…she turned to stare incredulously at Ian a moment then continued ranting and pacing…a son who wants to live with harlots, murderers, gamblers, and God only knows what else."

Pablo Eduardo Zala could be very patient when necessary, and he knew that it would now be required if he was to get out of Mexico alive, with so many people trying to collect the reward being offered for his capture—or his head. He was tempted many times to steal a horse, but knew that would make people think that maybe it was the deadly 'Culebra' that stole it. He was still healing from his wounds and did not want to try dodging people trying to kill him. The thought of his severed head being delivered to Mexico City however, made him smile.

Two months after the incident with Patrick and Broderick's armed escort, a tall, berry and tobacco juice brown-skinned, black-haired young man walked into California. He stayed east of the mountains and entered between Yuma and San Diego. Another two months of performing small jobs in exchange for food found the now light skinned Pablo working on a small sheep ranch not too far from Luis' South Ranch.

Six months after being wounded during his narrow escape, he was fully recovered and possessed the information he had been seeking. The brothers and sister of the two men he had planned to kidnap lived on a sheep ranch three hundred miles north. His new plan was working out. *Patience,* he thought, *I must be patient. This rich old man they call Uncle Luis on the big horse ranch will pay me a fortune to get his little niece back.* A sinister smile crossed his handsome—now pale again—young face. He rode north on the old nag he had negotiated for from his Mexican employer before saying, "I must go north to find my family."

A couple of months before Simon left to go in search of his friend's killers, a pale smiling young man approached Sean's sheep ranch. In flawless Spanish he asked Manollo if he had a job for a man that knows how to handle sheep.

Manollo, ever cautious asked the stranger, "Where did you learn such perfect Spanish?"

The man smiled, "From my Mexican daddy I learned the language, but the fair skin I got from my English mother. It makes many people wonder how this gringo can speak our language so well." His laughter was friendly and unguarded so Manollo, like many others, was taken in.

He started work that same day then moved into the bunkhouse that night. Ian came a little later to see if the men wanted to play a game of cards. The stranger gladly accepted a seat in the game. Sometime before midnight Ian left and headed for the main house. *There is no way to read that new man's face.* He continued thinking about the man as he lay in bed. *His moves are always the same and his expression never changes while he holds the cards.* He looked out the open window; *I think I can learn much from his manner.*

Pablo let a month pass as he worked hard on Sean's ranch. His eyes never missed a thing, and soon after arriving he noticed that the homely young girl went riding her horse almost every day to the big oak tree beside the small stream about two miles from the house. *Perfect place to get her alone and knock her out then head for those caves I found.* He walked among his sheep and watched as she rode toward the tree. His thoughts were sinister and deadly. *I will kill her as soon as we are in the caves then leave the ransom letter on the porch one night.*

A week later he put his plan in motion as soon as he saw Aleena leave for her favorite thinking spot. Everyone was gathering sheep for shearing on the south end of the ranch. He ducked down among the sheep and disappeared over the nearby hill.

A pair of black Apache eyes had been watching him from the moment he spotted the tall white man standing with the sheep. He now moved stealthily along the ridge so he would not be seen, but kept peering above the rim often to be sure he was still with the man he followed.

Pablo cautiously approached the area near the creek, so she wouldn't have a chance to scream.

The Apache approached Pablo as quietly as a spider moving across his web.

Aleena leaned back against the huge oak and dreamed of going off to school like her two oldest brothers. *I'll never be a beautiful teacher, but I'll be the best teacher my students ever had.* Her mind was walking along beautifully paneled hallways somewhere far away, so she never heard Pablo approaching behind her.

Pablo's mind was busy spending the fortune that he knew was going to be the easiest money he had ever made. He didn't hear the soft footfalls of the Apache moving in behind him. All that came from his mouth was a grunt as the tomahawk went into his back. He turned in time to see Pomada Estido closing the five feet between them, but not in time to prevent the long blade from entering his chest to slice his heart nearly in half. He was dead while still hanging on Pomada's blade.

When Aleena heard the commotion behind the tree she jumped up and looked in time to see one man running toward another one. As her brothers had taught her, she instantly turned and ran toward the horse grazing nearby. She was in the saddle about the same time Pablo's life ended. Her screaming brought her father and three brothers galloping toward her. When she explained what she had seen, they spread out and approached the tree as Sean heard a familiar voice call out from behind a boulder.

"Señor McKannah, it is I, Pomada Estido."

"I recognize your voice Pomada, c'mon out." He looked at the dead man that Manollo had hired awhile back lying spread-eagled on his back with blood all over the front. "Who is this guy?" He turned to the diminutive young half-Mexican/half-Apache, "And what the heck are you doing way up here?"

As Sean explained to Bella what had happened earlier, she held Aleena so tight that she couldn't move and when she tried, her mother held her even tighter. Her mouth hung open as the story unfolded.

"Pomada," Sean said, "visited a ranch near Luis' South Ranch that raised sheep. A young woman he liked lived and worked there so he went as often as possible. On one trip he saw a tall white man tending the sheep. He said there was something familiar about the man, but he couldn't come up with anyone like him that he knew, so Pomada dismissed it. On the next trip he saw the man again, and this time he couldn't take his eyes from him. The white face stayed with him. He said he suddenly awoke from a sound sleep with the man's identity. He was the one that got away from the ambush that Emiliano told us about. Pomada grabbed his gear in the middle of the night and rode to the sheep ranch and quietly woke up the owner. When he was told that the man had quit and headed north, Pomada said he somehow knew the man was heading for our ranch." Before he could continue, Bella spoke for the first time.

"What in God's name did he want here?"

"I think Jesse figured it out," Sean answered. "He thinks that gang was gonna grab Patrick and Broderick to get a big reward for giving them back."

She looked at her only daughter then at Sean. "He was going to grab her for the same reason?"

"Yep, I reckon so." Sean waited a moment before continuing, "Pomada pushed his horse until it was useless, then stopped at a ranch and told 'em what was going on, so they let him have food and a new horse. He rushed on and arrived a short time before that guy went to grab Aleena. He left his horse over near that dry creek-bed and came in on foot."

"Oh thank God and thank God for sending Pomada," Bella repeated several times, "where is he so I can thank him for saving our daughter?"

"He's already gone."

"What?"

"Yeah. He said Uncle Luis and Aunt Carmen plus Maggie would be worried sick 'cause they won't have any idea what happened to him. He's gonna return the horse those good folks let him use then ride his on home.

Tears ran freely down Bella's face as she hugged Aleena. "Thank you God for looking after our precious daughter."

Sean left the house thinking, *Thanks Pomada, for coming on the run.*

"We've got all five thousand sheep culled aside for the trip to Yerba Buena," Sean said to Issabella, "and four men are looking after them till we get ready to leave."

"When do you plan on leaving?"

"Manollo has eight good sheep men coming tomorrow, so we'll probably head out the day after that."

"Jesse going with you?"

"Yeah, he says he's scouted a trail better'n the one we used last time, and it has better grass and water along the way too."

She rolled over in bed and rested her still lovely face on the palm of her hand and looked intently at Sean. "While you're gone I plan to try to talk Ian out of following this crazy scheme of his to be a professional card player."

The green flecks in Sean's gray eyes sparkled, "Everyone thought me n' Frank were crazy to go up in the mountains looking for beaver, darlin', but if we hadn't done it we'd still be thinking about it." His smile made her stomach quiver a little like it always did. "A man's gotta try different things till he finds out what he's good at."

She reached out and grabbed his rusty red hair with her free hand. "We found out together one thing you're really good at, you wild Irish heathen."

"Yeah, we sure did, didn't we, sweetheart." He moved closer to her."

His work worn hands were already under her sleeping gown and caressing her as she turned to blow out the lamp.

She turned to him in the dark and met his lips with hers. After a long silent kiss she said, "Wait!" She sat up in bed and pulled the long gown over the top of her head, then moved her body close to his, wispering, "I love you."

Sean spent the next day going over everything with Manollo that had to be taken care of while he was gone. It was late in the afternoon when he was satisfied he had covered everything. As he headed for the main house, he noticed his daughter riding off toward the huge old oak tree where she recently almost lost her life. He stopped and watched her ride into the approaching sunset. Sean turned and went back to the barn to saddle a horse. "Take mine," Manollo said.

Sean hadn't noticed his foreman leaning on the fence watching. He stared at the man who had been with him since he started the ranch, and then let a grin spread across his face. "You even know what I'm thinking, doncha?"

The stout Mexican called Manny, by all but Sean and Bella, who always referred to him as Manollo, just smiled and turned back to watch the young girl that he had rocked on the porch as a baby, disappear over a hill.

Sean easily caught up with Aleena before she got to the tree. When she turned to see her father coming at a gallop her face lit up. She knew her father was a man's man and spent very little time with any female except her mother. That Sean would go out of his way to come and be with her a while before leaving made her happy.

"Where ya headin', sweetheart?"

"My thinking place."

"That big ole oak by the creek?"

"Yep."

"Me n' yer mom used to go there to have a picnic and talk when you were still in her belly," he said with a wide smile, "that's probably why you like it so much."

"Sure is a peaceful place."

They let the horses wander around looking for good grass as they sat beneath the tree together. Sean never knew what to say to females so he waited for his daughter to speak.

"When you leaving with the sheep, daddy?"

"Tomorrow at dawn."

"How long you think you'll be gone?"

"Mmmmm," Sean mused, "probably about three weeks. If all goes well we'll get 'em there in a coupla weeks then take about a week to get back home."

"Is Miguello going with you?"

"Yeah, Jesse asked Arianna, and she said okay."

She was silent for a long time then said wistfully, "That must really be som'n."

"What's that darlin'?"

"Being out on a trail drive like that with cooking fires, stars blinking, and wolves howling at night."

He turned and looked at the daydreaming expression on her face. His mind was racing with thoughts that had never entered it before. After a long silent pause he said, "I don't suppose a girl would wanna come along on a trail drive like that, would she?"

Her face lit up when she turned to him. "Oh daddy, I'd love to go with you guys. I could make breakfast, cook a pot of menudo better'n any of them guys, make biscuits, and and…

"Whoa girl," he said with a wide smile, "y'ain't gotta impress me, 'cause I already know all them things." He stood and reached for her hand, "Let's go getcher stuff ready for a trail drive, gal."

"Oh dear God, no." Issabella wailed when Sean told her that he was taking Aleena with him. "But she's just a baby."

"Jesse's taught that girl to ride better'n any of them Mexicans I betcha, and I never have taken much time with her. This'll be a great time for Aleena and her daddy to get to know each other."

The next morning Issabella helped their cook Angelina get all of the men fed that were going with Sean. When she saw her daughter in a pair of Jesse's trail pants and wearing one of his old leather hats she started crying. "Oh my goodness, I don't have a little girl any more."

Aleena went to her mother and hugged her. "Sure you do mama," she looked down with a grin, "she's just growing up."

Jesse's new route led them west of Chief Chalponich's village and north to Coyote Lake where they camped on the fourth night of the drive. When the sheep were herded into a grassy area that led all the way to one edge of the lake, Sean divided the six Mexicans into three groups taking shifts to keep the sheep from wandering off.

"This's a lot better than the route we took the last time," Sean said after getting a tin cup of coffee, before settling in next to Jesse at the campfire. "What're them things cookin' in the skillet?"

"Aleena's been collecting stuff," Jesse said. "She's been getting acorns and berries all day so she could make acorn cakes in that bacon grease." He nodded toward the sizzling pan in the fire.

Sean turned toward the supply wagon and smiled at his daughter, "Where'd you learn how to make them things, darlin'?"

"Angelina showed me how, that time Uncle Frank was coming to visit." She finished at the wagon and sat down beside Sean. "She said they were Uncle Frank's favorite treat, so she wanted to have some for him."

He put his arm out and pulled her close to him. "She's right 'cause I don't know anything he likes better." He leaned toward the fire, "Mmmm boy smells good too, and they'll be a nice little treat for us after that dinner you fixed." He turned to her and asked, "All this cookin' ain't too much for you?"

"Nope." She grinned, "I like cooking."

When Sean looked into his daughter's twinkling blue eyes he felt a pulling in his chest—as always. *Why couldn't she have been pretty like her mother and one o' them boys born homely?*

"Well," he grinned, "you're sure doin' a great job of it." He paused then added, "Maybe we'll retire Angelina and let you take over."

"Oh no daddy," her grin widened, "I'm gonna be a schoolteacher."

"Yeah," he said seriously, "that's what I hear. Whatever you decide to do darlin' I reckon you'll be great at it."

She was finally getting the praise from her father that she'd always wanted, so she leaned her head close and laid it on his shoulder. "I'll sure try to be a good one." She stood to begin turning the cakes, "Guess what we got to put on these?"

"Teeth," Jesse said with a wide grin as he walked toward the fire.

"Them too, but we got som'n really good that Manollo gave me for the trip."

"Bee honey." Miguello had been sitting silently staring into the fire, and blurted out, "I bet my dad sent some o' that bee honey he makes, huh?"

"Yeah," Aleena said, "but he doesn't make it, the bees do."

"I know, but daddy fixes it so we can eat it," his grin prevented her from pursuing the matter further, "and boy do I love that stuff."

The four Mexicans sat quietly watching the acorn cakes simmering. "Bien, bien, muy bien."

Aleena looked at the man and smiled. "I hope they're good," she replied in perfect Spanish.

When the two dozen small cakes were gone, the Mexicans were still saying, "Delicioso, muy sabroso."

"Yep," Sean said, "they really were tasty darlin', thank you. That was a nice treat for everyone."

"Especially with that bee honey on 'em," Jesse added.

Miguello nodded his head in approval as he chewed. "Can you show mama how to make them things?"

"Miguello, I bet your mom knows how to make 'em way better n' me."

"I don't think so, 'cause I ain't ever ate any before."

"There's still about an half hour of daylight left so while you guys are telling your stories I'm gonna go around those boulders and take me a nice long bath." Aleena gathered up her towel and a set of fresh clothes and headed for the boulders that bordered the edge of the lake about a half-mile away.

As she walked along the edge of the crystal clear lake, a set of black eyes watched her with growing interest.

Tolahta was on the other side of the lake, tending fish traps when Sean's sheep outfit arrived. He was from Chulponich's village, and was born twenty-five years earlier with a lot of his wiring crossed. The village of Yokut Indians tolerated him, but all knew he was crazy, and at times dangerous—especially when a woman was involved. He had scars from one end to the other from fights he had over grabbing someone else's woman. Many had repeated the same statement over the years, "One day he will kill or be killed over a woman."

Tolahta came stealthily around the lake to watch the camp from the same boulders that Aleena was now walking toward. He lay quietly as the sheep herders fixed and ate their food. His eyes were filled with only curiosity until the person walking toward him was close enough for him to see that it was a young girl. The black eyes now took on the same crazy look they always did when he watched a female. He quietly reached down and picked up a rock and waited.

The moment Aleena rounded the corner and could not be seen by the men at the cookfire, Tolahta grabbed her and clamped his hand over her mouth then hit her on the side of the head with the rock. Before she even knew what was happening to her, Aleena was out like a light and being carried swiftly toward the Indian's waiting horse.

The stories went around the campfire like they always do when men gather together. When the first two men were relieved from their watch it was after dark. One of the men said, "Where is that cook? I want to tell her how much I enjoyed those acorn cakes." He smiled and looked for her then continued, "Not since I was a child have I had them."

Sean looked around. "I think she's over in the supply wagon."

Jesse was on his feet and almost running to the small wagon where she slept. "She ain't here pa," he almost screamed.

As the men were looking everywhere, Jesse was walking slowly with an oil lamp following her track. He knew she had a habit of kicking a stone with every other step, so it would be easy for him to follow her. When he came to the boulder he saw the small spot of blood and his heart almost stopped. In ten minutes he saw that someone had hit Aleena and was running along the bank with her.

He was in the camp minutes later yelling, "Someone's grabbed her."

"What? What?" His father asked incredulously, "Grabbed Aleena?"

"Yeah," Jesse said as he quickly gathered the things he knew he'd need, "and I'm going after her." He looked at Sean hard and his father knew it would be useless to argue. "We let our guard down pa," he shook his head, "we shoulda kept an eye on her." He soon had his gear assembled. "Lemme take the Brown Bess, pa."

Ten minutes after arriving back in camp, Jesse was heading back along the bank of Coyote Lake. He had one of the small oil lanterns, but it wasn't lit as he swiftly returned to the spot that he had followed a short time earlier. With it lit he walked along the bank until he followed the man's track to the far side. He saw that the dry fish trap on the bank was only half serviced. *Musta been checkin' his traps when he saw Aleena.* Jesse inspected the trap better in the lamplight. *Crazy Tolahta. He's the only Yokut that would make such a poor trap.* He held the light closer to be certain. *Yep. I've seen these traps before when I was with Wampohnah.* He stood and looked around then began walking slowly back and forth until he spotted trampled brush where the Indian's horse had headed for the small line of low mountains a few miles in the distance. He stood motionless as he put the good memory he had inherited from his father to work. *Wampohnah took me to some big caves up in them hills.* He scoured his memory for any other caves or some other place the man might take his sister. When he was satisfied there was no other place he had been to in this area where a man could keep a person captive, he double-checked his thinking by following the track of the horse in the lamplight for a distance. It was heading straight toward the caves. He turned the lamp out and hung it on a tree limb, then set off at a slow trot. *Must be about ten miles from here.*

Early the following morning Sean said, "Young as he is, my son is as good a tracker as any man I know, so whoever took my daughter is probably in more trouble than she is, 'cause he's the toughest of all my boys." He looked hard into the distance where they had seen the lamplight last night then turned to his men. "We gotta get these sheep to the place they're gonna be loaded on the boat to Cuba so let's get at it." He turned to Miguello. "I want you near one of us all the time till we find out what's goin' on." He shook his head slowly. *Might be some kinda freak wandering around out here stealing kids.*

Before dawn was lighting the eastern sky behind the mountains, Jesse closed in. He had been moving forward during the long night. He was now cautiously and silently moving toward the entrance to the caves that he'd been shown by Wampohnah. Many months earlier his Indian friend was training him to track anything on two, four, or no legs at all. Jesse could now track a rattler across granite boulders. His hearing was alert to any sound as he inched forward. His heart almost leaped into his throat when he finally noticed the faint flicker of light coming from far within. *I was right.* Jesse ran his hands over the Brown Bess musket to make certain all was as it should be, and then moved into the caves.

"You be my wife now." The Indian with an oddly elongated, too-narrow head spoke in Spanish, after trying his native Yokut tongue.

Aleena's head hurt where he had hit her to knock her unconscious, and she had a headache so bad she was having trouble focusing on her abductor. Through the rag he had tied around her mouth she could only grunt and stare wide-eyed and terrified at the crazy Indian.

"Woo, woo, woo," he quietly grunted as he danced around the small fire. Then he pointed at her chanting in Spanish, "You my wife now—you my wife now."

Jesse took his time inching along the narrow entrance passage, but was inside as the sun began removing the shadows. He remembered that there were several passages leading to the huge main cavern. Once inside the mountain he stopped every few feet to listen. When he was satisfied, he moved ahead a little farther then stopped again to listen. After half an hour he finally heard Tolahta's chanting. The sound of his voice was Jesse's guide through the darkness to the main cavern. He stopped when he heard him talking.

"I go get more firewood so we be warm when we take our clothes off." His grin was so hideously lecherous that it made Aleena whimper beneath her gag. He checked the rawhide ropes binding her feet and hands then shoved her roughly down on her side to tie her hands and feet together behind her. She was unable to do anything but lay and await her fate. He walked away chanting, "Woo, woo, woo, you my wife now—woo, woo, woo, you my wife now."

Jesse held his breath, knowing the Indian was going to leave the caves to get wood. He hoped he would take the one he was now crouched down in with the Brown Bess ready. He heard the crazy man's chanting fade as he headed for the entrance.

"Woo, woo, woo, Tolahta has a wife now—woo, woo, woo, Tolahta has a wife now, woo…

When his chanting grew fainter, Jesse hurried to his sister and moved in front so she could see him in the dim light. Her eyes widened then tears began flowing as she squeezed them tight.

His knife quickly severed the binding then he removed the gag covering her mouth. In a whisper she said, "Oh Jesse."—Nothing more.

"I ain't messin' around with this crazy Indian," he whispered in her ear, "so you lay back down like you was." When her eyes showed her panic he said, "Trust me sis n' everything's gonna be fine."

Aleena had always trusted her brother so she did as she was told.

Jesse went into the shadows and readied the Brown Bess that his father had carried through the mountains when he was about his age. Jesse's fingers ran across the gold inlay on the walnut stock. *SEAN McKANNAH 1798* he said to himself. His eyes were adjusted to the dim light put out by the small fire, when he heard Tolahta returning—still chanting. He waited until the Indian tossed the wood he was carrying to the floor of the cave and was facing Aleena, which also made him facing Jesse. He squeezed the trigger on the old single shot muzzleloader. The huge ball roared down the almost four foot long barrel then crossed the fifteen feet to hit the Indian exactly where Jesse had intended—the heart. Tolahta was dead before he even had time to realize what the loud noise was.

Jesse could see that Aleena was still a little wobbly from the blow on the side of her head so he kept his hand on her arm as they left the cavern. He held the Brown Bess, which he had reloaded, in his free hand as he tried to follow the same path to the outside. Light was finally filtering in. "We're about outa here sis, and then we'll catch up with pa and the guys."

The pace he maintained while running through the night had tired him, so he was glad to see the Indian's horse hobbled not far away when they emerged from the caves. "Up ya go," he said as he hoisted her onto the horse's back then removed the hobbles and jumped up behind her. She hadn't said a word since he arrived to rescue her, but now turned toward him. "Jesse."

"Yeah, sis."

"I love you."

He put his arm around her and hugged, "I love you too, sis."

Jesse knew his father would follow the route he had drawn on the piece of leather, so he kept checking and rechecking his bearings, so they would not miss them. Jesse retrieved the lantern he'd hung in the tree, then an hour after dark Aleena spotted a fire in the distance.

"That fire up ahead's bigger'n it oughta be," Jesse said, "so I reckon that's pa giving us a light to head for." He was right, and awhile later he yelled as they approached the camp.

Sean held his daughter tight as Jesse told all of them what happened. When her brother finished his brief story she said, "Daddy."

"Yeah, darling."

"I bet Jesse coulda fought all those pirates with you when you were out on that ocean."

All of the men laughed and were silently thankful to have the little girl back safe.

Sean reached out and grabbed Jesse's arm. He squeezed it, "You did good, son, real good."

Sean saw to it that Aleena was never out of his sight as they continued toward what would become San Pablo Bay where James Poorsmith's new Hudson Bay Trading Company was located. It was north of the beautiful, natural harbor, adjacent to Yerba Buena. James had chosen the spot as the site for the new building because it was easy to load sheep, and later cattle onto ships for live transport to Mexico City, Cuba, and later the newly forming country of Australia.

Jesse scouted ahead and guided the men west of Coyote Lake, north past Mt. Hamilton, then on toward San Pablo Bay that tied into the Feather River.

"You only missed Simon by two days," James told Sean. "He was here Monday afternoon, and then headed for home that same night; soon as I paid him the reward money."

Sean smiled, "He got them guys, huh?"

"Yep, said he had to kill 'em both when they went for their weapons."

Sean let a frown cross his weathered red face. "Darn James, a thousand dollars is a lotta money for him t'be carrying."

"Ain't a thousand Sean," James said, "I added two hundred apiece for those two lousy killers m'self. He rode outa here with fourteen hundred dollars minus the cost of another one of those new revolvers." Before Sean could speak, James added, "Ain't nobody knows about the money he's carrying Sean, but if someone decides to jump that man, they're gonna find themselves in a heap o' trouble and will learn a hard lesson."

Sean looked at his friend a moment. "He really is a man, ain't he?"

"Sure is. He was a boy when he rode outa here after those guys, but he was darn sure a man when he rode back in."

During the first year that his two older brothers were getting their education at Harvard University, Simon was also getting his. His younger brother Jesse, and Jesse's Indian friend, Wahpohnah, were teaching him. During this time he was also practicing very often with his new revolver, and getting very good at hitting what he aimed at.

After a few weeks of showing Simon how to track an animal, then sneak close before realizing it was in danger, Jesse turned to him as he leaned back against a huge oak, eating an apple. "Why you wanna learn all this stuff all of a sudden Simon?"

"Cause I figure them lawmen ain't ever gonna find the guys that killed Elijah and his daddy, so I'm gonna go find 'em and bring 'em to the sheriff." He looked up and stared hard at Jesse, "Or kill 'em." Simon paused before adding, "Don't say anything to ma or pa."

"Yeah," Jesse agreed, "pa probably wouldn't say nothin' but mama would have a fit." They were both silent for a while then Jesse asked, "How long fore you're goin' off after 'em?"

"Whenever you n' Wahpohnah say I'm good enough." He continued eating on the apple until every piece was gone except the seeds, which he put in his pocket. He looked up at Jesse, "Ain't no hurry cause they been dead over a year now. Purvis Mole and Billy Mattick have killed some more people near Yerba Buena, so I reckon they'll stick around till I'm ready t'go after 'em."

Jesse looked hard at him. "You know who killed Elijah?"

"Yeah, when me n' daddy went to Mister Poorsmith's new place to get supplies last month, he showed me a thing he made up. It had their names and all on it, plus it says a reward of five hundred dollars each, dead or alive, is offered by the Hudson Bay Trading Company that he works for."

"Wow." Jesse exclaimed loudly, "That's a fortune."

"Yeah it is, but Mister Poorsmith said it's because they robbed n' killed one of the people that was running one of their outpost trading places. If they let 'em get away with it, then they'll just keep on doin' the same thing, and that means they won't be able to hire anyone to work in them outposts way out in the wilderness."

Jesse thought a few moments. "Makes sense. A thousand bucks, schrreee," he whistled.

One evening, Simon approached Manollo's house. He yelled, and waved at Manollo when he saw that he was sitting on the porch with his wife. "Hi ma'am, hi Manollo, can I come talk to you a minute?"

"Yes Simon, any time."

He removed the soft leather hat that she had made for him as a birthday gift when he turned thirteen. "Good evening, ma'am."

"Hello Simon, would you like a glass of lemonade?"

"Yes ma'am sure would. This here's been a scorcher May." After downing half of the cool drink he asked, "Ma'am could you do som'n for me?"

"If I can Simon, what is it you need?"

He stood so she could see him better in the lamplight. "See how I re-rigged this holster you made for m'new revolver?" He turned his left side to her. "I've tried it both ways and I can get this pistol out a whole lot faster if it's on the left side with the butt facing forward like this."

She held the lamp so she could see better. "Hmmm, yes. I can see how that could be. You want me to attach it there where you have it tied?"

"Well ma'am," he said, "and I reckon it oughta be leanin' forward a little more'n it is." He adjusted it so she could see."

"Hold it there," she said and got up, "I'll get a piece of charcoal to mark it right where you want it to be."

Two days later Simon stood on the same porch with the newly rigged holster hanging on the front of his left hip with the butt of the revolver available, left of the center of his flat stomach. "Ma'am," he said after removing the pistol several times, "this's absolutely perfect. What did you do to make it stiff so it'd stay right there like that?"

She smiled, "Manollo cut a piece of copper and I stitched it between the holster and the belt."

"Me n' Jesse are goin' over to the lake tomorrow. Would a string of big sunfish square us up on this?" He grinned knowing how much Manollo and his wife loved the sweet perch that were abundant in the lake.

She matched his grin, "Very nicely."

The two brothers had been sitting on the bank of the lake for about two hours the next day when Simon asked, "How many sunfish we got on that string, Jesse?"

"Eleven."

"Pretty darn good, and it ain't even time for 'em to start biting yet." Simon's coal black eyes, and cold intense stare scanned the lake. "This was a good idea you had Jesse, 'cause I needed to relax a bit."

"Yeah, y'sure been pushing hard to learn." He smiled at his tall, heavy built brother, "Wahpohnah says you're gonna be a better tracker than either of us."

A while later, Simon had his pistol out and pointing at the edge of the water so fast that Jesse hardly had time to yell. "Don't shoot! Don't shoot! It's Wahpohnah."

Simon lowered the barrel as the young Indian climbed from the water with weeds all over him. "What the heck're you doin' injun? I coulda shot you."

"Not really," the Indian replied in Spanish as he began removing the weeds, "you never pull the trigger till you're sure what you're shooting."

When Jesse explained that it was his friend's idea to give his brother one last test to see how observant he was, even while he was relaxing. They all laughed.

"I spent an hour closing that short gap Simon, and I thought sure I had you."

Simon grinned, "I was watching you since you come under that log over yonder." He pointed at a dead tree lying in the water fifty feet away. "I just didn't know who," he grinned wide, "or what it was."

They all laughed again, and then returned to fishing.

The return trip for Sean and his crew was uneventful. Aleena enjoyed cooking for the men with the fresh supplies they loaded the supply wagon with. Jesse was thrilled with the revolver like Simon's that his father gave him, and practiced constantly with it until he could fire and change to the next loaded chamber as fast as he had seen his brother do it.

When they reached the rise above the ranch a few days later, Sean stopped to take it all in as he did every time he returned. He turned to Jesse. "Sure is pretty ain't it?

8

~ Tracking killers ~

A few days before Jesse's fifteenth birthday, two Mexicans rode into the McKannah sheep ranch. Manollo listened to their story, and then said, "Come with me and speak to his father."

"Sean," Manollo said as he approached, "this is Señor Olando of the Mexican Federal Police, and his assistant Señor Malaga. Sean shook each man's hand. "Where you gentlemen from?"

The taller of the two middle-aged men replied, "San Diego de Alcala de Henares."

The older, gray-haired one who was obviously in charge said, "Yes, although everyone is starting to refer to it as just San Diego." He displayed a friendly smile as he removed his large sombrero and wiped sweat from his forehead and sweatband. "Very warm, for February."

"Yes! Let's sit on the porch and I'll have some lemonade brought out." Sean turned to Manollo, "Get one of the men to take care of their horses then please join us on the porch."

A little small talk and two glasses of lemonade later, Sean leaned forward. "Is there some way I can help you?" He addressed the gray-haired man.

"I hope so, 'cause now that Mexico has gained independence from Spain, the government in Madrid wants two criminals we had in our jail returned. They are to face charges of murder," he paused and raised his eyebrows, then twisted his mouth to form a grimace, "but unfortunately they escaped two weeks ago as I was arranging for their passage back to Spain."

Sean sat patiently waiting until the man continued. "We," he motioned to his assistant, "had a good tracker with us when we started. We were following the two men, and were gaining on them, but he became very ill yesterday so we left him in a village south of here. A woman who learned medicine from her Indian mother will treat him. A man in that village told us of your son, who the Indian's say is one of the best trackers in this area." He reached into his shirt pocket to remove a small piece of paper. "Jesse is the name he gave me."

Sean said with a proud smile, "After seeing him in action a while back on our sheep drive, I think they're right."

"Is he available?"

When Jesse responded to his father's call, and came walking through the screen door opening, the two Mexicans looked at the six-foot-tall, lanky young boy. Each had obviou surprise written across his face. "Yeah pa," he said then greeted Manollo before holding out his hand to the two strangers, "hi, I'm Jesse."

The gray-haired man took Jesse's hand and bluntly said, "I didn't realize you were so young."

Before Jesse could answer, Manollo spoke up. "This young man has been trained to track by his Yokut Indian friends, and he's been at it since he was a little boy. He can track a ghost across solid granite." After saying his piece he shifted back into the rocker and sipped his lemonade.

Señor Olando turned to Sean. "Señor McKannah, we would be very grateful if you would allow the boy to help us track and locate these two men."

Sean quietly sipped his lemonade as he looked into the eyes of the short, gray-haired Mexican policeman. He liked the way the man didn't shift his eyes away, as so many men do when directly confronted by an inspection stare as intense as Sean's. He set the glass down and spoke slowly. "I only have one child left, and she'll soon be a woman. Jesse's the youngest of my five sons, but he's not a boy. They're all men, so anything you wanna talk to him about, you can go right ahead." He leaned slightly forward adding, "Jesse'll decide if he wants to help you or not."

"Very well sir," the officer said then turned to Jesse. "We are in desperate need of a tracker to apprehend and return two dangerous men to the ship that will be leaving for Spain in about a fortnight. We were paying the other tracker two silver dollars a day, and will pay you that plus another dollar a day if you help us get them to the ship on time." He patiently waited for Jesse to answer.

After a few moments he asked, "What did they do to get locked up?"

Manollo smiled to himself. *Never jumps into anything until he knows what the deal is. Just like his daddy.*

"They killed our jailer," the tall officer said, "then killed a man, his wife, and their teen-age son so they could take horses and supplies from their ranch."

"We believe," the other officer said, "that they are trying to get into the high country north of here and out of Mexican territory."

Jesse looked from one of the officers to the other. Manollo smiled to himself again. *Just like Sean, he's forming an opinion of these two men before committing himself. Good!*

"What did they do to get locked up in the first place?"

"They stopped a coach travelling from a Hacienda just south of San Diego, and severely beat the passenger and his driver."

"It is happening very often these days," the tall officer commented.

"Yes, but it's going to be stopped, because the man they beat is related to some very highly placed people in the government of Spain." He looked hard at Jesse a moment. "You might even get a reward and commendation from the government if you help us."

"I'll help you catch 'em. When you wanna leave?"

Before either man could answer Sean spoke. "You're welcome to stay here overnight if you want."

"Thank you Señor McKannah, but no thank you. We can not let them get too far ahead of us." Officer Olando turned to Jesse, "We would like to get under way as soon as possible Señor McKannah."

Sean and Manollo both liked the way the two officers were already addressing Jesse as a man rather than a boy.

"I'll get m'gear then and be ready to go in ten minutes." Jesse went into the house to begin packing the few things he knew he'd need. When he returned moments later he didn't look like the same person the two officers had spoken to only moments earlier. Around his slender waist was a belt that had his new revolver in a holster, plus a long blade knife in a leather sheath. Hanging from a leather strap around his neck was a leather bag with ammunition and loading supplies for the Brown Bess his father had given him. "I'll go get my horse and we'll head right out and pick up their trail."

The two Mexican police officers were mounted and waiting when Jesse came from the barn on his horse. Sean walked out and handed the small, folding telescope that he'd carried since Captain Mullholland gave it to him. "You might find this handy, son."

Jesse turned it over in his hands as he inspected the ancient looking glass. "This's the one that old sea captain friend of yours gave you, ain't it?"

"Yep, I've had it a long time."

"Thanks pa." He turned his horse and followed the two men from the ranch.

The three men pressed hard and by noon the following day they located the spot on the escaped prisoners' trail where they had been forced to leave due to the health of their tracker. They were soon into heavy brush and trees, which made the trail difficult to follow. After an hour Jesse stopped them. "Make yourselves a camp here among these trees while I scout around for their trail."

"But Jesse, we are on their trail."

"I ain't so sure." Jesse galloped away.

An hour later Sergeant Malaga had coffee water boiling and a pot of beans simmering when Jesse rode in. After hobbling his horse to graze, he poured himself a tin cup of coffee, and then got a plate of beans and a couple of tortillas from the huge pile the cook from the ranch sent with them.

Both Mexicans waited for him to speak. "Found their fresh trail," he said after washing down a mouthful with coffee.

"You mean we weren't following their trail?"

"Nope. The one we were following was a false trail. These two guys are good. They figured you'd be back so they laid a false trail then cut south."

"South?" Olando exclaimed.

"South?" Malaga echoed.

"Yep, smart move. They've led you this way on purpose is my guess, so you'll think they went up into the far north country." He paused to finish his coffee. "When you lost the trail they hoped you'd think they were gone for good up into that wild country, and then you'd go on back to where you came from." Jesse scooped the last of his beans into a tortilla.

"Where do you think they're heading?"

"Well, if it was me I'd go south like I was gonna slip into Mexico to maybe catch a boat. Then I'd cut east when I got down to that flat country where daddy and Uncle Luis' ranch men went to find the horses." He saw the looks on their faces. "Sorry, you probably don't even know my Uncle Luis."

"Is Señor Carvojol your uncle?"

"Yes, do you know him?"

"I bought this horse and three others from him." The small policeman smiled. "Almost all of our officers ride horses from El Cielo de los Caballos."

"Horse Heaven," Jesse smiled back. "Yes, it is a wonderful horse ranch." The smile left when he continued, "My mother's brother Frank runs it now because Uncle Luis is very ill."

The other policeman said, "I am very sorry to hear that. I have also been to Señor Carvojol's ranch, and liked him very much." He patted his horse's neck. "This horse also came from there."

Jesse wiped his mouth to remove the salsa then divided the rest of the coffee between their three cups. "Let's get this camp cleared up and get after those guys before they kill any more folks along their trail."

Awhile before dark Jesse stopped and slipped from his horse to inspect a pile of horse droppings. After poking in it and moving some aside he wiped his knife on a nearby bush and replaced it in the leather sheath. He got on hands and knees to get his nose close to smell the pile. "Yep." He said after he was back in his saddle, "That grass still smells fresh as new-mown-hay." He pulled his father's folding telescope and scanned the country ahead. "They stopped back yonder a'ways," he motioned with a nod of his head at the trail they just came down, "to let their horses graze on that gophergrass we rode through."

"How far do you think they are ahead of us?"

"Not over half a day, because they think they fooled you and are taking their time."

"Can we catch them before nightfall?" Sergeant Malaga was lighting a thin cigar.

"I wouldn't light that thing if I was you." Jesse turned in the saddle to look at the officer. "I can smell one o' them stinking things from a mile away if the wind's blowing toward me like it is them guys." He nodded in the direction that he felt certain their prisoners were.

The tall thin Mexican frowned and was about to say something when his boss said, "Put it away."

"Sergeant," Jesse said, "those two guys are not newcomers to the wilderness so let's not give then an edge if we can help it." He waited a moment to see if the man was going to comment, but when he returned the cigar to his pocket Jesse continued. "Yes, we could catch them before night but we'll move closer to 'em so I can go in and observe their camp, then we'll strike at dawn when they think they're alone."

An hour before dark Jesse pointed, "Let's stop there for the night. I'm purdy certain that they're only about a mile ahead in that stand of trees down in that shallow valley." He pointed down through trees from atop the hill he'd chosen for their camp.

After hobbling their horses so they could graze, the two Mexicans began digging out supplies for the night. Jesse spoke softly, "I'm gonna slip down near them, then hobble my horse and slip in to see what their camp looks like and be certain they haven't met up with anyone else down there." He sat and replaced his boots with the moccasins his sister Aleena made him for his last birthday. He removed his revolver and placed it over his saddlehorn. After checking the edge of his long hunting knife he turned to the captain. "We can't have a fire tonight so I'm gonna take a few tortillas to chew on during the trip to their camp." He didn't want to tell two grown men that they couldn't start a fire, but he figured this would let them know not to. "Do not forget. Sound will carry a long way down into a valley like that." He turned and was silently moving toward the fugitives below as the sun dropped behind the mountains in the west.

Two hundred yards from the escaped men's camp, Jesse hobbled his horse. Even with the leather bags on its hoofs he didn't want to chance being heard. An hour later he was within fifty feet of the small fire where the two men lay sleeping in blankets. He silently eased the telescope from his leather bag and put it on first one, then the other of the motionless men. He kept moving it back and forth. He'd look at the spot where boots made lumps beneath the blanket, then at the hat covering their head. He scanned the entire camp then returned to the sleeping men. He had a funny feeling about the camp he was watching.

Jesse lowered the telescope and let all of the facts run through his mind. He cautiously turned his head and looked in the direction of the camp that the two policemen were in. There was no sign of a fire but something was still nagging at his mind.

~ The two policemen were about to learn a hard lesson ~

With Sean's help, Simon primed and loaded all five cylinders of his new cap and ball revolver. He turned to his father, "Pop this's as nice a gift as I reckon I'll ever git in m'whole life, thank you." He then took aim and fired, re-cocked, re-closed the pan and cover, then used his fingers to rotate the cylinder that brought the next loaded chamber into position. He fired again then repeated the process. After firing it five times he turned to Sean, "Dad, I bet I hit that cactus ear all five times. Let's go have a look."

He was wrong, but four out of five wasn't bad for a man firing a new pistol for the first time. He had been practicing with his friend Vasquez Olomo, who came to work for his father three years earlier, when he was only nineteen. The young man liked Simon and his family who treated him like a son, so he was always ready to let the young boy practice firing his old flintlock pistol.

"All that practicing with Vasquez has made you a good shot son."

Simon was surprised because he thought he and his friend had gone far enough away from the ranch so no one would know he was learning to shoot a gun. *I shoulda known nothing escapes dad's eyes around here.* He looked at the back of Sean's shirt as he followed him back to the table. *Or anywhere else he goes.*

"Son, I didn't buy the holster with it because I didn't think it was made right. I asked Manollo's wife to make one for it the way it oughta be for around these parts. She took the measurements from it when I first got it, so it should be ready soon."

"That's great, pop. She's the best at makin' leather things I ever saw."

A few days later she saw Simon and yelled for him to come to her house that day after work. When he departed Manollo's home later that evening, he was wearing a hand tooled leather belt with the holster an integral part of it. On the other side resting on the hip was a removable leather bag that held slugs, wad, and powder. Walking across the open field toward his home he already looked like the man that would become one of the most famous man hunters in early nineteenth century Western America Lore.

Had his friend's killers known of the tenacity with which he held to an idea, and the vengeance that burned within because of the sheriff's inability to capture them, they would have left the area long ago.

"Why do you come out here n' shoot so much Simon?" Aleena loved no one on earth like her brother Jesse, but she was also very close to Simon. Like Jesse, he never made fun of her dreams no matter how silly they seemed to him.

"Cause I always wanna hit what I aim at, sis." He turned his intense black eyes toward her and smiled, "Wanna give 'er a try?"

"Nope, I'd rather read a book."

He finished reloading all five chambers. "Change yer mind, lemme know."

"I won't, 'cause I hate guns."

A few days later Simon had accumulated all he thought he'd need so he sought out his father. "I'm gonna go find those guys that killed Elijah and his pa." Sean had always appreciated his son's abrupt manner because it was much like his own when his mind was made up about anything serious. He remained silent as he studied his son a moment. "I figured as much when I saw you spending so much time with Jesse and Wahpohnah this past year." He reached in his pocket and removed an oilskin pouch. "I made you this map of the Indian camps up in the mountains above Yerba Buena that I spent time in, and the names of the men that were the chiefs back when I was with 'em." He handed it to Simon. "They'll remember me and help you if you need any."

Simon tucked it into the small leather bag which held his fishing line, fire flint, beef jerky, and the few other items he knew he'd need. "Thanks dad. I don't wanna say anything to mom 'cause she'll just get upset. How 'bout you tellin' her after I'm gone?"

"Yeah." Sean answered, grinning. "I'll tell her you've gone off into the mountains to practice your tracking skills n' it won't be telling her a lie."

"Thanks dad. I'm going to Mister Poorsmith's first. Can I give him an order for you or tell him anything?"

"I'll be goin' there with the sheep soon m'self." He watched as Simon, wearing his newly rigged holster with the pistol's handle facing foreward, turned and headed toward his horse, mounted the saddle, and rode out of the ranch without a look back. Sean remained motionless; watching until his son was beyond his sight. *I got a hunch those two guys are in trouble with that boy after 'em.* Sean took a couple of steps then turned back hoping for one last glimpse of Simon. He knew he'd turned north and was already in the canyon so he headed back toward the barn. *He's young but I don't reckon he's a boy any longer.*

Jesse lowered the telescope to rest his arms and to also let his eyes take in the entire camp at one time. Tiny nerves were marching up the back of his neck like silent soldier sneaking up on the enemy. He brought the scope back up to the man nearest him and forced himself to leave it on him for a full minute. Thousands more joined the tiny, silent soldiers. *Som'ns not right here,* he thought, *I've never seen a person lay so long without movin' something.* He folded the scope and put it back in his bag then fumbled around below him until he had a good sized pebble in his hand. *I don't often miss goin' through that hole in the side of the barn,* he thought as he prepared to throw. He let the rock go and prepared himself for anything that might happen if the man should yell. It hit right where he aimed. Nothing—no movement. He located another pebble and repeated the throw. "Damn!" He said aloud as he ran for his horse. *They fooled me.*

He ran as hard as he could and still keep an eye out for the two men in case they were hiding nearby. *They fooled us all.* He quickly unhobbled his horse and removed the padded hoof-bags. Once in the saddle he angled away from the camp the Mexicans were in. *I'll go around and come in from the rear.* Three hours later the moon was lighting his way as he approached his own camp from the north. *Those Mexicans don't know much about this business, and I let 'em down. Darn! I forgot that there's plenty o' guys out there that's as good or better'n me.* He ground his teeth together. *Please God, make Olando and Malaga be okay when I get there.*

Jesse hobbled his horse again a half-mile north of his camp and silently moved in on foot. The scene in the telescope was horrible. Captain Olando lay on his back with his arms straight out. The moonlight made the blood all over the front of his fancy shirt glow in a reddish black color. The gaping wound in his neck was grotesque even at the distance Jesse was from the body. He knew Sergeant Malaga had met a similar fate by the way his body lay.

Jesse's survival senses were now at their peak as he strained to hear any foreign sound. He had his pistol back around his waist and the Brown Bess was at his feet. He picked up the musket and checked the entire camp. He remained alert so it would make it impossible for them to slip up on him in case they were hiding and planning to kill him also.

After an hour he said to himself, *I'm sorry I letcha down amigos, but I guarantee you that I'll make 'em pay for doin' this to ya.* He left the campsite as silently as a snake leaving a gopher hole. When daylight arrived, Jesse had already located their trail.

When Simon arrived at James Poorsmith's new building he looked up at the sign that took up almost the entire front of the brand new building.

HUDSON BAY TRADING COMPANY

He was still looking at it when he heard his name. "Simon McKannah, what brings you all the way over here?"

"I'm tired of waitin' for the sheriff to catch the guys that killed my friend and his daddy, so I'm gonna go get 'em."

The seriousness of the young man's manner, plus the matter-of-fact way he stated it, as though it was already a fact that they were going to be caught by him, prompted James to invite him into the back room.

"Simon," he said after the door was closed, "there're some folks around here just as bad as those two, and will send word to 'em in a hoofbeat if they know what you're up to." He paused a moment to look intently at his friend's tall fifteen-year-old son. He was well on the way to the two hundred and fifty pounds he would carry well on a six-and-a-half-foot frame. His size would also lend believability to the legend he would become in future years. James thought; *sure don't look like a kid.* "C'mere Simon and look at the drawings I've made of those two guys."

Simon looked the drawings over good. "That's what they look like, huh?"

"Yep, best I can recall from the times they were in here getting supplies before this all happened."

"Ain't nothin but a coupla kids," Simon said as he picked the drawings up one at a time again to look hard at each one's. "What the heck's the matter with someone that kills a little boy and an old man just for the few coins in their pockets?"

"Just too darn many people moving into this area all of a sudden. Simon, you know about the five hundred dollar reward the company's offering for each of those guys dead or alive, don't you?"

"Yessir, you told us when me n' pa was here awhile back for supplies."

"If you can get those two guys," he paused and thought a moment, "in say a month from today then I'll add two hundred dollars for each of 'em m'self." When Simon said nothing he added, "I've got three outposts up in the mountains where those two are suppose to be staying. If they're not put out of action soon, the people running them ain't gonna stay up there and it's gonna cost me and this company a bundle of money."

Simon turned away from the window from which he was looking at the big sailing boats in the harbor, and looked at James. "I'll get 'em Mr. Poorsmith. You can count on it." He motioned toward the mountains with his head. "You said you have an idea where they're stayin up there most of the time."

"Yeah, I do, there's a small settlement of mostly outlaws and the like in the timber country above Clear Lake. It's called Coleman's Bluff, and it's about ten miles northeast, above the lake."

"Well," Simon said, "I reckon I can find it easy enough." He turned to open the door to the main part of the supply house, "Let's get my supplies and I'll be on m'way." He stopped abruptly and turned, "You got any more of these revolvers?"

"No, but I will have though by the time you get back, 'cause your dad's ordered two more, and I added another six to the order."

"Hmmm, must be for Jesse and Ian, 'cause I told him how good these things are once you get used to 'em. How about holding another one for me when they get here, okay?"

"It'll be waiting on you, Simon."

An hour later he was heading into country he had never set foot in, searching for two killers that had already murdered nine men and two women; that the sheriff in Yerba Buena was aware of. He rode his horse into the early sunrise a young boy. He would ride out later as a man with two dead men behind him that started the living legend passed on by the men who saw it.

"Mama," Ian said, "this is Mr. Hamilton." He turned to the stocky, middle-aged man as he introduced his mother. "Mr. Hamilton this's my mother Issabella." Ian turned toward his father, "Daddy, you've already met Mr. Hamilton when we were in Yerba Buena that last trip."

"Yes," Sean said as he took the man's offered hand, "at James Poorsmith's supply house. Good to see you again, Mr. Hamilton."

"Just Hunter, Mr. McKannah, that's what everyone calls me." His handshake was firm and accompanied by a sincere smile. "Mama wanted to name me Jedediah, but daddy told her no. He was a professional big game hunter and hoped I'd become one too." His smile broadened as he added, "They were both disappointed, because I hate killing animals." He released Sean's hand and offered it to Bella. "Mrs. McKannah I want you and your husband to know that Ian's going to be with good company, because I plan to make the Bayview Hotel and Casino the nicest place in the west." He gently shook her hand before releasing it.

"How about just Bella and Sean from now on, Hunter?" She liked his direct approach and saw nothing to alarm her in his intense gray eyes.

"Okay! Bella it is." He turned, "Sean, I realize that Ian's still young, but from the two previous discussions I had with him I believe he's a very mature young man." He turned to Ian and smiled before returning his eyes to the young man's parents. "And God willing, he and I will have a long and profitable relationship."

As they all walked toward the coach, Sean noticed that the two tough looking men seated in the driver's seat had not stopped scanning the surrounding area since the coach arrived. *This guy knows how to take care of himself.*

Hunter T. Hamilton opened the coach door and waited until Ian had hugged his mother then shook hands with Sean. After following Ian inside, he lowered the small window. "We'll keep in touch and look for you to stop by when you're in to see Mr. Poorsmith. And Sean, your money will not spend at the hotel." He grinned wide then added, "But the casino's another story altogether." He leaned close to the opening and told his men to head for home.

Dust swirled around them as Sean and Bella stood watching. The coach soon disappeared in the west.

After an hour of casual conversation to better get to know the young man who was going to work for him, Hunter finally said, "You've been playing mostly Primero with your father's Mexican ranch hands, haven't you?"

"Yessir, but we sometimes play a game called Brag that Angelo Baranaja learned from an Englishman that stayed awhile with Uncle Luis at South Ranch."

"Ah yes," Hunter smiled, "Brag. I played it when I was in London. Well Ian, what I have planned will keep you busy learning a few new games. New to you that is, because they've all been around a long time."

"I'm looking forward to it. What kinda games are you gonna have in the casino for the people to play?"

"Now that the casino is completed we're changing our plans a bit, because we actually have more room than we expected. We still plan to have several Poker and Blackjack tables operating, but we now plan to have two dice tables and a roulette wheel in the main gambling area, and a separate room for the big money gamblers who wish to play Chem de fer. I'm also considering a separate area in the main hall for a few of the games that I learned as I traveled through Europe." He paused to light a cigar. "Have you heard of a game called Spoil Five?"

"Nope."

"The reason I ask is that it's an Irish game, and I understand that your dad's from Ireland." Ian explained how young his father was when he left Ireland. "That's tragic," Hunter commented, "he certainly must be a tough man to have gone out on his own at such a young age."

"Tough as they come, Mr. Hamilton."

"Well, Spoil Five is one I might put in, and there are others that are easily learned. There's Boston, Vint, Plafond, Skat, Ombre, and a game that's getting very popular called Euchre."

"Phew! Sounds like I've got m'work cut out for me."

"We have a seventy-five mile trip ahead so we might as well use the time constructively." Hunter removed a deck of cards from a compartment below the seat. "Blackjack is going to be a big attraction, so I'll show you how the deal goes and the odds that the house has in its favor."

By the time it was too dark inside to continue, Hunter was very impressed with Ian's ability to master the odds and be able to recite them back, plus he could handle the deck with the skill of any dealer he had yet seen. They each settled into their seat for some rest, as the coach rolled along the bumpy trail toward what would become San Francisco's South Bay area.

It was a little after midnight as the four-horse-team pulled the coach into the recently cleared and leveled area where future customers would have their drivers park the coaches.

Simon located the first Indian village on the map his father had given him. The sun was high and his arrival was followed by several sets of black eyes. The upright manner he sat his horse as he approached the village, plus holding his hand out to indicate in sign language that he meant the Indians no harm, soon provided him with an audience. He walked the horse along the row of bark-covered shelters that were partially underground. A group of older men clothed only in breechcloths were assembling ahead of him, so he climbed from the horse and addressed the only one wearing an elaborate necklace. In Spanish he said, "My father lived among you long ago before I was even a thought in his mind, and he asked me to bring you his greeting." He held their stare without blinking or moving a muscle for what seemed like minutes until the one with the necklace spoke in good Spanish.

"What is your father called?"

"Sean McKannah and his friend Francisco was with him." Again he silently waited as they spoke among themselves.

"Was you father's hair always on fire?"

"Yes. He was given it by his father who got it from his father." He pointed west. "All of his family where he came from across the big water had hair that was on fire."

The one with the necklace was obviously the chief. "I remember him well, because he was the first man with flaming hair I had ever seen." He motioned for Simon to follow, "Come, we will sit in the cool of my lodge and drink sassafras tea." The Indian stopped at the lodge's entrance, and turned. "Your father was also a very honorable man." He pulled the flap back, and as Simon entered he added, "Not many white men are."

As one of the chief's women prepared the tea, he asked Simon where he lived. When Simon explained, he asked why he was so far from his home all alone.

All of the Indian men listened intently as Simon explained his mission. When he was finished, the chief said he had heard of the two evil men from his brother who was chief of another tribe of Miwok who lived in a village not far from the place where the men were. "When two white people that traded supplies with my people, were killed inside the little house they kept the supplies in, some white people came and said we did it." He shook his head from side to side. "It could have started a war except a white man wearing the skins of animals came from the forest to say that he saw two white men kill the two traders."

Simon finished the tea then stood. "I must go now because the longer I am away the more my mother will worry."

The chief also stood. "It is good that you are concerned about your mother.

Sometimes they worry themselves into the ground." He led the way back up the short set of earthen steps to the clearing.

"Can you point the way I must go to find the place where the white men stay?"

The old man turned and gave a command to one of the younger men with him. He headed to the other end of the village running, and soon came back with a boy about a year younger than Simon. "This is my grandson Hwotahka. He will lead you to my brother's village, and then my brother will tell you how to find the place where the evil white men stay."

Simon thanked the chief then followed the boy who stopped for only a few minutes to gather the things he would need for the trip higher into the mountains. The boy set a brisk pace on his small pony and Simon followed close behind.

Simon and the Indian boy reached the Miwok village in three days. The boy explained everything to his grandfather's brother then turned to Simon. "I will stay here a few weeks to visit with my friends I have not seen in a long time." He smiled then turned to leave, but turned back and said sincerely, "Good luck."

Simon returned the smile, "Thanks, gonna need a little."

Early the next morning Simon was nearing the little settlement called Coleman's Bluff. He moved cautiously through the last half of the day, fearing the settlement of crooks might have guards posted along the trails leading to their hideaway. It was long after dark when he saw lights in the distance to indicate that he was coming to their little settlement or some other gathering of people. He hobbled his horse then moved exactly as his brother's Indian friend Wampohnah had taught him. He silently moved ahead step-by-step, weighing each footfall as if an enemy was waiting behind every tree and boulder. Two hours later he was within earshot of the laughing men and women gathered around a big fire in the street between what looked to Simon like ramshackle huts and tents thrown over frames.

One by one he studied each man until he was certain he knew which was Purvis Mole and which was Billy Mattick. When he heard the short little man stutter he knew it was Billy. He studied the other five-foot-tall man as he strutted around the fire bragging to the two women that Simon could see mingling with the men. When he was finally able to spot the white streak of hair that ran down the middle of the one man's head of brown hair, which had earned him the nickname 'skunk', he knew he had spotted both of the men he had come for. He remained lying silently nearby as he watched their every movement.

He thought again of the last thing that James Poorsmith said to him before leaving. *Simon, because your Sean's son, lemme tell you something. If you come back and tell me those two rotten scoundrels are dead, that'll be good enough for me. I'll pay you the reward straight away, son.*

Simon wanted to hear what was being said, so he inched forward until he was close enough to the campfire to hear the men talking. "Hey Skunk you n' Billy goin' with us down to Yerba Buena when we leave in the morning?"

"Dammit Lemuell, I tole ya t'quit callin me that."

"Well dern, Purvis everyone calls ya Skunk."

"Yeah, I know, and a bunch of 'em's gonna get their guts spilled out on the ground if they don't stop." Simon watched as the little man glared at the huge, bearded man that was talking to him.

"When ever you think you're man enough t'climb this mountain Skunk, you just git that blade out n' come on." The man glared back at Purvis until the little man turned away. "Here," the big one said as he handed the bottle toward Purvis, "have another drink n' don't be so dern touchy." He watched as Purvis drank from the earthen jug. The huge man repeated his question. "So, you n' Billy goin' with us or ya staying up here alone?"

"Ain't goin' and ain't stayin' either." He drank again from the jug. "Me n' Billy're goin' over to that trading shack north of 'at 'ere Injun village west o' Clear Lake. We wanna see if they got a load o' furs in. If they do, were gonna take 'em and head up into Canady till folks fergit about all the darn posters what got the drawins of me n' Billy on 'em."

The big mountain man laughed as he took the jug Purvis held out to him. "If they ever offer any real money fer yer carcasses there's gonna be a lotta folks lookin' for you two fellers," he lowered the jug and added with a grin, "and I just might be one of 'em, Skunk."

Simon saw the little man shift slightly as he brought up the barrel of the shotgun. The mountain man was already drinking from the jug again when it went off. The two women ran away screaming, and the men that had been talking to them leaped back. Purvis already had his flintlock pistol out. "You fellers just relax, an ain't gonna be no trouble." He motioned with the pistol barrel toward the giant with only half a head. "I been tellin' him t'quit callin' me Skunk."

One of the men spoke cautiously. "We been tellin' him too thet he oughn't t'be callin' you that, Purvis, 'cause we's all friends around here."

Billy Mattick began stuttering badly as he moved toward the dead man, "Bbbbbrrrokkke tthe jjjuugggg o' lllikkker."

"Here," another of the men said as he reached down to get another jug, "likker's one thing we've got plenty of."

The thin, nervous little man took the jug and returned to where he had been sitting. "Gggggood."

If these guys knew about the five hundred dollars on each of their heads, there'd be hell t'pay around this camp. Simon watched as Purvis calmly reloaded his shotgun. *That's a guy to watch closely, 'cause he's crazy.* He listened as the men continued drinking whiskey and talking.

"You guys still going down to Yerba Buena?" Purvis asked.

"Yep! There's s'pose to be a big ship comin' in and our girls're gonna lure them sailors out to us so's we can knock 'em in the head n' take everything they got." He grinned as he accepted the jug from Purvis.

Oughta be a reward on all these people, Simon thought as he watched. The men dragged the dead man into the woods then coaxed the two women back to the fire. As they drank, laughed and talked, Simon was fixing the trading station James Poorsmith had told him about in his mind. *That's gotta be the one these two guys are going to, because James said the only other one's way up north of here.* He watched awhile longer then decided to take a gamble. He silently backed away from the group then cautiously returned to his horse and began heading toward the trading station north of Clear Lake.

When he came to the lake he stopped and got grain from his saddlebags for his horse. As the horse ate, it suddenly came to him that he hadn't eaten in a long time himself so he opened the other saddlebag that contained his own food rations. Simon removed three pieces of jerked beef and a crumbling biscuit. With the horse hobbled, he stretched out next to the lake and slept until a couple hours before sunrise.

It was still early when he arrived at the trading post, but the sun was already shining through the trees. He hailed the man sitting on the edge of the plank porch, telling him that he brought news from James Poorsmith. The man kept the long muzzleloader in his hand, but waved Simon on with the other.

After a complete explanation of what he was doing there so early, the man asked, "You pretty sure them guys're headin' this way?"

"That's what they said."

The man remained silent, as he looked the young boy in the eyes. He saw something that gave him confidence. "Me and m'brother in there have been planning to get on outa here, 'cause of those two crazy killers, but if you think you can capture 'em we'll stay awhile." He shook his head slowly, "We been takin' turns during the nights and daytime too to watch for them guys, and lemme tell ya son, we're both 'bout worn down to a nub."

Simon looked around, "I ain't got no way o' knowing when they'll show up so you guys just stay in there with your weapons ready while I check out this whole area, so I'll know which's the best place t'see 'em coming."

The man just shook his head and went inside without another word, as Simon began to survey the entire area surrounding the outpost. When he was satisfied he had located the best position to await their arrival, he removed the tack from his horse and turned it into the small corral with the outpost horses and two mules. He then chose a limb from a bush a good distance from the building so it wouldn't be noticed missing and began brushing his tracks from the area. He brushed his tracks out behind him as he moved toward the high rise just beyond the clearing. It was only a short distance from the trail he was certain they would enter on. He removed his long bladed belt knife and ran it across the stone he carried in his pocket then checked the revolver. He settled in for what he hoped wasn't going to be a long wait.

Simon reviewed everything he had learned about the two men he had watched as they drank whiskey and talked at the campfire during the previous night. Purvis Mole carried the short shotgun everywhere he went, even when it was just to go into the woods to relieve himself. He carried a flintlock pistol shoved down into his waistband, and a large handled knife carried in some kind of rig slung over his neck and beneath his left arm.

Billy Mattick only carried one weapon. It was a huge knife with a blade longer than the one Simon carried, which his Uncle Francisco gave him for his twelfth birthday. The handle on Billy's knife was so big that Simon thought it looked ridiculous hanging on the tiny man.

He remembered what James told him the one witness that identified the two killers had said. 'I hid up in the loft of that trading post where I worked when they killed the man and his woman. The stuttering one slit the throat of the man as the other guy shot the woman with a shotgun. That stuttering one then jumped a'straddle of the dying woman and kept stabbing her and was stuttering so bad I couldn't understand a word he said.'

Simon recalled the sheriff's description of how his friend Elijah and his father had been killed. 'The old man had been shot in the face with what musta been a shotgun, and the little boy's throat was cut, and then stabbed a buncha times.' *That stuttering one's crazy as a loon too, so I can't let him get that knife out of his belt.*

The sun went past straight up and was beginning its journey to the western horizon. *Hope I ain't figured these guys wrong.* Simon waited and kept mentally checking all other possible routes into the clearing where the trading post sat. He was thinking that it must be a couple hours past noon when he heard a horse whinny. The noise came from the direction he had been certain they would enter from, so he slipped down from the spot where he'd been waiting, and moved a little closer to the trail. He was still well hidden behind a series of boulders that had bushes growing among them. When he could hear the horses walking slowly toward him he removed his revolver and waited.

"There's smoke comin' outa the chimney," Purvis said loud enough for Simon to hear, "so them guys're here."

"Wwwisssh ttttheeeey wwwas a wwwoman ttttoo," Billy stuttered. The horses stopped just before entering the clearing—just as Simon had figured they would. He peered cautiously through the brush and saw the two killers tying their horses to bushes.

"C'mon Billy n' be quiet 'cause we wanna surprise 'em."

Simon saw that Purvis had the shotgun in his right hand, which was on the side to him so he tensed as the men approached.

The explosion startled both of the men and Purvis screamed as the slug tore through his arm, sending the shotgun to the ground. Simon had the cylinder revolved to the next loaded chamber when he stepped out and told Billy, "Don't pull that knife out," as he pointed the pistol at him.

"Yyyyou ain't gggot nnno mmore bbbbullets tttto ssshooot," he stuttered as he pulled the knife out and charged Simon. When Simon described the incident to James Poorsmith, he said that the look on the young guy's face was one of absolute disbelief—even after the slug had entered his forehead just above the eyes.

As Simon was moving the cylinder to the next chamber Purvis was pulling the old flintlock from his waistband. He was still in the process of bringing it up when Simon took a step forward and shot him in the chest. The man was knocked to the ground but was still trying to bring the gun barrel up. Simon had revolved the next loaded chamber into position and fired another slug into Purvis's brain from less than two feet. Both killers lay still as Simon revolved the cylinder again and looked from one to the other. He held the barrel close to Purvis's chest as he reached down and took the flintlock from his hand, then walked to Billy and did the same as he picked up the huge knife. He kept an eye on them as he got the shotgun from where it had fallen then he stood and looked at the blood covering the ground around both men.

"They both dead?" The man was yelling from the porch.

"Yeah." Simon heard the man call to his brother then both men came to look at the bodies.

"Yep." The brother said, "Them's the two that was nosin' around awhile back before we saw them pitchers Mr. Poorsmith sent up."

"That's a darn good job y'done there son," the other man said, "after we bury 'em let's have us a drink of good whiskey to celebrate."

"Don't use the stuff. After they're in the ground I'm gonna take this knife and shotgun with me then head on home." He removed the belt and sheath that Billy had carried the big knife in. "You can keep the pistol and their horses."

Later that afternoon the two men watched as Simon saddled his horse then led it to the porch where they sat. "I'm heading on down to let James know that them two guys are dead." He climbed into the saddle but before leaving asked, "Anything you want me to tell James?"

"Yessir." The older of the two brothers said, "Tell Mr. Poorsmith that we'll be stayin' now that them two fellers're dead, so he can send another wagon load of supplies to trade for furs."

"I'll sure do that," Simon answered and then turned to ride south out of the mountains.

"Wouldn't want that young feller chasing me," the younger brother said as he watched Simon disappear into the forest.

~ In the coming years, a lot of men would wish they hadn't allowed themselves to get in exactly that situation. ~

Manollo and his crew had constructed a large arched entrance to Sean and Issabella's ranch. Simon had taken the old route back to the ranch, and was setting on the west fence that the arch was attached to when Aleena drove the supply wagon through. Her big smile brought one to his face to as he waved. "Growin' up aincha, sis?"

Jesse was riding beside the wagon and heard Simon, so he answered. "Big brother you don't know the half of it." He then looked at Simon's waist. "Carryin two of 'em now, huh?"

Simon put a hand on each of the front facing handles after crossing his arms, "Don't mention 'em, 'cause mom's been upset ever since Arianna made this other holster."

"Sure makes you look like a mean hombre." Jesse grinned and followed the wagon.

Sean reined up when he came to Simon. "Sure was glad to hear you got them two guys without gettin' shot'r anything, son. Got yourself a nice chunk o' money gettin' 'em, too." He leaned forward and rested his forearms on the pummel. "What you plan to do with it, son?"

"Ain't got but half of it left, dad."

Sean grinned wide, "Ian got you in a card game already, huh?"

Simon's black eyes twinkled. "He sure tried, but no pa, I gave half the money to Mrs. Ledderman so she can keep her little spread working."

Sean wasn't really surprised, even though he had no idea about his son's plan all along to give her half of whatever he got for capturing or killing the two men that killed her husband and Simon's best friend. He looked hard at Simon. "That's a heck of a fine thing to do son." He started to move on in behind the men but stopped and turned. "Simon, we'll go over and help her when she needs it. You keep a check on her n' let me know."

"Okay pa, I'm sure she'll be needin' some now with only them two girls to help her."

Simon hadn't said anything to anyone except Ian since he came home, so Sean asked Manollo to get a big fire going after everyone had eaten supper so they could all get together and talk.

Sean had his arm around Aleena as he stood and looked into the fire. It was the first time a female had ever been with the men when they had a fire and talked, so she was excited. "I asked Aleena to be here so she can hear all about her brother's adventure up into the mountains to get those two killers, plus I want her to tell the story herself how Jesse found her after she'd been grabbed by a crazy Indian from Chalponich's village."

After both stories had been told to a silent audience, Simon spoke. "Dad I ain't told mama nothing about this yet 'cause I know it'll upset her."

"I already broke it to her son, and you're right."

"Pretty upset huh?"

"Well, I ain't planning on goin' in till she's asleep." Sean grinned, "But son,

I know that woman well, and by tomorrow she'll be proud of what you did."

"Daddy," Aleena said, "I'll go on in and be company to mama while she's upset."

"Okay darlin', but don't say a word about you being grabbed by that crazy injun." He winked at her adding, "I'll ease that'n to her after a while."

"Dad." Ian said after his sister had left the fire.

"Yeah son, what's on yer mind?"

"Y'know that guy that came here before to have sheep and cows delivered to that new slaughterhouse in Yerba Buena?"

"The one that's building a big hotel there?"

"Same one," Ian answered.

"What about him?"

"Well, he heard I'm a good card player. He's gonna put in a casino for gambling, and a big dining room for his customers to eat at and…" He hesitated a moment trying to find the right words, but his father spoke first.

"Son, if that's what you wanna do then do it or you'll always regret it."

Ian grinned as Simon said, "Pa, Ian said he'd bet a ten dollar gold piece you'd say som'n like that, and was willing to give three to one odds."

9

~ *No escape* ~

The two escaped men pushed their horses for the first half of the day, and then slowed to a walk. "Where ya reckon we oughta head?" James Calvin spoke apprehensively to his companion.

Riff Colter was a man that demanded respect and was always in charge of whatever he was involved in. More than one man had ended his involvement with Riff by catching a bullet in his back because he didn't go along with the diminutive, sociopathic criminal's plans. All of his decisions were like his responses—slow and deliberate.

He finally answered his tall, skeletal-thin follower, who appeared more cadaver than a live human. "We'll head south till we get below the mountains then cut east."

After ten minutes of silence, James wanted badly to ask where they were going to go then, but he knew better than to break in on his boss' thoughts. He leaned toward him when Riff finally spoke again.

"We'll stay north of where those Apache spend most of their time, and hope we don't run into any of 'em. We're gonna go past a few small sodbustin settlers that we passed when we come across here last year. We'll stop at a couple of them sorry little shacks they live in and get what we need before headin' on across that desert country. When we get through Apache country we'll head south to the ocean and get us a job on one of those big schooners we saw."

A lecherous sneer spread across James' face. "I need me a woman, so I hope them injuns ain't burnt them folks out since we was here."

Riff grinned as he turned toward James. "A woman sounds purdy good t'me too, but what I really want is a coupla young kids, so we'll have trading stock in case we run into some Apache." He paused in thought a moment before continuing. "Plus a coupla kids'll get us passage on a ship somewhere without us having to work our way there."

"If it's a girl kid," cruelty and desire filling the cadaver's voice, "can I have her for awhile?"

"Nope." Riff turned in his saddle to glare at James. "Them ship captains ain't interested in kids that've been ripped all up by an old rogue like you."

James settled back into his saddle with disappointed thoughts. After a period of silent sulking he grinned lecherously. "How about if it's a boy kid, can I have him awhile?"

Riff turned in his saddle to stare intently at his partner. "You're a sick old scoundrel." He shook his head and glared at the man.

James didn't understand why Riff was always in such a bad mood, but he knew when to keep quiet, so he rode along in silence for an hour before speaking. "You think some other Mexican policemen'll be coming after us?"

After a few minutes of silence, Riff answered. "By the time they've found 'em and loaded their bodies on their horses and took 'em someplace to get buried, we'll be too far ahead for them or anyone else to pick up our trail."

James' spirits picked up at the thought of finding a ranch with a woman. "We'll be able to spend some time with the woman then won't we?"

Riff turned again to look at his only remaining gang member.

"You sure do like to kill 'em slow, doncha?"

"Yeah." James' eyes were almost closed in anticipation when he answered, "Sure do, but not till I'm done with 'em."

During the first few days of their sea voyage, the two young McKannah boys emptied their stomachs into the water boiling along the side of the sailing vessel. They attempted to cope with the ten-foot-high seas, so close together that it reminded them of the trail to school near their home. It never leveled out long enough to allow a person to settle into a comfortable position. They wobbled from cabin to gunwale, each wishing they had never heard of Harvard. Patrick lay in his bunk thinking about the last days at home in an attempt to keep his mind from dwelling on the rolling seas that his body was having difficulty adjusting to. He recalled the last days with his father as he and Manollo showed them more about the coach.

"See these two places kinda stickin' out?" Sean said as he pointed to the two boxed-in places on each side where the drivers would sit. "Reach inside."

When Patrick felt the shotgun he said, "Hey! This's neat. How do we get 'em out?"

"Grab hold," Manollo said, "and lift, then pull it out butt first."

When Patrick had the gun out he looked into the area that it came from, but couldn't see in the darkness of the barn. "Reach up in there," Manollo said. "You'll feel a hole for the barrel lined with rabbit fur to keep it from banging around."

"Dern," Patrick said, "that's pretty neat. The gun shoves up in there then the butt goes down in the bottom huh?"

"Yes!" Sean answered, "There's one on each side."

"Lemme see that thing."

After Patrick passed the shotgun to his younger brother, Broderick stepped down and looked the weapon over carefully. "How big a chunk o' lead does this thing shoot?"

Sean pulled a small piece of leather from his shirt pocket. Luis had written all of the information on it and gave it to Sean when he delivered the guns on his last trip to North Ranch. "Says right here, .16 gauge Theo, uhhh," he stammered and pulled the leather tag closer to his eyes, "Uhhh Theo, uhhh phi, dern this writin's small."

"Lemme see that, pop." Broderick held his hand toward his father, who was struggling with great difficulty as he stared at the alien words. "It says here, .16 gauge shotgun made by Theophilus Richards—London 1813." He looked up at his father, "Boy pop, these things're almost brand new." He handed the piece of leather back then sighted along the length of the nearly four-foot-long gun.

"Uncle Luis said they came into Mexico City while he and Aunt Carmen were visiting there last year. Remember the old sea captain I came here to California with?"

"Sure do," Patrick said loudly from the coach seat, "was it him that brought 'em?"

Sean chuckled, "Come back from the ground to bring 'em if it was," he grinned up at Patrick, " 'cause he's been dead a long time now, I'm sure. No, but it was a ship bringing stuff from all over the world like we did.

"Gonna be a ship like that to take us to Harvard?"

"No, but I hope it's a captain as good as Captain Mullholland."

"Hey, pa."

Sean looked up at his oldest son, "Yeah?"

"I know you named me after that sea captain, but who'd you name that after?" He motioned toward his brother with a nod of his head.

Sean grinned as he glanced at Broderick. "One of Luis' Mexican hands couldn't remember the word maverick that we called several of the horses we were breaking, so he called 'em a broderick and yer ma liked the sound of it." He shoved the piece of leather back into his pocket. "Me n' Manollo will show you how to load 'em before you leave. Lift up that seat lid under the pillow on the other side and get that box out."

When Patrick handed the wooden box down to Sean he said, "C'mon down and look at the stuff in here."

Back on the ground Broderick joined Patrick as they watched Manollo open the box. Broderick said, "Powder and shot for the gun, huh?"

No stupid, Jesse thought as he pressed his eye to the crack in the overhead floor, *it's another spare wheel.*

"That and more," Manollo replied as he laid the items out on the wooden bench. "Powder flask," he named the items one-by-one as he removed them, "shot flask, fine grain powder flask for priming, wads, and spare flints." When he had them all back in the box he said, "We'll go through everything again tomorrow when you boys shoot 'em."

"How far is it to the place we get on the boat?"

"Luis says it's about twelve hundred miles from here to Matamoros then east about four hundred to Rio Bravo, and then a short distance to the coast where the boat'll be waiting."

"Schrreee," Broderick whistled, "long ride."

"Won't be too bad," Sean replied, " 'cause you're stopping at Uncle Luis' South Ranch for a week with him and Aunt Carmen before you head on into Mexico."

"When you figure we oughta be leaving?"

"Monday mornin' at dawn. Jaime and Alejandro are gonna go to Uncle Luis' with you then bring a dozen or so of those new horses back with 'em."

"You getting in the horse business, pa?" Broderick asked.

"Nope, just getting'new riding stock for the ranch hands."

"Well little brother," Patrick grinned at Broderick, "we only got three days to say goodbye to the gals around here so we better get on with it."

Can't be too soon for me, Jesse said to himself, *good riddance.*

Two hours before dawn on Monday morning the entire family was gathered in the big kitchen—even a reluctant Jesse.

Patrick was reading from a piece of paper that Sean had written the route on. "After we leave Uncle Luis' South Ranch we go to Nogales in Mexico, then through Chihuahua, Matamoros, Monterrey, and Rio Bravo then on to the coast." He looked up at his father standing beside him. "Do these towns along the way have friends of Uncle Luis' in 'em if we have problems?"

"Well, maybe not exactly friends like me n' Manollo here, but they'll all have people who'll know who he is and will be more than willing to lend a hand."

"How long you figure it'll take them to get to Matamoros from Uncle Luis' ranch?" Issabella asked.

Manollo answered her. "We figure they can make a hundred miles a day by changing to the spare horses four times a day and letting them all rest half an hour each time."

Issabella had heard all of the information from Sean, but wanted to hear it again to calm herself. When the idea had first come up for the boys to go to the recently created Harvard University Law School in the east, the idea was for them to ride horses all the way, with only two of the ranchmen riding along for protection. She realized how dangerous it would be and was sick with worry. When Luis said he could arrange for a ship to pick them up near Rio Bravo, Mexico and would also have an armed escort all the way from his ranch to the ship, she was relieved, even though she knew the trip could still be very dangerous.

"Well," Issabela said, "it's three hundred miles to uncle's ranch, then you told me about sixteen hundred miles on to Rio Bravo, so with the stay at his ranch you boys oughta be on the ship and heading for college in about a month from today."

"Give or take a few weeks," Patrick grinned, "depending on the senoritas we meet along the way."

Manollo's estimate was accurate because by dusk on the third day after leaving Sean's ranch, the coach with Patrick, Broderick, and the two ranch hands as drivers pulled into Luis Carvojol's South Ranch.

Luis Carvojol enjoyed the two young men and let them visit with his wife, their Aunt Carmen, with no disturbance until the afternoon prior to their departure. "Come sit with me in my study please."

After the three men were seated, with each holding a cut crystal glass of his imported brandy, Luis Carvojol held his glass up and proposed a toast. "Here's to a successful trip, a profitable learning experience, and a career of enjoyable adventures in this wonderful new country."

After each had sipped the exquisite golden elixir, Patrick, the articulate McKannah, lifted his glass again toward his uncle. "I would also like to propose a toast if you don't mind, Uncle Luis."

Luis had always enjoyed the company of his first-born nephew, and smiled at the tall young man with his mother's deep, sea green eyes. "Of course, Patrick."

Patrick smiled back and spoke in the commanding voice that would carry him far in future California politics. "If all that you said comes true, then it will be the result of your kindness and unswerving faith in the McKannah family." He raised his glass higher then added, "To an uncle and friend with no equal, Luis Javier de Carvojol."

"Yes," Broderick added as he raised his glass.

Luis sipped with the two young men before answering. "Thank you, and I will add that you both always gave me many reasons for my support." After another sip he said, "Now let us get down to the business of getting you both to the coast, and on my friend's vessel near Rio Bravo."

The two McKannah boys refused his offer of another glass of brandy, which pleased him, and leaned forward, to listen.

The route you will take is about sixteen hundred miles to the coast where you will meet the vessel. I have arranged for you to take four rest stops of two days each at haciendas owned by acquaintances of mine. The first will be in Nogales, then Hermosillo, Chihuahua, and Monterrey. At each stop the coach will be thoroughly checked and any necessary repairs will be made. While we're on the subject of repairs I had one thing changed that has been worrying me."

"What was that uncle?"

"I never liked the way those two shotguns on each side of the driver were not available to the passengers inside. I had a removable panel installed, so each weapon can be reached by you or whoever is riding inside."

Patrick shook his head slowly up and down. "Very good thinking uncle, it never crossed my mind."

Luis smiled, "Let us hope you never have the need to remove those panels." He reached into a drawer of the table his glass was sitting on and removed two sheets of paper. "Patrick, you're the oldest so you carry these." Luis handed his nephew the papers while explaining, "This document states that you and Broderick are my nephews who are on a very important mission for me, and should not be detained for any reason. There are many small towns that have greedy officials that might attempt to charge a fee to allow you safe passage through their area." He leaned back with his glass and smiled. "If my name is not familiar to whoever might detain you, then that seal from the Governor of Spain should convince them to be courteous." He pointed to his map of Mexico. "You will go on through Rio Bravo without stopping, because there are too many greedy men there, and you might have problems. Check the carriage before nearing that town so you can go swiftly through with no need of stopping."

"You don't leave anything to chance do you?" Broderick commented as he looked over his brother's shoulder at the document and map.

"I try not to, which is why I am sending my six very best men with you. They are all equally good at what they do, but two will do the driving and the other four will scout the trail ahead and guard the rear as you pass." He finished his brandy then stood. "You will be leaving early in the morning so come with me and I will introduce them to you now."

They followed Luis out of the hacienda and into the yard. "Emiliano," Louis called to the tall thin man walking toward the huge barn.

"Yessir."

"You've met my two nephews?"

"Si, I told them about the horse adventure many years ago when I was with their father."

Patrick smiled, "I didn't know it was you that was going with us Emiliano, I'm very glad."

"Are the other five nearby?" Luis asked.

"Yessir, come." The Mexican horseman turned toward the barn.

Two hours before dawn the next morning, a huge breakfast was served for all, then with little ceremony Luis Carvojol's custom designed forerunner of the California Stagecoach was heading south toward Mexico. The two young men inside, and the six Mexicans outside were aware that they were setting off on a long journey that could prove very dangerous unless they were all extremely cautious.

The captain of the boat had orders from the owner to see to it that absolutely no harm came to his friend's two young nephews. During their first of the three days on Key West, while the vessel was loaded with Cuban rum and sugar brought across the Gulfstream by small trading boats, the boys didn't mind the company of the two stout, muscular young men that went everywhere with them. As they departed the boat on the second morning they saw that the same two men were coming with them. After reaching the little village center which was teeming with activity, a lot of which was the many whores negotiating for the money the sailors brought to the isolated little island, Patrick said, "Are you two gentlemen going to remain with us every moment we're here?"

The larger of the two dark young men smiled. "Yes, unless," he turned and pointed toward the waterfront, only a short walk away where the tall masts of his floating home were plainly visible, "we want our heads hanging from those."

Patrick turned to his redheaded brother, "I wonder if Uncle Luis' influence reaches all the way to Harvard."

"He has friends everywhere," Broderick answered, "but Harvard is too far away for even him."—They would eventually learn more lessons about their uncle's far-reaching influence.

"Well gentleman," Patrick smiled at their two escorts, "let's go find that bar you said sells the best rum in this little village."

The crude sign above the driftwood door had the owner's name carved in it. JOLLY'S was dug deeply into the wood. When the four entered the building, the two McKannah boys were surprised. "Wow." Broderick said softly, "Jorge, this place is even nicer than you said."

"Thank you for the compliment, Mister McKannah."

Both boys turned to see a slightly built man about their father's age smiling at them. He held his hand out, "Joliette Bromesierre welcomes you to Cayo

Hueso."

Patrick took his hand, "You already know our name?" He held the man's hand until he answered.

After looking down at his hand—firmly trapped in the tall, redheaded man's huge paw, he smiled even wider. "This far from civilization sir, I find it to my advantage to know as much as I can about the happenings on the Island of Bones."

"Nothing wrong with that amigo," Patrick said as he released the delicate hand, "I like t'know what's happening around me too." He stared intently into the pale gray eyes then added, "Especially when it has my name attached to it."

The French Canadian had been thrown off his ship two years earlier for cheating at cards. He was seldom rattled, so he smiled patronizingly and invited them all to join him for a drink at his personal table. When the owner of the most active bar on the island left to attend to business one of their escorts said, "Seems like you sized Jolly up quick, Mister McKannah."

"No problem there, as long as you keep one eye open all night when you're sleeping in his camp."

"Yep," the other man said, "you got him right.'

Two hours of Cuban rum later Broderick stood, "Let's walk off a little of this rum and find someplace cooking some turtle like we had yesterday."

"Mmmm yes, tortuga." Their escort responded. "I could live here just for those turtle steaks."

They all returned to JOLLY'S after stuffing themselves on green turtle steaks and fried doughballs stuffed with meat—they had never heard of conch fritters. "I could've eaten a dozen of those delicious little cakes," Broderick said as he filled his glass with rum.

"You did little brother," Patrick answered, smiling.

"Phew, no wonder I feel like I have a watermelon in m'belly."

An hour later Patrick said, "Let's go back to the ship and take a nap so later we can look for those beautiful girls they must have hidden someplace." Broderick agreed, and as they stood to leave, one of the drunken fishermen turned from his table of friends to address the two young men he had been watching and listening to.

"Why bother looking for girls little boy? With that pretty red hair you can have all the fun you want if you come with us." He turned his homemade chair toward them and rubbed his crotch.

Before Patrick could answer, Broderick said with his quick tongue and even quicker mind, "You better save what you have in your hand there for your mother and sister or they'll have to come find me tonight."

The man's growl sounded like a wounded animal as he leaped from his chair. His lunge carried him straight into Patrick's fist as it loosened a few teeth with the first punch then he removed two of them with the next. A rabbit punch sent the drunken fisherman to dreamland for the duration of the brief scuffle. Scuffle is all it could be called because it didn't last long enough to be considered a fight.

Two of his drunken friends jumped up to help their comrade and before the two escorts could react, Patrick had then both in a vice-like grip beneath each long arm that was the result of years of wrestling his brothers, and anyone else who would accept his challenge. He lunged for the narrow doorway, but found it to small to accommodate the three of them so he dropped the two unconscious drunks after their heads hit the door jamb, then he casually walked on out. Broderick and the two men followed.

"Y'know," one of their escorts said, "I think we have wasted two days watching over you two." They all four laughed as they headed for the boat.

During their last day on Key West, the two McKannah boys had no more luck finding the hidden maidens than they had during the previous two. They enjoyed walking around the island meeting the wide mix of people living there. They spoke in Spanish with the Cubans and Mexicans who had migrated there for one reason or another—often to escape a hangman's noose where they came from. They used the French they had learned at school to converse with the few French people from a place they had heard of called New Orleans. There were quite a few blacks that spoke a language they didn't understand and figured it wouldn't matter if they did because they spoke so rapidly they would never be able to keep up anyway. They were from a series of islands called Bahamas, and were their very favorite people because they seemed to enjoy life so much.

"Hey mon," one old Bahamian woman asked them as she fried the fritters they liked so much over an open fire in a huge pan, "Whachew puttin' on dat hair what makin it pretty red like dat?"

Broderick took another cake and paid her for all four of the men's lunch then answered, "It's our own color hair and we got it from out daddy."

"Hmmm," the old woman replied, as she looked hard at Broderick. "I dunno mon, dat hard t'believe. How bouchew comin' in de room wit me den I fine out for m'self if dat real all over." She grinned wide; displaying the one remaining tooth she ate with.

"Not me darlin', I only like boys, but my brother here," he pointed to Patrick, "loves nothing better than older women."

"Uh huh, dat soun' good t'me darlin', juss you wait till I put dis pan on de side dese hot coals, an we gone git it on, mon." As she prepared to go with him, Patrick headed on along the oyster-shell street shaking his hands, "No mama, not today." Broderick and the two men had to rush to catch up with him.

"Brother, you're really getting old, letting a gal slip away from ya like that."

"Ain't that atol little brother, I'm just getting choosy in m'old age." They all laughed and headed for JOLLY'S.

"Good day, Jolly." Broderick said as they entered, "Our friends been around looking for a re-match?"

"Two of them won't be around looking for anything again. They're dead, and the third leaped through that window so fast I missed and blew one of the hinges off."

"Darn! What happened?"

"They woke up and found their money gone, and said that I must have taken it because I was the only one here. When they decided to see if I had it, I shot two of them and would have got that other one but he was fast on his feet," he grinned, "especially when the shooting started." He placed six loaded pistols on the bar one by one and smiled. "I am always ready for those kind." He replaced the weapons below the bar-top and poured the four men a drink on the house.

As they walked toward the boat later that afternoon Patrick said, "That Joliette's a guy to be careful around."

"Don't plan t'run into him again," Broderick commented.

On the deck were six green turtles, lying on their backs with their front flippers bound together with wire. "What're those for?" Patrick asked one of the senior seamen.

"The captain hired a run-away slave to cook them for us on the way to Boston Harbor. He wants to go to Canada where he has friends and thinks he can make it to there from Boston. The captain had him bring some to his cabin last night and cook it. He says it's the best and most tender he has ever had, so I guess we're gonna eat well on the next leg of the trip."

The captain waited until daylight to give the order for the sails to be raised. Both McKannah boys were on deck watching the little island disappear astern as the ship headed into the Gulfstream to pick up the northern running current.

"Well little brother," Patrick said, "the captain says no more stops till we're at the dock in Boston."

"I'm ready for some solid land beneath m'feet, Patrick."

"Yeah, me too."

Jesse tracked the two men for six days without closing the gap more than about a mile. They were heading toward his Uncle Luis's South Ranch, and even though he had never actually been out on the land himself, he knew it well. His father's stories about the horse catching days were his favorite, and he absorbed details that most would miss. The details of the surrounding country were unrolling in his mind as he recalled the stories told over and over during the winter months.

He was laying plans in his mind as he rode along the trail the two men were leaving. *They're gonna go right through Boulder Arroyo day after tomorrow so that's where I'll take 'em.*

That night Jesse used the light from a full moon to go over the Brown Bess.

The gift from Captain Mullholland to his father, when he decided to go into the northern mountains trapping with his Uncle Frank, was the young man's most prized possession. Jesse loved the weapon and practiced with it at every opportunity until he was the best shot in the family with the British manufactured Short Land Pattern 1777 Musket.

Even though he knew the 42" barrel was clean, he still removed the rod and ran a cloth once through. His father had explained the one big flaw with the weapon. "The black powder clogs the barrel and touch hole so bad that the soldiers used a ball a wee bit too small so it didn't get stuck in the barrel. Keep her good n' clean so you can ram a ball with a small chunk of cloth around it down in 'er and she'll run true for a hundred yards."

Jesse knew that was an exaggeration, but with a lightly oiled cloth on the ball he could hit one of the six inch clay targets he made, at thirty of his paces. As he shoved the ball and cloth down the barrel, he closed his eyes so he could feel it as it went along the inside of the smooth, but pitted-with-age barrel. When he was satisfied that the Brown Bess was as good as he could make it, he ran his hands over the gold inlay. *That ol' sea captain sure musta liked my pa.* He then started cleaning his new revolver. When he was finished, he laid his head on his saddle and looked at the bright moon while thinking about the two killers and his plan.

I'll swing wide tomorrow and get ahead of 'em early so I'll have plenty of time to lay my ambush. If I don't get both these guys then I'm sure a few more good people are gonna die.

Jesse stayed with their trail till noon the next day then began moving in a large arc to the south to get around them. Before nightfall he spotted the arroyo from the vivid descriptions used by his father as he told his stories. He continued slowly after dark, and when he arrived at the entrance of Boulder Arroyo, the moonlight allowed him to see exactly where he would set his ambush.

James Calvin asked cautiously as the two men slouched in their saddles, "We goin' through that place with them big rocks in it again?"

After a lengthy pause, Riff Colter turned a sneer toward his follower. "Would you rather go all the way around?"

"Might not be such a bad idea, Riff." He turned in the saddle and looked behind. "That darn place gave me the creeps when we come through it on the way out here."

"Just keep in close t'me and if one of them spooks jumps out atcha I'll blow a hole in his sheet with this shotgun I took from that Mexican lawman." He laughed hard and shook his head from side-to-side. "You're sure a spooky ol' skeleton, ain'cha?"

James remained silent awhile then asked, "How about them Apache?"

After fifteen minutes Riff still hadn't responded so James repeated his dread, "How about them Apache?"

Finally Riff turned toward him. "I tole you before when we come through there, that I was tole they don't go into this country around here because a buncha Mexican soldiers about wiped 'em out one time when they come west too far."

James was still turning regularly in his saddle to survey their rear trail as they approached the entrance to Boulder Arroyo. He pulled the nearly ancient flintlock pistol from his waist rope and checked it. *Riff orter had let me have one 'o them pistols he took off'n them dead Mexicans. Nuts! He's got 'em both in his saddlebags and that shotgun too. If'n I was sure certain that this ol' pistol would fire I'd shoot him in the back then take all them guns and trade with them boat fellers m'self.* It wasn't the first time that James Colter had such thoughts about the men he'd teamed with, but he never could get up the courage to do anything about it—and never would.

Jesse held his breath as he put the sight on the shoulder of the man holding the long barreled shotgun across the saddlehorn of his horse. Before the cloud of black smoke cleared he was standing with his pistol pointed at James who was trying desperately to control his horse.

The .77 caliber lead ball hit Riff on the inside edge of the clay target that Jesse had in his mind when he pulled the trigger. It missed the target he aimed for by less than an inch and tore one lung to shreds as it plowed into the man's spine. Riff's final moments on earth were looking into a blinding sun as he tried in vain to move. He was relieved when the sun started going down behind the mountains moments later as everything started getting dark. He didn't realize that it would never get light for him again.

"Get both them hands up in the air," Jesse yelled as he leveled his revolver at James. James didn't say a word as he finally gained control and swung his horse around to flee. He had moved about ten feet from where Riff lay when he felt the lead enter his back. He tried to keep his hands on the reins but his fingers seemed to belong to someone else. He had no control of his body as it began sagging from the saddle and fell to the ground.

By the time James Colter was falling, Jesse had the Brown Bess reloaded. He knew that the British soldiers were suppose to be able to reload and fire four times a minute so Jesse practiced until he could send five lead balls down the barrel every minute for three full minutes.

A moment after James hit the ground the Brown Bess was reloaded and pointed straight at him. Jesse kept it there to see what the man was going to do. After looking at first one then the other, he was certain that the fight had left them. He picked up the shotgun then removed the old flintlock from the dead man's belt. He then retrieved the other man's old flintlock and headed toward his horse, which was hobbled a quarter-mile away, and later returned cautiously to the arroyo entrance.

The two men lay just as he had left them, so he got down to look at each. Riff was still staring at the sun but it was plain to Jesse that he was seeing nothing. He then walked toward James. He could tell by the expression on his face that he was alive. After asking him a few questions, but getting no answers, he lifted an arm and let it go. When the other arm and both legs dropped like logs, he knew his bullet had busted the man's spine. Jesse positioned one of their horses and loaded the dead man across the saddle and securely tied him. Jesse then got James' horse. He knew the man was still alive as he loaded his carcass across the saddle and secured him, but didn't think he'd make the journey to his Uncle Luis's South Ranch—he was right.

The trip took Jesse until dawn the next day. The tower guard alerted Frank that someone was approaching from the east leading two horses. Frank and Victoriano Madera rode out to meet the person, each holding a musket and wearing pistols in leather holsters.

Frank's fondness for his youngest nephew was apparent from the day Jesse was born. He saw his best friend, Sean McKannahs' fierce determination in Jesse at an early age, as the boy constantly battled his older brothers. He smiled when he saw who it was. "Find those guys like that or did you make 'em that way, Jesse?"

"Been trackin' 'em for quite awhile." He looked haggard when he spoke. "Maggie fixed breakfast yet? I ain't et much in a coupla days."

"She is making a big breakfast right now," Victor answered, "so we can all go look for horses that broke out last night." He grinned at the young man, "You want to go with us?"

"Yeah, I reckon I will if you need me."

"Ha, I make a joke, amigo. You look like you join them two if you don't get rest soon."

"I am pretty dern tired."

Frank rode around to look at the bodies. "Are both of them dead?"

"That skinny one was alive when I left, but I reckon he's dead now."

Frank lifted James' head to look at it then let it fall. "Yesiree, dead as a cat's rat."

Jesse rested all that first day and at the noon meal he told Uncle Luis, "I'm heading back home sir, so mom and dad won't get t'thinking som'n bad happened to me."

Before Luis could respond Frank said, "Everything is going very well here at the ranch Uncle Luis, so if you don't mind me being gone for a while I'll take Victor and the coach and return Jesse to Sean's ranch so I can visit with them all for a while.

"Very good idea. Yes, and I'll see to it that the two Mexican policemen's bodies are located and returned to their families. You go north and visit as long as you like." He smiled at Frank, "Because of all your help, El Cielo de los Caballos is running very smoothly." Another grin and he added, "With the exception of a few wild horses that wished to be free again."

"They will all soon be back in the corral, uncle. They smelled the free wind from the east and couldn't help themselves."

"Ah, yes. They all have the wild genes in them. That is why they are such a magnificent animal."

Frank smiled and nodded his head at the man he loved as a father. He knew that the man's health was failing and didn't really want to leave him, but he wanted badly to see his sister and his old friend Sean.

During the long trip to Sean and his sister Issabella's sheep ranch, Frank listened as Jesse brought him up to date about all that had happened during the two years since he'd been north for a visit. Frank did the same for him, since it had been five years since Jesse had come south with his father. "Do you think Uncle Luis will die soon?" Jesse asked, after listening as Frank explained about his uncle's bad health.

"I'm certain he will not last much longer. His doctor comes regularly from San Diego to check his lungs, then he tells me what to expect." He paused awhile to look out the coach's window. "I guess a man makes his mark on the land and then he goes back to it."

"I always liked Uncle Luis," Jesse said, "but I never really got to know him good. Mom and dad are sure gonna be sad." He turned to Frank "Do they know that he's real sick?"

"Yes, they've known for a while that he's not doing well, but they don't know that he's so bad that they won't have him much longer." He turned toward the window and was silent.

Jesse knew that Frank and his parents were very close to Luis, so he sat in silence as the coach rumbled along with his horse trailing behind.

10

~ *Born gambler* ~

Issabella held her son Ian's hand as they walked toward the huge old oak tree beside the creek that had become the discussion and parting place of the McKannah family. Each silently thought of the past-present-and-future as they closed the gap between the ranch and the tree. Issabella dreaded getting there because she was aware that when they returned to the ranch, Ian would prepare to leave the following morning.

Her thoughts at the moment were of her two older sons in college so far away. *Seems like only a short time ago since I walked to the tree to say goodbye to Patrick and Broderick, and it's been two years.*

Ian's mother had developed a closer bond with Ian than with any of the other McKannah boys. His thoughts were of her as they strolled along toward the creek. *My God I hate leaving mama, but I just gotta see if I can really be a gambler. Patrick and Broderick ain't gonna be able to come home to visit like they thought, and Simon's talking about going after those guys that killed his friend, so mama's really gonna be hurting terrible with four of us gone.* His seventeen-year-old mind was in turmoil when his mother broke the silence.

"You know I always hoped you'd become a preacher or a businessman, Ian." It was said more to herself than as a confrontational statement to her young son. He didn't know how to answer, so they walked the remaining few yards to the tree in silence.

She squeezed his hand hard before letting it go. "But darling, whatever you think you have to do in this world is what you must do." She turned her beautiful eyes toward him in the direct stare she used when her concern was at its peak, and then smiled. "Took your father a lot of talking to convince me that you boys aren't children any longer."

"I reckon it's pretty tough," Ian said, "to see your kids all go off like we're doing mama, but there's just so darn much out there in the world that we all wanna see n' do."

"Do you remember the story I told you about your daddy going off to find those wild horses in Indian country for Uncle Luis?"

"Sure do mama. We boys have talked about it many times."

"Well I was so in love with that boy," she turned to look directly into Ian's blue piercing eyes, "and that's all he really was, a boy, so much that I asked Uncle Luis to please make him stay at South Ranch and do something else." She turned her gaze to the river then continued; "He told me that if I tried to hold him down I'd lose him forever. He said that a man must do many things that a woman will not understand, but if she really loves him she must allow him the freedom to test himself and just hope and pray that he comes through his adventures in one piece." Her intense stare was now boring into Ian's eyes. She finally smiled. "That's exactly what I've been doing with all of you." She reached out and took his hand again, "Especially you Ian, because I've known for a long time that your love of cards and gambling would probably take you away. I hope this man you're going to work for is honest and you do well."

They spent an enjoyable hour in the shade reminiscing about the more pleasant events that had occurred between them before returning to the ranchhouse.

Later that night in the room they shared, Simon asked Ian, "When are you going to Yerba Buena?"

"When Mr. Hamilton stopped here in his coach last week on the way to Uncle Luis' North Ranch to talk to Manny about buying some more cattle, he said he'd be back here on Saturday."

"Dern," Simon said, "that's tomorrow; you heading on to Yerba Buena with him?"

"Yes." Ian grinned, "He said we can tie my horse to the rear of his coach and I can ride inside so we can talk."

"That coach he was in is one that Uncle Luis' guys built ain't it?"

"Yeah. He figures it all out and draws the pictures and everything, and then

Miguel and his guys build it."

"They've changed 'em a lot ain't they since Patrick and Broderick went down into Mexico in that little one?"

"Yeah, they make 'em a lot fancier now with soft seats inside n' better springs on 'em so they ride smoother. Daddy says there're so many people waiting for one that it takes a year or so to get it. Manny now has a crew of new men that do nothing but build 'em."

"They're sure nice with all that carving and stuff on 'em but I wouldn't wanna go nowhere in one m'self. I like being on my horse where I can see everything around me."

"This'll be the first time I ever rode in one," Ian said, "and I ain't gonna like it either. It'll feel strange not being able to see who's coming up behind us."

Simon grinned again, "By the looks of those two guys with that feller you're goin' off with, I don't reckon you gotta worry about that."

"Yeah, they were a coupla tough looking guys, especially that big one."

Jesse rode silently beside his father as they headed toward Yerba Buena. Even without a herd of sheep it would still take them four hard-riding days to get there. There wasn't another person on earth that Jesse would rather be with than his father. It seemed there was always so much to do that he seldom found time to just be with him and talk. He loved it when Sean would tell the stories about his younger days when he was riding with Uncle Luis' Mexican ranch hands, and especially when he was in the mood to talk about the days when he and Jesse's mother were young. Jesse had met one of the Ledderman girls at a party recently and had many questions to ask, but knew he must wait awhile. *Daddy's sure missing Ian and Simon.*

He was correct about Sean's silence. He kept his emotions inside rather than allow them to run rampant, as his wife Issabella did. He still thought often of Patrick and Broderick being in the east at Harvard Law School. Even though he had known they were going to accept Uncle Luis' offer to go east to get their education, he still dreaded the day they'd actually leave. He only had to close his eyes to see the carriage and men guarding it pulling out on their way to South Ranch. *Darn, seems like Ian and Simon're just little boys, and they're already off in the world to make their own way. Heck, I guess I was about their age when I headed off into the mountains with Frank. Hmmm! How old was I anyway? How old are those boys? Lemme see, Ian's older'n Simon and Simon's…*Sean struggled to figure out how old the two middle boys were, but finally gave up. "Jesse."

"Yessir."

"How old are you now, son?"

"I'll be fifteen next month, on February twelfth."

"Fifteen?" Sean turned in the saddle to look hard at his favorite son—something he would die without revealing—then repeated, "Fifteen?"

"Yep." Jesse grinned, "We're all growin' up, pa."

"My God, I thought you were about twelve, or maybe thirteen at the outside. Well fer cryin' out loud, no wonder them boys was itchin' to go off n' see the world. Lemme see then," Sean removed his leather hat and rubbed his head, sweaty even with the chill in the air. "That makes Ian uh, hmm, lemme see." As he was trying to get their birth times lined up in his head, Jesse spoke.

"Ian'll be seventeen in April pa, and Simon's gonna turn sixteen come May." He didn't want to embarrass his father so he added, "I been working on memorizing all kindsa things pa 'cause Mr. Adderly says it's good exercise for the brain."

Actually, Jesse only had to learn something, and it was with him forever. His two older brothers, who were attending Harvard University's newly formed Law School, could use his natural ability to learn and remember facts. It was this natural ability that would eventually save his life more than once. When he becomes WHITE BUFFALO, and lives amongst the Salish Indians, Jesse would bring back knowledge filed away many years earlier.

I guess I can remember stuff the way pa can remember all the details about the land he travels across. When Sean commented on the good weather they were having for this trip, Jesse knew his father's mind had left his brothers behind so he began the conversation he was dying to get into.

"Pa."

"Yeah, Jesse."

"Am I too young to be having serious thoughts about a girl?"

Sean turned in the saddle again to look hard at the son he still considered a boy. "Well son, I was a bit older'n you when me n' yer ma got married," Sean paused to stare a moment at Jesse, "but I reckon you're a lot wiser than I was at your age. Have you met a girl you're feeling serious about?"

"You remember Simon's friend Elijah, who was murdered?"

"Sure do, I liked Mr. Ledderman."

"Well pa, I went to their ranch a while after Simon took Mrs. Ledderman half of that reward money, and I met them two sisters of Elijahs'." He fidgeted in the saddle a little before continuing, "I, uh sorta took a shine to that older one, pa."

"Gee," Sean commented, "they still seem like kids t'me." He grinned at his son, "But you still do too, and we darn sure know that's a pile o' sheep poop. How old are they son?"

"One's a year younger'n me and the other one's almost a year older'n me. She was already fifteen last May."

"A sucker for older women, huh?" His father turned his charming Irish grin toward Jesse. "I reckon," he was now serious; "you're old enough to know if you got real feelings in your heart for this gal, son."

Their conversation about women and the way they thought differently about things than a man popped up spontaneously every now and then as the two men rode on toward Sean's meeting with James Poorsmith in Yerba Buena.

The following day the two men rode toward the small rocky area where an old mountain hermit was holed up nursing a wound received when he tried to run off a badger. His good hearing compensated for his poor eyesight so he heard them long before they were within view. He remained hidden as they passed almost close enough to touch. He was very relieved to see them disappearing into the distance. He waited until their sounds diminished then returned to the sunny area that he was enjoying when he first heard their approach.

The moment Jesse and his father entered James Poorsmith's new trading post, Jesse's heart skipped a beat. "That's Mrs. Ledderman's horse in front pa," Jesse said pointing, "and that's Maura's horse beside it." He was grinning when Sean turned toward him.

"Maura, huh? That's an Irish name."

"Her ma's Irish pa. She married Mr. Ledderman when her folks died on the boat coming to Yerba Buena."

"Dern, I ain't sure if I ever met Mrs. Ledderman. Me n' Emil did some business a few times, and I liked that hard-headed old German." He reached up and rubbed his jaw, "Darn shame what happened to him n' that boy o' his." He shifted in the saddle, "She comes all the way here with just a young girl?"

"I don't think so pa. I reckon them other two horses belong to her Mexican ranch hands." Jesse now turned to Sean, "Y'know that reward money Simon gave her n' them girls?"

"Yeah I sure do. Me n' your ma was real proud that he'd do som'n like that."

"Well, I guess it was enough for her to get that ranch goin' pretty good, 'cause she's got two Mexican families livin' there n' workin' it with her."

They rounded the corral and approached the front of the new trading post. "I been so darn busy lately, I don't know anything about what the other folks around us are doing. I remember when your ma went over to her place n' stayed a few days when it happened."

"I reckon she's a pretty tough woman, pa." Jesse got down from his horse and tied the reins to the rail. He was already opening the door before Sean finished tying his. Sean smiled, remembering his enthusiasm when he and his Bella first met.

There wasn't time for socializing, so Sean conducted his business with James then spent a short time talking to Mrs. Ledderman while Jesse talked to Maura. "Well ma'am, I'm really proud that you think so highly of our son there," he nodded toward Jesse, "he's been a right fine boy his whole life. I'll tell his mother what you said."

The young girl was standing near the door and talking to Jesse. "When will

I see you again, Jesse?"

"Mama's tryin' to talk daddy into having a big party and when she sets her mind to som'n," he grinned and the girl felt shivers run up and down her spine, "she always gets her way. I reckon you better start getting your party dress all cleaned up." Another of his charming Irish grins and she thought she'd faint, so she held to the huge barrel of pickles. "I see pa's ready to head home so I'll ride over n' tell you when that party's gonna be, as soon as I find out." He turned and followed Sean out to their horses.

As soon as they were back on the trail, Sean broke the silence. "That's a right nice little gal Mrs. Ledderman brought with her."

"You'll know how right you are daddy when you have a chance to really meet her n' talk a little."

"Well, that shouldn't be too long from now 'cause your ma's planning a big party at our ranch." He kept a stone face, but wanted to laugh when Jesse almost fell from the saddle when he whipped around.

"Really? Eeyow," he yelped as his foot slipped from the stirrup, almost dumping him to the ground. After composing himself he said, "I knew she was wanting to but I didn't know for sure if there was gonna be time enough to have it."

They talked about the party and who they'd invite as they moved toward their ranch. When they approached the same area they had come through days earlier, their path was a little closer to the old hermit that had watched as they passed. His wounds were healing and this time his senses began sending signals to his brain. He peered out of his cave to see the two men approaching. He ducked back in and looked around for a way out. He knew he had been lying in too small a place, but the sun was hitting it just right and he wasn't expecting anyone to be coming through his territory. No matter how well he squeezed back against the wall he was still exposed. When Sean's horse was almost right on top of him he jumped out. It was partly due to anger and partly because of fear.

When Sean's horse saw the huge rattlesnake lunge out, it instinctually reared up and did a backward dance to get away. It saved the horse from being struck in the leg, but Sean was caught off guard and thrown over the rear and onto a boulder. Jesse saw the rattler strike toward his dad's horse so he drew his new revolver and fired at it. The slug missed but it was enough to convince the snake to take off in the opposite direction.

Jesse got down and went to his father who was groaning, while still lying on the boulder he'd landed on. "You hurt bad, pa?"

"I ain't sure yet, son. Right now I feel like some Blackfoot shoved a spear into my back, but maybe it'll be okay after a while."

It wasn't okay. Jesse finally got his father back on his horse and they slowly continued toward their ranch. It topped all of the grueling ordeals Sean had been through. The pain in his lower back prevented anything other than a slow walk on horseback. At the end of the first day Jesse realized that it was going to be impossible for his dad to continue on the horse. Sean ate a small amount of jerky and hardtack then lapsed into a pain-riddled stupor from which he only periodically rallied. By dawn on the second morning, Sean was lashed to a travois that Jesse had made during the night. It was tied to Sean's horse, and Sean was tied to it. Jesse had a tether from his horse to the horse pulling the travois, so that there was no chance of it running scared with his father bouncing along behind. He had learned well from his Native American friends.

The pain was still intense, but lying down rather than sitting in the saddle allowed enough relief for Sean to rally from his delirium. Jesse was glad to hear his father's voice in the late afternoon.

"Jesse."

He turned in the saddle and looked down to see his father's head twisted enough to look up at him. "Yeah pa?"

"Ya done real good son. Ain't near as bad as it was up in the saddle. How long've we been on the trail like this?"

"We're closin' out the first day of draggin that rig pa." There was a long silence as Sean sorted through his pain-racked brain.

"Bout two days t'home I reckon," he finally said.

"I'm gonna cut 'er down some by draggin on through the night, 'cause you're gonna be just as miserable stopped as you will movin'." There was another long silence before Sean spoke.

"I s'pose yer right, but whadaya say we stop for a few minutes so I can pee n' get som'n t'eat and drink."

Jesse was very happy to hear his father speaking lucid again, after the delirious babbling the first day as he slumped in his saddle. He stopped both horses and tied his to a thick tree limb. "I only padded under your back with the blankets pa, so you can get 'er out n' pee down through the crosslashings." He began getting out the necessities for a quick lunch. Thirty minutes later his smokeless fire had the tin pot of water and venison jerky simmering. Fifteen minutes later they were heading toward home again.

A couple of hours after dawn, a slumped Jesse entered the ranch dragging his father, as their ranch hands ran alongside. Bella and Aleena were all of his family that remained at home, since Ian and Simon had also gone off to pursue their own futures. Bella looked up at her son, who looked older than his father did as he looked back through tired, worried eyes. She said nothing except, "Go get the sick room ready Aleena." The young girl's training prevented her from uttering a word as she spun around in mid-stride and ran back to the house.

The year following Sean's injury brought two major changes to Jesse's life. He suddenly found himself in complete charge of the ranch. Sean steadfastly insisted that he'd be back on his feet in no time, but a visit by the doctor making his once-every-two-months rounds convinced him otherwise.

"Mister Sean McKannah," the portly little bald headed doctor said, "you've damaged at least one and maybe two of the vertebrae and discs in your back." He paused letting the Irishman that he knew to be spontaneously hotheaded with a fiery temper, digest what he'd just said. Finally he continued, "Do you understand what this means about your immediate future, sir?"

"I know that there's a lot of pain in my back, but I've had some pretty bad pain before, so I reckon this'll pass and I'll be up n' around in a week'r so."

The doctor was silent as he packed his few tools back into the small leather valise and pulled a chair to the bedside and sat. "That's not how it's going to be this time, Mr. McKannah. Let me show you what's happened inside your back." He opened a notebook that had drawings of the human body in it. "This is your spinal column, and this is," he pointed his pencil to the spot and began explaining the situation to Sean.

Fifteen minutes later he closed the book. "The only way you'll get back to work is by allowing the swelling to go down, and hopefully the disc or discs will heal themselves." He was surprised that the crusty redheaded man was silently listening to every word and had paid close attention to his diagrams. He knew the man was in severe pain and must realize the seriousness of his dilemma. "This will require complete bed rest for at least six months, with you on the floor and not in this soft bed. You absolutely must teach yourself to lie on your back with your knees up. Here, let me show you." The doctor got down on the floor and stretched out on his back then pulled his knees up.

He turned to Bella who had stood silently in the corner watching and listening. "Mrs. McKannah, if you could make a thick pillow to go under his knees it will help immensely." He rolled over and struggled to his hands and knees, then slowly got to his feet. He turned to her again, "Can you prepare a palate of thick blankets and horse pads on the floor so he'll be as comfortable as possible?"

"Yes, and I'll have that pillow for his knees made by this evening." The concern for her husband's painful condition was etched deeply into her normally radiant Spanish face. She was more concerned about the fact that Sean lay silently listening with no argument. That told her for certain that he realized the desperate situation he was in.

When the doctor left the ranch, Sean reached beneath the cloth that covered the crock jar on the table beside the bed. There was a covered bucket beneath the bed for him to relieve his bowels in, and the jar was for his kidneys. After emptying his kidneys Sean replaced it on the table, and then swung his legs over the edge of the bed. He gasped as the pain went through his lower back, but he grimaced and lowered his legs to the floor and slowly stood. *A man can't keep lettin' others empty his night bucket. I'll just slowly go outside and empty this pee jar, then come back n' get that slops bucket and empty it in the outhouse too.*

Before his right foot moved to follow the left one that he'd carefully shoved forward, the entire room started flashing as though it was on fire. An involuntary cry rushed from his lips as he crashed on top of the crock—now broken. He lay gasping in pottery shards and his own urine.

Aleena was near enough to hear his cry and came running. "Oh daddy, oh my God." She ran from the room and yelled for her mother. Jesse was just tying his horse to the rail nearby and came running. He entered the sick room just a step behind his mother. Aleena was already at her father's side holding his head and wiping the sweat from his pain furrowed brow.

"Take it easy pop," Jesse said, "we'll have you back in bed in no time atol."

"Aleena, go get a bunch of towels and a bucket of warm water." Bella then got down on her knees beside Sean. "Heading out to check on the ranch, big fella?" Her radiant smile warmed him as he looked into her eyes.

"Nah, I was just gonna see if I could still leap over the hitchin' post without touching it." It was a very weak smile she saw in his eyes.

"Okay tough guy, let's see if you can handle this." She smiled as she dabbed the sweat from his forehead. "Jesse."

"Yeah, Ma."

"You n' me gotta roll him over outa this broken pottery, and get him cleaned up. Go around and hold his hips and legs as steady as you can, and we'll just move him half way at first." When Jesse was in position she said, "Easy now over we go." Sean didn't make a sound but they could both hear his teeth grinding.

Aleena arrived with the blankets and water just as they had him on his side out of most of the mess. "Go get the pan and mop so you can clean this area up." The young girl spun around on one big foot and was gone.

"Okay Jesse, let's ease his nightshirt up and get it off."

Thirty minutes later Sean was once again clean, dry, and stretched out on the floor in a fresh nightshirt. "You're gonna have to lay there a while," Bella said, "till I get some thick blankets to make a place on the floor for you."

"In our bedroom?"

"Nope. Doc said not to move you till he's had a chance to look you over again, 'cause it might paralyze you if we moved you now."

After getting Sean settled on the floor palate, Bella removed the linen from the bed he'd been lying in prior to his fall. "I'll be right back."

"How y'feelin now, pa?" The concern on Jesse's young face was obvious.

"A whole lot better." He smiled up at his son. "Ain't this a helluva situation for a full grown man t'be in." It wasn't a question; simply a bitter comment. "Jesse."

"Yeah, pa."

"I wancha t'know how proud I am to have a son like you to step in and take charge like you're doin'."

"That ain't any problem atol pa." Jesse was embarrassed for his father and didn't know what to say. He was also worried because he knew his father. "You gotta forget all about the ranch, pa, and just get well. I'll come to you whenever there's anything I don't understand. Som'n I'm gonna do as soon as ma gets back with her bed stuff is put that big ol' bell on the wall outside and run a rope in here for you to pull in you need som'n."

"Darn good idea Jesse, but whadaya mean, bring her bed stuff in here?"

"She's movin in here to be near ya, pa."

"Aw nuts."

"What's the matter, pa?"

"Nothing I reckon, but she's gonna hafta go out when I gotta git up n' pee or poop."

Jesse was silent for a long spell then said, "Uh pa, doc says you're gonna have to use that thin little pan for quite awhile, so you don't bugger up your back any more'n it already is, and somebody's gonna have to help you with it."

"Oh my God." Sean squeezed his eyes tight and shook his head. "Jesse."

"Yeah."

"You reckon that old rattler'll still be there when I get back on my feet?" He was grinning when Jesse looked down at him.

"Indians say they live n' die in the same little area sometimes, so he might still be there." He was grinning too, happy to see his father kidding.

"Ah, wasn't his fault. I'd do the same thing if some big critter like that horse o' mine came stomping through the yard."

During the next six months other changes happened in Jesse's life. He realized that he was a natural at running the ranch. He'd always loved working with his father but left the decisions to Sean and simply did the tasks that he was given. Something else very important to this young boy; forced to quickly becoming a man—he was in love. When everything was going smoothly and the ranch hands had the sheep under control, he would ride the short distance to the Ledderman ranch to visit with Maurah Jenna Ledderman.

As winter rolled into Northern California, Sean was feeling much better. During the doctor's third visit, Sean received good news. "Mister McKannah, I'm truly surprised that you've been following my instructions. It's paying off for you too because there's no way you could walk around this room as you just did if those discs in your back hadn't fused back together." As he was placing his tools back in the small leather bag, Sean spoke.

"Took me a while to figure out that you were right, doc. The only way I was ever gonna get back on m'feet was to let 'er heal up, but lemme tell ya, wasn't easy lying here like a dern lump on a log all this time." He continued walking slowly around the small room.

"I'm sure it wasn't, that's why so many of my patients with similar injuries have wound up paralyzed or simply unable to do anything for the remainder of their lives."

"Am I ready to get back to work now?"

"Yes," the doctor replied, "but at a very slow pace. You're obviously capable of using good common sense, so you should be able to do almost everything you want and need to by spring." He looked intently at Sean over his new spectacles. "That word I just used is the key to your future Mr. McKannah."

"Yeah, I caught that word—almost."

"Once a back is injured it will never be as strong as it was. Start off at about ten percent of your normal activities, but do not lift anything heavier than a feather for at least another year. Before I leave I'll give you a small book of diagrams and instructions that will explain how you must lift and carry anything once I'm certain you've healed completely." He picked his bag up and said, "If your daughter will follow me to my buggy I'll give her the diagrams." At the door he paused to look hard at Sean again. "One mistake like lifting something as small as the slops bucket you've been using, and you could wind up back on the floor for another six months." The doctor paused, as he looked over the top of his glasses then added, "Or longer, he paused—much longer." He stepped through the doorway saying, "C'mon young lady let's get him that booklet then see if your mother has that coffee ready."

On a brilliant Sunday afternoon in January, Sean and Bella looked up from the books they were reading as they sat on the porch. Riding toward them was Jesse and Maurah. The young woman had visited the McKannah ranch previously with Jesse. As they tied their horses to the rail, Bella called to them. "How about some hot coffee?"

"Sure ma, it's a pretty day but a wee bit chilly out in that breeze."

"Yes ma'am," the young woman said, "I'd love a cup." She climbed the steps and sat in one of the many rockers, as Jesse sat on the porch railing. He held to the post and began swinging his legs.

Sean noticed nervousness in both of them, but remained silent. Bella soon arrived with the tray of cups and accessories, followed by her Mexican cook carrying the pot of coffee. Once they all had a cup in their hand, Jesse nervously cleared his throat.

"Uh Mom, Dad." He cleared his throat again, "I uh, I mean we uh, that is me and, er I mean Maurah and me uh," he cleared his throat a couple more times as he struggled to find the words. The young Irish-German woman laughed as he stumbled across his tongue then spoke. "We want to get married." Her radiant smile brought one to Jesse's parents.

"Well," Sean said with a huge smile spreading across his face, "I'm sure glad you told us Maurah, because I don't think Jesse woulda ever been able to get it out."

The news came as no surprise to Bella, because she'd seen the obvious signs on their previous visits together. She set her cup down and went to the young girl with her arms open. "I'm so happy for both of you." She hugged Maurah then turned to Jesse, "When do you two plan to have the wedding?"

"Uh, gee uh," Jesse stammered and looked at his bride-to-be.

Maurah smiled at her soon-to-be mother-in-law. "We'd like it to be in May before ma and her helpers get too busy with the ranch."

"May is a wonderful time for a wedding."

"Yep." Sean added, "May's the best time. Won't be busy 'round here either." He leaned toward the couple and asked, "Where you figure on living?"

Jesse spoke up. "We're hoping we can live in the big room upstairs 'till I can get us a house built over on that hill yonder." He pointed to the small hill near the tree beside the river that his sister loved.

Sean followed his pointing arm even though he knew exactly what hill he was referring to because that was where he wished he'd built his house. "Darn good location for a house son." He turned to Maurah, "You like that location too?"

"Oh yes," she answered enthusiastically. "We've walked all over that little hill and I love it."

"Good!" Sean replied, but Bella knew what he was thinking because she tried to get him to build their house on the hill. He chose a spot that he thought would be better suited to his expanding ranch, so she didn't press her desires for the hilltop house. Uncle Luis had suggested the spot their home now sat on, and she felt he was probably correct. She was extremely pleased that her son and his wife selected the hill for their home.

"Is the wedding going to be at your ranch?"

"Yes ma'am," Maurah responded, but Jesse spoke before she could continue.

"We just want a very small wedding, Ma. Nothing like the one you n' Pa had. Just gonna be her folks over there n' my family here. I'd really like to have Uncle Frank come but now that Uncle Luis is dead I reckon he'll be busy running Horse Heaven, and lookin' after Aunt Carmen."

"Yeah. I don't think we'll see him for quite awhile. When Manollo sent us the news of Luis' death, he said Frank hasn't been to North Ranch either for a year because the horses keep him so busy." He shook his head slowly in thought. "Luis was the best man I ever knew and he was like a daddy to your Mom. We couldn't even go south to visit him before he died because of this back o' mine.

Sean was taking a big liking to Jesse's girlfriend. "Maurah."

"Yessir."

From this day on I'm either Dad or Sean and this's," he nodded toward his wife, "Mom or Bella." He looked hard at her. "That okay with you?"

She stepped forward and leaned down so she could put her arms around his neck. "Thanks Dad. I haven't had one in a long time." She released him and hugged Jesse's mother saying, "I'm so happy to have you for a second Mom."

By the time May rolled around and the wedding was near, Sean was getting around much better. His friend Manollo Calaveras' son Miguello was working for him now. He was married and had his own small house that he built a short distance away on a plot of land that Sean deeded to him. When Sean was finally able to get up and move around, Miguello began working on a leather back brace for his boss. As soon as Sean was on his feet in the morning he strapped it on. The doctor checked it to see how he was doing and approved of it.

Sitting beside Bella in the small coach that Frank had his crew make for he and Bella, Sean said, "I don't think I could make it over to the Ledderman ranch without this coach and brace that Miguello made for me."

Jesse and his new bride stayed two days after the wedding at the Ledderman ranch, and then moved to his parent's ranch and set up the large upstairs room as their temporary home. Jesse had already carried all of her large possessions up to the room after arriving from a trip to visit her, and returned with his buckboard loaded. After helping her get the balance of her things upstairs on the day they arrived, he immediately climbed on his horse and headed out to check on the ranch.

Even though Sean was getting stronger each month, as his back healed, he was still only able to ride around in the spring-axle carriage that Frank sent. He was only able to drive around for two hours in the morning and two more in the late afternoon. Sitting on the porch with his wife, Sean said, "We had a mess of darn good kids darlin' but I reckon Jesse's the only one who ever had any interest in ranching."

"Many people," Bella replied, "aren't lucky enough to have one good kid out of a litter and we've got six." She turned to Sean, "You're right, all of 'em are very good kids."

Two months after moving in, Jesse came down holding Maurah's hand one morning. They entered the kitchen area where Sean and Bella were sitting at the tiny table sipping coffee, and watching as their cook Angelina prepared breakfast for the ranch hands. The two young lovers just stood silently smiling and looking back and forth at each other. Finally Bella said, "Okay kids, what's up?"

"Nothing, grandma." Jesse said grinning.

A brief pause, and then she yelled, "Oh my God!" Bella screamed so loud as she jumped up that Angelina screamed too, looking around wide-eyed.

"What is missus? what is missus?"

Bella put her arms around Maura then motioned for Angelina to come to her. When she had the Mexican lady in her hug too she said, "I'm gonna be a grandma, Angel."

Angelina was a tall skinny friend of Manuello's wife, and began cooking for them as soon as her husband and his friends finished their house. He also worked on the ranch and they were more like family than hired help. Angel smiled wide saying, 'Nino' as she pointed at Maura's still flat belly.

The baby was born on February 15th. The nine-pound boy would eventually have his mama's red hair and green eyes. A true Aquarius, he was always busy watching everything going on around him. When he spotted Sean standing next to the bed looking down at him, he didn't move his eyes from him for a long time. "That little feller's my kindred soulmate," Sean said as he just stared at his grandson.

Francisco de Rivera Santiago sat on the porch thinking of the man who had stepped in and taken the place of his parents. Frank also remembered him as the best friend he ever had. "I wish" he said quietly aloud, "that Sean and Bella could have come when I sent word of your heart attack." He leaned back in deep thought. *They both loved you very much, Uncle Luis.*

Speaking Sean's name carried his thoughts to his best friend. *I hope that coach I had Miguel and his men build helps you get around.*

He returned to the parlor and approached his still-grieving aunt. He took her frail hand and held it for a long time before speaking. "Aunt Carmen, God has a special place for men like Uncle Luis, so I know he's very happy now."

She moved her head very slowly to look up at the young boy who had come to her as a son. She never saw the man he had become—always the boy. "Yes," she said in a weak voice, "he was a good man." Her vacant gaze returned to the closed door that she had not been able to walk through after Frank brought her the news.

When it became obvious that Luis Javier de Carvojol's remaining time on earth would be very short, Frank had given orders for the grave to be dug. What little means were available to prepare a body was done, but to last long enough for a wake and service was not possible for the people in the outlying areas. Luis died early Monday morning and on Tuesday his family and more than a hundred workers followed his casket to the family plot. Frank walked slowly behind the carriage with his arm around his aunt's shoulder. As the dirt hit the casket, thunder roared across a perfectly clear sky.

All looked questioningly at the sky. Frank spoke in a voice loud enough to be heard by all. "Uncle Luis is being announced at the gates to heaven." Few doubted it even after it began raining before all were back to work.

11

~ *Night flames* ~

The tragedy at the McKannah ranch occurred when Ollie—as all referred to the new McKannah boy—was ten months old. It was a cold December day not long before Christmas. The downstairs fireplace had been roaring all day. Before retiring for the night Sean had stacked it full of wood and closed the damper quite a bit to keep the fire burning all night. The fireplace in Jesse and Maurah's upstairs apartment was also burning. A noise awakened Jesse sometime in the wee hours. He lay a moment listening. *Sounds like a woman screaming—must be a Cougar.*

Jesse heard it again, so he quickly dressed and grabbed the belt attached to the holster holding his revolver. At the bottom of the stairs he grabbed the Brown Bess that always sat in the same place—ready to fire.

He eased the door open and stepped noiselessly onto the porch in his longjohns and leather moccasins. The moon was full, and he could easily see the barn and corrals holding their breeding sheep. He silently listened for the mountain lion then stealthily rounded the barn. He paused at each corral as his eyes searched. Twenty minutes later he was at the farthest corral, which was a hundred yards from the house, when he heard a noise. His keen eyes were penetrating the darkness for the source of this strange new sound. He turned slightly and his peripheral vision caught sight of the flames.

"Oh my God." He screamed as he began running.

~ The house was on fire ~

Years of fires had slowly worked on the stone and mortar of the fireplace that rested against the wooden house. Small pieces of mortar flaked away with each new blaze. Finally, a fatal chunk dropped to the hearth below and exposed the now tinder-dry wood. At first there were only small flames, but as soon as the flames reached more of the dry wood, a blaze burst to life and quickly began consuming everything in its path. When Jesse reached the house, his father had begun to investigate the strange noise that awakened him also, and was helping Bella get out.

"Jesse," Sean screamed, "stay with your mother. I'll get Maurah and Ollie out." He turned and disappeared into the burning house—forever.

Jesse helped get his mother, who was slightly burned, to the Mexican ranch hands. He then turned to go help his father, who he expected to come out with his wife and young son. The flames were by then reaching high into the sky, lighting everything as though the sun had risen early—Jesse knew that his father, wife, and son were gone.

A bucket brigade was quickly established but it was in vain, and soon Jesse yelled. "There's nothing we can do about the house so keep an eye on the bunkhouse and barn in case they catch fire." He stood with the bucket dangling from his hand as his dreams of a future went up into the sky.

Two months later, Jesse and his helpers had a section of the barn walled off for his mother, sister, and him to live in. He was very busy getting everything arranged for the comfort of what remained of his family. He worked tirelessly, and didn't grieve openly for his departed family—but nights was another story. Every night for months he lay in the dark thinking about them—seeing the flames—hearing their cries.

Winter finally lost its grip and slid into the past as spring began, and the charred remains of the house were cleared. The intensity of the fire consumed almost all of the bodies. Miguello Calaveras, Jesse's young friend who Sean had made next in charge, beneath Jesse, informed his crew. "If you find a bone or any part of his family, do not say a word." A few were found but Jesse was spared that knowledge. By late summer Jesse was making plans to build a new house for his mother and sister to live in. Word was sent to Patrick and Broderick at Harvard informing them of the tragedy, but Jesse told them that nothing would be accomplished by them coming home. "I'm gonna build a small house where the other one was, and I'll take care of Mom and Aleena."

Simon was in pursuit of an escaped man who had murdered a lawyer and a judge. The lawyer had failed in the defense of the escaped man's brother on a murder charge. The judge the escaped man killed had convicted him and he was sentenced to hang. Messages were sent out but so far they hadn't heard from Simon.

Ian was now in charge of the hotel's casino in Yerba Buena, where he'd gone to work. He came as soon as he received the message Jesse sent with the traveling Tinker who often stopped at the ranch. It took the Tinker a month to make it to the city because of so many stops to sell his knives and other items. When Ian arrived home, the rubble was already cleared. He stayed a few days to comfort his mother and sister, and talk to Jesse. "Ma sure doesn't look good."

"I know. Her burns weren't too serious, but she's grieving bad for pa, and it seems like she's getting weaker by the day."

"Maybe once you get the new house going she'll perk up?"

"I dunno," Jesse said—gloom etched into his young face. "I think maybe she's wanting so bad to be with pa that she'll just will herself to be with him."

"Sis," Ian said as he held his sister, "you stick real close to ma so she'll have someone to talk to while Jesse's busy."

"I will, but she hardly ever says a word."

Ian finally had to get back to the hotel. As his coach and two driver/guards rumbled toward the coast, a black cloud of despair hung over the McKannah ranch behind him.

~ Issabella Magdelena Ruiz Santiago McKannah died in August ~

Jesse paid the doctor extra to make two special trips in June because his mother had lost so much weight. "I can't find a thing physically wrong with her Jesse," the doctor said. "I think she just doesn't want to live without Sean."

Bella weighed less than seventy pounds when Jesse found her early one morning. She had been so weak that she was not able to get out of bed for many days previously, but when Jesse approached her dead body she had Sean's spare leather back-brace clutched over her chest. She was smiling for the first time in a long time. "She somehow got up and walked to that far wall over there," Jesse said to his sister as he pointed at the far end of the huge barn, "climbed up, and got Pa's spare brace."

The two McKannahs stood looking down at their mother for a long time. Finally Aleena broke the silence. "She's smiling for the first time since the fire."

Two weeks after they buried her, Jesse called all of his help to the barn. "Miguello, this's hard for me to do, but I gotta get outa here so I'm selling this place." He remained silent so the news could sink in. Finally his childhood friend spoke.

"I understand Jesse." He nodded toward the men with him who had all worked many years for the McKannahs. "We all understand. This has been a good life but much has happened, much has changed." He paused as he looked at his friend and slowly shook his head, "And we must all change with it."

Jesse went to Yerba Buena to discuss the situation with his brother Ian. "I can't stand being around that place, Ian. Everywhere I look I see Mom, Dad n' my wife and baby. It's like living in a ghost house and the ghosts come to see me every night." Even though he was a young man, Jesse wasn't prone to fear ghosts and the like, but too much happened to him in a very short time. He needed time away from the memories, so he could heal.

Ian sat quietly with his brother in the room he'd arranged for him to use during his visit. Finally he spoke. "That's some of the best cleared land around Jesse and a two-hundred-and-twenty-thousand-acre chunk with a clear title oughta make it easy to sell."

It was. The few important papers Sean kept in a steel box in the stone root cellar had survived. A month after talking to Ian, a coach with three friends of Ian's boss arrived to look at the property. By nightfall they made a deal with Jesse, who Ian agreed should go ahead and handle the sale. The men spent the night in the bunkhouse, and then departed for Yerba Buena at dawn. It was Tuesday and Jesse was to meet them at a bank on the following Monday.

"Sis," Jesse said to Aleena, "are you certain that you wanna to go to that town where Patrick and Broderick are going to school?"

"Yes, I'm sure. That letter they sent said they'd get me into a good school where I can learn to be a teacher, and that's what I really wanna be."

"Okay sis if that's what you want then we'll get you on a boat heading that way as soon as possible." He hugged her a long time. "I'm gonna ride over to the Ledderman ranch, you wanna go along?

"Sure, what are we gonna do over there?"

"I want her to have the sheep and Ian said he was certain the others'll feel the same way."

When Jesse and Aleena pulled out of the McKannah ranch on Friday morning, everything they owned was inside the small coach. They arrived at the hotel Sunday evening exhausted. Ian immediately arranged a room for them until all negotiations were completed. A bit of good luck finally came their way. A freight schooner belonging to Luis' friend was in the port offloading cargo. When approached, the captain recognized the name McKannah. He said Luis Carvojol was his employer's very good friend, and that he had also met Senor Carvojol once, many years earlier. He was saddened to hear of his death, just as his boss would be. “The young lady is welcome to accompany my wife and I to Massachusetts.”

Jesse was so happy to hear this unexpected information that he blurted out, “Wife. Your wife is with you?” His main worry lately was his sister traveling alone.

The captain understood the young man’s concern about his sister and smiled. “Not at the moment but we’ll be picking her up in Mexico, soon after we leave here. She accompanied me on the last trip from Spain and is staying at her sister’s home for a long awaited reunion.”

“Boy-oh-boy captain, that’s great news. I’ll admit I was sure worried about her traveling alone. Just tell me how much and I’ll go to the bank and get the money right now.”

“And have me flogged when I get home? No sir! There will be no charge. My wife will also be quite thrilled to find that she will have a traveling companion.”

Several days later the vessel was loaded and ready to begin the return trip. Jesse was lecturing Aleena again. “Be sure to give that letter to Patrick when you get there sis, ‘cause it explains which bank here in Yerba Buena has everyone’s share of the ranch money. Be sure to send the bank a letter when you know which bank there in Masta, Massa, I can never say that word, in Harvard where you want your share sent.”

“Harvard’s the school silly,” she smiled, “and the town the bank’ll be in is Boston Massachusetts.” She lifted her long bony arm and pointed a thin finger to her head. “I had it all in here the first time I was told brother dear, and that was a long time ago.”

Jesse was very embarrassed to be scolded by his younger sister—even moderately, although he knew she was just teasing him. “Well sis,” his turn to grin and tease now, “you are still just a kid, y’know.” He was covering his embarrassment and his sister knew it so she made no comment.

“Well old man,” she grinned then put her arms around him, “looks like they’re just waiting for me, so I better get on that thing before they leave without me.” She was now holding Jesse as tight as she could.

“I love ya little sister,” he said while hugging her, “and I’m sure gonna miss having you to talk to.”

“I’ll miss you too, but we’ll have years to talk once I’m teaching school back here.”

She was wrong, but neither could possibly have known the tragic events that would affect their futures.

Jesse watched as the schooner’s crew began raising her sails, and she slowly eased out of the harbor. Aleena stood on the stern behind the man at the huge spoke wheel. She wasn’t waving any longer—just watching Jesse. Without realizing it, he sat on the same boulder where his father had sat while waiting for his friend Frank’s ‘ugly’ sister to arrive from Mexico, many years earlier.

Lord, Jesse silently prayed, *you've sure taken a lotta people outa my life lately, but I reckon you know what you're doing.* He sat with his arms around his knees and watched as the schooner's sails filled with wind. He continued watching as the ship left the harbor and headed out into the Pacific Ocean. He finally stood. *Time to go find that chunk o' land east of here that the bank guy told me about.* Jesse bought supplies at James Poorsmith's Hudson Bay Trading Post because he planned to stay long enough to look at the entire piece of land before he bought it. "I think I've been through that chunk o' land," James said. "If it's the one I'm thinking of then it's a good location for a small cattle ranch."

"I hope you're right." After loading his supplies into the coach, he checked the rope holding his horse to the rear. "I'll take this off big fella," he said softly to his horse, "as soon as we're away from this darn city. Then you can just follow along." He climbed up to the driver's bench and headed east.

The sun was directly overhead, so his first night was spent about ten miles inland. By dawn the next morning he and his horse had already eaten and was moving east again. He was anxious to see the land that might become his new home. When it was light enough, he removed the paper from his pocket, which the banker had written on, and read it to himself. *Go east for about fifty miles until you see where the lakes run into a big river. Follow that river and if it ends at a pretty good size lake about forty miles from the first one, then you've found the property we're selling for a family that went back east. The land begins at that lake and goes west. The river runs right through the middle.*

Jesse angled a little northeast, as he had been told, and on the fourth day located the first lake. He turned southeast and followed the lake until he came to the river. It was late, so he made camp. At dawn he was following the river east, and four days later arrived at the other lake. *This's gotta be the land that's for sale.* One week later he was heading west again, and planning the ranch he would build. All of the paperwork was completed soon after arriving back at the bank. "Begin your house near the middle," the banker suggested, "so you won't be off your land. A government man will come out one day and set the legal boundaries."

"Hello Jesse." James yelled from the corral when he saw the coach pull in.

"Hi Mr. Poorsmith," he yelled back and waved.

"Get that land?"

"Sure did," Jesse grinned, "and it's even better than I hoped it'd be. Now I gotta get supplies to take with me and a list of stuff for you to send as soon as you can."

"Okay! Just yell 'em out while we're getting the stuff to load in the coach and I'll make a list."

"How 'bout you n' me making a deal for that coach, James?"

"Don't reckon you'll be needing it anymore, huh?"

"Nope! I need a good two-mule wagon to pull stumps, drag logs, and carry stuff when I come back here to get my cattle after I build some corrals."

"See that buncha mules over in that corral?"

"Yeah, I'll go look at 'em but I don't know much about mules." He headed toward the two dozen or so mules in the smaller corral. When he returned, James was inside making a list of the items he thought Jesse would need. He looked up when Jesse entered. "Whadaya think?"

"I think they all look alike."

"You mean kinda like women?" James was grinning.

"You mean ain't no two o' them critters alike either?"

"I could tell you all I know about mules n' women Jesse and you still wouldn't know much about 'em. You just gotta get yourself one n' learn as you go."

"Well, I had me a really good woman, so maybe I'll be as lucky with mules."

"Luck," James said, "has a little to do with it. It's mostly the same as it is with women. It's how good you treat 'em that really counts." He handed Jesse the list, "Here's some things I think you'll need and you can keep adding to it as we go."

It took until almost dark to get everything loaded, so Jesse slept in the back room of the trading post. Before James arrived the following morning, from the nearby cabin that he shared with a Flathead Indian woman, Jesse was heading east again in his new wagon being pulled by two very large mules. He stopped when they were a few miles inland and turned his horse loose to follow. Rather than run off a short distance as it did the last time it was free of the rope, the horse moved cautiously ahead and walked slowly along beside the strange looking animals, occasionally glancing at them.

A month later a supply wagon entered Jesse's camp in the middle of his new property. The driver was a young man about his age, who smiled and waved. "Right where that bloody Englishman said you'd be." The tall thin man set the brake and climbed down. "Arliss O'Reilly," he said with his hand out, "and either you're Jesse or that bloody pommy gave me bad directions again." His grin was so sincere that Jesse was also grinning as he pumped the offered hand.

A friendship was beginning that would last until another tragedy hit the McKannah family. It was many years in the future and would change Jesse McKannah's life completely.

Jesse McKannah would become a living legend among the local Indians, and they would ever after know him as WHITE BUFFALO.

MANY YEARS LATER

12

~ The search ~

Jesse McKannah left the Muddy River outpost on the third day after arriving. He was trail ragged, and bone weary but had to locate the lone survivor of the massacre at Green River. A week later he was talking to the old Indian who hid when he saw the two white men enter the little homestead. "I just didn't like their looks. I could see a cloud of evil spirits around them, so I hid. They didn't even get down from their horses when they started shooting. Them was really nice white people, and they killed them all then went into that little cabin and got what they wanted. Them two men dragged all those bodies inside and set it on fire. When I went and told the soldiers, they thought I had done it, till it happened again to two trappers down near Red Canyon while they had me locked up."

Jesse had the old Indian describe the two men several times, until he was sure he would recognize them when the time came.

He headed south toward the Uintas Mountains of Utah. The spring air still had a bite to it, so he began to feel revived as he urged his horse toward the two-mile high range. He hoped to locate the camp of the two men he had pursued through the hot summer and on into the freezing winter of 1848.

Jesse had waited at his cattle ranch, southeast of San Francisco, for word of the arrival of his sister Aleena. She was traveling with two good guides, along with about eighty other people who had made the decision to start a new life in California. His sister had always been good about getting word to him somehow, so when nothing came after a few months, he told his foreman and good friend, Arliss O'Reilly, "Keep things running till I get back. I'm goin' back down their trail, now that it's thawing." He had been told that George and Jacob Donner were good trail men, and would get them through. When news of the Donner tragedy reached him though, he began preparing to leave immediately and see if she was one of the forty-seven survivors.

"How long'll you be, Jesse?"

"Long as it takes."

His foreman had been with Jesse for over twenty years. He knew the tall, hard as granite man better than anyone else alive, so as he watched him ride toward the sunrise he thought, *everything better be alright or there'll be some more dead people on that trail 'fore he comes home.*

The story Jesse was told left him with hope that she was alive and doing well.

"She dropped out with two other women and their husbands," a surviving woman told him. "There was another couple that had a cabin there near Green River, east of that Muddy River outpost, so they decided to build a small one themselves and stay right there until they could move on in springtime." She spat a wad of tobacco off to the side then added, "More'n once I wished I'd stayed with 'em. I'm sure a lot of them that froze to death wished they had too."

The first night up into the Uintas, Jesse spotted a campfire and hailed it. "Hello the camp."

"Yeah, how many are ya?"

"One man on one horse."

"Okay, c'mon in, slow like."

He tied his horse to a tree limb, and then approached the camp. The two men were squatting on the ground beside a small campfire.

"Where ya headin'?"

"Lookin' to meet up with a couple of guys I know. S'pose to be up around Kings Peak."

The one that asked just mumbled and returned to his coffee cup. The other man said nothing, and stared at Jesse across the fire.

When neither man offered him a cup of coffee Jesse said, "I'll bed down over against that boulder if it's alright with you folks." When he got no answer he walked his horse to the rear of the boulder and tended to it before stretching out beneath his horse's blanket with his head on the saddle.

He felt a kick against his boot, so he opened his eyes, and saw that it was beginning to get light.

"That saddle and horse don't belong to no trail bum." The one that was silent the night before spoke now with a leering grin. "We figure you to be carrying folding money dude, so ease on out from under that saddle blanket and fork it over."

~ Jesse's saddle blanket suddenly had a hole in it ~

Just as suddenly, the leering man holding the pistol did too—in the center of his chest.

The other man was still clawing at his pistol when Jesse threw the blanket aside, and took quick, but deadly aim. The man still had his hand on the pistol in its holster when the .44 hit him just below his breastbone. The two men didn't fit the description the old Indian had given him, so he saddled his horse and headed on up into the Uintas without a glance at the two dead bodies.

Thirty years earlier, for a short while, Jesse had taken a job as trail burner and tracker for the Hudson Bay Trading Company. He was young, but James Poorsmith, who ran the post at Yerba Buena, recommended him. He was good then, and was still good, so he was having no trouble tracking the two men. Catching up to them was another story—they were movers.

After several months, their trail took him north to Bear Lake where he thought he'd finally found the two men. He hobbled his horse near grass a half mile away, and went in after dark. Through the small, folding telescope he carried, it became obvious that none of the four men around the campfire were the men he was searching for. As he had done many times in the past months, he hailed the camp awhile later. "Hello the camp."

"Who are ya?"

"A tracker, can I come to the fire?"

"You alone?"

"Yep."

"C'mon in then."

After tossing him a cup and motioning toward the coffeepot, one of the men asked, "Whacha trackin'?"

As he poured himself a cup, he described the two men.

"Them's the two that're up on Mud Lake."

The one that Jesse noticed take a drink from a jug when he first stepped out spoke up. "Don't tell this dude nothing. How do we know what he wants to get up with them fellers for?" He stood up and glared across the fire, "Just what the hell you wantin' them two guys for, anyway."

Jesse saw that the man didn't carry a pistol, but had a trapper's knife on his side, with a blade at least a foot long. His eyes had not left the man from the time he stood. He lowered the cup, "That ain't any concern of yours. Sit back down if you have work to do tomorrow."

"Smart aleck tin horn dude," the man grumbled drunkenly as he reached for his knife, and came around the fire at Jesse.

Jesse had learned young, that even though he was deadly accurate with a pistol, always aim for the largest place to put your bullet. The drunk's body was huge, and made a good target. The long knife was barely out of its sheath when the .44 struck him in the heart. He was dead before he hit the fire.

Jesse jumped up as he revolved the cylinder and swung the barrel on the three other men, but none had moved a muscle.

"Mind if I drag him outa the fire 'fore it goes out?"

"Go ahead, but you other two keep your seat."

Many miles away from the area where Jesse was tracking Aleena's killers, Patrick and Broderick looked up from their studies when a young man entered the apartment they shared on the Harvard campus. "That boat your sister's on is entering Boston Harbor. I've been watching through this telescope all morning, just like you paid me to do." He lifted the long, leather-bound, glass. "This thing really brings it right up to you."

The camp at Mud Lake was a week or so cold when Jesse arrived, so he began looking for sign. It eventually led higher up into the Uintas. Once again he ground hobbled his horse and was moving silently toward the small fire he'd spotted. Two hours later he watched through his small telescope as the two men moved around in the camp. While they sat at the fire he got into a position to get their faces in the eyepiece. *Deep scar running down from the forehead and across the missing eye's socket.* He moved the scope to the other man. *Bald as a river rock and the left ear cut clean off. Boys, this ain't gonna be a good night for ya.*

A while later when he stepped silently into the firelight across from them. He had the .44 in his hand.

Both men were as bad as they come, and were wilderness wise. They made no move at all as they watched the tall, muscular man standing in front of them. When they realized he wasn't going to speak, the earless one asked, "What is this, a hold up?"

"No, Carmine, I'm just here to tell you and One Eye Amos that you made a mistake back at Green River when you didn't kill the Indian too."

"What Indian?" The man with one eye blurted out.

"The one hiding in the wood shack," Jesse said, as he slowly moved the barrel onto the man. "The same one that told me who slaughtered my sister."

"Hey mister," the earless one said in a pleading voice, "you got the wrong men."

"You might be right. I understand there's a lot of one eyed, earless freaks like you two wandering around up in these mountains."

"Well listen now," One Eye said, "we can show we wasn't nowheres near that place if you'll take us in so's we can prove it."

Jesse had waited too long to be cheated out of his revenge. He knew these types of men as well as he knew his horse, so he returned the .44 to its holster. "Okay, get on your feet and let's get ready to ride."

His feet were spread wide and to anyone watching he would appear to be relaxed and waiting for the two men to assemble their gear. There was however, a spring inside of him wound tighter than a hangman's noose.

"Okay Amos, might as well get ready to ride," the earless one said. It was a pre-arranged signal the two desperadoes had used for a long time to get themselves out of a bad situation. As they simultaneously began to get to their feet, both went for their pistols at the same time.

Jesse's first .44 slug went in Carmine's stomach just above his navel. The man's gun never cleared leather. One Eye Amos was quick enough to get his out of its holster, but not quick enough to get off a shot before he too felt the .44 enter his gut.

As the two men lay writhing on the cold spring ground, Jesse picked up the overturned cup and poured himself some coffee. He watched and listened to the two men as their moaning ceased and the thrashing slowed down to twitches. He poured himself another cup as he waited for their agony to end then said aloud, "This doesn't help you a bit sis, but it sure makes me feel better."

As Jesse began the long trip back to his ranch, he let his mind ramble back to his younger years with his sister.

Jesse Devon McKannah was known as a quiet boy who loved nature far better than the classroom, and proved it often with his many absences. He was also known for a very violent temper when anyone harassed him or anyone he cared about. He cared more for his homely little sister than he did for his four brothers combined. Constant combat with the four older brothers was transforming the husky young soon-to-be twelve-year-old into what the other kids were calling, 'The toughest kid in California.'

The boy with the busted nose had recovered enough to run screaming toward the schoolhouse, but the remaining two fourteen-year-old boys were giving Jesse 'a good run for his money' as his father would say. When one felt loose teeth in his mouth, he too ran for the schoolhouse. Now alone to face—*that crazy Mick with those weird eyes*—the third boy prepared to join his departed friends. A hand in his disheveled hair convinced him that he wasn't going anywhere just yet. "Tell her you're sorry."

The boy began crying and felt a blow on his bleeding ear. “Tell her,” the voice now growled in his ear.

“I, I, I’m sorry.” As soon as Jesse released his handful of hair, the boy ran to join his friends.

“You wanna stay out here n’ live like a wilderness pioneer the rest o’ your life, wild boy?” Patrick knew his little brother had a good head on his shoulders so he was constantly trying to get him to accept his Uncle Luis’ offer to give Jesse a good education. “If you’d put as much effort into your schoolwork as you do tryin to be a mountain man, you could follow Broderick and me to Harvard and learn how to be a lawyer.”

Ian and Simon, Jesse’s two other brothers, walked around the corner of the house as his mother came with a small basin of water. “What happened Jesse?”

“Patrick n’ Broderick beat me with an axe handle.” Before the boys could comment he added, “Only way the two of ‘em could whup me.”

“Hooligan,” Patrick commented as he stretched out in the porch rocker. Broderick just shook his head and went to the end of the porch to stretch out on the wide wooden top of the railing.

“Well Jesse,” his mother said, “I’m proud of you for standing up for your sister.”

A few days after the fight at school Jesse went up the stairs to Aleena’s room and tapped on the door lightly.

“Yes.”

“It’s me Aleena, can I come in?”

“Sure Jesse, c’mon.”

He walked to the small bed his father made with a canopy that Issabella sewed a frilly cover for. Aleena looked at the brother she adored, “They’re right, cha’know.”

“About what?”

“Asking Santa Clause for a new face. I have every year since I was old enough to know how ugly I am.”

“You ain’t ugly, Aleena.”

She squeezed his hand then swung her spindly legs over his head to the side of the bed and onto the floor. “Aunt Carmen always has said I’ll get prettier as I get older, ‘cause all women do, but what really happens is my face gets a little longer and my ears stick out a little farther.” She pulled her hand from his and stood. “I’m almost as tall as Patrick and Broderick already,” she lifted her foot, “and look at the size of my feet. She held it up for a long time then grinned, “Won’t need snowshoes when you take me hunting in the mountains this winter.” She swung her legs back over his head and leaned back against the headboard. “That’s enough of this poor little me stuff.”

Jesse never knew what to say when she talked about her ugliness. He knew she was not a pretty girl but he didn't see her as ugly. He remained quiet until her mood passed. One of the things he admired about her was the way she could always shove her troubles aside and move on.

"Do you think Patrick and Broderick will really go off to Harbors, or where ever it is, to become lawyers?" She pulled her legs up and wrapped her long skinny arms around her knees, then looked directly into Jesse's eyes. It was another of her traits he admired. Most everyone he knew, especially his brothers, would look away if he stared hard at them—not Aleena.

"Well," Jesse said, then paused to think a moment about her question. She admired the way her brother acted so mature when she asked him anything. "Patrick told me that Uncle Luis is gonna set them up to go to a school back east called Harvard, where they can teach you to be anything."

"Even a school teacher?" The young girl perked up and swung her legs over the edge again and looked hard at Jesse.

"Well," another long pause so she waited patiently until he finally answered, "I s'pose they could."

"Really? Where is Harvard? Would Uncle Luis send me there? Who would I live with?" Her troubles forgotten she rambled on. "Would you come and be a lawyer while I learn to be a school teacher? We could…

"Whoa sis, you still got a few years of school to do here fore you can even think about stuff like that."

"Why not," she grinned at him, "better than thinking about my barn door ears getting bigger and my gourd nose having birds making nests in it."

Jesse loved to quietly slip into the area where the men were working, without them hearing him until he was seen sitting silently watching. He would just smile when one would say, "Hey Chico, where you come from?" He moved quietly through the huge barn door and into the shade, and then stood to let his eyes get adjusted to the darkness. He waited until all of them were bent over sheep shearing off the wool then climbed to the top of the stall Sean was working in, and sat silently watching. He never tired of watching his father squeezing the huge shears. He could tell when one of the four men would be starting a new sheep at the same time as Sean and would try to beat him finished. They never let on that they were racing to beat Sean, but he could tell they were by the way they kept glancing at his father. Jesse knew that each man wanted badly to beat his father, and he loved the way his dad just kept his head down and squeezed the shears; never once glancing up to see what was going on around him. Jesse smiled when his dad's sheep was shoved through the opening into the pasture and he began piling the wool. The other men were mumbling something quietly in Spanish as he finished.

"Darn boy," his father said when he looked up and saw Jesse sitting there so close to him, "you're getting more injun all the time."

Jesse suspected his dad always knew when he slipped in, but never let on.

Jesse always tried to be there unheard and Sean always acted surprised—he never was.

"When ya gonna let me shear one o' them sheep, daddy?"

Before bringing another animal in for shearing Sean said, "Lemme see your hand." It was the same routine every time, but the young boy always held his hand out to his father. Sean put his huge hand against his son's then looked carefully at the comparison. "Hmm, gettin' close but still got a way to go." He smiled as he looked up at the boy's battered face then returned to his work. After finishing another sheep he said, "Been fightin' again?"

"Nah, just wasn't paying attention and ran smack into that ole crab apple tree."

Jesse loved the way his father never got upset about things like a little fight, a small cut on the hand, or a bruised knee like his mother did. After watching him shear another two sheep he asked, "Okay if Aleena goes to Chalponich's village with me tomorrow?"

Without looking up Sean said, "Yeah, I don't see why not. Ian told me there's no school till Monday so he n' Simon are gonna camp over on the river and do some serious fishing."

"Yeah, Mr. Adderly gave us tomorrow off so we could have three days."

"Must be time to start a new batch of home brew, huh?" He grinned up at Jesse who returned the grin with a shrug of his wide shoulders. "Whacha gonna do over there?"

"Wampohnah's gonna make a cattail boat and said I could help him so I can learn how."

Over the clicking of the shears Sean said, "He's a good one to be learnin' from 'cause his daddy's the best boat builder there is around here."

"Was Chalponich the chief when you first met him?" Jesse loved to hear his dad's stories of his youth when he was trapping and living in the wilderness. He used every opportunity to get him talking about those days.

"Lordy no," he answered while squeezing the shears, "when we were both younger, his grandpa was chief of the Yokut Indians and later his daddy was, till he got some kind of infection and died."

"That when he was made chief?"

"Yep, and he's really doin' a good job too." He looked up after stacking the last pile of wool, "Tell him I said hello and will be over that way 'fore too long." Sean bent down and began clipping the next sheep.

Jesse waited a while to see if his dad would continue talking about his wilderness days. When he didn't Jesse said, "See you at dinner pa," and jumped from the railing.

"C'mon sis." Jesse was shaking Aleena's skinny arm, hanging from the bed like a winter-bare limb from one of the cherry trees behind the house.

"Huh, wha, uh, mmm, wha."

He shook it a little harder, "Wanna sleep or go with me?" He'd left her sleeping before and thought a little threat would get her on her feet. When she just mumbled again he said directly into her huge ear, "You go ahead and sleep sis, I'll see you later and tell you all about the Indian village." He had been promising to take her with him for several months and thought now was a good time, because it would keep her mind from the taunts of the kids at school.

"Huh?" She bolted from the bed as if it was on fire. She strained in the darkness to see, "is that you Jesse?"

"No," he responded with a growl, "I'm the Leprechaun of the forest come to drag you off into the wilderness and devour you."

She was hopping around on one leg, trying to get her britches pulled on beneath her nightshirt when she answered. "Boy, you must be a starved little bugger, 'cause there sure ain't much meat on these bones."

"Don't wake ma or she'll be up n' tryin to keep you from goin'. I'm gonna get us a coupla slices of butter-bread." He went stealthily back down the stairs to the kitchen. When Aleena tiptoed in with her boots in her hand he had the two thick slices of bread heavily slathered with homemade butter. He nodded with his head toward the back door then they silently slipped out.

He lit the kerosene lantern and saddled both horses, then was about to blow it out when a voice came from the darkness. "Where you kids going this early?"

Aleena jumped then yelled, "Jeez Manollo, you scared the crap outa me."

"I'm sorry Miss Aleena," the stout, neckless Mexican said, "but I'm always up at this time and saw the light out here." He looked at Jesse, "Your folks know you're going off today?"

"Yep, but we don't wanna wake ma, 'cause she's apt to change her mind and not let her go." He indicated his sister with a nod then added, "That's why we were being so quiet."

Manollo Calaveras came to Sean from Luis' North Ranch. When his father was made foreman Manollo said, "I can no longer work with him." Sean hired him as a regular ranch hand to tend the sheep and do whatever else was needed. After a year he had taught himself to shear sheep, and tend to their diseases. "He can spot a sick sheep even before the darn thing knows it's sick," Sean told Issabella.

"Did he tell you he has a wife in that little village west of here?"

"No," Sean looked at her, "how do you know?"

"He talks to me when he's not busy." She smiled at her husband. "He's a shy, aloof man but he's also very nice when he gets you figured out."

He removed his cap and scratched his already graying red hair, "Must not o' figured me out yet cause he hardly ever says anything 'cept okay to me."

"He's a little afraid of you, ya big wild Irishman."

"Now why in the heck would he be scared o' me?"

"That ain't what I said." She stared hard at him. "I said he's a little afraid of you. He's got a job that he likes and you're so wild at times he's afraid you'll blow up n' fire him."

Sean approached the man later and told him that he doesn't fire anyone except "Them that I catch stealin' from me." He reached for the Mexican's hand for the first time in the year he'd been with him. "I'd like you to be my foreman and build yourself a house and bring your family here too."

Manollo observed the youngest McKannah boy and knew he would never lie. "Where do you plan to go today?" Satisfied with Jesse's answer he said, "Have a good time," and reached for the lantern. "I'll put it out after you get into the yard." He put the lantern on the nail and closed the barn doors then looked at the two young people riding west in the twilight of a coming dawn.

Even though they were both born in the same year, he in early February and Aleena a day before New Year's Eve, she still thought of him as her much older, much wiser, brother. It was partly because he never laughed at any of the things she would ask him or talk about, and partly because she knew their father talked to Jesse about things he didn't with the older boys. She also knew he was a lot like their father, which was why they got along so good and talked to each other often.

As they rode slowly toward the Indian village she asked some of the many questions that were always in her head. "Did daddy really find a buried treasure when he was young?"

"Well," Jesse answered, "in a way I guess, but he had buried it himself."

"Really?" She turned wide-eyed to him, "where'd he get it?"

"Potatoes."

"Potatoes?"

"Well, not all of it. When he was with that old sea captain he sold seed potatoes like we plant every year. When they'd get to a new country he'd get down on the dock or where ever he could and sell 'em to the farmers and people."

"Hmmm," she rode along silent for awhile then said, "that's strange, people givin' ya gold for potatoes."

"Depends on how hungry y'are, sis."

"Sure musta sold a heck of a lot of 'em huh?"

"Yeah, but that ole sea captain gave him a pile o' gold when daddy left the ship to go trapping."

"Hmmm, why'd he bury it?"

"In case somebody knocked him in the head or som'n, they wouldn't get all of his gold."

"Where'd he bury it?"

"Big ole tree up in the mountains somewhere."

"What if somebody woulda killed him? All his gold would still be there."

"Nope, he showed Uncle Frank where he buried it."

"He really likes Uncle Frank, huh?"

"Yep. Guess they been kinda like brothers."

"That's som'n I don't understand."

"Whazzat?"

"Well, Frank's mama's brother, right?"

"Yep."

"Uncle Luis is mama's uncle, right?"

"Right again."

"How come we call 'em both, Louis and Frank, uncle?"

"Well sis, sometimes a person just gets a nickname kinda thing and everyone just always calls 'em that. Even them guys that have worked for Uncle Luis so long call him Uncle Luis instead of boss or som'n like that."

"Mama says we're gonna go down and see him and Aunt Carmen pretty soon, because he's been sick."

"Yeah, I know. Hope so, 'cause I really like it with all them horses n' stuff."

"Me too, because Uncle Frank is always so nice to me."

On and on the questions came as they moved slowly east—a young girl emptying her inquisitive mind into her mentor's lap. Two hours of easy riding put Jesse and Aleena into the Yokut camp of Chief Chalponich. "Hello wild Irishman," the slender, six-foot-tall chief of the small band of Yokut Indians greeted the two young McKannah children. Sean had told him to set up his camp anywhere on McKannah land they wanted. Several years at the nearby mission had given him a second language. He was fluent in Spanish and used it whenever he had an opportunity. "You come to hunt eagle feathers again with Wahpohnah?"

"No," Jesse answered in Spanish, a language he and his siblings were all fluent in, "I am going to learn how to make a tule boat today."

The tall Indian walked to Aleena's horse and reached up for her. His easy, natural way made her immediately comfortable so she slipped into his strong hands and was set on the ground. His warm smile made her warm inside as he spoke. "This beautiful princess must be the sister you said you would one day bring."

"Yes," Jesse answered, "she is Aleena."

"Ahh leen yaa," the chief repeated.

"No," Jesse said, "Ahhh leee nahhh."

Chalponich repeated it perfect then several of the women that had crowded around began saying it. "Ahhh leee nahhh." The chief's youngest wife took Aleena's hand and said in Spanish, "Come, I show you my new baby."

The young girl had never had so much attention and loved it. She turned toward Jesse and smiled. "Go ahead and enjoy yourself sis, 'cause me n' Wahpohnah will be all day on that boat." He turned back to the chief. "You know where Wahpohnah is?"

The dark man with eyes that sparkled like coal black diamonds pointed. "He is at the river cutting tule for his new boat."

Jesse saw Aleena entering one of the chief's tents and knew no harm would ever come to her among these honorable people. He asked Chalponich where he could hobble their horses. When they were secured and chewing what grass was available on the cold December day, he started toward the nearby river at a trot. He saw the pile of cattail first, and then the fifteen-year-old Indian boy saw him and yelled in Spanish, "Ready to see how we build our little river boats?"

"Sure am, what do you want me to do?" He had been coming to this village since they settled here on his dad's ranch three years earlier. Even though Jesse was over four years younger than the Indian boy, the two became instant friends. With his Indian friend teaching, Jesse had become a good trapper and trail-sign reader by the time he was ten years old. Now at almost eleven he was good enough to locate Wahpohnah in the surrounding terrain, regardless how carefully he covered his trail.

They took turns trying to elude the other, and when Jesse found him the first time after a six-hour hunt. The Indian boy was proud of him. At the fire that night he told all of his father's braves about Jesse's skills. Two-dozen accomplished trackers shook their heads up and down as they looked across the fire at the young, redheaded, white boy and grunted their approval. It was the proudest day of Jesse's young life. That knowledge would return to serve him well and save his life in the not too distant future.

"Start laying the tule out straight," the Indian boy said, "and I'll be up in a minute."

His friend, during the last trip to the village several days earlier, had already told Jesse that the cattail must be laid out in small piles so he could choose from them. By the time Wahpohnah came out of the cold shallow creek, Jesse had six piles made from the reeds that had been tossed on the bank.

"Yes," the Indian said, "very good. Now I can begin selecting the ones for the center and the others for the outer part. When I throw them over there," he pointed to a spot nearby, "get all of the cut ends even." He began quickly going through the piles Jesse had made. "Okay" he said, "that's enough in that pile, now start another with this length." Again he began tossing reeds at Jesse's feet. After another thirty minutes he said, "That's enough for the centers, now we'll get two piles of these longer ones." In a little over an hour they had the reeds separated into four piles and began tying them together.

"First thing you must do," Wahpohnah said, "is fit these shorter ones into the middle of the long tule. Then when we tie them all together we have two pieces big like this in the center," he patted his muscular torso, "with ends tapering off to the size of my leg." He walked to a pile of thin strips of rawhide and returned with several, "I will show you."

Jesse helped hold the cattail reeds as Wahpohnah gathered them together with all the shorter ones in the center, and then tied them with the rawhide rope. Jesse watched intently as the young man kept shuffling the reeds into position and moving slowly toward one end while tying the bundle every foot. He now understood why it was so important to get the reeds in the correct position as the bundle began tapering to a very small tip. His friend returned to where he had started and repeated the process until he reached the other end. After an hour of tying, he finally stood, stretched and rubbed his back muscles.

"Hard on the back, huh?" Jesse commented.

"Yes, and my uncle has made two of these in one day." He shook his head from side to side, "He is older than my father."

"Wow," Jesse exclaimed. "Is he the one that no one can beat at wrasslin'?"

"The same one." He held out a muscled arm. "The muscles in his back are bigger than my arm." He grinned at Jesse, "Tough old man." An hour later he finished the other bundle, then pulled them together for inspection.

Jesse marveled at how the two bundles were exactly the same. He asked, "Have you ever eaten those yellow things they bring up from Mexico called bananas?"

"No."

"Well that's what these things look like 'cept these're more pointed at the ends. I'll bring you some next time my uncle brings 'em so you can try some."

Wahpohnah sniffed the air. "Smell that?"

"Sure do, and my stomach did a flip."

"Auntie Looteenah is making pigeon soup and acorn berry cakes. Let's go."

"Mmm, mmm," Jesse rubbed his stomach, "I'm ready."

When they walked into the eating area, Aleena was already eating with her new friends. "Hello," Wahpohnah said as he looked at her. "Who is this white princess joining us today?"

Before Jesse could answer, one of the girls her own age said, "Ahhh Leee Naaa. She his sister."

The handsome young Indian stepped to her and took her hand. "Hello Ahhh Leee Naaa, welcome to my father's camp."

Aleena blushed and felt pretty for the first time in her life. As her brother and friend walked away after eating, she watched Wahpohnah. *I wish I could have a boyfriend like that some day.*

When the two boys were back near the river, Wahpohnah straddled the two bundles and told Jesse, "Help me pull the ends of these two bundles together tight as I tie them." Jesse put his arms around them and squeezed as his friend tied them tight. They turned around and repeated the process.

The Indian went to a tree and cut a small straight limb then gathered several long pieces of one-inch-wide rawhide. "These pieces of rawhide must be shoved through the center every two handwidths." Jesse watched as he attached the rawhide strips to the end of the stick and carefully worked them through. "Now we tie them so when you shove the reeds aside to sit in the boat these will keep the bottom part together and you will sit on them."

When it was completed he told Jesse, "Pick it up on one end."

"Wow. Much lighter than I thought it would be."

"Yes, but it will get heavy after it is in the water a long time, so you must put it on the bank and let all the water leave before continuing to where you are going."

"Are you gonna go down the river to try it out?"

"No, you are."

"Me? Oh boy, yeah, I'm ready." He sat down and began taking off his boots.

"Better take off your britches too cause you'll want something warm to put on when you get out."

"I ain't got anything on underneath 'em."

"Ha," his friend laughed, "no matter. We all swim naked in the warm time. You don't have anything that will be a surprise to anyone here."

After dragging the reed boat into the shallow creek, Jesse climbed on top and snuggled down into the area between the two bundles. Wahpohnah handed him a paddle made of a round, heavy vine covered by animal skin and attached to a short pole. "Paddle up against the flow so you won't have a hard time coming back." He squatted and watched his young white friend begin the struggle to master the watercraft. He was once again pleased to see Jesse in good control before rounding the bend in the creek a couple hundred yards upstream. He watched thinking; *he will always be able to survive in the wilderness.*

It was late in the afternoon when Jesse and Aleena started home. As the horse plodded along, Aleena bombarded Jesse with questions, and as always he patiently answered them as best he could. "How did daddy meet Chalo, uh Chalpo, uh," she looked at Jesse who responded with a smile.

"Chalponich, Chal just like a challenge, pa just like yellin' for your pa, and nick like when you nick yourself with the kitchen knife."

"Chal pa nick," She said slowly. "Got it, Chalponich. Anyway, how did they meet?"

"When daddy and Uncle Frank were trapping up in the mountains, Uncle Luis asked them to come to his ranch," he turned and looked at her, "the one near ours where they make all that wine. Well, they was comin' around the end of Coyote Lake…

"Where's that?"

"That lake," he patiently said, "north of our ranch where daddy took me hunting last winter."

"Oh yeah, I remember you telling me about it."

"Anyway, about the time they came outa the woods at the end of it they saw Chalponich's horse…

"Was he chief then?"

"No, he was just a hunter for his tribe, his daddy was chief."

"Oh."

"Well, his horse reared up when a great big ole rattler struck at it, and Chalponich fell off n' busted his leg. It was a new horse he was breakin' in so it just ran off. Daddy and Uncle Frank fixed his leg with some sticks and let him ride daddy's horse while they rode double. They carried him to his camp, and they been friends ever since."

"Gee," she said wistfully, "daddy's really done some neat stuff, huh?"

"He sure has," Jesse answered, and then turned to look at her again, "when you're a little older I'll tell you about the time…

The gunshot startled both of them. A huge mountain lion fell from the tree they were about to go under, and they had to fight to keep the horses from running. Jesse later said, "It was a good thing I taught her how to control a horse when it's scared."

"Look," Aleena said as she pointed ahead.

Jesse followed her pointing finger and saw Manollo running toward them. Jesse looked at the lion laying dead on the ground not twenty feet from them, then at the ranch foreman who was almost to them. "Manollo, what're you doin' out here?" He looked at the lion then at his sister who was still trembling.

"I follow you when you leave." The Mexican looked up and grinned. "Good thing, huh?"

"Boy-oh-boy," she said with a shaky voice, "it sure was." Her mouth hung open, as she looked down at a lion that weighed more than her.

"That was really a great shot Manollo," Jesse said as he looked at the small hill he had seen the man come over right after the shot. "Must be at least a hundred yards."

Manollo looked back then shook his head, "Maybe half that far." He prodded the lion with his rifle barrel then bent down to open its mouth. "See here Jesse," he held the head so the boy could see, "this lion was shot by someone a while back and broke its jaw. It didn't heal right so it must have had a real hard time finding something to eat." He stood back up, "It was gonna have an easy meal out of little sister today."

When she said, "Poor cat," both men's lower jaws dropped open.

"Throw your rope over that limb Jesse, and I will gut it so we can take the meat home."

"We're gonna eat it?" Aleena asked, as her eyes bulged open.

After Jesse backed his horse slowly up to pull the heavy cat's front legs off the ground, Manollo looked up at Aleena before beginning. "Once you've had puma meat you don't want to eat deer or bear, because puma is much, much better." He pulled the razor sharp knife from his belt and in two minutes had the animal skinned and gutted.

"Want me to ride over the hill and get your horse?" Jesse asked.

"I didn't ride because I knew you would see me following you." Manollo looked up and grinned, "I didn't want to spoil your day."

"You walked all the way?" Aleena's mouth dropped open again.

"I always walk when I am tracking." He grinned again and lifted his moccasin-covered feet, then patted the leather water pouch on his shoulder. "I was prepared."

Jesse nodded at his sister, "Move your horse over here so it can carry the meat on it while you ride with me."

She climbed behind him, and then watched as Manollo maneuvered her horse beneath the lion's carcass. As Jesse move his horse slowly ahead and lowered it, Manollo balanced the cat's carcass onto the horse's front shoulders, just in front of the saddle. The horse was still leery of the lion but the Mexican had a way with animals and talked soothingly to it the whole time he was tying the carcass on. When it was secure he leaped easily into the saddle. "Okay, let's head home to some good eating tonight."

Jesse had never eaten puma before either but he acted like he had, and smacked his lips. "Mmmm boy, can't wait."

"You can have my share too," Aleena said, "it looks too much like my cat Hazel for me to eat it."

On the ride home Aleena took advantage of her time with the Mexican she had known and admired as long as she could remember. "Your daddy is Uncle Luis' North Ranch foreman ain't he?"

"Oh yes," he answered, "even more now. He runs the entire ranch, winery and all."

"How come you didn't stay there instead of coming to work for daddy?"

The two hundred pound Mexican was silent a moment before grinning at the young girl. "I love my daddy like you love yours but when he became the foreman he gives me a pain where I touch the saddle."

Jesse laughed and responded while still chuckling, "Mine does that too."

Aleena grinned, "Yeah, he does get kinda bossy now n' then." She rode with her long skinny arms around her brother for awhile then asked, "Why did you follow us?"

Manollo turned a very serious face to her. "Very, very strange thing happened as you were riding away. The sun was beginning to shine on the clouds and I saw a small one above you with blood dripping from it. I ran and put my leather moccasins on and got my water bag and rifle then followed."

She silently contemplated his words for a moment. "Good thing." She looked hard at the dead animal bouncing on the horse's neck and asked, "Would it really have eaten me?"

"Yes," Manollo said simply without turning to her.

"Hmmm, maybe I will eat some of it."

When they entered the yard, Issabella had been worrying all day about Manollo's disappearance, and when she saw them she saw the bloody corpse but not her skinny daughter behind Jesse, she came running from the house screaming, "Oh my God, what happened?"

A big ear popped from behind her son then a smiling face followed, "Manollo killed a lion that was gonna eat me, mama."

When she heard her daughter, Issabella became so weak that holding to the fence was the only way she kept from collapsing. Sean heard his wife scream and came running from inside the barn with the pitchfork still in his hands. He stopped at the group. "Mmm boy, puma for dinner tonight."

Later that night Jesse saw his father standing with Manollo and a couple of the men watching a small campfire. His mother and sister had already gone to bed so he joined them. When the opportunity came he said, "Daddy, mom ain't gonna let sis go ridin' with me any more." He paused then added, "That ain't fair atol, 'cause she loves it and didn't do anything wrong."

Sean put his arm around his youngest son's shoulder. "Manollo's got a darn good idea son, and you let me handle yer mom," he looked at Jesse, "she's just upset now; she'll settle down in a day'r two."

Jesse was anxious to hear about whatever idea the foreman had, but remained silent. After several minutes passed, Manollo finally spoke. "I told your father I think you should be taught how to handle a gun and not leave here without one."

"Yeah," Sean responded, "good idea I reckon, whadaya think son?"

"Yes sir, I been wanting to take one but didn't know if I oughta ask."

"Well," Sean said, "yer gonna be eleven next month, so it's time."

"Not next month daddy, my birthday's February twelfth."

"Hmmm!" He looked confused then scratched his graying red hair, "Oh yeah," he smiled, "next month's Aleena's birthday."

"Uh, nossir," Jesse said quietly, "her tenth birthday's just after Christmas on the thirtieth."

Sean put the cap back on and pulled it down tightly. "Dern, I ain't ever been able to keep all them days straightened out in my head. Anyway Manollo's right, so tomorrow we'll clean up that ole Brown Bess then I'll show you all about it." He yawned and stretched then said, "I'm going to bed." He turned and headed for the house.

Jesse turned back to the fire and listened to the men's stories about their adventures in the wilderness. One-by-one the three men left to go in the bunkhouse, leaving only Jesse and Manollo at the burned down fire. Manollo glanced around to be sure they were alone then spoke softly, "You should have seen that lion, Jesse."

The boy didn't look up for a minute but the statement didn't surprise him; he'd been thinking the same thing since it happened. He finally looked at the

Mexican that had been instructing him about the wilderness since he was old enough to understand. "I know."

"That's all that matters. I'm tired and going to bed too. Goodnight."

Before the man was out of earshot Jesse said, "Thanks for getting daddy to let me carry a rifle."

Manollo kept walking but turned his head, "It is time."

Before Manollo took a couple more steps Jesse called to him, "Manollo."

He stopped and turned, "Yes?"

"Thanks for keepin' an eye out 'cause one of us mighta got killed."

The Mexican grinned even though he knew the boy couldn't see it, "Knowing you as I do Jesse, it mighta been the lion." He continued on to his house.

Ian and Simon returned from the river, late Saturday afternoon, with a large string of fish. As they cleaned them at the bench near the garden, so the discarded parts could soak in water to be used as fertilizer, they listened as Jesse and Aleena gave them a blow-by-blow of the incident with the lion. "Wow." Ian, the diminutive, blonde, blue-eyed McKannah boy that looked out of place among his tall, robust brothers said. "That's too dern close for comfort, sis."

"Thank God for Manollo," Simon chimed in.

13

~ *New tragedy* ~

Jesse slept a few hours after he passed north of Death Valley and was into the foothills of the Inyo Mountains. He trusted his horse Paloma with his life, so he dozed when the trail was wider and less hazardous. The spring air still had a bite to it, and the trail was getting risky. When he came into the ten thousand foot break between White Mountain Peak and Mt. Whitney, he made camp to rest himself and his horse.

When he came out of the mountains two days later, he cut southwest toward the San Joaquin Valley, then turned northwest and headed for his ranch. He was dead tired from almost a year of searching for his sister's killers, but he felt good. He was almost home.

Jesse McKannah could almost smell the coffee that he knew his foreman and friend of twenty years, Arliss O'Reilly, would have on the stove. He felt good as he walked Paloma to the crest of Stirrup Mountain, the four-thousand-foot rise that overlooked his twenty-thousand-acre ranch. When he approached the clearing where he had first viewed the valley in which he would eventually build his ranch, an icy hand reached inside his chest and grabbed his heart.

~ The ranch was gone ~

He sat as frozen, as would the men who viewed the Little Big Horn disaster thirty years later. He looked at the devastation for a full five minutes then took out his telescope to get a closer look. *Ashes*! Little else remained. *Even the fences and corrals were pulled down.* The big hacienda that he, Arliss, and the ranch hands built; log-by-log—stone-by-stone, was reduced to ashes. The windmill they built to supply the hacienda with fresh water was on the ground destroyed. Even the stone chimney that Arliss insisted on constructing himself had been pulled down. *No life at all! Not a dog or a cat—nothing*! He moved the eyepiece back and forth across the obviously man-made devastation. *Been like this a long time.* M*usta been right after I left the valley.*

Jesse removed the saddle then rubbed down Paloma. He got grain from his saddlebags to feed the horse then turned it out to graze. He went to the artesian well that supplied the small stream running toward the ranch. Jesse returned with a drink in his hat for Paloma, and then as it grazed, he squatted among the trees and looked out over what he had once considered his paradise-found. His steel gray eyes took on a cold hard sheen. "Jack Hannan," he said quietly. "If you're behind this, you're a dead man."

As he lay next to his tiny smokeless fire that night, he thought about his next move. He recalled what Wovokatah, his Indian trapper friend, taught him many years earlier. *Always observe your enemy's camp from every angle. Then when the time is right, go in with your guns firing.*

The following morning he stretched to his six-foot-plus frame and bent down to stretch the muscles in his back. After running a hand through the full beard he'd worn most of his life he reached up and felt the head of gray hair that had become quite long over the past year.

Days later, when Paloma entered the booming town of San Francisco, the man in the saddle was clean-shaven, and had a head of short dark hair. A little ash black from the fire had made his eyebrows and hair a nice color, and also made him appear much younger. San Francisco was not a small town, but it was still small enough that Jesse wouldn't go unnoticed for long looking the way he had when he arrived in the area above his burned ranch the previous week. He was well known in certain circles as, 'that hard nose Irish rancher holding out against Jack Hannan'.

They were right. Jack Hannan planned to own the entire north end of the San Joaquin Valley, and Jesse McKannah had become the burr under Jack's saddle. The last time Jack and his men rode out to the ranch to make another offer, Jesse looked coldly at him as he spoke. "Jack, you didn't have enough money fifteen years ago, and you still don't."

The short, big-bellied man in the carriage had become San Francisco's land baron and was used to getting what he wanted. He leaned forward as he spoke, “I shoulda shot you back then when we didn’t have no law out here and you just a cow puncher.” He chomped down on his two-dollar cigar and squint his eyes to small slits in a futile attempt to look tough.

“You can still do it, Fat Jack, if you can get it done before those six rifles cut you n’ all your men to rags.” Jesse knew the chunky little man hated to be called Fat Jack, so he never called him anything else. He also hoped he or one of his men would be foolish enough to raise a weapon. He stared at the man a long moment. “If you’re running short of grit today then get off m’land, ‘cause them boys o’ mine back there got plenty and they’d love to give you some that’s been stickin’ in their craw.”

After stabling Paloma in the southernmost part of the city, he rented a horse on the pretense of wanting his to have a rest. He then headed north into the center of the city. He knew exactly where he was heading, and whom he intended to see. He tied the strange horse outside of the Silver Ingot Saloon, and walked the quarter mile to his destination. He had removed his spurs and placed them in the saddlebags on Paloma. His boots were hung over the saddle at the stable, and he now wore the moccasins he preferred in the woods when stalking wild game.

The only visible weapon was the long knife on his side. His reserve, custom built, short barrel, Colt .44 was facing butt forward in the homemade shoulder holster beneath the buckskin jacket. There was nothing on him to make noise or rub against anything to alert his prey.

Jesse positioned himself to watch Jake Faggon’s second story window. The huge man had worked for Jesse when he first started building his ranch, but when he was caught selling a few steers for gambling money, Jesse fired him saying, “You’re darn lucky I’m lettin’ you live, Jake.”

Jesse knew the man well. One of his pleasures was to leave the lights on so all could see that he was entertaining one of the girls from the dance hall downstairs. He stood patiently in the shadows across the street and waited for the girl to leave.

A half-hour after he arrived, the girl came down the outside stairs. Before she was on the street, the light in Jake’s window went out. Jesse gave him another half-hour to get sound asleep before he slipped silently into his apartment.

Jake Faggon came awake as the knife at his throat made a slight slicing motion. “Oh my God, what do you want? Money? I got plenty. Please don’t cut me.”

“If you cry out Jake, half your words’ll be floatin’ in your own blood.”

He recognized the voice in the darkness immediately. “My God Jesse, whadaya want outa me?”

“I know there were at least six of you out at my place burnin’ it when I was gone. I’m startin’ with you, and if you don’t tell me the truth, I’ll slit your throat then go to the next guy till I find out who put you up to it. You got five seconds to decide if you wanna live or die."

"Jack Hannan, Jesse. I didn't want nothin' to do with burnin' you out and killin' all them men, but he said if I didn't he'd have me tossed in the fire with 'em. I swear on my mother's grave that's the truth, Jesse. I. . . . ." The gurgling noises coming from Jake's throat lasted only seconds, and could barely be heard beneath the pillow Jesse used to keep the blood from splattering all over him. "I lied, Jake." He spoke quietly as he stood to leave. "I planned to kill you when I came through the window."

He stood inside the window until he was certain there was no one to see him leave. Not a living soul knew he was even back in California. He intended to keep it that way.

He had been to Jack Hannan's big house down near the bay once when it was first built. This was back when Jesse thought they could be neighboring ranchers and friends. He spent two hours carefully circling his enemy's camp. When he finally climbed the tree that had a limb to put him on the second story roof overhang, he had figured out which window would be easiest to enter unseen. He watched Jack through a window as he removed his jacket and put on a housecoat, so he knew where his bedroom was. He knew Jack always kicked the girls out when he was ready for sleep. All he had to do now was get in the house and wait.

The window opened easily and silently. He stepped in and closed it before stepping into the shadows of a corner in the long hallway. Jesse then turned the gaslight in the hall down a little and waited in the shadows. Two hours later he silently opened the bedroom door. He didn't know what time it was, but he knew it was not too far from dawn when he moved toward Jack's bed.

He considered waking Jack to tell him goodbye but remembered another of Wovokatah's lessons. 'Slip into the enemy's camp and silently send him to the other world'.

The knife went deep as the pillow went down. He held the fat man until the thrashing stopped then wiped the blade on the bed covers. He looked down at the man he couldn't see in the darkness and said quietly, "That's for you n' the boys, Arliss."

Awhile later, Jesse was back on Paloma and heading north toward the wilderness. "Kinda old to start trapping again ain't we old pal?"

As Jesse began the long trip into the mountains, his thoughts, as they often did, wandered back to his younger days.

Aleena sat beside Jesse beneath the huge tree next to the river near their home. It was their favorite place to sit and talk without their brothers or anyone else disturbing them. "How far do you think Patrick and Broderick have gone by now?"

"Well," he said quietly. "It's been ten days now so I s'pose they're about to Chihuahua."

"How do you know about all those places if you've never been there?"

"Pa and Manollo put together a better map than that first one. They took down all the rigging n' stuff from that south wall and laid out the course they're gonna take all the way to that ship they're goin' to Harvard on. A lotta Manollo's men have been way down in Mexico and know about where all those towns are, so pop and him put a mark where they're each at, and the name beside it."

"Jesse," she said in a quiet voice. "Do you really think I could go to a school like Pat and Brod are going to?"

He turned to her and saw the sincere look on her young face and knew she was dreaming about her future. "Sis, anything you really wanna do I'm sure you can do it." He smiled and reached out to squeeze her hand. "Still thinking about being a teacher?"

"Yes," she replied quickly. "That's all I've been thinking about lately."

"Well, I can tell you one thing for sure sis, if you really wanna be a teacher, then I'm sure Uncle Luis will help you. But sis, are you certain you wanna go all the way to that town where Pat and Brod are going to school?"

"Yes! I'm sure. That letter they sent said they'd get me into a good school where I can learn to be a teacher, and that's what I really wanna be."

Jesse moved farther into the mountains, putting San Francisco and the two men he'd killed behind him. He settled into Paloma's saddle as he recalled the letter he received from his brother Patrick, describing their trip. He smiled at the memory, just as he had when he first read it.

> Hello wild boy,
>
> Brod and I stood in the bow of the sailing vessel as the captain brought the ship into Boston Harbor. We moved back next to the forward mast (That's what the sail is attached to) when the men came to the bow to drop the anchor. Look at the size of that town, I said as I moved to the rail. Brod followed me and didn't say a word. Finally he said, I knew it'd be bigger'n anything we've ever seen brother, but this's just incredible. He said; remind me to thank Uncle Luis when we see him, because we would never have brought that coach if he hadn't absolutely insisted on it. Whoeee! Broderick yelped like he always does. He scanned the buildings that stretched out of sight in both directions then said, can you imagine trying to get around in a place this big without it? Yeah I can, I answered. On a horse, and I don't imagine these

ladies are used to riding double like them gals back home. Speaking of horses, Broderick said the boat's First Mate told him where we could buy a good horse trained to a coach harness. He lived near here for a few years, shoeing horses for a living, before he went back to sea to get away from a nagging woman. Well, I said, let's make that the first thing we do. Y'know what I think the second thing we oughta do is, Brod said. I turned to him and said find a pub. You catch on quick for an old man, he answered with one of those goofy grins he makes. We both laughed as we relaxed after that long sea voyage and waited for the ship to come to rest on her anchor. (Don't know why, but a ship's always referred to as HER or SHE)

The elderly man at the HORSE & HARNESS said he'd have to see the coach, and then build a harness to fit it and the horse. The First Mate on our ship had directed us to his place. He said the old man is the best at what he does in this part of the country. Could you arrange to have the coach brought here from the pier? I asked the old man. She already there? He asked us. Yessir, I replied. They loaded it on a barge and brought it to the pier first thing, to get it outa their way. The old man finished the shoe he'd been hammering and tossed it into a bucket of his secret tempering fluid. I can't tell you how much it'll cost until I see the coach, he said, but it ain't gonna be cheap for an all new leather harness and all the rigging. He relit his long stem pipe and looked silently at us as he puffed.

I'd counted on the need for some up-front money and removed several twenty-dollar gold coins from my money belt before leaving our cabin on the ship. I pulled my hand from my pocket and held that old man's stare without blinking. You know how good I am about that. The man's face was emotionless as he watched me lay five of the coins on the work bench then say we're not here looking for a cheap job, sir, what we want is a good job. I put the remaining coins back in my pocket and continued staring at the old man. He put the coins in his pocket and asked you want me to write you a receipt? Nope, I answered. I might cheat you, he said with a wry smile now crossing his face. Broderick spoke for the first time. Only once, he said with that intense stare of his. The man musta saw a slight glint of sardonic humor on Broderick's face and decided he liked the two young men that he thought talked funny. Ha, ha, ha, Jesse we could hardly understand that guy. Come back in two days n' we'll see then how much more you owe me when she's rigged and ready. He turned and grabbed another shoe from his forge and began hammering.

I had refused to pay the buggy man that took us to the HORSE & HARNESS saying; we don't want to get stuck here, so you wait on us then take us someplace where we can spend a few days until we get our coach rigged. The young man tried to complain but we just turned and disappeared into the big building.

We were back in the buggy and Broderick asked, is there a place to stay that's near a pub where we can have a couple of beers? The young man turned toward us. Yeah, he said, but it's always full of bloody Micks. I thought, seems like he would have noticed our red hair, and smiled as Broderick spoke to the guy. What's a bloody Mick? The driver turned again and said, Damn Irish. He stopped before another word fell from his lips as he suddenly noticed the bright red hair on both of us. Brod was scowling as he grabbed the driver's arm. The horse continued clopping down the cobblestone street as he was yanked into the rear with us. Broderick McKannah, Brod said as he held the man's face so close he could feel his breath. Now you say it. It was all I could do to keep from laughing when the man just stared in disbelief as Brod shook him like a doll. He said, Broddik Mc….then Brod shook him and repeated his name. The man said it perfect. Then Brod shoved him in my smiling face. Patrick McKannah, Brod said and the driver got it right the first time. Then Brod threw him up front. I mean that, Jesse. He actually threw the kid up and into his seat, and he almost fell from the carriage. I forget sometimes just how strong ole Brod is. The buggy driver regained the reins as Broderick leaned up and said, I suggest you remember those two names even if you forget your own, you pompous English fool. Now take us to a nice friendly **IRISH** pub. Brood heavily emphasized the word Irish.

Five days later we followed the directions Luis had given us before leaving. We secured our coach in front of the building and entered. A young man at the desk directed us to the Dean's Office then went back to his stack of papers. We knocked then looked at each other as a woman's voice said, yes come in. I looked around the tiny office, as Brod asked, are you the Dean of Harvard? The middle-aged lady smiled slightly then said, hardly. Do you gentlemen have an appointment? I handed her the pouch of papers Luis told us to present to the Dean. We were told to give the Dean these. Very well, have a seat please. She walked down a short hall leading to a large door and knocked lightly, then entered without waiting for an answer. She returned after several minutes. The Dean will see you gentlemen now.

We waited after knocking until a voice said come in. We were both surprised to see a very small man about Uncle Luis' age seated behind the largest desk either of us had ever seen. Patrick, the man said after looking through the papers I gave him, and Broderick McKannah? He held his hand out and smiled real friendly like. Yessir, Brod answered. The Dean then took my hand. You're the older McKannah boy, correct? Yessir, I said, I'll be nineteen soon. Have a seat, the Dean said as he returned to his own. Did Luis ever tell you that we went to school together at the University of Madrid? Nossir, I answered, not a word. The dean said, two years before I came here to get my degree I tried to talk him into coming with me, but he has heavy family ties there in Spain. He leaned forward on his arms and spoke as though we had been friends for a long time.

Boys this's going to be pretty rough on you two for the first year because you'll have a lot of catching up to do. (That turned out to be an understatement, Jess) He paused to let his words sink in. Jess, back home they told us that Brod and me were the two smartest young men they had ever encountered. We headed off for Harvard thinking we were prepared to enter law school as soon as we arrived, so we looked questioningly at each other. The Dean picked up a large leather pouch. See this, he said then continued without waiting for our answer, it's from your uncle and was on the ship with you then was brought to me the day you arrived. He removed the contents and selected one page from them. Your uncle states here that he has the highest confidence in you two men. He also realizes you will be far behind the other men entering law here at Harvard so he has sent authorization for funds to be made available for you both to be tutored privately until you have caught up with the other students. He looked straight at us. What is your reaction to that? He knew it came as a shock to us, so he waited patiently as we absorbed this new information. I finally spoke. We have learned to accept Uncle Luis' advice in all matters sir. So if that's what he says we should do, then that's the way it'll be.

The Dean smiled. Seems to me that his confidence in you is justified, gentlemen. He shifted more papers then said, you are aware that other funds have been placed in a bank in Boston for your needs? Yessir, he told us that before we left. He lifted another letter from the pile then said; He has also authorized an additional ten thousand United States dollars to be placed in our safe here at the university and gave me Power of Attorney to disperse it in the event of an emergency. Brod said, well I'll be darn, and sounded like a hick. I said to the Dean, Uncle Luis tries to cover everything that might come up. He was always that way, the Dean said, and then stood. Well gentlemen let's get your enrollment taken care of. We followed him out to the woman's office to begin filling out the papers that would officially begin our long schooling to become lawyers.

I'll keep in touch as often as I have time.

Your brother,

Patrick.

During the period when Patrick and Broderick were beginning to think they might actually live through their schooling nightmare, Jesse was learning to stalk the most allusive prey that lived near his home, Wahpohnah. He told his Indian friend, "I wanna learn how to track animals and sneak up on 'em like you do."

"Then you must first study all of the animals around here so you will know how they do things, where they go, how they think." He liked the young white boy and was very impressed with his willingness to come often and work side by side with him and others of the tribe to learn about living off the land. He was also impressed with the boy's natural abilities. *He will do very well in the wilderness*, the Indian thought, as he watched from his hiding spot that he'd camouflaged. He continued watching Jesse as he went over the slight hill and into the ravine ahead.

When the arrow, tipped with a padded end, hit him in the back it startled him so much that he almost fell from his perch. When Wahpohnah told the story to the braves sitting around the fire that night, they all solemnly nodded their approval.

"How did you know he was in the tree?" Chalponich asked.

The young boy's heart was pounding after being addressed by the Yokut Chief. He knew it was a great honor to be sitting with them, but Jesse never dreamed Chalponich would ask him to speak—even if the chief was the father of his best friend.

He waited a moment to gain control of his breath and voice, but his words still came out squeaky. “When I approached the tree, I thought it would be a good place to watch for deer.” When all quietly watched and listened, he cleared his throat and continued. “As I passed the tree I spotted two small leaves lying on the ground. They were still green and there was no wind blowing so I wondered what might have knocked them to the ground. I circled and watched from the bushes and after a while I saw Wahpohnah move.”

Several fast Yokut words that Jesse couldn’t understand were passed around the fire, and then Chief Chalponich spoke. “I have learned two good things here.” He scanned the faces of his men as they nodded their heads. “One is that a white man is not as clumsy in the wilderness as we thought.” He grinned now as he looked at his son. “The other is to remain still when being stalked by a warrior such as this.” He pointed to Jesse who knew at that moment that he’d never get a bigger compliment in his life.

Jesse knew that Jack Hannon’s associates would figure out who had paid their meal ticket and another of their kind a visit, and canceled their bright futures. Even though they probably wouldn’t follow his trail, he didn’t want to be spotted by one of them. He headed northwest out of San Francisco, went around the big lake south of Black Rock Desert, and then cut north toward the sparsely settled Oregon Territory.

Two weeks later he was camped on Lost River, south of Klamath Lake. Except for the summer mosquitoes eating him alive, it was a good time to be there. One day after rigging a trap in the river, he was eating fresh fish. He looked at Paloma grazing nearby, and spoke to his horse like an old friend. “You been doin’ good all along aincha? Good grass to eat and fresh water everywhere. Wish that grass’d keep me glued together like it does you. I gotta work hard just to get some’n to eat every day.”

The rabbits he caught in his traps weren’t the highest quality, but he skinned and cured the pelts anyway. The list of things he knew he’d need was growing longer as he thought about it. “Y’know Paloma,” he said one evening as he watched his small fire, “we could go back to riding range.” He paused a few moments thinking then added, “Thirty dollars and found. Hrummph.” He grunted, “Nah, let’s go trapping.” When the horse snorted and pawed the ground he said, “What do you know about it? You weren’t even born when I was trapping.”

Over the next few weeks he worked his way northwest to Portland. He had been there a few years earlier to order some breeding cattle to be sent by boat to San Francisco. He knew he could get everything he’d need at a fair price, and anything bought in the wilderness would be outrageously expensive.

He arrived at dusk to look out over the Oregon city, and waited until dawn to remove the thread from his saddle blanket. Jesse looked all around to be sure he was alone then removed the thread and took out enough money to get his supplies, then re-sewed the balance inside the blanket.

During the next four months Jesse trapped the Little Sanpoil River west of the Columbia. He started setting his traps twenty miles north of the dogleg in the Columbia and continued north for ten miles. As the first cold winds of fall began sending winter signals through the area, he decided it was time to bring down his pelts and head for Portland. He climbed the trees he had his pelts hanging in, to prevent bears and other animals from getting to them, and untied the lines to lower them to the ground. By noon he had his two mules loaded and was talking to Paloma. "Not bad for a guy that's been ranching twenty years, huh?"

"You kin keep talkin' to yer horse, but if'n you make a move for that hog leg on yer hip, I'll cut you in two with this here shotgun."

Jesse had not seen a white man in the months that he'd been up in the mountains. The only humans he saw were a few small bands of Nez Perce that passed through the area where he was trapping, and they just solemnly observed him as they continued on their way. He had become carelessly relaxed, and by the tone of the voice behind him, it might very well cost him his life.

"Mister, your life depends on how careful you can get rid of that gun. All we want are them skins, so if'n yer careful you can go back to gittin' more after we leave." Jesse now knew there were at least two of them. "Get rid of it right now, and be dern careful."

"I'll unbuckle it n' let the whole rig go down on the ground," Jesse said.

"Do it," the first voice said.

"Now step back away from the mule, and face that tree with both yer hands on it."

Jesse held one hand on each side of the tree and waited for the next move the two men would make. He never heard it coming, but an hour later he sat up and figured it out. *Musta hit me on the back of the head with the butt of that shotgun.* He rolled over and sat against the tree letting his head droop between his bent knees. After about ten minutes of clearing the fog from his brain, he suddenly realized it was too quiet. He raised his head, but couldn't focus right away. He squeezed his eyes shut as hard as he could, then slowly opened them to a thin slit. "Oh no. Dear God, no. You low down dirty thieves." He got shakily to his feet and walked the few yards to Paloma. The horse was lying on its side—dead.

Few emotions he had experienced could hold up against the anger he now felt rising like a volcano inside. As if the lump on the back of his bloody head wasn't even there, Jesse went right to work. He removed the saddle from his dead friend and hoisted it into the tree where his pelts had been concealed until a short time ago. He went to the boulder and removed the small rock, then reached in to get his short barrel .44 in the shoulder holster, and his spare knife. After putting the rig on, he took one last look at Paloma. "They'll wish they'd put that bullet in me, old friend."

He followed the tracks of his two mules for only a short distance to see which way they were going. "They must have canoes over by Twin Lakes," he said aloud as he thought out their moves. Without another second of delay he was off at a trot. *I'll settle this with you two somewhere down on the Columbia. If not, I'll see you in Portland.*

The men had opened his saddlebags, and found nothing but horse grain. They left them tied to the saddle, so Jesse carried them with him. After he had eaten the grain, he dropped the saddlebags on the ground without breaking his steady stride. The grain kept his strength up, and little pools of water he found along the trail relieved his thirst. He carried the folded blanket with his money in it lying over his shoulder. Before noon the next day Jesse had the dogleg in sight. Upon reaching a high spot, he had a good view of the Columbia, in the direction from which they would come. He was breathing deep but not with difficulty when he said aloud, "I think I beat you murdering thieves here." He headed down toward the spot he chose to confront them.

Jesse knew their canoe would be forced into the bottom of the dogleg, so he went along the river to a place far upstream. Before he climbed into the river he wrapped his gun and boots in the horse blanket then secured it with his belt. The horse blanket helped keep him afloat as he fought his way across. He then positioned himself on the bank so he would see them coming, pulled his socks and boots on, checked his .44, and shoved it back into the holster beneath his armpit. Even though the blanket was wet, it kept him from shivering as he waited.

Two hours later he realized, with a smile on his face that his efforts had paid off. *Here they come*, he thought—but not as he suspected. There were two canoes. He hid in the brush and watched as they approached. *Still only two men but I'm gonna hafta to be satisfied with the one for now.* He saw that the front canoe was going to land right in front of where he was hiding, so he concentrated on the other one which was at least a hundred feet behind and would probably be out of pistol range when he saw what was happening to his friend. Jesse wanted to know what he looked like so he strained his eyes to spot details. *Red hair, red beard, very tall, very skinny. . .hmmm, that guy's left-handed.*

He watched as the front canoe headed to a landing spot not twenty feet beyond where he was crouched down behind a boulder. He remained as motionless as a deer on alert, when the canoe's nose shoved up onto the sand. When the little man got out and turned his back to him, Jesse sprang like a hungry panther. His barrel was no more than two inches away as he released the cocked hammer to send the .44 slug into the thief's brain. He helped the man on his way down the Columbia with a shove, and then reached for the shotgun lying in the canoe. By the time he brought it up, the other man was leaning over in the fleeing canoe and paddling hard. He knew it would be a wasted shot, so he repositioned the pelts and got in the canoe. When he was out in the middle of the Columbia, the other canoe was a hundred yards downstream and moving fast into the upward reach of the dogleg. Jesse's eyes were focused on the man's back as he paddled with relentless abandon. For three hours he kept the canoe ahead of him from opening the gap too much, but the twenty mile trek to the river, combined with a lack of food began to take it's toll. As darkness began to cast its cloak over the river, Jesse had to accept a fact. *I'll never catch you on this river, but you better not stick around Portland, you thieving horse killer.*

By the time Jesse found a place along the river to make a camp, he was shaking from a combination of exhaustion and rage. When the fire finally began to drive the chill from his body, he rigged a drying rack to hang Paloma's blanket on. When he went to the canoe with a burning torch to get a few pelts to sleep beneath, he searched for the holster and revolver they had taken from him. "Good," he said when satisfied that it wasn't there. "Bet you've never seen a gun that fine it your worthless life, so I know it'll be strapped to your hip when I cut you in two with your own shotgun."

The burning torch cast eerie shadows on his haggard face as he looked down river. *I'll be seein' ya somewhere down the road, Red—to even the score for Paloma.*

It took a few of hours to dry Paloma's blanket and get the chill out of his bones. He finally stopped shaking and put the fire out. After gathering a pile of leaves, he lay down in them and put the blanket over his upper body. He was startled when he opened his eyes and realized it was starting to get light in the east. *My God, I never slept like this back when I was trappin'.*

He groaned as he rolled over to his hands and knees to get up. *I didn't ache like this either.* He remained motionless for a few minutes as he surveyed the area along the river, and the sandy beach where he had stranded the canoe full of pelts. After satisfying himself that he was alone, he gathered the blanket and shoved the .44 back in the shoulder holster. Jesse was already thinking about the possibilities of the next several days as he splashed water in his face.

Less than ten minutes after opening his eyes, he was paddling downstream. Two hours later he spotted berry bushes growing along the river, so he stopped the canoe among them, and ate as many as he could hold. He took out the oilskin map of the Columbia River that he bought in Portland. *Gotta cut north, on up a ways, and go around Rufus Woods Lake, then west to Lake Pateros.* As he rolled the map back up Jesse said aloud, "Down hill to Portland all the way then." He laid his hat beside him and filled it with berries then began paddling.

Half an hour after heading out into the Columbia, all of Jesse's tiredness was gone. His muscles no longer ached as he shoved paddle after paddle of water behind the canoe. His eyes missed nothing along the bank on either side. *Never know what might cause that redheaded, horse killin' thief to hole up along here some'rs.* Jesse's eyes narrowed at the thought of catching up with the tall, skinny, redheaded man that had half of his pelts. *You take one break too many along here Red and we'll settle this before we get to Portland.*

Jesse McKannah's beard and hair were growing back out, and he looked the part of a mountain trapper. To an observer he would look like a man casually heading along the Columbia River toward Portland to sell his furs and stock up for another winter in the mountains. A better eye would see that this man was driving the canoe ahead at half again the speed of most men. The bearded mass of muscle was certainly driven. Not to pay back the dead man's redheaded partner for stealing his pelts—not for trying to split open his skull with the butt of the shotgun he now carried at his feet—it was for killing his horse. When they put the bullet in Paloma's head, they had set the stage.

~ Red would die before the curtain came down ~

Jesse figured the man ahead of him to be a shiftless type that stole what he could when he could. He pulled steadily on the paddle. *You've sat in on a game that's way outa your league Red, and I have a hunch you'll be cashin' in your chips 'fore too long.*

Jesse stayed on the paddle until the moon was winning the battle with the sun—darkness was rapidly shrouding the river. When he realized his strokes were getting weak, he pulled under a tree and tied the canoe so he could rest. *I can't move at night or I might go past him. I gotta get some food if I'm gonna keep up this pace.* The berries he'd picked were gone, so he scooped water to drink then dozed off.

The following day's dawn was casting spears of light against his back as he approached Rufus Woods Lake. "Gonna get a heckuva lot easier," he said quietly, "once I get past this lake. But I gotta find me some food."

An hour later he was past the lake and there on the edge of the river squatted an opportunity for food—he hoped. Jesse had come into contact with a few small groups of Nez Perce, and even though they were a warlike tribe of Native Americans, he had traded with them without incident. He was far from fluent in their tongue, but he could get his needs across with the few words he'd learned, plus sign language.

The three braves and two women remained motionless as he brought the canoe to a stop and indicated that he wished to talk to them. After a few moments of quiet observation they motioned for him to come and sit at their fire. When one of the women poured him a gourd full of coffee, he thought for a moment that he'd either shout or cry. With so much on the line, he stoically accepted it. When she saw how he looked at the soon emptied gourd, she refilled it as soon as he sat it down. The first thing he asked was if they could provide him with food in exchange for pelts. The oldest of the three men stood and went to the canoe. When he returned, he made the sign for yes.

Then Jesse asked if the redheaded man had been seen coming along the river. The same man who had inspected the pelts signed *Yes, he stopped early this same morning.* Jesse had to control his emotions. He wanted to shout and run to the canoe. Instead he asked if they had traded with him too.

He watched as an elaborate series of signs were made by all five of them. He thought he understood, but he indicated that he wasn't sure of what they said. The older man used very basic signs to tell Jesse that the man was sick. They didn't know what was wrong with him, but they wanted nothing to do with white man's sickness, so they ran into the woods and watched. The Indian signed, *the redheaded man had a fever and was pale as dried fish. He was too sick to get out, so he screamed at us, and headed on down the river.*

Jesse signed that he must catch up with the man so he could stop him from spreading the disease. The trade for food was completed in a few minutes and he was again heading down the Columbia. The run to Lake Pateros was a breeze compared to what he'd put behind the canoe, so he was able to concentrate on the shoreline on both sides. He thought the man might be too sick to continue, and would hole up somewhere along the river if he could find a spot to conceal the canoe. Jesse had no intention of allowing that to happen. He knew he'd have to stop at dark again to keep from passing the man, so he pulled hard to cover as much water as possible.

As darkness began robbing him of his sight, Jesse decided not to risk going past the redhead and pulled up onto the first accessible bank. After securing the canoe, he gathered enough dry wood for a small smokeless fire. When the gourd full of water was hot, he dumped in a small amount of the coffee beans he'd ground against a rock. As what he considered the greatest aroma on earth permeated his entire senses, he began to chew on the dried fish. He couldn't hold in the sigh that escaped. *My God this is wonderful.*

After consuming the small piece of fish, he re-wrapped the rest. *Probably over four hundred miles to Portland, so this'll have to last a while.* He took the gourd of coffee and walked to the river's edge and looked back in the direction he'd come from. He allowed his eyes to adjust then searched for any sign of life in the darkness. He turned his attention downstream and did the same. His breath caught, and his eyes automatically narrowed when he saw the fire in the distance. He studied it for a full five minutes to be sure his eyes weren't playing tricks on him. *It's a fire all right. Small, but definitely a fire, about a mile down river.*

He added a little wood to his fire so it would continue burning, and a moment later he was quietly paddling toward the fire. *If it's not Red, I'll come back to my camp and wait till morning.*

A hundred yards from the fire, Jesse silently pulled the canoe to the bank and tied it to a limb. He checked the .44 then opened the shotgun to insert a shell into each of the two barrels. There had been a shell in each barrel when he came into possession of it, and four were lying in the canoe. He had wrapped them all in the oilskin map to be certain they'd work when needed.

He spent the better part of an hour closing the short distance from his canoe to the fire. There in front of the fire sat the redheaded man with both arms lying flat on the ground beside him and his head hung down like a ragdoll. Silently Jesse moved up behind the man then put the shotgun to the back of his head.

The man was half-dozing and half-delirious, but it startled him upright anyway. "Wha. Huh. What. Who are you?" He tried to turn and look at whoever was behind him, but Jesse closed the six-inch gap with a thrust. The barrels made a thud as they connected with the man's skull.

"Ow. Mister, take it easy, willya. One o' them goldang Nez Perch injuns shot me with an arrow a while back, an I'm havin' a bad time of it."

"Ain't nothin' like what's gonna happen if you move one of your hands, especially the left one."

"Yer that feller me n' Chirpy took the skins from, ain'cha?"

"Yep, and you know som'n? That lump's still on the back of my head."

"Well heck man, we couldn't just leave ya standin' there, now could we?"

"Your mistake was killing Paloma, and hittin' me. Shoulda took Paloma and shot me."

"That's what I tole that stupid darn Chirpy." When he said it, he turned slightly to the right.

Jesse had noticed the barrel of his own .44 laying beside the man when he first slipped up on him. When the man turned to the right he let his left hand ease to the handle of it. He knew the man standing behind him would make a move when he brought the gun up, but at least he'd have a chance—he thought.

He was dead wrong. Both barrels exploded, one behind the other, taking the man's head and a shoulder off.

Thirty minutes later his body was heading toward Portland—without the canoe. The man's canoe was tied behind Jesse's. "That one was for you Paloma."

Seventeen-year-old Ian McKannah landed against the railing and could easily have fallen to the patio below if not for his good balance and lithe movements.

The huge man he was fighting was one of the original guards that his employer had brought to his father's ranch. For reasons unknown to Ian, the brute had disliked him from the moment they met.

When Ian was eleven-years-old, he once looked up at his brother Simon. He was standing atop stacked hay in a wagon that their father Sean was pulling across the field with horses. Simon's punch had followed an argument and Ian went sailing through the air, but landed perfectly on both feet.

"Yer like a bloody cat," ten-year-old Simon said as the wagon rolled on, "always landing on yer feet."

The punch Ian just took on the jaw was not the same kind that Simon, Patrick, Broderick, or Jesse regularly pummeled him with. They were his brothers. This was a man twice his age, a foot taller, and a hundred pounds heavier. There was only one thing about Ian that could even the odds.

~ He was a McKannah ~

A year prior to Ian beginning his job as dealer at the Bayview Hotel and Casino, his brothers, Patrick and Broderick, were heading south through Mexico to rendezvous with the vessel that would carry them across the Gulf of Mexico. They would sail through the treacherous Straits of Florida to the Atlantic, then on to Boston, and Harvard University. As they rode south, a war was brewing at home. One they too had fought in many times.

Ian Brennan McKannah was engaged in a 'battle-to-death' with his younger brother, Jesse. At least that's what any stranger watching would think. The five McKannah boys bare-knuckle boxed and wrestled as survival training, and often just for the fun of it—much the same as grizzly bear cubs. Just as Jesse was certain that Ian had made a bad move, Ian ducked, stepped in, and swung a hard right uppercut at his jaw.

Earlier, prior to departing for Harvard, Ian's oldest brother Patrick spent a couple of hours alone with his younger brother. "You're always going to be fighting bigger guys than you, so listen up little brother and I'll teach you how to use your small size as an advantage."

As Jesse learned that day—It worked. Ian, now facing a deadly opponent, saw an opening. The huge brute that was using Ian's face as a punching bag, had underestimated the young Irishman facing him. If he saw something to alarm him in the intense blue eyes that never blink, he had waited too long. He had made an error that he would not be allowed to correct and would forfeit his life as payment. When the man's next swing came toward him, Ian executed one of his trademark moves—which many others would eventually also pay dearly to see. He ducked down low at the perfect moment and came inside then up toward the man's jaw. It was an uppercut that actually lifted the man off his feet and carried him just high enough against the flimsy wood railing to send his body falling toward the patio stones, thirty feet below.

It was the first of many incidents that would create a mystique around the small young man. His eyes never blinked when his intense stare was directed at someone that he considered an opponent—in a wagering game or otherwise. By the time they realized that Ian was evaluating them, it was too late. They always paid for their lack of attention—one way or another.

This was not the first incident that the seventeen-year-old had been involved in during his year with the Bayview Hotel and Casino. The coastal city named Yerba Buena was in the beginning stages of a boom that would last many years. Ian was hired because of reputation, and his age did not bother Mr. Hamilton. "Our clientele will not take this young card wizard serious until it is too late, and by then their money will be in our vault."

London England hotel owner, Hunter T. Hamilton, made a trip to the newly formed city in 1816, and turned to his valet. "Walter, this will soon be the largest city on the pacific side of this country because of that natural deep harbor." He nodded with his head toward San Francisco Bay.

Hunter's keen eye for business was correct. When he returned in 1818 he had secured unlimited financing with the powerful hotel owners in London. By Ian's fourteenth birthday the hotel was nearing completion. Hunter began asking about potential card dealers among the drinking pubs along the waterfront that had card games in the rear.

James Poorsmith had just delivered a load of supplies to the hotel when he overheard Hunter asking a man about an old card player he'd heard about. James waited until the man left before approaching Hunter. "Mr. Hamilton, I know where the best person with cards I've ever seen lives."

"Bloody good news that is, James. Where might I locate this bloke to talk a wee bit with him?"

James told Hunter that he would draw a map to the McKannah ranch and bring it with the next load of supplies. A week later, the map was delivered. "Here's a letter of introduction from me. Sean McKannah is a very good man but not too keen on strangers if he doesn't know what they're up to." He purposely didn't mention that the man he was referring to, as a great card handler, was only a young boy barely in his teens.

Ian's fascination with cards began at a very young age. "I was hiding up in the loft," he told Hunter a few months later, "and was watchin' the Mexicans playing cards. I think I was eight-years-old." A frown crossed his youthful face. "Hmm, maybe I was nine." Through the grin Ian flashed at him, Hunter saw the glint of steely confidence deep within his youthful eyes. "After that I never missed a chance to be up there when they played. I studied everything they did and memorized every game's rules. I kept after them to let me play but they just laughed. When my dad's foreman, Manollo Calaveras, said it would be okay if they kept the stakes very low, I started playing with them."

"How old were you when you started wagering?"

"I was twelve when the ranch hands introduced me to the game called primero. I was thirteen when I began playing with them for money and it was love at first deal.

"Yes. We don't play it in London, but I'm familiar with the game." The tall, thin, quiet spoken gentleman grinned at Ian. “As you know, I don’t gamble, but I understand everything there is about the various games. Our British game, Bragg, is also called Poker here in this country. It’s very similar to the Spanish game of primero.” He turned to Ian again. “Did you play for a sizable amount of cash?”

“To the ranch hands it was just pocket change, but to me it was the beginning of my dream. Me n’ my brother Simon bunked together in the same attic bedroom, and we talked a lot about our future. ‘Yer dream pot’s buildin’ up pretty good there, gambling man,’ Simon once said to me.” With a smile Ian turned to his employer. “I kept adding my winnings to the lard tin I kept under my bed.”

“Beat them often did you?”

“Yessir, but mostly because they were playing for entertainment and I knew it was what I was gonna do for a living. I studied ‘em really close, and pretty soon I knew what cards they were holding just by the way they acted.”

“Ha, ha, ha, ho boy, that’s bloody good.” He patted Ian lightly on the back. “Those blokes were cheating themselves and didn’t know it, huh?”

“Yep. I figured that even if it was small money, it was gonna take me all the way to Yerba Buena where I heard there were fools just aching to pass good money to a man that can read the table signs.”

“I’m starting to wonder if you really can read those fellow’s minds?” Hunter gave Ian a sly smile and winked.

Earlier, back at the ranch, Ian had stretched out across his own bed and grinned at Simon who said the same thing. “Nah, I ain’t readin’ anyone’s mind. I’ve just been learning what the others do when they get certain cards in their hands.”

Simon admired his brother’s abilities, but didn’t really understand them. He held his fellow man at arms length, always a little leery of their motives. He now pursed his lips as he ran his fingers over the beginnings of the full beard he would wear for his entire life. “How’s that?” He asked.

“Well,” Ian said, “every time Alejandro gets a good hand, he starts biting the corner of his mouth. And when he’s trying to bluff everyone into thinking he’s really got a good buncha cards, by betting the limit, he starts licking his lips. Just a little with the tip of his tongue between ‘em, but I noticed that he does it every time.” For an hour Ian explained how he’d built himself an edge to win against the ranch hands.

Simon listened intently then asked, “How ‘bout you? Ain’t them guys able t’read sign on you too, the way they read sign out on the trail?”

“I reckon they’ve tried,” Ian said, with a devilish grin. “But I’m teaching m’self to keep the same face and movements no matter what kinda cards I’ve got in my hand.”

“Hrrumph!” Simon grunted with a wide grin. “Looks like the proof’s in that lard tin under yer bed there

14

~ Fire on the mountain ~

By noon, the day after Jesse settled the score with the redheaded thief, he knew he'd been forced to make some changes in his plans. Towing the canoe full of pelts behind the canoe he was in proved to be an almost impossible task. He was totally unaware of the wild passages that awaited him on the Columbia. He'd been told that it was a pretty easy run, once he was around the dogleg where he settled the score with Red's partner. This kind of information was often passed on to what the mountain men considered to be 'greenhorns.'

Jesse pulled into a small sandy area and redistributed his skins between the two canoes, and shortened the towline. An hour along the river and he knew he had to try something else. It was starting to get dark by the time he located a spot to camp, so he pulled the canoes from the water and emptied them both.

After starting a small fire, Jesse carefully counted out twenty coffee beans and ground them against a nearby stone. As his gourdful of water heated, he thought about the journey down the Columbia River. After a meal of dried fish, topped off with fresh coffee, he sorted through the hides until he located a large deerskin. He sat by the fire and began cutting it into inch wide strips. With a dozen strips around his neck, he positioned the two canoes side by side and began lashing them together. *I oughta be able to control them both if it don't get too wild down yonder.*

Jesse carefully reloading the skins then rolled up Paloma's blanket and lay it next to the fire. He placed his hat on one end and tossed a few skins on the feet end. He then went into the brush to lie down on a few of the skins he'd tossed there earlier for that purpose. He lay facing east so that when his eyes opened, he'd be able to tell if it was getting light.

When he saw streaks coming through the trees, he knew it was time to get moving. After loading his bedroll in the canoes, he drank the cold coffee from last night's ground beans that he left soaking.

Thirty minutes after opening his eyes, Jesse was on his way down the Columbia again. By noon he was almost exhausted from fighting the twin hulled canoe rig. *I'd trade half of these skins and both of these canoes for one sorry ole mule.*

He worked all afternoon on his latest attempt to make the two canoes manageable. Another night similar to the last couple and he was once again out in the Columbia at daybreak. This time he was able to keep the two canoes heading in the direction he wanted with a minimum of effort.

The previous afternoon he had securely lashed the two canoes end-to-end. Then after trimming two long narrow lodgepole pines with his knife, he lashed them to each side. They extended almost from the end of the front canoe to the rear end of the second one Jesse was sitting in. They were lashed in several places and worked against each other so that when the canoe bow tried to turn off course on its own, the other pole kept it in place. By noon, Jesse was able to control the rig almost as good as if it was only one canoe. He was still under the mistaken impression that the Columbia was going to be an easy ride to Portland, and felt as though he was going to come out of this nightmare all right after all. He actually began to hum a favorite tune to himself quietly as he headed slowly into the arms of one of the wild northwest's most deadly stretches of water.

He was chewing on a piece of dried fish when he first noticed the smoke. At first it was only a wisp coming over the tops of the trees. He was traveling a stretch where the trees all came to the edge of the water, so he could see nothing in the distance beyond. As his Viking-like affair rounded a bend in the river, he saw more smoke. This time it was a sheet-like layer coming over the tops of the trees. There was no doubt in his mind that there was a forest fire somewhere not far away.

The next bend took him the opposite direction as the last and there it was. He could see the flames jumping above the tops of the trees in several spots. He looked ahead and realized it was there too. *That fire's big but it'll never jump the river along here. It's too wide.*

Just as he began maneuvering his double-canoe rig to the other side of the river, he saw a group of people ahead on a tiny sandy clearing. He could see the fire was going to be on top of them soon—they had no place to go. *Why ain't they swimming for the other side?* Soon he was close enough to see why. Half of them were very old, and the other half very young. By the time he reached the stranded group, he recognized them as Flathead Indians. Some referred to them as Salish or Sanpoil. These were Flatheads. He had traded with them a few times up in his trapping area. Even though they were warriors, he had gotten along okay with them.

By the time Jesse got close enough to sign with them, he could feel the heat from the fire. The children were all quiet, holding to each other, but he could see the fear in their dark eyes. There were three old men, two old women, and a dozen kids about six or eight years old. Jesse signed for two of them to hold the front and back end of the long rig, as he frantically threw out the bundles of skins. He suddenly realized he'd just thrown the skin overboard that he'd wrapped his Colt and holster in. The fire was almost on them, so he quickly got the children into the front canoe. One old woman's tunic actually caught fire before she could get in the canoe. The others splashed water to put it out as Jesse pulled hard to get the canoe away from the blaze, before it caught the canoes and all of them on fire.

He heard the old woman in the front yell something at the children when they first pulled away, but until now didn't know what she was telling them. He now saw that every one of them was reaching into the water and paddling with their tiny hands, and the old people in his canoe were doing the same thing. *Mighta made the difference*, he later thought, *darn sure mighta.*

They continued down the river until they were beyond the worst part of the fire, then sat and watched as it burned itself out without jumping the Columbia River. Realizing that it was getting into late afternoon, Jesse signed to the old man, that he figured to be in charge of the little band of Indians. '*Where should we go?*'

He watched as the Indian signed, '*We have people down the river and inland that will help us and you too.*'

Jesse looked around, and then answered in sign. '*I have a knife. Let us go to the bank, and make another paddle.*'

The old man grinned then pulled a long knife from beneath his buckskin shirt. '*I too have a knife. Yes! We will go much faster.*'

While they were cutting a small sapling for the paddle handle, one of the women was weaving thin branches for the paddle head. Another was weaving a long, thin paddle head. When they were both finished, they covered them with the few remaining skins that he had been sitting on. They sewed them together with thin strips cut from another hide of the deer that Jesse killed for meat while he was trapping. As Jesse and the old Indian attached the paddle head, one of the other men and the women attached the other long skinny paddle head to a longer piece of the sapling. When they went to the double-canoe rig and began attaching this long paddle to the rear, Jesse finally saw what they had made—*a steering rudder will help,* he thought.

Even though it was getting late, the old Indian signed that they could safely travel on the river for a while after dark to get to a good place to camp for the night. Only minutes after heading back down the Columbia, Jesse understood the wisdom of making the rudder. With the old man paddling in the front canoe with the children, Jesse paddling in the rear, and another to the rear of him steering, their long vessel went swiftly and smoothly down the river.

It was midnight when one of the women slapped him lightly on the shoulder and pointed toward shore. He followed the lead of the front paddler and pulled into a recessed area of the river. It turned out to be a small lagoon-like area with a sandy beach. After the children gathered dry wood for a campfire, Jesse pleased everyone when he produced matches to start the blaze. They were again pleased when he opened the package of dried fish and signed that the women should divide it equally among the children. Exhausted, he laid his head on Paloma's blanket to find that sleep had been waiting just around the corner. He was snoring lightly in moments.

At dawn Jesse awoke to a busy camp. He realized how deeply he had slept when he saw both canoes sitting side by side in the woods beyond the camp. They had been unlashed and placed upside down beneath the trees. After stretching the soreness from his body, he went to the river to splash water in his face and get a drink. When he returned to the fire, the old Indian signed for him to follow. Ten minutes later they were standing on top of a cliff overlooking a sight that made chills run down Jesse's spine.

The calm river they had been traveling on was now a wild, tormented beast. It leaped high in the air as it twisted among huge boulders in its race to the canyon far below. *If that fire hadn't stopped me, I'd be dead in that canyon right now.*

When they returned to the camp, one of the women spoke to the old man, who then signed to Jesse. '*Two of the older children have gone to get our people to come with horses. You will be much honored for saving our lives.*'

He signed back to the Indian, '*now that I have seen the river,*' he pointed to the cliff they had just returned from, *'I know that I am alive only because I stopped to help you.*'

The old Indian cupped the fingers of his hands and grasped them as he signed. '*One hand must always help the other.*'

It was almost dark when Jesse and the small group of Flathead Indians heard what sounded like a herd of horses coming their way. The older Indian spoke to the children who immediately began placing the wood they had gathered earlier onto the campfire. When it was blazing, the old Indian placed the pile of wet green branches and leaves he had gathered on top of it. A cloud of smoke rose straight up through the trees. Fifteen minutes later a band of Indian men entered the camp. Their ages ranged from young teens to one that looked like he could be the father of the old Indian with Jesse. He quickly counted them and saw that there were twenty, and each led a horse behind his mount. Two of the spare horses had packs tied across their backs and without a word the men leading them dismounted to begin removing the packs. To Jesse's hungry eyes, what began to take shape next to the campfire looked like a feast fit for a king. He had lost track of how many days it had been since he had enjoyed a real meal.

The old man that Jesse had thought too old to be out riding in the mountains, brought his left leg nimbly across the horse's mane, and in one deft movement leaped to the ground. He was perfectly erect as he walked to Jesse, who figured the man to be a couple inches taller than he was. The manner in which he placed himself in charge and issued orders to those who came with him made Jesse think he must be the Chief. The huge old Chief stopped in front of Jesse and removed his tomahawk, which was in an elaborate sheath fastened to a gold nugget studded belt.

When the Chief offered the elaborate gift to him, Jesse extended both arms toward him. He knew these were Salish Indians and were probably related by marriage to the Flatheads he was with. He was familiar enough with their customs to know that this gift of the Chief's tomahawk made him an honored guest as long as he wished to remain with them. When the Chief spoke to him, Jesse signed that he spoke very little of their language, but his signing was so good that the Chief began explaining.

'*You have saved the life of my brother and many of his people. To do this you cast away all of your possessions. The word will spread among our people, and you will be welcome wherever you travel among us.*'

Jesse accepted the tomahawk, belted it around his waist then tied the rawhide strands to keep it secure. He looked into the Chief's black eyes and signed, '*This is a great gift. I thank you and I know what an honor you have placed upon me.*'

The old Indian smiled as he motioned toward the food that was spread near the fire. '*Let us eat.*'

'*Yes,*' Jesse signed, '*it has been a long time, and I am hungry.*'

The meal was dried fish, dried venison, and several items he had never eaten, except the soft, pure white bitterroot, which he developed a taste for as a young trapper. The Indians considered the bitter tasting root a delicacy but knew that the white men they traded with did not care for it. When Jesse ate several pieces with gusto, they were very pleased. After an hour of slow eating Jesse took the tin pot the young boy had boiled the bitterroot in and went to the river. He rinsed it, then filled it with water, and returned to place it on the fire. All eyes watched as he ground the last of his coffee beans then scooped them from the small rock into the pot.

The old Chief leaned over the pot when it started to boil. He closed his eyes and breathed deeply of the aroma, then sat back as Jesse removed the pot. He filled one of the many small gourds they brought and handed it to the Chief. Jesse signed for all to get a gourdful of the liquid and was happy to see enough remaining for him also. No words were spoken as each savored the hot stimulating drink.

The Chief sat his empty gourd down and signed, '*It has been long since we have traded for the white man's bitter beans. It is a great treat for my people, and all here tonight will remember that you shared them with us.*'

The group broke camp before dawn the following day and headed for the Chief's home camp. The sun passed overhead and was two hours into its journey to the west by the time they arrived. *How in the world did those two children find their way here?*

The Chief insisted that Jesse ride beside him as they entered the camp. Jesse was surprised to see such a large group in the valley. He thought most Salish camps to be made up of fifty or so families, but there were at least two hundred ahead of him. They were living in tepees and woven mat-covered A-frames typical of the ones he had encountered farther north.

The Chief watched as Jesse signed, then answered in sign about the size of the camp. '*We are four tribes come together for a buffalo hunt on the great plateaus in the land where the sun comes from.*'

Jesse later learned that the four tribes were the chief's Sanpoil, his brother's Flathead tribe from north of the Columbia River, the Coeur d'Alene, and the Nez Percé.

The Chief continued in sign language, '*We have gathered in great strength this year to guard against our enemies. When I was young, our chief went to the plains with too few, and many were killed by Blackfoot warriors.*' He swung his left hand in an arc to cover the large group in the valley they were riding into, and then continued. '*This is many and when my brother's Chief brings his people from the north, there will be half as many again.*'

At the mention of the Chief's brother, Jesse signed, '*why was your brother and the little group away from their camp*?'

'*They left early in the morning to gather serviceberries. When they saw the fire, it was too late to turn back, so they ran to the river.*'

Jesse nodded then asked in sign language. '*Will your brother's people be alright*?'

The Chief turned on the bare back of his paint horse, and looked at Jesse. He was surprised to hear a white man concerned about an Indian. '*Yes, they have a camp in a large clearing next to a lake.*'

When they entered the huge camp, Jesse could see the distinct difference in the three groups. Each tribe had its own dress and living arrangements. They also seemed to remain in their own area of the camp. He watched as several women carried hot rocks from a fire to keep an earthen baking oven hot. *I hope there's cama lily in there*, he thought. It was one of his favorite foods.

He had seen the horses from the mountaintop before they descended into the valley, but hadn't realized how many there were until now. He knew that the Flathead were horsemen, and now realized that all of these Salish Indians must have aligned themselves with the horse. He looked out over the herd. *Must be almost five hundred horses, and somebody had to break every one of 'em.*

As they rode through the camp everyone smiled at him. Several young boys and girls signed to him, '*Thank you for saving The People.*' An old woman waited until he was beside her, then reached up and patted his leg while shaking her head and smiling.

An hour before dark a great feast began in his honor. He realized they must have begun to prepare for it as soon as the children he had rescued arrived with the news. There were many stone platters coming from many ovens, all piled high with food. He saw meat that turned out to be goat, plus cama, bitterroot, wild onions, wild carrots, parsnips, and a doughy pancake like treat filled with serviceberries. He had to be careful not to eat too much of any one item because many of the people brought him something to try; no doubt their own specialty. Everyone was pleased to see that he ate some of everything brought to him.

He noticed that one woman in particular kept bringing him food. She was a little on the chunky side, with a smile as kind and sweet as Jesse had ever seen on a female. She wasn't his age, but she wasn't a young girl either. *Somewhere between thirty and forty,* he thought after her forth trip. He began to watch her. He noticed that everyone moved back to allow her through, and smiled up at her when she passed. He sensed that she was either someone of importance in this tribe, or at least very well liked. He would later find out he was right on both counts.

During his first day in the village, he had seen only one unfriendly face. He first saw it when the chunky lady brought him the first platter of food. With each parcel of food she brought, the man's scowl got more pronounced, until he finally jumped up and left the feast. Jesse turned to the chief sitting next to him and signed, '*have I offended him*?'

The Chief raised his left hand to his chest then slowly moved it away from him, '*He is always a problem. He is called Bad Wolf.*'

An hour later Jesse said he was too tired to remain at the feast. They took him to a small teepee and gave him a bearfat candle to cast a tiny light to see by. After arranging the skins to sleep on, and choosing two to cover himself with, he was about to blow out the stinking candle when the teepee flap was quietly pulled back. The chunky lady slipped inside and with the smile he had admired still on her face, she removed her tunic.

Jesse awoke early the next morning and found himself alone in the teepee. Just as he had convinced himself that his exhaustion caused him to dream the events with the Indian lady, the teepee flap was pulled back and the sweet smiling woman entered. She was carrying a gourd full of water and a stone platter of warm food. She knelt down and placed them on the ground, then startled him by reaching under the skins and grabbing his manhood. When his mouth flew open, she grinned mischievously.

She signed. '*No Indian man ever be as good as you under the skins.*'

He smiled back and said, "You're sure good for a man's ego," even though he knew she couldn't understand him. He then signed to her. '*You are the first woman I have had for many, many moons. It was very, very pleasant.*'

Eagerly she signed back. '*For me too.*'

'*What is your name*?'

It took her several times before she made him understand her name.

'*Oh,*' he signed. '*Prairie Rose.*'

'*Yes,*' she smiled. '*And you are River Angel.*'

'*River Angel?*' he repeated in sign language.

'*Yes. That is what the children you saved call you.*'

'*How about Rose,*' he pointed to her, '*and Jesse,*' he pointed to himself.

After several attempts at each name, she finally came close. He laughed and reached up to place his hand on her cheek. Faster than he would have thought possible she had her tunic off again and was under the skins with him. Half an hour later as she lay in his arms, he said quietly, "That's how I'd like to wake up every day."

An hour later the two of them left the teepee and headed for the campfire where two women were already building up a blaze in preparation for the days cooking. Jesse could smell the sassafras tea in the bubbling pot, so he dipped himself a gourdful and squatted shivering near the fire. Winter was not considerate of his thin shirt. Rose began helping the women pile the stones for the ovens around the fire.

So quietly did the old Chief approach that he was beside Jesse before he heard him. After dipping a gourd of tea for himself, he sat it between his moccasins and signed to Jesse. '*Did you enjoy Prairie Rose beneath the skins last night*?'

Jesse was so surprised by the simple, matter-of-fact question that he paused for a moment before signing. '*Yes! She was correctly named. She is a true rose.*'

'*I named her that myself.*' The Chief signed as he smiled broadly.

'*She is your daughter*?'

'*No. She is from the Kutenai tribe. We found her when we went to dig cama. Blackfoot warriors killed her mother and father as they were digging. She was on the backboard in the bushes where her mother had placed her. The Blackfoot are so stupid that they did not see her. That was thirty-five summers ago. My wives and I have raised her as our own.*'

That answered his curiosity about her age, but Jesse had another question.

'*Is she married to Bad Wolf*?'

'*She married him two summers ago when her husband drowned on the river, but she left his teepee two moons ago and returned to our teepee. She said he never smiles and he beats her.*'

'*I do not believe a man should beat a woman,*' Jesse signed. '*I had a young wife many summers ago, but she, my baby, and my father died when our house burned. A woman is a man's great pleasure in many ways and should be treated with kindness.*'

'*Many men do not think that is so.*'

'*Only the small ones.*'

'*Yes,*' the Chief signed. '*No matter what size they are, only a small man beats his woman.*' He turned to Jesse and observed him for a long moment before signing, '*Are you going to marry my Prairie Rose*?'

Jesse paused a full minute before answering. '*I could not find a better woman, and a man needs a woman, but that decision must be made by her.*'

The Chief smiled wide then pointed. '*Her decision has been made. Did you not see her moving her belongings to your teepee as we spoke*?'

Jesse looked in the direction of the teepee he had been given. Rose was entering with the last of her possessions. The old Chief just smiled and nodded his head as he saw the smile spread across Jesse's face.

For the next few weeks Jesse helped break the wild horses that were brought to camp by the warriors of the combined tribes. Bad Wolf was among those men, who were out searching daily for horses, so Jesse didn't have to be concerned with him. Jesse had been breaking horses since he was a young man, so the Indians enjoyed watching him ride the wild animals to a standstill. The young braves would be thrown many times before finally subduing their mounts. Jesse had learned at a very young age that the best place to be was on the horse's back rather than on the ground, so he worked hard to learn how to stay there.

After enough horses had been captured, the warriors stopped their search and watched the breaking of the ones they had provided. Among the spectators, was Bad Wolf; a frown on his face as usual. As he saw the expert manner that Jesse rode the horses to submission his frown turned to a hard scowl.

Jesse noticed that Rose had not been among the spectators, and concluded that she had other things to attend to. When the horses were all broken and ready for use by the tribes, a celebration feast was planned. It would be the last before the migration to the plateaus for buffalo hunting. It was to be a communal affair with all of the tribes in attendance.

By late afternoon on the day of the feast, the fires were already burning. Many had gathered early to visit. Jesse sat beside the old Chief and sipped sassafras tea. When he heard "Jeffe," he turned to see Rose standing behind him. She was holding the most beautiful buckskin jacket he had ever seen.

"Por wimmer, to you nop be cole." She said in the broken English that Jesse had taught her.

He looked at the waist length coat in her hands and signed. '*I see now what you have been doing all this time. You are right. I will not be cold this winter.*' He smiled. '*Yes, you are the grandest rose of any prairie.*'

As silent and swift as an arrow, Bad Wolf stepped in and grabbed the coat from her hands and shoved her to the ground. He signed, '*I am your husband, so this is mine.*' Jesse immediately had his neck in one huge, powerful hand. When Bad Wolf's hand went to his knife, the old Chief gave a command and four braves stepped between the two men. One of them had prevented the knife being drawn from its sheath. Jesse released his grip on the man's throat as the old Chief stepped up. Jesse had learned enough of their language to understand most of what was said.

"We are too few," the Chief said to Bad Wolf, "and we are getting fewer all the time. There will be no killing among our warriors. You will settle this in the wrestling circle tomorrow."

Bad Wolf spoke through clenched teeth. "I am the best wrestler in all of the Salish tribes. Tomorrow you will be humiliated, gray haired old white man." He turned to leave with the coat still in his grip.

The Chief's loud command stopped him in his tracks. "Give me the coat. It and the woman will go to the victor tomorrow."

When Bad Wolf departed, and the two young warriors stepped away from Jesse, he went to Rose and asked, "Are you alright?"

She glared at her retreating ex-husband then turned to Jesse and smiled. "*Bad Pig has knocked me down many times. What is one more?*"

Later, as the feast progressed and the dancers whirled around the huge fire, Jesse kept looking over at the beautiful coat the Chief was inspecting. The buckskin outer garment had been carefully stitched together with rawhide. Then rabbit skins had been sewn to the inside for warmth. It had a removable hood, attached by rawhide, and was made of the same materials. The chief turned to Rose. "Daughter, you have never made anything as beautiful as this before."

She smiled radiantly at him then turned slightly toward Jesse and said in her language, "There has never been a man like him under the skins."

Jesse had worked as hard as Rose to learn his new language, and understood enough of what she said to make him blush. One of the women across the fire said with a laugh, "Ask him if he would teach my man." Jesse turned beet red.

The fire still blazed when Rose indicated to her new love that she was ready to go to their teepee. As she lay in his arms, she spoke in her new language. "You muff win Jeffe, or I kill seff. I nop go to Bad Pig some more."

He sat up, and in the glow of the smelly bearfat candle, said to her, "Two things I have loved doing during my life; riding wild horses and wrestling."

She blew out the candle and moved close to him.

~ Battle circle ~

Jesse awoke to a smell that had almost disappeared from his memory—coffee. He looked into Rose's smiling eyes, and then to the gourd of steaming liquid. His mouth hung slightly open as he leaned over to be certain his mind wasn't playing a cruel joke on his senses.

"Oh my God, it is coffee." He sat up on the skins and took the gourd from Rose and held it beneath his nose. "Mmmmm," he crooned then took a sip. Rose smiled contentedly as she watched him close his eyes as he continued to smell her gift.

"You rike?"

"Oh yes, I like very much." He took another sip then asked, "Where did you get the beans?"

Rose smiled widely. She was very happy with herself for pleasing him so much. "I know Nez Perce woman have them to trading. I go yesserday and trade Bad Pig's bag of yellow roots for the bitter beans."

"Won't Bad Wolf miss them and come looking for you?"

"No. I take them last round moon. He not know they gone. He very stupid pig."

Jesse lifted the gourd to her then toward Bad Wolf's teepee. "Thank you Rose, thank you Bad Pig." After finishing the coffee, Jesse followed Rose to the campfire. He sat close to it shivering slightly, wishing Bad Wolf had been off hunting horses when Rose presented him with the coat, so he could be wearing it right then.

Rose noticed him shivering and jumped up. She returned from their teepee and placed a large buffalo robe over his shoulders. He noticed that several of the older men around the fire were wearing breechcloths only, and some of the women only had light tunics on. He scooted closer to the fire while pulling the robe about him thinking, *no time to be proud, because this thing feels too good.*

Rose used a hooked stick to pull a small tin pot from the fire, and using a small piece of hide, lifted it and poured a gourdful for Jesse. He tasted it and turned to her. "This is good. Did you make it?"

"Yep." She liked the sound of the word and used it frequently. "Yep." she repeated. "I make for you Jeffe. You rike?"

"Yep. I rike." He mimicked her and smiled then signed, "Parsnips, carrots, onions, and venison. Right?"

"Almost." She turned a mischievious grin toward Jesse.

Before he could ask about the *almost* she was on her feet and helping put hot stones in the fire for the ovens. He heard a noise behind and turned to see the old Chief coming to the fire. He was glad to see him with a bigger buffalo robe than his over his shoulders.

After quietly sipping the gourd of sassafras tea that one of the women brought the Chief, he turned to Jesse and signed. *'Are you ready to enter the battle circle?'*

"Yes, Jesse signed, *'you are a very wise Chief to prevent your people from killing each other over something like this.'*

'With some of the young braves it is very difficult. With Bad Wolf it has always been hard to keep his killing knife in its sheath.'

'Has he always been a man of your tribe?'

'No. He is a Kootenai, like my Prairie Rose, and he has never been a real man. My sister married a Kootenai brave she met when we were all together trading horses. Her husband was killed in a war with the Blackfoot, and later she caught the white man's bad face disease and died, and left the boy with me. Bad Wolf was only ten summers when I took him into my family twenty years ago.'

So, Jesse thought. *I've got sixteen years experience on him. That's my edge.* He sipped his tea quietly as he thought about the wrestling match that would soon begin. *He's gonna have more energy that me. That's his edge. I'll have to use all of my tricks and throw him outa that circle as quick as I can.* Jesse knew about the battle circle from trading with the Flathead Indians in his trapping area. He once watched a friendly contest while trading coffee beans for cama and bitterroot. He knew that the only rules were no weapons and the winner was the first to put his opponent out of the circle.

The Chief sipped his tea then asked Jesse. *'Have you fought like this before?'*

'Many times. My father loved the sport, and insisted my brothers and I learn to wrestle. On my ranch we had a place to do friendly battle, but it was a square place.'

The Chief turned to him, *'Square? That is very strange. Where was your ranch?'*

'Far away.' Jesse pointed to the south.

'Why did you leave it?'

'I went looking for my only sister. A man who did not like me burned it to the ground while I was away. He also killed my best friend.'

'Did you go to the battle circle with him?'

'No. He was a man with no honor, and did not give my friend a chance—I gave him none.'

The Chief just slowly shook his head up and down. *'Did you find your sister?'*

'No. But I found her killers.'

'And did they go to the battle circle?'

'No.'

One of the women brought the pot of tea to fill both of their gourds. The Chief sipped his a moment, then signed to Jesse. *'Bad Wolf has fought many men in the circle, but none were great fighters. I think he is going to be taught a lesson this day.'*

The Chief did not move from the fire until the sun was high enough to warm the air then he stood. *'They will be waiting.'*

Jesse stood and smiled, *'Let us go and give them a good show.'*

The Chief smiled back then led the way toward the battle circle. He had developed a great liking for the white man who had saved his brother and the others, and was very pleased when Rose decided to take him for a husband. The previous evening, he had called his medicine man to the teepee. The two of them called upon their favorite spirits to go into the ring with the white man and defeat Bad Wolf. He had tried to love his sister's son, but as the years went by he realized that Bad Wolf was not a man of honor and would never be loved by anyone.

Before reaching the circle, they could see that many people were waiting to see the event. The crowd parted to let the two men through.

A tiny hand reached up and grasped Jesse's finger. Because of her one crossed eye he recognized her as one of the children he rescued from the fire. He stopped and scooped her up in his arms. As they continued to the circle she put her short arms around the bulging muscles of his neck. He had learned many of their words from Rose, so he understood her when she asked. "Will you beat the Bad Wolf, River Angel?"

"It's as good as done," he said quietly in her ear. Then he kissed her on the cheek and put her down.

Bad Wolf stood on the far side of the circle, naked except for a bark breechclout, over his genitals, which were tightly bound with what appeared to be white man's clothing material.

Rose sure as heck knew what she was doin' when she bound everything up real tight for me this morning. I'll be glad when this's over, 'cause I gotta pee.

Bad Wolf signed to Jesse. '*Braves do not walk around with babies in their arms kissing them.*'

'Only real braves can do that, Bad Pig.' He signed because he knew the man hated being called that, and Jesse wanted him flustered.

'*When I am done with you old white man, you will wish the Chief had let me cut your throat.*'

Jesse had looked over the circle when they first reached it. There was a small trench around it approximately six inches wide and the same depth. It was filled with small stones. He estimated the circle to be about fifteen feet across. He looked across at his opponent and signed, '*Bad Pig, the mighty lip wrestler.*'

When Bad Wolf stepped into the circle, Jesse could tell that the Indian had already lost his composure. He was shaking with anger as many spectators began laughing. *Good,* he thought as he stepped in with the young brave.

With no preliminary maneuvering or sparring, the Indian rushed in. Jesse fell to the ground and swung his legs like a scythe. They struck the surprised Indian on the shins and sent him sliding in the dirt. He lunged to his feet and found Jesse standing in front of him. Jesse grabbed the man's arm, spun him around, and brought it high above his back, forcing his head down into the knee that was coming up to meet it. Bad Wolf's shattered nose spew blood as he fell backwards with his feet high in the air. Before he had a chance to react, Jesse had both feet in a vise-like grip and was swinging the still groggy Indian around and around like a rag doll. When Jesse released him, his body landed two feet outside of the battle circle.

The assembled spectators cheered wildly. Many who hated Bad Wolf were making buzzing sounds with their tongues between lips. The man's face was already beginning to swell when he stood and faced Jesse. When the white man looked into the Indian's black eyes, he knew that a dangerous enemy had been created. It was one that he would probably have to face under more violent circumstances some day.

~ He was right ~

During the following two weeks, many preparations were made for the migration to the lower plateaus, where the Indians would hunt the bison. During this time, Jesse noticed that Bad Wolf was not in the camp, or at least he had not seen him. He'd been keeping an eye out for the man he now considered his enemy.

The Chief's brother finally arrived with his people, and was very surprised to see his old friend who had led the small group to search for serviceberries. He'd been certain that the fire consumed them all. When he learned of their rescue, he declared a feast in honor of the white man who was now living with his brother's tribe. Two days later Jesse was told there was to be a feast that evening in the old Chief's camp, and River Angel was to be the guest of honor.

As the sun disappeared behind the trees, Rose helped Jesse into his newly won coat. They stopped at her father's teepee to accompany him to the feast. Jesse could understand him good because of the language lessons in her tongue that Rose was pressing on him. "I'm glad you came for me Prairie Rose, but I would have gone without you. I love a good feast, and I know that old Dancing Bear will tell the story of the great rescue by the River Angel."

When Jesse finished eating, he felt someone moving in beside him. It was the cross-eyed little girl. Before the story was well under way he was surrounded by all of the children from that terrifying day at the riverbank. Jesse now felt truly honored.

As predicted, one of the old men that Jesse had rescued from the blazing forest stood and held his arms high above his head. It was a signal for all to be quiet. The feast had been in progress for several hours, so all present were willing to sit back and listen.

~ Dancing Bear began his story ~

For an hour the old Indian told his story while gyrating, wailing, and dancing about. At one point he even reached into the fire and threw a handful of flaming embers into the air to simulate the forest fire.

When the story ended, all the little voices began chanting, "River Angel." He smiled down at each one individually and looked around the campfire as everyone began chanting, "Hi-Eee-Yah" as they patted the ground beside them. He saw the Chief coming toward him carrying something.

Rose's father said quietly, "My brother has a gift for you."

The Chief was not as agile as his brother, so he came slowly around the fire. Jesse could see that it was a rifle he carried.

When he stopped in front of Jesse, Rose nudged him to stand. The Chief made a long speech that Jesse only caught parts of. When he handed Jesse the rifle his brother said, "He is learning our language, but he understands sign very well." The Chief then explained to Jesse in sign. '*The little pistol you carry in a sack under your arm is not a warrior's weapon. This is the finest rifle I have ever seen, and should be carried by a brave warrior. I was once a very brave warrior, but now one of my wives must chew my meat for me. So I give this to you because you returned my people to me.*'

Jesse leaned the rifle against him so he could answer in sign. '*I have only heard about these great rifles, but have never seen one. I thank you. I will carry it with pride.*'

A young boy carrying a small bag had followed the Chief. He stood silent as the Chief talked, but now stepped forward signing, '*We all thank you River Angel for giving us back our people, especially Roaming Eye, my sister.*' Then he stepped forward and handed Jesse the bag.

The Chief smiled. "Our young people will now dance to show the spirits how much we appreciate them helping the white man to bring our people home."

Jesse remained at the campfire to watch the dancers, and smoke a pipe with the Chief. The long days of preparation for the journey across Washington, Idaho, and into Montana to the bison plateaus, had worn him down. After an hour, he thanked everyone for a great feast and headed for his teepee with Rose. As they arrived, Rose lit their candle with an ember from her father's fire. Jesse asked her to hold the candle close so he could inspect the rifle. "Holy smoke," he mumbled as he turned it over and over.

"Wass madder?"

"Goodness, Rose, Nothing. This is the latest rifle there is. I only heard about them just before I went trapping." He held it up to his shoulder and sighted down the barrel. "It's a Sharps Drop Block Action. Look!" He opened the breechblock by lowering the trigger guard. "See here!" He pointed to the breechblock. "A paper cartridge is put here, then when you close it." He pulled the trigger guard back into place. "It snips off the end so it's ready to fire the slug in the barrel." He rolled it over on his lap to admire it. "A good shooter can load and fire several times while another person readies a muzzle loader for one shot."

Rose had only caught a word here and there, but she smiled with happiness that her man was so admired by her people that they would give him a gift so nice.

Jesse opened the breech. "Now if only I could find some cartridges for the buffalo hunt."

With that, Rose gave him the small package the young Indian had given him. "Maybe this, Yep?"

When he opened the package, he yelped. "Oh Lordy, look at this." He dumped a pile of cartridges out on the skins. "And shot too. Rose, they have given me the gift of a lifetime."

She understood what he was saying, but she wanted to make sure he understood her every word, so she signed to him. '*River Angel, what you have given everyone could never be equaled.*'

A few days after the feast, almost two hundred and fifty Indian families were on the trail. When Jesse saw how much had to be packed and carried, he understood why these people had so many horses. He and Rose had remained with her father near the rear of the migrating Indian train. He realized that he could not see the front of it, so moving closer to the Chief he said, "I am concerned that we are spread out so long. You said that there will be Blackfoot along the way."

"Yes, but not until we are farther along the trail. We have scouts out on both sides and our best warriors all around. When we are beyond these narrow trails through the canyons, we will come closer together.'

It wasn't long before Jesse understood what the Chief was talking about. The trail narrowed so severely that only a few horses could walk side by side. He peered over the edge to the canyon floor hundreds of feet below.

Most of the Indians used a rawhide harness to control their horses. It fit over the muzzle and the horse's head securing it behind the ears and around the neck. The horse is made to respond by pulling on either the left or right rein.

Jesse's father taught him to train a horse to follow his commands by laying the reins across the horse's neck. He had trained the horse that he was riding, which he also called Paloma in honor of his dead friend, to respond to the neck-rein technique. He made a simple set of rawhide reins laid back over the horse's head and attached to a round piece of rabbit fur that slipped loosely over its muzzle and a similar one behind the ears. It would stay in place, but could easily be removed by pulling the reins forward.

Jesse had adopted something he saw the Indians with rifles do. “Why do your braves all have a piece of rawhide tied to their wrist and to their rifle when they are mounted?”

“If their horse is shot from beneath them, they will not lose their rifle in the fall to the ground.”

He made a rawhide strap that day. Whenever he was on Paloma, his rifle was tied to him.

The long train of migrating Indians was emerging from a narrow area in the trail, and would soon be searching for a spot to camp for the night. Jesse was in the rear to keep an eye on a few of the older people who were having difficulty keeping up with the train. He was riding near the edge to keep them from getting too close to the drop off.

Ahead in the trees, Bad Wolf waited patiently. He had tied rabbit fur bags on his horse’s hooves to muffle the sound. After Jesse passed, he eased his horse quietly onto the narrow trail, and then abruptly kicked the animal in the flanks. It shot ahead as though it was a willing partner in the plot. Jesse heard a noise behind him, but before he could react, Bad Wolf's horse was slamming into him and Paloma. Paloma’s front hooves went over the edge as her head went down. Jesse was thrown over the horse’s neck, still holding the reins. He hit the rim of the drop off as he felt the horse go over. A slight tug and he knew the reins had slipped from the horse’s head as it pummeled into space. He felt helpless as he held onto the rawhide reins, and went over the edge himself—toward the canyon floor far below.

As soon as Bad Wolf saw that his collision sent Jesse over the edge of the cliff as planned, he turned his mount and fled back into the forest. A few of the old Indians turned on their horses and witnessed the tragic event but were helpless to do anything about it. They did see who committed the act and were quick to bring it to the Chief's attention, when he was summoned to the site.

Rose followed. When she realized what had happened, she went to her knees. Tears flowed down her full round cheeks as she began a quiet, mournful chant.

She began by asking the spirits to guide her warrior husband to the happy lands of plenty. Her father talked to those who had witnessed the attack by Bad Wolf.

The Chief then went to Rose, and helped her to her feet. “Come Prairie Rose. It will soon be dark. We must help these old ones off the trail.” Together they guided the old Indians down to a wide, grassy area where the others had already begun setting up camp for the night

15

~ *Survival—Revenge* ~

When Jesse felt the impact of Bad Wolf's horse, he intuitively knew he was going over the edge, and there wasn't a thing he could do to prevent it. When he felt his arm being stopped, his natural survival instinct kicked in. He would later determine that it was his new rifle that fell across two stubby bushes, and the rawhide line attached to his wrist was what stopped his fall long enough for him to start clawing for a finger and toehold. He felt the tug on his other hand as the rings holding the reins slipped from Paloma's nose. At that same moment, he felt the moccasin on his right foot touch a small ledge. The rifle was either letting go, or the bushes were pulling out of the flimsy soil on the cliff edge, so Jesse fought hard to get his body close enough to the small indentation in the wall. It was less than three feet deep, but it allowed him to huddle against the back, and wedge himself against the sides as the bushes went by on their way into the canyon floor.

He braced himself for the jolt of the rifle when it came to the end of the rawhide line that was attached to his wrist, and was relieved to find that it wasn't tangled up with the bushes, so he carefully pulled it to him. It took him a moment to release the death grip he had on the reins, so he could bring them to him also. He looked at the two round loops padded with rabbit fur that the reins were attached to, and imagined the poor horse falling to the floor below. *No more wrestling Bad Wolf, if I get out of this mess.*

Jesse hunkered back against the rear of his tiny shallow cave, keeping himself wedged tightly to the walls. He was dazed from the blow on the head that he got when he went over the horse. He remained motionless for about fifteen minutes and only half-aware of all that had happened.

So certain were the others above, that he had fallen to his death that no attempt was made to call to him. The Indians would not go to the edge to look over; fearing that the spirits might cast them into the chasm below to keep the white man company. By the time Jesse was getting a clear head, they were well on their way to the clearing beyond.

After checking himself to be certain that nothing was broken, Jesse looked up at a full moon. "Thank you Lord, for turnin' the lights up tonight, I'm gonna need 'em." The trail was only a little over six feet above his head, but it might as well have been a mile when he first looked up. There was nothing to grab hold of to pull himself up. *Those two bushes were all there was along here, so my luck's still holdin' out.* He turned and looked in the direction the others had gone—nothing. Not even a boulder to get a hold of. *They musta been certain that I fell to my death, and after saying a prayer for me, they all moved on.*

He turned in the other direction, and saw the tree for the first time. It was small, only about two inches in diameter and it was at least six feet away. He stood and pressed his body tight against the cliff while securing a good foothold on the edge of his small cave. To slip now would mean sure death, so he moved extremely slow and very deliberately. He had no intentions of letting anything, not even death, cheat him from dealing with Bad Wolf.

Standing now, the tree was only about four feet from him. He stood and surveyed the situation for a few minutes then with a plan settled in his mind, he carefully hunkered back into his tiny cave. He wedged himself against the walls again, and began checking his equipment in the light of the full moon. He removed the rawhide attached to the rifle and retied it, leaving a two-foot-long tail then tied a large knot in it. Next he checked every inch of the rawhide for abrasions—*none.* He then checked the knot around his wrist—*secure.* He went over every inch of the horse's reins—*in good condition.* He tied the rawhide on his wrist to one end of the reins, and carefully stood. He brought the rawhide into his hands one loop at a time until it was tight against the rifle. He then eased the rifle up until it was in his hand. He was now holding the rifle above his head in both hands, while keeping the rawhide rope looped over his thumb. *Gotta get this rifle to go past that tree and lodge itself.*

Jesse stood and breathed deeply to settle himself down as he worked with his toes to get a good secure footing on the little ledge; holding him precariously above oblivion. When he had the trajectory of his throw figured out, he placed his right hand against the butt of the rifle. A couple of slow feigning moves and he let the rifle go. It landed exactly where he had planned, and when he pulled it toward him it lodged itself against the small tree.

Now the difficult part. If that rifle lets go before I get a hand on that rawhide tail with the knot to pull m'self up and grab the tree, I'll be taking my last ride on Paloma. He reached as high as he could with his left hand and wrapped the rawhide around his right hand once. He took a deep breath, and eased himself out onto the face of the cliff, while pulling with all of his strength. He helped his right arm as much as he could with his toes digging into the cliff wall. It seemed much longer than the ten seconds it actually was until his left hand had the knot in the end of the short rawhide tail he had left for that purpose. One steady pull and he had the tree in his right hand. Jesse's great strength now allowed him to pull his body high enough to get a leg up on the trail. Soon he was lying flat on his back staring at the moon. "You can turn 'em down now Lord, 'cause I got a mean Indian to find and send to hell." He could hardly believe his eyes when a large, black cloud passed in front of the full moon, making it so dark he couldn't see the tree that just helped save his life. *A good omen*, he thought.

Jesse rolled over on his hands and knees, and then got painfully to his feet. He had abrasions on his hands and a couple of small cuts on his face, but except for aching muscles, he was in good shape considering what he had just come through. After stretching to rid himself of the stiffness, he reached down and picked up the rifle. He levered the trigger guard to check the cartridge. It looked fine in the dim light of the moon, now peeking through the clouds. Next he removed his pistol from the shoulder holster he'd made long ago to keep the weapon snug beneath his armpit. Revolving the cartridge cylinder in the moonlight, he was satisfied that it was undamaged, so he returned it to the holster. The last thing he did before setting out for the camp, that he knew would be nearby, was to untie the thong that secured the beautiful tomahawk in its sheath. He thoroughly inspected the weapon that he was becoming very good with. It hadn't taken him long to get the feel for the balance of the tomahawk, because one of the sports he and his crew had enjoyed on his ranch was throwing hatchets and the double-edged axes that they used to clear his land of the many trees.

After untying the two rawhide ropes he'd used to climb from the canyon wall, he cut two short pieces to bind them with after coiling each. He then secured the two ropes to the belt and doeskin bag that Rose had made for him to carry cartridges and shot for his new rifle. Jesse began walking east along the narrow trail. *With me out of the way, I'll bet Bad Wolf's in camp right now.* Jesse actually chuckled quietly when he thought, *that's gonna be one surprised Indian when I step out in front of him.* The grin quickly faded. *Your next lesson comes in lead, Bad Pig.*

In less than a mile, the trail widened enough to allow him to be less cautious, so Jesse picked up the pace to a slow jog. Within an hour he could see the glow of the campfires. As he neared the camp he was glad to see the clouds return, because he knew there would be guards posted, and he wasn't sure whether or not Bad Wolf had friends in the camp. Moving as silent as a light breeze across a smooth lake, Jesse went from tree-to-tree, stopping at each to search the area ahead. He moved to within a hundred yards of the campfire—as unseen as the ghosts who move through frightened men's minds.

Jesse moved silently to within twenty yards of the campfire and became part of the trees he was standing among. His eyes went from Bad Wolf to the body of the chief lying on the ground. He looked hard at Rose who was sitting at Bad Wolf's feet, and could see that she had been beaten. He looked back to the old Chief, and was relieved to see his leg move. *Thank God, he's not dead.*

Bad Wolf had Rose's hair in his grip and jerked it a couple of times as he spoke. Jesse studied his woman, and knew by her demeanor that she would soon strike out at her ex-husband. *I'm gonna have to make a move pretty soon or he'll kill her when she goes after him.*

A young Indian was standing on each side of Bad Wolf. One was holding a muzzle-loading rifle—the other a tomahawk in his hand with his arms crossed on his chest. He didn't recognize either man's dress, so he figured Bad Wolf must have recruited them from another tribe, after being defeated in the wrestling circle.

Jesse spent several minutes observing the Indians sitting around the campfire. They were either very old or very young, so he knew the Chief's young braves were either out on guard duty, or were visiting friends and ladies throughout the camp.

Once convinced that none of the others would side with Bad Wolf, Jesse decided what he had to do. As he made his plans he listened carefully to what bad Wolf was saying. "I am now your Chief. Other Kutenai will soon be here to join me. And you Prairie Dog are my wife to do as I say." He yanked Rose's hair as he looked down at her and laughed.

Jesse ran his hands all over the firing mechanisms on the rifle once again to be sure it was ready to send its slug into his target. He reached in under his arm and removed the rawhide thong that held the pistol in its holster. He removed the weapon to inspect it thoroughly one final time. Satisfied that it too was ready for action, he replaced it and untied the sheath cover to remove the beautiful tomahawk then slid it into his belt. The last thing he did was lift the wide piece of rawhide that had a hole in it to secure his huge knife—that was as much a part of him as one of his arms.

He surveyed the short distance between him and the Indians standing on the other side of the fire. *Three of 'em—no room for any mistakes*. He took a few slow, measured breaths. *A big edge is that I know I'm coming and they don't. Gotta cover as much ground as I can before they know what's happening.*

With the rifle held low, but pointed straight at Bad Wolf, Jesse stepped out from behind the tree and began silently walking toward the three men. He had covered half of the distance when one of the young men that Bad Wolf had brought with him, yelled. Before Bad Wolf had time to look up from Rose, Jesse's rifle slug hit him in the heart—he died before he hit the ground. Jesse let the rifle fall to the ground as he drew his pistol from the shoulder holster. The young Kutenai with the rifle was just bringing the barrel up when Jesse leveled his weapon and put a slug in his chest. The remaining young warrior had his tomahawk up and in position to throw, when Jesse's tomahawk hit him in the chest. He went down yelling and clawing at the object buried deep within him. Jesse followed the tomahawk so quickly that some would later swear that he ran to the man and hit him with it. The young Indian almost had the tomahawk out of his chest when Jesse's long knife blade entered his heart.

It was over in less time than it took Jesse to plan it. He turned to Rose, who was sitting on the ground staring at him like he was a ghost. He went to her and kneeled down. "I ain't as easy to kill as Bad Pig thought."

"Oh Jeffe," she said when she realized he wasn't a spirit come back to revenge his killing. "Oh Jeffe," she repeated, then put her arms around him, and buried her face in his chest.

He heard the familiar trilling calls that he knew would bring the tribe's warriors in a flash. He was surprised to see old Moccasin Woman across the fire making the loudest calls. No sooner had one of the young children brought the rifle Jesse had dropped, than a dozen warriors came running into the camp.

Jesse and Rose had the Chief sitting up, and were bathing his bleeding head. Dancing Bear had been sitting at the fire as the episode unfolded. He was now on his feet dancing, and telling the warriors the story. When he finished the condensed version that would later take three hours to tell, Jesse signed to the warriors. '*Bad Wolf said more Kutenai will come to join him.*'

Lame Wolverine was much younger than Jesse, but the two had become good friends. He was a little lame in one leg from a battle he won with a bear. Because of his ferocious attitude, he was given the name Wolverine to honor his courage. Only the very brave are ever given the name of the savage little pint-sized beast that has been known to run a grizzly out of his own den. He signed back to Jesse. '*They will die like them if they come to fight.*' He motioned toward the three bodies with his bow.

'*Like everything else with bad Wolf, it was probably just talk.*'

'*Yes'*, Lame Wolverine answered in sign, '*but I have sent word to all others in this camp to keep alert.*'

Jesse nodded his head, "That is very good thinking," he said in near perfect

Salish.

Jesse and Rose helped the Chief to his feet so they could walk him to his teepee. His wives were gathering the necessary items to attend to the wound he received from Bad Wolf, who hit him with the flat side of his tomahawk. When they sat him down, the Chief looked at Jesse. "Are you a ghost warrior?"

"No," he answered smiling at his friend, "just a hard white man to kill."

He looked at his daughter. "Tie yourself tightly to this man, Prairie Rose."

She grinned at her father; "We will be as one all night tonight."

"Ah yes, that is the way to keep him with you always."

Jesse looked at the Chief. "I was forced to kill Bad Wolf tonight."

The Chief pushed the wife who was dressing his wound away. "You have made the world a better place, and saved my life, because he would have killed me to become Chief."

Jesse turned to Rose, "Do you have any coffee beans?"

"Yep." She said in English, "You womp?"

"Yes, my lovely Prairie Rose, I womp."

As she went to her side of the chief's teepee to get them, Jesse turned to the old Chief. "Would you like a cup of the bitter bean water?"

"No. When these women quit fixing my busted head I am going to sleep, if the drums inside it will stop pounding."

"I am going to sit at the fire and drink some, then with your permission I will sleep in here and make my own teepee tomorrow night."

"Yes, and if I am not sleeping I will listen and feel young again."

Jesse leaned toward his friend and patted him on the knee. "You could still ride a young woman into the meadows of sweet dreams, old friend." He stood and headed for the fire where Rose was preparing the coffee.

The Chief turned to his three wives. "If any of you get a chance to go under the skins with that man, go."

The oldest of the three replied loudly, "Yes, I will." Her toothless grin caused the old chief to smile.

Jesse was pleased to see Lame Wolverine at the fire. After each man had a cup of coffee at their feet, Jesse said, "Any sign of Kutenai?"

Lame Wolverine sipped his coffee before answering. "No, and there will be no surprise visits tonight. Our guards are in the trees, and on the ground watching."

"Do you think they will come?"

"No. They will look from a safe distance, and see that all did not go as Bad Wolf had promised. Kutenai are like us, they do not mind a fight but they do not want to make war."

"Yes. I think Bad Wolf just found a few more like him."

"I think that is true, but not far down this trail we might encounter our enemies the Blackfoot. All they want to do is fight and make war."

"Are they many?"

"Not where we go, but they can call many of their people to come and fight if they think we have something worth fighting for."

Jesse finished his coffee before speaking. "I have traded with the Blackfoot, and I never felt good around them."

"That is the safe way to always be with them."

Rose kept her arm linked to his as he stood up. Jesse smiled. "I am going to the skins."

"And I am going up in a tree on guard duty. Sleep well, and thank you for saving our Chief."

Jesse was restless, even after he and Rose made love, so he lay awake in the darkness listening to her deep, contented breathing. He never knew which part of his past would suddenly begin opening inside his mind when he was relaxed but couldn't sleep. His brother, Ian, had sent Jesse a letter from San Francisco, and suddenly began replaying itself in his mind. He placed his arms above his head and folded his hands beneath it

Hello again, Jesse.

After the fight that I wrote you about with that guy up on the third floor, I was winded and exhausted. I very carefully leaned against the wooden rail and looked down at his body lying motionless below. That bloody fool MacAllister had considered me his enemy from the moment we met. After regaining my breath and composure, I wiped the blood from my swollen face and headed down the stairs. Dead? I asked the black livery attendant who was bent over inspecting the twisted carcass of my ex-bodyguard. Yassuh, he daid as dey come. The old man talked a lot like the blacks that Pat and Brod met in Key West. They can mimic them perfect, especially Brod. An dat ain no bad ting, cause dis fella ain nevah been good f'nothin but fightin an hurtin other folks. A lot of the black people around here are from the Bahamas and talk like that. Well, I commented, he won't be pounding on anyone else now. The old black man looked up toward the area where the fight had occurred. I was watchin you two fightin Mistah Ian, and I was scared Mistah Mac gonna trow you over dat rail. Phewee, dat sho was a punch you hit him with. You musta lifted dat big moose clear up above dat wood rail. He was looking me up and down as if trying to understand how a small man like me was able to accomplish such a feat. Not really Mister Cassidy, I told him, his upper body was so big that all I had to do was hit him hard enough to get him up and off balance, and then gravity did the rest. The man was silent a moment before answering me. Mistah Ian, you de onliest man roun heah what evah call me an all de ress us black folks, mistah or missus. You needs me to explainin what happened up deah, all you muss do is ax an I tell ever ting I see. Thanks Mister Cassidy, I told him, I doubt I'll need it because he had nothing but enemies, but I'll remember your offer. His old head nodded a few times then he added, Dunno why Mistah Hamilton keepin dat Mistah Mac roun heah so long? Because he was tough and could handle trouble, I said. Didn't do a very good job up deah, the old fella said and nodded with his wolly gray head toward the floor I had just come from. I got lucky, I said with a grin. A grin spread across his weathered old face, Uh huh, sho you did. He moved swiftly toward the stables in the rear as others started arriving to see what all the commotion was about. I stood watching as the hotel's domestic staff loaded the body on a makeshift stretcher and carried it from the open pavilion. Mister Hamilton arrived moments later and came directly to me. With a concerned look on his face he asked if I was badly hurt. I don't believe so, I answered, no thanks to that crazy Scotchman. I should have run him off long ago, he replied, then said come, let's go to my apartment and have some coffee. He gently laid his hand on my shoulder. I guess he'd begun thinking of me as a son to replace his only son, who recently died in a London carriage crash along with his wife. He said, I'm terribly sorry now that I didn't, because it would have saved you a lot of pain and aggravation. He motioned to one of the young girls who worked in the kitchen and asked that coffee be delivered to his apartment. Hunter's first floor apartment was only a short walk, and once I was settled into a chair I said, thanks boss, I don't think I coulda climbed those two flights of stairs. As he poured the coffee he asked me, how in God's name were you able to defeat a huge brute like that? I have my older brother Patrick to thank for that, and several similar fights, I told him. Mister Hamilton said, seems to me that some of those big men are actually pretty darn small inside and can only pick on smaller people, animals, and even defenseless kids. Several times I saw Mac kick dogs and heard stories about him throwing things at the hotel help's kids. I guess I mistook size for tough? I lowered the cup and grinned at him. Don't get me wrong boss, that was one tough fella, but

I've learned a few tricks to even the odds when they're stacked too high against me. I forced my left wrist back to an extreme position as I pressed my arm against my body to trip the device holding the blade in place. I caught the long thin knife's handle with my free hand as it was propelled out a couple of inches by a spring. I held it up saying, such as this but I hope I never have to use it. My God, that's incredible, he said, I had no idea you were even carrying a weapon. I told him that I'd only had it a short time. The last time the Tinker was here delivering our new kitchen knives I told him what I wanted and would pay him a bonus if he would not say a word to anyone about it. I slid the nine-inch-long, Tinker-Built knife back into the sheath that was strapped to my forearm until it made a click. I pulled the frilly cuffs, now bloodied, down over it and repeated, I'll be happy if I never take it from its sheath, but some of these gamblers are not like those gentlemen gamblers you have in England. Hunter quietly watched then asked me, why didn't you use it on that man? He beat you so badly that your eyes are swelling shut. I told him that I knew I could whip him fairly when he tired, and since he didn't have a weapon I didn't feel it'd be fair to use mine. Incredible. You actually felt that you would win? Hunter looked at me and just shook his head. Jesse, I don't think he's ever been in a fight of any kind, but don't get me wrong, he's a very good man. Yep. I told him, he was pounding me pretty hard at first but I saw his confidence starting to leave when I didn't go down as fast as he thought I surely would. That's when I started maneuvering him into the position I wanted him in. Incredible, Hunter repeated then said it again, absolutely incredible. He poured us each another coffee then asked me if I still planned to play cards with a buncha rich gentlemen from an Argentina ship that brought 'em to Yerba Buena to see our Casino? Yessir, I answered, Maria Alverista said to come to the kitchen in an hour and she'll have her son go into the woods for some medicines that will fix my bruised face. I grinned and said we don't want this bunch of men from down south to think we're a buncha darn savages, do we? Ha, ha, he laughed, these are men of immeasurable wealth but I'm certain that to build their cattle ranches and giant plantations, they've all been in similar skirmishes themselves. Jesse, I might get to see Patrick and Broderick before too long. Hunter Hamilton told me that a big hotel investor group here in Yerba Buena wants to buy this place. He bought property in New York City when he got off the boat the last time he returned from England. It's an area that's getting very famous and folks're coming from all over to go to the places there. He thinks that a good gambling house that doesn't cheat the people would do well there. I think he'd like to be closer to the ships that take him to his home in England, so I expect to be heading that way soon. I like it here but you know how I always liked to travel and am sure looking forward to seeing our brothers and Aleena. From your letter it sounds as though she's doing real well in that teacher's school. Darn, I sure wish we could all get together one of these days.

Love, your brother.

Ian.

A series of tragic events would make Ian's wish come true, but would be many years after he wrote the letter that Jesse was remembering.

16

~ *Indians on the move* ~

Jesse extricated himself from Rose's arms and legs. She had been so happy to see him still alive that she couldn't get close enough to him during the night. He rolled from the skins and covered her. After slipping into the soft buckskin pants she had made him, he located his moccasins then picked up his beautiful fur-lined coat and slipped quietly through the teepee flap. As silently as he could move, even through the woods, he still found himself looking into the eyes of the old Chief sitting near the small fire he had revived.

He poured himself a gourdful of sassafras tea. *Tough old bird; beat up 'n knocked out at night, then up 'n ready to roll before dawn.* After a sip he asked his friend, "How do you feel this morning?"

"Wonderful, Ghost Warrior."

"Ghost Warrior?"

The chief laughed quietly, "Yes, a couple of the young ones have already been here to the fire, asking if the Ghost Warrior will be here again today."

Jesse chuckled, “Maybe I should undress and put some of old Bread Woman’s white flour on my body to give them a scare?”

The Chief shook both hands in front of him, “Oh no. They would not stop running until they were old like me.”

“The sun will soon arrive, where will we go today?”

Before answering Jesse, the Chief said, “You are learning to speak our Salish language very well.”

“Rose insisted I learn Salish so I can speak to the many different tribes.”

“She is wise. We all have our own language, but we all speak Salish, also.”

As Jesse re-filled their gourds with tea, the Chief answered his question. “We will travel six days with poor camps at night, but then we will come to my favorite place in these mountains. It is only a small lake, but it is full of fish, and the ground is level all around. Our guards can see anyone approaching, plus we put sentries in the trees a long distance out. We will stay there and take a few days to recover from the first part of our journey. You will like it there, Ghost Warrior.”

“So that’s my new name, huh?” Jesse said with a grin.

“Yes. Look across the fire.”

Jesse looked in the direction of the Chief’s nodding head. There were at least half a dozen sets of little eyes on the other side of the fire. “Come, sit with the Ghost Warrior, and you will be safe until the sun arrives from its journey to the dark land.” Jesse patted his leg.

Roaming eye, her brother, and her five companions came around the fire to huddle close to the man who had saved their lives. The smallest child looked up at Jesse. “Did you fly up from the deep canyon, Ghost Warrior?”

“No. The Chief had the medicine man send good spirits to help me back from the dark place.”

All of the little eyes were wide with wonder because they knew he had been knocked over the edge into the canyon. Roaming eye spoke. “Did you see the spirit?”

“No, but I felt his wind as he brushed past me, then lifted me back onto the trail.”

“Were you afraid?”

“Yes. When I was alone, but as soon as the good spirit was there, I knew I would be saved.”

One of the older boys asked, “Will Bad Wolf come back too?”

“No. He has no one to send good spirits to him because he was a bad man all of his time here.”

“Good. He hit my grandfather when I was a little boy, and he still hurts from the wound.”

The boy asked about the spirits. “I am afraid of spirits; where did it go?”

Jesse lifted the child up onto his knee. “The good spirits went back to the medicine man, but when you are good you do not have to be afraid of the spirits. They always help the good people."

"But I am bad, sometimes."

"It is good to know when you are not being good, but that does not mean you are being bad."

"Mommy says sometimes that I am bad."

"Then tell her you are sorry, and that you will try very hard to be better."

"Okay." The little boy used the only white man's word he knew. He smiled broadly when Jesse repeated the word.

"Okay."

After the children left the fire, the Chief turned to Jesse. "The young ones enjoy being near you."

"I enjoy being with them too. They are innocent and full of wonder."

It was always amazing to Jesse when the camp came alive just after dawn. Everyone would have already eaten and were ready to break camp to begin the day's journey. The small light tepees that were used for traveling were held upright as the thin hide cover was wrapped around the poles. Once secured with rawhide, two and sometimes three would be placed on a travois to be pulled by one of the larger horses. The only large teepee was the Chief's. It would be loaded alone on a longer travois with the pots, pans, and assorted gear necessary to make a comfortable camp. Bed skins would be rolled into a compact package then tied to a horse with one on each side, as a comfortable place for the younger children to ride. While this was being done, new guards would go out to relieve the tired ones who had been watching for three hours. Thirty minutes after the first rays of daylight were coming through the trees, the Indians were heading east down the trail.

When the Chief pointed out the area to which they were heading, Jesse and Lame Wolverine moved ahead of the main body of Indians. They would go four or five miles in a straight-ahead direction, as two other teams from the other tribes moved out at an angle.

Twenty or more warriors would be covering the sides and rear, as the main group moved slowly ahead. There were many things Jesse knew he must learn about Indian life, but foremost was to learn the trilling signals they employed to let each group know what was encountered out beyond the main body of people. *I'll have to ask Rose if she understands those signals.* He thought a moment then smiled, *Of course she does.*

As the day moved slowly by, the two men continued covering the ground ahead. They searched for any sign of Blackfoot Indians, or any other potential enemy to the group of people behind them. Occasionally, Lame Wolverine would send a trilling call across the forest. To Jesse it sounded like one of the many birds he constantly heard as he scouted the terrain ahead. In the distance, a faint reply could be heard. "How do you tell one call from the other?"

"You start learning from the time you are old enough to go into the woods with your father or one of your uncles. There are many different calls, but it is all done with your tongue, and that is what takes so long to learn."

"Hmmm," Jesse mumbled, "maybe I'm starting too late in life."

"Yes. That is true, but you can learn the basic ones we use to alert our people."

"How will anyone be able to teach me and not make the other guards think it's a real alert?"

"Like this." Lame Wolverine sent a strange trilling sound out through the woods. "That is letting them know that I am now teaching one of the children how to make the signals."

For the next two hours, Lame Wolverine kept showing Jesse how to make the most common sounds that were used between the men out scouting ahead of the tribes. When the sun had dropped toward the western horizon, Lame Wolverine made a series of calls, and then waited for a reply. When it came from two different directions, he said, "I told them that we have found a place to camp tonight." He pointed to a fairly level spot down in a little valley ahead. "The camps will not be very good until we get to the lake."

"Yes," Jesse answered, "the Chief told me about the lakeside camp that he likes very much."

As Jesse was scanning the night's campsight he spotted a large buck standing in a clearing. It was about two hundred yards away and took no notice of the two men. He quietly told Lame Wolverine where it was. "We do not want to warn the Blackfoot that we are in this area, but The People need meat. Do not use your gun unless you must. I will see if I can get close enough to the deer to kill it with an arrow."

When the Indian slid silently from his mount, Jesse did the same and took the other horse's reins to tie both horses to a nearby tree. He continued searching the surrounding area for any sign of an enemy while Lame Wolverine moved toward the deer. After thoroughly scanning the woods, Jesse positioned himself so he could see the deer that was still in the clearing eating, and checked to be certain that his rifle was ready. He knew Lame Wolverine was one of the best stalkers in the entire tribe, but he was still surprised when he saw the big buck leap almost straight up in the air, and fall to the ground a short distance from where he had been eating. Lame Wolverine stepped out and waved, then made a long, shrill, trilling noise. *That didn't take him thirty minutes*.

They dragged the buck to the camp area and lay it on the side of the clearing. Lame Wolverine used his tomahawk to scoop out a shallow depression in the earth then with Jesse's help, lined it with leaves. When he gutted the deer into the leaf lined area he said, "The old women will make many tasty things from those."

They moved the carcass beneath a tree and Jesse stood on his horse's back to get on a limb. With him pulling on the rawhide rope and the Indian lifting, they got the big buck up off of the ground and hanging from the limb.

Jesse climbed down and helped his friend dig a large hole next to the deer, and lined it with leaves also. When the Indian train came into the camp area they found two men sitting beside a small smokeless fire with a beautiful deerskin, spread out on a drying rack, and a pile of fresh meat covered with leaves and ready for the women to begin cooking.

The next few days were uneventful as the Indians continued the journey east to the buffalo hunting grounds on the lower plateaus. Jesse McKannah and Lame Wolverine were a few miles ahead, scouting the area that the others must cross, when they came to a small cliff overlooking a wide valley. In the center was a beautiful azure lake being fed by a tall waterfall on the north end, a mile or so away. A breathy, "Ohhhh," came from deep within Jesse's chest as he stopped his horse Marble. He'd decided that Paloma was not a lucky name for his horses, so he named this one Marble. It was similar in color to the mantle he had bought in San Francisco for the fireplace at his ranch. He sat wide-eyed and silent as Lame Wolverine came up beside him. "That must be the lake the Chief likes."

"Yes. He was happy here for many years as a child."

"Oh. He didn't tell me that he'd lived here."

"For him it is a place of many happy times, but also bad memories."

"He lived here with his family?"

"Yes. It was a small tribe. His mother was a Sandpoil Flathead, so when they married, many of her relatives went with them to live in this new country. He always speaks of his father as a great hunter that did not like war. All he wanted was a place where his little tribe could live and prosper, but it was not to be. When Chief was young, ten summers I think? he was napping in the sun, next to the waterfall." He pointed toward the waterfall, still cascading into the lake after many centuries. "He was awakened by the yelling of the Blackfoot warriors as they attacked his tribe. He quickly ducked behind the waterfall, and waited until all noise was gone. He waited behind there until morning then cautiously came out to find his entire tribe dead and mutilated."

"Phew, I don't know if I could come back here or not. I was so saddened when I walked among the ashes of my ranch and friends that I think I will never return to that place."

"I feel the same way, but Chief and Medicine Man come to talk to the spirit family."

"The same spirits of his tribe are still here?" Jesse asked. He was sincerely interested.

"After eighty-five winters they are still here. He talks to each one of them."

Jesse turned on his horse's back and looked incredulous at his friend. "Eighty-five winters?" He blew a half-whistle sound between his teeth.

"Phreeeee, I thought he was spry for about sixty years. Ninety-five—wow."

Lame Wolverine smiled, "He is a man to use as a guide to follow through life. He is also strong like two men, and if he must fight, he will fight to win."

"And he probably would," Jesse added.

Lame Wolverine shook his head up and down, "Yes, he would." He grinned at his white friend, "One way or another. Bad Wolf and his two men jumped him after he pushed you over the rim. He knew that he could never have overcome him alone."

The Indian made a series of signaling calls then turned to Jesse, to explain what he had informed the other scouts. Before he could speak Jesse said, "You told them that we are at the lake, and will check it out, right?"

His Indian friend smiled while shaking his head up and down again. "You learn quickly, my friend."

"I have a very good teacher that will not let me rest until I have learned whatever she decides to teach me."

"You are a very lucky man to have Prairie Rose. She has been like an older sister to me, and has taught me much. You will prosper in her company."

"Yes, I'm sure that's true; I find things about her every day that amaze me."

"Did she tell you she will not stay in camp during the hunt?"

"No." He turned and looked quizzically at Lame Wolverine.

"She will ride among the beasts with us, and will kill as many buffalo as most warriors."

"What?" Jesse almost yelled. "Oh my God, just what I need. I must watch for Blackfoot while I'm trying not to get trampled by a herd of frightened buffalo, and now I must also worry about Rose riding right in the middle of the herd."

Lame Wolverine laughed. "Do not worry my friend, because she has been doing it since she was a young girl." He turned his horse toward the trail that headed down to the lake. "Come, let us scout the area around the lake before The People arrive."

An hour later they were satisfied that the only tracks in the area were made by wildlife, so the two men began cutting small limbs to construct a fish trap. When each had as many as he could carry, they went to the southern end of the lake where it spilled into several small rivers. They used stones to pound the stakes into the riverbed and by the time the tribe began arriving, fish were already starting to accumulate behind their trap.

By dark the camp was set up, and food pots were on the many fires scattered among the four tribes. It had been several difficult days of traveling, so after the guards were assigned their posts, many of the people were heading for their sleeping skins. Jesse felt himself trying to nod off and when he looked at Rose, sitting beside him asleep, he gently lifted her into his arms and headed for their small traveling teepee. Several of the old women watching made loud comments. "Ah, to be young again." Another said, "Why young? I would go with him now."

A tiny old woman that looked like she could be the Chief's mother spoke loudly, "Yes, me too."

The Chief grunted, "And do what?"

She turned and glared at the chief, "I would dream of sweet memories, you old grizzly bear."

Jesse was up as the moon began its decent across the second half of the sky. He slipped quietly out of camp and went a hundred yards into the forest before making his trilling signal. Lame Wolverine soon answered him. It took him fifteen minutes to cover the distance to where his friend was on guard duty. Other than the two signals, neither man made another sound. Jesse took his position among the boulders as Lame Wolverine silently headed for camp. Two hours before dawn another signal alerted Jesse that his replacement was on the way.

He slipped into his teepee and dropped his buckskin pants to the dirt floor. He removed the big coat, and then slid quietly under the skins. He stretched out on his back in the dim light, which the moon provided through the flap. He was surprised when Rose rolled over on top of him. There was enough light to see her smiling face looking down at him.

He was startled to see how light it was when he awoke. *Darn, I'm getting old; shoulda been up already.* He lay there alone for a few minutes thinking about Rose. *I'm a very lucky man to have another good woman.*

Even before his morning gourd of sassafras tea, he went to the fish trap. In the thirty feet of river in front of the trap, there were at least two hundred fish. He recognized several trout that he figured to be at least ten pounds. He turned when he heard someone coming up behind him. Lame Wolverine spoke quietly, "We are constructing drying racks, and even though we have seen no tracks of Blackfoot we are not going to smoke them. We will keep a smokeless fire beneath the fish until they are dried enough to store them." Lame Wolverine smiled, "We did a good job on the fish trap."

"Yes," Jesse grinned, "old Dancing Bear will spend a lot of time tonight at the fire, telling the story about our great catch."

"Yes and the fish will get bigger as he tells the story."

When Jesse learned that one of the Coeur d'Alene braves had a double-edged axe, he set out to locate the man. He told Rose what he wanted it for, and she surprised him again with a bag of coffee beans that weighed about a pound. When he found the man and asked if he would like to trade for the axe, the Indian said, "Yes, let us have birch tea, and talk."

Two hours later Jesse returned with the axe. After Rose finished praising him for his transaction, Jesse began filling her lap with coffee beans from his coat pocket. When the last bean was on her lap he said, "I put half of the beans in my coat pocket, then re-tied the bag. I told him I could only trade for half of the beans in the bag, so when he got them all he thought he had gotten the best of me."

She smiled as she put the beans in a buckskin pouch. "You did very well. The Coeur d'Alene are very wise traders."

He spent an hour working on the axe edges until they were as sharp as the knife he carried. He selected a tree a foot thick at the base, and began chopping. After selecting the best ten-foot section of the tree, he cut it from the rest and removed the bark, then used his horse Marble to haul it to the edge of the lake. After cutting a notch into the center, he rolled the log over to begin digging a hole a foot from each end with his knife. It was after mid day by the time he had a hole half way through on each end of the log. By now he had an audience of several children and a couple of old women. They all sat patiently as he boarded Marble to get more limbs from the tree at the edge of the forest.

When he located the several correct pieces and had them cut away, the children helped him carry them to the log. He laid the log in the position he wanted it then laid one of the two forked limbs a foot out from the notch. When he began digging with a shovel he'd made from a limb, one of the older children reached for the tool. He smiled at the boy as he gave it to him. While the boy worked on the hole, Jesse began shaping two, foot-long pegs to go in the holes at the ends of the log. He smiled at the four old women that were now watching. They smiled back and patiently watched.

When the boy had the hole as deep as he could get it, Jesse stood the forked limb in, and pounded it deeper with a large rock. He then began adding small stones with the soil and made it tight with a tamping pole. The children continued bringing small stones when Jesse went back to his project. He selected another two-inch limb from his pile, and trimmed it to match the forked one just buried. As the children brought the stones he added dirt as they tossed them in the hole, while Jesse tamped the mass solid. He continued until the hole was full, and the forked limb was rigid. When he was finished he had two forked limbs sticking a foot and a half out of the ground on each side of the log. As the children and the old women, now grown in number to seven watched, he began to carefully chop at each end of the log. When he was satisfied that he'd carved a good sitting place on the ends as well as he could with the axe, he finished the areas with his long knife.

As he began the process of fitting the pegs into the holes he had drilled into each end with his knife, Jesse had an audience of about thirty children, and a dozen old women. When the pegs felt fairly solid in their holes, he began slicing small wedges and driving them in around the pegs until they were as rigid as though they were actually part of the log. All that remained was to place the short crosslog on the forked limbs then position the half moon notch on the big log into position.

When he had the crosslog on the forked limbs, all eyes watched as he lifted the log, and placed the notch on it. The expression on the faces of the Indians was uniform—curiosity.

He smiled down at little Roaming Eye and motioned for her to come to him. He picked her up in his arms, and then placed her on one end of the log. He then placed her hands on the peg sticking up in front of her. He smiled at the little boy that always worked himself into the front of the others—regardless what was going on. The boy rushed to him and was soon placed on the opposite end of the log from Roaming Eye.

Jesse only had to show them once how to push up with their feet when their end was down. After that, squeals of joy could be heard for hours as the children waited their turn on the first seesaw any of them had ever seen. The old women were now smiling as they took charge to see that everyone got a turn on the wonderful toy the white man had made for the children.

As the children came from all over the camp to ride the seesaw, Jesse went to the area where the fish were being dried. The older children were cleaning what was left, as the women placed them on the racks to be dried. He turned to Lame Wolverine who was watching, "Is the trap filling up again?"

"No. I pulled some of the stakes from the center. When these are finished I will put them back in place."

"It looks like you have plenty of help here, so I am going to make something for the older children to play on when their work is finished."

"The word has spread," Lame Wolverine said smiling, "that you have made something wonderful for the little ones."

"Yes, it is a copy of one that my father made for us children."

Lame Wolverine looked up at Jesse. "You have not seen your brothers in a long time have you?"

Jesse shook his head slowly and pursed his lips. "No I haven't," he looked off into the distance then added quietly, "not for a very long time." As he began walking around the lake toward the huge tree that he had decided to use for his gift to the older children, his mind carried him back to the last letter he had received from Ian, many years earlier.

Hello brother Jesse,

I was very happy to get that letter from you. Your ranch sounds like a wonderful place and I hope to see it one day. Much has happened here since I last wrote you. Patrick and Broderick came to New York City to visit, and see the gambling hall that Mister Hamilton built from an old warehouse that was on the property that he bought a short distance from a place called Five Points. You would find it hard to believe how many Irish families live in this section of New York. We were accepted in California, but here it seems that no one likes the Irish. They are paid very poor wages and must live in shacks with very little hope of making a better life for themselves. For that reason, many are becoming involved in crime. Patrick and Broderick did not like it here and are happy that they will soon be heading back to California. You will be happy, I think, with this news about Aleena. She is doing so well at the teacher's college in Boston that she is going to stay and be one of their professors. She plans to write you a letter herself but wants to wait until she is certain that she can do a good job as teacher. Mister Hamilton has been very sick and has mentioned that he would like to sell me the gambling hall and property, so he can return to England. With the money I have saved plus what you put in the bank for me from the sale of mom and dad's ranch, I believe I can swing the deal. It will be a big gamble but that's what I do every day, so I think I'll take the chance and buy it if he decides for certain that he wants to sell. I hope all continues to go well for you and will visit your ranch some day. We will have much to talk about.

Love,

Your brother, Ian

17

~ *Five Points* ~

The young immigrant was fresh off the boat. The trip from his home in Sicily was the first time he had been away from his family in his nineteen years on this earth. If the new country was as open to opportunity as they had heard, the rest of his family would follow. The trip on the old schooner from Palermo to the Strait of Gibraltar made Andolo wonder if he had made a big mistake. The Mediterranean Sea wasn't the placid stretch of water he had heard about from the fishermen. In the winter of 1924 two storms rushed across Greenland, then raised havoc on the small country of Iceland before slamming into the North Sea. The first storm lost some of its intensity as it bruised France before heading into the Mediterranean. Mother Nature wasn't finished with young Andolo's seafaring venture. Her second storm rushed in behind the first so swiftly that the fishermen and seamen barely had time to prepare for it. Andolo lay prostrate in his hammock below decks—his prayers alternating between salvation and a swift death.

When the schooner anchored off Lisbon Portugal, her sheets, sticks, and rigging were very little changed after facing this latest, of hundreds of storms.

Andolo felt as though he had passed the test of manhood.

Satisfied that she had done her best, Mother Nature gave the old schooner and Andolo a calm North Atlantic to cross. All memories of frightening nights and terrifying daytime seas were replaced by dreams of adventure in Andolo's mind as he watched the harbor of New York City becoming a reality instead of the dream he had nurtured for three long years.

In less time than it took him to pack his bags back home in Palermo, he had a delightful young maiden on his arm and was heading toward an area where she said, "The pubs are gay and full of fun and laughter." Winking a painted eye, she added with a sly, sexy smile, "And there are rooms above where we can have a very good time together." Another smile and just one word sealed the deal. "Alone."

Arm in arm the two young people approached the area that was soon to be known as one of the most dangerous places in the world for a person to enter.

FIVE POINTS
New York City
America

The walk was long and tiring, so Andolo was more than ready when she suggested a shortcut to the cold beer waiting at the bar she had spoke of. Only several steps into the alley, but a million miles from home and family, Andolo suddenly looked down in shock as a long blade was shoved into his stomach. His mouth opened and closed silently as he looked into the cold black eyes beneath the filthy derby. As darkness began surrounding him he heard strange voices.

"C'mon O'Rourk, help me get the bloody coat off this bugger 'fore she's wet with blood."

"Soon's I get 'is shoes."

"C'mon lads, lemme 'av me quid."

That's Rosie's voice, Andolo thought while his body was tossed about as if it were a sack of bones. Nearly naked but not cold at all, he lay listening to their footsteps rapidly departing. Darkness surrounded him as the dream of a new life in a new country faded into oblivion.

Patrick and Broderick McKannah stood side-by-side on the bow of the freighter. The Dean of Harvard University had arranged for a trip to New York City so the two McKannah boys could visit with their brother, Ian. "Looks a lot like Boston Harbor," Broderick commented, "but this's a much bigger city."

"Yeah, and from what I've heard, these people are a pretty hard lot, so we'd best stick close to each other and keep our eyes open."

Awhile later, as the anchor was being dropped and the sails lowered, Patrick nudged Broderick. "Hey Brod, look at that small boat coming toward us. I swear that's Ian standing on the front waving his arms."

As the small launch approached the ship, Broderick's smile widened. "Yeah, that's our little brother, the gambler."

"Hello strangers," Ian called when the small rowing launch was next to the ship.

A short time later the two oarsmen pulled toward the shore as the three brothers chatted. "Gotcher own private yacht now, huh?" Patrick grinned as he spoke.

Their young brother also grinned. "It can be yours too for the same couple of quid it cost me to come out and get you two bookworms."

"How did you know we were coming in today?" Broderick spoke as he looked around at the different types of sailing vessels they were going past.

"Brek Swenssen is the dockmaster here, and he also comes to my place to gamble and watch the shows. I asked him to let me know when he heard you two were coming. He knows everything that happens between Boston and New York City if it happens on the water.

Broderick's head jerked around. "Your place? Shows?

"Yeah. Mister Hamilton," he looked at Broderick then at Patrick, "the man I've worked for since going to Yerba Buena, has been sick for quite a while and decided to retire back home in London. I bought the place here in New York City from him."

"We've been hearing a lot about that Five Points area." His oldest brother looked hard at him, "Is it as rough as we've heard?"

"Patrick, it's probably many times worse than you've heard, but my place isn't in that area. It's nearby because Hunter, that's Mister Hamilton's first name and what we all called him, knew that many people were coming to see that crazy, wild place. He figured that they wouldn't want to gamble or stay there after seeing how bad it is, so he bought an old warehouse not far away and had it rebuilt."

"Is it all Irish people," Broderick asked, "in that Five Points place?"

"No. There are Italians, Polish, Germans, Blacks and I imagine there's every kind of people on earth living in that area. For some reason though, our Irish kinfolk aren't welcomed here, so they find good jobs almost impossible to get. Because of that, the Irish immigrants that can't afford the cost to take a ship around to California get off here and settle in Five Points."

"We've noticed the same reaction to the Irish in the Boston area."

"Yeah Pat," Broderick turned toward his brother then back to Ian, "but we sure don't have a place like this Five Points that everyone's talking about."

"Ha." Ian laughed, "It's so bad that even the sailors that have been in places like dad and that old sea captain went, won't go down there."

"You don't have any problems with 'em?"

"Nope, none atol. They stay in that area, so if you don't wander in there, especially after dark, you won't have any problems. You've gotta be careful wherever you go here in the city, but I guess there's no other place like Five Points anywhere on this bloody green earth."

"Where you reckon we oughta stay while we're here?"

"Well, brother Brod me lad," Ian flashed his mischievous grin, "I've recently converted the top three floors to rooms, kinda like a hotel. If yer interested I s'pose I can work out a pretty good deal for you two soon-to-be legal wizards."

"And what kind o' deal might that be, little brother?"

Ian's eyes twinkled as he spoke. "How about all me legal work done free in me future?"

"Deal," Patrick answered, "you'd be getting that anyway and you know it, so we might as well save our money and stay with you."

"And now," Broderick said, smiling. "About those shows you mentioned, any dancing girls in 'em?"

"The best in the city and you'll be seeing them tonight. You'll also be meeting Mister John Quincy Adams and his wife Louisa." Ian smiled at them asking, "You do know who he is, don't you?"

Patrick commented, "I met him in Boston while he was visiting the Dean, who was his professor when he was in law school there. You must have quite a place to bring them to it."

"You'll be seeing for yourself soon because it won't take us long to get there in my new carriage."

"I never met the man," Broderick said, "but from what I hear lately, he's thinking about running to be president just like his father was."

"I wouldn't know a thing about it." Ian grinned, "you know me, brother Brod, I never get involved in politics. That game's too crooked for me. All I know is that Louisa loves the shows and he enjoys playing Poker."

"Doin' pretty good for yourself it seems t'me brother," Patrick commented, "new carriage n' all."

"I had three of them built so I can pick up the more famous of my visitors when they arrive."

Patrick turned to Broderick. "Brother Brod me lad, methinks this little fella's gonna be a good guy t'be knowin'."

"Yes, but don't forget how he is with cards and sit in on a game with the little bugger."

"Darn Brod. I was plannin on getting another carriage outa you fellas."

The three brothers were still chatting and laughing as they walked up the dock toward the waiting carriage.

A while later the carriage was moving along Chatham Street, just on the edge of the Five Points District, and approaching Chatham Square. They would soon turn onto Mott Street and head toward Ian's gambling club and show palace, that he'd renamed The Shamrock.

Ian had just finished saying, “My workers will be busy getting ready for tonight’s customers, so we’ll stop up ahead at Patrick Kelly’s Saloon for a cold beer.” The words were no sooner out of his mouth than two men jumped up on the sideboards of the carriage. Each had a flintlock pistol and pointed them at Patrick and Broderick. “Give us yer money ye rich bastards n’ be quick about it.”

As soon as Ian saw his driver’s hand coming around, he bent his wrist back, shoved his arm against his side, and caught the knife as it came out of the sheath on his arm. Before the pistol in his driver’s hand exploded and blew a sizable portion of the thief on the opposite side’s head off, Ian’s blade was in the other man’s throat as he grabbed the hand holding the pistol. The shot went up in the air as his body fell into the dirt road.

It all happened so fast that neither Patrick nor Broderick moved. After getting his nerves settled down, Patrick spoke. “You go through this every time you go for a carriage ride?”

“No.” Ian said as he wiped the blood from his knife’s blade on his handkerchief, tossed it into the street, and returned the knife to its hiding place. “Never had any trouble like this at all but with so many people coming here it doesn’t surprise me.” He grinned at his two brothers. “Those fellas mighta been following you two rich looking dudes from the time you left Boston, but waited until they were on their own turf to act.”

Broderick motioned with a nod toward the driver. “That’s the kind of companion that’ll help you become an old man, brother Ian.”

“He came from Yerba Buena with Hunter and me when we opened here. He’s half Modoc Indian and half Mexican.”

“And all big.” Broderick added.

“I ain’t quite certain that you need any help,” Patrick said. “Your reactions are as good’s ever, baby brother.” He pointed toward Ian’s ruffled shirtsleeve, “That’s quite a weapon you’ve got there.”

“Yeah it is, Pat. Remember the tinker that came to our ranch a coupla times a year?”

“Sure do, did he make it for you?”

“Yes. I had it made right after a guy at the blackjack table pulled a big hunting knife from his boot and stabbed the dealer. It started dawning on me that I was in a tough business.”

Broderick grinned, “A little different than playing with the Mexicans at the Ranch, huh?”

“Yeah, but it’s things like that and those two guys laying back behind us on the road that’s taught me to keep my eyes on everything.”

“Hey, speaking of teaching, guess what Aleena’s gonna do.”

Ian turned toward Broderick, “Marry a rich professor from that school she’s going to?”

“Nope. Better’n that, she’s gonna be a professor.”

“Well,” Patrick interrupted, “not right away. It’ll be a while until she’s actually a professor but she’s thrilled just to be getting hired to teach there.”

“That’s great news. She’s wanted to be a teacher since she was a little girl.” Ian stood and looked ahead. “We’re almost to Patrick Kelly’s Saloon, boys.”

“We don’t have weapons. Does he pass out pistols when you enter?”

“Y’won’t need ‘em in this place, because Kelly won’t allow any rough stuff inside. Anyone’s got a problem they hafta go out back and settle it then they can return to the bar.”

“Well now, sounds like my kinda watering hole.”

18

~ *Enemy tracks* ~

Jesse's Indian friend, Lame Wolverine, slowly shook his head up and down. "That is a good thing you made for the children, because they should have fun now, while they can. Their lives will become very hard, very soon."

Jesse asked, "Can I use that deerskin we got the other day?"

"Yes, come with me, it's in my teepee." The younger man headed off at a trot, with Jesse following.

Jesse made pegs to hold the skin to a tree so he could slice off one-inch strips. With the pile of strips at his feet a couple of hours later, he began to weave them into a rope. He laid three different lengths, side-by-side, so that when one ran out he could attach another to it, and there would never be a weak place in the finished rope. Hours later he reached the end of his material and stretched it straight, and was satisfied that it was long enough. He went into the woods and cut a one-inch limb from an oak tree, then trimmed the bark from it. After placing the two-foot-long piece of wood at the end of his rope, he wrapped and tied the buckskin ends to it. Before beginning the weave, he'd already made a large knot on the other end.

There was still plenty of daylight left, so he headed for the giant old oak tree he had spotted earlier hanging out over the water like a beckoning arm from his past. The older children were finished with their chores for the rest of the day and were aware that he was making something for them to play on. As soon as they saw him walking toward the big tree they ran to join him.

He turned to his group and asked, "Who is the best climber?"

The others shoved a tall skinny boy about eleven, forward. A short, chubby boy said, "He is called Squirrel, because he can climb trees like one."

"Okay Squirrel," he said as he put his hand on the young Indian's shoulder, "look up there." Jesse pointed into the tree. "See that place where two limbs go out like this?" He held his hand out and spread his first two fingers.

The boy pointed up, "There?"

"Yes. What you must do is carry this over your shoulder to that fork in the tree then place the stick so the rope will hang down. Use these two pieces of buckskin that I've tied to each end and secure it."

He watched as the boy lived up to his name. With no visible effort he was in the tree, and out onto the forked limb. While the boy was coming down, Jesse was removing his moccasins, britches, and the light doeskin jacket that Rose had just made for him. He fished in the end of the rope with the pole he had cut for that purpose, and as he stood naked, preparing to demonstrate his latest device for the boys, he heard cheering behind him. He had not seen the six old women that had quietly come to watch. *Too late now,* he thought as he grabbed the knot to begin his swing out over the water.

It was only ten feet from the end of the knot to the water, but it was a daring stunt to the young boys. They watched as Jesse let go of the rope at its farthest point and hit the water. He surfaced with a big grin. The first to go was Squirrel. He actually got back to get a good run before leaving the bank. When he let go, he gave a loud screech, and carried it to the water. Next to try was the chubby boy. He stood at the edge of the bank, trying to get up his nerve, when another boy pushed him off. He swung back and forth until he could no longer hold on then fell into the water. After swimming awhile in the cold lake, Jesse went to his clothes and dressed. From the time he came in view up on the bank until he was dressed, the old women clapped their hands, and hooted.

When he was again dressed he turned to his audience of old women, and took a bow, then straightened and extended both arms above his head. They loved it, and showed it by doubling their hoots and clapping.

By the time he arrived at the Chief's campfire he was freezing. *Phewee, I didn't think the water'd be that cold.* He gladly accepted the gourd of hot sassafras tea that one of the Chief's wives offered him. He removed his moccasins and held his feet toward the fire.

The Chief's youngest wife walked around and looked hard at Jesse's feet then asked, "Are all white man's feet blue?"

"Only when they swim in ice water," Jesse replied with a grin.

Rose and several of the other younger women returned just before dark. Each carried a basket of Cama Lily roots. "Oh boy," Jesse said when he saw what they carried, "I love those things."

"Yes, I know," Rose smiled, "that is why we went to get them. Tonight we will have a big feast of fish and Cama then Dancing Bear will tell the story about all of the wonderful things you have done for the children."

Jesse had not eaten all day, but had not thought about it until he saw the fish being cooked and smelled the Cama baking. When it was finished and passed around, he had to control himself to keep from eating like a starved wolf.

Roaming Eye sat between he and Rose, watching wide eyed as Dancing Bear told his stories. When he finished everyones favorite story about Lame Wolverine killing the bear, he began the story of Jesse building the wooden horse for the children to ride and the rope for the older ones to swing on. When he got to the part in the rope swing story when Jesse removed his clothes, he dropped his pants, and then leaped about the fire naked. To help with the story, all of the old women clapped their hands, and hooted even louder than they had at Jesse.

The stay at the small lake was extended to ten days because of the abundance of fish. A few of the younger men on the council wanted to keep moving toward the buffalo hunting plateaus, but the Chief overruled them. "We must take advantage of this gift the Great Spirit has sent to us. We have the fish in our hand, but the buffalo are only in our mind."

As the council broke up and everyone was leaving, one of the younger braves spoke quietly—he thought—to his companion. "Chief likes this place and just wants to stay awhile longer." When he heard the Chief's thundering voice, he froze in his tracks.

"**Dancing Feet**." The Chief's voice could be heard throughout their area.

The young man was wishing he could have his comment back to swallow unheard, as he turned. "Yes, my Chief."

"Do not chew your words like an old woman around her cooking fire. When you have something to say to a man you should go to him and say it while looking him in the eyes."

"You are right, my Chief. I should not have said anything. It is just that I am anxious to hunt the buffalo."

The old Chief stared hard at the young brave until the younger man looked away. "Instead of hunting the buffalo with your mouth, you should be hunting the deer with your arrows so the people can eat red meat and grow strong."

"Yes," the young brave quietly responded. "I will go hunt the deer this very minute." When he was ten feet away, and wishing he was a thousand, he heard the Chief's loud voice call his name again. He turned. "Yes, my Chief."

The wrinkled old face opened into a smile. "Good luck on your hunt."

The young brave smiled back, "Thank you."

When they were a far distance from the Chief's teepee, his companion turned to the young brave, "Our Chief is a great man; that is why he is Chief."

"Perhaps I will be Chief one day?"

His friend smiled, "Only after your lips have been sewn shut."

Dancing Feet smiled back, "Come and help me correct my error by bringing a large buck to the camp."

With the Indian Train back on the trail, Jesse and Lame Wolverine scouted far ahead. Jesse was getting good at the trilling signal calls, so he was doing most of the communication with the other scouts out on each side.

Lame Wolverine had told him earlier that their next major resting camp would be at Lake Coeur d'Alene, which was seven days away. Jesse calculated the distance they could travel in one day, and came up with an average of ten miles. It was going to be a rough seventy miles, but from what he had learned, the traveling would be easier from there to the plateaus, and they would be able to make half again as many miles each day.

On the second day of travel, Jesse returned from a short scouting venture to the south of the area that he and Lame Wolverine were traveling. "Come with me," he said as he turned Marble back in the direction he had just come from. Two hundred yards later he stopped and jumped down, followed by his friend. A few careful steps later he pointed to several horse tracks heading toward the main body of people.

"These were made only yesterday." Lame Wolverine said.

"Is our camp being scouted by Blackfoot?"

"Yes. No one else would be good enough to scout so close to a camp as big as ours. The Blackfoot are warriors before all else. They want to rule all of the land from sun to sun."

Jesse mounted Marble. "Let's go the other way and see if there are more."

A couple of hundred yards from their main trail they found more tracks. "I do not like this," Lame Wolverine said, "winter is not far away. They should be in their winter camp by now."

"We have many fine horses with us. "Perhaps they plan to surprise us when we camp at the big lake?"

Lame Wolverine pursed his lips in thought a moment. "You keep scouting, I must go back to tell Chief, so he can be thinking about what we must do, then talk to his other chiefs."

Jesse continued ahead, but went off to the side several times to search for more sign of the Blackfoot. An hour later, Lame Wolverine was back to tell Jesse what the Chief had said. "He has posted double guards to the sides and rear. He will call a council when we stop tonight to discuss a battle plan with the other tribes."

At the campfire in front of the Chief's teepee that night was his brother, chief of the Flathead tribe north of the Colombia River—the head Chiefs from the Nez Perce and Coeur d'Alene tribes—plus several sub-chiefs that dealt with battle plans when trouble was brewing.

After listening to two hours of talk about what could be done to defend their position when the Blackfoot attacked, Jesse turned to the Chief. "Would I be allowed to speak to this council?"

"All who are with us may speak to the council."

He stood and spoke slowly so all could understand him as he struggled with his new language. "The people in this tribe do not like war, and I do not either. I have wondered why men must do war on their neighbors, so I have read many of the white man's books to try to understand. I still do not know why, but I have learned a great deal about how wars are fought and won. If you great Chiefs would like, I will explain some of what I have learned, and maybe you will learn from it too."

The tall Chief of the Nez Perce stood. "We have heard the stories, and know that you too are a great warrior, so I would like to hear what you have learned."

The others nodded their heads.

Jesse began. "We do not know how many they are, so it might be like the soldiers from across the big water that were fighting the black men in that land. They were very few against great numbers; many more than the tiny bugs that come out at night to bite us. These few men defeated the many black men by using a very simple method of rifle fire." He paused to let what he had said sink in.

"How did they do this?" The Nez Perce Chief asked.

"They formed three lines of soldiers with rifles. The front line would fire then stoop down to re-load their rifles. The men in the second line would fire and do the same thing, and then the third line. When the third line had fired, the first line was ready to fire again, so they stood and fired, starting the whole process over. As practice, they dry fired without bullets until they were satisfied they had the system perfect. When the black warriors charged the little group they were met with a continuous wall of bullets."

Jesse sat back down to a deafening silence that lasted a couple of minutes as the Chiefs pondered what he had said. Then they all began talking so rapidly that he could not keep up with them. After ten minutes of talk between the Chiefs, they were suddenly silent and sat down. Jesse's friend, the old Chief turned to him. "They think it is a good plan and asked if you would help train the warriors who have rifles?"

Jesse stood again and addressed the Chiefs. "I will be happy to do anything to help The People survive. Let me add one thing. The men with bows and arrows could also be trained to fight like this."

The old Chief stood, "It is settled then." He pointed to the sky at a point above the western horizon. "We will stop every day when the sun is there, so the warriors can be trained in the white man's way of war. Our scouts will range farther out so the Blackfoot warriors will not see."

Jesse was relieved early each day by the night guards, so he could return to camp and train the warriors. By the third day, the warriors with rifles were so good at the dry runs that Jesse told the various Chiefs they could continue the training as he began with the men using bow and arrow.

Jesse sat beside the Chief one evening at the fire. "I do not think the Blackfoot will attack us on the trail."

"Why is that?"

"We have the horses too close to our group, with many guards. I believe they will wait until we are all set up in our camp by Lake Coeur d'Alene."

The Chief sat silent for several minutes. "Yes. The horses will be in a corral, so if they could make a successful attack and catch us off guard, they could escape with many of them."

"And a few of our scalps," Jesse added.

Each day that passed left a group of warriors better prepared than the day before. The warriors with bow and arrow were even more impressive that the ones with rifles. They could string a new arrow much faster than the Indians with the muzzleloaders could be ready to fire again, plus they had a small army of arrow makers supplying them with arrows without points. Instead of dry runs, they were actually firing arrows to get the feel of battle. When the time came, the killing points would be placed on those same arrows.

Reminds me of a ballet I saw in Portland once, he thought as he watched them fire and stoop to reload. He walked from one group to the other and was surprised at how much each was like a choreographed play. Fire-stoop, fire-stoop, fire-stoop. Up and down the three lines went, and each time throwing a wall of arrows that would be deadly when the killing tips were put on.

When the Indian Train arrived at Lake Coeur d'Alene, the Chief's were aware that they had been scouted the entire way, but not one of the Blackfoot had been spotted. "They are like ghosts in the forest," Lame Wolverine said to Jesse.

"Boy, they must be for us not to have seen 'em a time'r two."

"I have heard it said that Blackfoot warriors can stand motionless for an entire day and can see a fly move an arrow's distance away."

"I've heard similar stories, and I'm beginning to think they're true."

In years past, the horses were always put into pastures around the lake with ample guards to watch for raiding Blackfoot. The Blackfoot usually divided into several smaller hunting bands and had one or more Chiefs controlling the various aspects of the tribe. Small groups would conduct the raids they made against the other Indian tribes to steal horses, women, and sometimes a scalp or two. This time the Salish Chiefs all had bad feelings about being scouted for so long, especially Jesse's friend, the head Chief of the entire band of Indians.

"Did Lame Wolverine show you the little canyon?" He asked Jesse.

"Yes, it is a good place to put the horses while we rest and replenish our food so we can continue on to the buffalo hunting grounds."

The old Chief sat on his mount and surveyed the surrounding area. "We will set up our camp at the entrance to the canyon. There is no way out at the other end, so we can guard our horses and The People from attack. It will not be the pleasant stay as when we camp at the lake's edge, but I feel certain that the Blackfoot are going to attack us in greater numbers hoping they can steal our horses."

"I feel the same way Chief. We have many more horses than you usually take to the buffalo hunting grounds, so they have reason to come in greater numbers."

"Yes," the old Chief answered, "we are more people than ever before; so many more horses were needed." He paused and looked at the Indian wranglers who were herding the horses into the small canyon. "I wonder if it was a good idea to come as such a large group?"

Jesse turned to his friend. "An old Indian trapper friend taught me many things long ago. One was that when you are in the enemy's land, either go alone or with many warriors."

The old Chief just nodded his head and kept watching his group enter the lake area. "I must go tell the Chiefs what I have decided." He turned his horse to leave then turned back. "The People will not like it."

"You must do what is best for them."

"Yes."

Jesse watched, as the expert horsemen herded the nearly three hundred horses into the canyon. When the last of them had entered, the four groups of Indians began setting up their camps. By pre-arrangement, the larger Chief's teepees were set up side-by-side, facing the direction that any attack must come from. Behind them warriors would occupy the family tepees that would normally house individual families. After the evening food was consumed and guards were posted, then the women and children went to the teepees in the rear. The warriors had their weapons loaded and inspected. Before retiring for the night, each placed his weapon where he could get to it in the dark. Each man had his own personal plan and each man was part of a group that had a well-rehearsed plan of action. In the event of a surprise attack during the night—they would be ready.

Jesse had attempted to make a count of the warriors with weapons. The ten guards that were always out watching could be counted on to come into the fight as soon as the warning sounded. His best estimate of remaining warriors was twenty from each tribe, which meant that they had eighty armed warriors that could be in position within a moment's notice. He lost count many times in his attempt to count the rifles, but he concluded that about half had bow and arrow, and half had rifles. He looked at many of the rifles, and was impressed with the care the Indian warriors gave their old rifles. They were all muzzleloaders and some dated back to the previous century. He looked at a few of the more modern muzzleloaders that he knew would be more accurate, and wondered how they had come to possess them. He made a mental note never to inquire about it.

The task of catching and smoking fish, to supply food for the remainder of their journey, fell entirely to the women and children. The warriors remained close to the teepees where their weapons were stored.

Jesse and Lame Wolverine rode far in each direction searching for any sign of the Blackfoot—Nothing! They were continuously trilling the scouts in the distance for word of any enemy—nothing! They were in the sixth day at Lake Coeur d'Alene and it looked like their fears of an attack were unfounded. The warriors were beginning to get relaxed in the routine of the day, and also began slipping off into the woods with their women. Some left their sleeping comrades to join their women in the teepees.

Jesse noticed the breakdown in the readiness of the camp and talked to the Chief. "If I were an enemy planning to attack a camp like this I would wait until everyone was relaxed and convinced that nothing was going to happen, then I would hit them hard when they would least expect it."

"When would that be?"

"Dawn."

The old Chief sat silent for a moment. "Your words have been my concern for two days. I see what the young bucks are doing, and I wonder if the enemy's eyes are seeing the same thing?"

"Today I found sign in the woods that we are not alone."

"Then you think they are going to attack?"

"Yes."

"We will only be here two more nights. The women and children have almost enough fish smoked and have gathered roots enough for the journey. Tonight I will stop this foolishness and get our warriors back on alert."

Jesse sat by the fire and watched as the Chiefs casually moved among their warriors. By midnight there were no more men sneaking from teepee to teepee. He checked his Sharps rifle and curled up under a pile of skins that Rose had brought him earlier.

He was awake as dawn began creeping through the woods. He rubbed the sleep from his eyes and watched the open ground beyond the Chief's teepees. Nothing moved.

The young warriors stayed away from the women all day, and the night was repeated. Jesse sat at the Chief's fire, each noticing that the warriors were taking the warning serious. "I have something to ask you," the Chief said.

"Yes, my friend."

"When you came to my aid they said you shot Bad Wolf with the rifle, then you shot his friend that had a rifle, with your pistol. It was very daring to put the pistol back in the bag and throw the tomahawk, because he might have killed you."

Jesse removed the Colt from the shoulder holster, and opened the chamber. "Only three bullets left and I don't know when I will get more."

The Chief's eyes twinkled as a toothless grin spread across his face. "I thought you might say that it was to honor me that you put it in his heart."

"It was a good place for it to be, with you lying on the ground."

"Yes, he was the one who hit me."

Jesse turned and smiled at his old friend. "Good justice."

When the first rays of dawn began showing, the trilling signals started. The time it took the Indians to assemble would have impressed any army sergeant. Less than ten minutes from the first signal, the Blackfoot warriors charged. They came out of the woods a hundred yards away, running silently toward what they thought was a sleeping camp of tired old Salish Indians. The Blackfoot scouts had not been as observant as they should have been.

Facing them in the near darkness were eight groups in a wide arc across the front of the large teepees. There were approximately ten riflemen in each of four groups, and a similar number of bowmen in four groups. They had been instructed to wait for the order to fire, so their first slugs and arrows would send many enemies to the hereafter. Jesse was off to the side and appreciated the remarkable control each man showed in the face of a charging enemy.

The order to fire was not given until the Blackfoot were ten yards from the rifle barrels. The first volley knocked several to the ground. All the others were stunned and in a state of confusion, when the second wall of lead tore into their bodies. Arrows also began to take their toll as the bowmen fired in sequence. Nine volleys in half as many minutes and the brief encounter was over. Only a small handful of Blackfoot was left to run for the security of the woods. The Salish guards that were running to join in the battle met a few of them and brought their scalps with them into camp.

The Salish warriors scalped their enemies, and several needed finishing off. When the sun was up, Jesse counted fifty-three dead Blackfoot scattered in front of the teepees. He learned later that the scouts had killed four more in the woods. He found it incredible that not one of his people had been injured.

The Chief gave the signal to break camp and get ready to travel. He turned to Jesse. "Your teachings have saved The People."

"It was your braves who did the fighting, Chief. I did not even fire my weapon."

"Dancing Bear will tell this story many times around our fire, and I am sure it will be told around many other fires for a long time."

As the Indian Train headed down the trail toward the Bitterroot Range, Jesse looked back at the carnage. He wondered how long the story about the defeat of the powerful Blackfoot by the more peaceful Salish would be told.

He would have been amazed to learn that it would still be told a century and a half later.

~ California 1837 ~

Simon McKannah sat a moment looking down at the new trading post that the Hudson Bay Company had constructed only a year earlier. Word from James Poorsmith to stop by the new post had reached him by means of the mountain men who were trapping beaver for the company. Simon approached the mountain men's remote outpost a few days after killing the bank robber that he had been following. "Hello the campfire."

"Who are ya?"

"Simon McKannah, man hunter with a large empty hole back o' my belt."

"I've heard o' you, c'mon in n' fill that hole."

After tending to his horse, Simon accepted a tin cup of coffee and a tin plate of beans and hardtack. "Thanks, I been two days without a bite."

"I got a message for you from the main office in Yerba Buena." The man watched Simon chew and waited for him to answer.

"From Mister Poorsmith?"

"Yeah, he's wanting you t'find a man what killed the family running that outpost up in Bear Valley."

Simon swallowed and washed it down with coffee before answering. "That the one above Fat Woman Gap that's run by the family with the little blind girl?"

"Yep."

"He kill her, too?"

"All three of 'em, four actually, 'cause the wife was with child again."

Simon finished his beans and hardtack then accepted a refill of coffee. He shook his head slowly. "Too darn much of that kinda stuff lately. This guy I had to kill, robbed the new bank in Los Angeles, then even though they gave him the money he shot and killed a woman that was just visiting her brother who was the teller. Killed him too, and shot a young boy outside before ridin' outa town. Som'ns makin' people plumb crazy, I reckon."

"I reckon it's all these people comin' into this area," an old trapper across the fire said. "Warn't long ago I could walk these 'ere mountains from one full moon to the next n' never see another white man." He leaned forward to spit tobacco juice into the fire before continuing. "I run into someone pert'near every dern day now."

"You'll have to send that robber's belongings to Mister Poorsmith, so he can have my reward money put in the bank for me. I've also got seven hundred and forty dollars of the bank's money that you can give me a receipt for and send it to him with the guys stuff." He put his empty plate and cup on the pile with the others then got the bundle of money from behind him. Simon handed it to the outpost man, and then headed toward his horse. "If you'll count the money and get me that receipt, I'll get the saddle back on my horse."

"Y'headin' on up 'ere now?"

"Yeah. The colder the trail, the longer it takes me to catch 'em. Probably cold already. When did it happen?"

"About two weeks ago."

"Hmm! Pretty darn cold." Simon continued toward his horse, picking up his saddle on the way.

The trapper who had remained silent said quietly to the outpost man, " I sure wouldn't want that big feller after me."

The outpost operator agreed. "I hear he's never come back without his man." After a moment he added, "Or at least the guy's belongings.

19

~ On to the plateaus ~

During the first day on the trail, most of the people were still upset because of the attack at Lake Coeur d'Alene. The women and old people wanted only to be left alone to reach the buffalo hunting plateaus just north of what was to become Plains Montana. Many of the older people knew that this would be their last great hunt and were looking forward to meeting their lifetime allies in life—the buffalo. For centuries beyond their imagination these people had maintained an honorable relationship with the sixty million shaggy brutes that had supplied these true North Americans with almost every necessity to maintain a life in the harsh northwest. It had been five years since these tribes had gathered to make the long and treacherous journey to the country of their Flathead relatives, to hunt the great buffalo herds. As the days passed, the old people waited with pleasant anticipation for their first sight of the black masses of meandering buffalo. They were to be sadly disappointed.

After the shock of the attack by the Blackfoot wore off, the younger braves, who had never been in a battle before, began to boast about their bravery during the fight. Most were like Dancing Feet, and had also never been on a buffalo hunt. Their anticipation was in some ways greater than the old people. They too would be very disappointed.

Each night after the Indian Train made camp, the guards were sent out and the cooking fires lit—all would enjoy a well-earned rest and something to eat. When Jesse was presented a meal of bitterroot, he consumed it with such gusto and pleasure that the old Chief commented, "I have been around many white men and you are the first that has ever liked the bitterroot."

Jesse finished the mouthful he had been chewing before speaking. "When I was much younger, I was a guide and tracker for the Hudson Bay Trading Company for a while. I became a good friend of an Indian trapper named Wovokatah who loved the bitterroot and prepared it often. He also made a delicious meal with the cama lily. I hated to cook, so whenever he offered me anything I ate it. I did not like either at first, but now they are among my favorite foods." He turned to Rose who was sitting beside him. "My Prairie Rose often prepares them for me."

She smiled then beamed as the Chief spoke. "She is the best cook in this camp. You are a very lucky man to have her as your wife."

Rose scooted closer to Jesse and looked up lovingly into his eyes. "I am learning every day how lucky I am that this young woman chose an old man like me." He jumped back in surprise when she reached over and grabbed his crotch.

"Not old," she said with a wide grin. "You like young brave."

When Rose got up to help the Chief's wives clear the cooking utensils, the old Chief asked Jesse, "Have you ever heard the legend of how we got the bitterroot?"

"No."

"Long ago there was a famine. One old woman believed her sons were starving to death, so she went to the river to sing the death song. The sun heard and took pity. He sent a guardian spirit in the form of a red bird to comfort her with food and beauty. 'A new plant will be formed,' said the bird, 'where your tears have wetted the soil. Its flowers will have the rose color of my wings, and the white of your hair. Your people will eat the roots of this plant. Your sorrow will make it bitter, but it will be good for them. They will always survive as long as they can dig it. The people will say, our mother's tears of bitterness have given us food.' I believe that the old woman's death song saved The People."

The Flathead Indians were a relatively small tribe, but were known for their bravery, honesty, and general high character. Their territory was comprised mostly in the northern Montana lands. In five short years it would be their high character, combined with a friendly disposition toward the white men, which would lead them into a foul treaty with the young government of the United States. The treaty of 1855 would strip this noble people of most of their land, and place them forever at the disposal of their white neighbors. They would be herded onto a small reservation just south of Flathead Lake to wither like flowers struck down by a harsh winter wind.

But for now, the old Chief's relatives commanded vast reserves, so he and the others were looking forward to re-uniting for a great buffalo hunt. The young braves sat around his fire when invited—to hear his stories, and try to imagine the unending sea of bison he talked about. Dancing Bear had been on every hunt with the old Chief, so as the stories were told he would dance and portray the pictures into their eager young minds.

When a story about a particularly successful hunt was over, the Chief said, "As we hunted the great beasts we had to be on constant guard for attack by our lifetime enemy, The Blackfoot." A hush came over the entire group as Dancing Bear slipped the buffalo robe with head and horns over his body. He slowly danced around the fire, stopping to stare through the beast's eyeholes at each young warrior. The Chief began his story.

"The Flathead camp was pitched in Flathead Valley near the great river of their name. After the hunt, many gathered to hold races on foot and on horseback of long and short distance. They had the three valleys in which to camp and hold contests—the Bitterroot, Hell's Gate, and the Missoula. Their lives were in danger though, for enemy eyes were spying." At this point Dancing Bear jumped in and out of the fire, sending sparks high into the dark night to add drama to the Chief's story.

The old Chief took a pull on the pipe then passed it to Jesse before continuing. "It was a bright day as the men sat and told of the daring and dire incidents of their lives as they passed the pipe. Others of the tribe were scanning the green mountain steeps in front of them. They regularly looked to Mount Lolo, looming like an evening star to their west. Four buffalo bulls were observed grazing on the mountain." Dancing Bear was now on all four, appearing to all who watched, like a grazing buffalo. "All of the men were soon on their best buffalo horses in swift pursuit of the four bulls. Soon they stood where the bulls were, but could find no trace of them." With the agility of a young man, Dancing Bear threw the buffalo costume aside and was now portraying a confused hunter.

"When the terrible shape of human feet," the Chief continued, "was seen where the bulls had just been spotted, the warriors suddenly realized they had been tricked by the cunning Blackfoot." The many children who had been listening from beyond the fire had gathered close together as the story grew more frightening. They now moved back as one huge body when Dancing Bear went into a wild frenzy of antics to describe the terror and helplessness that the Flathead braves felt as they watched in horror while the enemy was slaying their friends and family.

"They whipped their horses mercilessly as they crossed the plain toward their camp. Before they could reach it, two hundred Blackfoot warriors had slain most of The People in the camp, and disappeared into the forest." With the conclusion of the story, Dancing Bear went slowly around the fire, and then disappeared into the darkness of the camp beyond the fire. Mothers and grandmothers then shuffled away the wide-eyed children to their individual teepees. The young men around the fire sat silent as the Chief stood. He turned to each in turn. "Do not be fooled by this enemy. They are the most powerful warriors ever to roam on these grounds we are going to. They have been our enemy since the sun was created by the Great Spirit, and can walk through our camp unseen or turn your arrows back on you with the powerful medicine in the bags they carry." With this warning, he turned and went into his large teepee.

Jesse took Rose's hand and stood. Together they headed for their own small teepee as the young braves remained at the fire, quietly talking about how they would bravely defeat the ghost warriors of the Blackfoot.

Dancing Feet removed a small bundle from his waist. "I too have a powerful medicine bag." He emptied the contents on the ground before him. His young friends, several still in their teens, leaned closer for a look. "This is a grizzly tooth my uncle Wild Horse gave me." He pointed to each item. "This is a fang from a big rattlesnake that my father killed." His friends had no medicine bag and were very impressed that a warrior so young could already have so much power and protection at his calling.

As Jesse lay beneath the skins he said, "I have never seen the big herds of buffalo that your father has described. I am looking forward to getting to the plateaus to see them." He too would be very disappointed, but not on this night as Rose snuggled her body next to him.

The next several days were uneventful as the Indian Train wound its way east. After crossing the Bitterroot Range of high mountains, they were finally in Montana. Three more night camps were made until they reached the land of the old Chief's eastern family. Jesse McKannah rode beside the Chief as they approached Rainbow Lake.

"We will soon come to a high rise," the Chief said, "and we will look down on a small lake with a vast plateau beyond. As far as we will be able to see there will be moving bison. The Great Spirit has placed them here to join with the Flathead in their struggle to survive."

"Yes," Jesse replied, "the buffalo supply many of the things The People need."

"And many things of great pleasure too. We have survived many long periods on bitterroot and cama because the guardian spirit of the old woman put everything in them that the people need, but there is little pleasure after many moons of eating them."

Jesse could tell by the old Chief's voice that he had the expectations of a small boy who was returning once again to the buffalo plateaus. "There is no food so pleasant to eat as a buffalo tongue. I could eat it every night at the campfire for as many passings of the sun as the Great Spirit would give me."

"And there is no meat so tender," Jesse added, "as a chunk from the rear of the buffalo."

"Yes, yes," the Chief responded with a smile, and a twinkle in his old eyes, "and the many wonderful things the women make for us from the parts inside the belly." He spurred his horse on and leaned forward as the beast climbed the last rise to the top, overlooking the lake and plateau beyond.

Both men were stunned by the vast emptiness before their eyes. Jesse's disappointment was from stories heard around campfires. The Chief's was from memories of days past. The disbelief came through in his voice. "Where could they have all gone?" His vision stretched for miles in every direction, but not a single buffalo could be seen.

Jesse watched as the Chief slowly turned his head from south to north, then back again. When the Chief's erect back sagged and he slouched back on his horse, Jesse had the feeling he was watching a cold winter's night fire die. Something vital to this old Chief's survival left him on that cool fall day when the millions of buffalo deserted him forever.

When Lame Wolverine left the trail to Flathead Lake to join the Chief and his friend on the rise overlooking the plateau, he was also shocked to see the empty plains beyond. "I think they have gone to the other side of the world," the Chief said.

The three men sat silently staring at the world below, suddenly empty of the one thing this small band of Indians would need to survive the cold winter—that would soon be upon them. Jesse broke the silence. "I think my people are to blame for this." When both men turned and looked at him he continued. "When I got my supplies to go into the mountains trapping again, I heard stories about large caravans of white men going into these buffalo grounds and killing thousands of the great beasts. I thought they were just stories. Until now I did not believe that anyone could be so foolish."

The Chief looked at his white friend, then back to the barren plains. "Why would the white man want to kill all of them?"

Jesse sat silent a long time, trying to find some logical reason for his own people to commit such a terrible crime. There was no answer, and yet the answer was sickeningly obvious. When he spoke his voice was so hollow that both Indians turned to him. "The white men do not use the buffalo. They do not eat it, make their homes from it, or sleep under it. They are killing your people by killing the buffalo."

"Why do the white men want to kill The People? We have always treated the white men with honor and made them welcome guests in our land."

"I think your land is what they want. White men are greedy for land and will do anything to possess it. In California where I had my ranch, small wars were fought over land. The man I sent to the other side burned my ranch and killed my friends so he could have all of the land. I fear that the white men have seen something in your lands they want, and will do anything to have it."

The Chief had not stopped scanning the terrain before him, as though he expected the millions of buffalo to suddenly re-appear. When he did speak it was as though he was speaking to the ghosts of his past, rather than the two men beside him. "Long ago when the white men first came into our lands, the Blackfoot asked all of the Tribal Chiefs to come to a peaceful camp to talk. Many did not trust them and would not attend, but I and several others went." He turned to Lame Wolverine, "Your father was one who went with me. It was a peaceful gathering of Chiefs that lasted three days. We of the Salish tribes did not want war and said we would try to get along with the white men. All of the Blackfoot Chiefs said their Great Spirits had told them of the arrival of men with no color, and no honor. On the last night of the camp, the great Chief of the powerful Siksika stood and spoke. 'If you sit at these white devils fire they will empty your rivers of fish, take the trees from your mountains, and run the buffalo from your land forever. We will not let them on our land without a war. It will be better to ride with the buffalo to the other world than to sit in a white man's camp and wait for him to bring us meat that has worms in it, as our people that live where the sun rises have done.' I wish now that I had believed his warning was true." The Chief turned his horse toward the approaching Indian Train. "Come, we must be with our people when they see that there will be no buffalo."

That night they camped near their Montana relatives on the shores of Flathead Lake. After all had eaten and the utensils were cleared away, the local Chief began his story.

After you were last here, the white men began coming to kill the buffalo. There were so many buffalo that we did not mind. Then two years ago they began coming in great numbers in large wagons. They killed many of them for sport and left them to rot. We used as many as we could, but there were too many. The smell was so bad that you could not sleep at night. We tried to move away from the smell, but no matter how far we traveled, dead buffalo lay everywhere. Then the white men came in great wagons and took all of the buffalo bones that lay everywhere. As far as our eyes could travel, the prairies looked as though they were growing forests of white bones. Still there were so many that we did not mind, even though we thought all white men must be crazy. The smell soon went away so we were glad—life returned to normal. A year ago we noticed that the buffalo were not as plentiful, so we became alarmed and talked to the white men about it. They told us that their white Chief was going to give us all that we needed in exchange for letting them hunt the buffalo, so we went to our camps and waited. No supplies came from the white men. Last year we ran a small herd over a cliff so we could get what we needed to be prepared for the winter. White soldiers came and took us to the white man's fort. They put us in little rooms with iron sticks on the windows. Several of our older people died after a couple of weeks. When one moon went all the way around and came back, they let us out. They said we could not run the buffalo over a cliff like that because it was not right, and if we did it again all who were caught would be hung from the neck for breaking the white man's law. We must work very hard now to get a few buffalo because nothing has come from the Great White Chief to help us through the winters. We used to dig cama, bitterroot, parsnips, carrots and onions to make the meals of buffalo more appetizing, but now it is what keeps us alive. As our teepee hides wear thin and tear, allowing the wind to blow through, and we must live together in fewer teepees. During the winter we must huddle together under the few skins we have, so we will not freeze. When I went to the white general at the fort he said that many of the white man's sleeping skins would soon be here to keep us warm this winter. When the sun comes tomorrow you will see that there are no more fat women and children in this camp. They are thin now because there is not enough to eat and if they are not kept warm in the winter I fear that many will not survive.

Jesse turned to the Chief of the local people. "In all of this time the Great White Chief has not sent you anything to help you get through these cold winters?"

"Nothing. I do not think he will send anything until we give him our land. He wants us to go to a place called a reservation. It is just south of where we sit tonight, but it is not a good place to live. The white general said as soon as we sign our land over to him we will have more than we have ever had before. As I watch my people get thinner and thinner I fear that it is what I must do."

Jesse's friend, the old Chief, spoke with bitterness in his voice. "The Blackfoot Chief was right."

One of the younger Chiefs said, "The Blackfoot still do not let the white men on their land without war, so the white men do not go there."

"Tomorrow," Jesse said, "I will go to the white general and see if I can get us some help for the winter that is almost here."

The following morning Jesse was given directions to Fort Connah and was told that the general's name was Angus McDonald. By noon he was able to see the fort in the distance. He was very surprised at the size of it. There were several small log buildings, a corral, and a small bastion. When he rode through the unguarded entrance he was not challenged for his identity or asked about his business. He saw people standing in front of one of the small buildings as others entered and left. Jesse tied his horse to one of the roof support poles and dismounted. When he asked if the general was inside, the men all smiled as one old timer said, "General Angus? Sure is." He stepped up on the porch, opened the door and stuck his head in. "Hey Gen'l Angus, someone here to see you."

Simon remained a few hours at the outpost where the family was slaughtered. He was tired and needed some rest, plus he wanted to look for anything that might help him track the killer.

When he kicked a pile of old rags aside he spotted the doll. He picked up the wooden doll that he'd carved for the little blind girl when he stopped a few months earlier for supplies. As he turned it over in his huge callused hands, tears began flowing down his cheeks.

He flung the doll into the woods, and then wiped his eyes. They now had a hardness that few men, who ever saw it, had lived to tell about. *You're staying right where I find you, mister.*

After resting awhile inside the outpost with the door secured, Simon fixed himself some food from the provisions inside the log structure. Before leaving the building, he peered through a hole in the door to locate his horse that he'd hobbled nearby. He was satisfied there was not another human nearby because of his horse's casual grazing, so he went out and began another search of the area.

He kept seeing the same odd bootprints, so he continued until he was in an area with soft soil free of grass and weeds. He squatted and looked carefully at the bootprints. Finally he stood. *That guy's got a bad foot or leg.* He looked back down, *foot I reckon 'cause he drags it a little and the toe points in.*

Simon took two steps back then walked across the area next to the bootprints. He returned to carefully look at his prints compared to the other man's. *He's a little guy, or at least he's not heavy. Even if he's as tall's me he don't weight half as much.*

He followed the bootprints into the woods until he located where the killer had tied his horse. Simon squatted again and looked at the horse's prints. He stood and looked toward the valley east of the outpost. *You'll be easy to follow you sorry child-killer, 'cause that horse's needed shoeing for a long time.* He returned to the outpost to get his horse ready for the hunt. *The local Indians'll take good care o' that horse after I take care o' you.*

Two weeks later Simon knew he was closing in on the killer, partially due to the signs he was reading and partly because of a feeling in his gut. He had another feeling nagging him. *I might be taking this guy for granted. He just might be better in these woods than I've given him credit for and knows I'm close on his trail. Better keep remindin' m'self to be cautious.*

Simon moved ahead slowly when he became certain he was very close to the killer. *He'll make camp on top o' that rise over yonder tonight.* He continued until it was very dark then quietly dismounted. He fumbled in the dark with his bedroll until locating his spare shirt and canvas pants. Two hours later, after pulling up large mounds of grass, his horse was moving toward the small fire in the distance. It was something Simon had taught the horse to do when he first got him. The grass man was securely tied to the stirrups and was slumped in the saddle as Simon silently stalked through the woods.

When the horse was within shouting distance, Simon's voice carried through to the camp ahead. "Hello the camp. I'm wounded and need help, can I come in?"

"Sure," a voice called back, "c'mon in n' I'll do what I can for ya."

The hair on Simon's neck bristled when he realized how close the voice was. As the horse continued toward the fire, Simon headed silently toward the area that the voice had come from.

His eyes were adjusted to the darkness of the woods, because he hadn't looked at the fire but once to get his bearings. In the moon's faint glow he spotted movement and silently moved toward it. His Collier flintlock five shot revolver was in his hand—ready to fire. The shadow he was watching was so close to the horse that he could have touched it when the flash of the muzzle lit the night. The horse, unaware that a man was next to him, reared then leapt ahead toward the nearby fire.

Simon's barrel was almost touching the man's back when it exploded. The man's scream was piercing but Simon stood and mechanically revolved the chamber so that another shot was available. The man was moaning as Simon felt around until locating the man's hands, neither of which held the pistol. He grabbed him by the long hair and began dragging him toward the fire. He had earlier assured himself that the killer was alone, so he dragged him straight into the camp. His pistol was ready in case he was wrong and the killer had met another man at this spot.

Satisfied that they were alone, Simon poured himself a cup of coffee from the pot at the side of the fire then retreated to the darkness to watch the man writhing and moaning on the ground. His thoughts were of the little blind girl as he watched. *I hope it takes all night for you to die.*

An hour later the moaning had ceased and there was no longer any movement. Simon went to his horse, which had remained nearby, and tended to it. He then went to a pot next to the fire and saw that it held jerked meat in warm broth, and a package of hardtack sat on a rock. With his back to a tree in the darkness, he ate the beef then dipped the hardtack in the broth, before drinking it. After wrapping himself in his horse blanket Simon dozed on and off until dawn.

After getting his horse some water and moving to a spot where it could get better grass, he returned and removed the killer's boots. He was surprised to see that one boot was stuffed with rags, because he had never seen or even heard of clubfoot. *Poorsmith'll be able to identify him with these boots.* He went through the pocket and found nothing, so he searched the man's gear until he located the money. He counted the gold coins the man had stolen after killing the entire family. After wrapping them in a piece of cloth to be turned in to Mr. Poorsmith, he looked down at the killer. *Forty dollars. Killed 'em all for forty lousy dollars.* He shook his head slowly as he headed toward his horse.

Jesse heard a thundering voice come from inside, "Well tell him to come on in lad, tell him to come on in—or is it a she?"

When Jesse entered, a huge man with red hair that dominated the upper half of his head, and a beard of the same color that rested on his enormous belly, stood and offered his hand. When Jesse shook it and told him his name, the huge man smiled wide. "Aye lad, it's the Scottish Highlands y'be from is it?"

"No. My father Sean came here from Ireland before I was born."

"Well lad, that's a pity it is, not to be born in Scotland, but I guess it's better bein' born 'ere than in Ireland to starve to death." He returned to his ample chair and sat down. "And what is it I can be doin' for ya, lad?"

"I've come with a group of Salish Indians from the western lands, to visit with their relatives and hunt buffalo. We are all shocked at how thin they are with no buffalo to hunt. What in God's name happened to the buffalo?"

"God 'ad nary a thing t'do wi' it, lad. Tis the work of those ignorant politicians back east. Decided a couple o' years ago, they did, to acquire these lands, so they tried to negotiate a deal with the local Indians. My wife's Nez Perce and her people wanted nothing t'do wi' any kind o' deal that would give away their bloody land. Those bloodthirsty Blackfoot felt the same way. He pulled open an old wooden drawer and asked Jesse if he'd like a drink of good Scots whiskey.

"Thanks, but don't use the stuff."

The huge man poured himself three fingers depth in a tin cup then returned the bottle to the drawer. "Don't use Scottish whiskey, eh?"

"Don't use any of it." Jesse spoke while looking the man straight in the eyes.

"Betcher daddy's proud o' that, 'e is by Jesus?"

"Nope, my brothers all drank a little with pa, and they all thought I was a bit of a sissy."

"Well now lad, I s'pose that's understandable."

"They changed their minds when I was sixteen."

"Thought better of it did they?"

"Yeah," Jesse grinned, "after I whipped all four of 'em on the same day."

"Four brothers in a single day, eh?"

"Nope." He said matter-of-factly. "A single hour. I was arguing with pa, 'cause he said that my sister was too homely to get a husband. He didn't know how close she was and she heard him. My brothers come runnin' when they heard us hollering."

The big, redheaded man sipped his whisky and just mumbled, "Hmmm."

"About all those buffalo?" Jesse reminded him.

"Well, some o' the bloody Indians wanted to make a deal with the skunks the gov'ment sent out 'ere t'steal their land, but most said no deal. One o' those bright boys had been out 'ere several times and knew 'ow much these people depend on the buffalo. He went back and proposed that the gov'ment send wagon trains out 'ere to kill off the buffalo so's the Indians'd 'ave to deal with 'em. At first they just kilt the beasts and let 'em rot right where they bloody well dropped, but another smart feller found out that the bones made one of the best fertilizers there is when ground into dust." He reflected a moment then added, "To make those darlin' little ole eastern lady's roses grow, I s'pose. Anyway, they started killin' more n' ever so they'd rot and make getting' the bones easier. They'd kill 'em then others'd come along and cut out the tongue n' salt it down to carry back east to them fancy new restaurants. The rest of those magnificient animals just went back into the ground. Sorriest bunch of imbeciles, ever I seen, and runnin' the gov'ment they are." He drained the tin cup and pulled open the drawer again. After filling the cup half way, he pulled a wicked, sneering smile across his face. "And lad, twas all designed by our own new government leaders, and all of those men were paid with nice new gov'ment gold," he took a drink then added, "mostly stolen from Indian land."

Jesse had taken a seat and was leaning back against the wooden wall as he listened to the sickening story the man was telling. "The Indians say you told them there would be supplies sent by the government, but they have never received anything."

"I used t'get the gov'ment promises in me left hand, and pass 'em to the Indians wi' me right—no more. A month ago I got a message from a passing trapper saying that a wagon train full of supplies for the Indians was on its way. If it ever gets 'ere I'll pass it out to 'em, but I keep tellin' 'em to dig plenty of cama and bitterroot while they can."

"They call you general, are you with the military?"

"By Jesus no, lad." He slammed the empty cup down on the desktop and opened the drawer. "At times I think the bloody soldiers're worse than those shifty crooks in the gov'ment offices." He poured a full cup this time then continued. "Sent a detachment 'ere a coupla years ago, they did, to enforce their laws. The man was a captain, but everyone referred to him as The General. He kinda liked it, so that's what he became. A small band of Flatheads ran a little herd over a cliff for the old people to skin and prepare. That pissant captain about 'ad 'imself a fit. Them sorry government turds had him brainwashed." He grinned at Jesse. "Which don't take much doin' with a full time soldier. He was convinced that all them buffalo belonged to 'is bosses back east." He took a good pull from the tin before continuing. "Lad, that little pipsqueak of a captain," he shook his wooly red head before continuing, "was only about this tall, even with those special boots he had made with extra thick heels." He held his open hand at the bottom of his neck.

"Was gonna 'ang every darn one of them Indians, 'e was. He was rantin' and ravin' about 'ow it was cruel to run a bunch of animals off a cliff to their deaths. Lemme tell ya lad, I 'ad to use all o' me Scottish charm," he grinned, "that's wha' we call arse-kissin in a pinch, t'get that little dimwit settled down so we wouldn't wind up with another war."

"What ever became of him?"

"Got 'im a big gov'ment job back east, 'e did, by Christ. I wouldn't 'ave given a hoot m'self if they'd made 'im the next president, just so they got 'im outa 'ere." He finished his whiskey then smiled, "Guess wha' 'appened when that little turkey left?" When Jesse remained silent, he continued. "These Indians started callin' me General. I did everything includin' threatening to 'ang the buggers if they didn't quit, but didn't do a bit o' good. Even me own wife refers to me as The General."

"So what do you think'll be the outcome of all this?" Jesse asked, now starting to like the robust Scot.

"Pre-determined long ago, lad. The Blackfoot and maybe the Nez Perce'll 'old out to the last, and probably die fighting rather than give in. The rest o' these noble people will eventually give this sorry gov'ment most o' their bloody land and sit off in a corner wi' jugs of gov'ment supplied whiskey and wait to die."

"Are all of the buffalo really gone?"

"Nah, there's a few left here n' there, but not enough t'make any difference t'these poor people."

"For the life of me, Mister McDonald, I can't imagine how anyone could kill off so many of any animal in such a short time."

"Angus lad, just Angus. Y'know, I've already 'eard it many times around 'ere, mostly from passin' trappers. Courageous buffalo hunters they call 'em." With that said he opened the drawer with a slam this time. After pouring another tin cup, full to the top, he continued. "Courageous me wide Scottish arse. These Indians co'be called that because they ride right in with the herd to make enough kills, but those," he dramatically emphasized the next words, "**Great American Buffalo Hunters**," he slowly shook his head from side-to-side, "were a disgusting bunch o' psychos, and drunken losers. Do you know what a buffalo does when you shoot 'im?"

When Jesse nodded that he didn't, the man went on. "Drops dead, 'e does, 'cause e's easy to kill. Know wha' the thousands standing around 'im do?"

Before Jesse could even nod his head Angus added, "They just look down at 'im. Pow—another one drops—pow another drops—and another—and another 'till they're all layin' there on the plains dead." He drank half of the tin of whiskey before growling, "Guess wha' the Great Buffalo Hunters do next?" He stared through slightly bleary eyes at Jesse.

"Go find another herd?"

"Yes. Y'got it right, lad. And they kept doin' it for months on end. Day in—

day out, winter—summer, matters not—boom-boom-boom, kill the bloody buffalo. 'ad a motto, they did, those **Courageous Buffalo Hunters**. 'A dead buffalo is a dead Indian.' I'll bet 'istory's gonna make 'eroes and great men outa those dregs of mankind."

Jesse stood and walked to the small window, propped open with a stick, and looked out at the barren terrain. He studied the two groups of men standing in the sun talking. He spoke more to himself than to the man at the desk behind him. "The men who are replacing these noble people, who I've just begun to get to know, sure are a sorry lookin' bunch."

"Lemme tell ya som'n lad," the voice behind him boomed, "those're the cream o' the bloody crop." He slammed the desk with the palm of his hand and laughed loudly as he pulled the drawer open again.

Jesse turned. "Think it'd do any good for me to go to the government men and talk to them?"

"Think y'could get through a ten-foot-thick stone wall by buttin' yer 'ead agin' it, laddie?"

Later that night Jesse sat at Chief's campfire, explaining what he had learned from Angus McDonald.

At the very moment that he and the others were discussing what must be done to survive the winter with no buffalo, a small band of Blackfoot warriors were carefully studying a wagon train camped for the night about fifty miles from where Jesse and the Indians sat. They had been watching it all day. Foolishly, the Wagonmaster, young brother of a senator back east, had not instructed his twenty wagons to circle for the night and make the camp secure. The Blackfoot leader of the small band of warriors thanked the Great Spirit for sending him and his warriors a fool. They would wait until the white men were asleep and the two guards were dozing on their feet.

The wagon train had been contracted by the government to carry supplies to the temporary Indian Agent, Angus McDonald, at the Trading Post called Fort Connah. The politicians back east had held off as long as possible, but they were now getting pressure from civic groups—especially in Montana, to help the starving Indians.

Several senators contacted friends, and before long a purveyor was found in eastern Montana that was processing buffalo meat for pet food. He was told to stop immediately and set up his processing plant to salt cure the buffalo meat as food for the Indians. The man was told that large barrels were being made locally, and would be delivered in two weeks. He began converting his machinery to handle the lucrative government contract that his uncle had assured him would last for many years. Within a month he was ready to begin filling barrels with what he thought was, *Much too fine a meat to be giving away to a bunch of savages*. Since the government was supplying him with the buffalo meat, he soon began culling the better cuts aside for his restaurant customers who were serving it as ‘Corn Fed Beef’ and the Indians got what was left.

After stopping to load five wagons with thin blankets that were made specifically for the Indians, the wagon train headed for the processing plant to pick up the barrels of salted meat. The nights were getting cold, so one of the wagoneers opened a box of blankets and removed one. After opening it, he then held it up to the fire to inspect it. “Hey Pekitt, look at this.”

His friend walked over and observed the thin sheet of material. “Goldang, man, I wouldn’t blow m’nose on one of them things.”

“I wouldn’t either, ‘cause you’d git snot all over yer hand.”

The second man took it from his friend and held it in front of the fire. “Boy, these things’re thin alright. Hope them injuns ain’t as cold natured as that skinny ol’ woman of mine.”

The wagon train made its way to the processing plant, where they spent two days loading the barrels of salted buffalo parts. When the barrels were secured, and the wagon carrying the wagoneers’ supplies was replenished, it began the last leg of the trip to Fort Connah.

The thirty men had worked hard at getting the twenty wagons across the Continental Divide. Before heading into the pass through the Rocky Mountains, they were looking forward to a two-day rest at Big Salmon Lake. Of the thirty men that twenty-three-year-old Wagonmaster Whorley Schittle had hired, only two were veterans who had made several trips across the vast terrain they were navigating. Purvis Stamp was over fifty and had made the trip so many times he lost count. A lifelong love affair with whiskey had prevented him from ever leaving the employ of other men, but he knew what he was doing.

Addis Stanford was twenty years younger than Purvis, but had made several trips across these same mountains, and on one occasion had even gone to San Francisco with a Wagon Train. The two men were hired as guides by young Whorley Schittle to keep the wagons on the correct trail. The senator’s young brother was very taken with himself in his first responsible job for the government and wasn’t about to let an old drunk tell him what to do.

As the train approached Big Salmon Lake, Addis rode alongside Purvis. “What did Whoreshit say when you told him we better circle these wagons tonight?”

The emaciated old man turned his ninety-pound body around to scan the area. “Said he didn’t hire me to tell him how to handle the wagons.” He spit a blast of tobacco juice that almost covered a front hoof. “Tole him this is Blackfoot country and ifn they see this goldang train they’s gonna think it’s guns a’goin to the army.”

Addis turned his eyes to watch as the train passed the two men. “Think he’ll circle ‘em up anyway?”

“Probably not,” the old man grinned through blackened teeth, “said his brother the senator tole him there'd be no trouble at all with the Indians, 'cause they knew it was food n' supplies we's bringin'."

"Hell's Belles," the younger man mumbled, "now that we all know thet everthang's gonna be alright we can get a good nights rest." He shook his head then tightened the chin string to hold his hat secure. "I better run on ahead and be sure ol' Whoreshit don't get 'em too close to the end o' the lake or we'll have a helluva time getting' these heavy wagons outa there."

The two men sat by the campfire as the sun fell into the trees. They were both thankful that the young wagonmaster had listened, and didn't get too close to the soft ground on the south end of the lake. They were very unhappy with the way he allowed the wagons to pull to a stop in a shallow arc instead of the circle that would let the men protect themselves in the event of an attack.

As the Wagon Train was bedding down for the night, a few days ride away, Jesse sat with the old Chief amongst a council of Chiefs that had been called to discuss the problem of their starving relatives. "We must begin now," the old Chief said, "to get the best trappers of all the tribes to start setting traps for anything that will feed our hungry people."

Eaglefeather, Chief of the Kootenai, stood and addressed the council. "Our people have hunted the buffalo for so many years that it will be very difficult to teach them to hunt small animals for food, but you are right. We must begin teaching them now or many will not be here next year to teach the young braves anything." Jesse asked if he could talk to the council, and all agreed because they liked the white man who was living among them. "I think it would be good to teach the people in the spring how to plant crops that will let them eat, even if the trapping is not successful, and the buffalo do not return. On my ranch I planted crops that gave us plenty of food every year and I will show The People how if you want me to."

There was much mumbling and discussion among the various Chiefs. The old Chief waited until they had settled down then stood. "The Great Spirit has turned the world on its side and all of the buffalo have fallen off. If we are to survive, we must change the way we have lived for many winters. Our white friend can get information that we cannot, so we should let him teach our people how to do whatever is necessary to survive.

As Jesse and the Indians sat around their Chief's fire and talked about the many problems they were facing, another group of Indians sat quietly in the dark; softly discussing their attack strategy. Cave Bear, the leader of the Blackfoot warriors spoke. "We must move as the shadows move with the passing of the moon until we are so close to the guards that we can smell their breath. When we are all in position, a signal will be given. Our first attack against the guards must be as silent as the falling sun so we do not alert the others. We can then kill many of them as they sleep, and risk few of our warriors. There will be many guns and ammunition in these wagons with which to fight the white men who are taking all of the land, so we must make this a successful attack.

As trail wise as Purvis Stamp was, he didn't hear the Indian as he stealthily moved into position only a few feet from him as he stood the first guard. The other man was half-asleep on his feet as another Indian stood only five feet away.

Both men died instantly when the Indians heard the signal. Eleven more died silently as they slept. Addis Stanford heard a noise that brought him to his feet only to die with a tomahawk buried in the back of his head. His brief scream alerted the others who stumbled sleepily from their bedrolls to face similar deaths. Whorley Schittle was so dumbfounded when he climbed from his special bunk in the supply wagon that he stood placidly like a lamb as he was slaughtered.

When the Blackfoot began opening the barrels and crates, they could hardly believe their eyes. After every barrel and crate had been busted open and the contents scattered among the corpses, the Indians set fire to everything.

When the warriors returned to their tethered mounts Cave Bear said, "Whoever was waiting for those supplies will never see them, so it was a good raid."

A warrior next to him spoke. "I am sad that it was not the rifles we sought."

"There will be many more wagons I am sure." Cave Bear had long before seen the signs of the future, so he shook his head then added, "Many, many more."

20

~ Creaking wheels of government ~

Three days after the massacre at Big Salmon Lake, no word had arrived at Fort Connah. Jesse was at the fort, talking to Angus McDonald about the supplies that were supposed to arrive any day. “Did the dispatch say what was on the Wagon Train for the Indians?”

After filling his tin cup half full of whiskey, Angus returned the bottle to the drawer. “Food n’ everything they’ll need t’get through the bloody winter. ‘At’s what the dispatch said, but I wouldn’t quit diggin’ bitterroot till it gets ‘ere. Those politicians’ idea of food might be a long bloody way from wha’ we consider eatin’ stuff, n’ Christ ‘imself only knows what ‘everything they’ll need to get through the bloody winter’ might mean.”

Two days after the Blackfoot burned the wagon train and killed the men bringing it, a pair of young men heading for Great Falls, hoping to get work on a Missouri River Boat, stumbled across the charred remains of the men and wagons. When they saw the condition of the bodies and the remains of the wagons, barrels, and crates that had PROPERTY OF THE US GOVERN-

MENT stamped on them, the two men changed their plans and headed south toward Missoula instead. The Montana town and mission was almost as far as Great Falls, but the trail to their original destination was through Blackfoot country. The various Salish tribes, who were all friendly with white men, controlled the land between them and Missoula.

"Them dern Blackfoot are on the warpath again," were the first words out of their mouths when they got to Father Pierre-Jean de Smet's mission. After hearing their story, he asked them if they would go to Fort Connah and talk to his friend, Angus McDonald.

"He's the temporary Indian Agent until the government sends one out to establish an agency. I have no means to contact anyone, but he may be able to have someone traveling east carry a dispatch."

Both young men agreed. "Yes. Yes, of course. The government's gotta be notified as soon as possible. We'll need soldiers out here soon to put down this uprising."

"Perhaps it was just a few renegades?"

"Oh no," the younger of the two responded, "it was a war party all right. Musta been a hundred of 'em, judging by the tracks we saw," he turned to his friend, "ain't that so, Bevus?"

"Yeah, sure's shit stinks. Oops, scuse me Father. Anyway, there was at least that many. Poor fellas didn't have a chance against that many."

"Put up a good fight though," his friend added, "you could tell by readin' the sign that they was assembled just like regler sojers."

"Well then, the sooner you can get to Fort Connah to tell Angus, the better we'll all be in case it really is another Blackfoot uprising."

"Our horses are wore out n' so're we, so we'll stay here tonight then head on up there come morning. Right now I'm 'bout starved to death."

The following morning, the two men departed and covered the sixty miles through the mountains in good time. Jesse was back at the trading post talking to Angus McDonald when the two young men arrived with the news of the disaster at Big Salmon Lake.

Before telling their story, Elwood Waggoner looked at the small group of little log buildings. "I thought this here was a army post?"

"Yeah," Bevus Ramp chimed in, "how come they call this place a fort?"

Angus McDonald had little patience with young people, or any people for that matter, but a trader with a small mule train had arrived the day before with two cases of Scottish whiskey, so he was in a particularly good mood. "Don't know m'self 'ow it came t'be called a fort. Neil McArthur started this bloody place for the Hudson Bay Company in forty-six then I took 'er over two years later. I named it Connen after a river back in th'old country, but Francois Finlay there," he pointed to a small Indian sitting on a huge barrel of brine pickles, "couldn't pronounce it. Called it Connah, 'e did, so that's what everybody else called it, n' it's been called 'at ever since."

"Well you better start makin' it a fort 'cause we got us a war on our hands." Elwood Waggoner was so excited he strung his words together so fast that both men had a difficult time understanding him.

"Did you say a war?" Jesse asked.

"Yep," Bevus Ramp answered, "with them dern Blackfoot, agin."

After listening to the two men tell their story, Angus nodded at a small cabin. "That mule skinner's 'eadin' for Great Falls this afternoon, so I'll 'ave 'im carry a message to the gov'ment office there n' they can get a dispatch off to those fools in Washington." He turned to Jesse who was sitting on the steps listening. "Bad news for these Indians, 'cause they sure as 'ell won't send another one till they sort this mess out."

"Mister McDonald," Bevus said.

"Yeah?"

"Where can we find that mule skinner? Maybe he'll let us go to Great Falls with him?"

"Wi' 'is squaw in that cabin over there, 'e is." Angus pointed at one of the tiny log buildings, "But I would n'go rappin' on 'is door, I were you."

Elwood looked at the building then turned a dumb stare at Angus. Finally he grinned through gray teeth. "Uh yeah, I gotcha, we'll wait'll he comes out to talk with him."

"Bloody good idea, y've 'atched, lad."

Later that afternoon when the log door opened and a giant man stooped to come out, they were glad Angus had warned them not to bother him. Jesse had left for the Indian camp earlier, so Angus stood alone and watched as the skinner and the two young men headed for the trail to Great Falls Montana.

"Ghost horses." The old Chief said when Jesse finished telling him about the incident at Big Salmon Lake.

"That's what I figured too, 'cause there's not gonna be a big war party of Blackfoot jumpin' a few wagons."

"Frightened men see many things that are not there, but why would the Blackfoot burn the wagons with all of the supplies? They could have taken them back to their camp."

"Puzzles me too, Chief. I'm gonna ask Lame Wolverine if he will go with me to the lake so we can look for ourselves."

"Yes. Now I must call a meeting with the chiefs so they can tell their people that no supplies are coming."

Jesse and Lame Wolverine were very cautious as they moved through Blackfoot country toward the massacre site. It took them three days to arrive at the lake. Small animals and vultures had done their work, so there was little left of the men—just bones. The Indians had cut the horses loose to take them back to camp and set fire to everything else before leaving. Many of the wagons were only partially burned and the barrels of buffalo meat were scattered about the scene. As enormous as the piles of meat had been, it was all gone; consumed by a wide variety of animals always looking for food. The crates of thin blankets had been busted open, but the material was still there.

"Come look at this."

Jesse took one corner of the thin material his friend was holding, and stretched it out. "I can see why they didn't take these with them."

Lame Wolverine just shook his head as he continued looking at the pitifully thin blankets. "I wonder what kind of food was in the barrels?"

"I found a few scraps. Looks like cow hide or maybe buffalo hide. At any rate it wouldn't have been any better quality than these blankets."

It took a few weeks for the dispatch to finally reach the hands of Senator Avery Schittle. It arrived only an hour before he was to attend a cocktail party hosted by Madeline Roosevelt, Washington's new hostess elite. He enjoyed a rapt audience as he filled the story with details that were missing from the dispatch.

"There were several hundred of the savages, and my brother held them off for days until his ammunition ran out—poor little Whorley." He shook his head slowly from side to side and hoped that a tear or two would come to his eyes, but he wasn't a crier—no such luck.

"Oh, you poor dear." An overfed, matronly woman about the size of one of the lost barrels of meat, said as she patted him on the shoulder.

Senator Schittle was still trying to get a tear out of his ruthless eyes when a waiter arrived with another tray of Russian caviar, and champagne.

The forty-year-old Senator, only two years in the nation's capitol, was already gaining a reputation among his peers—a glutton. He would eat only the finest foods supplied by the Washington elite that cater to the men who wield the power.

Bits of cracker, and an occasional Russian fish egg, that his prehensile little tongue missed, flew in the direction of his audience as he continued to enhance his tale. So attentive were the people gathered around to hear about the massacre that several didn't even bother to brush away the tiny bits of food that landed on them.

"Those ungrateful savages mutilated my brother and those courageous men who stood shoulder to shoulder with him to the end. And what were these men doing out there?" He took advantage of the timely pause to consume another twenty dollars worth of the world's most expensive snack. "They were carrying food, blankets, medicine and many other things that could have made life for those savages a little better." Another pause and another twenty dollars worth of fish eggs disappeared. "No more." He dropped his head and was certain a tear was going to find its way to his eyes. "They're not getting another thing from this government, nossir. We've taken care of those savages long enough. All that we've done, and what do they do?" He lowered his head again then almost screamed, but remained stoic as he thought, *it's working, I finally got it.* "Kill my dear little brother." As he said these words a tear ran down his cheek. Not much, just one big tear—it was a start. He was quickly learning about 'The ways of high society in the nation's capitol.'

The round little man dramatically wiped the tear from his puffy cheek. "I'm going to President Fillmore's party this evening, and I assure you that I'm going to brief him on this disgusting situation out west." After another cracker piled high with caviar he added, "And I'm going to ask him to consider awarding my brave little brother a medal."

When he had finally departed for another group being served truffles and mutton, imported from Scotland, one of the ladies who had stood motionless as he rambled on said, "How disgusting."

A gentleman, who had listened and watched, replied. "Yes, he certainly is."

With a look of cultured indignity, the matronly woman replied, "I was referring to those savages."

"Oh." He walked away.

A week after they left, Jesse and Lame Wolverine were back in camp. The many campfires throughout the Indian camp lighted the night sky, and they were a welcome sight to the two weary men. When Rose saw them she smiled and began preparing two large bowls of woodchuck stew from the large groundhog she had found in her morning run of traps. As Jesse sat and quietly ate, she stayed as close to him as possible. Lame Wolverine's wife, Gentle Breeze, came to the Chief's campfire as soon as she heard that her man had returned. She too sat close to her man as he ate. The old Chief sat contentedly smoking his pipe until the two men finished eating and were sipping a cup of coffee.

Rose had been trading animals from her traps for the precious beans to make Jesse the bitter, black drink that he loved. She poured Lame Wolverine a cup but didn't pour one for herself or offer Gentle Breeze one. She did pour the Chief a larger gourdful than even Jesse's, and carried it to him. He smiled gratefully up at her and closed his eyes as he smelled the aroma of the coffee that he also loved.

Jesse finally spoke. "Something is not the way it appears with this massacre. We backtracked the Blackfoot to see what we could learn. It's very strange, because they did not send a scout out to locate victims for their raiding. The warriors went to a location a little distance from the trail that the wagoneers were using and just camped to await their arrival. It was as if they knew the Wagon Train was going to come right past them."

"Yes," Lame Wolverine added, "they remained hidden and observed the long train of wagons until it had moved past, then they went to a place above Big Salmon Lake and camped again to wait. They knew where the train was heading, so we think they must have a white man helping them."

Jesse sipped his coffee and shook his head slightly.

The Chief remained silent as he thought about what he had just learned. Finally he asked, "How many warriors were there?"

"Ten," Jesse responded.

"And you said there were three times that many white men. Those must have been very fierce Blackfoot."

"No," Jesse answered, "the men with the Wagon Train were either very stupid, very lazy or maybe both. They took no precautions against possible attack and even left the wagons strung out in a line." He shook his head from side-to-side. "I don't know why anyone would send men like that with a Wagon Train." He finished his coffee. "Especially one carrying the junk this one was."

"Why would they go to so much work to send a load of bad meat, and blankets too thin to use?" The Chief inquired of Jesse.

"Old friend, I don't know, but I'll try to find some of the answers."

The following day he went to Fort Connah to talk to Angus McDonald. After listening to Jesse's information he said, "Lotta skimmin' went on in that deal. Probably allotted a hundred thousand dollars t'get supplies out 'ere." He pulled open the drawer and emptied the bottle into his cup before continuing. "By the time all the politicians took a chunk, there probably wasn't but 'alf of it left, and then everyone else got a piece. A wee bit for the crate n' barrel makers—a little for the meat processor—a chunk for the mill owner where those sorry blankets were made—and who knows what other greedy fingers dipped into the pot? Probably wasn't enough left t'pay a decent crew t'bring 'er out 'ere." He opened the desk drawer and brought out a new bottle of Scottish whiskey. After pulling the cork he poured his tin cup half full and continued. "So y'think 'em injuns was in cahoots with someone, huh?" He sipped and looked over the rim at Jesse.

"Yes. Those Blackfoot knew exactly where that bunch o' wagons were gonna be n' when they'd be there."

Angus finished his whiskey and leaned back in the chair, staring at the ceiling. Jesse watched as the huge man pursed his lips over and over, chewing on something that wasn't there. After five minutes he sat back up and opened the drawer again. When he had the tin full and the fresh bottle back in the drawer he said, "Betcha 'ey was after guns."

"I had the same thought, but I don't think they got any."

"Why's 'at, lad?"

"If there had been guns they woulda took one of the wagons to carry 'em, plus the way they busted open everything." He paused, picturing the scene again. "It was like they were mad about not finding what they were expecting to find."

"Hmmm," Angus mused, pursing his lips again. "Could they 'ave found a few rifles in those blanket crates?"

"Nope, don't think so, they were too small." Jesse turned and looked out the open window trying to make sense of a senseless situation. "Startin' t'look like more'n one somebody was messing around with this load o' supplies."

"Yeah," Angus answered, "somebody didn't want those supplies t'get 'ere for these Indians."

Jesse mumbled, "Gonna be a terrible time for The People if this's a really bad winter."

As the two men spoke, another group of men were speaking to their chief. "There were no guns, only rotten meat and blankets that were not even worth bringing to our camp."

The chief of the Blackfoot sat in his council teepee and listened to the account of the raid by his most trusted war chief, Hook. When Hook finished and sat back down, the chief spoke. "The old white trader you deal with told you there would be guns on this Wagon Train?"

"Yes, my chief."

"He has deceived you then."

"Yes, and he will pay for it."

The chief sat and pondered the situation before commenting. "We can never trust the words that come from a white man's mouth—they know not truth."

Over a thousand miles away many people in Washington were talking about the massacre at Big Salmon Lake. The two men most concerned were gathered in Senator Lester Falworth's private study. The senator turned to his lifetime friend, Congressman Paul Swope. "Can we trust that trader to keep his mouth shut?"

"Doesn't matter," the diminutive congressman replied with a grin, "the man I sent out there to set it up didn't tell the old fool anything. He told him there were guns on that Wagon Train of supplies for the Indians who won't turn loose of that land we want. He's been trading with those Indians with black feet for a long time, and they believed him."

"We don't want Schittle to ever learn anything, because of his brother."

"I never met his brother, Lester, but judging by that fat little eating machine, I doubt if his death was any great loss to anyone."

The senator poured them each another fishbowl of imported cognac, then said with a treacherous twinkle in his eyes. "I sure wouldn't wanna be in that trader's shoes when he meets with those savages with black feet again." He laughed heartily and drank his cognac.

Alvin Pissit had the best load of supplies yet for his Blackfoot Indian friend, Hook. He had been in California since the raid on the '*wagon train full of guns*', and he had paid a considerable amount, to have them put in the hands of his Blackfoot friends. He was bringing them knives made of Spanish steel, several of the new revolving cylinder pistols, and several other items that he knew they would like, especially coffee beans. He also knew they would be pleased with the rifles. He had acquired them cheap, and knew they would pay a very high price.

Hook's scouts brought the news that he had waited long for. "Stinky Mouth is coming to trade." He never let any of the white men he traded with come to his chief's camp, so he intercepted the old trader a few miles from it.

Alvin Pissit was always surprised at the way the Blackfoot could step out of the surrounding forest that he'd been traveling through. He wouldn't see a single sign, and then suddenly there they were. He held his hand up toward Hook. "Hola, old friend. I have… he was shocked when two young braves jumped into his wagon and threw him to the ground.

Hook slid from his horse effortlessly and walked to where the old man was being held against the ground. Two more to secure his legs joined the two braves holding his arms. Hook looked grimly down at the old white man and spoke in a dialect that he knew the old man understood. "You deceived me, Stinky Mouth."

All Alvin Pissit could think as he lay on the ground was, *why did he call me stinky mouth*? His eyes widened when the man he'd been trading with for several years reached toward him. He saw an object in the Indian's hand, but didn't know what it was.

~ He was about to find out ~

Hook was not a man to be lied to. He had a short steel rod with a bent-back pointed end that he used to dissuade his own people never to lie to him. His hook always worked. No one had lied to him for many years—that was how he earned his name.

Alvin Pissit screamed when the pointed rod went through his tongue. His eyeballs bulged almost out of their sockets as his tongue was pulled far out of his nasty mouth. Even with the Indians holding him tightly to the ground his body convulsed in spasms as the pains shot through his frail body. Alvin Pissit's screams turned to a gurgling noise as Hook pulled the tongue even farther out of his mouth, then leaned down close to say in a variation of his language that the old man did not understand. 'When a tongue tells lies it must be removed.' He very slowly cut it off. Hook took a bite of the tongue as the old man watched through terror filled eyes. He removed it from his hook then tossed it to his favorite warrior who also took a bite before passing it to his comrades. Each shook the bloody tongue at Alvin before holding it high over their mouth to bite into it, grinning all the time at the old man lying below on the ground.

He was still trying to scream through the bloody mess as the warriors tied him around the waist then tossed the rope over a tree limb and hoisted him off the ground. He swung slowly back and forth as several warriors readied their bows. Another warrior retrieved a tree branch lying nearby to prod Alvin so that the old man's body swung back and forth. The Indians circled him on their horses, shaking their bows at him, all the while screaming insults—none of which he understood.

Hook gave a command and as he went through the wagonload of supplies. His braves began having a good time trying to see how many arrows they could shoot into the swinging body before someone accidentally landed a fatal one—none did. "Enough, we must go." Hook leaped upon his mount's back, "Lower him until his feet barely touch the ground and the animals will have a good time."

The Indians released the rope until Alvin's toes were just touching the ground, and then retied it. Before departing, one of the braves laughed. "That is strong medicine you use my chief." He pointed at Alvin, standing supported by the rope, with many arrows protruding from his body. "You have made a porcupine out of a white man." They all laughed as they rode away.

Alvin Pissit's arrow riddled body swung slowly in a circle on his toes as if he was a ballet dancer. He was still conscious when a thin cougar with ribs showing approached. His only thoughts were still, *why did he call me stinky mouth*?

21

~ *Buffalo—salvation at a price* ~

Fall had only recently been shoved out by a hard northwest winter wind. Things were looking very bleak for the old Chief's people and his relatives too, when two young Kootenai hunters came into camp with the best news anyone had heard in a long time. They went first to their own Chief, who brought the two men and the news to the old Chief's Teepee.

Jesse sat with his old friend who listened as the two young men related the story to the Chief.

"We were tracking a small group of deer when we came to the small canyon at the north end of Hungry Horse Lake. We both saw the signs but could not believe our eyes. We went carefully forward to look and there they were—buffalo. A small herd of about two hundred animals were grazing on the floor of the canyon."

"Is this the Canyon of Death you speak of," the old Chief asked, "where we have fought the Blackfoot many times in years past?"

"Yes Chief," the younger of the two answered, "we have hunted there many times and know it well."

The old Chief turned to his white friend. "It is a canyon that you must leave the way you enter."

"That oughta make getting a bunch of 'em pretty easy, but we'll have to be quiet about it 'cause we don't wanna let the Blackfoot know what we're up to or we'll have a war too."

"Yes, and we must not let any of the white men know because even though the buffalo are on our land, they will stop us from taking them."

"That is true," the Kootenai Chief added, "we must plan very careful, but quickly before the buffalo leave."

The two young Kootenai were sent throughout the camp to ask all chiefs to come to the main Salish Chief's teepee. In less than an hour they were all sitting around a roaring fire. Tactics were discussed that they'd use to get enough buffalo for the winter.

The Nez Perce Chief spoke. "We should not take the women or children. If the Blackfoot see us we will have to fight them."

"I agree," the Pend d'Orielle Chief replied, "we must go in quickly and as silently as we can. We will not be able to take every piece of bone as we normally do, but we can bring back the hides, and the meat."

Each time-tested Chief offered something to the council and by midnight it was settled. Each group would select ten of their tribe's best hunters who had great stamina, so they could get there and back in as little time as possible.

After they all returned to their own camps Jesse said, "It is a wise thing you did, my friend. Sending each group a few hours apart will not appear suspicious in the event they are seen traveling north."

"Yes. My brother's Flatheads will be the first to leave, just before dawn."

"Lame Wolverine and I will choose the best eight men, just as you said, and arm them with the best rifles in our camp. We will be the last group to leave so we can watch for anyone following."

The old Chief slowly shook his head up and down. "All of the Medicine Men will be talking to the Great Spirit to ride with you. This buffalo hunt will help our people, and it will be the difference in living or dying to many of these people who we have come to visit."

An hour before dawn, the old Chief's brother's ten chosen Flatheads slipped quietly out of camp. They had decided that a second horse to carry the meat and hides home would look suspicious, so the men were on the strongest horses the camp had. Each would have to pull a loaded travois on the return journey.

At three-hour intervals another ten men would casually ride from the camp. The second group was Kootenai, then the Kalispell, Pend d'Orielle, Spokane, Nez Perce, and finally Jesse, Lame Wolverine and their eight Flathead braves. As Northern Montana's winter winds whipped through the Rocky Mountains, a long strung out train of Salish Indians headed for a small canyon fifty miles north. It held the answer to the survival of their starving relatives in the camp behind them.

The men dismounted at regular intervals and walked beside their horses to give the beasts a rest from their weight. They stopped every six hours to rest and let the horses eat grass. While the horses grazed, nine warriors slept as one stood guard at the best vantagepoint. After one hour the guard was relieved, and they headed north again. It was exhausting, but before dark on the third day the first ten men arrived to find the buffalo still grazing.

These ten young Indians had never seen a large herd of buffalo. They had heard only stories of the great black masses moving across the Great Plains and on the plateaus in these mountains. To actually see them below the bluff from which they watched was an indescribable event in their lives. They alternated guard duty and just lay silently and watched until there was no light remaining in the sky. It was to be the last large herd, if these pitiful few could be called a large herd, which any of them would ever see. The memory of it would last until they were old men.

Jesse, Lame Wolverine and their eight warriors finally arrived. No fires had been lit since the arrival of the first ten men, and now the seventy men gathered a short distance away to chew jerky and lay their plans.

The men knew that every Chief respected this white man's opinions, so when Jesse spoke, they all listened. All of these men from the western regions of the Salish Indians that were chosen to go on this mission were too young to have ever been on a buffalo hunt. They all knew that Jesse had never hunted the buffalo either, but they felt that his white mans knowledge and his skill with the fine rifle which the Chief of the Flatheads had presented him with, would insure success.

"We are going to take fifty of the animals," Jesse began, "when we have them all loaded and are ready to head home we'll send eight men out front to be sure we are not caught in a surprise ambush by the Blackfoot or the white soldiers. Lame Wolverine and I will remain behind with our eight braves. We all have rifles to cover the rear in case we are discovered and followed." He paused to chew on his jerky and allow the men to absorb what he had just said.

"Now," he continued, "about the taking of these animals. I have been told by many buffalo hunters I have talked to, that if a man is a good shot and can make a clean kill, these great beasts will not be alarmed when one of their number falls right beside them. Since the white man at Fort Connah supplied me with bullets for my rifle, I have practiced much and I think the sound from the rifle will remain in the canyon. If we try to chase fifty of them into the end of the canyon for the kill, I believe many will turn back and escape. I can move to a ledge I have located that will put me above and very close to them. I can kill fifty without disturbing the rest of the herd."

Those who had been chosen as leaders of their small groups nodded their heads. “Yes. It is a good plan. Those who came early have already cut travois poles, so while you are killing the buffalo we will be attaching the poles to the pulling harness on the horses.”

“Very good. Then, while you skin and cut up the animals, the eight warriors will be scouting the trail home, while those of us remaining will scout the surrounding area.”

Lame Wolverine spoke. “I feel the presence of the Great Spirit. Our Medicine Men have sent them to help us bring these supplies to our starving people. We will be successful,” he said with positive conviction. As the others began rigging the horses for the difficult journey home, Lone Wolverine took his eight warriors in an attempt to turn the buffalo back into the canyon if they attempted to flee. Jesse slowly worked himself into position to begin the kill as soon as it was light enough.

When the first buffalo dropped where it had been standing, Jesse held his breath. *No reaction at all from the others*. He quietly levered the trigger guard to send another shell into the weapon then took a deep breath and held it as he squeezed the trigger. Another great beast fell where he had been grazing, and still no reaction from the others. It saddened him somewhat to see such a magnificent animal die so effortlessly, but he knew what rested on his skills, so he continued until the fifty bullets he’d counted out were gone. Jesse’s skill with the rifle would become part of the legend of White Buffalo.

As he, Lame Wolverine, and their warriors scouted the area beyond the canyon, the remaining fifty men began skinning the buffalo and attaching the hides to the travois. When Jesse and his men found no sign beyond the canyon, they returned to where the men were almost ready to begin the trip home. He was amazed at how quick the men had butchered the buffalo and had the meat bundled on the buffalo skin travois. There was a large pile of meat and bones that could be used, but each horse was loaded with what it could pull, so it had to be left behind. There was still plenty of daylight remaining when the long train of horses, with the Indians walking beside them, headed south.

Jesse had been correct about the sound remaining in the canyon; not a shot was heard. What he could not have known though, was that a band of thirty Blackfoot warriors was returning from a raid on a peaceful group of Flatheads camped on Whitefish Lake. They would use the trail on the north edge of the canyon on their way back to their own camp. The breaking dawn revealed the buffalo below, they too were happy because it would make their winter much better. “Look,” one of the braves said as he pointed down toward the pile of meat and bones left behind several hours earlier.

Eye of Eagle, so named for his incredible eyesight, spotted the travois drag tracks leaving the canyon, even though Jesse and the others had removed all traces of their exit. Without a word, Eye of Eagle headed toward the trail.

~ It wasn't going to be an uneventful trip home for Jesse and the Indians ~

Jesse's eight scouts had headed south even before the skinning and the butchering began. These young men knew that their task was very important. If they did not cover the terrain well, their friends might walk right into an ambush. That would not only be a disaster for the hunting party, but would mean death for many of their people in the home camp. They were the best trackers among Jesse's new friends and were being led by Stalking Cat. He had been named that as a small boy of six, when his family realized he had extraordinary tracking talents. Until he was ten, they tried many different tricks to foul his attempts to follow warriors, but never once did they succeed in escaping his vigilant pursuit. Now at twice that age he was twice as good. As Stalking Cat's men scattered out two miles in each direction, moving slow and silent at his signals so they wouldn't be seen, he ran noiselessly through the forest behind them to double check their findings. After covering five miles of trail he was certain that no one was ahead in the forest. He sent his swiftest man back to the main party to give them the news.

Jesse, Lame Wolverine, and their warriors watched as the last horse-drawn travois left Hungry Horse Canyon. Lame Wolverine turned to the others, "Sleep for the two hours that we will wait before following. I am not tired so I will watch over you." He did not have to coax Jesse or any of the men—they were exhausted.

The sun had taken its daylight below the horizon only moments before Jesse's eyes opened as his friend's hand touched his shoulder. "It is time to follow." Each man came to his feet and rubbed sleep from tired eyes, then stretched to limber up sore muscles. Five minutes after being awakened, the small rear guard was moving along the same trail that the hunting party used. At the exit from the canyon and for the first two miles, the men used stout branches they had gone deeper into the forest to cut from trees, and swept away the tracks left by the horses and travois. They moved with a deliberate slowness to make the trail as hard to follow as possible and to remain at a distance of about two miles from the main group. When a moonless dark finally engulfed the forest, the trail became very difficult to follow, which pleased Jesse and Lame Wolverine.

"We know where we're heading, but if someone tries to follow it will be very difficult."

"Yes, but if the Blackfoot come upon our leavings in the canyon and decide to follow, they will find the trail."

"I've heard they're very good trackers."

"Very good," Lame Wolverine said with an ominous tone to his voice.

"Do they ever attack at night?"

"They are a very unpredictable people, but no, they usually prefer to be in a position to attack at daylight."

"Like they did at Lake Coeur d'Alene?"

"Yes, that's the way they like to attack, but I was told a story when I was young about a time when they attacked our people in that same canyon we just left by coming down from the top on ropes to attack the sleeping hunters at night."

"Hmmm," Jesse mused in the dark, "that's pretty unpredictable."

"We will be on guard until we reach our home camp."

It was pre-arranged that the main body of hunters would move for six hours, and then stop to rest and let the horses also rest for two hours until they arrived home. After six hours of travel Jesse said, "Let's take our two hours of rest. You get some sleep while I post our guards."

"Yes. I am very tired now." Lame Wolverine was soon asleep.

Eye of Eagle moved back and forth across the exit from the canyon, as his Blackfoot warriors stood silently watching. He seldom went out on horseback, preferring to move through the forest on foot when leading a war party to an attack. He and the twenty-nine men with him were as close to perfect human specimens as could be found on earth. When it was called for, they could move along a trail twenty out of twenty-four hours, and eat on the move. Their motivation in this life was to make war on their enemies, so they would be given a better life in the Dark Beyond, as described by the Great Spirit through their Medicine Men.

After twenty minutes of constant moving back and forth, Eye of Eagle gave a screeching eagle call and waited for his warriors to come over the hill to him. "Many horses pulling heavy loads." He pointed in the direction Jesse and the hunting party had gone. He and two of his best trackers moved ahead of the warriors as they started along the trail south.

Jesse and three men watched over the sleeping group for an hour then awakened another four to finish the watch. The twelve men began searching out the trail, moving slowly south toward home. Most of the Indians were chewing jerky, but Jesse was crunching the coffee beans that Rose had given him before leaving. *Ain't like hot coffee, but ain't bad, thanks Rose.*

The eight scouts in front of the main body of hunters were on the same schedule as the rest. They would scout the area in front of the advancing travois train for six hours, then post guards and rest for two hours. After a difficult night of looking for any sign of company, the morning sun was a very welcome sight. Stalking Cat was a good judge of time and distance. After almost eighteen hours of travel, he calculated that they had covered about one third of the distance to their home camp. *Very good, and still no sign of anyone in the forest with us.*

A couple hours before dawn, Jesse's group took another two-hour break to sleep. Lame Wolverine stayed on the two-hour watch with the other three men for the entire two hours. Something was pulling his eyes into the forest behind them, but he could see nothing. During the last hour, he slipped away and backtracked their trail for about half a mile—nothing, but the nagging feeling was still there. He could almost smell danger moving toward them. He returned and woke Jesse. "I have a feeling that we are being followed."

"See som'n?"

"No, but something in this forest is not right. Be very alert this day."

Dawn flooded the forest soon after they began moving again and it felt great, until Lame Wolverine pointed toward the sky. "Storm coming from the northwest."

The others had been so occupied with tracking the main group that they had not seen the storm building to their rear. Jesse turned. "Those're snow clouds."

"Yes. Let us hope that it does not come down too heavy for the horses to continue, but a light snow will cover our tracks"

Three hours later, Jesse and the others dismounted to walk beside their horses and give them a rest. Lame Wolverine pointed at the trail. "They stopped here briefly to tie more poles to the worn out travois. They stopped to add one whenever necessary."

"You figure we're making good time?"

"Yes, we will soon be half way to our camp where The People wait."

The clouds built throughout the day, and by evening it began to snow lightly. The movement through the night went as it did the night before, but just before dawn, Lame Wolverine silently woke Jesse. "We are not alone in the woods."

Jesse stood and stretched the stiffness from his forty-seven-year-old bones, as his friend woke the others saying quietly, "Remember what you have learned about sequence firing, because we are not alone."

Jesse and Lame Wolverine rode side by side in the rear of the group. "Did you see the enemy?"

"No, but I went far to the rear and listened to the forest. Something is not right. The tiny animals and birds are changed by something. It is the same when a grizzly comes into the area—everything sounds different."

"Could it be a grizzly tracking the meat on the travois?"

"No. A grizzly is not careful. He moves through the forest with no fear, but whoever is with us is moving very careful."

"Blackfoot?"

"Yes. They move in the forest like shadows." He and Jesse kept looking to the rear as they nudged their horses over the top of a small rise. Snow was now falling enough to put a small white cover on the ground. Lame Wolverine said, "We will tie our horses in that ravine and wait here." They hurriedly rode to the bottom of the ravine between the two small hills and tied the horses. Dawn was lighting the woods by the time they returned to the top of the hill.

"We will have an edge by holding the high ground."

Ten minutes later, the first of the thirty Blackfoot could be seen moving carefully across the ravine below. The twelve men on top of the hill were in position and watching the Blackfoot advance.

Eye of Eagle knew it was only a small rear guard he was advancing on. He expected them to make a temporary stop in an effort to slow his men down to give the main body of travois laden hunters time to get closer to their camp and call for reinforcements. He was confident that his thirty Blackfoot warriors would easily defeat this handful of men, and move on toward the main group. There was no way he could have known that he was facing eleven deadly accurate shooters that would employ a technique of sequence firing that he had never faced. There was also one white man with a new rifle capable of firing several times while the Blackfoot restrung their bows and loaded primitive muskets.

At twenty yards from the top of the hill they were advancing up, Eye of Eagle and his warriors were given a lesson in warfare tactics that would send shockwaves through the Blackfoot nation.

Jesse had a position off to the side so he could concentrate rapid fire at the enemy without interfering with the other eleven shooters. When he yelled, "now" four men stepped from behind trees and took quick, but careful aim and dropped four Blackfoot in their tracks. When the four moved back behind their trees to re-load, another four stepped out and repeated the action with the same results. There were now eight dead or wounded Blackfoot warriors. Lame Wolverine and his two shooters followed the other eight and dropped another three. During this time, Jesse had fired five times and dropped five. Eye of Eagle realized that he had walked his men into a trap of many warriors and must retreat with his remaining men. The men on the hill hooted at the retreating Blackfoot, as they raced across the snow-covered ground.

After finishing off the wounded and removing all the scalps, the twelve uninjured scouts returned to their duty as rear guard. It was snowing harder now, and they were cold and tired, but every brave was exhilarated by such a decisive victory over their ancient enemy.

Aleena McKannah was absolutely mesmerized by the handsome young professor. It was the first time in her young life that any man had paid particular attention to her. She was in her fourth year of teachers college, and they had been classmates and friends during the last few months at the school.

Joshua Elisha Panderholt arrived from New York City with his parents during the winter of 1826. His father, Maurice Pellet Panderholt, was transferred to Boston to assume the head position of the firm he worked for in New York.

Along with a substantially higher salary came many side benefits such as a huge house on Knob Hill, overlooking the harbor, and immense prestige—both of which Mrs. Panderholt accepted with enthusiastic pleasure. Her automatic membership in Boston's prestigious Knob Hill Ladies Society was the beginning of her climb to the top of Boston's *upper crust.*

~ It was also the beginning of the end to Aleena's dreams ~

Aleena's heart beat faster and her breath came in short bursts each day as she headed toward Professor Panderholt's classroom. Always particular about her appearance, Aleena now became fanatic. She weighed each piece of garb against the others she would wear that day, often going through everything that she owned before deciding which to wear—for Joshua. *Joshua*! *Oh, I just love that name.* She had never addressed him as anything except Professor Panderholt, but always thought of him as Joshua. Her dreams were greater than she had as yet ever dared to dream and her future had never been as bright.

On a beautiful, clear spring day she arose after a night filled with dreams of love and began following her classmates from the classroom when the professor called her name. "Miss McKannah." She thought for a moment that she would faint.

Regaining her composure, she turned toward him while holding her breath, and barely able to say, "Yes Professor Panderholt." When asked to remain in class a moment, butterflies began a ballet in her stomach. "Yes, of course."

After all other students had departed the room he spoke. "Please have a seat, I'd like to talk to you a moment if you don't mind." He was as nervous and self-conscious as a young man could be when alone in the presence of a young woman. To Aleena he was charming, handsome and intelligent. To the other girls in his classes he was dull, boring, homely and stupid.

When he began fidgeting with the papers on his desk, Aleena was surprised. She could tell that he was not at ease. *Could I have done something wrong?* Whenever he was in front of the class he was perfectly at ease and in total control. Now he was having difficulty looking directly at her. "Have I done something wrong, Professor Panderholt?"

"Oh no." He was suddenly looking at her with alarm. "Oh, dear me no, Aleena." He actually blushed then asked, "I hope you don't mind me calling you by your first name?" She was so taken aback by his tender, concerned approach that she also blushed.

"Of course not, professor."

"Well uh," he stammered, "perhaps you could refer to me as Josh, well uh, only when we are not in the classroom of course." He was now wringing his small, delicate hands together.

"Well uh," she was now also nervous, "yessir, of course, professor," she looked quickly around, then seeing that they were alone added, "I mean Josh."

His pale, child-like face erupted in a wide smile as he laughed. She giggled as he came around and leaned against the huge oak desk. "Josh and Aleena it is then." Another grin, "When we're not around other students, of course."

Her own huge grin, when she said, "Of course," bolstered his confidence and he felt at ease. It was his first encounter of any sort with a female other than his overbearing, domineering mother.

"Aleena, would you like to go for a walk and see what new colors have popped out on the trees?"

"Oh yes, I love walking through our beautiful campus park." She got her light jacket from the closet as he put on his coat that hung nearby. It was the last class of the day, so he locked the door and they walked side-by-side down the hall toward the main door. They made an odd looking couple. He very short and delicate, she very tall and gangly—both physically unattractive.

They spent a month, meeting daily for a walk in the park, a stroll around the lake, or simply sitting on the stone wall, talking about their individual plans for their future. "I hope one day to get a position at Harvard teaching English and poetry."

Aleena looked at the young man of her dreams, through stars that flickered about his handsome face each time she looked at him. "Oh Josh, you would be the best professor they ever had. I hope you get the job." Secretly she wished, *I hope you stay right here and marry me so we can have a dozen lovely children and be happy like mama and daddy were.*

"Do you still plan to accept the position they're offering you here, Aleena?"

"Oh yes, Josh. It's more than I ever dared dream for myself." She thought to herself, *but I'll go wherever you ask me to go.*

"Well," he said, "it's only about two hours from here to the Harvard campus, so if I do get that position we can still get together occasionally for our walks."

"Yes, I would miss them terribly Josh." Aleena loved the sound of his name and used it as often as she could. To herself she often ran their names through her head. *Josh and Aleena—Aleena and her husband Josh—Mister and Missus Josh Panderholt—Josh, Aleena, and their lovely children.*

"Well, we'll have many walks around that lake before then because I'll have to be in this position at least four years before I could even apply to Harvard."

Thank you Lord, Aleena thought as she looked at him.

Another month passed and the young couple placed many footprints on top of the ones they had already made upon the paths through the park and around the lake. They fed the swans so frequently that the birds came quickly across the lake as soon as they arrived. Love had exploded inside Aleena's heart and Joshua realized that he was also in love with the tall bright student who would soon be joining his ranks as educater.

"Mum's planning a garden party now that the weather has warmed a bit."

He took both her hands in his. "Would you like to go and meet my mother and father?"

"Oh yes Josh, I'd love to." *Oh dear Jesus, he really is serious about me. Thank you God, thank you Jesus.* She had prayed every night on her knees beside the bed, that Josh would fall in love with her.

"Wonderful. It's going to be next Saturday afternoon, so I'll pick you up in my father's carriage." He took her hand and held it tighter than ever before as they continued around the lake; he solidly touching the stones—she floating above them.

Aleena began the day of the party at dawn, removing one dress after another and holding them up to her long frame, now slightly over six-feet-tall. After hours of indecision she finally settled on the outfit that she would wear. She then spent two hours working with her stringy, bodiless hair. She did everything she'd learned and soon had her enormous ears partially hidden behind carefully sculptured hair. She stood in front of her full-length mirror practicing with her hands. After bending down, she straightened, and with a practiced movement had the ears back beneath her hair.

Aleena heard the campus clock strike one and knew that Josh would be arriving soon. One last inspection and she was out the door. As soon as she reached the bottom stone step, Josh's carriage rounded the corner. A huge black driver in full livery sat atop the ornate carriage, as another in less colorful attire came from the rear where he rode standing. Josh remained in the open carriage as the footman ran to Aleena, "Step right this way, miss." He gently held her hand in his callused, butterscotch colored hand as she boarded. The carriage started before he had the door completely closed so he struggled with it then ran along behind and jumped aboard his small protruding platform.

One lane was reserved for the Panderholt carriage, so Aleena watched in awe as they passed what seemed like a hundred beautiful carriages. *My goodness, his parents must be fabulously wealthy.*

After walking through manicured trees enclosed by white iron fencing, and passing groups of people accepting mint juleps; testifying to his mother's southern roots, they finally came to a huge woman dressed in frilly wear and sporting a gigantic hat. Although Aleena had never seen a Southern Belle, she knew from reading, that Joshua's mother was trying hard to portray one—and failing miserably.

Before reaching her small group, Aleena heard her call to a black servant in red velvet garb. "You there. Yes you, boy, come here and refresh this drink."

Aleena suddenly had a feeling of dread wash over her. She glanced at Joshua who was standing beside his mother, holding her hand. She realized that he was looking at his mother with adoring affection. Her feeling of dread intensified. The beautiful afternoon sky suddenly turned dark gray through the young girl's eyes, and a feeling of doom swept over her—with good reason.

The afternoon party went wonderful for everyone who attended—except Aleena. Madeline Aluvia Panderholt treated Aleena as though she was applying for a position in her household. Her obvious appraisal was so intensely inspective that Aleena had trouble breathing. Her three hours at the party were dragged out to a hundred, and she was grateful when Joshua asked if she was ready to go home. Once in the carriage she said, “Your mother doesn’t like me.”

“Oh nonsense Aleena, she’s always like that when she meets someone new.” He turned and smiled at her but the stars couldn’t be seen through the gray clouds around his head. “She’s really a wonderful person once you get to know her.”

I have a feeling that’s never gonna happen. She smiled at Joshua then turned and looked one last time at the large grassy area full of people. *I doubt I’ll ever be asked to return here.* Her intuition was always good—this time perfect.

“Who is that dreadful beanstalk you brought amongst my guests?”

“Why she’s, uh I mean Aleena is, uh,” Joshua was always in a state of distress when confronted by his mother. He began again slowly. “She’s a student, uh well not exactly just a stu… he was interrupted before completing the sentence.

“A student. She’s one of your damn students?” His mother’s harsh voice was always terrifying to the diminutive boy, who she’d always compared to his small, round, slightly effeminate father. “What in God’s name were you thinking?” She leaned down to stare at him as she continued in a much higher voice. “You invited an ugly little schoolgirl to my party?”

“Well, uh, she and I uh…

“Do you realize that every single person at that party today was carefully selected by me? I am trying to elevate your father to a position of prominence in this community,” she turned her attention to her husband standing placidly next to the fireplace, glancing through a book of poetry, “even though I fear it is a futile effort with him.”

She glared hard at her son then turned and abruptly threw her glass of whiskey against the wall. Turning back to Joshua she growled. “You and that ghastly beanstalk, what?” Her eyes bore into his mind intensely and he was unable to speak.

Finally he stuttered, “I, uh, we er uh, I like her very much mother.”

She literally screamed at the servant standing near the bar. “Get me another glass of whiskey.” She returned her glare to her son. “Impossible.” She glared at her son. “Impossible.” She repeated. “They must have switched babies the day you were born. You couldn’t possibly be from my loins.” She accepted the whiskey then pointed the glass at her husband. “Even with his sperm donation, my strong character would still have dominated. No. You’re mother must be some washerwoman or fishwife sitting near a campfire somewhere with my strong domineering baby." She downed the whiskey, threw the glass against the wall, and turned toward her husband. "Follow me Maurice, we've got to discuss this."

The little man sat his book down and waddled through the huge archway trying to catch up to his wife.

On Monday, Aleena entered Joshua's classroom with intense trepidation. He conducted his class as though in a fog, seldom looking at Aleena. She stalled until all of the students had left the room then said, "You look terrible Josh, is it because of taking me to your mother's party? She wasn't happy at all to see you with someone like me." She was now fighting to contain the tears that were trying very hard to fall down her cheeks.

In a voice barely above a whisper he said, "Mother is having my father use his influence to get me transferred to this school's other campus in New York." He looked up at Aleena then reached out to accept her hand. "I love you Aleena and would rather die than leave here."

"Please don't say that Josh." The tears won and were flowing down her unpowdered, blotchy face. "If you're transferred to another campus then I'll just transfer too."

He silently shook his head in agreement, and then as the bell sounded to begin the next class, they each went about their day.

When Aleena entered Joshua's classroom on Tuesday he wasn't there. The students all waited at their desks and worked at their assignments until the bell rang. Before reaching his classroom on Wednesday, a student approached Aleena. "Did you hear about Professor Panderholt?"

Something made Aleena's heart skip a beat several times and her voice quivered when she answered, "No."

"He's dead. Hung himself from a tree in the park there." She pointed to the area that Aleena had walked many times with the young professor.

Aleena was barely able to make it the few feet distant to a huge boulder to lean against. "Oh dear God. Oh no, no, no." She held her hands to her face and sobbed.

The surprised student asked, "You gonna be okay?"

Unable to stop sobbing, Aleena just nodded her head and watched as the girl walked away. She didn't go to any of her classes for the rest of the week but on the following Monday she was up and dressing for class. *No more men for me. I'm gonna be the best darn old maid professor these kids ever had to teach them how to be schoolteachers.*

~ She was ~

22

~ *A legend begins* ~

As the men began entering the home camp with their snow-covered loads of buffalo meat and hides, all welcomed them. Word was sent throughout the camp for the chief's to come for the division of the supplies. The tired horses were used to pull the travois loads to the various tribes then were thoroughlly rubbed down, and allowed to graze on what greenery they could uncover through the deepening snow. They had earned a rest.

The hunters were also treated to the best feast that could be supplied. Buffalo tongue was stewed with wild onions, parsnips, and carrots. The ovens were filled with cama and bitterroot, while acorn meal cakes were fried on flat rocks in the fire.

Dancing Bear had been interrogating the hunters since their arrival, and by nightfall he had enough of the details to begin his story. Those he lacked, he made up as he went along. He would get it straightened out later, but a great victory story was called for this night. Large amounts of sassafras tea were made to hold off the cold biting wind. The warrior/hunters sipped tea and sat beside their mates as Dancing Bear told of their cunning pursuit of the mighty buffalo. The children listened with rapt attention to the details of the hunt, but when he spread war paint across his face to begin the story of the attack by the dreaded Blackfoot warriors, they began moving closer to the adults. By the time Dancing Bear began the pantomime shooting, a dozen children closely surrounded Jesse and Rose.

Almost a hundred miles away at the Blackfoot camp on Horse Lake, Eye of Eagle and his few remaining men came into camp a day after Jesse and the Salish hunters returned to their camp. When the people saw that many of the men who had gone to attack the Flathead Indians were not among the returning warriors, a wailing rather than a victory celebration began. There was no feasting at the fire that night—only a death-dance to wish the departed warriors a safe journey.

The following day, Hook sought out his friend Eye of Eagle. "You are a great warrior that sees everything. How did this happen?" He was sincerely concerned about this incident that he could never have imagined occurring. Eye of Eagle looked intently into his friend's eyes as he answered. When he finished the account of the battle Hook asked, "Are you certain it was a white man, and not a Flathead in white war paint?"

"Yes. A white man with a rifle that makes its own bullets and it keeps firing without loading."

"Hook and most of the Blackfoot never made friendly contact with the white men they saw occasionally in their area. When they could, they attacked and killed them, otherwise they were avoided. None of the Blackfoot had heard of the new rifles being made, so this was a perplexing situation. Hook brooded about this devastating firefight that had cost so many warriors their lives. When he disappeared from camp a few days later, no one thought anything about it because he often went on trips alone.

Two weeks later he walked back into camp un-noticed, as though he had never left. He sought out his Chief to tell him what he had learned. "We have all heard the story about the Ghost Warrior who defeated our neighboring Blackfoot tribe, but we did not know if it was true. I have been to that Blackfoot camp and talked to the ones who escaped the deadly firing rifles that make bullets. It is true, my chief. More than half a hundred warriors were killed by only a few rifles, and a white man was their chief."

The Blackfoot Chief was in his seventieth year and had seen things that the young warriors had only heard of. He had become chief of this tribe of over five hundred Indians when he was still a young man. He was alone when he came upon a group of eight Flathead hunters and attacked them. When he returned to his camp he had eight fresh scalps on his lance. When he now spoke, his people listened. "It is White Buffalo. He has come back to save the

Flatheads, just as the Medicine Man said he would."

~ Forever after the Indians would know Jesse McKannah as White Buffalo ~

A couple of weeks after the hunters returned with the buffalo meat, Jesse walked from camp to camp, talking to the different tribes in a combination of their own Salish language—and sign. He saw that all were looking better and their spirits were high. They all spoke of the coming spring, and most said they were willing to learn how to grow food. He walked with Rose around the tip of Flathead Lake to the next camp, which was only a hundred yards away. He glanced at others walking nearby. *A full belly does wonders for a good attitude.*

Snow fell for two weeks straight and was three feet thick everywhere, with drifts several feet deep in places. Jesse watched as the old women huddled together while preparing the food outside. He recalled the first snow fort that he and his brothers had made on an outing into the mountains. He located Lame Wolverine. "Let's find five or six young men to help me. I will show you how to use this snow."

His project began with the two of them and five young warriors, but as they finished it three hours later there were a dozen young men and twice that many boys, all laughing and eagerly rolling big snowballs.

The five-foot-high wall of snow that was now around the campfire had an offset entrance where the one wall went past the other by six feet, so the wind would not whip through. The old women praised him, and were soon shedding some of their almost worn out garments. The fire usually took care of the snow that fell, but snow really wasn't the problem. The harsh wind had been cutting through their thin tunics, and now it was no longer a big problem as they prepared the food. He received much praise from all who worked at the fire.

Good news travels almost as fast as bad and when Rose and Jesse next visited the camps, they found that all had snow walls of some kind around the main campfires. As Rose walked beside Jesse she said, "You are going to become a legend to our people and will be in many songs and dances around the fires."

"They have treated me very good. I'm glad I can do something to make their lives a little easier."

"These people out here have had a very hard time since all of the buffalo disappeared. They depended very much on them." She paused a moment then added, "Maybe too much."

"No." Jesse exclaimed rather harshly. "They didn't disappear, they were slaughtered." He shook his head in disgust. "And they were right to depend on them for their survival. My God, there were millions of them, enough for thousands of generations to depend on." Rose was alarmed when he slammed his oak walking stick against a tree they were passing, splintering it. "And my own people are the ones who did it."

Hook left his camp the same day Jesse had decided to show the Indians how to construct a snow wall to hold off the wind. He was dressed warmly to travel in the extreme weather. The outer garment was made of white rabbit fur and made him, with his white-painted face almost invisible in the snow-covered forest. He'd been told the direction the Flatheads and their White Chief were heading when the shooting began, so he knew it was the big camp on the south end of Flathead Lake. He had scouted it many times, but realized it was too big to attack. He had planned to catch them out in smaller numbers, but now with this miracle gun that made its own bullets, he was unsure. He planned to scout the camp and see for himself. He moved steadily through the forest on snowshoes, even as the snow came down heavy, but when he was within a few miles he slowed his pace. He did not want anyone to know he was watching.

From atop a small hill, Hook saw smoke from the camp about two miles ahead. He huddled against a tree on the side away from the wind and slept—he would move closer after dark.

Hook spent half of the night moving from one area on the perimeter of the camp to the other until he finally spotted the White Chief. He moved close enough to throw a tomahawk and split the back of the White Chief's head open like a melon when Jesse stood, but remained silent and watched. *I wonder if my chief is correct and this really is White Buffalo returned.* He was pondering this when Jesse said to the old chief, "I am tired, so we will see you in the morning."

Hook was more perplexed now. *Why would a Great Spirit like White Buffalo be tired? Do spirits need women under the skins too*? As Jesse and Rose headed for their own teepee, Hook backed away from the campfire. *I will sleep awhile, and then watch this White Chief later.*

Before dawn the following morning, when Rose came from the teepee to prepare Jesse a gourdful of coffee from the beans she had been hoarding for his pleasure, Hook was no farther than fifty feet away. He had silently slipped close to the teepee and had watched the Indian girl and White Buffalo enter after leaving the fire the night before. Their teepee was on the edge of the trees so he felt secure as he lay in his white coat on a snow-covered ground, with snow coming lightly down. He watched her crush something in a stone mortar with a wooden pestle. *She is making a spirit potion to guard him against harm. I must be very careful.*

Hook remained in his position and listened to the Indian girl talk to White Buffalo in a language he was not familiar with. *They talk in spirit tongue* so *she must be his spirit woman here in the Land of Man.* As the snow slowly covered him, Hook lay and listened to Rose and Jesse talk and laugh as he sipped the coffee. Before the first slivers of dawn began slicing through the thick winter air, Hook retreated to a safer spot where he could observe the camp—more specifically, White Buffalo and his Spirit Woman.

Jesse carried wood into the snow wall around the fire for the women to begin the cooking. When the fire was roaring and the sassafras tea was made, Jesse accepted a gourdful from one of the chief's wives. Only a short time later, his friend Lame Wolverine came into the protected area. "This is a good thing you have showed us. Everyone now sits warm by the fire instead of inside their teepee, huddled in many skins, and smelling the stinky smoke from the little cooking fires inside. Many of the other camps have now made one."

"Yes," Jesse replied, "the wind coming down out of those mountains can run a grizzly back into his den."

His friend grinned. "It has run me back into my teepee many times, but often it was to my woman that I knew was waiting under the skins for me."

"What do you think will be the results of our defeat of those Blackfoot?"

"We are too many for them to attack us here, but they will not forget, so we must always go in larger numbers than usual." He looked up at the gloomy sky then added, "The story of our glorious victory at Lake Coeur d'Alene will have reached all of the Blackfoot ears by now, so they will be very cautious about attacking us under any conditions, but we must still remain very cautious."

Jesse stood and shook the snow from the warm jacket that Rose had made for him months earlier. "I promised the children a see-saw or wooden bucking horse as they call it, so I must get busy with the axe." As he went to the teepee to get the axe, Hook's eyes followed him.

Jesse entered the woods only a few feet from where Hook lay in the snow. The Indian pushed his face into the snow and waited for White Buffalo to pass. Even with the white war paint smeared across his face, Hook wanted to take no chance of being seen. There was much he wanted to learn about White Buffalo, and his Spirit Woman.

Jesse pulled the tree to the edge of the woods, so the cuttings could be used in the campfire. After two hours of cutting, he had the pieces he wanted ready to be taken to the lakeside site, where he had chosen to assemble the seesaw. He walked to the Kootenai camp to get the older boys that had volunteered to carry the parts. Four of the eight boys took turns carrying the main log, while the other four carried the smaller parts in turn. Jesse carried the two oak shovels that he'd carved with the axe and the long hunting knife he wore.

As the group of boys and Jesse carried their load toward the lake's edge, Hook was stealthily working his way along with them. When they stopped, he slid into a prone position where he could observe them. He was very curious what they were going to do with the tree parts.

Two of the boys began digging the holes where small fires had been tended since the previous day to thaw the frozen soil. They would bury the forked poles, as Jesse cut the half moon notch in the seesaw. When the boys had the forked poles buried and packed tight, one of the larger boys picked up the cross pole by himself. He had noticed several young girls watching and wanted to impress them with his strength. He was grinning at the girls when he turned to place the pole on the two forked sticks. The boy wasn't watching what he was doing, and Jesse was just straightening up from working on the half moon notch, when the pole hit him beside the head. It wasn't a serious blow, or even a painful one, but a small knot on the end had a sharp place on it. As luck would have it, that's exactly what made contact with the side of Jesse's head.

What Hook saw next made his heart beat faster—*Blood. How can that be?*

One of the young boys said, "You're bleeding."

Jesse took out a soft piece of rabbit skin and rubbed it. "Just a scratch," he said to the boy that had caused it. "I'll put some snow on it and it'll stop in a minute." He bent over and grabbed a handful of snow, and after less than a minute he showed the concerned children that it had indeed stopped bleeding. "See," he turned his scratched head toward them, "no more blood."

Hook's eyes were tuned in on Jesse—as a hawk watches a fieldmouse far below. He saw the blood a second time. *Spirits do not bleed. This is not White Buffalo.* His eyes neither blinked nor left their target for the next ten minutes while Jesse tied the crosspiece to the forked poles. Jesse laughed at the children's antics on the seesaw for a few minutes, and then turned to return to his camp. Hook's eyes followed him. *This is only a white man living with these Salish people and he is the man who was leading them both times when our people were defeated.* He lay and watched Jesse walk away as he pondered these thoughts. *Now I know I can kill him and then our trouble with these people will be over.* He carefully moved away from the children because he knew their eyes were much better at catching movement than older people. When he was on the other side of the small hill that he had come down to watch them from, he began moving into position to watch Jesse's teepee.

The afternoon sky began to darken as the sun started falling into the western trees. Hook had remained vigilant and motionless, his eyes never leaving Jesse and Rose's teepee. Finally the flap was thrown open and they came out. The old Chief was at the fire when they came inside the snow wall to sit with him. Hook's ears picked up Jesse's voice as he spoke to the chief in Salish.

"Rose and I are going to Fort Connah in the morning to see if I can get Angus McDonald to order us four of these new rifles with plenty of ammunition and take beaver skins as payment."

"Do you think he will do it? The white soldiers do not want us to have any guns at all."

"He knows we will use them only for hunting and to protect ourselves against the Blackfoot. Yes. I think he will order them for me."

"That would be good, because with four of those guns we will never be defeated by the Blackfoot."

"Yes! With four of these repeating rifles, and about twenty of the best shooters with muzzle loaders, firing in sequence as we have taught them, it would be a difficult wall of lead to come through."

"Dancing Bear," the chief said, "is going to put on a special show at the big communal camp fire tonight. Are you going to come and watch?"

"Yes." Rose answered with delight. "I want to hear all about my brave husband and how he defeated the Blackfoot almost single handed."

Jesse smiled and looked down at her. "Careful woman or you'll have my scalp hanging from one of these jealous young brave's belt, because they really did all the defeating."

"Never. Every one of them looks up to you as their great war leader."

The old chief smiled inwardly at Jesse's lack of self-praise.

"I'd rather have one of Lame Wolverine than two of me any day."

Lame Wolverine and his woman were walking in from the dark when Jesse made that statement. When his friend was inside the snow wall he said, "If it was two of you with those rifles or ten of me with these old muzzleloaders, I'd take you two."

Jesse casually lifted his beautiful drop-block action rifle and looked at it momentarily. "This is quite a weapon, and it can make an enemy think twice before attacking."

His friend produced a fine, large beaver pelt. "When you go to Fort Connah will you see if he will give me some of the white mans tobacco they chew, for this?"

Jesse took the pelt. "Sure. Rose and I are going in the morning."

Hook smiled. *I will be waiting for you, white man.*

Hook was already awake and watching Jesse's teepee when he saw the small buffalo-fat candle being lit. It had stopped snowing during the night and the wind had settled down to a light breeze. He was comfortable as he leaned back against a tree, chewing jerky and eating grain. He had buried two caches of food at equal distances during the journey from his camp to where he now sat. He would slowly consume all that he had left to build his strength for the task ahead today, knowing that he could locate his stashed rations even in the snow.

Jesse lay beneath the skins and silently watched Rose moving about in the dim light of the buffalo-fat candle. Before she could get into her buckskin winter pants, he said, "Come back under here and let me hold you."

She turned around to see his arms reaching toward her and a big smile on his face. She returned his smile as the buckskins fell from her hand and she slid into his arms. There was nothing on earth that she would rather do than have this white man who treated her like a princess every day of her life.

"You like me more than coffee?"

"I like you more than anything."

Rose closed her eyes as he put his arms around her. "I like you more than everything, too."

Hook patiently watched the teepee as dawn began flushing the darkness from the forest he was hiding in. Before it got too light he moved farther back into the trees, but remained close enough to see the teepee that held his quarry.

The teepee was fully flooded with morning light when Jesse opened his eyes again. He was looking straight into Rose's dark, almond shaped smiling eyes.

"What do you see, Prairie Rose?"

"I see good man."

When he made a move to get up from the skins, she put her arms around him. "Before, you want me—now I want you."

Half an hour later he said, "Phew! What a great way to start a day."

"Yes." She smiled as she lay in his arms with her head nestled against his chest, "Great day."

An hour after dawn had completely lit the camp. Hook further narrowed his already narrow eyes, and watched as the Indian woman came through the flap on the teepee. He saw her prepare the drink she had the morning before when he thought it was a spirit potion. As she returned to the teepee he thought, *Lazy white man sleeps late and has his woman feed him in the sleeping skins.* He continued chewing his jerky. *He will be easy to kill.*

When Jesse came to the fire, the old chief was eating warm leftover buffalo tongue stew. He asked Jesse if he would like some.

"Never turn down an offered meal, my pappy used to say, 'cause you never know when you'll get another one."

"Your father was a wise man. Has he gone on to the other side?"

"Yes. When I was just twenty-two summers."

"Did he go as a great warrior?"

"Yes. Greater than I realized at the time. Our home caught on fire in the winter night and even though he was burned from rescuing my mother, he returned to get my young wife, and my baby son."

"The flames took him?"

"Yes. And them too."

"Mmmm," the old chief mused, "only brave men enter the flames."

"True." Jesse looked off through the cold morning mist. "He would have done battle against any odds for his family." He reached out and accepted the gourdful of stew offered to him by the old chief's oldest wife. "Thank you."

"Has your mother gone to be with him?"

"Yes. A year later she just went to bed and died in her sleep. She missed him that much."

"It is better that way. One should not be alone on the other side. I have taken four wives much older than me so that I will have someone waiting when I get to the Land of Dreams. My young wives are pleasant to be with under the skins now, but when I go over, they will look for new husbands." He gummed the tender buffalo tongue while looking at the old woman stirring the day's food. "She will be the first to go over. She has been a good wife for more than forty winters, and will wait for me to come to be with her."

Jesse looked up at the gray overcast sky, "Yes, I'm sure you're right. My mother and father are together in the Land of Dreams."

As Jesse was finishing his gourd of stew, Rose came to the fire carrying a small bundle.

"Whatcha got there, lady?"

"Cama bread with dried serviceberries, for Angus."

"Boy oh boy, he's gonna hug you till air pops out."

"He tell me last time I bring them that he never have anything so good."

"You make?" The old chief asked.

"I can father, but not so good as Wahkoohani. I trade her rabbit fur bag for this. She likes to put her hands in one so they stay warm."

"Ah yes, she is the best to cook the sweet things. I tried to buy her as a wife many times, but her husband loves the cakes too much to sell her."

It was near ten o'clock when Jesse stood. "Let's get our horses and head to the fort."

Rose divided the sweet cakes into two equal parts and put them in the rabbit fur bags that rested across the horse's neck. Before she boarded her horse Jesse said, "Wear this." He removed the warm coat she had made him. When she attempted to protest he insisted. "I don't expect trouble on this short trip, but I don't want to be bundled up in the coat in case there is."

Rose laid the heavy coat across the horse's neck and removed her buffalo robe for Jesse. She deftly jumped up on the beast's back, then put the warm coat on and pulled the hood over her head. A stiff wind and light snow was already replacing the morning calm.

Jesse laid the heavy rifle on the ground then placed the buffalo robe over the horse's neck before leaping astride. After placing the robe over his shoulders he pulled the separate rabbit fur hood, which Rose had made for him, down over his head. After checking to be certain that the small .44-caliber pistol was snugly in the shoulder holster, and his knife secured, he pulled the rifle up by the rawhide rope that was attached to it and his wrist.

As they headed toward Fort Connah, twenty miles away, the snow began coming down heavier. Soon they looked like snowmen astride two horses moving through a winter wonderland.

Someone else was moving through the same snow shrouded terrain. Hook had never been to Fort Connah, but had scouted it several times to be familiar with it in case he ever wanted to attack. When he heard Jesse say that he was going there, he knew what route he and the woman must take. As Jesse and Rose left the camp, Hook was already two miles ahead of them on the only trail they could use. When he reached a high vantagepoint on the side of Bearfoot Mountain, he waited to be sure they were coming along the trail below. Soon he saw the two white figures moving slowly along the trail. He let a crooked smile run across his face. *I know where to ambush you now, white man.* The forty-year-old Indian now began a descending pace that would have exhausted a much younger man. He was driven by a need to revenge the Blackfoot warriors that he was certain this white man caused to die.

Jesse and Rose sat hunched against the cold wind that was now blowing at them from their right. His hands were cold but he held the rifle outside the buffalo robe anyway, with a piece of rabbit fur covering the breech. He glanced to his left and saw that Rose was securely snuggled into his warm coat. The snow and wind impeded Jesse's vision, so his eyes passed right over the Indian that was pointing the long muzzleloader right at them, only fifty feet away.

Hook took careful aim at the white man in the coat. Before pulling the trigger he thought, *I will kill the woman under the buffalo robe, after he falls. Her hair will also make a fine trophy.* He squeezed the trigger, but had to wait a moment for the smoke to clear before he could be certain that his ball had found its target.

Before the smoke had lifted from his weapon, Hook felt a horrible pain enter his chest. The rifle dropped from his useless hand. He had no idea what had gone wrong, but instinct spun him around and his feet were moving as fast as they could. The signal from his brain said RUN—ESCAPE.

Jesse heard the report of Hook's rifle and saw Rose jolted back and off of her horse. Pure instinct brought the rifle up and on target as his eyes registered the puff of smoke. A marksman of unequaled skill, he put a bullet right below the puff of smoke, and briefly saw the Indian stagger then turn and run. He instinctually wanted to pursue him, but he went to Rose first. She was lying on her back, upon the frozen ground when he got to her side. "I be alright," she said, "go get him."

Jesse removed the rope that held the rifle to his wrist and was after the Indian at a hard run. At the tree where the Indian had stood to steady his rifle, Jesse saw a lot of blood. *This guy ain't goin' far. Musta got him good in a lung.*

Hook was leaving a trail of blood that a blind man could follow, and he knew it. He had already lost so much blood he was getting dizzy. He was also confused by the events because he was certain he had set up an easy kill. The Indian knew it was useless to attempt to outrun anyone that might try to pursue him, so he pulled the tomahawk from his waistband and huddled against a large boulder. When Jesse rounded the corner and Hook saw who it was, he let the tomahawk fall from his hand. "So you truly are White Buffalo and cannot be killed."

Jesse had never learned the Blackfoot language, so he had no idea what the man was saying. He could have cared less as he stepped forward and put a .44-caliber bullet between the Indian's eyes. He returned the short-barreled pistol to the shoulderholster and began running back to the trail. When he returned to Rose and lifted her up, he could hardly believe his eyes.

~ She was dead ~

Jesse lifted Rose onto the back of her horse, and used all of the rawhide rope they carried to secure her. He removed the beautiful coat that she had made him, to make her body less bulky. In insisting that she wear it, he had caused her to be Hooks target instead of him. He threw the buffalo robe across Rose and put the warm coat on. It had started snowing harder when he first started securing her body and by the time he was ready to head back to camp it was coming down very heavy. He had stopped at her head and patted her straight black hair, "You're outa the cold for good now, darlin'." He stood a moment and just looked at her body, so un-natural lying across the horse. Tears froze in place on his face as he lead both horse's back up the trail until he came to a fallen tree. It would let him climb stiffly up onto his horse's back. He was so cold from the driving snow and wind that he had a very difficult time mounting.

When the two horses entered the camp a few hours later, Jesse could take no credit for it. He had simply sat on the horses back and let it find its own way home. The first person to see him return was a group of children making snowmen as he had taught them. Roaming Eye saw who it was, and ran to him. He was so cold that he could barely speak to her, so she held his foot and walked along beside. One of the older boys, who had helped with the seesaw, took the horse by the padded nose-ring and turned the horse toward the old chief's camp.

As the two horses were led through the camp, children came from every teepee along the way. There were over two-dozen by the time Jesse and Rose arrived at her father's large teepee. Word of his return had spread, so by the time he arrived at her father's camp, Lone Wolverine came running. As the old chief and his wives untied the ropes to let them take Rose's stiff body inside the teepee, Lone Wolverine helped Jesse get down from his horse. All of the children but one remained outside of the snow wall that surrounded the fire as Jesse leaned against his friend and slowly followed him inside. Roaming Eye held his hand and stayed as close to her River Angel as she could.

After Jesse had warmed his aching bones by the fire, he finally accepted a gourdful of broth from one of the old Chief's wives. For an hour the only sounds other than the crackling of the fire was the wailing of the women in the teepee over Rose's body. Jesse opened his coat and pulled little Roaming Eye into the warmth, and held her close to him.

After finishing his story, he turned to his friend Lame Wolverine. "Why would a crazy man be out in this kind of weather looking to kill the first person to pass by?"

The chief asked, "Are you sure it was a Blackfoot?"

"I've only seen a few of them. The way he was dressed I think he was."

Lame Wolverine spoke. "When the snow stops I will take a few good trackers and find his body, then we will know."

The Chief shook his head. "I want to know who killed my Prairie Rose."

The chief's words echoed through Jesse's head, so he pulled Roaming Eye closer to him and sat silently staring at the fire long after darkness had covered the camp. When he realized that the tiny girl was sound asleep, he picked her up in his arms and carried her to her own teepee. When Jesse returned, he asked the chief, "May I sleep in your teepee so I can be close to Rose for one more night?"

"Yes. The women will wail all night, but I will tell them to do it quietly so you can rest."

Jesse entered the teepee and went to where the women had Rose's body lying on beautiful deerskin hides. She was dressed in an all white doeskin tunic and was prepared so well that she looked like she was just sleeping. He stood for half an hour just looking down at her, remembering all of the fun and laughter she had brought into his life. Before turning to find a place to sleep, he spoke to the women. "You have made her look like the most beautiful rose to ever bloom on any prairie."

The women looked up from their wailing to see tears streaming down his face. The old wife smiled. *It is a very brave man who cries in front of women.*

Jesse went slowly to a pile of skins and lay down.

The next day, he insisted on going with the men that were to prepare Rose's burial place. Her father had chosen a spot near the lake, beneath a small cliff. The men dug through the frozen earth and created a depression about three feet deep next to the cliff. Later in the day, her body was brought from the teepee and carried the short distance to her grave. All but the very young and the infirm attended her funeral. She was not only the head Chief's daughter, but was also liked by every person in the camp. The men remained silent as she was placed into the shallow grave, but the women began a death chant to the spirits, asking them to guide her on her way to the other side.

Jesse's face was a frozen mask of grief as he stood and watched the young men gently place rocks on top of her body. When she was completely covered everyone began filing past and putting stones on top of her grave. As they went past they continued on to their own teepees. Soon there was only her father, Jesse and four strong young braves. The old chief gave them a signal, and the four men went to the top of the small cliff. Boulders soon began falling from the top as they worked them loose. In fifteen minutes the whole side of the little cliff began to crumble onto Rose's grave. The men continued until they could walk down and across her grave.

The chief turned to his white friend. "No animal will touch our Prairie Rose."

When they returned to the chief's teepee Jesse said, "I must walk alone in the woods."

The old chief didn't answer, he just slowly shook his head then went to the fire to smoke his pipe while he communicated with the spirits on his daughter's behalf.

Two days later it was already dark when Jesse once again walked from the woods and entered the snow wall to sit with the chief and Lame Wolverine. He had not eaten a bite, so gladly accepted the gourdful of buffalo stew from one of the chief's wives. After eating Jesse said, "I must leave this camp. My sorrow is too great each time I look at Rose's grave."

"Where will you go?" Lame Wolverine asked.

"West to the big water. I still have a lot of the white man's money. I took it from the bank where I kept it before they burned my ranch. Rose removed it from my horse blanket and sewed it into my new coat." He patted the warm coat that she'd presented him with, and that he had to fight Bad Wolf to keep. "I will buy new trapping supplies and go into the mountains to hunt the beaver. It will be better for me and others if I am alone."

The old chief removed the pipe he'd been puffing on. "You have been very good for The People, my white friend. They have many good things now that they would not have if you had not come among them."

"Many would not have their lives either." Lame Wolverine added.

"I know it is selfish that I go, but I take a young wife and she and my baby die—I ask my sister to come to live with me and she dies—I killed several men, but it did not bring her back—I married a lovely woman to spend the rest of my life with and she lies dead beneath those rocks at the lake—Even the horses I loved died beneath me. I do not want to kill another person or have one die because they are with me. I will go into the mountains and trap alone." He paused a moment then added, "And stay alone."

The Chief removed his pipe. "I have decided to remain here instead of returning to the land where you came to us. It will be better for our relatives here, and for our own people too. With the buffalo we now have, we can make it to the warm time and we will be strong again, so we will not be easy to attack. We will put the small seeds in the ground you got for us and grow food as you taught us. If you come down from the mountains, come this way and talk to us. You will always be River Angel to the children and Ghost Warrior to The People."

Long after the names, River Angel and Ghost Warrior were forgotten, Jesse McKannah would still be talked about around many campfires as:

~ White Buffalo ~

Legends and stories have a way of traveling great distances. When the killing of Hook reached the Blackfoot camp, it soon became a legend. Around spring fires, the storytellers danced and told of the brave warrior Hook, who went in search of White Buffalo. Jesse's presence, even as only a legend, kept the Blackfoot from further attacks on the Flatheads and their Salish friends. They too would soon be pressed together on a small piece of land called an Indian Reservation by the white men with no honor who lived in a place called Washington.

The following morning found Jesse McKannah moving through the forest toward Fort Connah.

23

~ *The Shamrock* ~

“So,” Kelly said to Ian McKannah, as he and the two men walked into his saloon. “What brings the young gambler into me place so arly in the day?” He leaned against the bartop on two huge muscular arms and grinned amiably at the three men. “Road dust in yer bloody throat n’ it’s a wash y’be needin’, is it?”

“Well, by the oath o’ me grandpappy’s favorite leprechaun, I do believe y’ve ‘it the nail right on the bleedin’ ‘ead Mister Kelly.” Ian grinned wide, “Hows ‘bout three of yer best Irish ales for m’self and me two brothers.”

“Well, by Jesus lad, and all this time I was thinkin’ the likes o’ you ‘ad t’be a one uva kind fella. I’ll just go in the back n’ open a keg o’ me finest fer the likes o’ three distinguished Irish gentlemen such’s yerselves.”

“Twas practicin’ fer the perfect Irishman, it was, that me dear mum n’ pop were doin’, and these two gentlemen standin’ ‘ere are the results o’ their practicin’.”

Before another word was said, a drunk who was listening at the end of the bar spoke loudly. "An' a sorry lookin' two they are indeed. Looks t'me like a pair o' bloody stage fairies y've drug in t'dance in yer silly rich folks pub up the bloody road."

Broderick moved so swiftly that he had the man by the front of the shirt and was dragging him toward the swinging bat-wing doors before the drunk could say another word. He flung him through them then followed closely behind. A brief silence was followed by a thud as his body was slammed down on the muddy dirt road.

"Ow. Stop that, ow. Quit, ye bloody fool, ow stop, oh no…

"'E won't 'urt the little bugger, will 'e?"

Ian grinned at Kelly as Patrick said, "No, but I bet he teaches him a good lesson about keepin' his mouth shut when 'e don't know who 'e's speakin' to."

A moment later, Broderick returned with the man's clothing, boots, and hat wrapped into a ball. He tossed them into the corner as he approached the bar. "Filthy little urchin decided to run 'ome n' take a bath."

Kelly came from the back with a huge pewter pitcher of dark ale, and after filling four mugs he raised his. "Cheers boys, this's from an old family recipe 'at's not equaled in this new country." After wiping foam from his lips he smiled. "And best of all gentlemen, she's on the 'ouse."

"Aye sir, and it's proud I am t'be meetin' a true Irishman."

"Ha." Kelly roared with a hearty laugh. "No true Irishman 'as ever in 'is bloody life bought a coupla strangers a free drink." He downed his beer. "Who are you two gentlemen, anyway?"

Ian grinned as Broderick stepped closer and said with his hand extended, "Me brother Patrick there is the gentleman sir, and I'd greatly appreciate it if you'd not be using that word when directing the conversation toward me." He also downed his beer then said as he held the mug closer for inspection. "I do believe you're correct about this ale. Will ya look at the bloody 'ead still 'anging t'the sides o' this mug." He held it first toward Patrick then Ian. "Stout stuff this drink, 'olds to a man's gut so 'e can go on wi' business. I'll be payin' for the next round, Mister Kelly."

"There'll be no more mister in 'ere now that we're close friends n' y've cleaned me place of rodents." He poured them all another. "An what's your name, lad?" He nodded toward Patrick as he sat the pitcher back down. "Ian drops in 'ere often but 'e never mentioned you fellas."

"You'll bloody well know why after you 'ear where they're goin' t'school n' what they plan t'do if they ever graduate." Ian leaned back against the bar and grinned.

"Oh bleedin' Jesus, don't tell me you two young gentlemen are gonna be politicians?"

"Patrick Oliver McKannah, soon to be Harvard graduate and California lawyer." He held out his hand to Kelly who paused a moment before taking it.

"Well sir," he said as he looked around, "as long as I'm not seen shakin' the 'and of a bloody lawyer, I'm pleased t'meetcha."

"Broderick Luis McKannah, brightest of the two McKannah legal wizards." He held his mug toward Kelly. "No reason t'wear out yer 'and shakin' mine. Another mug o' that wonderful ale will do just fine."

The bar owner smiled and nodded at Broderick. "Bloody poet, this fella."

The McKannah brothers split another pitcher of ale then yelled to Kelly who was busy with customers that they would be back in before returning to Boston. As Patrick and Broderick climbed into the carriage, Ian went to the front where the huge black man was sitting. "Here y'are, Gap." He handed him a full pewter pitcher of ale."

The huge brown face opened to expose a mouthful of perfect white teeth with a wide gap between the front two on top that made his smile even more pronounced. "Thank you," was all he said when he took the pitcher, but after Ian was in he turned to the three men and smiled with foam on his lips. "This a very good drink."

"I was wondering where he got an odd name like that."

"Ha." Ian bent forward and spoke to the driver. "Hey Gap, my brother thinks Gap's an unusual name."

Another grin from the huge driver, but he said nothing and turned back to watch the road ahead.

"Oh, I see." Broderick said, smiling.

Ian laughed. "Gap's a nickname he was given as a kid by the missionary that raised him. His real name is Abraham Jefferson Stanton but he prefers Gap."

"Gap it is then."

The trip to The Shamrock was without incident and when Gap turned in at the five-story, light green building, with dark green shamrocks painted on every available spot, Patrick nodded. "Yer not ashamed o' yer bleedin' 'eritage, are ye little brother?"

"Aye ol' timer, the Irish're getting' the leftovers everywhere but 'ere. In me Shamrock it's the best o' the beast is where we cut the O'Malley's and O'Shea's their steaks from."

"And the McKannah's?"

"It's workin' class the McKannah Irish are lad, so you'll be gettin' a bloody apron from me kitchen 'elp n' y'll be arnin' yer potato soup n' stale bread, just as all the rest o' me peasants do."

Broderick grinned, "Y'mean t'tell me you'd 'ave the lawyer who'll be representing the future president eatin' gruel with the domestic staff?"

Ian grinned at Patrick. "The lad still thinks in a big way, doesn't he?"

"Ever see 'im any other way?"

The three exited the carriage laughing and entered the rear double doors that were propped open to allow the many hustling people coming and going as they prepared Ian's Shamrock Hotel and Gaming Club for the evening's business.

Both of the older McKannahs noticed the casual manner that their younger brother was treated by everyone, and were pleased to see that his obvious success had not changed him in any way.

"Ian." a large burley man as old as their father called from a door like neither of his brother's had seen.

"Yes, Mac?"

"Take a look." He nodded his bushy red head toward the door.

"C'mon and have a look at our ice room," Ian beckoned with a nod.

"Mac, these're my brothers." He pointed first to Patrick then Broderick as he introduced them. "Boys, this's Shea MacHue my right hand man and bartender, bouncer, manager, and in a pinch a good chef, too."

Patrick extended his hand. "Pleased t'meetcha MacHue. Scotsman, I'm thinkin' ye be?"

"To the bone lad," he said as he pumped Patrick's hand then took Broderick's. "Scot to the marrow o' me bones." He opened the huge door that swung on monstrous hinges and stepped back as the three brothers entered.

"Wow." Broderick said as he looked at the roomful of ice blocks.

Patrick was silent as he looked around the room.

"I was at the docks when the ice ship arrived from Greenland," Mac said, "so I bought half the bloody load." A mischievous grin spread across his red face, "We'll be 'earin' from yer pal Kelly up the road, and a few other's I'm sure, but by Jesus lad," the grin got wider, "we'll 'ave ice t'last till the bloody lakes around 'ere are frozen again."

Patrick spoke as he looked around, "I noticed how thick that door is Mac, are the walls that thick too?"

"Walls, door, ceiling and floor're all this thick." He spread his hands indicating almost a yardstick length. "Hunter bought an entire shipload of poor quality English wool that a captain was about to carry back to the London owners n' by Jesus he got 'er at a bloody good price. 'At's what we used to pack between all of 'em." He waved his arm around his head.

Patrick's head was nodding as he looked around. "What's that small room there with the holes in it?" He pointed to a small room in the center.

"C'mon," Ian said before Mac could answer. "Lemme show you Mac's best idea yet."

He opened a thin door then stepped back for his brother's to look inside.

Broderick stepped in as Patrick leaned forward to better view the contents. Broderick walked to the end, several yards from the doorway as he looked at the hanging sides of beef, sheep, goats and pigs, plus many varieties of fowl. "What're these things?" He bent down to look into the box beneath the hanging pigs.

"They're called conchs and come from some islands south of here." Mac stepped past Patrick and picked one of them up. He turned it so they could both see the shell's entrance. "See this hard little thing?" He tapped the fingernail-like substance guarding the entrance. "On the other side o' this little thing is som'n so tasty you won't believe it's the same meat comin' from the nasty lookin' critter that our black island boy knocks out of this shell. Looks bloody well like those leeches the doctors put on you when you've gone n' got yourself a right nasty infection but just a wee bit larger."

"Yeah." Ian said, "When Stoop gets finished pounding on the meat that comes outa these shells, and fries 'em up all brown n' crispy," he smacked his lips, "mmm boy, you fella's will understand why we buy every single one that Stoop's daddy sends on the ship."

"How do they keep 'em from rotting till they get here?" Broderick ran his hand across the beautiful pink and white shell.

"Get 'em 'ere alive they bloody well do." Mac said. "They 'ave a shallow box wi' 'oles in it below deck where they place the critters, then all they 'afta do is pump sea water over 'em once a day. Only takes a wee bit o' seawater to keep 'em alive, till we git 'em in 'ere. Then we keep sprayin' a bit o' seawater across 'em and would ya believe, they'll stay alive several more days."

"Schrreee," Broderick whistled, "beats anything I ever saw. We ate these things in Key West when our boat stopped there on the way to Boston."

Patrick had the shell in his hand and was looking at every side of it when the conch reached out with its 'foot' and touched him. "Eeyow," he yelled and tossed the shell up but caught is as it was coming down. He juggled the shell like a seasoned circus performer as Ian, Broderick and Mac laughed.

"Watch it lad. Bloody poisonous critters they are an by Jesus their teeth're like a bulldogs." He was bent double as Patrick grappled with the shiny pink beast until he finally had it by the tip. He held it as the animal began getting longer until it was hanging almost a foot out of the shell."

"Will it come all the way out?"

"Stoop wishes they would, but no, Patrick, they need more'n a bit o' coaxing to get 'em out" Ian reached out and took the shell from him, "Look here, see these rings on the pointed end." He held it and pointed to the third layer of pointed protrusions that got bigger as they left the point and continued toward the large part of the shell. "Stoop knocks a hole right here on the third ring then shoves his sharp knife in and severs where the animal's attached itself. Sluuurp, out she comes." Ian made a noise that sounded to Broderick like the same sound that one of the crew made on the ship when he was eating raw oysters in Key West.

"We had conch in Key West when we stopped to get supplies, but is was made into little round balls and cooked in hot oil by the black people who lived there." Broderick raised his eyebrows, "And I believe I could eat two dozen of those delicious little conch critters."

"You did," Patrick said laughing, "and they're fritters not critters."

"I'll ask Stoop if he knows how to make 'em."

"How'd he get that name? He a stupid guy or is it just a nickname?"

"Stoop'll be here pretty soon 'n you'll see for yourself." As the words drifted toward Patrick, the back door opened and a seven-foot-nine-inch tall black boy stooped and entered.

"Good day lad," Mac said, followed by Ian's greeting to the tall black boy.

Both McKannah boys smiled as they shook the Bahamian youth's hand. "Ready to knock out some conch?" Ian asked.

"Yes mon, came in did dey?"

"Sure did," Mac answered, "and three of those small turtles, too."

"Same kine like dem lass one?"

"Yessiree. They're over in the corner with their flippers still tied."

"Dem's hawkbill turtle if dey de same kine. Gone be ver hoppy folks in dat dinner room, dis night."

"Good timing," Ian said, "because the future President of America might be eating with us tonight."

"What he name?" The young island boy was tying his apron on as Ian spoke.

"John Quincy Adams and he loved the turtle steaks your Aunt Meriam fixed him and his wife Louisa when they were here on their last visit?"

The black face spread into a huge grin. "Auntie bess cook in Nassau."

"I don't doubt it Stoop," Ian commented, "and we're very happy that you convinced her to come here and work with us—and that we don't feed the black people to dogs for sport, like she was told."

"She ver hoppy now, Mistah Ian," the smile spread again and his pearl white teeth flashed. "An now she knowin' dat dem white plantation folks juss sayin' all dat, so we all be fraid to leave. Dem folks wants us to stay workin' in dem field all time for dem coupla shilling dey toss at us now an again. Dey gone be more n' more black folks comin' here, bye n' bye." Before he went to work on the conch he turned toward Patrick and Broderick. "I hope you gennemens enjoy you visit, an I gone ax auntie to fixin' you de bess conch steak you ever been eatin'."

"Thanks Stoop, Patrick and I both loved the conch we ate in uh," he looked at Patrick, "what was the name of that place again?"

"Cayo Hueso."

"Island of Bones," the black Bahamian boy said, "but bout ever body callin' dat place Kee Wess now. I got uncle what move dere, an he woman cookin' dem ting for dem sailor fella now, an makin' mo money den ever see in she life."

"We liked 'em, so we'll be looking forward to your aunties'." Stoop smiled, waved and headed toward the ice room.

"Hey Ian," Patrick said.

"Yeah?"

"Where did you meet Mister Adams and his wife Louisa?

"Hunter sent me to Washington a while before he got sick, to talk with his friend in government about getting a grant to restore this building. Mister and Missus Adams were on the ship that stopped here. They were going to Washington too, so we got to know each other." Ian smiled at his oldest brother. "When I finished this place and was ready to open, I sent them a personal invitation to be my guests and it was one of the smartest things I've done lately."

"Pays t'have friends in government."

"Sure does. They've been like my own personal ambassadors for The Shamrock; recommending us to everyone they know in Washington."

"If he becomes president," Broderick said, "you'll have more politicians comin' to see that crazy Five Points place down the road than you'll have rooms and card tables enough for, when they come here to spend the evening."

Ian turned to Mac. "I'll be back shortly, but first I wanna show 'em the old Brandt Mansion while I have time."

"Sure boss, I'll 'ave 'er all bloody well ready t'go on time, so go on n' show yer brothers wha' we'll be workin' on t'please the buggers when they come wi' them gold coins burnin' bloody 'oles in their fancy silk pockets."

Ian motioned with a wave for Patrick and Broderick to follow him as he headed for the rear door. Once outside, he pointed toward an old five-story mansion sitting a hundred feet away on the property next to his Shamrock. "I said we didn't get the government grant for the Shamrock but we did get one for this old mansion. C'mon." He headed across the area between the two buildings, which was already being cleared and graveled to accommodate carriages. He waved to a couple of workers. "They'll soon have the entire property cleared of bushes and filled with stones for the carriages that are bringing guests to park."

"You own this, too?"

"Sure do, Patrick. Hunter and I worked hard to get the government to give us funding to renovate this old mansion, which once belonged to relatives of Benjamin Franklin. The inside's almost finished then they'll begin repairs and painting on the outside."

"Is it going to be a gambling place, too?" Broderick walked around the corner ahead of them.

"No Brod, this'll strictly be a hotel for the very wealthy, who want fine accommodations and security while they're visiting Five Points during the day, and The Shamrock during the evening." He grinned, "Plus rich people just love to tell their friends that they stayed in a famous person's home."

"Did Benjamin Franklin really live here?"

"Don't really know Pat, but we gathered enough documents to prove that he was here a lot as a kid, then later as a young man."

After showing them the inside of the one-hundred-and-twenty-year-old mansion, they returned to The Shamrock. Ian had an employee take the two McKannahs' to their rooms as he left to assist Mac prepare for the evening patrons.

When they entered their third-story room, Broderick pointed at the porcelain tub sitting in the corner. "Boy-oh-boy am I ready for that." He turned to the boy and asked, "Can I have warm water brought up?"

"No need for that, sir." The boy went to a small narrow door behind the tub. He opened it and yanked a rope several times. After only a moment, a small bell rang and he began pulling the rope as the two men watched. When the dumbwaiter arrived with a bucket of water, he secured the rope then dumped the warm water in the tub. Several dumbwaiter trips later the tub had enough water in it for a bath. He brought up another bucketful and sat it on the floor. "That's to rinse with sir and when you're both finished just leave it in the tub and someone will come up and pour the water from the tub out the window into the field in the rear."

Patrick walked to the window to shove it open. "No need for that lad, we're not gentlemen lawyers yet, and we remember well how to earn our way."

Broderick asked. "Does each room offer warm water this way?"

"No sir. Only the rooms in the rear, so the tub water can be dumped out the window. Well then gentlemen, if you want more water just do as I did and jiggle the rope so the bell down in the boiler room rings, and up she'll come."

The boy left, and Broderick sat on the bed to remove his shoes. He turned when Patrick spoke. "Shall we flip a coin to decide who goes first?"

"Why certainly, brother. Yer always full o' good ideas." He pointed toward a large set of drawers against the far wall. "Get one o' those twenty-dollar gold coins I placed there with me pocket junk, and that's exactly what we'll do."

By the time his brother reached the dresser he heard the splash that woke him to the fact that his ever scheming younger brother had once again fooled him. Patrick turned to see Broderick sinking into the tub as he removed his shirt and tossed it to the floor. "Noticed the water was getting cold and figured it'd be a bloody shame t'waste it."

"Seems I'll never learn."

"Sure looks that way old man," Broderick grinned, "but don't be worryin' yerself 'cause there'll always be a need for a straight-laced, somewhat slow thinking lawyer.

Patrick stretched out on the bed and worked his shoes off. "I'm too tired anyway so dump the water out the window when you're finished n' I'll take a bath after I rest a bit."

Three hours later they were dressed in their finest evening clothes and walking down the stairs. At the second floor landing, the door opened and a pretty young woman wearing nothing but her silk panties abruptly stopped to look first at Patrick, and then at Broderick—whose mouth was hanging open.

"Oh my, who are you two big hunks of male beast?"

"Ha. Mitzy, you hit those two right on the head. Beasts. Yes by Jesus that fits those two fellas perfectly." Ian came walking across to the open doorway laughing. "Close your mouth Brod, y'look like that crazy Indian that Jesse killed to get sis back." He laughed again when his brother closed his mouth but still had his eyes locked on the girl's ample breasts. "Mitzy, these two flashy lookin' blokes are me backwoods brothers who have never seen anything like you in their entire boring lives." Ian smiled as he introduced his brother. "Broderick McKannah, Mitzy MacCreah." He waited until his brother shook off the effects of seeing the gorgeous, naked young girl, before introducing Patrick. "Wait'll you two fellas see her dance." He turned to her and inquired, "Lissie sewing up that hole in the dress?"

"Yes. That's where I was going when I bumped into these two beautiful creatures." She smiled at each then continued on her way.

"Little brother," Broderick said as he held the door open to watch her climb the stairs, "I do believe I followed the wrong path."

Ian laughed loudly. "She'd leave The Shamrock for a Harvard lawyer without even telling me goodbye."

Broderick's eyes opened wide. "Y'don't say." He leaned into the stairway trying for a last glance.

"Not a gonnabe lawyer, Brod. A lawyer with his office open and people bringing him bucket's full of gold coins."

The next day, Patrick and Broderick were discussing their meeting with John Quincy Adams and his wife Louisa Catherine. "At our own Harvard Debater's Club I often heard Mister Adams called Old Man Eloquent," Patrick commented, "and now I understand why."

"I never heard that," Broderick said, "but it certainly fits. He's a brilliant conversationalist."

Patrick shook his head slowly from side-to-side saying, "I don't speak my own language as well as he does several foreign languages."

"We all understand one language though, and that goes for him, too."

"What's that Brod?"

"Good lookin' girls. Did you notice how those big muttonchop sideburns were wigglin' when Mitzy and those gals were dancing?"

"Nope, sure didn't."

"Well brother, I sure did and so did Louisa." He chuckled, "Bet he caught hell after they got to their room last night."

"Maybe it was the money he lost playing poker with his friends that she was mad about?"

"How do you know he lost?"

"While you were busy watching Mitzy, I was watching him play cards." Patrick turned toward his brother. "By the way, you still hadn't come in when

I fell asleep last night. Where'd you go?"

A grin that Patrick had seen many times spread across Broderick's face. "Mitzy said she hadn't had any sleep for two nights because her bedframe had busted and the mattress was all cockeyed, so I volunteered my services."

"And did you get it fixed for her?"

"Sure did and it only took a minute. Pulled it out of that frame and spread it out on the floor."

"And did she get a good sleep last night?" Patrick was unable to refrain from laughing before he finished.

"She had a very good night, but she didn't get much sleep."

24

~ *New frontiers—New adventures* ~

By the time Jesse made it to Fort Connah, the snow was coming down heavy. The little group of log buildings was a welcome sight, as was the opened door with Angus McDonald's big frame in it. When Jesse stomped the snow from his feet, Angus roared, "What the bloody 'ell brings you 'ere in a storm like this?"

An hour and several trips to his desk drawer later Angus said, "That's a lousy way to wind up what looked like a pretty darn good life you 'ad goin', lad." He silently sipped his whisky for awhile before asking, "Whacher plans now?"

Jesse was standing at the window, watching the snow building against the side of the log building across the dirt street. He remained silent for a long time, as though rolling the possibilities over in his head before responding. "Go west to Portland I reckon and get supplied for the coming trapping season, then head back up into the high mountains."

Angus had been dealing with men on the move all of his life, and detected a tone of uncertainty in his friend's voice. After emptying, then refilling the tin cup and putting the bottle back in the drawer he said, "Heard about the gold being dug outa them hills in California?"

Jesse turned away from the window. "I heard some folks talking about it a coupla years ago while I was in Portland getting trapping gear."

"Well, sounds like they found a bloody big pile of it just a while back, somewhere near San Francisco."

"How do they get the stuff outa the ground?"

"Ain't got any idea," the big Scot replied, "but I reckon they just dig till 'ey find a batch of it then put it in a bucket or som'n, and start diggin' som'rs else." He took a sip from the tin cup then added, "I figure one of 'em'll come through 'ere one of these days n' tell me all about it."

"Got me curious now, Angus, so I'll ask around when I get to Portland; oughta be someone there that knows som'n about it."

"I got me a full load o' beaver pelts n' a few buffalo 'ides in that log shed across there that's needin' t'go to Portland. Ain't 'eard a bleedin word from Alaine since 'e went to see that squaw o' his a few weeks ago."

"Alaine?" Jesse said. "Don't think I ever met him."

"Canadian frog 'at hauled for me all summer." Angus took a short trip outside to relieve his bladder. When he came back he said, "Aw, e's not a bad sorta fella, but every time I need the bloke, I've got no idea where 'e is. Bloody frogs're all that way—can't rely on 'em." He held the tin cup to his lips for a long time watching Jesse, who was once again looking out at the storm. Finally he said, "'ow about me hiring you to take 'em pelts to Portland?"

Jesse turned from the window and looked at Angus. Finally he said, "That might work out good for both of us."

Over the next three days Jesse went over every inch of the wagon on which he'd be carrying the beaver pelts to Walla Walla, Washington. The storm had started letting up early on the third day, but Jesse wanted to rebuild the spare wheel and check out a few more things on the wagon before leaving.

"Alaine ain't ever bothered with any of that stuff," Angus said. He was impatient to have the beaver pelts on their way.

Jesse never even turned to look at him as he continued greasing the final wheel. He finally said over his shoulder, "I ain't Alaine."

"Oh yeah, sure. 'Ell's Belles lad, ain't no hurry."

"Well then," Jesse said as he hoisted the wheel back up onto the spindle, "I'll just let this go, and come in your cabin and talk with you."

Angus snorted like a mad bull and slammed the wagon shed door as he left. Jesse smiled as he secured the wheel to the spindle. Later, when he entered Angus's log office, the big man was in a good mood but a little wobbly. "So 'ow's she look now, lad?"

"She'll make it fine now, but that wagon would never have got outa

Montana in the sorry shape it was in."

"I appreciate your 'ard work lad, I truly do." He drained his tin cup and stood. "And to show you I do, I've som'n for you." He wobbled across the room to the wooden locker standing on the dirt floor, leaning against the log wall. He produced a key and opened the door, then reached in and produced a fine leather holster on a bullet filled belt that had one of the new .44 Colt revolvers in it. He turned and reached out to hand it to Jesse who just stood and looked from the pistol to Angus. "Take it lad. I've a better one than this in me drawer over there."

Jesse took the belt and swung it around his waist. After buckling the belt he removed the weapon. "Angus, this is a finer pistol than the one I told you I tossed in the river." He returned it to the holster. "Thanks Angus, take the price out of my pay."

"Not on yer bloody life, lad. It's a gift, and there's no strings attached, just a gift. I don't know of another man to put it t'better use."

"Thanks Angus." Jesse lifted the revolver half out then let it fall back down into the holster. "Feels right. Feels good too. Sure been awhile."

"Y'said you're leavin' in the morning?"

"Yep, first light. Will Huff Allen be up n' ready?"

"That 'e will. He don't look like much lad, but 'e ain't a slacker. Knows the country between here n' Walla Walla, Washington like nobody else I know. You can count on 'im in a pinch too."

"You said it's two hundred miles to Lewiston, on the Idaho border?"

"Yep, then an easy hundred more to Walla Walla. 'At's where you'll hire a guide n' take the pelts on to Portland by cargo canoe. Huff'll bring supplies back for us in the wagon."

"Hope this snow didn't build up too much."

"Nah, this's a freak storm 'at rolled in early. We won't start gettin' real snow for another month'r so."

Jesse had met Huff only once, when he and Rose came to the fort for talks with Angus. He was a tall, unusually thin man, with friendly blue eyes. Angus said he didn't talk much, so he didn't know a thing about him. No words were spoken as he and Jesse hooked the two horses to the wagon then tied the two spares to the rear. Huff climbed into the driver's place on the wooden bench, and positioned the reins in his hands then sat there silently as Jesse said thanks and goodbye to Angus.

They were an hour out on the trail before Huff spoke. "Y'reckon you'll be comin' back later?"

"Maybe someday, but for now I'm goin' trapping back up in the high mountains."

"Sorry 'bout your lady. She was really nice to me. Didja know she snuck me some o' them cakes she made Angus?"

"No, but it don't surprise me none. She was a good woman that was always helping or doing som'n for someone." There was no more talk for a while as the two men bumped along the well-worn trail to Lewiston. Jesse wondered; *how does he know about Rose? Angus ain't the type to say a word to anyone.*

A good distance down the trail, as if reading Jesse's mind Huff said, "My mama's sister lives with them folks you got the buffalo for. She told me about your lady." He paused awhile then added, "Said everyone liked her."

"Your mama's a Flathead?" Jesse asked.

"Nope. She's dead. She was a Spokane and married an Irishman that lived with the Kootenai."

As they bounced along, Jesse tried to figure out how old Huff might be. *Bet he'll never see sixty again.*

"Don't remember much about her," Huff offered, "she died of the fever when I was just ten n' that was over sixty years ago."

Dern, he must be able to read a man's mind. He turned and looked at the old man. "You been living with 'em ever since?"

"Nope, m'pappy took me to be raised with his kin over in Yerba Buena."

"They changed the name to San Francisco, didn't they?"

"Yep."

When the old man said that word, a feeling of sadness swept over Jesse. *Rose really loved that word, yep.* He smiled slightly at the memory of her.

The farther they went along the trail, the less snow there was. "Angus was right. That musta been a freak storm that came through behind us."

"Yeah. Hope the real stuff holds off till I get back with the supplies."

"Something I'm curious about Huff, how come I don't take these pelts on down to Walla Walla by canoe on the Snake River? I was told it gets pretty big right around Lewiston."

"Could I reckon," Huff answered, "but she gets pretty wild in a few places, and the only place I can get decent supplies to take back is in Walla Walla."

"It don't matter none, I was just curious. Ain't got no place to be in a hurry anyway. Gonna have about three months to kill in Portland till the weather'll let me head up into the mountains.

"If I was young as you," Huff replied, "I'd be on my way to where they're gettin' all that gold."

Jesse didn't answer, but he'd been thinking about doing exactly that.

Ten days after pulling out of Fort Connah, Jesse and Huff came to a good spot to camp for the night. It was a narrow ravine that in the spring would have been a death trap with melting snow causing flash floods. Huff said, "Ain't gonna be no water running through here for awhile."

The horses were rubbed down and put on long pickets to graze on what grass they could 'hoof up' to supplement the grain they'd been given. After a meal of hardtack, beans, and jerky, the two men sat at the campfire talking and drinking boiled coffee.

Huff finished chewing his mouthful of jerky, and swallowed it before

asking Jesse, "Where bouts was yer ranch them guys burned?"
"You familiar with the Calaveras River?"
"Yep. Sure am. Runs north of Stockton outa Lake Hogan."
"That's her. I had twenty thousand acres between there n' Comanche Lake."
Huff was chewing on another chunk of jerky, so he didn't answer for awhile. After he finally swallowed he said, "You said had, Jesse, didja sell the land?"
"Nope. Still own the land. When daddy's house burned, we sold his land; over two hundred thousand acres, to a lumber outfit outa Fresno. Me 'n Simon was livin' in the barn, planning to build a small house and let mom live there with us, but when she died, all of us brothers decided to go our own way. I took my cut of the money and bought that twenty thousand acres."
"Hmmm." Huff mumbled several times as he sat sipping coffee. Finally he said, "If my calculations are correct Jesse, that big gold strike's only 'bout fifty miles north of your land."
"No kidding?"
"Yep. Som'rs on the South Fork River, near a place called Coloma."
"Ain't that som'n? I was on that river when I was just a kid. Went up there with pa to buy some beef cattle, I think. Boy, I mighta been walking right across millions of gold nuggets." He turned a smile toward the old man.
Huff smiled a nearly toothless smile. "Might be millions on that land of yours; oughta check it out."
"Might do that. Yeah, might just do that while I'm waiting for spring to come around."
Jesse wasn't at ease sleeping up in the wagon even though it was warm on top of all the beaver pelts, so he let Huff have it all to himself. He scraped the snow away from the wheel of the wagon and draped a buffalo hide over it to hold off the wind. After placing another buffalo hide on the ground he opened up his bedroll and lay looking up at the sky. *Probably have to face a few of Jack Hannan's old buddies, but they were all a pretty sorry bunch. Heck yes, soon's I get the supplies ordered I'll go have a look-see at that land o' mine.*
An hour before dawn, Jesse's dream was vivid. He was on the African prairie and there were thousands of animals passing by in a thundering herd. Elephants, zebras, lions, tigers, giraffes—buffalo. He could even feel the ground beneath his feet moving. "**Buffalo**." he screamed out loud, and was wide-awake on his feet listening. This was no dream; his subconscious had alerted him. "**Huff**," he screamed, and was glad to see the old man climbing down from the wagon. "**Stampede**."
The rumbling noise was getting closer and all Jesse could think of was the narrowness of the ravine they were in. Whatever was coming had to run right over them. In the second it took him to figure out what to do, he looked up into the ravine and could see in the moonlight a black moving mass against the snow.

~ Coming their way ~

Jesse sprinted to the nearest picketed horse and leaped on its back. As he was pulling the picket peg from the ground he saw Huff hobbling toward the edge where there were a few trees. *He ain't gonna make it*, he thought as he grasped the picket rope in his right hand, and buried his heels in the horse's flanks.

As the horse neared the old man, Jesse locked his heels against the horse's belly as tight as he could and reached down to grab Huff as the horse went by. The jolt almost knocked him from the horse, but his heels were locked so tight that he was able to hold on for the few seconds that it took to reach the safety of the trees.

At the moment the horse went into the tree area, the herd of buffalo went thundering by. Ten minutes later the sound was almost gone and the herd could no longer be seen.

"Well," Huff said, "took a lifetime but I finally seen it."

"What's that?"

"Night stampede of buffalo."

"Whadaya think set 'em off like that?"

"A grizzly probably come out to get him an easy meal n' set 'em to running. I wouldn't have made it on these worn out old feet Jesse. Thanks."

The two barefoot men climbed on the wagon horse and headed back to their campsite to see what was left. When Huff saw the three other horses gone he was relieved. "Horses pulled their pickets n' run with 'em. We'll be able to find 'em when it's light."

"Which ain't long," Jesse commented as he looked east at the pale light flushing the darkness from the sky. He walked the horse to the overturned wagon and helped Huff down then dismounted. "Let's see how bad this wagon's damaged."

By the time the sun had climbed far enough above the horizon for them to see what they were doing, the two men realized the wagon was not broken, just overturned. "Gonna hafta remove all four wheels before we turn 'er over, or we're apt to break a couple of 'em when we do. While I'm doin' that, how 'bout you rounding up the horses."

"Sure thing," the old man answered as he walked to the other side of the wagon. "Willya lookit this, m'boots're still hangin' on the side of this thing." Huff sat down and pulled the knee-high leather boots on as he talked to Jesse. "I always hang 'em up on the wagon so scorpions and snakes'll stay out of 'em. Good thing,'cause I sure ain't no barefooter."

"I do too, but when she went over, mine musta got buried under all these bales of pelts, 'cause I don't see 'em anywhere." He got down and began pulling the tied bales of beaver pelts out from under the wagon. "I'm gonna dig till I find ‘em though, ‘cause m’feet’re already freezing.”

“Darn good thing we had these Long Johns on,” Huff said, as he stood and stomped his feet into the boots before climbing up on the horse.

“Yeah man, shouldn’t take me long to get these wheels off, so when you get back with the horses we’ll get this thing right side up, and find our clothes.”

“I don’t reckon they run far.” Huff turned the horse in the direction the buffalo had gone.

Two hours later Jesse had the four wheels off and had tied a beaver pelt around each greased axle. He looked up and saw Huff coming with the three horses in tow. The old man arrived a few minutes later. “See ya found yer boots.”

“Yeah, but the main thing is the toolbox stayed together. Don’t know what I woulda done without it.” He walked to the other side and began laying two ropes out on the snow. “I tied these on the wagon, so let’s see if we can turn her over without tearing up anything.”

Huff put two of the horses on pickets, and helped Jesse rig the ropes to the other two. They dragged bales of beaver pelts around to the place where they knew the wagon would fall. “These oughta keep the wagon from hitting too hard and breaking something, plus we won’t hafta to lift it too much higher t’get the wheels back on.”

Jesse knew Huff was good with horses, so he stood back out of the way while the old man talked to them as they strained against the ropes. When it finally started coming up, the two big workhorses easily brought it on over. Jesse held his breath until the wagon was on top of the bales and he could see that there was no damage done. “Wooeee, Look here,” Jesse yelled, as Huff put the two horses on pickets beside the others.

Jesse had already put his pants on and was buttoning his shirt when Huff started digging through the wagon for his clothes. “Oh boy, here they are. Now if I can just find that canvas coat.”

“Mine’s still hangin’ right here on the side of the wagon where I put it.”

“I was laying on mine, so it’s gotta be buried down in here som’rs.”

The sun had passed overhead, and was almost to the western horizon when the two men had the wagon ready to travel again. Huff had a fire started and was making coffee as Jesse was cutting wild carrots, parsnips, and onions into a pot of melted snow. “Glad I dug these up the other day when you spotted ‘em Huff, ‘cause I need something to go with the beans n’ jerky tonight.”

“Kinda wish we’d had time to hook up n’ move the heck outa this ravine.”

Jesse stood and looked around. “I think we’ll be alright.” There was a hint of doubt in his voice. “Surely those darn buffalo won’t come thundering back?”

“Probably not, but I’ll betcha neither one of us sleeps too good tonight.”

An hour before dawn Jesse had a small fire going, but Huff was right, he hadn’t slept much. He was just filling the pot with snow to boil for coffee when he noticed the old man climbing down from the wagon. "See you slept in your clothes too."

"Yep, m'boots too. Never been bit by the same snake twice."

"How come y'reckon those buffalo didn't run right on up over the wagon?" Jesse measured out enough beans into one of his socks to smash for coffee.

"I s'pose them first few just kinda run right up onto it fore they even saw it, and the rest musta figured it was easier to follow the others on around than climb up over 'em." Huff slipped into his rabbit fur vest then pulled the heavy canvas coat over it as he continued talking. "I heard about one of them scientific fellas that found the bones of a thousand buffalo at the bottom of a cliff. Indians'll cut out what they need before they run 'em over a cliff, so all them critters musta followed one dumbass buffalo over the darn cliff." He walked over to the fire as Jesse was pounding the beans on the wheel with a piece of flat iron from the toolbox. "Ain't no kinda cow too darn smart."

Jesse poured the pulverized coffee beans into the pot of boiling snow. "Kinda like people, they'll follow the biggest darn fool in town sometimes."

As the two men drank coffee, the remaining vegetable stew was heating in another pot. "How much farther to Lewiston y'reckon it is?"

"I figure we're about two thirds there." Huff answered as he softened some hardtack in his stew.

After coffee and breakfast, the two worked together and hitched two horses to the wagon. Just as dawn began to light the trail ahead they pulled out, with the two spare horses trailing behind.

Four days later they pulled into the small town of Lewiston, in Washington State. "We'll let Winslow Jeffries lock up the wagon, and take care of the horses till we're ready to head toward Walla Walla day after tomorrow."

"You said he's honest n' we can trust him to look after these pelts?"

"Ain't just that he's honest," Huff answered, "which he is, but nobody'd think of messing with anything Winslow is lookin' after."

"Good deal, 'cause I could sure do with a hot bath n' a good sleep."

"Soon's we leave Winslow's stable we'll stop by Angie's. It's a good hotel, a saloon, and bootlery, and the best place for you t'stay while we're here."

"How bouchew?"

Huff turned toward Jesse and grinned. "Got me a gal I stay with when I'm here in Lewiston."

"Riding life's wagon right to the end of the trail, huh?"

"Yep, I don't reckon I'll be coming this way again."

There's that word again, funny how Rose got such a kick outa the word yep. He still missed her, and had to shake his head a little to get the thought of her out of it. "I think you have the right idea, Huff. Have a good time while you're here, 'cause I think it's all over when the lights go out."

"Yeah, That's the way I got 'er figured m'self."

It was late afternoon when they pulled up in front of the biggest stable Jesse had ever seen, and before the wagon had stopped, the biggest blackest Negro he'd ever seen came out of the open double doors. "Well howdy Huff," came a thundering greeting from the black giant. The man walked to the wagon and stuck a hand out that could have made Angus McDonald's disappear. "How ya been old timer?" Jesse liked the sincere smile that spread across the man's face as he shook Huff's hand. Before Huff could introduce Jesse, the big man was leaning over toward Jesse's side with his hand out and the same big smile on his face. "Howdy, I'm Winslow Jefferies."

"Jesse McKannah."

The man turned back to Huff. "How long this time?"

"We'll leave out before dawn, day after tomorrow."

"Hauling beaver?"

"Yeah, nice batch of 'em, too."

After grabbing the lead horse's harness, the black man led them to a spot on the side of the gigantic barn. Jesse just sat and watched as the man turned the two pulling horses into position, then untied the two spares. After leading them into a stall he returned and coaxed the two horses backwards as Huff walked along holding the wagon's steering tongue. Jesse was impressed at how easy he made backing a wagon up using the horses, and he said as much.

"Been doing this for fifty some odd years now, so oughta be good at it, huh?" He unhooked the horses, and headed them toward a stall. "Have a good trip with this weird snow storm?"

After Huff explained about the buffalo stampede Winslow said, "Darn, that's really odd. I'll check all the tack tomorrow and replace any that's damaged and put it on Mr. McDonald's bill."

"Preciate that, Winslow." Huff said with a wave, "We're goin' over to Angie's and get Jesse a room with a bath. See ya tomorrow."

The big man waved back, "I'll be right here."

As they walked to Angie's place Jesse said, "See whacha mean, ain't nobody gonna mess with that mountain of black iron." Before they got there he asked Huff, "You say there's a boot place here, too?"

"Best darn boots you'll ever find. A guy came to town about ten years ago. He's twice as black as Winslow, and ain't near half his size. Had him a coupla suitcases full o' material and tools to make boots with. Made a couple pair right out on the porch of Angie's hotel then slept under the trees out back. Them guys raved about those boots so much that Angie talked him into staying here. She had a little shop built inside the hotel, and had a real nice room fixed up for him to live in out back."

"Wonder if he'll have a pair that'll fit me?"

"Probably will, 'cause when he ain't working on a special order he makes 'em up in regular sizes to sell to folks just passing through."

"I've walked through these old boots three times already, n' keep patching 'em with buffalo hide. It looks like we're running outa buffalo, so I'll see what he has."

As soon as they walked through front door of Angie's, a woman taller than Winslow, and twice as big came at a trot from behind the long bar. "Huff, you old beanfart, how ya been?" Jesse looked on as the little man disappeared for a moment, and was relieved when she only held out her hand after peeling Huff from her body. "I'm Angie, stranger, what's yours?"

"Jesse McKannah."

"Gonna spend a few days, Huff?"

"Just tonight n' tomorrow night, then gotta head on to Walla Walla, but I'll be comin' back through in a few days to spend another two with Mabel Ann." He looked around, "She in?"

"Sure is n' she'll be thrilled to see you. She's upstairs workin' right now, but won't be long. Boy is she gonna be happy to see you Huff, 'cause she ain't had an all-nighter since you was here in the summer." She looked at Jesse. "Want a room with its own tub Jesse or y'wanna save a few bucks n' share one with a couple other guys?"

"Gimme one with a bath n' I don't even care if its got a bed, 'cause I'm probably gonna be in the tub all night—lordy it's been awhile."

"Two nights'll be ten bucks and another two if you want a girl to come up for a while tonight." Her fat red lips parted, and he saw the grayest crooked teeth he'd ever seen.

Jesse told Angie that he didn't want one of the girls to come up. "Well, if you change your mind just gimme a shout n' I'll send one of my little angels up to rub yer back," the red and gray grin again, "or whatever ya want rubbed, haw, haw, haw." Her laugh almost made Jesse laugh, but he controlled himself. *I got a hunch you don't wanna make this woman mad.* He responded with a grin, "I'll do that."

"How 'bout a coupla beers darlin'," Huff said, with his toothless grin looking up to where his lady was earning her living.

After putting them in front of the two obviously trail weary men, she asked, "Hungry?"

Huff's hungry eyes were watching the second story landing, so Jesse answered. "Lordy, yes. Anything ya got'll be great, n' plenty of it."

"A man after my own heart," she said as she headed toward the kitchen. "Maybe you 'n me'll get together later?"

Not really. I wouldn't get on that for all the salt in Seattle. When she returned about ten minutes later he thought, *this's gonna be a good stop.* She set two tin plates bigger than any he had ever seen, full of a wonderful looking stew with vegetables, and two huge two-inch-thick slabs of bread smeared thick with butter.

"Plenty more back there, if you're still hungry. C'mon, drink them beers n' I'll getcha two more."

They ate in silent concentration, enjoying every bite, not knowing when it might happen again after they left. Huff was wiping out his plate with the last of his bread when one of the three doors on the landing opened. By the grin on the old man's face, Jesse knew it was Mabel Ann. He watched as she came down the stairs. As soon as she saw Huff she yelled, "Hey there you horny old devil, you come all the way just to try to ride old Mabel into the dust again?" Her grin was a red obscene mess as she came over and planted a wet smear of red grease on Huff's face.

Old is right, bet she's his age. No thanks, I'll rub m'own back.

Jesse didn't ignore the bed altogether, but he did spend a lot of time in the tub that he kept adding hot water to from the kettle over the fireplace. Midnight had just slipped into the room by the time he finally dried and climbed into the bed. It was well after dawn when he climbed reluctantly from the soft warm mattress and featherbed. After washing the sleep from his eyes, he slipped into his stiff canvas pants. *Gotta get them other buckskins washed so I can get these stiff, stinky things cleaned.* He put on the shirt he'd bought in a Lewiston dry goods store the previous day then looked down at the worn out boots. *Hope I can replace you two today.*

He sat down with the coat that Rose had made him, and began opening a seam with his long hunting knife. When it was large enough to slip his hand inside one of the several pockets that she had sewed his money in, he removed the flat piece of rabbit skin she sewed it in to keep it from getting wet or wadding up and be noticed. He sat looking at the package a long time then said quietly, "I sure miss ya, girl."

After putting part of the money in his pocket, he pulled open the flap he had added to the rear of the shoulder holster when he made it, and put the balance of the bills in there. After adding a short length of sewing thread to the one he'd cut, he began sewing the coat's seam. Jesse checked to be sure the open seam in the coat was not noticeable then slipped the holster over his left arm, and adjusted the .44 until it felt in place. He swung the loop around his back and slipped his right arm through it, then pulled the tie-down piece of rawhide to his belt, pulling the holster down, as he snugged up the rawhide to hold it in place.

After swinging Angus's gift around his hips, he put the coat on and headed for the stairs. He was intercepted by what was not long before an attractive twenty-year-old, but now looked fifty. "Hi handsome, how 'bout you n' me spending a coupla hours riding in the brush this morning?"

Jesse didn't want to insult one of Angie's ladies, especially with a hole in his gut that a saddle could be stored in, and her down there cooking. He answered with a smile. "I'd love to darlin', but a Sioux warrior left m'scalp n' took that to hang around his waist." He continued to the stairs, following the smell of bacon.

"Oh my God, that's terrible. Oh lordy, you poor man."

He gave her a sad glance. "Yeah, that's what I thought at the time, but I've got used to sitting down to pee."

The old, young woman just stood watching his lean frame going down the stairs and shook her head slowly, "Poor, poor man." She shrugged her shoulders as she opened her door and disappeared inside the room.

Huff looked up from a tin plate still piled high with flapjacks after several minutes working on it. Another tin plate of bacon was on the table beside a second tin mug of hot coffee with a small tin cover keeping it hot. "Whatcha carryin' your boots for?"

"Didn't have the heart to put m'feet in 'em after seeing those new ones through that bootlery window yesterday. Angie said the guy'll be here this morning so I can get a pair of new ones." He pulled the chair back and sat down, "This coffee?" he asked pointing at the tin covered mug."

"Yep. Heard ya moving around up there, so I tole Angie to fix you a mug, and then fry a buncha eggs to go with the flapjacks. Hey, here they come now."

When Angie set the platter of eggs on the table, and the plate of flapjacks in front of Jesse he said, "What took ya s'long, Angie?"

She grinned down at him. "Ain'chew a devil in the morning. Damn, wish t'hell I was twenty, thirty years younger." She grinned as she headed back to the kitchen.

And three hundred pounds lighter, Jesse thought, but kept a straight face.

Huff watched her sway across the room. *Wish that big ole gal'd give me a crack at that.*

About the same time that Jesse finished breakfast the boot man arrived. He was at least as old as Angie, and blacker than Winslow Jefferies. He walked straight toward Jesse. "Hello stranger, I hear you're looking for some boots."

"Sure am." He held out his hand, "Jesse McKannah."

The very erect, well-dressed Negro took the hand and gave Jesse a firm handshake. "Ruben Folberg, pleased to meet you, Jesse."

An hour later, Jesse walked out in a pair of soft, handsewn, leather boots. Huff was sitting in one of the many rockers on the porch. "Darn good lookin' boots, amigo."

"You can't tell, but he musta wore these a month to make 'em this soft. They feel like gloves on a hand. Best thirty dollars I've spent in a while." Jesse sat beside huff in the other rocker.

Two dusty, filthily dressed men sitting a short distance away didn't move a muscle, but both silently registered the words. *Thirty bucks cash money.*

Huff smiled. "Nah, that ole black man just knows how to tan leather so that it feels like you could wrap a new baby in it. I asked him one time where he learned to work leather like that. He said he started as a slave when he was five years old. Had to carry buckets of piss all day to pour over the hides and if he didn't have enough to cover 'em everybody got whipped, including him. If a slave was caught pissing on the ground instead of in the tanning buckets they got beat bad n' sometimes killed if his master was drunk or in a bad mood."

Jesse just shook his head. "Escaped?"

"Yep. About fifty years ago. He was through here a long time back and remembered how well everybody treated Winslow, so when his wife died he came here to see if he could get a little boot business started. Now he says he's thinkin' about going back up to Canada, 'cause he's got too darn much business for a man his age."

"He's kidding, ain't he?"

"Hell's Belles, I dunno? How old you reckon he is?"

"Mmmm, at least sixty, maybe a little more."

"Well, you count 'em up. He was twenty when he escaped from Alabama then he lived in Canada for fifty-five years, and he's been here about ten."

"Holey moley, he's over eighty-five n' still makin' boots."

"You noticed how straight he stands, dincha? Bet you was surprised when he shook your hand too, huh?"

"Yeah, and he dresses n' talks like a real gentleman."

"Guess what he was up in Canada."

"Bootmaker for the King, or whatever they got up there."

"Nah, nothing fancy like that, a lawyer." Huff waited for a reply, but continued when Jesse just waited. "A preacher and his family took him in and educated him. He says he had as many white people come to him as black."

"Strange world, huh? A black, bootmaking lawyer out here in the middle of nowhere." Jesse stood, "I'm gonna walk over to Winslow's and see if everything's gonna be ready to go tomorrow, then I'm gonna soak in that tub a few hours." He stretched his back then walked down the three steps from the porch to the muddy street where the melting snow was making it worse by the hour. Huff also rose and headed for the bar to see if Mable Ann was around. No one paid any attention, but the two grungy men that had listened to every word also got up and casually followed Jesse toward the stable.

It was a casual pastime that a lot of men killed time doing, so nobody noticed when the two men that had casually followed Jesse to the stable, began a game of slice the pie with their hunting knives. They seemed to be very involved in their game, even though neither said a word. What they were really doing was listening to what Jesse was saying to the stable man.

After inquiring about the wagon and tack, Jesse followed Winslow inside where he handed him one end of the main harness. "Give her a good yank while I hold this end."

When it broke in his hand Jesse said, "Darn, I thought it was good but guess I didn't check close enough, huh?"

"They woulda done fine till you had to really lay back on 'em, but you can see what would have happened then."

"Yep. Learned som'n today. I'll be a lot more careful when I check the gear. Thanks Winslow, that coulda caused me a world of grief. I'll send Angus a letter tellin' him the whole deal."

"Don't bother. I always do that with every customer so they can keep up with what it costs them, and when to do a little maintenance."

"They oughta let you keep up with it for 'em, and just pay the bill. All these trading companies are making a fortune I think, especially the one that Angus works for."

"Some of 'em do let me make repairs as I find them, but there are a few that try to get the very last mile out of every piece of their equipment." The huge man headed for the open doors. "It usually costs them guys twice as much in the end."

When the two men heard the black man and wagon guy coming, they quickly resumed their game.

Jesse asked Angie to have the water boy fill his tub with hot water then joined Huff at the bar for a beer. When he saw that the young boy had made two trips, he told Huff he'd see him for supper then went to his room for a long soak.

After supper, Huff smiled and waved as Mabel came into the bar. Jesse stood up as she sat down, excusing himself for being too tired to join them for another beer. "You enjoy the evening Huff, and I'll drive for the first leg. Goodnight Mabel, see ya for breakfast, Huff."

A little after dawn the two men thanked Winslow for everything he did on the wagon and pulled out with the two spare horses following on leads. "See ya in a coupla of weeks, Winslow." Huff yelled over his shoulder.

Before Jesse and Huff had even got out of bed that morning, the two grungy drifters had slipped out of town and were now standing beside their horses on a hilltop stand of trees. They watched as the wagon passed below them. "C'mon Emmit," the tall skinny man with a dirty gray beard and mustache said, "I know right where they gotta go across the Tucannon River."

"Yeah, Hollis." The short man with a red handlebar mustache, which looked like it had last week's breakfast still in it, said. "And we'll be waitin' for 'em." When he grinned, it made his friend Hollis Canfield shudder. *A possum wouldn't poke his nose in that mess.*

The trail between Lewiston and Walla Walla was much better than the one they had been traveling on, so Jesse and Huff made good time the first day. Huff was at the reins when it began getting dark, so Jesse asked him, "Gonna push her on a ways further?"

"Yeah, I think we're a little over half way to where we gotta cross the Tucannon River, but I wanna be sure, 'cause I've knowed it to get warm n' start thawin' the snow after an early storm like this last one." He spit a stream of tobacco juice out on the side of the trail. "We wanna get on the other side before dark tomorrow while it's nice n' shallow in the place where we're gonna cross."

The two drifters were only a few miles from the spot Huff was talking about when they made camp that first night. "Hobble these horses over there, Emmit, and I'll start us a fire." Hollis didn't like Emmit Brady, but he was the only man that had ever let him be the boss, so he put up with his foul ways and smelly breath. *Hell, I ain't gotta kiss the little dwarf or sleep with him.*

Emmit tied the two horses to a small bush near the spot where Hollis was putting the sticks together for a fire, and removed both saddles. He then walked them to the small flat clearing in the trees to hobble them so they could graze. It never crossed either man's mind to fill a saddlebag with grain for their horses.

The fire was burning by the time Emmit returned. "Boy Hollis, you're sure good with that sparkin' stone. I ain't never learned how to make one of them things work."

"Just stick with me, Emmit n' you ain't gotta learn anything, 'cause I'll do all the thinkin' and tell you what to do n' how to do it."

After the fire had burned down to a hot bed of coals Hollis said, "Get that little pot outa my saddlebag there n' fill er with clean snow from one of the drifts against these trees."

"Sure thing boss," the little man said, and jumped up.

Boss. I sure like the sound o' that.

A while later Emmit said, "Lookit there, boss, it's boilin' already. Man you sure know how to get a hot fire in a hurry."

"Yeah, I do. Now get that jerky meat outa your saddlebags and just put three pieces in the water."

The little man returned quickly because he was hungry. "I'll put four of 'em in, boss."

"Golldang it, Emmit," Hollis yelled, "what did I just tell you to do?"

"Well uh, you said to put three chunks o' jerky in the water, but I figured I'd put two for each of us."

"Yeah sure, just put the whole darn package in there n' when it's gone we'll just starve to death, you moron."

"Uh well uh," Emmit stammered, "I'll just put one for each of us in there then so we'll have enough to last till we get to your injun friends."

"Here Emmit, look at these." Hollis held up three fingers. "That's how many you put in the pot. One for you, 'cause you ain't gotta do nothin' but what I tells ya. Two for me 'cause I gotta do everything, like getting the fire going, and all the thinkin' too."

Emmit stood a moment and looked at the four big pieces of smoke-dried meat then returned one to the package. "You're right boss." He put three pieces of meat into the pot then put the package back in the saddlebags. "You're right, boss, a guy can't think when he's got a naggin' hunger in his gut."

"That's right, and if I don't plan everything out just right we wind up behind bars again for a few more years. Now go get our two tin cups so we can have us some o' that broth."

After the broth was gone, along with one piece of his jerky, Hollis said, "Now you can get some more wood n' build up this fire." He sat back against the tree and chewed on his other chunk of jerky.

When the fire was blazing Emmit said, "We gonna waylay these two at the same place we did that guy last week, or last month, or whenever it was?"

"It was three months ago you dumbass and yes, 'cause it's close to where we'll swap that wagon to them injuns for a big canoe n' take them beaver pelts down the Snake River to Rufus over in Oregon."

"How long you knowed that Rufus guy?"

"Rufus is a town, Emmit. I tole you that a bunch o' times. I know a guy over there what owns a trading post, and he'll buy anything we bring him." He finished his jerky then added, "And he don't give a rat's ass where we get it. Hell, he says he'll even buy scalps for them eastern folks what like to have that kinda stuff sittin' around their big fancy homes."

Emmit's eyes lit up. "Hey, let's kill these two n' scalp 'em."

"Dammit Emmit what's the matter with you? You're always wantin' to kill somebody. What the hell is it with you? Can't wait to get your neck in a hangman's noose?"

The fire went out of the little man's eyes. "Nah, I don't wanna hang, but I got m'knife razor sharp," his eyes began to shine again as he removed the long knife from its sheath, "and I just wanna see what it feels like to slice somebody's throat." He let out a gurgling kind of chuckle as he returned the knife to its sheath.

Sick son-of-a-bitch. Probably gonna hafta kill him too, one o' these day t'keep him from gettin' me strung up beside him.

As the wagon rolled along, Jesse and Huff chatted about many different things to pass the time. "How'd your daddy n' mama meet, Huff?"

"She saved his bacon."

"No hell, kept the Indians from killin' him?"

"Nope, he hit a sunk rock out in the Columbia River and dumped his canoe over. Pappy couldn't swim a lick n' he was drowning for sure till mama jumped in n' yanked him out. He appreciated it so much, he gave her me."

The other two men watched from the trees on a hilltop a half-mile away. "We'll wait'll after dark n' they got 'em a good fire, 'cause they'll be all relaxed n' tired, plus that cracklin' fire'll keep 'em from hearing any noise you might make while we're slipping up on 'em. Soon's we get the drop on 'em we'll take their guns n' hides, then haul ass for the Snake River. Time they get to anyplace they can talk about it we'll be on our way down the Columbia."

"We're gonna hafta hook up the horses," Emmit whined, "why don't we jump 'em in the daytime whilst them horses're still hitched?"

"Because there's too many people passing through here these days. That's why, you donkey-brain dumbass. Somebody sees us n' first thing you know there's a posse chasin' us again."

"I still think we oughta just ride up n' shoot 'em both."

Hollis shook his head. "It's that third word you used Emmitt. That's what keeps getting' you in trouble."

"What's that?"

"Think. You ain't any good at it, so quit doin' it. Lemme do the thinking, and you just do what I tell ya t'do."

When Emmit grinned, Hollis could smell his foul breath all the way across the fire. "Yeah, you're right Hollis, you're the boss."

"That's right Emmit; I'm the boss of this outfit."

"How long you been knowin' Winslow?" Jesse asked Huff.

"Mmmm lemme see," the skinny old man mumbled as he rubbed his chin, "bout sixty years I reckon. I think he said once that he was just fifteen years old when he come to Lewiston, and we're the same age, so I reckon that'd be 'bout right."

Jesse turned and looked hard at the tall, much too skinny old man holding the reins. After a long look he said, "You mean to tell me you're about seventy-five-years old?"

"Born in seventy-seven and we're just about to get shut of fifty-two, so how much is that? Must be about seventy-five, 'cause Winslow said he wants me to come to his seventy-fifth birthday party when I come back through."

Jesse shook his head from side to side several times. "Huff, you're really something."

The old man turned a big grin Jesse's way. "That's what Mabel Ann says."

"Winslow got himself a wife'r any kind o' family?"

"Buried two of 'em," Huff said, matter-of-factly, "both injuns. First one was a Flathead, but it's been so long I don't hardly remember her. Died of the fever I think." Another long stream of tobacco juice hit the side of the trail then he went on, "Second one died just a few years ago of that coughing disease. She was a Pend d'Orielle—real nice lady." He paused a long time, so Jesse kept silent and waited. "Yeah, a real nice lady. She was a medicine woman that come to town to doctor folks when they was real sick. Lived in a camp out on the Alpowa Creek, if I remember correctly. She was about forty when he married her, and they was a real good team. She worked right there with him till she got too sick to get outa bed." He paused a moment before adding, "Bet he still misses her."

"He got any kids?"

"Yeah, two boys. One went back up to Canada with his tribe, when the gov'ment started stealin' their land n' hangin' 'em for killing buffalo. The other one lives right there in Lewiston and works with Winslow. He does all the shoeing, and he's the best at it I ever saw. No doubt he'll stay right there n' run the business when ole Winslow kicks the bucket."

"Don't guess I saw him."

"You mighta, and didn't know it. Don't look much like his daddy. Got his mama's looks, plus he don't have a lot to say. He could walk right up behind you on a sunny day n' be standing in your shadow n' you wouldn't even know he was there—real injun.

As Huff eased the wagon across the Tucannon River, Jesse shivered. "Brrr, sure ain't gotta worry 'bout any flash floods, 'cause it's gettin' colder by the hour."

"Yeah, I'm glad we got here to cross this river 'fore dark. Nothin' but smooth sailing on into Walla Walla now."

After the wagon was out of the river, Huff continued to a flat area in the center of a large stand of trees. "I camped here a few times 'fore goin' on into Walla Walla. Nice 'n level and plenty of dead wood layin' around for a fire."

As soon as Huff had the wagon stopped, Jesse was on the ground unhitching the horses. After he had the pulling team hobbled, he returned and got the two spares and hobbled them too. He went to the horses and let each eat some of the grain he carried for them in his hat. When he got back to the wagon Huff already had a fire going. They both stood around it for ten minutes warming up, and then Jesse got out the coffee beans as Huff filled their pot with water. While Jesse pounded the beans in a clean sock, Huff got out the other pot and filled it half full of water. As the two pots heated, Huff began digging through their supplies for the rest of the wild vegetables that Jesse dug up along the way. Fifteen minutes later the two men were sitting around the fire drinking coffee and waiting for the stewing vegetables and jerky to cook tender.

It wasn't quite dark when the two drifters on top of the hill, just north of the wagon, saw the fire begin blazing. They remained behind the boulder and watched. "Dang, it's gettin' colder by the minute. Wish we was sittin' next to that fire."

"Me too," Emmit commented, and mumbled, "oughta go down there n' kill 'em so we can."

"What?"

"Said we oughta go kill 'em."

"Dammit Emmit, I swear I'm gonna get shut o' you 'fore I get m'neck in a noose."

Emmit was cold because the only coat he had was a thin, worn through, canvas windbreaker, so he was a little more aggressive than usual. "Aw hell Hollis, there ain't another living soul 'roun here for miles, and if anyone heard the shots they'd think someone got 'em a dinner deer juss afore dark."

"Tell you what Emmit, soon's we get to Portland you can get your own gang n' be the boss, but long as you'n me're together, I'm the boss." He glared at the smelly little man before turning his attention back to their prey.

"You think we'll be about three days getting to Walla Walla, huh?"

"Yeah, if we don't run into any more buffalo stampedes."

"You gonna get supplies n' head right on back to Lewiston and spend time with Mabel?"

"Hell no," the old man grinned, "Got a gal in Walla Walla too. She'd have a fit if she found out I was there 'n didn't spend a coupla days with her."

"Darn if I ain't startin' t'look forward to my old age, Huff."

"Hey son, don't wait'll you're old like me, get at it now while ya can." He went to the fire and pulled the pot of stew out with a small steel hook. After testing one of the carrots with his knife he said, "She's ready."

"Me too."

Thirty minutes later the stew was gone and the fire was blazing again. Both men sat huddled against the wind, sipping coffee.

"Let's go Emmit, and for cryin' out loud, be quiet. Don't fergit to pull your bandana up over your face when we get to that tree I pointed out." Hollis carefully picked his way through the dark toward the wagon. Emmit pulled his bandanna up over his face so he wouldn't forget, and followed close behind.

Jesse got up and put another few branches on the fire then settled back down against the boulder that was blocking some of the wind. Huff had just finished the last of his coffee when a voice came from the other side of the fire.

"You boys freeze right where y'are or I'll blow a hole through ya. Easy now, just keep calm n' do like I say n' we'll be on our way afore ya know it. Ain't no reason for anyone to go gettin' hisself kilt over a buncha dead beavers."

Jesse was trying desperately to see the man speaking, but the fire's smoke prevented it. He and Huff knew they were in a real bind, so neither man moved a muscle.

"You there Bones, stand up."

"Me?" Huff asked.

"That's right, stand up nice n' easy. And you dude, my partner's got his gun on ya, so don't move nothin' or you're both dead. You got 'em covered, Shorty?"

"Sure do Hollis, uh Slim."

In that moment Hollis seriously considered turning and shooting Emmit, but he was afraid the big guy could get his pistol out and shoot him before he could turn back around. "Where's your gun, bones?"

"Don't carry one. They're too damn heavy n' I ain't never been a good shot, noway."

"Okay, lie down on the ground, face to it."

After tying Huff's hands behind his back, Hollis took his pistol back out of the holster and turned to Jesse. "Now real slow n' careful dude, stand up."

Jesse was looking at the smaller of the two, as the skinny man tied Huff. He saw that he was a nervous type who kept moving his eyes back and forth from Jesse to his partner. *If I get a chance to make a move I'll get that skinny guy first cause this short guy'll be all messed up when it happens, and I'll probably have time to cancel his contract too.* He kept his hands out from his body as he slowly stood.

"Smart man. Now turn around n' face the other direction then be real, real careful n' unbuckle that gunbelt n' let it fall." After a moment of silence Hollis said, "Okay, do it now."

Facing away from them was the best thing that had happened to Jesse since the two bandits arrived. As he kept his right hand out to the side, he reached in with his left hand and unbuckled the belt holding the holster with the .44 revolver, which Angus had given him. The short barrel .44 was hanging right there beneath his left armpit, and the big coat was open enough to allow him to get to it when the right moment came.

"Hold your gun on him Shorty, while I get that belt."

Jesse heard the short man take a step or two toward him as he heard the skinny man reaching down to get the gunbelt.

A ninth eye in this little scene was open as the tenth eye was lining up the glittering point at the end of a five foot long barrel between the white vee just ahead of the eye. When the glittering point was exactly in the vee, and pointed right at Hollis's heart—the trigger was pulled.

Jesse was startled when he heard the explosion, but he instinctually reached for the short barrel .44. He wheeled around to find the little man standing with his mouth open, and holding a pistol pointed at the ground. He turned to look at Jesse about the time the .44 hit him in the chest. He was barely on his feet when the second slug hit him in the stomach. Reflex muscles were making his arm with the gun jerk, so Jesse stepped toward the falling man and pulled the trigger again. The last slug hit just below the left eye, and since he was falling backward the bullet exited from the top of his skull. Jesse turned the barrel toward the skinny man lying on the ground, but he could see that he was no longer a problem. He looked out to where the shot had come from as a voice came through the darkness. "Mahatma Jefferies here, Winslow's son."

"Hey Hat," Huff yelled from the ground, "c'mon in, boy."

Jesse watched as a man at least six inches taller than he was and twenty pounds lighter came through the darkness carrying the longest rifle he had ever seen. The man didn't look like he had an ounce of Negro blood. *He looks a lot like Lame Wolverine*. Before Jesse could say a word, the man explained.

"Daddy saw them two guys watching you, and when you pulled out they followed, so he told me to keep an eye on you."

"Thanks amigo." Jesse said as he nodded his head.

"Gotta ask you something," the tall, skinny man said.

Huff yelled, "Before this damned palaver gets goin' could one o' you untie me fore I freeze to death laying here."

"Oh heck, I'm sorry Huff." Jesse leaped across the burned down fire and sliced the rope holding Huff's hands behind his back. "Y'okay?"

"Am now. Damned good timing, Hat." He grinned at the man leaning casually on the long rifle. "Still's spooky as ever out there in the dark, aincha?"

The half-Indian/half-Negro smiled, "Got any coffee?"

"Sure gonna get some going." Jesse answered, then got the pot and filled it with water. As it heated, he helped pull the two dead men away from the fire.

As they waited for the coffee Jesse said, "What didja wanna ask me, uh whaja say your name is?"

"Mahatma. Odd name for a half Negro/half Indian, huh?"

"Yeah it is, ain't ever heard it before."

"A man from India was visiting my mama's camp before I was born. He thought the Indians he'd heard about here in America were his kind of people and he wanted to visit them," he grinned warmly, "mama said he was one of the nicest men she ever met, next to papa, so she named me after him." He leaned over to offer his hand. "Everybody just calls me Hat though, what's yours?"

"Jesse McKannah." He shook the man's hand then looked at Huff. "You sure meet some mighty good people, Huff."

The three men sat around the campfire for a couple of hours talking, and winding down from the events they'd just experienced. Jesse asked Mahatma, "You never did say what you wanted to ask me, Hat."

"Well, I was watching everything for quite awhile. When they left their spot up there on the hill I followed them down here and saw everything that went on. I saw you drop your pistolbelt, so what the heck did you shoot that little fella with?"

Jesse opened his coat and pulled the short barrel .44 caliber pistol from the shoulderholster. "This pistol has saved my bacon a couple of times since I had it made. Here, take a look at it."

After looking the pistol over, he handed it back to Jesse. "Where'd you get it made?"

"Went to San Francisco a few years ago, and a gunstore had these new Colt revolvers for sale, but they would take an order for something special like this as long as it didn't change the basic design." He opened the cylinder and filled the three empty chambers. As he went to put it back in the shoulder holster, Hat leaned forward to see where it was going.

"That's really neat, did it come with it?"

"Nope, made it m'self. Saw one of 'em in that shop, but it didn't look good to me, so I kinda remembered how it was put together then went home n' made m'own."

"What keeps it from flopping around?"

Jesse stood and removed his coat so the man could see how it was held in place with the loop around the back, and over the other shoulder then tied to his belt with a rawhide tong. "Son-of-a-gun," Hat said emphatically, "that's really a slick weapon."

"You shoulda seen the one I threw into the Columbia River." After telling the Indian about the incident with the fire and his time with the tribe, the tall man turned and looked at him for a long moment. Finally Hat said, "You must be White Buffalo."

Jesse's quizzical, unknowing expression prompted the Indian to explain. "My mama's people are talking about White Buffalo, who came back to save the The People, and avenge the Blackfoot. You're s'pose to have single-handedly wiped out a hundred of them, and killed their War Chief, Hook."

Jesse was having a hard time keeping Rose out of his thoughts, so when Mahatma mentioned the Flathead tribe she came drifting back through. After a moment he shook her from his mind. "Well, a bunch of Blackfoot got killed when they attacked us at a lakeside camp, but all I did was set 'em up in an organized shooting group. Those Indians I was with came through like a bunch of seasoned soldiers."

"Well, I know how my mama's people build a whole life around stories like that, so I bet you'll still be the center of stories told by the medicine dancers a hundred years from now and you'll still be White Buffalo."

"What was that other guy's name that I'm suppose to have killed?"

"Hook," Mahatma responded. "Never ran into him, but I've heard a lot about him; a real scary guy. Actually he sounds like he was crazy, if you can believe the stories you hear."

"Don't think I ever ran into him," Jesse said. "The only other time we had trouble was with a bunch that followed us, but we peppered 'em pretty good n' they took off for home." He filled their cups with coffee then added, "I killed some crazy guy that attacked me n' Rose the day she was killed, but later when we went to get his body to see who he was, it was gone. Maybe that was Hook?"

"I guess we'll never really know, but you're gonna be in Indian campfire legend from now on." Hat sipped his hot coffee then added, "Which is fine as far as I'm concerned, 'cause mama's people don't have much to look forward to these days. A good story that just keeps getting better n' better as it's told will help keep their minds off their worries."

"Son, I got som'n to ask you m'self." Huff poured them all more coffee.

"What's that, Huff?"

"I've tried to make a night shot at deer when I was hungry for meat n' never have hit one, but you plugged that beanpole dude right in the heart." He leaned forward to look the Indian right in the eyes. "What the heck's your secret for lining up on 'em when it's nighttime?"

Mahatma pulled the long rifle in to him so Huff and Jesse could see what he was pointing to. "See that sparkling thing on the tip of the sight?" Both men leaned over to see it better. "Yeah, I see something sparkling in the campfire light," Jesse said.

"Yeah, me too."

"Those're real diamonds, and all it takes is a bright star to make it shine enough to get it lined up in this vee here." He pushed the rifle back out and pointed to a vee-knotched rear sight on top of the long barrel, just ahead of the striker. "I smear a little white celebration face paint on it, and when I get that sparkling diamond in the white vee, it hits what I've got it on." He stood and handed the weapon to the old man. "Here Huff, go over there behind the wagon in the dark n' sight in on one of them trees out there. Careful though, 'cause I rammed another load in her 'fore I came in here."

As Huff headed for the wagon to see what it was like, Hat turned to Jesse. "On a starry night like this, it really sparkles."

"How 'bout when it's dark?"

"I just put a little white paste on the diamond. Don't work as good, but it works."

"Where do y'get the diamonds?"

"Mama used to dig 'em up out near where her folk's camp is. Never got any big ones, but she loved the way they sparkled. She smashed them into tiny little pieces, and glued them on about everything she wore." He pulled a chunk of buffalo horn from his waist bag. "She made this buffalo hoof glue and that's what I use to stick them on the end of the barrel. Daddy says it's the best glue in the world. He makes it up and sells it to folks around town." They both looked up when Huff spoke.

"Jesse you gotta go look at this." He handed the gun to him.

When Jesse returned, he handed it back to Hat. "I wouldn't have believed it if I hadn't seen it m'self."

"Yeah." Huff agreed. "That's som'n, ain't it."

"If you guys don't mind," Hat said as he stood, "I'll ride on into Walla Walla with you and see if they're gonna be sending daddy's supplies pretty soon."

"Sure thing." Jesse replied.

"Dang right," Huff said loudly, "after what we been through, who knows what's on the last leg o' this trip." He paused then said, "Speakin' o' last trips, this is it for me."

"Really?" Jesse said, leaning ahead to look past Hat, and at the old man.

"Yep, was already thinking about it, but this little trail opera settled it for me. I'm gitting too old to be lying on the cold ground with m'arms tied behind me, so this's m'last wagonload."

"I'm going up n' get m'horse." Hat tied the strings holding his coat together in the front. "I'll bring those guy's horses too, so we can tie them on till we get to a rim up ahead in the morning. We'll dump 'em over into the ravine. If a lawman came through and saw them, he'd be looking all over to find a murderer."

"When you get back you can sleep up in the wagon if you want, Hat." Huff offered.

"Nah, you guys go ahead n' I'll hobble the horses and sleep awhile out there in the bush." Before he walked away he turned, "There's plenty more of that kind around these days." He nodded at the two bodies

The following morning Huff was building a fire as Jesse pounded coffee beans on a wagon wheel. Hat yelled before walking in then went to the fire. "Mmmm, feels good; getting pretty darn cold."

"Yeah, bet I'll be facing deep snow before I get this last load of supplies back to Angus."

"If you don't mind, I'll ride back to Lewiston with you." Hat suggested.

"Mind? Hell, I'll put you down as driver n' you can make a few dollars off ole Angus."

"Great. I ain't against makin' a dollar when I can." He slapped his arms then held his hands out to the fire. "I can go on to Fort Connah with you if you want, and visit some of my kin."

"Hot damn, Jesse. Didja hear that?"

"Sure did Huff. Takes a load off m'mind too." He looked at the withered up little man. "You're beginning t'feel like family, we been through so much together."

After broth, jerky meat, and coffee, the three men got the two bodies up on their horses. Jesse secured them so they wouldn't fall, then Hat said. "That rim's only about five miles ahead. How 'bout we leave the saddles laying there for the Indians to find then turn the horses loose?"

"Sure thing. They'll put 'em to better use than those two sorry bastards ever did."

A couple of hours later, Huff waited on the trail as Jesse went with Hat to dump the two bodies into the canyon. When they returned he asked, "Didja say some words when you sent 'em on their way?"

"He sure did," Hat replied with a grin. "Rot in hell, you sons-a-bitches."

As the wagon rolled along, Jesse's mind wandered back to scenes from his younger days—almost forgotten. He recalled seeing the three riders coming over the hill then begin riding toward his new ranch. He didn't have to watch them long before he knew exactly who they were. He turned toward his foreman, Arliss O'Reilley and yelled loudly, "Hey Arliss, you've been hoping to meet my brothers so looks like you're gonna get t'meet three of 'em."

Patrick, Broderick and Ian stopped at the corral Jesse was working on. They were all grinning, but Patrick's wide grin exceeded them all when he spoke. "Well little brother, don't look so darn surprised, I sent word that we were coming."

Jesse maintained an artificial scowl as he answered. "Yeah y'did, and James Poorsmith had it waiting when I went for supplies." He paused a moment then added, "Last year."

"We had a slight delay," Broderick said as he dismounted. "We got stuck in Boston after we got our Law Degree, until Ian got his deal all set n' sold his place. We figured it best if we all headed home together."

"Hmmm. I was wondering who that tin horn dude there with you was." He looked at Ian who had also climbed down from his horse. "Darn Ian, you've muscled up pretty good. Lifting them dumbbell weights these days, are you?"

"Nope, dumbbell Irishmen. Gotta get 'em up off their feet if ya want 'em to land in the street instead of on the porch." His smile was sincere as he grabbed Jesse's hand. "Been awhile, huh?"

"Too darn long."

The four McKannah brothers were soon standing in a knot, their arms entangled as they did a jig around in the corral. When they stopped, Jesse saw that Arliss was still leaning against the rail, so he pointed at each as he introduced them. When he was finished he said, "Boys, this is my best friend and ranch foreman, Arliss O'Reilley."

Broderick was the last to shake the man's hand. "By Jesus I do believe we Irish are gonna take over this bloody new country.

Arliss had a warm, sincere smile, and it won the three brothers over immediately. "An' if we do, I bloody well 'ope we do a better job of it than we did in th' old country."

Patrick said, "Sending those damn Brits home from here with their tails between their legs was a bloody good start."

"I'll drink to that," Broderick said as he looked at Jesse. "Y'do 'ave som'n for a buncha traveling Irishmen to wet their whistles with, doncha?"

"Not a bloody drop, boys, I still don't use the stuff." Jesse paused a moment to enjoy the look on each face then added, "But Arliss keeps a few gallons of som'n in the bunkhouse that keeps the rodents out."

"Snakes, wolves, bears n' everything else 'roun here, 'cept the darn ranch hands." Arliss grinned and motioned with his arm, "C'mon n' decide for y'selves if it's that rough or we just 'ave weak critters hereabouts."

25

~ Walla Walla—good rest stop ~

A little before noon, on the third day after leaving the camp at the Tucannon River, Jesse and Huff entered Walla Walla, Washington. Hat was on his horse behind the two spare horses that were tied to the rear of the wagon. Huff pulled the wagon to the rear of a huge log building that had a sign hanging from the porch overhang.

OMAR CHADWICK
Wagon train outfitter—Trapping supplies—Hotel—Saloon.

Jesse read the sign aloud. "Whoever Omar is, he ain't missing a trick is he?"

Huff chuckled. "Wait'll you see the short, fat, baldheaded little guy with bulgy eyes n' thick wet lips. That and his dark skin makes him look like a real sleaze, but he's as honest as they come. Came out here from back east som'rs, New York City I think, and had this hotel built. Then he started getting supplies for the folks that wanted to go to California when that gold rush first started. He gave everyone a good deal n' backed everything he sold. 'Fore too long he was the only one gettin' any business atol." He brought the wagon to a stop then turned to Jesse with a grin, "Don't spread it around, but guess what his real name is?"

"Moneybags?"

Huff laughed. "That too. He n' I got a little too deep into the whisky barrel one night after he closed, and he told me his name's really Sheenie Schwartz. He left a nagging wife n' a bunch o' kids behind, and he don't want her finding him." He laughed as he climbed down from the wooden seat. He heard a thundering noise and turned to see two huge hands on the end of two of the biggest arms Jesse had ever seen on a woman, or a man for that matter, coming straight at the old man. Before he could react, the arms were around Huff's scrawny chest and his feet were almost snatched out of his boots.

"I seed ya comin' around back here n' come a'hoofin'."

Jesse was looking down from the seat at the top of the gigantic woman's head—which wasn't far below. *Ole Huff don't take to no regular size women.* When he climbed down and was on his feet, he was looking up at an old, but pretty face with the nicest smile he'd seen since Rose's, and it was at least a foot above his.

The smiling giant turned Huff loose. "Hi, I'm Annalina Simolina."

Jesse was relieved when she held her hand out instead of moving in for a hug. "Jesse McKannah," he said as he shook the middle three fingers, which was all she had on the huge right hand.

When she released his hand and held hers up she said, "Lost m'thumb n' pinky to a mountain lion when I was younger." She returned her attention to Huff, "Been gone to dern long ya old bag o' buzzard bait, where ya been?" She was looking at Huff with a cocked up eyebrow, but Jesse could tell it was a putt-on. As tall as Huff was, Jesse noticed he had to look up at this woman.

"Spent some time visiting mama's folks' camp up north o' here, then went back east to look around. Been haulin' dead beaver n' stuff for that Hudson Bay Company." He stepped back and looked her up and down. "Damned if you don't take good care of yerself, woman."

"Can't say the same for you," she smiled and shook her big head, "you look like you was dragged behind that wagon most of the way. My God Huff, don't them trading company folks ever feed ya?"

"He eats like a starved horse, Annalina."

"Anna," she answered Jesse with a smile, "just plain ole Anna." She noticed Mahatma sitting quietly on his horse at the rear of the wagon and walked to him. "Ain't you the fella that came with Huff the last time he was here?"

"Yes ma'am," he said as he removed his floppy, black felt hat, "Mahatma Jefferies."

"That's right," she said with a wide grin, "you're that Indian sorta injun, ain'cha."

"I think that's what mama had in mind," Hat replied with a grin, "but m'pa wouldn't go along with it; he's blacker'n Huff's soul."

"That's right, I remember now, your daddy's a Negro isn't he?"

"Yes'm, sure is, black to the bone."

"Remember what it was you said awhile ago, gal?" Huff nudged her.

"What's that?"

"Som'n 'bout eatin'."

"Hey, you guys hungry?"

"Starved." Jesse answered.

"Could eat on a buffalo at a flat out run." Hat smiled.

Huff rubbed his flat midsection. "Gonna take some vittles to fill this hole in m'gut, gal."

"Well then, let's get Chobie out here to take care of this wagon n' horses, so I can feed you fellers." She wheeled around and went inside the stable. A couple of minutes later she returned, followed by a big grinning boy that Jesse could see wasn't as mentally developed as his body was.

"Hi Mr. Huff." The boy said loudly in a monotone voice as though he had memorized the words just before coming out. He stood close to Anna, and looked expectantly at Huff, but didn't look at the other two men.

"Hiya Chobie, how ya been?"

"Really good Mr. Huff. Mr. Omar lets me drive him around in his buggy."

"Hey, that's great Chobie, where ya been going?"

"We went all the way to the Indian camp where them Indians he gets the dead skins from live." Jesse noticed that the boy got very excited just thinking about his great adventure. "Boy, that place is really something. I might go out there to live when I get growed up."

"Sounds fun," Huff replied, "but right now Chobie I needja to get these skins all packed up to go in the canoes to that big city."

"Yessir, Mr. Huff. I'll wrap em real good in that stuff, so they won't get wet if it rains."

"That's good Chobie, and don't forget to put my mark on every side."

"Yessir n' I'll feed n' rub these horses down really good, too."

"Attaboy. Couldn't make it around here without you, Chobie."

Huff turned to Anna, who was talking to Hat. "What was that you said about feedin' some fellers?"

Jesse almost fell down laughing when the big woman scooped the tall scrawny man off his feet, slung him over her broad shoulder, and headed out of the alley.

"C'mon boys," she yelled over her shoulder, "I'll feed you two while I'm stuffing this turkey."

Even the laid back Indian laughed when Huff looked over her shoulder at the two men, and wobbled his eyebrows.

"Looks happier'n a hog in a mud hole don't he?"

"Yeah he does." Hat said with a grin.

"Tell you the truth, I kinda envy that old man." Jesse commented as they tagged along behind.

By late afternoon all three men had eaten their fill of the gigantic meal Anna prepared, and were standing at the bar having a beer, when Jesse noticed a man come from the rear. *This's gotta be that Omar guy.*

The dark skinned little man came directly to Huff. "Heard you was in town Huff, how you doin' these days?"

"Great Omar, lemme introduce you to Jesse McKannah."

After they shook hands, the bald little man turned to Mahatma and held out his hand. "Metcha before, ain't I?"

"Yessir. M'daddy's got the livery stable back in Lewiston."

"That's right, he's the blacksmith too, ain't he?"

"Yessir, that's him."

"I met him when I went over awhile back to see if I could get that bootmaker to move over here n' work for me. Helluva man he is. I saw him throw a guy he caught stealing something farther than most men could throw a possum."

"Yeah, m'pappy's always been a powerful fella."

Huff rubbed his flat midsection, "Gonna take some beer to fill this empty hole."

Omar looked at the skinny old man. "I can sure take care o' that problem." He went behind the bar and poured everyone a mug of beer.

After three beers Huff said, "I'm sticking around for a few days, but Jesse says he wants t'get on down to Portland with Angus' pelts. Gonna be a problem gettin' him a canoe?"

"None atol." Omar turned to Jesse, "When you wanna get going?"

"Gonna rest up today n' tomorrow then head out the following morning if that works for you?"

"Your canoe n' guide'll be sitting next to the dock at dawn, right behind here. You want a second paddler or you wanna paddle yourself?"

"I'll paddle."

"Good, that's settled. I'll send the bill to Angus with Huff when he leaves." He turned to the old man, "You gonna want one of my men to go along with you?"

"Nope. Hat here's gonna be driver on the return trip n' I'm gonna letcha know right now that I ain't takin' any more loads anywhere."

"Finally gonna quit traveling, huh?"

"I didn't say that."

"Gonna become a man of leisure travel, are ya?"

Huff downed his beer. "Yessiree. Man of leisure travel. Hey, I like the sound o' that. Matter of fact I'll buy us all another beer to celebrate my new status." After their refills were on the bar, he picked his up and held it out to his three friends. "McHuffy Olin Allen—leisure traveler."

"Been wondering how you come to be called Huff?" Omar said with a grin; "Took me fifteen years to find out." He took his beer down in one long drink, then told his bartender to bring them all another one on the house. "Between you Irish, and the Indians, there shouldn't be a poor Jew in America in another twenty years."

"Your right there," Huff said with a big grin, "we're good for the economy of this wonderful new country 'cause we're spenders, not savers." He finished his beer then picked up the one Omar had provided. "First free beer in fifteen years n' I'm gonna really enjoy it."

"You better," Omar replied, "because you'll be dead when the next free one comes around."

Before Omar said he had to leave, Huff asked, "Were you able to get all of the things Angus ordered?"

"Everything but one item," the fat little man said with a straight face.

"What was that?"

"Scots whiskey. They said there won't be any for a year at least." There was still no expression on his face.

"Oh crap." Hat, you're gonna hafta to go alone, 'cause I ain't about to tell Angus that." When he heard Omar laugh, he turned and grinned. "You fat little mule turd."

"Got him ten cases, so he'll be fit to live with for a few months."

Jesse relaxed and enjoyed the town the following day then said goodbye to Huff that evening. "Might not be goodbye," the old man said with a twinkle in his eye. "I just might come west n' see if you got rich diggin' that gold off your land."

"Be looking for ya, Huff." Jesse waved and headed for his hotel room, and a hot bath. After he was settled down into the warm water, he laid his head back against the tub and wasn't surprised when his sister Aleena visited his memory.

The last letter Jesse received from Aleena began running through his mind—as it had so many times since he lost her. At first he tried to shake it from his head, not wanting to think about how frightened she must have been during her last moments on earth. The last couple of times she visited his memory, he allowed her written words to play themselves out; feeling a connection of sorts to the sister he'd loved as long as he could remember. He smiled as he recalled the opening words of her letter.

Hello big brother,

Okay! You asked for it, so here I come—big feet, big ears and all. Oh yeah, big love too for the man who loved me more than all the people I ever knew. You've been the brother that every little girl on earth dreams of having, and I want you to know how lucky I feel to have been blessed by God with a brother like you. Okay, enough of that teary stuff or I'll start crying and won't be able to finish this letter. I'm leaving within the hour to pack the few possessions I'm bringing with me into the wagon. The family I'm going with, Mister and Missus Rhoell, will be waiting at the church in nearby Quincy. Mister Samson, the black man I told you about in my last letter, is taking me in my small carriage and will help me load everything. He doesn't know it yet but I'm giving him and his wife—oh yes, forgot, she's driving there with us—the carriage and Mister Whip. I wish you could have come for a visit and witnessed that horse pop flies from his rear end with that tail of his, so you'd know why I named him that when I first bought him.

Mister Samson has treated that horse wonderful since the day I got it, so that's one thing I won't have to worry about. I'll miss them both, his wife especially because she's been like a mother to me all these years. I'll miss Whip too.

I'm certain you'll be wondering about the people I'll be traveling with so I'll tell you all about them. The Rhoell family is younger than me by about ten years, and has gone to the same church that I attended, since they arrived from Germany several years ago. When I mentioned to them that I was soon retiring and had been invited to live at your ranch, they explained that they also wanted to go west. Even though they said it was too much, I insisted on paying for half of the cost of the wagon that we'll all live in as we travel. You will be very impressed with it when we arrive at your ranch. It has a canvas cover over it that will keep everything and us dry. There are areas inside for Hilde and I to sleep and Gunter will sleep beneath the wagon. We will be traveling with four other wagons and will meet the other people who are going west with Mister Donner's group. They will all be gathered at the Elderville Baptist Church, where Mister Donner's men will tell us more about the trip, and what to expect. There will be about one hundred of us going in perhaps as many as fifty wagons. The Rhoell family, and probably everyone else, is very concerned about the Indians, which they thought were all wild savages. When I told them about Wampohnah and the many other friends you and I had among the Indians, they were very surprised and relieved. I'll try to talk to the others and perhaps dispel some of their fears as well. As I told you in my letter many years ago, I did not like the ocean voyage very much—ha ha ha—because I was seasick so much, but I am looking forward to the trip across our beautiful country. Perhaps I will teach at the new school that you told me about? If I do, then I'll be able to tell the children all about the places we will pass through. Oh Jesse, I am so very excited about this wonderful opportunity to cross the country. I've dreamed about this trip since the day that I decided to return home. Actually, since you offered me a home to return to. Thank you, darling brother. I can't wait to be with you again. I will keep a journal as we travel, so you will be able to one day read about our adventure. Samson has arrived with the carriage so I must close this letter. Time to head west, so wish us luck and include us all in your prayers each night.

Your loving sister,

Aleena.

Jesse absentmindedly splashed the tub water back and forth with his left hand as he pressed his eyes with the right. After all of the time that had passed since he knew he'd lost his only sister, he still felt a wrenching pain in his heart when he thought of her. *You'll always be right here in my memory, sis.* He began scrubbing his back with the coarse long-handled brush.

The morning Jesse wanted to leave, he was at the dock behind Omar's hotel an hour before dawn, just as he and the Flathead Indian that was to take him and Angus's pelts to Portland had agreed. Laughing Bear was not what Jesse expected to see when Omar first told him his name. He expected to see a huge, bear of a man, but when he came to Jesse's room later that first night to discuss the trip, he opened the door to a very small, smiling Indian about his own age.

The canoe guide was friendly and casual, but before he left, Jesse could tell that he'd been given a good man to get him the two hundred miles to Portland, Oregon. The man not only wanted to get the time Jesse planned to leave, but he also wanted to size up the man that he was going to spend time with. Their first meeting only lasted ten minutes, and when Jesse shook the Indian's hand he thought, *Good man, that's exactly what I'd do. See what kind of man I'm gonna be dealing with for a coupla weeks or longer on the river in a small canoe.*

It was a cold, clear morning, and Jesse thought his imagination was working overtime when his nose sent a signal to his brain—COFFEE. *Impossible* he thought, but Laughing Bear reached out with a cup in one hand, and a pot in the other. "You drink this nasty tasting, bitter water?" Jesse couldn't tell in the darkness, but he had a hunch the Indian was smiling.

"Only when I've got a cup of it in m'hand." He was about to ask where he got it, when the Indian volunteered.

"I have a key to the kitchen, so I made us a pot to start this journey off right." He set the pot on the dock then added, "I think it's gonna get pretty cold before we get to Portland." He glanced at a gray starless sky under a full moon. "Got all the signs."

As they drank coffee Jesse asked, "How long you been doing this kinda work, Laughing Bear?"

"Since Omar opened this place. Mmmm, lemme see, must be more'n ten years now." He took a sip of coffee. "How about Jesse n' Bear? much easier."

"Sounds good t'me, Bear. I've been on the Columbia farther up, but never down here, how is it?"

"Pretty good once we get around The Fishhook, below Umatilla. First we gotta get down the Walla Walla River, and that's the worst part of the trip. Twenty-five miles of rocks, logs, and all kinds of tricky little places to work our way through, then another thirty or so to The Fishhook." He finished his coffee then offered Jesse some before filling his own cup again. "Soon as we finish this we can get going. It'll be light before we get to the first rocks. You got much stuff to put in the canoe?"

"Nope, Just this Sharps, some ammo, and two wool blankets."

"Good. You oughta see the junk some of these people wanna drag along. Creates a problem sometimes, 'cause I've only got so much room in that canoe. One lady from back east somewhere talked her husband into them both going on to Portland in my canoe instead of on the stagecoach." He laughed quietly then continued. "She had a stinking old buffalo head that some Indian sold her and she wanted to take it in the canoe. Whoever sold it to her didn't prepare it right and it was really getting ripe. Her husband finally talked her into letting him pay the freight charge to let the stage take it." He laughed again, "My son found it beside the stagecoach trail about a mile outa town. Jesse, two trips in a row like that n' I'd give this up. By the time we got to The Fishhook they woulda paid me a fortune if I coulda got 'em on that stage somehow. Boy, what a couple those two were." He laughed hard when he said, "I was actually having thoughts about scalping, and stuff like that. I won't be surprised to see her husband come through with another woman one of these days, 'cause without her I think he'd be a pretty nice fella." He poured the remaining coffee into Jesse's cup. "I'll go put this back and lock up then we'll leave."

It was noon before they got to a place where they could stop and have some jerky and hardtack. When Jesse finally had a chance to observe the man more intently, he realized he didn't look at all like an Indian. His hair was dark brown, but he had the palest blue eyes he'd ever seen in a man's face. After finishing his jerky he commented, "You're not full blooded Flathead are you?"

"Ug," Bear said with a wide grin, "these damn blue eyes give me away every time. My mama's a Flathead, and papa's a Swede. You probably met them both at the hotel. He's that huge bartender with the white hair, and mom's the head cook."

"Don't think I met her, but can't miss your dad; that's a big man."

"Yeah, and he's as good as he is big. Well, let's head on to that dogleg near the Columbia. We'll camp there tonight then head on out into the river at dawn." The two men picked up their paddles and resumed the trip toward Portland.

Camp the first night was a cutback on the Walla Walla River about five miles from the Columbia River. There was a coarse sandy beach to pull the canoe up on, and Jesse put together a small fire while Bear secured the canoe. By the time Jesse had pounded coffee beans, and had water boiling, Bear had put together a lean-to rig from poles stashed in the woods from previous trips. Jesse helped him cover it with a large piece of canvas then asked, "What's this stuff on the canvas?"

"Bear fat," the Indian answered, "it'll keep the rain or snow off in winter, and bugs won't come near it in the heat of summer stinks too bad I get a few of the local boys to help me put it on when I buy a new one, but if their mothers find out first, they won't let 'em help me."

"Why's that?"

Bear chuckled. "I lay it out on the ground and have the kids put big globs of bear fat on it, then they use their feet to slide around on it for an hour or so to work it into the canvas. They love it 'cause the more they work the stuff into it, the slippery it gets. Pretty soon they're slipping and sliding all over it. When they get done they've got bear fat from one end of them to the other, and their parents won't let 'em in the house for a few days." He laughed out loud. "It's only done on the hottest days of summer so the stuff'll thin out and go into the material, and the boys love it. They swim all day there at the dock and sleep right there to, till the smell's gone." He pointed at the canoe, "I have the beaver pelts covered with one also."

"I noticed you have a shotgun."

"Yeah, twelve gauge. I've had a little trouble the last year or so. Must be the changing times. Ain't had to kill anyone yet, but I've had to back a couple down. Hard telling what mighta happened if pop hadn't bought me that shotgun awhile back. It's a mighty convincing chunk of iron in a heated conversation."

"A guy donated a ten gauge to my cause awhile back and I really liked it."

"Ain't got it anymore?"

"Gave it to a Flathead friend o' mine back in Montana when a Chief gave me this Sharps as a gift." When Bear inquired about the reason Jesse was given such a gift by a Chief, he listened intently as Jesse briefly explained about his time with the Salish Indians.

The Indian stared at his white companion for a few silent moments then said almost reverently. "You're White Buffalo?"

"That's what they kept sayin' before I left," Jesse grinned, "then a friend of Huff's said the same thing."

"Small world, huh? I only heard the story recently when I spent a week at mom's camp. The Medicine Dancer told the whole tale one night at the fire, and I've never seen my people so caught up in a story." He looked hard at Jesse then said with a friendly smile, "Brother, you're on your way to becoming a permanent part of Salish legend."

Jesse sat staring into the fire for a few moments. "Y'know Bear, I don't think I could be associated with a better bunch of people anywhere on this earth." The two men sat beneath their buffalo robes talking as the fire burned down to a glowing bed of coals. They awoke before dawn to a changed landscape.

"Snow," Jesse said loudly, "I woke up during the night n' saw it.

"Oh well, what the hell, it's that time o' year."

"Sure is, and it'll be Christmas pretty soon."

"Day after tomorrow," Bear replied.

"Didja get me a present?"

"Darn right. When you hire Laughing Bear you get nothing but the best of everything." He reached into his supply sack. "Yep, it's still there. I'll give it to you when we get the fire going."

Jesse smiled, and then ten minutes later he was warming his hands over the re-kindled fire when Bear said, "Here's the Christmas present I promised you."

Jesse watched closely as Bear reached into the canvas bag. He barely kept from spilling his precious re-heated coffee when the Indian handed him a wriggling rattlesnake with its rattles singing a deadly tune.

Bear was laughing uproariously as he held the wooden snake in the air for Jesse to see.

"Holey moley, lemme see that thing." He inspected the toy closely in the firelight. "You make this?"

"Gotta do som'n when there ain't any work."

"This's really something. All these little sections pinned together so it moves just like a real snake. Hell, for a moment I thought it was a real one." He looked it over again more closely. "It's the paint job that makes it look so real."

Jesse could tell that Bear was proud of his artwork, and appreciated the praise. “I spent a lot of time on this thing last winter.” He held it up and made it wriggle in the firelight.

Laughing Bear wasn’t up and moving about early on the second day. He was usually finished preparing the canoe for the day’s journey, before it was daylight, so Jesse asked him why. “We have five very difficult miles to get from the Walla Walla into the Columbia River, and there’s no room for mistakes.” He turned a slightly mischievous grin toward Jesse, “I was just getting a little extra rest, because then the real ride begins.”

Jesse filled his cup again. “I know how that river can get ‘cause I’ve been through a couple of hairy sections m’self.”

Laughing Bear raised his eyebrows, and looked seriously at Jesse. “Wait’ll you see this section we’ll soon be coming to.”

The Indian looked up and grinned again. "You probably ain't seen anything like it." After a sip of coffee he grinned. "Remember the lady with the buffalo head?"

"Yeah."

"Well, she had the easiest trip of all my passengers." He looked at Jesse with a deadpan expression.

"How's that?"

"When we pulled out into the Columbia, she passed out. Every time she came around a little, she'd look out at that wild river all around us and pass out again. She was off in Dream Land that first day n' I was starting to think it was gonna be an okay trip after all, but she was able to stay awake after we got around Umatilla." He finished his coffee then shook his head, "Damn shame."

Jesse did as he was told and moved his fur padding around so he would be as low in the canoe as possible. Laughing Bear did the same thing. "Once we start getting the pull from the Columbia there won't be much paddling—just steering. The roughest place here in the Walla Walla will be the last half-mile. Keep a sharp eye till we're out in the middle of the big water, then just listen for my instructions as we approach each funnel where the big boulders have pinched the water flow, 'cause it gets wild through them."

About an hour after the sun was penetrating the snow on his back, Jesse could see the wild water just ahead of their canoe, and knew that the Indian hadn't exaggerated. Wild was an understatement for the area where the Walla Walla entered the Columbia. *It feels like we're actually being pulled by a rope or something. Hell, we are. That big river's trying to suck all the water outa this creek.*

Moments later, Bear yelled above the roar of the river. "Watch it now Jesse, gonna feel like she's eating us for breakfast when we enter."

To make things worse the snow was coming down harder by the minute, making visibility worse. A few minutes after Bear's yell, Jesse felt the front of the canoe suddenly jerked to the left and he knew they were in the Columbia. "Big funnel coming up," he heard bear yell. There it was, dead ahead, two boulders the size of Omar's hotel with a pass about fifty feet wide between them.

Before he had time to think about it, they were through, and half paddling, half steering their way into what was quickly becoming a raging white wall of water just ahead of the canoe.

An hour of tense steering through a white world, with only glimpses of the bank on each side, was shattered by Bear's yell. "Funnel right ahead somewhere."

Jesse's brain was on full alert and immediately registered the 'ahead somewhere.' *Oh brother*, he thought but before he could even think about what to do there it was. Jesse paddled, as he was told, while Bear steered through the narrow pass into the relatively calm water beyond. *This guy's the best river man I've ever seen, but I bet he doesn't get too many repeat riders.*

The next hour passed uneventful, even though it was still a treacherous ride capable of turning a landloving man's hair gray. After the entrance into the Columbia then passing through two funnels, it was almost relaxing to Jesse. The snow kept falling at the same rate, making the river a white road interrupted occasionally by enormous boulders, and offering brief glimpses of the banks on each side.

"Gonna make a sharp left turn not too far ahead," Bear yelled, "then a few paddle strokes and a hard right."

Jesse nodded his head that he'd heard.

"Very wild through there, then we're gonna drop down through some rough water."

Jesse nodded again. *If it's gonna get rough, then this must not be rough to him.* The thought had just exited his mind when he saw the gray and black mottled, granite wall directly ahead of the canoe.

"Push us off with the paddle," Bear yelled, above the roar of the water being squeezed between the two giant boulders.

Jesse had already reversed ends and was pushing as hard as he could with the handle end of the paddle. There were two spare paddles but it was a long way to Portland, and Jesse didn't want to break the water end on one of them. He was able to keep the front of the huge canoe away from the boulder with the help of the water rushing between it and the granite, but he was unprepared when the canoe swung so radically to the left that it leaned hard over. Just as he was about to extend his body out to counterbalance the tipping canoe, Bear's end of the giant canoe, which had suddenly become very small, followed him around the corner and remained upright. *Hard right coming up,* he reminded himself and there it was. He reversed paddle ends again and pushed hard against the boulder on the left side. The canoe didn't lean this time, so Jesse breathed a sigh of relief. It was a false sense of relief because a slight opening in the white wall, partially due to the huge boulders blocking the path, revealed no water ahead of the canoe. Jesse and his end of the long canoe were extended out into a white foaming oblivion. A brief moment later he was falling. *Water, I hope you're still there.*

Bear's end had never left the security of the water, plus he'd been through here so many times that he knew what to expect. He and his father had constructed the giant canoe of the finest materials the forest provided. After cracking one of their first canoes on a trip to Portland, while loaded down with furs, they sold it cheap and returned by stagecoach to Walla Walla. Since then they constructed a new canoe each trip. They used stronger materials, and reinforced it to withstand the rigors of a-river-gone-mad. Bear's father had retired to the kitchen of Omar's hotel, but he was still Bear's partner in the construction of a new canoe for each trip. The two industrious men were accumulating a tidy sum from the sale of their huge cargo canoes and no longer had to search for a buyer because they now had a waiting list.

When Jesse's end hit the water he was certain he would turn to see Bear in his own half of the split-in-two canoe, adrift somewhere behind him.

Bear smiled at the wide-eyed man in the front of his canoe, but maintained a constant vigilance to steer through the rapidly descending rapids. Ten minutes later they were in a widening area that was relatively smooth. "Let's pull to the side here and have a rest and something to eat." Bear pointed with his paddle to a basin on the side with a sloping beach-like area where the canoe could be secured.

When the canoe was tied at each end, and the two men were standing on solid ground Bear said, "It got a little tense there for a while, huh?"

"Tense?" Jesse replied loudly, but with a humorous lilt to his voice. "You couldn't have driven a horseshoe nail up my ass with a blacksmith's anvil hammer. Injun, you're sure good at whacha do for a livin'."

"Thanks," Bear said with a grin, "had some pretty scary trips till I learned about the bad places on the river."

"Hope they're all behind us."

Bear looked straight at Jesse, and then raised both eyebrows with mock questioning. "Well uh, there's a little wild water till we get past Umatilla."

"Ought oh. I'm getting to know that look."

"I'm gonna get a fire going. Want some coffee n' jerky?"

"In this snow? I gotta see this." Jesse watched the Indian go to the granite cliff. He followed him, and watched as he removed some well-placed branches that concealed a small cave in the solid rock wall. He crouched down to follow, but once inside he was able to stand. It was roomy enough for the two men to stand, so Jesse watched as Bear swept the walls with a fresh branch he'd busted from a bush outside.

"Found a rattlesnake in my firewood one time." Bear kept going around the small cave until he was certain they were alone. "Darn near got me too, so I been careful since then." He removed a small package from under his jacket, and began to unwrap the beargrease-covered canvas to reveal a small amount of dried grass, leaves, and twigs. Jesse watched as he began repeatedly striking his fire-flint against a small piece of steel into the center of a small amount of the dry material. In moments a tiny bit of smoke emerged from the center as Bear blew on the pile. Flames soon jumped from the pile, so Bear added small pieces from the firewood he'd stashed in the cave.

Ten minutes later, Jesse and Bear had their cold hands out of the wet gloves and had them against the fire's warmth. Bear left for a moment then returned with the coffee, jerky, tin mugs, and a small pot. After putting everything down but the pot he went back outside for some snow to melt. As it melted he made another trip to fill it, while Jesse crushed the beans. "Snow's letting up some."

Bear was unwrapping the jerky when he felt the first rumblings in his feet. He looked at Jesse, who he could tell had felt them also. Both men froze momentarily. Another tremor transmitted its warning through the earth into their feet. Not a word was said, but each man quickly gathered what he could hold and went swiftly to the canoe. They untied both ends in a rush, and were no sooner in it, paddling to the center of the river when boulders began falling from the cliff directly above where they had been standing only moments earlier.

The two men paddled furiously to the center of the river, then looked back once they had the canoe heading downstream. The small cave in which they had been about to enjoy a rest and a cup of coffee was gone—buried beneath a mass of boulders. Ahead, they saw boulders the size of stagecoaches hitting the river exactly where they were. A small boulder bounced from a rim above, and landed only a few feet from Jesse's right paddle, but he paid no attention to it. Bear had yelled moments earlier, "Paddle like hell, the river widens out right around that bend ahead."

The two men had the huge canoe going as fast as they could, and still manage steering as boulders hit the water all around them. Jesse could see the bend that Bear pointed to but suddenly the water right ahead was funneling into a whirlpool as the earth cracked open on the riverbed. "Pull hard," Bear yelled, "and hit it right in the middle."

Jesse was calling on muscles he hadn't used in years as he thrust the paddle fore and aft. He felt the canoe stop suddenly as though a giant hand had grabbed it. He continued to bury the paddle, thrusting the water behind, and knew Bear was doing the same. Just as suddenly as it had been stopped, the canoe began moving ahead then finally shot forward as if it had been given a shove from behind by an unseen force. Both men knew their lives probably depended on getting around the bend ahead and into wider water, so they continued paddling furiously.

Just as the canoe was entering a funnel that opened into the wide water, another crack opened below and the water went berserk. Jesse was raised out of the water and high into the air, and then felt a shudder go through the long canoe. He didn't know what else to do so he brought the paddle in and held on to the sides. A moment later he was glad he had gripped the sides because the canoe was going down faster than he was. It hit with a sickening, crunching sound a moment before Jesse hit the canoe bottom with his own bottom. "Pull," Bear yelled, "we're almost there."

Before the words were out of the Indian's mouth Jesse had the paddle buried and was pushing water behind him. The earthquake was getting worse as boulders rained down all around them, so they headed for the relative safety of the center of the river. They were soon in the middle where the Columbia was about three times as wide as any part they had yet traveled on, and it was now obvious that the boulders would not reach them. "Phew, close huh?"

"If that wasn't, then I never wanna get close." Jesse laid his paddle aside and looked around for the torn, busted areas in the canoe, that he felt certain must be everywhere. After finding the vessel in about the same shape as it was before their ordeal, he turned to his guide. "Bear, you and your pop oughta quit everything and just build canoes." He looked around again. "This is one helluva boat."

Bear looked around himself. "Papa says a lotta guys have lost it because they build the canoe too tight. Gotta make them strong, but so they can move when they have to, otherwise they tear apart trying to."

Jesse continued looking around at the inside of the undamaged canoe as it headed down the river with Bear's one paddle steering as he took a breather. "Wouldn't expect anyone to believe it." He shook his head, "I sure wouldn't if I hadn't seen it." He turned to Bear. "Ever been through one o' them before?"

"Been through plenty of grumbling-ground times, but that's the first time on the river," he grinned at Jesse, "and the last, I hope."

"We used to have them pass through the area where my ranch was, but this is the worst I can remember. Man, did you see the size of some o' those boulders?"

"Not really. I was concentrating on a path through the water, and praying to the Great Spirit."

"Musta heard ya."

They still encountered some wild water, even after the earthquake had subsided, but after what they just came through, it seemed mild. About two hours before dark they came to an Indian camp a few miles from the trading settlement of Umatilla. "Let's stop and see if they're alright," Bear said. "I have relatives here."

As the two men maneuvered the big canoe toward the shore, Jesse asked over his shoulder. "Are these Flatheads?"

"No, it's a Umatilla tribe that a couple of girls from my mother's camp married into." He brought the canoe to a makeshift landing with poles pounded into the ground near the river's edge, then held it steady as Jesse got out to tie both ends. As they walked toward the camp Bear said, "One's my cousin, and I think the other's a second cousin." He grinned at Jesse, "Or som'n like that."

They were met by a group of men with solemn faces. Bear spoke to the men as Jesse signed a friendly greeting. "Bad trouble," Bear said to Jesse, "my cousin and some of the other women were gathering wood thrown up by the river along the wall over there when the ground began rumbling." He pointed to a high cliff a quarter mile away.

'Let's go see if they're still alive,' Jesse signed.

When the men looked frightened Bear said, "They're afraid the ground spirits are mad and wanted sacrifices." He turned to listen to the Indians. "They are afraid the spirits will demand more if they interfere."

Jesse turned a severe face to the dozen or so men then signed *'Go sit with the women, and I will go see if I can find anyone alive.'* He turned abruptly and began running toward the cliff. When he arrived he stopped to catch his breath, and heard a noise behind. "You shamed them good, White Buffalo." Bear was panting, but still was able to flash a grin.

Jesse began throwing the smaller boulders into the river as he called out, hoping to hear a voice answer. Bear was doing the same thing and before they had moved too many, there were about fifty men from the camp helping. Ten minutes later a body was found, crushed by numerous blows. A moment later another was found, then another, then a fourth. Jesse raised his arms to quiet the crowd. When there was silence he again heard a tiny voice over next to the cliff. He scrambled over the boulders and began throwing rocks aside. Soon he could hear it again, but stronger. Now there were several men moving the granite debris, and moments later they saw a hand waving from behind a huge boulder. Another ten minutes of moving rocks and they could see the face of a woman trapped in a crevice, but otherwise unhurt.

"Ahatta," Bear called to her, and then turned to Jesse. "That's my cousin." Fifteen minutes of rock moving and she was free. Bear asked her how many of them were here when the ground rumbled, and she replied five. "There's no more to look for," Bear said as he helped his cousin over the rocks. They left the others to retrieve the four dead bodies, and headed for the camp.

After escorting his cousin to her family's teepee, Bear returned to the fire to tell Jesse, "Her husband's running traps in the mountains and she's fears for him."

After accepting a tin cup of tea from one of the many women tending pots of food around the big fire Jesse said, "Might not be a bad place to be when stuff starts falling." He looked around the fire at the faces staring at him then turned to Bear, "Are they all pissed off because I pointed out what a bunch of sissies they were being?"

"No, I just told them that you are White Buffalo."

"Don't tell me that story's already this far?"

"Sure is," Bear grinned then said seriously, "it really isn't just a story to them Jesse. The ground rumbles, women are buried, and who comes from the river through a snow storm to rescue one of them?"

Slightly embarrassed, Jesse looked up at the sky. "I didn't even notice that it started snowing again."

When the food was finished, everyone took a portion and headed for the shelter of a teepee. Bear said, "C'mon were invited into the chief's quarters." Jesse got a plateful and followed him into the giant teepee a short distance away. Once inside he was surprised how warm it was. It had been a while since he'd been out of the weather, so he removed his coat. One of the chief's wives took it and hung it so it would be dry the following morning.

There was a good size fire in the middle, so both men sat next to it warming their hands. “If this snow lets up by morning,” Bear said, “we’ll keep on moving toward Portland.”

“Sounds good t’me. Hope they won’t be offended if we don’t stay for the burial?”

Before Bear could answer, a booming voice entered just ahead of a huge Indian. “Hell no.” The man spoke in perfect English. “They’ll be so busy wailing, those squaws won’t even see you leave.”

Jesse looked up at the smiling face of a huge Indian. A hand the size of a small snowshoe came down at him. “Hi, I’m Chief Walks Alone. So you’re White Buffalo?”

Jesse started to get up, but the huge hand held him in place. “Relax. Hello Laughing Bear, have you brought us some funny stories?”

“No, but I brought you a gift.” Laughing Bear reached into his bag.

The huge Indian hadn’t seen his small friend for almost two years, so he was surprised when he was told he had a gift for him. He leaned toward Bear to see what he’d brought him, but half-jumped, and half-crawled away when the little Indian held a live rattlesnake out to him. The Chief’s wives gasped when they first saw the snake but began to giggle when they realized it was not real.

Bear draped the wooden snake over his head and sat grinning as the chief bent way down to have a closer look. Finally he grinned, “You little peckerhead. One of these days I’m gonna dry you over a fire and sell you to a trading post as a souvenir.” He turned to Jesse, “How long you gotta be on the river with this character?”

“Too long already. I swallowed a whole chunk of jerked beef because of that wooden snake.”

“Beef? Beef? Where did you get the idea that meat was beef?”

Jesse turned a cautious eye to the little Indian then said with a grin. “Oh well, whatever it is, it’s good.”

“Not whatever,” Bear said with a poker face, “whoever.”

As Jesse sat staring at Bear trying to figure out if he was kidding, the chief said, “Wood? Let me see that snake.” After inspecting it for five minutes, he handed it back then turned to Jesse. “What’s your name?” After Jesse responded he said, “Jesse, this guy and his dad are probably the most talented of all the people I know, but I can’t get them to listen to me.” He turned back to Bear. “You and Sven could be rich in five years just making canoes, but with stuff like this in the Portland shops being shipped all over the world,” he shook his Buffalo size head, “you guys are missing the boat.” He turned back to Jesse, “Been to Portland in the last couple of years?”

“Nope, been almost three I think?”

“Wait’ll you see it now. Shops everywhere, and they’re shipping goods all over the world, especially Indian stuff." He turned to Bear again, "You n' your pop make it, and I'll be your agent and we'll all get rich." The huge, gregarious Indian turned back to Jesse. "Is any of that White Buffalo stuff true?"

"Only the part about me wanting to find a place that to visit me, someone's gotta come through two hundred miles of wilderness to find me."

"Getting sick of people, huh?"

"Started getting sick of 'em when they burned my ranch, killed my best friend, butchered my little sister, and killed the loveliest woman I'll ever find." He paused a moment at the memory of Rose. "And I been gettin' m'fill of 'em ever since."

The chief looked into the fire. "I understand. I was educated at a mission south of Portland, with several other Indians. I spent a lot of time later, back east in Washington, trying to work things out with this new government so my people don't get screwed too bad by these phony treaties they keep shoving beneath the noses of the Chiefs. They don't understand one damn word of English, and they trust the white men because they all want so badly to have a better life for their families." The morose, almost pleading look left his face and was replaced with a wide grin. "I don't have any problems getting along with people at all. Hell, I go see the Chinese when I'm in San Francisco, and have more black friends than white ones, but Jesse I'm sure getting sick of dealing with those politicians who have a different face every time you see one." He smacked the fire so hard with the stick he'd been poking around in it that sparks flew out in such a rage that his wives all jumped up and hollered. He yelled back, "Yes, yes, I'll not burn down your home."

Shock registered on his face when Jesse answered him in perfect Salish; a language very close to his own. "You understood what I said?"

"My woman taught me to speak Salish."

At that moment a voice raged just outside the chief's teepee. "Hey White Buffalo shit, why you hide under my chief's blankets?"

"Ah damn." The chief growled as he rose from the dirt floor. "Moon Dog's been in a whiskey bottle again." He headed toward the flap, but Jesse had risen quicker, and grabbed his arm.

"Let me go out and see what he wants."

He said it with such intensity that the chief said, "Fine, but I will go out too." He pulled open the flap and held it for his white visitor to go through.

Jesse didn't know what to expect as he went through, but what was waiting with a whiskey bottle in one hand, and a red umbrella in the other, wasn't on his list. The short thin Indian before him was wearing a squaw's tunic, and had women's beaded knee-length moccasins on. He hadn't been carrying the umbrella when Jesse confronted the group of men about searching for survivors, but he recognized this man because of a long scar across his face, and also because of his eyebrows—there were none. The whole specter stopped Jesse dead in his tracks.

The Indian tried to sign to Jesse, thinking he hadn't understood his yell, but almost fell while doing it, and had to collapse the umbrella to lean on, even though it was snowing very hard.

In Salish Jesse said, "Are you the camp news boy, or the snow fairy?"

The young Indian staggered a little as he turned the whiskey bottle up for a drink, then looked as hard as he was capable of, at Jesse. "Have you come to steal my people's land, White Buffalo dick?" He regained his footing and swung the folded umbrella at Jesse in a slow, wide arc. So slow that Jesse casually ducked as it passed over his head.

As he was still in a ducked position, Jesse saw Walks Alone grab the young man by shoving his hand between his legs from behind as he pivoted after his wild swing. The chief then grabbed him by one shoulder. Several long strides later Moon Dog was flying over the cargo canoe, the whiskey bottle still in his hand. The chief turned and was walking back before he hit the water.

"Can he swim?"

"See him drop his umbrella?"

"Yeah, I did."

"We go through this about once a month. C'mon, let's go back to the fire. That'll cool him off for a while."

"I'm gonna check the canoe," Bear said, "go ahead, I'll be right in."

Bear was gone for almost an hour, so when he returned, Jesse turned to the chief after Bear had settled in next to the fire, and was warming his hands, "Tell him about the men that're hitting freight loads up ahead."

Walks Alone finished the piece of jerky he was chewing then turned to Bear. "A small gang of men has been stopping cargo canoes as they slow down to go around Beaver Island. They wait till the canoes are in that shallow area, then they throw ropes with hooks on them and snag the canoe, or the men; whatever they hit. They pulled Horse Trader from his canoe a few months ago and drowned him."

"Your brother Horse Trader is dead?"

"Yes, Bear. Then they beat his helper very bad before he ran into the forest."

"How long has this been going on?"

"More than a year now, but they must leave, and then come back when they have sold the furs they steal, because several canoes will pass through with no trouble."

"I was through here with a load for Omar awhile back, but I didn't stop because I had a lady and her husband with me." He turned to Jesse. "That Buffalo head gal." He returned his attention to the chief. "I won't go past here again without stopping to find out what's going on down river."

"You ought to. I know what's happening between here and Portland."

"Anyone tried doing anything about it?" Jesse inquired intently.

"Who?" The chief asked, sarcastically. "My warriors are typical of what's around these days, with this government subsidy supply program, plus whiskey being supplied by traders. They all think we're gonna get a big money deal from the white government for our ancestral lands, and they'll never have to hunt again." He shook his head with a sad slowness that Jesse sensed was the beginning of defeat.

"You say they work from an island down below?"

"Yes, Beaver Island, about twenty-five-miles from here. It lies right in the middle of the river, but hard bottom on the north side makes it the only place to get around the island. The other side is as wild as anything you'll ever see on this river." When the chief saw the look in Jesse's eyes he turned, "Tell him, Bear."

"Remember that last passage as the ground shook?"

"Yeah," Jesse grinned, "when your end was twenty feet up above and behind me with almost no water under my end of the canoe?"

"That's the one. Well, that would be like a cruise on a lake compared to the water that goes around the south side of Beaver Island."

Jesse looked hard at Bear then the chief. Finally he said, "Som'ns gotta be done about that lousy bunch of, thieving murderers, or honest guys like Omar will go broke trying to get furs down the river."

"I've tried to get a group of warriors to go with me and wait to ambush them, but these people were never warriors in their best days, and their best days are gone."

Jesse turned to Bear. "Will the water let us get outa here early tomorrow?"

"Yeah, it's a pretty calm ride from here on, at least until the snow starts melting in the spring."

"Well, let's hit it about an hour before light, Okay?"

"Sure, your boss's paying the freight."

"Whacha got in mind?" The chief asked Jesse.

"Dunno, but I'll come up with som'n before we get there."

The following morning Jesse and Bear slipped quietly from the chief's teepee, and went to the canoe. They removed the canvas cover that Bear had rolled over it to keep the snow out, and after folding it; Bear used it for a seat. He steadied the long vessel as Jesse untied both ends and got into the front. Under a bright moon the two men headed for Beaver Island.

Jesse paddled without saying a word, so Bear figured he was thinking about the possible situation ahead, and what to do about it. He remained silent and paddled. As the sun rose in the sky, snow began falling heavier. Except for the passage around the island ahead, the worse part of the river was behind them, and the trip was pleasant in spite of the snow. Jesse finally turned back to Bear. "How close can we get to Beaver Island without those guys seeing us, if they're waiting to waylay someone passing?"

Bear had been picturing the island and all of the area surrounding it, so he responded immediately. "About two miles from it we come to a right bend where the forest comes out to the river. Until we go around that we won't even be able to see the island and they won't be able to see us."

"Good, we'll pull in there then, and make some plans."

As they approached the jetty of land concealing Beaver Island, Bear said quietly, "That's it ahead."

Jesse didn't even turn around, he just shook his head to acknowledge that he heard.

Bear silently brought the canoe to a stop against the bank beneath the trees, and waited for Jesse to speak. "I'm gonna go ahead on foot while you wait with the canoe. Is there anything that'll slow me down between here n' there that you're aware of?"

"No! Should be easy going all the way to where they're waiting, if they're here." He watched as Jesse checked the short-barreled pistol he carried under his arm then did the same with the one in the holster on his waist. Bear steadied the canoe as Jesse got out with the long Sharps rifle. After opening the Drop-Block Action breech to double-check it, Jesse placed a hand briefly on the tomahawk, then the knife. Bear wasn't surprised that he didn't remove them to check, because he'd spent an hour at the fire last night sharpening each.

"Have that shotgun ready and listen for gunfire, then come on around." He turned to go, but then looked back with a grin. "Hopefully, it'll be me doin' the shootin'." He turned and headed up the mountain and into the forest.

Bear watched him silently moving through the trees. *They won't even see White Buffalo coming, in that rabbit fur coat.* He had already checked the shotgun, so he pulled a chunk of jerked dog meat; his favorite, from his supplies and began chewing.

Jesse moved swiftly through the trees as he went up the mountain. When he was certain that he was above anyone that might be waiting to ambush a load of furs, he headed toward the area behind the island. When he got glimpses of the island ahead through the trees, he began to move slower, and more cautiously. The last hundred yards took an hour, but his caution paid off. The guard watching the approach of potential prey from the river was just below him. Jesse lay in the snow and slowly moved his eyes across every inch of the terrain surrounding the guard, who lay on a bed of pine branches spread out on a ledge twenty feet below.

After satisfying himself that the man was the lone guard, who was to alert the others of the approach of their next victims, Jesse stood and began to close the distance between them. He had the long Sharps rifle in his left hand and the tomahawk in his right, as he eased first one moccasin-covered foot, then the other into the snow.

When the razor sharp tomahawk hit the unsuspecting guard's neck, he didn't make a sound. Jesse held his knee in the man's back as blood flowed from the nearly severed head. When the twitching stopped, he lay beside the body and surveyed the area.

A hundred feet below, two men sat at a small smokeless fire, talking quietly but animatedly with their hands. Jesse watched them for a couple of minutes, and then began sweeping the entire area with his eyes—searching for sign of other people. Almost satisfied that these were the only two men left of the gang of murderous thieves, he began one last search. He started on the far left of the camp area, and locked his eyes onto one small section. After intently watching that one area, he moved to the one next to it. Back and forth his eyes went for almost an hour. Jesse was finally satisfied that only he and these two men were in the immediate area. *There's soon only gonna be one of us.*

Bear heard one shot, then another that came too quick to be Jesse. He pushed off and began the trip to Beaver Island, uncertain what he would find. Furious paddling brought him to within close range in minutes. *Damn*, he thought when he saw Jesse leaning against a tree at the edge of the forest. When he moved the canoe closer, Jesse grabbed the front and placed three holsters; with pistols on belts loaded with cartridges. He climbed in then shoved it out using his long rifle's stock. When he turned to place his rifle behind him in the canoe he spoke quietly. "There won't be any more problems around here for awhile."

There was enough daylight left for the two men to get a little farther toward Portland. "There's a good spot just ahead where we can camp for the night."

Bear maneuvered the canoe to the area beneath trees hanging out over the river. "Good spot to stop and we oughta get some protection from this snow under these branches."

Bear grinned at him, "Hope I have better luck with this fire than I did with the last one."

Jesse grinned back, "Ain't a cave here is there?"

"Nope, and if there was, I wouldn't go in it."

"Know whacha mean. Grumbling ground'll break a guy of camping inside these mountains, huh?"

"Broke me of it."

After tying the canoe and covering it with the canvas, the two men went about making a camp for the night. Jesse pounded coffee beans while Bear got a small fire started. Jesse had the beans in a pot of water by the time the fire was going good, and Bear was getting the other pot filled with water to make a stew.

Jesse watched intently as Bear began putting ingredients into the small pot. When he held up a piece of pure white root about the size of a quill he asked, "You eat this stuff?"

"Like a grizzly comin' out in spring."

Bear shook his head as he cut several pieces of bitterroot into the pot. "Are you sure you weren't stolen from an Indian camp?" He turned a smiling face at Jesse. "White men usually can't stand this stuff."

"Wondered about that m'self till one day I looked in a mirror and saw my pop's face in there lookin' back at me."

He leaned way over and asked, "What else y'got in there?"

"Parsnips, cama, and, uh, beef."

Jesse looked at the fresh chunks of meat that Bear was putting into the pot. "It sure don't look like any beef I ever saw." He grinned.

"Special kinda beef that they raise around here; small n' tasty. Walks Alone's old woman gave me this stuff." He turned and picked up the bag so Jesse could look inside. "Look what else she sent."

"Oh my God," Jesse said with enthusiasm, "what kind are they?"

"Chokecherry cakes." Bear wobbled his eyebrows.

"Mmm, mmm, mmmmmm. Be sure to thank 'em for me when you stop next time." Jesse sat back and waited for the pot of stew to finish. "What's the deal with that young guy with the red umbrella, and the shaved eyebrows?"

"Moon Dog went a little crazy when his lover drowned a couple of years ago. They had a fight while they were drinking, and Dancing Squaw, that's what they called him, but I don't know what his real name was, ran to the water and tried to get into a canoe. He fell in, and went right to the bottom; couldn't swim."

"So he's one of those guys that loves men, huh?"

"Yeah. Moon Dog was really a pretty nice young man. Drank too much whisky, but always very friendly n' helpful." He shook his head. "Sure is a mess now."

"I'm kinda curious, Bear; where'd y'stay for an hour last night with it snowing so hard?"

I went to my cousin's teepee after I checked on the canoe. Her best friend was there too, and after she was sure Ahatta was okay, she asked me if I wanted to see something in her teepee?" He looked wide-eyed at Jesse. "I'm a very congenial kinda guy like my Swedish papa, so I said sure." He continued sipping his coffee until Jesse could stand it no longer.

"Okay, so what did she show you?"

"Oh, it wasn't anything new. I'd seen a lot of 'em before but," He shook his head from side to side slowly, "I ain't ever seen one jump around like that, though."

Jesse chuckled, "Gonna have another look at it?"

"Jesse, I ain't ever passing that camp again without stopping."

The Colombia was a smooth running river when they left the camp, so Jesse began daydreaming about his brothers again. He remembered the day that he spotted his brother Simon riding toward his ranch.

Arliss yelled, "Rider approaching."

“Nothing to worry about Arliss,” Jesse yelled back, “ain’t another man alive that sits a horse like m’brother Simon.”

Arliss came down from the roof where he was flashing in the new chimney he was building. When he was next to Jesse he said, “Bet he has a hard time finding horses big enough.”

Jesse just laughed and waited for his brother to get close enough to hear. “Hey there rider, you one of those traveling minstrels come t’give us some entertainment.”

“Nope. Been trackin’ some no count Irishman posing as a cowboy.”

Jesse turned to his friend, “Guess the law’s caught up with you, Arliss.”

“Figured they would some day.” They waited until Simon was at the porch and off his horse. Arliss stepped forward and held his hand to Simon. “Arliss O’Reilly n’ I’m pleased t’finally be meetin’ ya.”

Simon shook his hand. “That Mick’s been talking about me, huh?”

“Talks about you McKannah boys all the time.”

Simon turned to Jesse. “Howdy brother, nice spread you have here.” They embraced each other then climbed the steps to the porch. Jesse said he’d be right back and headed toward a small building nearby as Arliss and Simon began talking like two old friends.

Moments later Jesse returned with a crock jug. “Figured you’d like to try a sip of Arliss’ special corn water.” He sat it down and went inside for two tin cups. When he returned he saw the jug tipped up to Simon’s lips. He handed one to Arliss and the other to his brother.

“Good as anything paw ever made.”

“Arliss, that’s a helluva compliment ‘cause our dad’s was suppose to be the best there was in this part of the country, and he didn’t start making it or drinkin’ it either till he got all busted up n’ ached all the time.”

As the two men sipped the whiskey, Jesse went to the coffeepot that was on the stove constantly as the men worked. He returned to the porch and asked, “Have a hard time findin m’ranch?”

“Too damn easy Jesse, you’ve made a few enemies in Yerba Buena.”

“Yeah, there’s one in particular that wants to buy me out, but I keep turning him down. He thinks he can call the shots any damn way he wants to, and it really sticks in his craw that I won’t even talk to him about it.”

Simon looked over the rim of the cup as he sipped. “You picked a good spot for your house Jesse. How long y’been here now?”

“Going on ten years.”

“Raising cattle?”

“Yep,” Arliss cut in, “best darn eatin’ beef anywhere around ‘ese parts.”

“Y’got good hands workin’ for ya?”

“Sure do. All but one’s been with me from the start, and he’s been here about seven years now.”

Simon just shook his head up and down slowly. “Good!”

After finishing the cup of corn whiskey, they went inside to look at the new chimney Arliss was building. “We just kinda threw that one over there together,” he pointed to the fireplace on the other wall, ‘till I could gather enough stones to build a good one like we did in the old country.”

“You born in Ireland?”

“Sure’s leprechauns steal a man’s liquor at night when ‘e sleeps. Worked wi’ m’pop building ‘ouses till I was nineteen. Died of an ‘eart attack ‘e did, poor ol’ fella, and mum died o’ grief a short while later. A pompous English bastard owned the house they lived in an’ ‘ad me thrown out. I ‘opped a ship n’ headed for new places. Liked this country when first I set eyes on it.”

“I’d love t’see the old country, but doubt I ever will,” Simon said as he inspected the chimney closely. “Best stone work I’ve seen.”

An obviously pleased Arliss began pointing out all of the methods he used to construct not only a beautiful piece of work, but also one that would work well. They eventually returned to the porch for some coffee and more conversation. “Y’been tracking someone?” Jesse asked.

“Yep. I signed on with an outfit east of Uncle Frank’s horse ranch in Texas. A guy murdered two of our men, so they asked me to track him and bring back his boots.”

“Gettin’ close to him?”

Simon nodded toward his horse. “Those’re his boots that’re tied behind my bedroll.” Arliss had heard Jesse’s stories about his brother and never doubted him, but seeing the cold impartial manner of the huge man had him watching Simon with awe.

“I think I’ll stay with this outfit. A fella named Daniel Parker's talking about making it a regular law outfit. If he does, we’ll all get paid pretty well and be called Texas Rangers.”

26

~ *Stagecoaches* ~

The balance of the trip to Portland was uneventful, with the exception of a few heavy snowfalls. After pulling into the fur trader's warehouse, Jesse stretched his legs and turned to Bear. "I'm swearing off canoes for awhile, 'cause these old legs don't like bein' cramped up like that for s'long."

"Tell you the truth Jesse, I been thinking about what Walks Alone has been telling me for quite awhile."

"Quit haulin' freight n' just build these canoes?"

"Yeah, I'm not as young as I thought. Didja hear these bones crackin' when I just got outa that darn thing?"

"No," Jesse grinned, "mine drowned yours out."

The Indian stretched his back and looked around the trading company's yard. "Lotta these guys around here have been wanting me n' pop to build them a canoe ahead of the guys that've been waiting for their name to come to the top of pop's list." He took a long section of his braided hair in each hand, and rested them on his chest, as he looked around at the men busy with their chores. "Offered a lot of extra money to be put first too, but pop said no, everybody's gotta wait their turn. Y'know Jesse," he turned and looked hard at him; "with some help from some of the men from mom's camp we could make two of these a month."

"How 'bout getting them down here?"

"That's som'n pop n' me'll have to work out."

Jesse remained with the beaver pelts while Bear went into the trading company office. He returned a short time later accompanied by a short, bald headed man with an accent that was alien to Jesse's ears. He walked with a swagger that should have belonged to a seven-foot-tall man. He came directly to Jesse with his hand out and a big friendly smile on his face. "G'day mate, Jeff Holbrook."

"Jesse McKannah." He shook the small man's hand. "These furs are from Angus McDonald, at Fort Connah."

"Righto. Bloody good man, that fella. Got a dispatch on the stagecoach awhile back saying to expect you two blokes."

Jesse's surprise was obvious. "Stage coach stopping at Fort Connah now?"

"First bloody trip brought me that dispatch, mate."

"They'll be haulin' these pelts over land from now on then, won't they?"

The little man looked at Bear. "Bloody well will, if they can get close enough to your price, 'cause they'll get here much quicker, mate."

Bear turned to Jesse. "Knew it was coming." He grinned, "Wanna order a canoe?"

"Nope. Swore off of 'em."

Jeff Holbrook turned toward Bear. "You making these canoes to sell?"

"Thinking about it. Especially now that it looks like I'm gonna be out of the fur hauling business."

"When y've time, let's talk about canoes, mate. If you decide to build the bloody things I can sell all you can deliver."

The three men unloaded the pelts and carried them into the warehouse a short distance away. The company man cut the bales open, and counted the pelts. He gave Jesse a receipt for the merchandise and a voucher for his pay from Angus that could be cashed at the bank. "Come on over to the office, mate." He turned to Bear, "You gonna buy a horse again t'sell and ride back, or take the bloody stage this time?"

"No market for horses now. Damn Blackfoot are sellin' stolen horses to everyone. Even the stupid settlers that they'll probably be scalping next month are buying them from the thievin' bastards. Now that I'm a businessman, I might as well take the stage back, and you can start taking orders from these trappers who want one of our canoes."

"Bloody good show mate," the man said enthusiastically, "I wrote my fair dinkum cobber back 'ome and tole 'im about your fantastic vessels. He wants one shipped to 'im straight away, or as soon's one's available. You tell me 'ow much and I'll pay you in advance today."

An hour later the two men were standing at the canoe. Jesse got in and handed up bear's shotgun, then his own rifle. He climbed out, and took another good look at the huge canoe. “I got a hunch you n’ your daddy are gonna have so many orders you’ll have to train some of your people to work with you.”

“Starting to look that way, huh?”

“I got his prices for the supplies I’ll need for the coming trapping season, but they seem a little high. I’m gonna look around and get some other prices before I order the stuff.”

Bear held out his hand, “I’m glad that I’ll be able to tell my grandchildren that I traveled with White Buffalo.”

“Well,” Jesse grinned, “don’t pump ‘em too full of wild tales.”

“No need to. I’ll just tell ‘em the true story about Beaver Island.” He grinned wide then added, “Som’n I been wanting to ask you.”

“Sure.”

“When you went in there, I heard two shots so close together that I was sure one musta come from one of those guys?” He looked quizzically at his new white friend.

Jesse just grinned back at him. “I’ve been practicing, ever since I got plenty of ammunition from Angus.”

Bear just shook his head. “Where you headin’ when you get your supplies ordered? It’s gonna be a while before you’ll be goin’ up into the mountains.”

“Going south to see what’s been happening since I left my spread.”

“Good luck. Look me up if you get back to Walla Walla.”

Before turning to leave, Jesse called to him. “Where in the heck is that little guy that talks funny from?”

“It’s a place called Australia. I don’t know where it is, but he says the Indians there are as black as Hat Jefferie’s daddy.”

“Yeah, I heard about that place from my daddy.” He pointed in the direction of the Pacific Ocean. “Out there som’rs, I think.”

Bear looked west with his lips pursed. “Wonder if Jeff’s friend plans to come here in one of my canoes?”

“If he does, my bet is he’ll make it.”

Two days later, after shopping around, Jesse returned to Jeff Holbrook’s office and placed his order for the supplies that he wanted. He asked if they could be assembled and ready by mid summer. After learning that they could, he paid for them and headed back to the hotel where he’d rented a room. He planned to catch the noon stagecoach to San Francisco, California.

As he stood in the sun behind the five other men he would be making the trip with he received strange looks from a couple of them. He had looked at the clothes in a couple of the shops, but didn’t like the looks of anything he saw, so he was still in his buckskins, knee length moccasins, and the rabbit fur coat that Rose had made him. The two pistols, the tomahawk, and the long hunting knife he wore weren’t visible, but the long rifle was almost as intimidating as the solemn man holding it. All five of the men were younger, and dressed in business suits. Jesse ignored them, realizing he had nothing in common with their type.

An hour into the trip, he was bored with the attempts each man was making to impress all of the others, with comments about their business dealings, and subtle statements about their wealth. "I think 1852 is going to be a year that will go into the history books because of all of the gold that is being mined in California." The others nodded their agreement at the fat man who made the statement. He looked at Jesse, "What do you think, Mister uh, Mister? Mister?"

Jesse looked hard at the superficial little man then finally said, "What I think is that you should have to pay twice the fare of a normal size man." When he continued to stare, the fat man turned red, then turned his watered down conversation toward the other men in the coach.

Just before dark the stagecoach pulled into a small town and stopped. The driver informed his passengers that they would be there long enough to get a bite to eat while he picked up packages and the mail. Jesse walked across the street to a livery stable, and yelled for the attendant. "Yessir," a black man walked from the back.

"You own this stable?"

"Sure do, whacha need?"

"Can't handle those stagecoach folks any longer, 'cause they're a different kinda people since I was last in one. You got a good horse with complete tack for sale?"

"Got two right over here, c'mon."

Awhile later, Jesse was walking his new horse to the rail next to the stage, when the passengers came out. The fat man was picking his teeth with an ivory toothpick, as Jesse tied the horse. "Not continuing with us, Mister, uhhh?"

Jesse turned from the door. "I've still got some good years left, and I'm pretty sure that what's on that stage's contagious."

All five men stopped dead and looked concerned; first at Jesse then at the stage, and finally back at Jesse. The fat man, who had obviously designated himself the leader of the five travelers asked with alarm, "Contagious? What's contagious?"

Jesse was cold, and in a foul mood after a few hours of listening to him blow, so he slowly looked at the fat man, then at the other four overfed men. "Fat and stupidity." He turned and entered the warm room.

One long wooden table still had food sitting in plates, so he asked the old man behind the split log bar on the other side of the room, "Okay if I eat?"

"Sure thing, that's what I cook it for. Fifty cents for all you can hold in your gut, but no saddlebag filling though unless you wanna pay another fifty for some extra to carry with you."

After eating two plates of what the man called pig stew and half a loaf of homemade bread, Jesse gave the man a dollar to cover another loaf of bread he wanted to take with him. He laid the saddlebags that were half filled with grain for the horse out on the table, and tore the loaf in half, stuffing one in each side above the grain. Before he closed the second one, the old man yelled, "Catch."

Jesse caught a pound chunk of homemade cheese. "Thanks, that'll taste good about midnight."

"Gotta get somewhere in a hurry?"

"Nah. Them folks on the stage just got me aggravated n' I gotta ride it off."

The toothless old man grinned. "Know whacha mean son, I'm gittin' two stagecoach loads of 'em a day."

Jesse rode south through the lightly falling snow until about midnight. His disgust for his fellow travelers had fallen by the trailside as he contemplated going back to the twenty thousand acres of land where he once thought he'd spend the rest of his life. *Wonder if anyone's squatting on it since I took Jack Hannon outa the picture?*

When he saw a wall of granite with a small stand of trees on the end, he decided to camp for a few hours in the lee of it. As soon as he pulled in he knew it would be a good place to rest. He pulled the saddle from his horse and rubbed it down before giving it grain. "That wind was trying to cut us both in half, huh boy?" Jesse ate a chunk of the bread, and a small piece of the cheese, and then rolled up in the horse blanket and canvas that the stable owner had included with the tack. His pistol was in his hand and the rifle was beside him. The tomahawk and knife lay nearby.

When the winter sun cast its first rays the next morning, they fell on Jesse and his horse as they were continuing south. A little before noon he stopped at a small cave, created by one of the many earthquakes that rumbled through the area. After a few minutes of searching inside he found what he had been looking for. He hadn't thought about Wovokatah in a long time. *You taught me a lot old friend.* He tucked what he'd found inside his inner coat pocket then secured it with the rawhide lines.

Jesse moved steadily along the next day, occasionally walking to give his horse a rest from his weight, and stopped only long enough to sleep a few hours after tending his horse. He was anxious to get back to his spread to see if there might actually be gold in the creek that ran through it. The pace he was keeping was more to burn off the built up tensions he still had from the trip down the river. *I've never sat in one position for so long in my life.*

When he finally felt himself all settled down he started looking for a place to camp for the night. He reached forward and patted his horse on the neck. "A good night's rest'll do us both a lotta good."

An hour later he found the perfect place. "Good grass for you to graze on, and this little cliff to keep the wind off me." After hobbling the horse, he carried the saddle back to the cliff and gathered enough wood for a fire while it was still light enough to see what he was picking up. By the time darkness had sealed off the winter sky he'd tended his horse and eaten some jerky. After finishing his coffee he placed the canvas over the pile of brush that he had earlier molded, and then shoved his boots under one end after slipping into his moccasins, and laid his hat on the other. He picked up the Sharps rifle and headed for the ledge twenty feet away on the other side of the trail.

After moving a few rocks and a dead tree limb, he stretched out in his warm coat, on top of the horse blanket. He lay quietly, only glancing at the fire a short distance away, so his eyes would be used to the darkness. Sleep finally took control.

The sound of horse hoofs was not loud, but a couple of years in Indian country had tuned Jesse's senses to any new sound—especially at night. He was instantly wide-awake listening. *Three horses.* When they stopped he was already sighting down the barrel of the rifle. It had crushed diamonds on the front sight and white on the V sight near his eye. He was always amazed how easy he could get the target in the sights. *Thanks, Hat.* By the faint glow of the fire he knew it hadn't been very long since he'd gone to sleep. *Probably saw the fire a couple of hours ago n' been homing in on it ever since.*

It had been silent for several minutes when suddenly two men walked into his camp down below. It shocked him a little when both men fired point blank into the 'sleeping man' with shotguns. Before the men fired, he already had the glittering diamonds centered in the white grove on the rear sight—in the middle of one man's back.

He was knocked over the fire and into the cliff wall when Jesse's first slug hit him. The second man turned and jumped around in confusion but before he could run, Jesse's second slug hit him in the chest.

Aware of a third set of horse hoofs earlier, Jesse reached into the inside pocket of his coat and removed the sleeping lizard. He had already rigged it as Wovokatah had taught him. A foot long piece of rawhide was tied snuggly around its belly just ahead of the rear legs then was tied to a short peg. He shoved the peg into the ground in the middle of the pile of dry brush he'd carried to the cliff with him. He then slid silently out of the coat, and placed it over the rifle, with the barrel sticking out. He bunched the coat up so it looked like someone was lying beneath it, then moved off about fifteen feet and lay motionless. His own eyes were adjusted to the near darkness so he knew that the third man's were also adjusted. As he listened to the lizard making faint sounds, as it searched for an escape, he could make out the shape of the coat. It was a half-hour before he heard the first alien noise—a careless foot touched a dry twig. A few moments later a shadowy shape passed the tree that Jesse was laying next to. *You ain't putting any holes in Rose's nice coat.* He squeezed the trigger. He could tell the man was hit by the grunt he made, but he turned toward Jesse anyway. Jesse's Colt .44 fired twice more, and sent the man over the top of the little cliff.

Jesse put his coat back on, and placed the lizard back in the pocket. "Thanks for the distraction, little amigo." He replaced the three spent cartridges in the pistol and reloaded the rifle before working his way back down from the cliff.

He checked the one he shot first. With the barrel of the Colt shoved into the man's neck he checked for a pulse with his finger—nothing. He cautiously moved from one to the other and when he was sure they were all dead, he held the canvas up to look at it in the fire's faint glow. *Don't look too bad, just a few holes. Better in it than me. I'll check it closer in the morning.* He arranged it again with his boots poking out and tossed a few chunks of wood on the fire before dragging the three bodies into the darkness, and then returned to his cliff for some more sleep.

Jesse was awake before light the following morning, and by dawn he had coffee made and was boiling water for some jerked beef and broth. As the coffee and broth simmered he released the lizard then went to his horse with some grain and the canteen of water. He gave it first the grain, and then he poured the water into his hat for the horse to drink. "Good fella," he said as he patted the horse's neck and rubbed its nose.

Before getting a cup of coffee, he rolled each body over to see what they looked like. After looking at the first two he went to the one that come to finish him off. When he rolled the body over he saw that it was a Mexican. *Ain't a one of 'em over twenty.* "Shoulda stayed at the fiesta," he said aloud, and then headed for his coffee and breakfast.

Later that day he stopped in a small town named Winchester. He tied his horse at the rail in front of a wood slab building about the size of the tack room back on his ranch. A large smiling man was standing behind two barrels with a plank across them. It was a bar with several bottles of whiskey on a shelf behind. "What'll it be stranger, good rye or rotgut?"

"Don't use the stuff; got any coffee?"

"Sure do. Don't use the likker m'self." He produced two clay cups and joined Jesse for a cup of strong, tar-black coffee.

"I followed the tracks in, does the train stop here?"

"Yep, sure does. Been running from Portland to San Francisco for almost a year now and won't be too long 'fore they tie into another train outfit from the east. Gonna be able to go all the way to New York City on a train when they get 'er all hooked up."

"Well I'll be darn. Wish to heck I'd thought to check that out before leaving on this horse." He finished the coffee with a shudder as he looked into the cup. "Where's the ticket shack?"

"Yer in it," the man grinned. "I was about to get outa here m'self when they offered me a deal to gather the mail and sell tickets for the train." He leaned aside so he could look out the window at the horse rail. "Gettin' the horse a ticket too, or wanna sell it?"

"Two tickets to San Francisco, and I'll stay in the horse car with m'horse." He looked hard at the too-friendly man. "Had all the people I can stand for awhile. How long 'fore it gets here?"

The bartender/ticket agent pulled a round watch from his pocket. "Little over an hour."

When Jesse leaned the Sharps rifle against the bar, he pulled his coat open and removed the leather pouch where he carried a little of the cash—the balance was still sewn inside the coat. The man's jaw dropped a little when he saw the long barrel Colt .44, the smaller pistol hanging in the holster beneath the armpit, the biggest knife he'd ever seen, and a tomahawk that he'd only heard of, hanging from Jesse's belt. "Got a general store where I can get m'horse some grain for the trip?"

"Uh yeah," he answered, a little apprehensively—now certain that he was in the presence of a very dangerous man. "Right across the street in the lobby of the hotel. They sell everything from grain to haircuts." As he watched Jesse leave he thought, *Bet he's got scalps in his gear.*

After paying for the coffee and the tickets, Jesse headed for the door, but turned. "If that train's early **don't**," he emphasized the last word, "let it leave without me n' m'horse."

"Yessir," the man said eagerly.

Jesse was waiting with his horse when the train stopped to pick up the mail, and get a little food for the crew. The boxcar assistant unlocked the door and slid it open. He asked Jesse to help him pull two ramps from the car. The first was attached to the side of the boxcar and the second was fitted to the middle of the first so the grade wouldn't be too steep for a horse. When his horse was inside and secured in a stall, Jesse helped the man shove the ramps back inside. When he started to close the door Jesse said, "Hold it, I'm riding with m'horse." He pointed to the padlock and said emphatically, "**Don't put that on**."

"Got to, it's the rules."

"The new rule is nobody gets in that car as long as I'm in there, unless they belong. Gimme that lock and I'll hang it up inside." He stared hard at the young man. "We'll put it back on the door when I get where I'm going."

The young man looked toward the engine for someone to tell him what to do, but realized they were standing there alone and the train was about to start moving. Reluctantly he handed the lock to the tall, bearded, hard-staring man; dressed more like an Indian than a white man.

Once inside, Jesse removed one of the spare lengths of rawhide he carried around his waist. After tying the door so that it would remain open about two feet, he went to his horse. "Look over there fella," he pointed to the three horses in stalls at the other end of the car, "company for you n' peace for me." He poured grain in the feedbag, and then piled straw for him to lie on. By the time the train had developed a steady clicking rhythm Jesse was asleep.

When the train stopped early the next evening Jesse leaned out the door to look around. When he saw that it was just a few buildings along the tracks, he walked to his horse to give it a reassuring pat on the back of its head. While rubbing its ears, he heard a noise at the open door. With the Colt in his hand he moved swiftly to it and saw two hands laying flat at the doorway, ready to propel the man they were attached to into the open car. When his boots came down on the hands with his entire weight, the man screamed. "Eeeeyooooow, get off m'hands, oh, oh, get off. Please!"

Jesse looked down. "Son, there's already four horse's asses in here n' I don't need another one." He stepped back as he saw a burly railroad man grab the young man by the back of his flimsy jacket and toss him into the briars and bushes behind him.

He looked up at Jesse and grinned. "How's your trip going?"

"Great. My fellow travelers ain't said a word the whole time."

Jesse settled back against the wall as the train picked up momentum. As he'd done many times during the past few years, he began thinking about his brothers. He recalled the last time he saw Patrick and how he'd described Broderick's successful career as a Los Angeles lawyer, plus his own law practice in Sacramento.

Jesse, ole Brod's got himself a big new building in Los Angeles that you could put that small place he started with over in a corner somewhere.

Pat, I'm sure you remember how he used to faint back a bit in a fight like someone was comin' up behind and as soon as we'd glance back, he'd wallop us with a good punch?

Sure do Jess. He got me more'n once with that ploy.

Me too, and after a coupla times I never doubted that he'd do good at whatever he decided on, 'cause I knew he'd do whatever it takes to win. I admired him for it even then.

I did too, Jess, but it was sure hard being the settled down older brother n' trying to lead a maverick like Brod on a leash.

You got him tagged right there Pat. That boy was one helluva maverick, wasn't he? Mom shoulda named him Maverick, but som'n about the word Broderick musta sounded good to her. He musta settled down a lot though 'cause he's sure's hell doin' good at that lawyering game. He set up Uncle Frank a contract with some big outfit too, didn't he?

Yeah, but it was Simon that brought the deal to Uncle Frank. When the outfit he was with officially became the Texas Rangers they wanted the best horses they could get, so naturally Simon thought of Uncle Frank.

I didn't know that. He still supplying them with his horses?

Yeah, and probably will as long as he's alive n' raising horses. Brod'll still be setting up the contract, too. He always drops everything when it comes to family.

The conversation finally got around to Patrick, so Jesse listened intently as his brother told the story about the Mexican he saved from a rope.

I was in my Sacramento office preparing my speech in preparation for my bid to be the congressman for Northern California, when Manollo Calaveras insisted he be allowed to talk with me. I heard the ruckus in the hall so I opened the door and recognized him immediately. He hadn't changed a bit, just a little older like the rest of us. I had to grab my secretary to keep her from punching him. That gal is two hundred pounds of total loyalty. He refused the seat and went directly to his problem. He said the San Francisco police came to the small town his friend's son lives in and arrested him for murder. Manny said that the young man was tending sheep with over a dozen men during the time the murder occurred, and had been for several days prior. One thing about a Mexican that stands out above almost all others, Jess—they don't lie. A hundred of them might beg and plead for his life but not one would lie to get him released. I listened to Manny explain that all they had was the fact that an eyewitness said the killer had a long scar on his face and was a Mexican. When he was done, I told my staff to put everything on hold until I returned. A dozen people were yelling, pleading, and saying they needed me to remain in Sacramento, as Manny and I headed for San Francisco. I talked to the boy in jail, and then told the authorities that if as much as one hair on his head was disturbed they would all be in cells before I got finished with them. The sheriff knows me well enough to know I don't make idle threats. He assured me that he'd see to it that the boy was not harmed until he went to court. Really pissed him off though Jess, 'cause he was a Mexican hater and had planned on hanging that boy. The Mexicans were creating such a hullabaloo that he decided to hold off till things settled down, but he sure hated to see me walk into his office that day. Manny stayed with me for three days while I rode around to be certain that the boy was innocent. We stayed in Mexican homes every night and were treated better'n we would have been in a fancy hotel like that one Ian owns now over in Carson City, Nevada. I stayed with him awhile back, and Jess lemme tell ya, the food we had in those Mexican homes was better'n his. Anyway, once I was certain he was innocent, I started building a defense. The first thing I did was see to it that we had as impartial a jury as we could get, and Jess that was no small task. We finally did though and the first thing I showed them was the affidavits from fourteen men that stated he was with them the entire time the murder happened, and that they were never closer to San Francisco than fifty-five miles. Five of those men were not Mexicans, so that helped us. When it came time for the eyewitness to identify the killer she saw, I had a little surprise for her. I had located seven Mexicans about the same age as my client Jaime, and each had a scar similar to the one on his face. You know how young hot-blooded Mexican boys are with their knives, so that didn't take us too long. When the seven boys walked into the courtroom with Jaime in the middle she just looked at them with her mouth hanging open. The jury was only out an hour when they returned a not guilty verdict. The best part Jess was about a month later a twelve-year-old boy came home after dark and heard a noise inside his mother's bedroom that didn't sound right. He got his dead daddy's shotgun and climbed out on the roof and went around to her window. He saw his mother tied to a chair and her face was bleeding, where the guy had beaten her. That boy didn't bat an eye when he took good aim and waited till the guy was in the right position. He let him have both barrels, and I'm glad he aimed for the body like his daddy taught him. There was that Mexican lying on the floor for the police to see the scar on his face. That eyewitness took one look and said it was definitely the man she saw kill the old man that Jaime had been accused of murdering.

Ian built that new place over in Nevada about two years ago. He thinks that town will grow and he plans to own most of it when it does. Jess, I don't know how much he got for that place in New York City, but I can tell you for sure it was a small fortune. He started buying up everything around him and 'fore long he owned the entire block of buildings. Some big manufacturer from England wanted to start a new factory in New York and bought Ian out. The place he has now is a hotel and gambling casino with a big restaurant. He's got stagecoaches that meet the trains in three places and he's working on a deal to get the railroad to bring rails for their trains into town. I'm handling the legal negotiations with the railroad lawyers and I think he's gonna get it.

When Aleena gets here Jess, she's gonna love your ranch. We're all happy that she can live here with you, 'cause you were always her mentor and very best friend.

Jesse looked out the partially open railroad door. He could almost see his brother Patrick, riding back toward Sacramento, and him standing on the front porch of his beautiful ranch house. Jesse wished that he and his sister Aleena could have grown old there together.

Except for the frequent stops, the trip was pleasant and uneventful. It allowed Jesse to unwind from the tensions of the past several weeks. The railroad man told him that the next stop would be the San Francisco station, so as soon as the train began slowing down he saddled his horse. "Good trip huh, fella? Bet you'll never cover so much ground in so short a time again in your life." He cinched the saddle, shoved the Sharps into the leather scabbard, put the bridle on its head, then stretched and rubbed his back. "Ain't slept so much in years n' I noticed you was catching up on yours, too."

After he helped the man set the gangplanks, he opened the stall gate to walk his horse down to the ground. The man watched as Jesse climbed into the saddle then turned toward town. "Take care of yourself." Jesse raised a hand to acknowledge that he had heard.

27

~ Old enemies ~

A couple of hours later, Jesse was at the State Bureau of Land Records. The moment he walked into the office, the small bald-headed man in spectacles working at a desk in the rear of the room almost dropped the stack of papers he had been sorting. He forced himself not to stare, but he kept glancing at the tall bearded man in mountain trapper clothing. *That's gotta be McKannah. Mr. Greely said he'd be back one day.* As soon as Jesse left the office, the man jumped up and grabbed his coat. "I've gotta take care of something, I'll not be gone long."

"You better not," the matronly woman at the counter said over her glasses, "you know what Mister Ashworth said."

MisterAshworth can kiss my ass. He rushed to The Joshua Greely Finance Institution. He arrived out of breath, and could barely explain to the young lady at the desk that he must see Mr. Greely at once. The tall, hard-looking man who always sat in the lobby stood and approached the little man. "You'll see him when he's damned good n' ready, Hamp." He pointed at a chair, "Sit down." He opened the door to the caged working area with a key from a ring of many then closed it behind him. He knocked on the large door in the far corner and explained who it was. Another cruel looking man opened the door. The man from the outer office approached the fat, barely five-foot-tall man with a huge brush mustache and muttonchops sideburns. The top of his head was bald with long hair hanging down the sides and back of his head. He was standing at the large picture window overlooking the city. "Hamp Peavus here to see you, boss."

He nodded and motioned with his fat, stubby-fingered hand that the visitor could be brought it. The banker demanded to be addressed as boss by all male employees, and as Joshua by all female employees. He didn't turn when he heard the man enter; he simply talked to the window. "Yes Hamp, what brings you all the way over here this time of day?"

"Guess who just walked into the land office?"

The man that opened the door had moved in close behind Hamp and now smacked him beside the head with his hat. "This ain't no damn kiddie school with guessing games you little mole, spit it out n' get the hell outa here."

Hamp was almost knocked down but came up explaining, "I was just trying to…

This time there was no hat in the man's hand when it landed against the side of Hamp's head. "Git up off the floor n' spit it out."

Hamp got to his knees, and before he was even on his feet, he was speaking. "Jesse McKannah just left the office."

"There. That wasn't so hard, now was it?" The man had Hamp by his collar, escorting him to the door. He released him growling, "Now git back over there n' keep your beady little eyes open." He closed the door then sat back down on the wooden chair. He turned a cold eye to the man who brought Hamp in. "Git back out to the lobby, Darvis."

Darvis Anka had one burning ambition in life—get Jerome Scanlon's job—by killing him. He knew the kind of man Jerome was, so he nodded his head and exited the room.

Jerome lit a cigar, "You were right, Joshua. Took awhile, but he's back." Jerome was the only man that could call Joshua Greely by his first name without so much as a glance from the banker. When Jesse had killed Jake Faggon and Jack Hannon, Jerome used his muscle and hired guns to catapult the diminutive little Joshua Greely into the top spot of Jack Hannon's crooked operation. Jerome knew the little man could be handled like a puppet, while he maintained control of the crime syndicate that Jack had started—and he now controlled.

The fat little man turned and picked out one of the cigars from his humidor. After lighting it he puffed quietly for a few moments.

Looks like a damn circus freak with a dog turd hangin' out his mouth."I'll go find Sheriff Pascal and have McKannah arrested on murder charges." He adjusted his gunbelt then added, "Oughta be able to have his neck in a noose pretty quick. We can then get movin' on that land of his."

Jesse was checking into a hotel when a small man approached him. "Excuse me, señor."

Jesse turned to find a Mexican standing with his hat in his hands.

"Yes?"

"I worked in the house with Issabella McKannah a very long time ago." He had a huge, friendly grin when he said "That was your mama, right?"

"Miguelo?" Jesse said with a quizzical expression on his face. "Miguelo Calaveras?"

"Si Señor, you remember me after all these years?"

Jesse took the man's hand and pumped it repeatedly. "Why sure I remember you Miguelo, we spent years together as kids. Your family still living on that river next to my place? The one that was named after them?"

"Si, and still growing vegetables, but now they are pretty big and shipping them all around the state."

"Just a minute Miguelo, lemme finish registering, then we can sit over there and get caught up." He turned back to hotel clerk and finished putting his name in the book. "Got plenty of hot water available?"

"Yep, all ya gotta do is turn it on. Got us a big boiler in the basement to keep hot water for cowpokes like you." He smiled as he took Jesse's money then handed him a room key.

The two old friends talked for an hour then the Mexican stood. "I must go now or my wife will be worried why I am gone so long. We are visiting friends here in the city. Can I come by tomorrow and talk some more?"

Jesse commented that he'd love to get together the following day then watched as the man headed for the door.

"Don't move so much as a muscle McKannah, or you're gonna be laying on the floor in two pieces."

He felt hands removing his gun belt, and then felt the muzzle of a pistol against his neck. "Take the coat off." A knife sliced the straps holding the shoulderholster then did the same to the belt holding the tomahawk and knife. "Now step damn slow away from that pile of weapons and the coat then put both hands behind your back." Jesse felt the steel handcuffs go on his wrists. As he was turned roughly around to be escorted out the door, he saw two men holding ten-gauge, sawed off shotguns. He also noticed Miguelo silently watching from the shadows.

After Jesse was securely locked in a cell he had visitors. They came as one group through the rear entrance to the jail. "Came back into town to pay for your crimes, huh Jesse?" The fat little man stood well beyond the bars and grinned malevolently.

"No Squirrel," Jesse remaining stretched out on the steel bunk on the one-inch-thick, vermin infested mat, "just wanted to see if you'd got big enough to piss over the first fence rail yet." Jesse had watched the fat little man grovel beneath the feet of Jack Hannon and his henchmen for a long time. He knew how bad he hated to be called Squirrel, or any reference made about his short stature. "Guess you never will."

The fat little man tried his best to stretch himself to a high stance in his size-six, hand-tooled, lizard-skin boots with extra thick soles and extended heels. He placed his thumb inside the belt that matched his boots, and moved a little closer to look at Jesse through the bars. "Well hotshot, we'll see how tall you are when they tighten that noose around your low class Irish neck." He leaned forward a little and grinned. "Probably do the same dance that Mick foreman of yours did."

A man like Joshua Greely couldn't rile Jesse, but he couldn't resist the urge to humiliate the cocky little man. "Why you," he said as he lunged at the bars.

Joshua Greely jumped back so fast that he smacked his head against the wall, knocking himself down, and almost out.

"Why you," Jesse calmly repeated, "couldn't spare one of those cigars could you?" He looked down at the boy-like man in the silk business suit, thrashing about on the filthy floor, trying to get back on his feet in the clumsy boots. "Ain't changed a bit Squirrel, you're still groveling at other people's feet."

Jerome Scanlon grabbed Joshua by the arm, and helped him to his feet. He looked hard into the little man's eyes, then nodded at the door, "Go get yourself some coffee, we'll be right out."

Joshua turned and stared his best mean stare at Jesse, who just smiled and slowly shook his head as the little man did as he was told.

Jerome turned from Jesse to Sheriff Raymond Pascal. "Go keep an eye on him." Without hesitation the sheriff also did as he was told. The tall, two-hundred-pound-man with eyes black as coal turned to Jesse. "You got one way outa this McKannah. Sign that land of yours over to my company and I'll see to it that the murder charges are dropped." Both deadly eyes focused on Jesse. "And they'll stay dropped as long as you keep the hell outa my town."

"I'll think about it." Jesse lied, stalling for time.

"Well, don't take too long. I got a federal judge coming to try you as a special favor to me, and he'll be here in a few days."

After a brief attempt to match Jesse's deadpan poker-stare, Jerome turned to leave, followed by his right hand man. Jesse waited until the two men were almost to the door. "Hey Darvis, I see you're still suckin' hind tit."

Darvis Anka turned and almost had his revolver out, but Jerome's steel grip closed around the man's wrist. Since the two men were stalled at the door Jesse asked, "Why'd you hang Arliss O'Reilly?"

Before Jerome could stop Darvis from shooting off his mouth he said, "Because that damn Mick bastard wouldn't die, even with four of my bullets in the son-of-a-bitch." He grinned pure malevolence at Jesse then followed Jerome.

You damn sure better hope they hang me or you're a dead man, Darvis.

Miguelo Calaveras had watched the arrest of his childhood friend, from the concealment of the shadowed columns outside the hotel. As soon as the sheriff left with Jesse, he ran all the way to a friend's house. When he was inside he was speaking in such rapid Spanish that even they couldn't quite make out what he was saying. He finally slowed down, and explained the situation.

His friend asked, "Is this the McKannah from Sacramento that saved the Mexican field worker from the murder charges?"

"No, that's his older brother. This is the youngest McKannah. We must get word to his brother immediately because this sheriff is part of the evil gang here in town, and I have a bad feeling for my old friend."

Within an hour a young Mexican man was on a fast horse, rapidly putting the lights of San Francisco behind him as he galloped toward Sacramento—over a hundred miles away. The entire Mexican community along the way responded to the name McKannah because they had all heard how the lawyer, who was running for congress, had defended a poor Mexican field worker for nothing, and proved his innocence. They did not hesitate to provide the message carrier with food and a fresh horse, every eight or ten miles. The trip was made in record time.

He saw a Mexican newspaperman setting up his small business and got the directions to the house. An hour before dawn he was pounding on Patrick McKannah's door. The door partially opened, but there was no one standing there. A voice came from the darkness behind the heavy wooden door. "What do you want?"

After a brief explanation, a tall man with rusty colored hair and mustache stepped from behind the door with a pistol in his hand. After checking the area around the front of the house, he motioned for the young Mexican to enter. The young man had never seen a man with green eyes, and couldn't answer at first.

"C'mon in son," Patrick said, "who sent you?"

When the young man explained about Miguelo Calaveras' message, Patrick smiled. In flawless Spanish he said, "Yes, I remember him and his family well." He took only a moment to think about the situation then looked hard at the young Mexican. "Are you ready to go to work for me right now?"

"Si, señor."

Patrick went into the next room and returned moments later with a handful of gold coins. "Do you know the route to Carson City, over in Nevada?"

"Si, señor."

"It's a few miles farther than the trip you just made. Can you continue with no rest?"

"Si señor."

Patrick handed him more money than he'd ever seen in one pile. "Here is two hundred dollars pay for the tasks that you will need to accomplish. Guard it with care, and listen to what I want you to do." He paused to stare hard at the man again. "Go to the Silver Slipper Hotel and Casino in Carson City. My brother Ian owns it. Tell him what you just told me, then ride south to Los Angeles, and talk to my brother Broderick." Again he looked hard at the young Mexican, "It's over five hundred miles, and he'll want you to go on to Texas. Can I count on you to accomplish this?"

"Señor McKannah, you have helped my people many times. We all know your name and respect you very much. Yes, I will make the journey or die trying."

Patrick liked the no nonsense way the young man made the statement. "Come inside and eat something amigo, then be on you way."

The young Mexican wasn't a mile from the house when Patrick McKannah was on his own horse. As he swiftly headed southwest, the elder McKannah was formulating a plan.

The kind of reception the young Mexican got along the trail to Carson City made the young man think, *Every Mexican in this country must know this man*. It was after dark when he arrived at the Silver Slipper, so he felt uncomfortable approaching the man at the desk. *I hope I don't get shot. I must look like a bum.*

"Yes, what can I do for you?" The man behind the desk leaned out and looked down at the Mexican in dirty clothes.

After briefly explaining, he was admitted to a room in the rear of the hotel. A small man about his own height met him. He was thin like his brother, but didn't look anything like him—until the young Mexican looked into his eyes. They had the same hard piercing stare. *This is another McKannah.* After explaining the reason for his intrusion, he realized that this man had not blinked once—he was still staring hard at him. *Perhaps he can't blink?* Ian McKannah smiled and blinked. "Are you up to heading right out toward Los Angeles?"

"Si, señor McKannah. I have gone five days with very little sleep. A little food, and I will ride south."

Ian slowly shook his head up and down. "Good man," He replied in good Spanish then gave the young man directions to his brother's Los Angeles business. "Wait here a moment." He returned with a handful of gold coins. "Take these and Godspeed, amigo."

The young man raised both his hands in front of him. "Oh no, señor. Your brother in Sacramento gave me gold already."

Ian just stood there a moment then turned to his assistant as he put the coins in his pocket. "Take him to the kitchen and get him anything he wants to eat now, and something to carry. Then Charles, have two good men see to it that he gets out of town and on his way." Before they left the room Ian said, "Oh Charles, tell them to be damned sure he isn't followed." Before the young man was even finished eating and packing a few food items for the long trip, Ian McKannah was on his horse, heading southwest toward San Francisco.

Long before the young Mexican messenger arrived in Los Angeles, two more McKannah men were in San Francisco; setting the stage for a confrontation with the criminal power structure that one of them was very aware of. After assuring themselves that Jesse was in no immediate danger, Patrick and Ian quietly began collecting the information they knew they would need.

It was noon when the young Mexican located the huge office building. He read the sign, quietly aloud. Broderick McKannah—Attorney at Law. He liked the easy nature of the tall brother with the same rusty hair as his older brother, and he loved the neat little goatee beard that he wore. He couldn't realize that the sparkling green eyes were very deceiving. This brother was cold and calculating when the stakes were high. And family was always at the top of his list. "You're in luck amigo," he said in the same flawless Spanish than his older brother used, "you won't have to go to Texas. My brother just arrived to have me do some legal work for him.

The young Mexican messenger sat in the office, as Broderick McKannah told his Mexican secretary that his partner was to handle all business for awhile. "I'll be gone for a few days—maybe longer." He turned to the waiting Mexican, "My brother Simon will be back soon, then we'll go find a stagecoach for hire to take us straight through to San Francisco. I'll have your horse stabled, then I'll ship it to you later, amigo."

"That is not my horse Señor McKannah. The many horses I used to get here were loaned to me along the way. This last one belongs to a farmer in Acton."

Broderick paused, then looked up from the papers he was arranging for his secretary. "You come from good people amigo; they know how to look after each other and their friends." He pursed his lips slightly and nodded his head. "My family will not let this go unnoticed. Tell Angelina where it belongs and she will see to it that the horse is returned to its owner."

The young Mexican was reading the Mexican newspaper that the secretary had brought with her to work when the door opened. He turned to see a huge, two-hundred-and-fifty-pound-man at least six and a half feet tall looking hard at him through intense eyes. His face was enclosed in a full beard, which joined long hair the same color. "Buenos Dios señor," the young Mexican said with a smile.

Simon McKannah nodded and continued into the rear of the office where his brother Broderick was packing a valise. As he walked away from him, the young Mexican couldn't take his eyes from the twin Colt pistols that rested easily, slightly forward of the man's hips in plain well used holsters—butts forward. *Mexican cross-draw pistols. This McKannah must be the Texas man-hunter we have all heard so much about.*

When the two brothers came from the back room, Simon went straight to the young Mexican. "You did a good job getting here this quick, thank you." He held out his hand. The young man took it, but suddenly felt like a child when his hand completely disappeared inside the man's huge hand.

Broderick soon joined them. "She'll have that horse back to its owner by tomorrow. Let's walk across the street and have them hitch up a team to a small stagecoach, while we get a bite to eat. When the three men got to the front of The Pacific Stagecoach Line, Broderick pointed at the diner a few doors down. "Order us dinner n' get us something to eat along the way. I'll make arrangements here n' be right over."

The small Mexican followed Simon in, and sat quietly as he ordered their meal from the old man behind the counter. "Ain't long on time, but we gotta have three plates of food n' a bag to take with us, amigo." The old man remained silent, but nodded his head. "For here," Simon began, "three plates of them two pound sirloins, with potatoes n' some kinda vegetable." He looked at the old man, "Got any fresh bread?"

"Sure do. Just came outa the oven awhile ago."

"A loaf for now n' three to take with us." Simon paused a moment, thinking about the long trip. "Put three more 'o them sirloins in that bag to go, n' cook 'em all well done." When the old man nodded and turned to go in the back Simon added, "Can you put us together three jugs of that sweet tea?"

"Sure can."

An hour later, the stagecoach was moving steadily north toward San Francisco. Broderick hired two drivers to handle the six-horse team they would need to get to their destination quickly. They would change teams of horses three times at stops along the way. The two drivers could alternate resting, so the stagecoach could keep moving. The two McKannahs didn't have any of the details yet, but they knew that things were desperate for Patrick to go to so much trouble to send word for them to come immediately.

Once the coach was on the trail heading north, both McKannahs settled into separate corners and were soon sleeping. The young Mexican was miserable. He had never seen pieces of meat as large as the ones the cafe owner sat in front of the three men. There wasn't an ounce of fat on the young man, but he wasn't thin, because he came from a good family and ate regularly and plenty. As he sat there in misery, he wondered why he attempted to eat the entire piece of meat and all the potatoes and other things brought to him. *That big gunfighter put chunks of meat in his mouth as big as a meal for me in my home. Ohhhhh me, why did I try to eat as much as him? Oh my, even the skinny one ate the whole thing like it was a snack. Ohhhhh, my poor belly.*

The trip for him started miserably, but during the first horse-team change, he was able to slip into the bushes and get rid of a few pounds of it. He slept the rest of the night.

Within hours of arriving in San Francisco, Patrick had Mexican spies everywhere. He was soon advised that Jerome Scanlon was calling in a favor from a Federal Judge in Patrick's town of Sacramento. He was to come as soon as possible to try a case for Jerome and his syndicate of crooks. There was only one place he could arrive, so Patrick had several men waiting to notify him the minute the stage arrived. In the meantime he was gathering all of the information he could about every member of Jerome's gang.

Jesse told his brother Patrick, years earlier about Jack Hannon's efforts to purchase the twenty thousand acres that his ranch sat on. Patrick had met Jack and Jerome only once, but warned Jesse. "Be damned careful around those guys; both look like they were thieves the moment they crawled out of the the cradle."

Jesse told Patrick that he'd known Joshua Greely for many years. "He failed at everything he tried until he became Jack Hannon's bookkeeper. When I took care of Jack Hannon, Jerome Scanlon took over and Joshua was made the puppet frontman for The Joshua Greely Finance Institution. That was Jerome's front for grabbing land from unsuspecting patrons of the company. Joshua is still a failure, he just doesn't know it."

His informants told Patrick that Darvis Anka was no more than a thug and had done everything for Jack Hannon from killing to arson. He had also committed rape, child abuse, murder, and kidnapping on his own. Many times, charges had been brought against him, but Sheriff Raymond Pascal had not seen evidence enough to arrest the man. *If this situation gets rough,* Patrick thought, *he'll be the first to go 'cause he's a bad one.*

Patrick had never met Sheriff Raymond Pascal, but he knew his older brother, State Representative Julius Pascal. He had an office two buildings away from him in Sacramento. Julius started as a good lawyer, but had left all scruples and moral conduct behind as he struggled up the political ladder. He arranged for his brother to be made Sheriff of San Francisco, not as a favor or from brotherly love, but as a tool he planned to use in the future. Patrick was aware that Sheriff Pascal was a chip off the old family block—crook to the bone.

As Patrick waited for the arrival of the federal judge, he wondered, *Quite a few bigshots might owe Jerome Scanlon a favor; wonder who they are?*

Ian had been busy since his arrival, gathering information in the saloons and gambling halls around town. When he was satisfied that he now saw the entire picture about his brother Jesse's arrest, he paid a local judge a visit. Judge Arnold Armbrister was a regular customer of Ian's. He loved to gamble, and he loved to play upstairs with the ladies on his occasional 'business trips' away from San Francisco—and his family. The short, rotund Judge turned paler than usual when he saw who was at his door. “Good evening judge,” Ian said pleasantly, “I’d like a few minutes of your time.”

The judge attempted to maintain his composure. “We have guests Mr. McKannah, could it wait until later?”

Ian put his hat back on. “Why certainly judge, I’m pretty busy m’self. Tell you what I’ll do, I’ll give Yellow Rose the message and have her bring it over next Sunday morning.” He paused, as he stared hard at the profusely sweating little man, “Just about church time, so she’ll be sure to catch you in a free moment. Goodnight.” He turned, but before he had taken the first step, the judge spoke.

“No. Please, please, Mr. McKannah. How rude of me. Do come in; we can use my study.”

Once inside away from the eyes and ears of the Judge’s guests, Ian dropped all courtesy. “There’s a crooked federal judge coming in from Sacramento for a Kangaroo Court then hang my brother for something he didn’t do. He’s gonna be persuaded to turn around and go back. I think me n’ my brothers can handle this situation just fine, but in case it gets outa hand we want you to go right now and get the necessary papers made up so it’ll be legal for this federal judge to temporarily assign you to handle this case. I’ll send a man by in an hour to get ‘em.” He stared hard at the now almost soaking wet little man. “If they’re not ready, I’ll have a lady come by awhile later.”

“There’s no need to send anyone, I have pre-notarized forms right here in my desk for just such emergencies.” He turned to go behind his giant walnut desk and Ian followed him closely—Ian was not a trusting man.

Ian climbed back into the coach. *Crooked devils have every corner covered.* As the small coach with Ian McKannah inside was pulling away from the judge’s expensive three-story home, another larger six-horse-team stagecoach was pulling into town with Broderick, and Simon McKannah inside. All the players were in town now, and the game was about to begin.

28

~ Leave nothing to chance ~

Patrick left word with the Mexicans who were waiting for the stage from Sacramento with the federal judge in it to arrive. "I'll be at the Parisian Review. Do not let that Judge leave until I'm there."

"Yessir, Mister McKannah." Miguelo Calaveras had assumed control of the Mexican end of the operation and was assigning men and women tasks and sending out eyes to watch everything. "I have a very fast horse standing by with a trusted rider to find you as soon as he arrives."

Miguelo's spies had located Sheriff Raymond Pascal only moments earlier and Patrick now climbed into the small coach he had reserved to be with him as long as he needed it. Ten minutes later it pulled up behind the famous nightspot.

Two, ten-dollar gold coins later, he was standing outside a door on the second floor as the young man turned a key in the lock. Patrick's pearl handled Colt was obvious as his coat hung loosely open, as he stepped through the door. It immediately caught the attention of the two naked young girls astride the sheriff. "Grab your clothes and get out," Patrick commanded. When they had their clothes in their hands and were at the door he added, "If you two're enjoying your life, keep your mouth shut." He had never removed his eyes from the sheriff. Like his brothers, he was not a trusting man.

"I'm gonna explain something to you while you're getting your clothes on, Raymond."

When the nearly bald headed little man with bushy white eyebrows longer than his remaining hair, finally got into his silk pants, he looked at the tall thin man staring at him. "How do you know my name?"

"Your brother's got an office a short distance from mine. My name's Patrick McKannah and I might be the governor of California before too long, so listen up."

The name McKannah hit a nerve. Sheriff Pascal hadn't liked the idea of locking up Jesse in the first place, because he was aware that his brother was running for congress and was reputed to be a shoe-in for governor if he wanted it. He listened carefully as Patrick explained.

"The first thing we're gonna do is go to the jail and release my brother into my custody. Then you can do whatever you want, but I'd suggest you take a vacation until this's settled with Jerome Scanlon. You're dealing with very dangerous men, Raymond." He stared at the sweating man who was struggling with shaking hands to close the pearl buttons on the silk shirt. "Jerome won't bat an eye when he puts a bullet in you after turning Jesse loose, so if you wanna live to ride your brother's coat tails into Washington, you'd better make yourself scarce for awhile."

Jerome Scanlon also had spies everywhere, and one of them was listening at one of the peepholes to the room Patrick was in at this very moment. The young man that unlocked the door for Patrick quietly left the building and headed for Jerome's office.

Patrick and Sheriff Pascal entered the coach that was waiting in the rear alley, and headed for the jail.

Miguelo's sentries had been on the trail waiting for the stage to arrive with the two McKannah brothers on board. Patrick knew exactly how his brothers operated and told Miguelo that they'd hire a stagecoach to get to San Francisco as soon as possible. When they sighted the stage, two Mexican riders came alongside and one yelled, "Misters McKannah."

Ian knew what Patrick was going to do when he found the sheriff, so he headed for the jail after leaving Judge Armbrister's house. He waited in the shadows until Patrick's coach pulled into the alley. Almost immediately after the two brothers began talking, a Mexican rider arrived with the news that the federal judge was being detained.

"Go with the sheriff and see to it that Jesse's released," Patrick said to Ian. "This won't take long n' I'll be right back."

Miguelo's men were doing their job well and before the stage carrying

Broderick and Simon had gone far, another Mexican rider came beside it to inform the two men that their brothers were at the jail.

As the stage headed for the huge four-story jail building, Patrick's coach was speeding toward the stagecoach building where the federal judge from Sacramento was being detained by a small army of Mexican civilians under the command of Miguelo Calaveras. When he approached the stagecoach, the judge yelled through the window of the door which had been tied shut the moment he arrived. "What the hell are you doing here, McKannah, and why are these savages keeping me prisoner?"

"Well I'll be darn, Anseth, you're the last person I thought would get involved with a crook like Jerome Scanlon." He smiled up at the now visibly upset man that he'd known since their early days as lawyers.

"What the hell's going on, Patrick?"

After a brief explanation, Patrick finished by saying, "Anseth, I ain't gonna stop a federal judge from executing his duties, but if you get involved with this crooked set-up, you'll probably lose your career at best." He paused to let the statement sink in, and then continued. "At worst you'll get killed by the same man you're here trying to pay off your debt to." Again he looked up at the judge, "My advice to you is to sign these papers and get back to Sacramento. I'll eventually find out why you came running, but as long as you keep outa my hair, we'll forget this night ever happened." Ten minutes after Patrick had arrived he was watching the stagecoach leave with the passenger never touching San Francisco dirt. Before the judge's stagecoach was even out of sight, Patrick was back in his and heading for the jail building.

It didn't take Patrick long when this mess was all over to get the sordid details about Judge Anseth Pillman's vacation orgy, and the death of the teenage whore he'd gotten too rough with.

Jerome's spies had also done their work well. His secretary had told her friend Carmolita, "Always keep your eyes open, and when you have information that will help Mr. Scanlon, bring it immediately to me." She smiled at the young girl. "You can see how I have used different bits of information to gain favor with him. When he is in control of San Francisco I will be his wife and if you have been of help to me I will see to it that you have my job." She smiled again, "And then you can begin your rise to the top as I have done."

That was how she saw her relationship with Jerome Scanlon. How it actually was became obvious when he answered Darvis' question one evening over drinks. "Why in the hell do you keep messing around with that damn beaner, with all these gorgeous white women around?"

"Information Darvis, information is the key to success." Jerome answered. "That bitch ain't got a thing to offer me, but she keeps me informed of everything that's going on in the Mexican community." He finished his drink then grinned at the huge man beside him who was combing his greasy black hair. “When I’m finished with her you can take her on a little trip to the desert like you enjoy, and cut her throat when you’re finished with her.”

Darvis Anka’s dark eyes glowed as he contemplated the things he would do to the woman when she was passed on to him—as the others had been.

The young man from the Parisian Review was a familiar face in Jerome Scanlon’s building. He was admitted immediately into the rear office. The young man shivered inside when he saw what always looked to him like ice forming in the man’s black eyes as Jerome flipped him a twenty dollar gold coin. As he was leaving the building, Jerome’s secretary’s friend was just entering.

Jerome was buckling on his pistol belt when he stepped through the door from his office. He watched the young girl leaving and asked his secretary. “She bring you any worthwhile information?”

“Yes. Two more of that man’s brothers have arrived from Los Angeles.”

Jerome paused momentarily to digest this unexpected bit of news then opened the humidor on his secretary’s desk to remove a fresh cigar. As soon as he’d returned the tip cutter to his pocket he held the cigar to the waiting light in her hand. He looked hard at her through the cloud of smoke. She looked back with a coy, sexy smile. *You’re on your last stack of tortillas, bitch.* He then turned to Darvis. “Get a dozen of our men and meet me at the jail building in about half an hour.”

Darvis left to gather the men. *Don’t know why the son-of-a-bitch even bothers to put that gun on, ‘cause he ain’t nothing but a stinkin’ businessman now.*

Jerome turned and went to Joshua Greely’s rear office where he was having one of his phony business meetings with the young girl that worked upstairs in the records department. “Get back upstairs to work.” Joshua snapped at the girl then turned to Joshua. “Get that fancy new rifle of yours with the sighting scope on it, and maybe for once you can be of some use.” He turned and went back to his secretary. “It’s getting dark so tell everyone to wrap it up and go on home.” He turned when he heard Joshua coming. He almost laughed when he saw the little man carrying the leather case almost as long as he was tall. “Been practicing with that thing?”

“Sure as hell have.” The little man lied through his big, brush mustache. The two men more closely resembled cartoon characters—something that was becoming very popular in the local paper. Except one was very deadly in his attitude toward all living things, and the other could be just as deadly in his innate incompetence.

Thirty minutes after unlocking the cell door, which allowed Jesse to walk out, Sheriff Raymond Pascal was on his horse and heading south toward San Luis Obispo to catch up on some fishing and spend time with a ladyfriend he had been neglecting.

Winter darkness closed in very quickly, concealing the movements of many men silently slipping into position around the jail building. It was to be a night that would be described over and over through the years—especially south of the border.

Jerome Scanlon had instructed Darvis Anka to have his men slip quietly into place where they could concentrate fire on the jail building, but could not be identified by any bystanders that might happen to be in the area. "I'm hoping I can get this McKannah bunch to swap their brother's freedom for that piece of property we found the gold on, but if not I want 'em all dead when this night's over." He took a few puffs on his cigar before adding; "I'll worry about getting the deed to that property later." He sent Darvis on his way to assemble the men for the night's confrontation.

Darvis climbed into his saddle. *I'm hoping there's plenty of gunfire, 'cause I'm gonna put a bullet right in the middle of that bastard, Jerome's back.* A sinister grin spread across his face as he turned his horse. *Then we'll have a real man in charge of this outfit.*

"Pretty quiet out there Patrick," his brother Broderick commented, as he looked around the edge of the window and into the area below, dimly lit by gas operated streetlights. "Whadaya think they're up to?"

"Getting re-enforcement's into position, I reckon."

"We'll have to cover all bets here boys," Jesse said, "he's a rotten to the core, no good murdering son-of-a-bitch, but he's no fool. He'll try to get me to sign that property over to him, and if that doesn't work, then he'll give the guys that're sure to be sneakin' around out there right now, orders to blast us out with gunfire, blow up the building, or burn it down." Jesse's grin brought a smile to his brothers. "Probably all three."

"Nice friendly bunch you've been hangin' around with since I last saw you, little brother." Ian's grin could be seen across the dimly lit room.

"Can't all be wrapped up in that church life like you are, Reverend Ian."

Broderick snorted then laughed. "Reverend Ian McKannah's Silver Slipper Revival." His grin was wider than his brothers. "Praise the Lord and pass the dice."

Simon McKannah had been through many similar scenes in a twenty-year career as a successful man hunter, so he was spending all of his time watching the area below. "How many guns'll he have down there, Jess?"

"A good, fair fight to him's about three to one," Jesse responded, "in his favor."

"No doubt," Patrick commented, "he knows there are five of us in here, so we oughta figure on at least fifteen men out there trying to kill us if we have to make this an outside shooting."

Jesse grinned again, “Damned fool’s outgunned and don’t even know it.”

Broderick laughed softly. “Remember the time we started kickin’ ass over in Clovis at that square dance?”

“Sure do,” Ian answered, “one of them guys told Jesse to go home n’ nurse on his mama and quit botherin’ their girls to dance.”

“Who hit that big som’bitch?” Broderick asked.

“I did.” Ian replied.

“Bullshit,” Patrick chimed in smiling, “Jesse knocked that guy out colder’n a cucumber with one punch.”

“No kidding?”

“No kidding?”

“That’s right,” Patrick answered both of them.

“Well,” Broderick said with a casual tug on his rusty red goatee, as his eyes twinkled, “as I remember it we bloodied up about a dozen of those Clovis boys that night.”

“You’re right,” Patrick said with a serious scowl at his brother, “but not a one of ‘em had a gun.”

“Hey, Jesse.” The call came from Jerome, somewhere down below.

“What’s on your mind, Scanlon?” Jesse yelled back while standing back from the opened window.

“I got plenty of witnesses that place you at Jake Faggon’s murder, and Jack Hannon’s, too. You’re gonna hang if you don’t work out some kinda deal with me. A federal judge friend of mine’s on his way here right now to try this case for me. You’re up shit creek without a paddle, Jesse, so whadaya say we git together down here n’ work this out?”

“I already sent Anseth Pillman home with his tail between his legs.” Patrick yelled back.

Jerome turned and grabbed the little Mexican by the throat. “What the hell do I pay you for, you piece o’ shit little wetback?” He began slapping the man back and forth across the face. “That’s the kind of information I pay you bastards to supply me with.” He stopped slapping the man, and began punching him until his hand was almost as bloody as the Mexican’s face. As quiet as he thought he was being, the sound still carried up into the building.

“I think you struck a nerve with that one.” Jesse said.

Jesse yelled out the window. “I’ve got a better idea Jerome, you come in here n’ tell me again why you bastards hung Arliss and killed my ranch hands.”

Jerome gritted his teeth so hard that those around him could hear the gnashing. *That stupid Darvis and his big mouth. When the shootin’ starts I hope I get a chance to put a bullet in that big bastard.*

“Hey Mr. Scanlon,” Patrick yelled out the window, “another thing you oughta know. That sheriff you thought you had in your pocket.” He paused to let it work on Jerome's mind. "Me n' his brother go way back. I talked to him about getting involved in a federal court case that's gonna put all of you guys behind bars for a long time." Since there was no word coming from down below he knew he had an audience. "Another judge was assigned tonight, and we've got a solid case against you n' a bunch of the men that work with you. The best thing you can do is either make a hard run for the Mexican border right now, or walk away before this gets outa hand. You can sit down with me tomorrow to see what we can work out to keep you from spending the rest of your life in prison."

Unknown to any of the McKannah brothers, Miguelo Calaveras had been quietly placing men all around the area. When he sent the word out, a hundred rock solid ex-revolutionaries quietly slipped into the area—well armed. These were men that had fought for their freedom under conditions that would have been intolerable to most men. Some had even fought against the world's best guerrilla soldier—Apache.

Eyes accustomed to seeing things in the darkness of night that most gringos would never see, were watching. One old Mexican spotted a long piece of pipe being slowly shoved out from behind a damaged carriage sitting across from the jail. He began moving noiselessly toward it to investigate.

Joshua Greely had taken his new hunting rifle to the desert to practice with on only a couple of occasions in the year he had owned the weapon. He was amazed when he hit every object he put in the crosshairs of the newly invented sighting scope. As he now searched through it for the man behind the voice in the jail, he spoke quietly, but aloud. "As soon as I get you in this scope McKannah you're a dead duck." It was his extreme misfortune that the old Mexican, now standing a foot behind him with a razor sharp field knife, understood perfect English. "Ah, there you are, now I'll just…It was the last thing he would ever say.

"Starting to look like this's gonna drag out awhile," Broderick said. "How much ammo we got in here?"

"I grabbed a full crate of forty-fours before I left home," Patrick answered, "and it looks like that's what all of us are using."

Jesse patted the Colt that was back on his hip. "Glad to get this back, but I'll bet I never see my tomahawk, Sharps, or shoulder holster again." He shook his head, "Thieving snakes."

Darvis Anka came looking for a fight, not a negotiation, and he was getting very impatient with all of the talking. *That damn Jerome's gonna try to work out some kinda deal with these guys*. He studied the window that the voices came from. Darvis turned to the three men that were staying close to him as he'd earlier instructed them to do. "Next time one of 'em starts shooting his mouth off, let's start shootin' some lead back at 'em." A sinister grin also spread across the faces of the other three men. They each began lining up their sights, along the barrels of their guns, at the window in the jail building.

"Soon's the shooting starts Jerome," Patrick yelled, "there's gonna be a crowd here, and…the first bullet hit close to his head and knocked a large chunk of wood from the frame. Several more hit the outside of the building but before any of the five men inside could get into position to return fire, a volley of gunfire began that sounded like another revolution had started. The five men intuitively went prone on the floor and waited for the firing to stop. After what seemed like a long time, but was actually only minutes, Patrick said, "Those bullets ain't coming in here or hitting the building, either."

"What the hell's going on down there?"

"One of you guys call the cavalry?" Broderick said with a grin.

"Sure as hell sounded like it," Ian commented, "musta been a thousand shots fired by somebody down there."

There were actually only about three hundred shots fired, and almost a quarter of them found their mark. The City Coroner would later testify that there were thirteen dead bodies with a total of seventy-four bullet holes in them, and one very small man with his throat slit.

"Hey, Señor McKannah, you can come out now because they are all dead."

"That's Miguelo Calaveras."

"Miguelo."

"Si Jesse. We have checked them all, and it is safe to come out now."

When the five brothers came out, they found only Miguelo standing in the street. Not another sign of life was anywhere. "I think these men," Miguelo stated as he looked around at several of the bodies, "got themselves into their own crossfire, and killed each other."

"That must be it," Jesse said, "sure wasn't any gunfire coming from us."

"I must go Jesse," Miguelo said, "my wife will be worried until I return." He turned and began walking away, but gave a little wave when his childhood friend said, "Muy gracias, amigo."

29

~ GOLD ~

The San Francisco City Coroner issued a statement to the newspaper that the assailants at the jail building apparently got into each other's crossfire and all thirteen men were killed. It also stated that an argument must have occurred between one of the men and Joshua Greely, whose throat was slit. ACCIDENTAL HOMICIDE was written on the folder and it was shoved into a file not to be opened again for many years.

Judge Arnold Armbrister saw to it that all records of Jesse's arrest were destroyed. Before Ian left for Carson City he told the judge about a new young girl from Canada that just began working for him at The Silver Slipper. The old judge's eyes twinkled. "Be lookin' for ya." Ian smiled.

While walking through the dead men, Jesse saw his tomahawk on the belt of one. When he rolled it over he was surprised to see it was Darvis Anka. "Phew, musta been several of 'em shootin' at you. Didn't recognize ya." He was pleased to see the hunting knife that he'd carried his entire adult life, attached to the same belt the tomahawk was on. He strapped the belt on and continued walking among the dead men. The blonde hair brought Jesse to Jerome Scanlon. He was staring sightlessly at the full moon overhead, but what caught Jesse's eye was his own custom made, short barrel Colt pistol that was still in Jerome Scanlon's hand. After removing it, he removed the shoulderholster and inspected it for bullet holes, but found none. "Good shooting, amigos." He looked at the repair where they had cut it from him. "Hmmm, musta used a good shoemaker to repair this." With the holster firmly snugged beneath his left armpit he shoved the .44, which still had all six shells in it. *Sorry bastard didn't even get off a shot.* He looked more closely at Jerome's dead body. There was a very nasty hole where one bullet made its exit. He rolled him over and raised his coat. *One shot right in the back.* He stood up and looked around. *That was ole Darvis back there behind you, Jerome. You musta pissed him off somewhere along the line.*

Jesse continued looking through the bodies but didn't find his Sharps rifle. When he got back to where his brothers were standing he opened his jacket front to display his finds.

"How come you didn't get yourself a few scalps, wild boy?" Broderick had always loved to kid his younger brother and was grinning widely.

Jesse returned the grin. "Still have room on my lance for one more rusty ole red scalp, white man."

"C'mon boys," Patrick said, "let's go get a beer n' talk awhile. Been a long time since the five of us have been together." Ian led them to a small Mexican cantina he often visited when he was in the city.

They ordered beers for everyone except Jesse who asked for a cup of coffee. Before the beer was gone, an old Mexican man walked to the table. "Señor McKannah?" He looked from one to the other.

Patrick spoke first. "We're all McKannahs. Can we help you?"

The man motioned to a young boy who came forward with Jesse's Sharps. "The boy found this rifle when he and some boys let their curiosity get the best of them when they went to see the dead bodies."

Jesse stood and took the offered rifle. "Muy gracias, Señor. I sure would have missed this gun." He dug a twenty dollar gold coin from his pocket and handed it to the boy, who smiled wide and followed the old Mexican from the cantina.

Two hours of beer and several cups of coffee later, the five brothers had brought each other up on the travels and happenings of one another. "What are you going to do now, Jesse?" Patrick inquired.

Jesse wasn't quick to answer questions, but he always had an enormous respect for his oldest brother so he replied, "Been thinking about it while I was in that cell."

"Them fellas were putting knots in a rope for your hanging party and you was still planning out your future, huh?" Broderick had a grin on his face as he pulled the goatee to a point.

"Wasn't planning to attend that party. I'm goin' over east of here to where they discovered all that gold. I wanna see how they go about gettin' it outa the ground." He took a sip of his coffee as he thought about his plans, some of which were being made up as he spoke. "When I think I know how to do it, I'm gonna go look around on that spread of mine. Any of you guys wanna come in with me? We'll be full partners."

"No suuuuh ree," Ian said with emphasis. "I've heard all the stories and I know how they get that shiny stuff outa the ground. Work, work, work, n' more work." The short little blonde brother grinned at Jesse. "I found a much better way to get the gold," another grin, "I dig it outa their pockets."

Patrick smiled. "My law practice keeps me very busy, plus running for congress," he paused and pursed his lips in thought, "or the governorship of California. Ain't decided which, but it's eating up all my spare time. Thanks for the offer, but no thanks." He pulled the gold watch that his father removed from the man he had to kill when he and Frank had Issabella with them enroute to Luis's ranch. "Time for me to be getting on back to work 'fore too long, anyway."

"Same here," Broderick said. "I've been busier'n a one legged tap dancer lately."

Jesse looked at his tall, powerfully built brother. "Well Simon, I guess that leaves just you n' me to split all the gold between us." He grinned knowing his brother would never consider anything that would take him away from his Texas Rangers for long.

The big man's black eyes stared hard at the brother that was only a year younger than him. They softened as he spoke. "Hope you find a ton of it Jesse, 'cause you can have it all to yourself." He pulled out the huge knife that he'd taken from the body of Billy, up in the mountains years earlier. He checked the edge, then before replacing it, he grinned at Jesse. "I'm gettin' back on the trail of a man wanted for killing a Texas Ranger."

"Tell you what though little brother," Ian said as they prepared to go back to their own lives. "That place they found all this gold at is on the way back to Carson City, so I'll ride along with you."

The April thaw was well under way by the time Jesse had learned all he thought he'd have to know to search for gold. He swore to himself that he'd not let gold fever get into him like most he met, but he planned to satisfy his curiosity about the possibility of gold being on his property. With a newly purchased wagon full of supplies, he was having one last store-bought meal when he heard a familiar voice behind him. "Jesse? Well I'll be doggoned." He turned to see Huff Allen closing the door behind him.

Jesse placed his boot against the chair on the other side of the small round table and shoved it out. "Sit n' get a bite to eat Huff; darn it's good to see ya."

As the two men ate, each brought the other up to date.

"Dumped that load of supplies n' headed right back here soon's I got everything settled," Huff said, "and I came on a fancy stagecoach this time." He flashed a toothless grin. "Couldn't get this dern gold outa my mind after you n' me was talkin about it."

"Well Huff," Jesse said quietly, "wanna go in with me n' see what we can find on my property?"

The old man just looked at Jesse a moment. "You said partners Jesse, but you know how old I am. Hell I could never work as hard as you."

"Huff, you said you did this for two years. Because you didn't hit it rich don't matter, you know how to go about lookin' for it and that's what counts."

"Well," Huff Allen grinned, "let's get the hell outa this mess o' people n' get to lookin'. How far is it, anyway?"

"About fifty miles for you, but a little farther for me, because while you're setting up camp I'm gonna go see if a friend of mine would like to come in with us."

As Huff began setting up a work camp beside the river that cut through the property, Jesse was on his new horse heading south toward a small Mexican village on the Calaveras River. The following morning he returned with a slightly built Mexican he introduced as Miguelo Calaveras.

By July, Jesse had forgotten all about the trapping supplies he'd bought in Portland. They all knew that they had stumbled onto a river of gold. By October, they had stashed a fortune in gold nuggets, and kept using Jesse's remaining cash to purchase supplies, so word wouldn't get out. Huff had located what would turn out to be one of the largest veins of gold in the entire state. By early spring the three-man-operation had grown to thirty. By the beginning of fall, 1854 it was over a hundred. They were all Mexicans and all had been hand picked by Miguelo. Each man had participated in the rescue of the McKannah brothers in San Francisco.

In the summer of 1855, Huff came to Jesse. "I'm ready to start spendin' some of the money I've got in the bank, Jesse." His friendly blue eyes still twinkled as he looked at Jesse. "If you don't mind, I'm gonna pull out n' go have a little fun." He grinned with his new store-bought teeth showing, "While I still can."

"Huff, I'm doin' the same thing. Been thinking about it a while now and I got more money than any man oughta have at one time. I'm letting my brother Broderick set this entire mining operation up as a co-op for all the men that work in it, with Miguelo as president."

"That's pretty darn generous, Jesse. Y'know you'll be makin' rich men outa these Mexican field workers."

"Never met a bunch o' men that deserved it more."

"You're sure right there, ain't a slacker in the bunch."

Jesse gave the old man a penetrating look. "And Huff I wouldn't be here if not for them, because I have a hunch that every last one of 'em was at the jail that night."

Huff pulled off the same old leather hat he'd worn since Jesse met him, and scratched his head. "Told Miguelo yet?"

"Nope, gonna talk to him tonight."

"Whacha gonna do when you leave here?"

"Been thinking a lot about those Flatheads that I lived with. Our own damn government's stealing their land n' treating them like unwanted foreigners. They're the original Americans and thy're being treated like dirt." Huff could see the muscles in his jaw working. "I'm going back and see if there's anything I can do with all this money to help 'em."

"I'll probably be runnin' into ya, 'cause there's a lotta good folks I wanna see back there, too."

Miguelo Calaveras sat across from Jesse with his mouth hanging wide open. "And I told Broderick to have you show him where you want a thousand acres on the Calaveras River to start that town you've always dreamed of, then deed it to you."

Finally Miguelo spoke, but quietly and shakily. "My God, Jesse. Do you really realize what this means to me and these people?" Tears began flowing down his brown cheeks. He wiped his eyes before speaking again. "That ten percent you'll get will keep you rich, but Jesse you are making every one of us richer than we ever dreamed about." More tears—more wiping. "When you come back for a visit, it will be to the finest little town in California."

Two days later, Jesse McKannah embraced his childhood friend, then climbed into the saddle and headed toward San Francisco to board a stagecoach. Over a hundred and fifty men began tapping their shovels and tools against the mining equipment as their benefactor rode into the sunset. They kept it up long after he was out of earshot.

Jesse went to the bank in San Francisco and explained what his plans were to his brother Patrick's friend, the bank president. After getting the details on paper for the bank to begin preparing the proper forms, he withdrew a significant amount of money and headed for the hotel he'd checked into. The hotel wasn't the finest in the newly prosperous town, but it was only a short walk to the stagecoach line office, and only three buildings from the livery stable where he always left his horse when in town on business. He dropped off the rabbit fur jacket that Rose made him at a Chinese laundry that assured him they could make it look like new. He was very happy when he saw how the cleaned jacket looked. In his hotel room he began opening up the inside pockets to stash his money. When he was finished, he held it up and looked to see if there were any bulges. Satisfied that there wasn't, he laid it on the bed and began running hot water in the tub. He sat deep in the steaming water and relaxed. *A tub with hot running water right in your room. Boy, this modern world's gettin t'be some'n else…wonder what's next?*

The following day he dressed in his new buckskin trousers and soft linen shirt, then buckled his gunbelt over the strap holding his knife and tomahawk. After adjusting the shoulderholster he slipped into the light jacket he bought the day before. Jesse picked up the suitcase that held Rose's coat plus a few personal items then went back to the bank and signed all the papers to be sent to Patrick for approval. He walked to the livery stable and called. "Hey Rodolpho." He greeted the young Mexican teenager that cared for his horse on every visit to town, and then said. "I'm heading off to see some old friends, and I'll be gone quite awhile, so how'd you like to have my horse?"

"I love that horse Señor Jesse," the smiling boy replied, "but I'm saving my money to go to college, so a horse will have to wait."

"I don't want a dime for him, Rodolpho. I just want to be sure he gets a good home. Him and all the tack, including that rifle and scabbard."

The young boy just stood and looked from him to the horse then back at Jesse, who was grinning. "That's a gift to a very good young man that will always do well. Thanks for taking such good care of him."

"Oh Señor Jesse, thank you. Oh my God," he said, with tears running down his face. "I never dreamed of having a horse such as this." He put his arms around the huge horse's head, and hugged it sincerely. "What name did you give him?"

"Never did give him one, just called him horse or boy." He handed the boy a paper of ownership he'd had legalized at the bank then turned to leave. A few steps later he heard the boy say, "Paloma." Jesse stopped dead in his tracks then turned, "What did you say?"

"Paloma," the smiling boy answered. "I will call him Paloma because he is the same color as my pigeon."

"Good name." Jesse turned and walked out of the stable. *Unbelievable.* He stepped into the summer sun and turned toward the stage station. *Absolutely unbelievable.*

He was in no particular hurry to be anyplace specific, and he remembered the beautiful country between San Francisco and Portland. He bought a one-way ticket to Portland so he could spend some time there before getting another ticket east. He enjoyed the warm days of just watching the changing scenery, and even enjoyed the conversation of his fellow travelers. When he arrived in Portland he went straight to see Jeff Holbrook at Oregon Fur Traders. "Still got m'order," Jesse asked with a grin.

"Bloody right you are, cobber. When we take your money we consider you family, mate."

"I've had a change of plans. Can I trust you to pass that stuff along to some trapper that's had a bit o' bad luck?"

"If 'at's what y'want mate, 'at's what y'get." He watched the man walking away toward town. *Strange bugger 'at one is, by Jesus.*

The ride to Walla Walla, Washington from Portland, Oregon was so much different than his trip on the river that he could hardly believe it was in the same country. *A lot of work has already been done to make these stagecoach trips comfortable. Yeah, I'll definitely recommend this over the Columbia River trip.*

The stage pulled into the area behind Omar's Chadwick's hotel. The first person he saw when he stepped down was Annalina Simolina—all six-foot-ten-inchs of her. She was smiling as usual as she looked in the coach after the other passengers had departed. "That old billygoat ain't with you this time?"

"No Anna, but I look for him to be passing through here 'fore too long." He couldn't believe she remembered his name after such a short time together, but then he thought, *hell, I remembered hers.*

She linked her arm in his, "C'mon, I'll fix you some grub." As they headed for her house she asked, "How long you staying in town?"

"Four hour stop, the driver said."

"Plenty of time to catch me up on whacha been doing."

After finishing a huge meal, he told her about him and Huff's good fortune. She roared, "Good on you boys," and smiled sincerely, "couldn't have happened to a coupla better guys."

"Som'ns been bothering me since I metcha, Anna."

"What's that?"

"How'd ya lose those fingers to a mountain lion?"

"Ha." She roared again with laughter. "M'own damn fault. Found this little cougar cub after someone shot her mother. I raised that little sucker with a darn bottle n' nipple, so she thought for sure I was her mama. Followed me everywhere I went, which wasn't a problem at first but," she roared with laughter again, "did that little gal grow up fast. Folks'd about crap their britches when I'd come into town with that big cat walking right beside me. Back to my missing fingers, though. I was drinkin' with ole Huff out around the campfire one night n' forgot about ole City Kitty, which's what I called her. She was layin' beside me chewing on a piece of meat I'd tossed her. Well, like a stupid dern drunk'll do, I reached down to pat her on the nose n' missed. My hand landed right on that chunk o' meat. Rrrrrowwwwww." Anna sounded just like a snarling cougar. She then held up her hand that was missing the thumb and pinky, and grinned.

"Shoot her?"

"Hell no, you crazy? That was my baby. No, me n' ole huff taught her how to hunt n' get along on her own, and then we took her into the high mountains and turned her loose. We camped there a week watchin' her n' sure enough along came one o' you horny guys."

"Think she's still around?"

"Nah. That was," she pursed her lips and wrinkled her brow, "over twenty years ago."

"You n' Huff go way back, huh?" Jesse listened to an hour of stories about her and Huff Allen, then said goodby and left to try to find Laughing Bear. He saw what must be his canoe building business across the river. Several Indians were busy, but no Laughing Bear. He went inside to the bar, and there was Swen, pouring drinks for the stagecoach passengers.

"Hi Swen, remember me?"

"Sure do. Lemme see now, mmmm, uh, McKeller, McKettrick, McSom'n," he said with a wide grin.

"McKannah."

"That's it," the huge, white haired Swede said, "Jesse McKannah." He reached out with his oversize paw and shook Jesse's outstretched hand. "Didja see m'boy's canoe building business across the river?"

"Yeah, but I didn't see him."

"He's in Portland talking to some business guy about building a hundred of those canoes."

"Man, that's great. You guys have a great piece of work there. What are they gonna do with that many?"

"Gonna build four different sizes so they can be put inside each other, then they're gonna ship em over to Australia on one 'o them big boats. Pretty neat, huh?"

"Darn sure is."

The Swede grinned. "Bear came up with the idea to build 'em so they could be stacked inside each other. The businessman who's buying them is gonna have a special wagon built, and two of his men are gonna come and get ten at a time when Bear has 'em ready. Pretty dern slick, huh?"

"Sure is, but it doesn't surprise me a bit. Bear's a smart fella."

Omar Chadwick spotted Jesse standing at the bar and came directly to him.

They spent the rest of Jesse's time talking about his plans to expand his hotel to better accommodate the steadily increasing flow of travelers on the new stage route.

While waiting for the stagecoach to be ready, Jesse noticed Chobie looking at him. "Hi Chobie," he said as he walked to the slightly retarded young man. "Still driving Mr. Chadwick's carriage?"

"Hello Mister McKannah," the boy smiled a little crookedly. "Yessir, I'm still taking him where he wants to go."

"That's good Chobie." Jesse smiled, and then boarded the stage. He waved at the young man standing with a smile on his face and waving. *How in the heck did he remember my name?*

The trip to Lewiston, Idaho was as bumpy as he remembered, so he and the other passengers were happy when they pulled into Winslow Jefferie's Livery Stable. He was first out of the stage, so he walked inside to talk to the old black man. Mahatma came from a side stall. "Jesse, that you?"

"Hey Hat, didn't know if I'd find you here or not."

"Gotta be here all the time now, 'cause we put daddy in the ground last year."

"Sorry to hear that."

"Time to go. He was almost eighty I think. He had a pretty good life, so he didn't seem to mind leaving."

"What happened, just get sick?"

"Nope. Healthy as a fall bear till that black stallion in the stall over there kicked him in the chest."

"We're only here for about an hour, Hat. That boot man still over at Angie's Hotel?"

"Sure is, and he's there right now. I just came from there a while ago."

Jesse told Mahatma that he'd see him somewhere down the trail and headed for the hotel. "Howdy, Ruben." Jesse greeted the tiny little black man that he knew had to be nearing ninety. "Still makin' boots?"

"What else can I do? They won't let me practice law down here. I know you?"

"Bought a pair of your boots a few years ago and I'd like another pair if you got a pair in my size."

The little man looked briefly down, "Size eleven. Yeah, I got a couple of new pair that I just recently finished. C'mon over here and see what you think."

"Eleven, huh? Man-oh-man, that's a heck of a memory."

"Memory my black ass," he grinned. "Sonny I can watch a herd of people go across the street and tell you what size every one of them are wearing." He grinned up at Jesse, "Oughta be able to, 'cause I've shoved about a million pair of boots and shoes on people's feet." He shoved a box of leather aside and pointed to a beautiful pair of plain leather boots. "Best pair I ever made, I

think."
Jesse paid him after trying them on, then opened his suitcase and placed them inside on top of his dress pants and shirt. He noticed Angie's huge body moving around inside the lobby, but carefully avoided her and headed for the stagecoach that was already putting people on for the trip to Missoula, Montana.

The trip was uneventful, and Jesse was glad to be finished with stagecoach travel for a while. He spent what was left of the day locating a good horse then choosing a saddle and gear. He bought a set of double saddlebags, and after putting his few things in them, he laid the empty suitcase on the store's porch for anyone who needed it, and headed for Fort Connah, a short ride away.
Angus McDonald was no longer there, but his replacement was very happy to see the man that Angus had told him about. He was from Dublin, Ireland and loved his liquor as much as Angus. Jesse smiled as the man poured himself a glass of good Irish whisky from one of the two bottles Jesse had brought for Angus. "Mmmmm, lad that's real whisky n' I bloody well thank you for it."

The two men spent the entire night talking about the plight of the local Indians. At dawn Jesse climbed on his horse and headed north. It was a short ride to the new reservation where his old friends now lived. The night's conversation remained in his head. *Signed a treaty with the government giving them all of their millions of acres in exchange for a little piece of ground to whither away on while eating white man's food, and learning white man's ways, and drinking white man's whiskey.*

He stopped the horse to look out over the vastness of the area. Jesse shook his head slowly and turned the horse toward the new reservation on the south end of Flathead Lake. "Eighteen fifty-five wasn't your best year people," he said aloud. As the horse walked slowly ahead he thought, *I don't know what I can do Rose, but I decided to come and see if I can help.*

THE END

The author appreciates feedback at→ magersrick@yahoo.com

ALL PRINTED BOOKS BY RICK MAGERS ARE AVAILABLE AT:

amazon.com

~ O ~

ebooks & 100+ short stories available at:

theebooksale.com

~ O ~

AVAILABLE NOVEMBER 2010

THE McKANNAHS

~ together again ~

... a sequel ...

Ride one last time with the McKannah boys when they rally around Jesse as he fights desparately to right a wrong done to his Native American friends.

The reader will also learn what *really* happened to Aleena McKannah.

Made in the USA
Charleston, SC
05 April 2011